Keep Me Close

and

Betrayal

Clare Francis is the author of seven previous international bestsellers, *Night Sky*, *Red Crystal*, *Wolf Winter*, *Requiem*, *Deceit*, *Betrayal*, and *A Dark Devotion*. She has also written three non-fiction books about her voyages across the oceans of the world.

CLARE FRANCIS

Keep Me Close

and

Betrayal

PAN BOOKS

Keep Me Close first published 1999 by Macmillan
Betrayal first published 1995 by William Heinemann Ltd

This omnibus edition published 2002 by Pan Books
an imprint of Pan Macmillan Ltd
Pan Macmillan, 20 New Wharf Road, London N1 9RR
Basingstoke and Oxford
Associated companies throughout the world
www.panmacmillan.com

ISBN 0 330 41510 7

The author and publishers would like to thank The Society of Authors
on behalf of the Estate of John Masefield for permission to
reprint the extract from 'Sea Fever' by John Masefield.

1 3 5 7 9 8 6 4 2

A CIP catalogue record for this book is available from
the British Library.

Printed and bound in Great Britain by
Mackays of Chatham plc, Chatham, Kent

Keep Me Close

For Vonnie

Chapter One

———

LEADEN SUMMER rain had seized the city. As the taxi inched along the humid streets, Simon felt a nervous dread. To see Catherine at last, to face the full extent of the damage, to get the whole awful business sorted out one way or the other! After the long hours at the hospital, the calls to the police, the sleepless nights, he felt as though he had been waiting for this moment for ever, though it was just – he knew it precisely – four and a half days.

The interminable journey also gave him more than enough time to brood with growing misgivings on the white roses that sat so obtrusively on the seat beside him. He had bought them hurriedly from Moyses Stevens at considerable expense, but now the arrangement seemed too formal, the roses too white, and he couldn't suppress the suspicion that they would be seen as glaringly inappropriate, more suited to a wedding or a funeral. The realisation irritated him excessively because with just a little more thought he would never have made such a ridiculous mistake.

Out of long habit, he reached for his mobile and began to make calls from the list he kept on the small white cards that fitted so neatly into his breast pocket. The list was long, it always was, yet after two calls he found himself staring blankly through the misted window at the streaming streets, the phone forgotten on his knee. A moment later he switched the thing off altogether, impatient with the cab's impossibly slow progress. At this rate there was a risk of getting to the hospital at the same time as Catherine's family, a prospect that filled him with dismay.

He called to the driver to try another route, only for the cab to enter a street that was completely blocked. As his frustration soared, the sweat sprang against his shirt, and he felt a familiar flutter high on his cheek: his certain visitor in times of stress. Removing his spectacles, he propped his elbow against the window and, finding the exact spot and angle, pressed two fingers hard against the dancing muscle until it subsided.

The cabbie cut down another side street; they began to make progress. Reaching the hospital at last, Simon resolved the problem of the flowers by thrusting them into the hands of some fellow arrivals, a shambling overweight couple bearing chocolates for some unhealthy relative. They stared at them with lumpen distrust, but he didn't waste time with explanations they wouldn't begin to understand.

The hospital was modern and showy, with expanses of steel and glass and the inevitable atrium. He followed the now familiar route along a suspended walkway past intensive care to the ward with the unpronounceable, vaguely African name. At the last set of doors he paused and, setting down his briefcase, peered critically at his outline, silhouetted in the glass. He smoothed his hair and flicked a hand over his lapels and viewed first one profile then the other, and saw a version of himself that was entirely as it should be: well-groomed, soberly dressed.

Typical of the shambolic way in which the hospital seemed to be run, there were unfamiliar faces at the nursing station for perhaps the fourth time that week, two pudding-faced girls, neither more than eighteen, both engrossed in paperwork and determined not to notice him. It was necessary to speak decisively before one of them would look up, and then in his general agitation he stumbled over Catherine's name, almost saying Langley instead of Galitza.

'Are you family?' the girl demanded curtly.

'I'm Catherine's solicitor,' Simon explained, producing his card. 'As well as a close—'

'Sorry, family only.'

'That's correct,' he agreed slowly and calmly. 'But – as I was trying to explain – I'm a close friend of the family and I have permission to see her. So long as the family haven't just arrived – have they? In which case I'll wait.'

The girl examined the card doubtfully. 'We've no instructions. I'll have to check.'

'But it was Sister Jones who called me,' Simon said with tight lips and a degree less patience. 'It was she who told me Catherine had regained consciousness. She knows I have permission to visit her.'

The girl was wavering. He tried to loosen his expression into something a little more friendly. 'You didn't say – have the family arrived yet?'

The girl went to check with the other nurse. 'No, but they're on their way over.'

'I'm aware of *that*. I was the one who contacted them, you see.'

A small exaggeration this – Simon had never attempted to contact Alice and by the time he'd got through to Duncan the old boy had already heard from the hospital – but it was enough to win the nurse over.

The nurse led the way down the corridor to Catherine's room and slipped inside. Through a chink in the curtained panel Simon could just make out the dark outline of a chair and a mass of shadowy flowers, but nothing of Catherine herself. He wasn't sure what to expect. It had been a couple of days since he'd last glimpsed her in intensive care, stretched out under bright lights amid a morass of equipment and wires. She would still be attached to tubes and machines that bleeped, he imagined, possibly to some even more disturbing apparatus which did not bear thinking about. But would she be drowsy or wide awake? Confused or coherent? When he'd made the hurried call to Duncan, the old boy had been too busy going through the motions of fatherly relief to provide any useful details.

The nurse reappeared. 'She's very drowsy. She's not up to much, but she's agreed to see you.'

The L-shaped room was dim, the blinds drawn against a day that was already overcast. Closing the door softly behind him, Simon waited in the angle of the room until his eyes had adjusted to the gloom. His nervousness came rushing back. His tongue felt thick, his shirt clammy against his back.

Soundlessly he moved forward into the pool of muted artificial light. Catherine lay flat under a thin coverlet that revealed the slightness of her body. He couldn't immediately see her eyes; her head was low, there was some sort of contraption under her chin and around her head, and wires and weights at the bedhead. Tubes were strapped to her arms, and two more emerged from beneath the coverlet and looped away through the bed frame, one to a machine on a stand that showed a green light, the other to a transparent bag half-filled with – he quickly averted his eyes.

He took a few steps towards her, the tension fluttering like a tribe of butterflies in his stomach. 'Hello, Catherine. It's Simon Jardine!'

A faint sound: gasp or sigh.

As he advanced into her field of vision her eyes swivelled down, searching for him, squinting uncertainly. Her entire head was held in a rigid cradle, he realised, a sort of surgical collar, but larger and sturdier than any he'd seen before, extending from her chin up and around the back of her head, like some bizarre Elizabethan ruff.

Her eyes narrowed again, she couldn't seem to focus on him, and, depositing his briefcase on the floor, he forced himself to move closer still, to the very edge of the bed.

'Simon?' Her voice was dry and cracked.

'Hello there.' In attempting to smile he felt his cheek give way again: a sharp shiver. 'How are you, Catherine?'

Her gaze widened, she looked at him with something like fear. 'Ohh . . . *Ohh . . .*'

For a moment he thought his heart would give out, it was beating so violently.

'Something's – happened?' she gasped with an effort. 'Something . . . Tell me . . .'

'It's all over now, Catherine. Nothing to worry about. You're in safe hands.'

She seemed to have trouble in understanding him, and he repeated the reassurances.

'But Ben? Pa?' she whispered. 'Has something—? Are they—?'

'They're fine. Really!' He produced a fiercely cheerful tone. 'Absolutely fine!'

'Fine?'

'Yes! I promise!'

She closed her eyes and gave a long ragged sigh. 'Ohh ... I thought ... Ohh ...' Then, with a fresh wave of anxiety, she whispered, 'But where – are – they?'

'Oh, they'll be arriving any minute now, I'm sure. I just happened to be the nearest, that's all!' He heard himself laugh awkwardly. 'Your father's definitely on his way. He'd just popped home for a wash and brush up. I spoke to him as I left. He was just turning round to come straight back. And Alice – she'll be in after work, I expect. So you see?'

'But – *Ben*?'

'Oh, bound to be in soon! Been in twice a day, most days, sometimes even more.' *Covering for Ben again*, he thought with a burst of anger. *How often have I had to do that?*

She frowned at him. 'So why ... are you ... here?'

He blurted, 'Oh, I just thought I'd drop by, that's all!' *What a ridiculous thing to say*, he thought unhappily. *I'm sounding like a complete idiot.* This was his fate, it seemed: always to feel off-balance with Catherine, always to feel hopelessly awkward. 'No, it was more that' – he selected a more considered tone – 'I came to help out.'

'Help . . .?' The idea seemed to add to her general air of puzzlement.

'To look after all the tedious things that Ben and Duncan don't want to be bothered with—'

But he had lost her. Her eyes were ranging back and forth in a slow incessant searching of the walls and ceiling. Finally she murmured, 'Where is . . . this . . . again?'

He gave her the name of the hospital.

'The doctor . . . said . . . an *accident*.'

'Yes, you bumped your head. You had us worried for a while, I can tell you, but you're okay now. You're in the very *best* of hands. We've made sure of that!'

The words came faintly, like small breaths. 'My head . . .?'

'A nasty crack.'

'But it's not – it's . . .' She lost this thought, or abandoned it, and after a moment her gaze came back to him. 'A car . . .?'

'No. It was a fall, a nasty fall.'

'*Fall* . . .' She took this in slowly, with renewed bafflement.

He thought: No memory, she has no memory at all. He could hardly believe it.

He leant over her so that she could look up at him without strain. He saw that the whites of her eyes had a jaundiced tinge, from medication perhaps, or some internal damage, while the irises, which in healthier times had been such an intense blue, seemed almost bleached of colour.

There was a terrible intimacy in being so close to her, in witnessing her defencelessness; he shuddered softly, with pity and wonder, and something like longing.

He said gravely, 'It happened at home. You fell from the landing.'

'Oh . . .'

'In fact . . . during a burglary.'

Alarm and confusion passed over her face, her mouth moved loosely. 'Burglary . . .' Then, with another stab of anxiety: 'Ben wasn't . . . there? Wasn't . . . hurt?'

'Hurt? No! He got a couple of bruises, that's all. Nothing serious. They discharged him almost immediately. Four days ago now.'

'Four . . .' She frowned, though he couldn't tell if it was the thought of the lost days or the burglary that troubled her.

The odd thing was that there was no visible bruising. Nothing to show for the fall but the dulled eyes and a deep pallor. In the sepulchral light her skin looked so white and smooth and polished that she might have been an alabaster effigy. Only the area beneath her eyes revealed the slightest trace of colour, a faint smudge of violet-blue far below the surface. The effect of this terrible perfection was dreamlike, hypnotic, and he could not look away.

'You wouldn't – *lie*?'

She had startled him. 'Lie, Catherine?'

'About Ben.'

'*Ben*? Oh – absolutely not!'

'You would – say?'

'Of *course* I would say, Catherine! How long have we known each other, for heaven's sake? How long have we been friends? Good God!' The laugh came again, a jarring sound that seemed to jump unbidden from his mouth. 'No, he's perfectly okay. Promise. Tough bastard. Grappled with the burglar and got a black eye for his trouble. And then – well, two stitches. On the cheek.'

The two stitches seemed to provide the authenticity she craved and for the first time since Simon had arrived she became almost calm.

Bending still lower, Simon whispered, 'Catherine, the police have asked if they can come and talk to you.'

Her expression was almost childlike in its incomprehension and it occurred to him that she was probably dosed up to the eyeballs with sedatives.

'Police?'

'To ask if you can remember anything about the attack. But, Catherine, you don't have to see them if you don't want to. Just tell me and I'll keep them away for as long as you like!'

'Attack . . .'

'They just want to know if you can remember anything.'

'But I— No . . .'

'You don't remember anything?'

'No . . .'

He nodded sympathetically to give her more time. 'What about – oh – arriving at the flat? Nothing about that?'

A faint furrow sprang up between her eyebrows as she agonised over this.

'Or going upstairs?'

'No.' Then, as if his words had only just sunk in: '*Attack?*'

He hesitated, wondering how much he could say without planting memories in her mind. 'Well, we don't know exactly what happened of course, but it seems that the intruder attacked Ben, then – well, who knows, he may have pushed past you, something like that. Anyway, somehow or another – you fell.'

'Fell . . .'

He left it for a moment before prompting gently, 'You'd just come back from France.'

'France.' It wasn't a memory but a repetition.

'The intruder was already inside the house.'

Clearly disturbed at this, she began to breathe in snatches. 'No – nothing – nothing—'

'It's all right,' Simon interrupted hastily. 'It really couldn't matter less. Please don't worry yourself about it. Plenty of time for all that later. *Plenty* of time! I'll tell the police not to come. I'll tell them not to bother you.'

'Yes, I . . . can't . . . can't . . .' She stared past him, the confusion chasing over her face like shadows.

'It's all right. It's all right.' He repeated the words over and over again because he couldn't think of what else to say, and because it thrilled him to be soothing her in this moment of fear and need, whispering to her like a lover in the night.

Her eyes became opaque, then closed altogether. If it hadn't been for the rapidity of her breathing and the slight crease between her eyebrows she might have been asleep.

Simon straightened up with the sense of a task completed, if only for the time being. She could recall nothing. It was a miracle, a blessing. No police, no hassle, no flashbacks, no nightmares. According to the information he had garnered from various medics concussion victims rarely recovered lost memories of events immediately surrounding a trauma.

Waiting quietly, he remembered the time he had first seen Catherine – when was it? – three years ago. No, he could be more precise than that – two years and eleven months ago – at Ascot. He had understood immediately why people should talk about her, why they should describe her as pretty, lovely, striking. Simon himself had had no hesitation in calling her beautiful, though then, as now, he would have found it hard to say exactly why. She had good eyes – extraordinary eyes – arresting, oval with a slight upwards tilt at the corners, and her hair, when it wasn't scraped back and dead-looking like this, was a rich browny-gold; yet her nose was by any standards rather long, while her mouth was a little on the wide side and very full. There was no one feature that could be described as exceptional, and yet taken together they had what his mother would have called an *effect*. From that first glimpse Simon had found it impossible not to be gripped by the sheer improbability of that brilliant face.

Later, when he'd had the chance to observe her, he'd become intrigued by her vitality, the way she moved and talked and held her head, by her low supple laughing voice and the warm conspiratorial glances she threw at those around her. She was the most vivid person Simon had ever met. He was in awe of this, and envious too, because, though he worked hard at every aspect of his life, enjoyment wasn't something that came easily to him. Watching Catherine sometimes, he was both fascinated and disturbed by the idea that such enjoyment of life could be acquired or learnt, that if he could only devote more time to the study of it he might be able to find the secret. But in his sombre and lonely heart he knew there was no secret, no trick, no easy way; it was simply that some people loved life and others had to take the promise of such things on trust.

Her hand lay on the coverlet, white and slender and smooth as a child's. He stared at it. He pictured himself taking it, squeezing it gently, communicating reassurance and affection, perhaps even managing to leave his hand resting lightly on hers for some moments afterwards. He imagined it, almost persuaded himself to do it, but in the end it was too enormous an undertaking, and it was a relief to hold back.

The emergency staff had removed the wedding ring, he noticed. He remembered Catherine wearing it for the first time. The wedding seemed very distant now, but it was just – Simon had to think – yes, eight months ago. Remembering her then, luminous and vibrant, it seemed strange to be looking down on this diminished shadowy version of Catherine, uncharacteristically subdued, confined, devoid of everything that had made her so alive.

Who would love and value her now? he wondered emotionally. Who would warm to someone so still, so changed? Not Ben's circle of acquaintances. If Simon's understanding of her medical condition was even half right, Catherine was going to need friends rather more substantial than that.

He found himself thinking: And Ben won't be much use either. *Love is not love which alters when it alteration finds.*

A mechanical hiss broke the silence: it took him an instant to realise that it was some sort of device for redistributing air around the mattress. When he looked up again it was to find Catherine watching him through half-closed eyes.

He smiled hastily, inanely. He felt his cheek tremble. He glanced away. 'Amazing flowers.'

There were flowers along the length of the window sill, at least six vases, and several more on the floor, as well as the large arrangement next to the chair, and, propped between them on every available surface, cards, several dozen of them. A few of the arrangements were striking, with unusual mixtures of flowers, foliage and dried grasses. From fellow garden designers, presumably, or, more likely still, grateful clients. He noted fleetingly but with satisfaction that the two all-white flower arrangements looked quite out of place.

'Could you ... move them ... please,' Catherine murmured.

'The flowers?'

'The white ...'

He looked at her sharply, thinking for a ludicrous moment that she had read his mind. 'Yes – rather too funereal, aren't they?' He gave a bright bark of a laugh. 'Or matrimonial! Shall I move them away?'

'Nearer.'

He felt a stab of heat in his face, as if she were making fun of him. 'Nearer?'

'I love ... white.'

This time he managed to turn his laugh into a sharp cough. 'Of course.'

It was no easy job. The sill was so crowded that he had to move two vases temporarily to the floor before he could rearrange everything satisfactorily.

Catherine's eyes followed him back to the bedside. 'I
– don't *see*—' For some reason she was suddenly close
to tears.

'What don't you see, Catherine?'

'Why' – her voice cracked with open resentment –
'*you* – came.'

His chest tightened, a sharpness burned his eyes.
'Why I came?'

Her face contorted. 'Go away,' she cried bitterly. 'I
don't want you here. I want my family.'

Steadying himself, he put a hand to his glasses and
settled them more precisely on his nose. 'I understand,
of course . . . But someone had to liaise with the police,
you see. And I thought it was the one area where I
could be useful. Give Ben and your father one less thing
to worry about.'

A single tear slid from Catherine's eye. 'But where –
are they?' she cried pathetically. 'I want them here.'

'They'll be here any moment now.' With Catherine's
rebuff still echoing painfully in his ears, Simon reached
for his briefcase. 'I'm sure you'll want to rest,' he said,
mustering his dignity. 'You'll want to sleep.'

The door sounded. Simon braced himself, but it was
only one of the ancillary staff.

'More flowers, Catherine!' she called gaily. 'What a
popular girl you are!' She brandished them in the air
before plopping them on top of the television set and
sweeping out of the room.

Simon took a step towards the door. 'Well . . . I'll be
off then.'

'They wild?'

'Sorry?'

'The flowers.'

Simon gave them a cursory glance. 'I wouldn't know, I'm afraid.'

She lifted the fingers of one hand: a summons. Dutifully, Simon put his briefcase down again and, fetching the flowers, held them just above her where she could see them. They were arranged in a posy, a mass of tiny blue, white and pink flowers, set in a halo of leaves and miniature foliage, supported by an outer layer of cellophane.

She touched them, she seemed to lose interest, but just as Simon thought it would be safe to slip away she gave a soft cry. '*Oh*, but they – look like—' There was an envelope pinned to the cellophane; she raised a hand towards it.

He unclipped it and took out the note. 'Do you want me to read it for you?'

She blinked slowly in agreement.

He turned the note over and glanced at the signature. 'It's from someone called Terry.'

Her eyes widened, she made a harsh sound of annoyance. This reaction was so unexpected that Simon went back to the note for an address or some other clue to Terry's identity. There was none. Then, with sharpened interest, he realised precisely who it might be. If it was indeed Terry Devlin, then the man certainly had a nerve. According to Ben, this was the man who, having been shown great kindness by Catherine's family in his youth, had repaid them by acquiring the debts on their house and throwing them out.

However, it was another, largely untold story that had taken a far deeper hold on Simon's imagination. While it was generally known that Ben and Terry Devlin had worked on a deal together, the cause of their falling out had always been something of a mystery. Certainly it was not a subject that could safely be raised with Ben. But if the hints and rumours Simon had picked up were even half correct, Terry Devlin had achieved the unique distinction of having played Ben at one of his trickier games and outmanoeuvred him. Simon had always ached to know how Devlin had achieved it.

He began to read aloud. '*Dear Catherine, I am so very sorry to hear that you are in the hospital. I trust they are looking after you well. I hope these flowers from Morne will bring a little colour to your room. They were fresh picked this morning from the meadow just the other side of the bridge—*'

Catherine made a faint sound that he couldn't interpret.

'Shall I go on?'

She closed her eyes. It wasn't a request to stop.

He continued, '*The meadow is completely covered in wild flowers every May now (last year there was a lot of marsh marigold, this year ragged robin and cranesbill). I think the land there was always trying to be a flower meadow and just needed to be left alone for a while.*'

Simon felt the irritation of having been mistaken. This was obviously a gardening crony or former colleague.

Seeing that Catherine was slowly losing the battle to stay awake, he rattled rapidly through the descriptions of seeding and grazing, and slowed down only for the last bit. '*Now, you take care of yourself, Catherine. We all wish you a speedy recovery. With fond regards, your devoted friend, Terry.*'

He glanced up to find that she had drifted off. He stood and watched her for a final moment, transfixed by her helplessness. With a rush of feeling, he thought: I will care for you when the rest have drifted away, I won't abandon you. But no sooner had he allowed this thought to fill him with secret pride than it became confusing to him, and he shrank away from it.

He had been here too long. Hurriedly he deposited the letter and flowers on a chair and, scooping up his briefcase, went softly towards the door.

He was beginning to think he had escaped the family when the door swung open in his face and he was confronted by Alice, followed shortly by Duncan.

'What the hell are *you* doing here?' Alice hissed.

'Simon, old chap,' Duncan murmured, looking puzzled.

'Well?' demanded Alice.

With an arrow-like gesture of one hand, Duncan cleared a path for himself and, muttering, 'Where's my girl?', shouldered his way into the room. A moment later Simon heard him call in a broken voice, 'My dearest darling girl—'

'*Well?*' Alice's tone was uncompromising.

Simon gestured her towards the corridor. It was a perfectly polite gesture, in fact he inclined his head as he did so, which was about as polite as you could get, but Alice was not one to let manners or self-control interfere with her temper, and she stood square, blocking the doorway with her plump frame, so that Simon had no choice but to squeeze past her into the passage. He pulled tight against the wall, but she moved to block him further or possibly to provoke him because first her arm, then, as she turned, her breast, brushed against him, and he had to suppress the urge to thrust her away.

Following hard behind him, yanking at his sleeve, she hissed, 'I suppose this was *Ben's* idea!'

He didn't answer immediately, which only seemed to enrage her further.

'How dare you!' she growled. 'How *dare* you!'

'Perhaps when you're a little calmer I could explain—'

'*Explain!* You sneak in here, like you sneak in everywhere, you go and *bother* her – and you think there's anything to *explain*!'

'The alternative was the police,' he replied in measured tones. 'I'm sure you wouldn't have wanted them to come and bother her.'

'At least *they* would have had the decency to *wait*! At least they wouldn't have barged in uninvited!'

Alice was a tall girl and several stone overweight, with a small nose and thin lips that were lost in the broad fleshy cheeks and frame of thick dark hair. Her complexion was the colour of dough and there was an unhealthy puffiness beneath her eyes. Her manner matched her temperament, sullen and irritable. Now, with her chin thrust out, her eyes glittering shrewishly, she looked positively ugly. If she had been anyone but Catherine's younger sister, Simon would have retreated without another word.

'Who gave you the *right*?' she flogged on. 'That's what I want to know! Who said you could just waltz in here?'

'It was your father, actually.'

He had caught her there, and she didn't like it one bit. Her eyes narrowed, her lips formed a jagged line.

Simon pressed home his advantage. 'He asked me if I would deal with the police – and that's exactly what I've been doing. And why I came here today, to see if it was necessary for them to bother her—'

'But you're a bloody *tax* lawyer!'

Her voice was strident, it could have commanded a hunting field. Glancing up the passage, he was aware of people looking in their direction.

With a conspicuous demonstration of restraint, he lowered his voice to a murmur. 'That's not right actually. I'm a commercial lawy—'

'But *money*! You deal in *money*!' From the way she said it money might have been one of the most noxious substances known to man.

'What I deal in are situations. This is just another situation.'

'Ha!' She wagged an exultant finger. 'Exactly! Just *another* situation you're fixing for someone else! For *Ben*, perhaps?'

This was the sort of emotionally charged, illogical argument that Simon found profoundly unpleasant. Recoiling, he lifted a splayed hand, in truce or farewell, however she cared to interpret it.

Alice chose to redirect her ire. 'What I want to know is why *Ben* isn't dealing with the police. *He* should be the one dealing with them – not *you*.'

'As I've said, your father thought—'

'Where the hell *is* Ben, anyway? God – Catherine's in this place, desperately ill, and Ben's vanished. Where's he been for the last few days, for Christ's sake?'

He put her right. 'He's been dashing in and out most of the time actually. But now – I can't tell you where he's gone.'

'Can't or *won't*!'

'Actually – can't.'

She searched his face for the lie, then, backing down, gave a grudging shrug. 'Well, he damn well *should* be here.'

'I agree.'

'When did you last speak to him?'

Simon selected his words with care. 'Not recently.'

'It's unbelievable! He doesn't even answer his mobile. Not for *me*, anyway. What about you?'

Choosing to interpret this question loosely, Simon gave a minute shake of his head. In fact, he'd managed to make contact a couple of times, but Ben had been so uncommunicative, the conversations so brief that they hardly seemed worth mentioning, particularly to Alice, who in her present mood was unlikely to believe anything so obvious as the truth.

'Just *incredible*!' Alice gave a harsh contemptuous sigh before fixing Simon with a cold eye. 'So why have *you* been dropping in the whole time, then? Oh, don't think I don't know – the staff have told me. At dawn, at *night* even. I assumed you were reporting back to Ben, but now you tell me you're not.'

'Actually I've been coming in to find out how Catherine was,' he replied solemnly.

'Oh, have you?' Her eyebrows shot up in an ironic expression of surprise. 'Really? Now why should you do that?' When he hesitated, she declared, 'You always were a creep, Simon. Right from the beginning. Wheed-

ling your way in, getting to know people who might be useful to you. Oh, don't think it hasn't been *obvious*—'
She broke off with a dismissive gesture.

Simon felt the coldness come over him that marked his moments of deepest bewilderment and humiliation.

'Anyway,' Alice went on, 'the point is, you've been talking to the staff about Catherine!'

He said very quietly, 'Only to ask about her health.'

'That's what I mean. Getting information that wasn't any of your business. Well, whatever you've heard, whatever they've said, it's not to be passed on to anyone else. Is that absolutely clear?'

'I wouldn't dream of it.'

'No talk of her condition. No talk of – *problems*.'

'Of course not!' he retorted, letting his indignation show. 'What do you take me for? Quite apart from anything else, I'm bound by client confidentiality.'

Another raised eyebrow. 'Well, that's something, I suppose. Assuming you stick to it, of course. Assuming we have the faintest idea of who you're acting *for*.'

Simon felt a shudder of rage. It was only with the greatest effort that he managed to control his voice. 'I'm acting for Ben while he's away. And for your father. And for Catherine of course, if she needs me.'

'Well, she doesn't need you.' Alice loomed closer and he could see the faint dampness on her forehead and the darkness in her muddy-green eyes. 'And you're not to see her again without our permission. Is that quite clear?'

My God, he thought savagely, *she'll be asking me to kiss her arse next*. He stated stiffly, 'I will return if asked to do so. As indeed I was *today*.'

'Quite.' She gave a tight little smile, and he had no doubt that Duncan would be strictly forbidden to issue any more rash instructions.

'Well, I think I'll go and see my sister now.' She added pointedly, 'If she isn't completely exhausted, that is.'

Simon managed to hold on to his expression until he was some distance up the corridor, when he was over-taken by a shiver that caught his breath and clouded his vision. My God, what had he done to deserve that?

Ben said it was lack of sex that made Alice so spiky, though being Ben he put it rather more bluntly than that. In his more unabashed moments he also said that she resented being fat and plain in a family of attractive people. Yet Ben had been referring to Alice's normal chippiness, a carping banter that could almost pass as humour; he knew nothing of this particular and malicious delight she reserved for Simon. Alice had attacked Simon before – twice – and, then as now, he had racked his brains as to why he should provoke such hostility. He had never to his knowledge given her the slightest cause to dislike him, had never overstepped the mark in any shape or form, indeed had taken care to be polite and pleasant, going so far as to ask after her interests (she watched polo, was pro-hunting, and went skiing in Val D'Isere). No, it couldn't be anything he had said or not said.

As for *using* people . . . as for *wheedling* his way in . . . This thought stung him to the core. Was this what Alice was telling everyone? Worse, was this what they were believing? Was this what Catherine herself thought of him? The idea was especially painful because it was so unjust. He had *never* promoted himself in any inappropriate way, had never been anything but meticulous in his dealings with other people. Away from the office, he was like everyone else, he drank with his friends, went to the races with them, supported their charities, and now and again dropped in a bit of business. Everyone did it. Not only was he no worse than anyone else, he was a great deal better. The suggestion was outrageous! He had nothing to reproach himself for.

It came to him suddenly that there was something far simpler behind Alice's attack. The answer was so obvious he couldn't imagine why he hadn't thought of it before. What she really loathed was the idea of being indebted to him. She couldn't stomach the fact that he had saved her father from his own excesses, that by taking control of Duncan's tinpot wine company Simon had rescued him from financial disaster. It was nothing personal at all.

He allowed himself a last burst of indignation and relief before pushing thoughts of Alice firmly to the back of his mind. The heat had gone from him, the sweat on his shirt felt cold on his skin. He found a washroom and splashed cold water on his face before going to a quiet spot overlooking the atrium and dialling Ben's mobile. As it rang he pictured Ben squinting at the phone, reading the caller's name on the display before deciding whether to answer it.

'About to call you,' came the laconic voice. From the background babble, Simon guessed he was speaking from a large public place, a hall or concourse.

'Where are you, Ben?' Simon used a neutral tone. 'Everyone's wondering. I'm at the hospital. Catherine's come round. She's asking for you.'

'She's come round? Well, thank God for that! They said she would, didn't they? Still – a relief. And she's okay, is she? I mean, cheerful and all that.'

'She needs you here, Ben.'

'Look, I just can't make it. Not for the moment. Just can't. Cover for me, will you, Simon? It's a bit urgent.'

'What's so urgent exactly?'

'Plenty!' Ben snapped in a rare show of nerves. Then, in a more subdued voice: 'Got to be somewhere, that's all. Just getting on a plane now. Won't get back till late tonight – no, at this rate, *tomorrow*. Yes – midday, I should think. Just tell her that nothing, absolutely nothing in the world would keep me away but wild horses. Tell her exactly that, will you? Wild horses. She'll understand.'

'What about a quick word on the phone? She'd love to hear—'

'No!' he cut in. 'Look, I would, I really would, but it'd be too difficult to explain. She'd only get upset. Make herself ill or something. Better for you to tell her. Really. Much better.'

Simon said firmly, 'I need to know one thing.' He didn't add *before I agree* but that was what he meant. 'Is this anything to do with the business? Anything I should know about? Because if it is—'

'Course not! I'd bloody tell you, wouldn't I, if it was.'

Summoning all his courage, Simon took a flier. 'Nothing to do with the Polska CMC deal?'

'*No*.' He sounded incredulous. 'How could it be?'

In his thoughts Simon echoed: That's right, Ben, how could it be? 'In that case,' he said aloud, 'is it anything I can help out with?'

'No, thanks.'

'As a friend, I mean?'

'Nope. Look – got to run. They're calling the flight.'

'Can I at least tell Catherine where you've gone?'

'No,' he said in the brisk disparaging tone he always used to halt discussion. 'Just tell her I'll see her tomorrow. Okay?'

The connection went dead.

Pocketing his phone, Simon tried to remember a time when he had known Ben so rattled. Not for years, not since they had first started the business and gambled everything on the Qatar deal. On second thoughts, not even then; no, in all this time Ben had never had it this bad.

Avoiding a passing trolley, Simon crossed the corridor to the nursing station and, taking some blank paper from his briefcase, used a free end of the counter to write out Ben's message to Catherine. As he underlined *wild horses*, he became aware of a woman marching up to the desk and casting vainly about for a member of staff. Simon recognised the tall, sharp-featured blonde immediately. She was a girlfriend of Catherine's called Emma Russell, in advertising, or maybe it was PR – yes, PR for an up-market china shop – and her father was the managing director of an independent Midlands brewery.

'Hello, Emma.'

She stared at him uncertainly. 'Oh . . . hi.'

'Simon Jardine.'

Though they had met at least three times before, it was clear she hadn't placed him. He suppressed the small flutter of resentment that was apt to stir in him at such moments.

'Cheltenham Gold Cup, lunch in the marquee,' he prompted lightly.

'Oh *yes!*' she exclaimed, springing to life. 'You work for Ben. Tell me—'

'*With* him—'

'What?' Blinking briefly at the interruption, she rushed on impatiently, 'But how's Cath? Is she all right? Tell me—'

'She regained consciousness a few hours ago,' Simon reported gravely. 'She's out of intensive care.'

'Oh, thank God for that!' Emma spread a scarlet-nailed hand against her chest in an extravagant gesture of relief. 'Thank *God*. I hadn't heard anything since Monday, and what with trying to get an earlier flight and the rush – oh, thank God!' Slowing down a little, she asked, 'But what are they saying? Is she going to be all right? Will she—' She moved closer and, resting her fingers lightly on Simon's arm, fixed him with an intense rather disconcerting gaze. She had large round eyes, hazel-brown, with brilliant whites and thick lashes. Despite her height, or perhaps because of it, she tilted her head forward so that, though her gaze was level with his, she seemed to be peering up at him. 'Someone told me she'd hurt her back, that it might be serious, that' – her voice faltered – 'it might be *broken*. Is it true?'

'I don't think the doctors know anything definite about anything yet. Too soon.'

'But it's *possible*?'

'Really – no one knows.'

She removed her hand rather crossly. 'Well – what *are* they saying, then?'

'Her skull's fractured, she was badly concussed, but

there are no blood clots, which are the dangerous thing apparently.'

'But are they reasonably happy with the way things are going? Do they think she's going to be okay?'

'They won't commit themselves.'

Giving up on him altogether, she narrowed her mouth and glanced away. 'Can I see her? Is it allowed?'

'Duncan's with her at the moment. And Alice. Best to ask them.'

'Oh, if they're both in there I'd better wait, hadn't I? It'd be too much to have me as well, wouldn't it?' Increasingly fidgety, she glanced around several times before grunting, 'Anywhere to smoke in this place? I've just had eight hours on a plane and a perfectly awful time in New York. The fascists there scream at you if you so much as light up in the *street*.' Another scan of the pristine white corridors and, with a sharp sigh of resignation and a pursing of her mouth, she abandoned the quest.

As if to keep her mind off nicotine, she began to speak in a rush that emphasised her high rather breathless voice. 'I only found out when I happened to call someone from New York. They told me she was on the critical list. I couldn't *believe* it. Tried to phone Ben, left dozens of messages – he never called back. I realised he must be here night and day, of course, but that only made me more frantic. Imagining the worst. So I phoned everyone I could think of. Finally got through to Jack and Amy Bellingham – you know, the restaurant people – and they told me Cath was here, in intensive care, and that she'd broken her spine and fractured her skull and the doctors weren't sure if she was going to make it. Well, you can imagine – I was just devastated.

I mean, from the way they were talking it sounded so *desperate*. And when they told me she'd been *pushed* – well, for God's sake! – is it true? – did this maniac really *push* her?'

'All that anyone knows for sure is she fell.'

Emma shuddered visibly and screwed up her eyes. 'Where? How?'

Even now, four days after the event, Simon had to take a slow breath before he could bring himself to relate it. 'She was found on the hall floor, underneath that railed landing. The banisters gave way. She fell across a large wooden chest – they think it was that which broke her back. Her head met the floor.'

Emma clasped a hand to her mouth. 'That hall – it's stone, isn't it? *God!* It's too awful to think about! Too ghastly!' She dropped her face into her hands amid curtains of hair and gave a long strangled moan. Then, lifting her head abruptly, flipping her hair back from her face, she cried, 'And this *person* – this *animal*, this piece of *scum* – he did it on purpose, did he? To get some sort of ghastly *kick*?'

'There's no way of knowing.'

'But how did he get in? Where was Ben?'

Taking care, as always, to be precise, Simon outlined what he'd been told by the police. That there were signs of a break-in, that the house had been ransacked, that Ben had been found stunned and confused, that when he'd been able to talk to the police some hours later he'd told them about finding an intruder.

Emma listened attentively with her head on one side and her arms hugged tightly round her waist. She had a slender, narrow-hipped figure, almost boyish, with a thin face that emphasised the childlike roundness of her eyes. She was dressed entirely in black, in a well-cut trouser suit rumpled from the journey. Her hair was straight and shoulder length and very blonde. Every few minutes she pushed it back from her face in what was evidently a nervous mannerism. She was probably the same age as Catherine though her angular rather pinched face made her seem older, more like thirty-two or -three.

'I always said it was a dodgy area,' she muttered. 'It's not really Notting Hill, is it? More like North Kensington. Anyway, I thought they were still meant to be in France. I didn't think they were back till this weekend.'

'Something came up.'

She declared disgustedly, 'With the bloody business, I suppose!' Then, in a voice hardly less contemptuous: 'And of course the police haven't caught this *person* yet, have they?'

Simon shook his head.

'No, *too* much to hope for. The police are *useless*! I got robbed last year *right* outside my door, and they were completely pathetic. Didn't want to know. Tried to fob me off with Victim Support. I mean, the woman was absolutely sweet and all that, but it wasn't tea I needed, it was transport – and *rapido*. I ended up missing the most fantastic party—' She broke off with a small sidelong glance at Simon and added a little defensively, 'I hope they're making a hell of a lot more effort over *this*.'

'The guy in charge seems reasonably efficient. Bright, too.'

Emma eyed Simon. 'You've met him?'

'Wilson? Very much so. Talk to him twice a day,

sometimes more. I'm liaising with them, you see. On behalf of Ben and Duncan. To take a bit of the load off their shoulders.' The last comment had sounded almost boastful and he frowned at the lapse.

Emma was looking at him with new interest. '*Liaising?* I hadn't realised. In that case you'll know if they've checked—' She paused abruptly, her eyes slid away. 'No,' she said after a moment, as if taking herself in hand. 'No, perhaps . . .' Then, attempting to strike a different note, she asked casually, 'Where's Ben? Is he around?'

'He had to go away.'

'But he'll be back soon?'

'Not immediately, no.'

'You mean – *away* away?'

'Yes.'

She gave Simon a mildly resentful glance, as if Ben's unaccountable absence was in some way his fault. 'But I can get him on his mobile?'

Simon made a doubtful gesture. 'I rather think he's out of reach. But I'm expecting him to call later. I'd be glad to pass on a message.'

Emma exhaled sharply, almost petulantly, and it occurred to him that she wasn't one to bear the trials of life with good grace. 'It'll wait,' she muttered.

Overtaken by a fresh attack of restlessness, she flicked her hair back, though now, as before, it fell forward again almost immediately. 'Do you think they'll be in there much longer, Duncan and Alice?' she said fretfully. 'Or shall I put my head round the door?'

'It might be an idea.'

But she made no move towards Catherine's room. Instead, agitating her hand, she paced off across the corridor.

A wall clock showed a quarter to five. If he got a move on Simon realised he might be able to catch DS Wilson at his desk before he knocked off for the day.

Returning to the message for Catherine, he picked up his pen again and added '*He sends tons of love*' and was immediately worried that *tons* was too breezy, even by Ben's standards, that *much* or *deepest* love would be more fitting.

He'd just decided to leave the love measured by weight when Emma came back. Leaning both forearms on the counter, she said, 'It was definitely a burglary?'

'Sorry?'

'The police – they think it was just a burglary?'

Her choice of words made him look up. 'Well – yes. Things were stolen, the house was ransacked.'

'It wasn't a stalker then?'

He stared. For an instant he thought he must have misheard her. 'A stalker? Why do you say that?'

She gave a sharp sigh, as though the whole matter had become altogether too much for her. 'That's what I wanted to talk to Ben about, you see, to ask him what he thought – whether the guy could have had anything to do with – well, *anything*. Look, it was probably nothing – Cath only mentioned it once, she didn't seem to take it seriously – but it's been on my mind, I kept thinking about it on the plane, that this *breather* might have turned out to be a complete *psycho*. You know, followed her, waited for her. I mean, it often starts with calls, doesn't it? And then they go on from there, get obsessed. But if it was just a burglary, then—'

Simon interrupted, 'Are you saying someone was stalking Catherine?'

'No – well, not then – no, it was just calls. But that's what I wanted to ask Ben – if anything else had happened, like anyone had started hanging around, or if this guy was just, you know, a sad anorak in a phone booth.' She threw up a hand. 'But, look, how do I know? It was probably nothing. It might have stopped weeks ago—'

Simon couldn't get to grips with this at all. 'Let me get this straight, someone was making nuisance calls to Catherine?'

'Yes.'

'Threatening calls?'

'Well – not quite. I think Cath said that he only ever spoke once. After that he never said a word. That's why she wasn't too fazed.'

'There was nothing else apart from the calls?'

She said touchily, 'Well . . . no.'

'He never bothered her in any other way?'

'Not that she ever—' Emma pushed a palm against her head in a gesture of stupidity. 'I'm crazy, aren't I? If this guy had shown his face, Ben would have said something, wouldn't he? If anything had happened to frighten Cath, he would have told the police.' She gave a long groan. 'I left my brain on a bar stool somewhere, didn't I? I really hadn't *thought*.'

But Simon wasn't listening, he was too busy trying to see how the police were likely to interpret this information, how it might affect the course of their investigation. 'Best to be on the safe side,' he said finally.

'What?'

'Best to tell the police. They should know everything, decide for themselves what's important.'

She shrugged, but she was relieved all the same. 'You think so? Well, in that case—' Her eye was caught by something over his shoulder. 'Oh, there's Alice!' She gave a tentative wave and prepared to move off.

Simon put the message into her hand. 'Could you read this to Catherine?'

Emma waved more strenuously to Alice and mimed greetings. 'Sure.'

'And the police may want to talk to you. Shall I call you—'

But she was already hurrying off. Just when he thought she would leave without a word she spun round and, pointing the edge of the folded message at him, sighting along it like the barrel of a gun, called, 'Got it now – you're the one into ballerina gear!'

Simon had long since taught himself to arrange his mouth into a smile whenever this subject came up. 'Ben's little joke,' he called back.

But she was already striding off and didn't hear.

Avoiding Alice's distant and frosty gaze, Simon turned away to find the pudding-faced nurse leaning over the counter, holding out a phone to him. 'A friend of Catherine's, wanting to speak to someone.'

Simon looked at the wall clock, then his watch; time was running out to see Wilson. He took the receiver hastily with a brusque, 'Yes?'

'Yes, hullo there. This is an old family friend of Catherine *Galitza*.' The soft male voice hesitated slightly over her married name. 'I wanted to know how she was.' The accent was muted but unmistakably Irish.

'I'm not at liberty to give out information over the phone.'

'I just wanted to know if she was conscious yet.'

Simon said grudgingly, 'She is.'

'*Ah.*' It was a cry of relief. 'And the operation went okay?'

'Operation?'

'Wasn't it yesterday? To stabilise the spine?'

Whoever the man was, he was astonishingly well-informed. 'Who is this?' Simon demanded.

A slight pause. 'My name is Terry.'

Simon pictured the flowers and the note, saw Catherine's reaction. 'Terry who?'

A more conspicuous hesitation. 'Devlin.'

He'd been right after all. Simon felt a brief satisfaction before his thoughts skidded off in several directions at once, all disturbing, all intriguing. How in the world had Devlin got hold of this information? Why on earth should he want it? Could he be planning to use it against the family in some way? Simon couldn't help thinking how furious Ben and Duncan would be when he told them about this call.

Now he retorted, 'The information you want is confidential.'

'I appreciate that, Doctor. I just wanted a general indication of whether she'd got through all right.'

'I'm not a doctor.'

'*What?*' There was a stunned pause. 'But the girl said— Who *am* I speaking to then?'

'This is the family solicitor.'

Another pause. 'Your name?'

'Simon Jardine.'

The silence drew out. Devlin's voice said very coldly, 'I was misinformed.'

A click and he had rung off.

With a glare at his watch, Simon strode rapidly out of the building into the last of the rain and, failing to find a cab, arrived at the police station a good twenty minutes after DS Wilson had left for the day.

Chapter Two

———

TERRY DEVLIN spent the rest of the afternoon in a state of angry self-reproach. The call had been a complete misjudgement, the blunder with the lawyer nothing less than excruciating. What had he been thinking of? Why couldn't he have waited? It would only have been a matter of an hour, two at the most. The wages of impatience. Now Duncan and Alice would know he had phoned, would be appalled at his intrusion. Daring to call himself a friend of the family! Presuming to ask about Catherine's operation! Having by some despicable underhand means managed to find out about it! They would be deeply offended, and who could blame them.

Just an hour or two. Why, oh why, couldn't he have shown a little patience?

He snapped instructions into the intercom, heard the imperious note in his voice, and moderated his tone abruptly. He was leaving, he told Bridget, would she cancel the rest of the day and summon the car immediately. Please – this more reasonably. If she would be so kind – this contritely.

Bridget came in, wearing her uncompromising face. 'You have an interview with the *Sunday Independent* starting in two minutes.'

'Can't it be put off?'

'I think that would be unwise since the journalist is waiting just outside and the time and venue have already been changed twice.'

He gave in with a shake of his head. 'All right. But nothing after that.'

Bridget asked if he would like the last two meetings of the day rescheduled for the morning.

'No. Tell everyone to go ahead without me.'

This was unheard of, not Terry's style at all, and he saw Bridget hesitate and eye him cautiously, like someone who has found herself in a cage with an animal of uncertain temperament.

He sighed and raised an upturned palm in a gesture that was partly an apology, partly an expression of helplessness, and she gave a rapid nod of understanding. Terry's daughter had been seriously ill, the recuperation slow, and during the months of his wretchedness and inattention Bridget had of necessity become a master of flexibility and improvisation, as well as a holder of forts, large and small. Then, just when his daughter seemed to be recovering and Bridget and the rest of the staff had thought life was settling down again, this new and terrible anxiety had overtaken him, a crisis whose cause he couldn't begin to explain to her, nor indeed to anyone else who found themselves on the receiving end of one of his unprovoked bursts of ill temper.

'And you mentioned you had a seven-thirty appointment this evening,' she said. 'Will you still be keeping—'

'You bet!' Terry cried with such ferocity that Bridget's eyes rounded momentarily. He repeated more reasonably, 'You bet.'

She plucked up courage to ask, 'Where is the meeting, so Pat will know what time to pick you up?'

'The Shelbourne.'

He saw her eyebrows lift in unspoken surprise.

'Shall Pat pick you up from home, then, at seven ten?'

'Seven twenty.'

'You want to be late?'

'I want to be late.'

Moving on from this topic with something like relief, Bridget asked, 'Will you want to freshen up?' This was her way of saying he needed to comb his hair and make himself presentable.

Obediently, Terry went through to the adjoining bathroom and faced the glass. He saw a man who looked weary, unhealthy and overweight. Since he had given up all pretence of taking care of himself some four years ago, these were conditions he richly deserved, though this didn't prevent him from feeling disappointment at the speed and relentlessness with which his body had given up the fight. Three extra stone had fixed themselves to his midriff and surrounding areas, his knees were creaking under the strain, his eyes had grown pouches and his skin had taken on a patchy uneven tone. His hair was beginning to grey and recede and if he was being ruthlessly honest there was a bare patch on his crown which, having been the size of a fifty-pence coin, was gaining currency by the day. His doctor told him the usual things doctors were paid to say, that he should drink less and eat less and take exercise. In the meantime, he looked nearer to fifty than forty. However, it was not his age or weight that preoccupied him as he looked in the glass, but the unprecedented doubt and uncertainty he saw reflected there. Maeve's illness had pulled him up short. Catherine's accident had shaken him. It seemed that fate was trying to bring him down off his high perch, and for the first time in his life he felt he had lost confidence and direction.

'It's a feature article,' Bridget reminded him when he emerged, washed and combed. 'For the main body of the paper, to mark the opening of The Kavanagh. Being a feature, you're to expect all sorts of questions.'

'I don't want all sorts of questions.'

'Anne did warn you.'

Anne was the PR girl. He hardly remembered the briefing, but then there was no accounting for the things that passed him by these days.

'Anne will be sitting in. She'll fend off anything unsuitable.'

The journalist was a tiny girl clad in tight black trousers and skimpy top with cropped blonde hair, and so young that she might have been Maeve's age and straight out of school.

His smile appeared mechanically; he had long since learnt to hide most emotions – certainly indifference and impatience – behind a smile. Assuming the rest of his required role was more difficult, however. From the time that the business world had started to take notice of him, some fifteen years back, he had been content to take on the various guises allotted to him by the press. First it had been the boy from the bogs on the up and up, the cheeky chappie who never missed a trick; then, following a round of acquisitions, he had become the daring young entrepreneur with the Midas touch; latterly, by a mysterious process of metamorphosis, he had grown into a pillar of the business community, a champion of the New Ireland. Not that he must ever fail to mention the rockier moments in his career, nor his humble beginnings, nor his gratitude for all that life and a booming Ireland had given him. He had learnt that so far as the press was concerned no cliché was so overblown that it should be left unprinted. Local boy made good. Rags to riches. Golden touch. Sometimes he felt like a living banality.

From the start it had always been easier to give them what they wanted, a Terry Devlin who was confident, outgoing, provocative, quick to joke and quicker to laugh. Over time this simplistic and distorted version of himself had become a habit as well as a shield. But today he could summon neither the energy nor the will to step into his role, and he faced the young journalist with an empty smile fuelled by an empty heart.

The journalist went straight to the large west-facing window at the far corner of his office to gaze at the view.

'That's why I chose this site,' he said, coming up beside her. 'It's the only place you can look straight along the river for such a distance – a mile in fact. The only place you can see five bridges in a row.'

Below them, the Liffey was a pale grey beneath an insipid May sun. The water had the smooth stagnant look of a canal. From this vantage point the bridges, one behind the other, seemed to number more than five and to crowd the river.

'Wasn't it the land prices that attracted you? The fact that this was a derelict area?'

'That too, of course.'

'Two birds with one stone?'

He broadened his smile. 'And why not?'

'And you can see The Kavanagh from here, can't you?'

'Just the top storey.'

'But gratifying all the same, I imagine.'

'Nice to keep an eye. Know it's still there.'

She turned to face him. 'But you're pleased with it?'

'It's the best hotel we could build.'

'Was that your purpose, to build the finest hotel in Dublin?'

'Well, it has five stars.'

'That wasn't quite my question. I meant the hotel that would be acknowledged as the finest in the city?'

'It's intended to be the best you can get anywhere.'

She tried another tack. 'Would you describe yourself as a proud man?'

'Without wishing to split hairs, in what sense do you mean?'

'A man who is proud of his achievements.'

'Ah, in *that* sense – yes. Overall.'

'Only overall? So there are things you're not so proud of?'

'Inevitably.'

She smiled ingenuously. 'Such as?'

Scenting danger, the PR girl moved forward, ready to catch his signal.

'Well, as you will have garnered from the press cuttings I have made a few mistakes in my time.'

'Business or personal?'

He made a gesture as if to award her marks for trying. 'Business. I would only count my business mistakes to a stranger.'

'But to yourself?'

'To myself?' He made a show of considering this. 'I think I could be relied on to count all my mistakes, honestly and without favour.'

'You have regrets?'

'Everyone has regrets.'

'What are your main regrets?'

'Business or personal?' And he offered a cautionary smile to show that this was just part of the game and he had no intention of answering anything to do with his private life.

'Both.'

'In business I would say that I have most regretted misreading situations. Misjudging them.'

'Does that happen very often?'

'Not often, but occasionally.'

'With serious results?'

He shrugged. 'With less than satisfactory results.'

'Are you a forgiving person?'

The question took him off-guard and he must have let it show because she quickly rephrased it more forcefully. 'Do you forgive people who have let you down?'

'Forgive? It's usually irrelevant by the time ... I don't concern myself with holding grudges, if that's what you mean.'

'Is that because you can afford to, or because you have a forgiving nature?'

He thought about that for a moment. 'Rivalry is perfectly natural, and you could say that rivalry is based on not forgiving or forgetting that someone managed to get the better of you last time, and making darned sure that you are the one to get the upper hand at the next opportunity. Men are naturally competitive. It's one of things that makes the world go round.'

'But if someone hasn't played fair?'

'Fair has many interpretations.'

'Done the dirty on you. Tried to cheat you.'

Immediately, he thought of Ben Galitza. 'I would not forget,' he said solemnly. 'No, I would not forget.'

'Forgive?'

'I wouldn't lose sleep over it. Life's too short. One must move on.'

'Indeed? People say you don't move on. People say you never forgive.'

'I can't answer for what people say.'

'So you don't care what they say?'

'I care very much what certain people say, people I respect.'

'And in your personal life? Do you forgive and forget there?' She was fishing unashamedly, though more in hope than expectation.

'By definition, that is personal.'

She nodded philosophically. 'Would you say it's necessary to be ruthless to achieve success?'

He laughed briefly but without humour. 'It's a fine word – *ruthless*. The ruthless businessman. The ruthless operator. The ruthless bastard. Those words always go together somehow, don't they? But I wouldn't say they were mutually dependent. And certainly not something to aspire to.'

'But the description might be apposite none the less.'

'It might. But I don't think it's necessary to be ruthless. Rather, *meticulous*. Or, if I had to be described by an adjective beginning with R, *resolute*.'

'So, you never give up.'

'I'm single-minded certainly. So long as I believe the prize to be worth winning.'

'You've never remarried, Mr Devlin. No prize worth winning among the ladies of Dublin?'

He didn't attempt to answer this, nor to laugh it off. Instead he gestured her towards the conference area. 'Why don't we talk about hotels now?'

The girl had the cheek to answer, 'I thought we were.'

On the journey home, Terry kept going back over his day and found little to ease his agony of mind. At some point after they had crossed the Liffey, Pat asked him if he would like to go round by The Kavanagh, a detour they generally made once or twice a week. But Terry was in no mood for discussions with the hotel staff, nor with anyone else for that matter, and told Pat he would go straight home. So they went on past Trinity and the Castle, towards the southern suburbs, and he was aware of little else until they were turning in through the gates and Pat was confirming that he'd bring the car round again at seven twenty.

Bridget must have phoned ahead as usual because Mrs Ellis was waiting at the door, one hand restraining Conn, who was struggling to break free and jump against his chest like the crazy dog that he was.

'Well, here you are again, Mr Devlin,' said Mrs Ellis, meaning that he was home once more at a reasonable time. 'And will you be wanting dinner?'

He explained that he would be going out again at seven twenty, he wasn't sure how long for, and would find something to eat along the way. 'But for Maeve . . .?' He knew that Mrs Ellis needed no reminding, but he couldn't help asking all the same.

'She's sleeping now,' said Mrs Ellis, 'but she said to wake her at six and that she might fancy some salmon for supper, though to be on the safe side I've prepared those vegetables she likes, the kind for stir-frying.'

For someone schooled in the Irish–French cookery tradition – her own incontestable description – a stir-fry represented something of a departure not to mention a challenge, and he made a point of thanking her for taking so much trouble.

Over the last few months whenever Maeve was at home and sleeping like this he would often go upstairs and look in on her as he used to do when she was a small child. Today, however, he headed straight for his study, partly because she would be waking soon and he didn't want to disturb her prematurely, partly because Fergal's call, now thirty minutes overdue, would be coming through on his mobile at any moment and he didn't want to take it in a place where he might be overheard.

Conn, the black thief, slunk in through the study door before Terry had the chance to shut him out and limped on his three and a half good legs to his unofficial perch by the bookcase, where, in an attempt to keep a low profile, he curled up immediately and feigned sleep.

Terry sat heavily at the desk and thought: Well, what is to be salvaged then? What can be done that won't make everything worse?

Duncan Langley would have heard about his call by now, perhaps Alice Langley too, and would have drawn their own conclusions. There was nothing that could be done about that. But Catherine herself – he could only pray to God that the family wouldn't tell her. It was too painful to imagine how she would judge him. She would think he was prying in the most gratuitous way, or – he flinched at each new thought – having the gall to patronise her, to take some sort of perverse satisfaction in her tragedy, or – most unbearable of all – that he still had 'feelings' for her and in some demeaning way was trying to win her favour.

Four years ago, in a burst of madness, he'd written her a letter, a foolish outpouring born of loss and loneliness and what he'd imagined at the time to be love. The letter had embarrassed her; it had very rapidly embarrassed him. She had delivered the only reply she could have made, also in the form of a letter, which he'd promptly consigned to the bin, as he very much hoped she had done with his. His phone call today had been nothing to do with this particular aspect of the past. If Catherine thought otherwise, there was nothing he could do to put her right. And yet, and yet . . . the demon pride would not be subdued. It pierced him, and he stung.

For a moment he could see no way forward. He stared at the photographs on the desk top, cased in bulky green leather frames, and felt that everything he held dear had slipped away.

Most of the photographs were from way back: a picture of his late wife, taken a few months after their marriage; a formal shot of the wedding itself, the two of them looking so young and nervous outside the church; then a series of Maeve, as a fluffy-haired baby, as a schoolgirl in uniform with a cheeky spark in her gypsy eyes, and most recently as a student nurse, looking serene and lovely in her natural unaffected way.

These pictures stood to the left. To the right was a picture of his most successful horse, Hellinger's Dip, a sprinter with three wins to his credit; and next to this, a landscape photograph of Morne, which had been Catherine's childhood home and was now, largely by chance or so it felt, his own, though he could never bring himself to think of it in that way. The photograph dated back to the late sixties, a time when Lizzie, Catherine's mother, had herself been a young woman there, and Terry, a feckless boy of eight or nine, had passed the gates every day on his way to school or more likely to snare rabbits, and had known the place, inevitably, as 'the big house', though by Ascendancy standards it wasn't big at all, a long way short of a mansion, more a modest English vicarage. In keeping with his memories of that time this was a distant view, taken from a hill a half mile away, the house a compact oblong sheltering in its verdant demesne, a rolling upward-sloping landscape of gardens, fields and woodland, which from this high angle looked larger and more impressive than its thirty acres. He had found a print of this photograph in an attic and had it blown up, partly because it was a fine picture, but also because he was a nostalgic man and it showed in all its leafy glory a patch of ancient oak forest to the south-west of the house that had been cut for timber a few years afterwards and then abandoned to hazel and scrub.

The small snap next to this was taken many years later. It showed Catherine and Alice sitting on the terrace at Morne, with Duncan in riding clothes leaning rakishly against a wall, and Lizzie standing with a tea tray she had just picked up from the table. Catherine was just eighteen then. Typically, both she and her mother were laughing.

The tea had begun awkwardly, he remembered. It

had soon become clear that the invitation had been Lizzie's alone, that Duncan regarded it as a familiarity too far. For Duncan, Terry Devlin was still the ungrateful odd-job man who, at considerable inconvenience to the family, had stopped turning up with any regularity some four years before. Even in the days when Terry had managed to get back every month or so to do the light repairs, Duncan had failed to grasp the fact that he was busy running two pizza restaurants and fitting out three more and could no longer drop everything to fix a loose slate.

Fragments of that day had stayed with Terry. From old habit, and perhaps a sense of irony, he had walked round to the side of the house and presented himself at the back door. He had an image of Lizzie welcoming him into the kitchen with a small cry of delight, of the two of them exchanging news secretively before they could be interrupted.

The weather had been fine enough for them to sit on the terrace, which neatly avoided the awkwardness of choosing drawing room versus kitchen. He remembered Catherine appearing from the garden, a figure grown taller and fuller and astonishingly self-possessed. Humming some pop tune, she strode past him into the house with a sidelong glance, a lift of one eyebrow and a brief careless hello, the effect of which would have been splendidly sophisticated if she hadn't pulled a larky schoolgirl grimace at the last moment. Alice's arrival was a more muted affair involving a silent approach, a flop into the remotest chair, downcast eyes and a series of monosyllabic responses. When Catherine reappeared, it was to take centre stage, with the recital of a series of extravagant tales, unashamedly featuring herself and her escapades, told amid excessive laughter and much twisting of her head and arching of her neck and other postures intended to beguile. Some might have judged her rather too full of herself, and there was no doubting that she enjoyed an audience, but Terry put her exuberance down to an understandable excitement at being young and pretty and fancy-free, and the discovery that in a troubled and gloomy world vivacity set you apart.

When they had finally exhausted the subject of Catherine, she fixed him with a challenging look. 'So, Mr Devlin,' – it had always been Terry before, and now she put a droll stress on the *Mr* – 'everyone says you're going very well, raking it in with all these restaurants. How nice to be rich!'

'Ah. It's the bank that's rich. I just keep them in profit.'

'You're *going* to be rich, then!'

He laughed. 'Well, I'm going to avoid being poor, that's for sure.'

'So, how will you spend it all? Cars? Houses? Planes?'

'I hadn't thought that far.'

She gave a cry of mock horror. 'Of course you have! Don't be so ridiculous! You've planned a Ferrari, a mansion in the country, a string of horses, enormous parties. Oh, please say you've got it all planned!'

Lizzie was eyeing her daughter tolerantly but also a little wearily.

Alice, staring fiercely into the garden, muttered in a tone of disgust, 'Oh, for God's sake.'

'I think I've got everything I want for the time being.'

'But that's hopeless!' Catherine groaned. 'I expected bigger and better things from you!'

Terry pretended to search his mind. 'I do have a new car on order.'

Catherine shot forward in her seat. 'A Porsche? No, no—' She flapped a delaying hand. 'A Merc convertible?'

'An Alfa. And not even the top model, I'm afraid.'

Alice murmured, 'He's already *got* an Alfa.'

'Have you? Have you?' Enjoying this flurry of her own making, not wanting it to end, Catherine wrinkled up her nose in disappointment. 'And you're getting *another*? Oh, how boring!'

It was then that Terry became aware of Duncan. For most of the meal Duncan had worn a distant inattentive expression, overlaid by the slightly glazed smile that was so characteristic of him. Now he was watching Terry with a glimmer of interest.

Later, while Lizzie and the girls were carrying the tea things into the house, Duncan launched into a monologue about European Community grants and interest rates and business conditions. 'Things are going pretty well already, of course, and are undoubtedly going to get better, but I've decided we'd be wise to tie up with an outfit in Britain, spread the risk, if you like.'

Failing to see the logic of this, Terry murmured non-committally, 'Aha.'

'People are getting far more confident about wine, you know. Bulk buying's going to be the big thing, no doubt about that, and we've got a real chance of cornering the market. This tie-in's going to let us negotiate the best possible terms.'

'What sort of volume are you handling, Duncan?'

'Oh . . . pretty large, pretty large.'

Terry found himself having doubts about this. In the same instant, he had a good idea of where the conversation was leading.

'You offer wine in your pizza places?' Duncan asked.

'Most certainly. We try to cover a reasonable price range. Not just plonk.'

'And who does your buying?'

He described their arrangement with a major wine importer.

'Well!' Duncan tapped the arm of his chair. 'We might be able to do something for you, you know. At least as good as they can, and probably a lot better. Why don't we talk? Never know, could be something in it for both of us.'

'Delighted.' As Terry handed him a card, he couldn't help wondering if his diplomatic skills were going to be up to the situation.

Duncan smiled magnanimously. 'Glad you're doing so well, Terry. Always nice to see a local chap getting on.' He stood up and surveyed the view. 'Well, must go and deal with the horses. Oh, yes!' He held up a forefinger, as if the matter had just come back to him. 'Terrible trouble finding anyone to repair the boiler. You wouldn't know of a good plumber by any chance? The chaps round here can't seem to handle it.'

When Terry phoned around he discovered that, in company with most other tradespeople in the area, the local plumbers were not prepared to call at Morne because of a long-standing problem with unpaid bills. In the end he sent one of his contract plumbers down from Dublin at his own expense.

It was a year later, when Lizzie had her first brush

with cancer, that Duncan touched him for a personal loan.

So, he asked himself again, what is to be salvaged?

With a troubled heart, he drew out some paper, picked up his pen and began to draft a letter.

He began *Dear Cathy*, only to cross this out and replace it with *Dear Catherine*. Formality seemed more appropriate in the circumstances.

I trust you will not feel I have overstepped the bounds of our acquaintance and what I hope, despite everything, to be our friendship, but I should tell you that I have phoned the hospital several times to ask how you were, and trust that you will not take this interest in your wellbeing amiss, but accept it as an expression of my continuing concern and affection . . .

No, no! He'd started from entirely the wrong angle! No, this sounded terrible! Crass! He ran a line through the words and, crushing the page into a ball, threw it into the bin.

Taking another sheet, he stared at it for some time before starting again.

Dear Catherine, I trust you continue to make progress. I hope you will not mind if I phone the nurses now and again to ask how you are (I have in fact called once or twice already). I realise that I may be overstepping the bounds of what you may regard as . . .

With a sigh, he dropped the pen and slowly tore the page into small pieces. Never had he felt the cost of his misspent schooldays more keenly. Over the years he had taught himself to write business letters in a reasonably proficient manner, he could argue contracts and figures any day, but *this* – how to strike the right note, how to communicate one thing without letting slip another, to convey regret without guilt, concern without anger – it was beyond him.

Abandoning the letter, at least for today, he called Bridget and asked her to arrange for another posy to be made from the final flush of May flowers at Morne, put on ice and flown to London as soon as possible.

'Will there be a note?'

He hesitated. 'Not this time. Just a card, saying it's from Terry.'

'With best wishes?'

At first he said no, thinking that it sounded too impersonal, then changed his mind: detachment was more appropriate. 'Yes, best wishes.'

Before ringing off he asked for the messages. He noted there was nothing from London, no delay to the evening meeting.

On impulse, he said, 'Tell Pat seven thirty for the car, would you?'

He would be fifteen minutes late because he could not bear the idea of having to sit and wait for Ben Galitza for so much as a single second, certainly not in the hotel that was probably the most public place to meet in all Dublin, and certainly not in a hotel that wasn't one of his own and where he wouldn't be able to busy himself talking to the staff. The Shelbourne had been Galitza's choice, and while Terry was in favour of neutral ground, he would have preferred somewhere more discreet.

The call had come through to Bridget first thing that morning. Thoroughly startled, heart in mouth, he had taken it immediately – expecting what, for God's sake?

News of Catherine? News of the police investigation? Fury? Accusations? Apologies? If the call hadn't taken him so completely by surprise he would have remembered that this was not Galitza's style at all, that Galitza had a breathtaking capacity for insensitivity. The voice had wrenched Terry back three years, to the joint venture on the west-coast hotel that had gathered so much speed so quickly that it seemed nothing could stop it. The voice was the same: cool, clipped, succinct. Catherine was 'recovering', Galitza had replied to Terry's enquiry, before going straight on to the matter in hand. He would like a meeting. As soon as possible. He would fly over. Terry had agreed immediately, which came as a surprise to neither of them. Whatever else, Galitza knew his man.

He hadn't said why he was coming of course; but then he hadn't needed to. Terry had never had the slightest doubt as to his purpose. The question was, how much would he have the nerve to ask for?

At ten to six Terry checked the battery and signal strength on his mobile and replaced it on the desk before him. Fergal was now almost an hour late with his report. In his general anxiety, he wondered if something had gone wrong, if Fergal had been caught or warned off. But he knew that this was to fall victim to paranoia, to overlook Fergal's experience and his infinite capacity for caution.

As if on cue a phone rang, but it wasn't the mobile, it was the house line. He answered it all the same.

'It's Dinah.' Her voice was smooth and warm as ever.

'Well now, how are you?' he asked, with as much affection as he could muster.

'Oh fine, but what about *you*?' This was her way, always to turn the subject round to him, to ask after his welfare.

'Not a great day, I have to say.'

'I'm sorry,' she said. 'And how's Maeve?'

'Oh, so-so.'

'And the food? Is she managing a bit more?'

'A little more, you know.'

'I got the phone number of that doctor everyone recommends so highly, the one in Howth. Would you like it? He's meant to be a marvel.'

'Perhaps . . . would you hang on to it? Maybe in a week or so.'

Dinah left it there. She never pushed her ideas, never tried to impose on him. In this, as in so many other ways, he could not fault her. Terry knew that if he had more sense he would persuade himself that he loved her, in so far as he understood what he meant by that nowadays; he would tell himself that she would be a good thing for him, that in her calm and accomplished way she would make him comfortable and content. Yet he retreated from the idea, some deep and stubborn part of him could not accept it, and this knowledge brought a weight of guilt. Sometimes when he stopped to think about it, it seemed to him that guilt had become the overriding emotion in his relationship with Dinah. He felt it now, corroding his thoughts.

She said, 'You'll be busy then, with Maeve.'

'Yes. I'm sorry. Perhaps next week.'

'Of course.' Her tone, as always, was light and without reproach. 'Now tell me, do you like the curtains? You must say if you don't, because if you don't I can alter them, change the trimmings or whatever.'

His mind was a blank. 'The curtains?'

She laughed softly. 'You obviously haven't been into the drawing room.'

'Give me a moment.' He picked up the portable extension and, almost tripping over Conn who dashed past him to the door, took it across the hall to the room that she called the drawing room but which he'd always been happy to call the lounge. He stared in astonishment at the mass of drapery bunched around the bay window and adjacent french windows. The curtains were huge and richly shaded in deep red and cream, with ornate curved pelmets and long tassels and great loops of fabric caught back from the windows.

'My goodness.'

'Do you like them?'

He had no idea what he liked or might be persuaded to like; no idea what was appropriate for a house such as this. In truth, he'd been quite happy with the way the room had looked before. It was only when Mrs Ellis pointed out the need for some new chair covers and a lick of paint, that he'd realised it'd been nine years since anything had been done, since two years before his wife's death. Friends had recommended Dinah for the work, and the next moment, or so it seemed, he'd found himself dining with her and signing up for a total refurbishment.

'Well, have a think about it,' she said.

'I'm sure they're fine,' he declared, though even as he said this he knew the decor was too rich and heavy for his taste and that if he had any courage at all he should tell her. Following on from this came the knowledge that he owed her other far more important truths, and that here too he was a terrible coward. He should tell

her what a poor prospect he was for her, how through
no fault of her own he was not husband material, but
the time never seemed right, in these troubled times
least of all.

'You sound rather down,' she said.

'I am a little.'

'You don't want me to come over for half an hour?'

This offer was made in a spirit of generosity, he
knew, but he refused it none the less.

'Terry,' she said with uncharacteristic hesitation, 'I
hate to mention it when you've so much on your mind,
but the holiday, it's getting late to book. Are we still
on?'

He had forgotten, or had chosen to forget, that in
three weeks they were meant to be going to Royal Ascot
for a couple of days, then on to the South of France for
a short break. 'Oh heavens, Dinah, I don't know . . .'
She made no sound, but he knew she would have been
planning for it, would have bought a hat, an outfit.
Steeling himself to take the sensible option, he said,
'Look, perhaps it would be safer to count me out for
the summer, until things get clearer.'

She said evenly, 'Of course.' Then: 'We could always
keep it to Ascot, couldn't we? Just a couple of days.'

'Best not. Too chancy—' He heard a distant ringing
and realised it was his mobile, back in the study. 'Speak
later!' Cutting Dinah off without chance of reply, he
hurried to answer the call before the message service
picked up.

'Sorry I was a bit delayed,' said Fergal in his unhurried tones.

'Nothing wrong?' asked Terry, clambering breathlessly into his chair.

'No. Fine.'

'So?'

'So – she's regained consciousness.'

It was on the tip of Terry's tongue to admit that he already knew this, but he checked himself. He didn't want to confess to having made the call.

'And she's lucid,' Fergal continued, 'which is a good indication for brain damage, by which, of course, I mean *lack* of brain damage—'

'She's talking?'

'And seeing. There's a question mark over the hearing – may be damage to one ear. But the other's fine.'

Terry shuddered with relief and anguish.

Fergal went on in his soft educated voice, 'They operated yesterday afternoon, as planned, and they're pleased with the way it went. They've also done a further round of X-rays and CT scans, so they've got as clear a picture as they're going to get for the moment—'

'What *is* the picture?'

A moment while Fergal phrased his answer. 'It's as they first thought – the spinal cord is damaged.'

'For certain?'

'For certain.'

'The operation – they couldn't fix it?'

'Spinal cord damage can't be fixed, Terry.'

Fergal never referred to him as Terry – never called him by any name at all in fact – and the unexpectedness of this only served to drive home the dread finality of his words. Terry heard an escape of breath and realised it was his own. 'Oh dear Lord,' he murmured.

'But they can't say what the effects will be, not yet—'

'Can't say or won't say?'

'Can't say. It's a bit complicated, but I can take a shot at explaining it if you like. After I got the information I went and checked it out with a doctor friend of mine. I think I've got it straight.'

Terry made an effort to clear his mind. 'Okay – go ahead.'

There was the leafing of paper as Fergal looked at his notes. 'The spine is damaged in two places, in the neck and in the thoracic region. The injury in the neck, at what they call C5/6, is a simple fracture of the vertebra – a hairline crack to you or me. It isn't likely to be a problem. The bone should mend itself over time and the scans suggest the spinal cord is undamaged. Just *suggest*, mind you, because here's where the uncertainty comes in – they won't know for sure about any effects until the body gets over the trauma and the swelling goes down and any natural healing has taken place. Then—'

'Healing? I thought you said . . .'

'I didn't say there wasn't any healing,' Fergal replied in his patient way. 'Just that damage to the spinal cord itself can't be mended.'

Terry hadn't entirely followed, but let it pass.

'Now the second injury is at the point known as T9. Here the vertebra suffered a comminuted transverse fracture. This means the bone was shattered and the spine was partially dislocated – I'm not sure that's the right word – put out of alignment, if you like. The operation fused the spine with screws and metal plates, so no further injury can occur. It's here that the scans show damage to the spinal cord, but again the doctors can't tell what the effects will be until the swelling goes

down and the body has had a chance to recover generally. And that takes months, sometimes many months.
There are different types of damage to the spinal cord,
like to the front of it, the back of it, the side of it, and
different degrees of damage, partial, complete, etcetera,
and only time will tell what's what. Oh, they'll be
transferring her to a spinal unit as soon as it's safe to
move her, by the way. No date yet, but in two weeks,
something like that.'

'But the outcome? What are they saying? What do
they think?'

'That's what I mean – it's too early to say yet, they
have no way of knowing.'

'Come on,' Terry protested. 'They must have their
views. I mean, privately.'

'Privately?' echoed Fergal with soft irony, as if the
information he'd already obtained hadn't been exclu-
sive enough. 'The only opinion I got was sort of third-
hand,' he said reluctantly, 'a junior source, if you follow
me. Not to be taken as totally reliable.'

'Yes, yes – and?'

'There'll be some degree of paralysis.'

'She won't walk again?'

'They can't know, Terry – that's what I'm trying to
say.'

'But it's probable?'

Fergal didn't answer and Terry took his silence to be
an answer in itself.

After a moment, Fergal said, 'I'm still working on
the police side of things. That might take a bit longer.
Starting from scratch there, if you understand me.'

'Of course.' Terry added, 'You've done fine. Thank

you. And Fergal? I want to extend the brief. Can we have a look at Ben Galitza?'

'When you say a look, are we talking surveillance or general intelligence?'

'General intelligence. For the moment anyway.'

Terry had only the vaguest idea of how Fergal obtained his information, and took care not to get any the wiser. Fergal had come from Cintel, a corporate intelligence agency Terry used from time to time. One day he had simply presented himself to Terry and asked to work for him on 'a one to one' basis because, as Fergal had put it, he wasn't really a corporate man, thereby implying that he didn't regard Terry as much of a one either. By degrees Terry had gathered that in Fergal's more misty past, before a flirtation with the priesthood, a short-lived marriage and what might have been a breakdown, he had been a lecturer in French at Trinity College, Dublin.

By any standards he had done an outstanding job this time round, and Terry said again, 'Thank you.'

'Have you had any more thoughts about the best way to play it with the police?' Fergal asked.

'I've thought.'

'You want to leave things as they are?'

'I do.'

Fergal made no comment on this, but the very fact that he'd asked was enough to send a small wedge of doubt into Terry's mind, and as soon as he'd put the phone down he sat staring out into the garden, raking over the pros and cons until he had satisfied himself once more that he had made the right decision.

Hearing a movement upstairs, he roused himself to

go and see Maeve. He wondered how it would be with her this evening: whether her day would have been good or bad, whether she would eat more than a token mouthful for supper. Most of all, he wondered how he would present the day's news to her without giving himself away. He poured himself two fingers of Jameson's and, downing them in one, poured another smaller measure and polished that off as well. As he started up the stairs he made a conscious effort to relax his features so that when Maeve looked into his face she shouldn't read too many of his troubles there.

He met her coming out of her room, and went to embrace her.

'How's my darling girl?'

She came into his arms and said, 'Better today, thanks, Dadda.'

'There's my girl.'

'The iron seems to be doing some good.'

'Your mother had the anaemia too. Runs in the family.' He shook his head. 'They should have spotted it before.'

He held her at arm's length. She did look a little better. He thought he could see a touch more colour in her cheeks, though the flesh itself was still drawn against the bones, her upper arms were still little more than matchsticks under his hands. For once he tried not to dwell on the doctors' incompetence, on the terrible hours when he thought he had lost her, and keep his anger focused on more worthy targets.

'Shall we go to Morne at the weekend then?' he said in a cheerful tone. 'Get some air into our lungs, take a walk or two in the garden. What do you say, my darling?'

Her face wore the exhausted look that had become so achingly familiar to him over the last four months. Sometimes he wondered if he would ever see her eyes bright again.

'If you like,' she said.

'Oh, I think a little walking would do us both good, wouldn't it? Your father most of all!' He tapped the bulge of his belly, which was something of a joke between them. 'What does the nurse say?'

She dropped her head abruptly, and his heart sank when he realised that in his thoughtless way he had said the wrong thing. 'Not too late to go back to college,' he said coaxingly. 'They're keeping your place—'

'I won't go back, Dadda. I won't.'

'But you were made to be a nurse, darling girl. You'd be the best nurse in the world.'

'No.'

'Is it England that's the problem? We could always find you a college in Dublin, so you could live at home—'

She raised her head and her eyes were brimming. 'No.'

He managed a smile. 'If that's what you want.'

He linked her arm through his and, covering her hand where it lay on his arm, walked her downstairs.

'Is there news?' she asked.

'News?'

'Of *Catherine*.'

'Indeed! I was going to tell you the minute we got downstairs. She's regained consciousness. I just heard a moment ago—'

With a gasp Maeve stopped and turned to him, and

for a moment her face came alive. 'She's going to be all right then?'

'Well, she's talking and hearing and seeing, so it's all looking good from that point of view.'

'What else?' she demanded hungrily.

'Well . . . she's off the danger list.'

'But what are they saying?'

'It's early days yet. You know – very early days. They need to wait and see.'

Instantly her mood plunged. 'What do you mean, they need to wait and see? There's something wrong, isn't there? Tell me.'

'Darling girl, they're investigating. You know better than anyone that sometimes they don't always find the problem straight away.'

'So there *is* something wrong! What is it? Tell me!'

She was taking great gulps of air and he hastened to calm her. 'Remember, darling, the fall was a terrible thing. Her body needs time to mend. Quite a while. There'll be rehabilitation, physiotherapy – all the usual things.'

Maeve shook her head and murmured, 'No, no . . .'

He persuaded her to continue down the stairs. She moved jerkily.

'I must go and see her,' she said.

'When you're better, darling girl. When you're better.'

'I can't bear it. I can't bear it. She was so kind to me, Dadda. So kind.'

Flashes of memory came to him from the long summer at Morne four years ago: a glimpse of Catherine taking Maeve off to show her something, a dress or it might have been shoes; then a picnic in the walled

garden, Catherine and Maeve sitting on the grass talking companionably as though they were of an age, not
eight years apart. Inevitably more painful and personal
memories followed, of the weeks of his folly and the
mortifying letter, but he shut these firmly from his
mind.

He walked Maeve into the small sitting room, to her
favourite chair facing the TV. She pressed herself into a
corner of the chair and drew her legs up under her. 'She
was so very good to me. So good, Dadda.'

Terry heard the crack in her voice and thought: Dear
Lord, please don't let there be tears tonight.

'If they're talking of rehab and physio, there must be
something seriously wrong,' Maeve cried. 'I know it. I
know it!'

'Hand on heart, darling, they really don't know.'

'But she fell! She fell!'

'We have to wait and see. That's all we can do.'

'I can't bear it, Dadda.'

'You can't take all the worries of the world on your
shoulders, darling girl. You must think of yourself.
That's your first duty.'

But there was no soothing her during these periodic
plunges into despondency and Terry wondered if he
should cancel his meeting with Galitza. He asked, 'You
have been taking all your pills, darling, haven't you?'

But she had turned her face away from him, her
head was pressed into the back of the chair, and he
knew he must attempt to cajole her out of this mood or
lose her to anxiety for the rest of the evening. Sometimes he wondered if he shouldn't try to shake her out
of it, literally take her by the shoulders, if it wouldn't
be a kindness, but he couldn't bring himself to do such

a thing, not when she had been so dreadfully ill, not when he could still remember in every terrible detail the night in the hospital when she had almost slipped away. Instead, he perched on the side of the chair and, threading an arm clumsily round her shoulders, rocked her gently, whispering softly, 'There, there, my darling girl. It'll all be fine, you wait and see.'

She murmured, 'I'm so sorry, Dadda, I'm such a nuisance to you.'

'A nuisance? That you could never be. Never!' Saying this, he remembered with a surge of emotion the only time he had felt truly frustrated by Maeve's dependence, the only time she had actually prevented him from doing anything he dearly wanted to do, and that was four days ago when he had longed with every instinct in his body to go to London and find out what had happened to Catherine and, while he was about it, to take Ben Galitza apart with his bare hands.

She was quieter now and he dared to hope that the worst might be over. He talked about the summer ahead, about the things they would do together, how he was going to take time off, a month or more, and spend it with her at Morne, how she was to invite friends, as many or as few as she wanted. When he finally ran short of words, he hummed softly to her, a poor rendering of 'Some Enchanted Evening'.

The thin summer light began to deepen imperceptibly, bringing the brilliant yellows and blues and golds that dominated the room into glaring focus. In keeping with his schizophrenic existence one inconsequential corner of Terry's mind was deciding that he really must ask Dinah to tone the colours down a bit, while another colder and more determined part was rehearsing the conversation he would have with Ben Galitza, speculating not only on how much money Ben would dare to ask for, but how much Terry would agree to give him and the heavy price that he would force him to pay.

At seven thirty he said quietly to Maeve, 'Now I have to go out for a while, just an hour or so. But you'll have to promise me you'll eat something while I'm gone. Will you? Otherwise I'll worry about you the whole time I'm away.'

She turned her face to him and fixing him with a beseeching gaze asked, 'You'll make sure Catherine's all right, won't you, Dadda?'

'Why, yes . . .' He hardly knew what to say. 'Of course I will.'

The light in her eyes faded as quickly as it had come.

Terry bent down to embrace her and felt the chill breath of uncertainty and doubt on his cheek.

Before leaving he turned the television on for her and commanded Conn to stay beside her chair. When he paused at the door to say goodbye Maeve was already staring dully at the screen.

Chapter Three

———

'IF YOU wouldn't mind.' Simon indicated the unlit cigarette poised between Emma Russell's fingers.

'Oh.' She looked around her with a show of exaggerated puzzlement as if a car was a perfectly natural receptacle for cigarette fumes. Then, in a tone of sudden understanding: 'Oh, it's *new*, is it?'

'No, I just don't want it smelling of cigarettes.'

She made a face and, closing her lighter with a snap, dropped the cigarette back into the packet. 'You must work *incredibly* hard to keep it this way.'

'I'm sorry?' They were crawling through the unlovely end of Earl's Court in a slow line of early-morning traffic that promised to last all the way to Notting Hill. The rain had stopped in the night but the sky was still heavy, and a dankness hung in the air. 'I'm sorry?' he said again.

'Do you ban feet?'

He glanced across at her, not quite sure of the spirit in which this remark was intended. 'I get it valeted every week.'

Her mouth twitched in a small knowing smile, as if he had just confirmed an accurate and rather unflattering picture of himself.

Irritated by this, and by the fact that he'd put himself

to considerable inconvenience by offering to pick her up and drive her to the police station on what was going to be an extremely busy morning, he said, 'I get a man to look after it for me, if you really want to know. I have to. I simply don't have the time for that sort of thing. I run three companies. Three very demanding companies.'

'Aha.' She was in the midst of an enormous yawn.

'And while we're on the subject of getting things straight,' he said in the slow steady voice he used to explain things to people who weren't too quick on the uptake, 'I don't work *for* Ben – the two of us are *partners* in a company that trades with Eastern Europe. We set up the company together. As *partners*.'

'Oh . . . right.'

He wanted to add crossly: And moreover there is no ballerina gear in my flat, there is nothing faintly out-rageous in my closet, only the costume my mother once wore when she danced with the Rambert, which Ben just happened to see hanging in the spare room when he invited himself to stay three years ago, when, having been kicked out by his then girlfriend at two in the morning, he was partaking of my hospitality, the shit.

He wanted to say all this and more, but he'd learnt from bitter experience that it would do him no good. If you tried to explain something like that, something that had grown into a huge joke, people weren't interested in the truth, they only wanted to roar with laughter and say how brilliant it was to be a cross-dresser, particu-larly such a cultured one – ah, the quips came thick and fast when people were having fun – and that he wasn't to be ashamed, not for a moment, not when it was so fantastically amusing to picture him in pink tulle. These people were shits as well, just like Ben. The secret was not to let it rankle, not to give anything away, but to rise effortlessly above it.

He did this now, saying smoothly, 'I know DS Wilson will appreciate this very much.'

'I still don't see why it can't wait,' Emma said peevishly, stifling another enormous yawn. 'I'm desperately jetlagged. My body's screaming: Three in the morning!'

Simon felt no remorse for having dragged her out. It served her right. She had started grousing as soon as he'd called and told her the police wanted to see her, had griped about having only just got to sleep a few hours before, had demanded to know why *they* couldn't come to *her* later in the day, for Christ's sake. Simon had bitten back the impulse to say that nobody was getting much sleep at the moment – certainly not him: four hours last night? five? – and that when it came to Catherine surely nothing could be too much trouble. Instead he had explained very firmly that everything of the remotest importance to the investigation had to be followed up immediately, that DS Wilson couldn't get away from the police station to see her, and – in an effort to humour her – that her information could be immensely valuable. Emma had finally agreed, though not without a series of resentful sighs that had caused him to grit his teeth. Devoted to Catherine? She had no idea what devotion meant.

Emma's litany of complaint was bringing an unattractive shrillness to her voice. 'Well, I hope they're not expecting a statement,' she said. 'I'm not going to hang around all day.'

'They just want to hear what you have to say.'

'But that's the point – I haven't *got* anything to say, have I? Not really. Why can't they talk to Ben, for heaven's sake? He'd be able to tell them much better than me.'

'I'm sure he will, once he gets back.'

She shot him a curious look. 'Yes, why *is* he away? There's nothing wrong, is there?'

'Like I said, he had to rush off.'

She shook her head and murmured admiringly, 'Ben!'

This reaction had a dreary familiarity for Simon, who had yet to meet a woman who wasn't prepared to forgive Ben behaviour that would be judged totally unacceptable in anyone else.

They stopped at some lights.

'Why didn't she get the calls traced?' Simon asked.

'Mmm?' Emma had leant her head back against the seat and closed her eyes.

'Why didn't Catherine dial 1471? Or get an intercept put on the line.'

'Didn't take it that seriously,' Emma murmured groggily.

'She told *you*, though. She mentioned it to you.'

After a while she muttered, 'I don't think you can get an intercept on a mobile, can you?'

They were moving off again and Simon was forced to look at the road. 'The calls came on her mobile?'

'Mmm.'

'You didn't say that.'

Reopening her eyes, Emma peered blearily ahead. 'I definitely said it was her mobile.'

Letting this pass, he asked, 'How long ago did it all start?'

Emma pressed her forefingers into the corners of her eyes, the scarlet talons like tears of blood. 'November?'

'And they've been going on all this time?'

'Haven't a clue. You see? I'm really *not* the person to ask.'

'And Catherine had no idea who this guy was?'

Emma's golden hair swung around as she slowly shook her head.

'Someone who had her number at any rate.'

'Oh, that could have been anyone, couldn't it? You know how it is in her line of work.'

He didn't know, and said so.

'Well, all her *clients* would have had her number for a start, wouldn't they? *And* all her would-be clients. *And* her suppliers. *And* all the little men who lay paving stones and build arbours and plant trees, who might have got the hots for Cath over the nasturtiums, or whatever it is that turns garden people on. And then there's the TV. Once you're on TV – well, you're inviting weirdos, aren't you?'

Remembering the three or four rather serious-minded programmes on garden design that Catherine had made for a minority network, Simon failed to see how this followed. 'Weirdos?'

'Sad people. Men in anoraks. People who get fixed on someone they see on TV. That's how I got on to the idea of a stalker. Though come to think about it, far more likely to be a wanker, isn't it? An anorak who wants a quick thrill with a soggy newspaper cutting.'

Simon winced. He could never get used to the way some women talked, the coarseness of their thinking, the ugliness of their language. 'But her number – how would he have got hold of it?'

'Oh' – she spun a hand through the air – 'a thousand ways.'

'Like?'

'Oh *God*—' She couldn't believe she was having to explain something so obvious. 'Well, he could phone the TV producers saying he wanted Cath to design this massive park for his stately home and could he have her number please, *or* he might phone the owners of one of the gardens in the programmes and say he was longing for a divine little knot garden just like theirs and what was the number of that clever little designer person, *or*—'

'I think I've got the picture,' Simon interrupted caustically, not taking kindly to being talked down to in this fashion. Staring glassily ahead, he maintained a firm silence and when he next glanced across it was to see Emma fast asleep with her head wedged against the window.

She groaned when he woke her. 'Shit. I hope this doesn't take long.'

The lobby of Notting Hill police station was built to withstand the assaults of an ungrateful public. The duty officer sat behind reinforced glass, and when Wilson appeared it was through a heavy steel pass door that swung shut behind him with a deep thud.

The sergeant was a lean wiry man of about forty with a straight back, a rapid handshake and an intense manner that suggested honesty, energy and dedication. His mouth shaped itself into a brief professional smile. 'Good of you to drop by, Miss Russell.'

'I wouldn't have called it *dropping by* exactly.'

Wilson looked mildly enquiring. 'Weren't you on your way to the hospital?'

She frowned at him. 'I wasn't on my way anywhere.'

'Good of you to come in specially, then.'

As the implications of Wilson's remark sank in, Emma threw Simon a suspicious glance.

Studiously ignoring this, Simon told Wilson he would go and wait outside in the car. 'Though I'd be glad of a brief word afterwards, if I may.'

'Sit in, if you like,' Wilson said. 'I'll find us some coffee.'

Simon said appreciatively, 'If that's all right. Thank you.'

'Dropping by!' hissed Emma sarcastically as they followed Wilson to an interview room.

Seated in front of Wilson with a coffee and a cigarette, Emma went through one of those transformations that left Simon wondering not for the first time at women's disconcerting ability to change moods at the drop of a hat. The petulant child vanished, replaced by a sympathetic and amenable woman, Catherine's dearest friend who was anxious to help in any way she could.

The story was much the same as before until Emma said, 'Sometimes he called twice a day.'

'Were these regular times?' Wilson asked.

'Oh, I don't know about that. Except . . . I think Cath said usually in the day. Yes,' she declared with greater certainty, 'the day.'

'What about weekends?'

She scooped her hair back from her forehead and tapped the ash thoughtfully off her cigarette. 'She didn't say.'

Wilson was about to ask another question when

Emma interrupted with a wave of her hand, a slow dipping of splayed fingers that accelerated into a flutter as she summoned up a half-buried memory. 'Yes – there was something else that stuck in my mind – something I couldn't work out at the time. Not sure I can now, really, but anyway – she said it was someone really *sad*. No . . .' She went trawling through her memory again. 'It wasn't so much sad . . . I think she said it was a very unhappy person. Yes, a very *unhappy* person. Now in one way I thought, yeah well, it would be an unhappy person, wouldn't it? But then I got this feeling she was talking about someone in particular, that she knew for sure that this person was unhappy, if you see what I mean.'

Wilson gazed unblinkingly at Emma. 'Knew for sure? But you say Catherine didn't know who this person was?'

'That's right. I mean – not a name.'

There was a pause in which Wilson seemed to be waiting for Emma to go on. 'You're suggesting', he said eventually, 'that though she had no name for this person, she knew something about him? Something to make her think he was unhappy?'

'Yes, that's what I'm saying. Yes.'

'The caller only ever spoke once, is that right?'

'That's what she told me, yes.'

'So it was from this one conversation?'

Emma raised a shoulder and turned her mouth down in a Gallic shrug. 'I suppose so.'

'Catherine didn't tell you what he said?'

'No.'

Wilson went through the motions of asking more

questions but it was obvious he wasn't expecting to learn much else and, winding things up briskly, he thanked Emma for her time.

When they reached the front hall Simon managed to catch Wilson's eye and gesture him to one side. As soon as Emma had gone ahead, Simon said, 'I was just wondering if you had any news that I could pass on to the family.'

'Nothing as yet, I'm afraid.'

'No leads?'

'Not really.'

Simon wondered if Wilson's air of efficiency was a cover for ineptitude. He was, after all, still a sergeant. 'Nothing from the labs?' Hearing himself say this Simon thought not without a certain pride that he was beginning to sound like a criminal lawyer.

'Nothing concrete,' Wilson replied carefully. 'However, there is one thing we are particularly keen to establish, and that is the identity of the man who called the ambulance.'

This was the man Simon had come to call The Good Samaritan. 'A neighbour?'

'Seems not. We've checked them all.'

'Not Ben Galitza?' Simon knew that it wasn't Ben, but he needed to play the part of the dispassionate professional.

Wilson shook his head. 'Barely conscious when the ambulance arrived. No, we're thinking along the lines of a passer-by. Saw the open door. Looked in. Spotted Catherine lying there.'

Simon had a vision of darkness and blood and silence, of a man rushing into the house and dropping onto his knees beside Catherine, staring down at her in horror, taking off his jacket and laying it over her. 'You think he might be able to help, this man?'

'Might have spotted a person leaving the scene. Could have been the very thing that made him go into the house – seeing someone running out in suspicious circumstances, leaving the door wide open.'

Simon nodded sagely. 'The call was taped, presumably?'

'Indeed.'

Well, tell me, you bastard. Don't force me to ask. 'Any clues there?' he enquired solemnly.

Wilson shrugged. 'Some.' For a moment it looked as though he wasn't going to elaborate, and Simon had to stifle the cry of frustration that sprang into his throat. Then Wilson was saying ruminatively, 'An educated voice – decidedly. Calm sort of type. Very businesslike. Very factual. And informed on medical matters, in the sense of having done a first-aid course, I would say. Something of that nature.'

Educated, calm, businesslike. This image flew around Simon's mind, seeking shape and substance. 'The ambulance crew saw this person, presumably?'

Wilson gave a sigh. 'Indeed they did, but according to them he disappeared so smartish that they can't give a description. For which read: they didn't take a real look at him, didn't ask his name, didn't see him go.'

Wilson moved purposefully towards the main doors and Simon was forced to follow.

'No description at all, then?'

'Nothing worth having. The three of them might as well have clocked three different people.'

Wilson led the way out into the street.

Simon said, 'If this man had seen someone running away, surely he'd have reported it by now.'

'You'd think. But people don't always realise the importance of what they've witnessed. Believe me.'

Simon made a gesture, as if to defer to Wilson's superior knowledge. 'You'll keep me in touch? You've got my number?'

'Yes, indeed.' Wilson turned as if to hurry away, only to think better of it and strike an awkward pose of informality, hands thrust into his pockets, face lifted to the sky. 'Ah, sun.'

A few yards away, Emma was leaning against the wing of Simon's car. Seeing her heavy shoulder bag lying on the bonnet, bristling with studs and buckles, Simon tried not to think of the scratches it would make when she dragged it off.

Wilson appeared to make up his mind about something. 'Look, there is one other thing,' he said in a low confidential tone, 'but I will ask you not to mention it to the family at the present time. No point in upsetting them, if you understand me.'

Simon felt a surge of tension. 'Of course.'

Wilson thrust out his chin. 'There would appear to be a somewhat' – he searched for the word – '*bizarre* factor in all this.'

Simon thought: Dear God, what's coming now? Will I be able to stand it? Outwardly he didn't move, didn't alter his expression of grave concern.

'I can't give you details, of course. But suffice it to say that we found some articles that give us reason to believe that the assault had overtones of – how shall I say? – a sexual or psychotic nature.'

Simon felt a rush of heat, his heart seemed to lift in his chest.

'No reason why your average burglar shouldn't be a bit of a psychopath, of course. On the side, so to speak. Or a fantasist, or any of these things they get off of the videos nowadays. But there we are, we have to take it into account.' Simon must have looked as startled as he felt because Wilson added, 'See what I mean – best not to mention it to the family.'

'When you say, *articles* . . .?'

'Well, I can't give details. You understand.'

But I don't understand, Simon wanted to argue. 'Of course,' he said. 'I'm just – shocked.'

Wilson was on the point of leaving. Desperate to detain him, Simon almost reached out to grab his arm. 'You're not saying she was sexually assaulted?'

'No – no evidence of that. It's just that this man appears to have been a bit – well, *sick*.'

Sick? He couldn't begin to think what he meant by this. His imagination roared off in a dozen different directions, all of them wild and disturbing and hopelessly mixed up. *Found some articles? Sick?* Feeling his cheek jump uncontrollably, he turned it away. 'So you'll be looking for someone with a . . . record of this sort of thing?'

'Let's just say we'll be keeping an open mind as to whether this person broke in with burglary or assault in mind.'

Simon almost laughed. 'So these calls . . .?'

'Oh, yes. Could be very significant.'

'I see.' With that, Simon was finally lost for words.

He had intended to drive straight to the hospital and leave Emma to pick up a cab there, but he was so agitated, his mind so numb, that he found himself driving her all the way back to her flat in Chelsea. At one point she asked what Wilson had told him during their huddled conversation. He fumbled for an answer, muttered something that made little sense and was unable to finish.

'You *are* in a state,' she remarked. 'What is it, for God's sake?'

He said with a break in his voice, 'They think he might have meant to harm her. Might have intended to, right from the outset.'

Emma absorbed this with a heavy sigh and a shake of her head. After a while he became aware of her watching him. She said, 'You think a lot of Cath, don't you?'

He couldn't answer, except to give an anguished nod.

'Ah, Mr Jardine. You've got me into a lot of trouble.' Sister Jones spoke in the weary tones of someone who is far too tired to get angry.

Simon looked suitably mystified, though having an idea of what was coming he felt the first stirrings of injured pride.

'The family say you're not representing them at all. They say we shouldn't have let you in to see Catherine. They say you aren't to be allowed to see her again.'

This pronouncement bore the stamp of Alice's vituperative little mind, but Simon was wounded all the same because Duncan obviously hadn't stood up for him. Even allowing for Duncan's erratic grasp on loyalty, he counted this an outright betrayal.

'They're under a lot of stress,' he said in a forgiving tone. 'I think everything will get sorted out as soon as Catherine's husband gets back.'

'But he *is* back.'

'Here?'

'Here.'

Startled, Simon looked at his watch. 'When did he arrive?'

'Oh . . . ten minutes ago?'

Simon covered his surprise with a brisk nod. Trying not to think of the work piling up at the office, he stationed himself by a window overlooking the atrium, which also offered a view of the passage leading to Catherine's room, and settled down to wait. He tried to work out where Ben could have got to last night that enabled him to fly back to London, get through the airport and into town by ten fifteen in the morning. Not Warsaw – Simon knew the timetable off by heart. Zurich? Paris? Guernsey? Not far away, that was for sure. But it must have been one hell of a panic to send him rushing all over town for three days and then off on a plane, one hell of a panic to make him leave Catherine's bedside. But listen, he wanted to say to Ben's face, what's so serious that you can't tell me about it? What's so momentous, so overwhelming that it doesn't involve me or the business in some way? Times are hard, Ben, remember? We've had a bad year, we lost the Polska CMC deal, we're seriously broke, if we're going to be in a panic about anything it should bloody well be the business. Listen, Ben – at this point he would look him dead in the eye – if you can't trust me who the hell can you trust, for God's sake? It's me, I'm your partner, remember?

There were seven messages waiting for Simon on his mobile; with the fifteen calls already listed on the white card in his breast pocket and the three meetings scheduled for the afternoon it was going to be a nightmare of a day. He needed no reminding that, yet again, he was shouldering most of the load. When it came to Duncan's wine company, this wasn't a problem. Since Simon had knocked it into shape and installed a half-decent manager it more or less ran itself. RNP was a different matter, however. RNP was a hands-on company that relied on vast amounts of time, effort and nurturing. How often had he said to Ben, *We're in the nurturing business*? Nurturing contacts, nurturing deals, nurturing the possibility of deals. In an average year, if he and Ben gave it their best shot and had a bit of luck, they managed to pull off four or five medium-sized deals. The simplest were straight sales, a shipment of grey-market Levi's from Detroit to Hungary, a cancelled order for amber from Poland to Singapore. But more often they were three-way deals, cash at both ends and a trade in the middle: a consignment of Laotian teak marooned by bankruptcy in Singapore that they traded to the Poles for a warehouse of glass, which they sold on, strictly cash on delivery, to a discount warehouse in Chicago.

They had decided right at the beginning that they weren't going to get involved in any deal so big that the whole business had to ride on it. Far too risky; they wouldn't let themselves fall into that old trap. For the first three years it hadn't been hard to stick to this policy for the simple reason that nothing very large had come their way.

Then they had got wind of the Polska CMC deal.

Simon thought briefly: I had a life before the Polska CMC deal, a life that was my own, running smoothly, going my way. The remembrance of what he had lost brought a shiver of bitterness.

Like all the best mistakes, they had been lured in effortlessly, by degrees. It had begun like any one of a dozen deals. There was a tip-off, a contact, they talked their way past the middlemen to the man in possession of the goods at Polska CMC, they got a feel for the price. A cancelled order for generators, twenty 2000-kilowatt machines originally destined for German hospitals. Dollar signs flashed huge and bright. Suspiciously huge, of course. But Ben wouldn't listen. He wanted to give it a go. *What's the harm*, he said, *we can only lose the deal*. So they had waltzed off to Warsaw with their double act, Ben the talker, the front-man, the Polish-speaking ideas man with the anglicised Polish name and the charming manner, Simon the detail man, specialist in small print and bank transfers.

Slowly but surely they had got sucked in. Slowly but surely they had neglected their other business until the other deals had melted away. Negotiations had spun out, months and months of suffocating red tape and back-slapping dinners and rousing toasts and appalling women with dubious hygiene and slobbering lips looming up in seedy Warsaw nightclubs; months and months of getting a feel for the way the wind was really blowing under the vodka-fired camaraderie, months of fine-tuning the terms and renegotiating the 'special payments'. All this while tying up the other end of the deal with the South American broker who'd found buyers across the continent and probably off it too. Getting the money in the right place at the right time was always an art form, but with this deal it was like writing a score for a hundred-piece orchestra, the web of transfers between Warsaw and Switzerland and the Caymans, banks and front companies in Panama and El Salvador and Monaco, the timing of it all, the bonds, the guarantees.

Three months ago it had been in the bag, signed, sealed, first bank transfers due any day. But as Simon should have known – did know deep down, but chose to ignore – it was precisely when something was almost in the bag that it leapt out and savaged you.

Now, as he attempted to revive the business, Simon wasn't sure whether it was his imagination or he was just suffering a general loss of heart but new deals seemed much harder to find.

He was finishing a call to Bahrain when he saw Ben emerge from Catherine's room and walk briskly down the passage towards him. He noticed Ben was wearing business clothes, a dark blue Armani suit he'd acquired a couple of months ago in Milan to add to the twenty or more suits already in his wardrobe, and a dark open-necked shirt. As he got closer Simon noticed he was unshaven and that his shirt was not as crisp as it might have been, which suggested that, against all habit and instinct, Ben had gone travelling without a change of clothes.

'Oh hi, what are you doing here?' Ben demanded vaguely, swivelling to a halt.

'I came to find out how Catherine was.'

'Oh, she's all right,' he said carelessly. 'So what's the latest?'

Simon shuddered with disbelief, he almost cried out, *How can you say she's all right? How can you stand there as if nothing's happened?* Then he remembered that they were all in shock, and that Ben simply had an unusual way of showing it.

Mechanically, Simon began to summarise events at RNP while Ben stared past him into the atrium, listening with the inattentive, faintly bored expression that Simon knew so well. His face was mending quickly, Simon noticed. The bruising around the left eye was still a rather bright shade of blue-black but the swelling had gone down, and beneath its strip of transparent plaster the gash on his left cheek, sealed by the minuscule stitches, seemed to be healing neatly. In no time he would be back to normal: unmarked, unblemished, the handsome man with the winning ways. Simon found himself thinking, *All bloody wrong*, and just as quickly pushed this thought from his mind, because if you allowed yourself to get consumed by the injustices of life you could go mad.

'So Bahrain could be a goer?'

As they talked Simon tried to gauge Ben's mood. With Ben this was never easy, since it was necessary to separate the person he chose to show to the world, a Ben who might be engaging, flamboyant, boyish, provocative, lost – he kept the most mawkish of these fronts for women – from the other Ben, the 'real' Ben in so far as this could ever be pinned down, the person who might be in a quite different and more prosaic mood, frustrated, annoyed, displeased, bleak. Simon saw the real Ben more often than most, saw him in his rare unguarded moments, between meetings, between phone calls, when for the odd minute or two he dropped the pretence that every moment of life must be lived to the full, at speed and with maximum enjoyment, and revealed a side of himself that was more sombre and altogether less straightforward.

The Ben he saw now – the outer Ben – was a man bearing tragedy intensely but bravely, with restraint and a kind of gruff bewilderment. As so often, his appearance had somehow come to match his mood, and he was looking Byronic, with his bruised face and unshaven chin, his grey eyes narrowed by fatigue, his light brown hair seemingly wavier and wilder and wind-blown. Yet for all his suffering, there was a light in his eye, a glimmer of something that, if not quite confidence, was pretty close to it – resolution perhaps – and, unless Simon was very much mistaken, relief.

Was the panic over, then? Had Ben, the master escape artist, done it again? Simon wanted to laugh aloud.

Instead, seeing an opportunity, seizing it hastily, he said, 'The cash situation's getting to be a real problem, Ben.'

'Yeah?' He was staring out into the atrium again.

'We have to decide. We could go on half salary until August, we could—'

'Look – I don't think I can deal with this now.'

'Later then?'

'Not today. Not this week.' Reading Simon's expression, he protested in a tone of self-justification, 'Got to look after Cath, haven't I? From now on, that's the only thing that matters. Look after her *properly*, Simon! Whatever it takes. Come what may. The full bit. Be there for her, one hundred per cent!' He nodded emotionally, caught up by his own fervour. 'It's the whole world for her from now on! Nothing but the best.'

Simon thought: He really seems to mean it.

'I'm afraid you're going to have to fill in for me, Simon. I mean, I'll do what I can, when I can – you know that. But Singapore, Warsaw – I just won't be able to make it. And Bahrain . . .' He gestured with upturned hands.

'I can do Bahrain and Warsaw, of course,' Simon replied. 'But Singapore – I won't have time, Ben. It's going to take a week just to—'

Ben cut him short with a rapid jerk of his fingers. 'Well, just do what you can, eh? What you can.'

When Simon didn't reply Ben made one of those comradely gestures he usually kept for business contacts, a complicit touch on the arm accompanied by a rapid uplifting smile.

'What about the cash problem?' Simon asked before he could disappear. 'Shall we go for the half salary?'

'Sure, sure.'

'But will you be able to manage?'

He appeared to consider this seriously for the first time, he gave a light-hearted shrug. 'I'll have to, won't I?'

Ben had always been a big spender, living up to his income and generally well beyond it, getting stuck into his half of the profits well before the end of the year. If he had savings Simon knew that they couldn't be large. The house had been bought with Catherine's only inheritance and a large mortgage.

He said, 'If it's a problem, I could always look into the chances of getting the Bahrain money up front.'

'Christ, no. We'd get stinking terms! No, no – let's cross bridges when we damn well come to them.'

A cash crisis was hardly a bridge to leave to the last

minute, but Simon knew better than to push the issue when Ben was in one of his more impatient moods.

'So, is that it, then?' Ben asked briskly.

'You got my message about the police all right? To say I was taking Emma Russell to see them this morning?'

He pulled an elaborate face. 'What?'

'I left a message at about eight—'

'Why the hell did you take *Emma* to the police?'

'Well, she told me about the nuisance calls and I thought she should go and tell Wilson—'

'What nuisance calls?'

'The calls that Catherine had been getting on her mobile.'

Ben screwed up his handsome face still further into an exaggerated expression of incredulity. 'For God's sake, what are you talking about?'

'I thought you knew. I thought you'd just forgotten.'

'I've never heard of any calls! Never! This is rubbish!' He was angry.

'Well, according to Emma, Catherine had been getting calls for some time, since about November. Sometimes as often as twice a day.'

'Look, you don't know what you're talking about,' Ben retorted in a shoot-the-messenger tone. 'Emma must have gone and got her wires completely crossed.'

'She seemed fairly certain.'

'For heaven's sake, Cath would have told me about something like that. If it was in the slightest bit *serious*, I mean.' He glared at Simon. 'And you went and took Emma to the police with it! Jesus, Simon, you might have waited, you might have talked to me first. Really! For God's sake!'

'You weren't around. I thought it was the right thing to do. And the police do seem to think it could be important. They're certainly taking it seriously.'

'That's all we need! Emma making a drama out of a crisis. Jesus! I'll have to go and sort it out with the police, I suppose. Tell them they've been sold a load of cobblers.' He gave a heavy sigh of forbearance. 'Oh, and speaking of dramas' – he jabbed a finger at Simon – 'Alice tells me you barged in on Cath when she was barely conscious. For Christ's sake, what's wrong with you? Have you gone mad?'

Simon took a deep breath. 'I didn't barge in on her, as you put it. I simply had a very quiet word to establish if she had any memory of the attack, so that I could keep the police away. I thought that was the idea – to make sure she wasn't hassled by them. Now if I've done the wrong thing, then excuse me!' He put a hand to his chest, his voice shook with aggrievement. 'But if I may remind you there's been no one else around to organise anything, to deal with the police and sort everything out. You were very glad of my help at the beginning, if you remember. Getting the locks changed and tidying up and everything else you couldn't deal with. And that was quite apart from the *business*. Now, don't get me wrong – I was *glad* to help, more than glad. I'd do anything, anything at all, you know that. But when you *disappeared*' – he emphasised the word mercilessly – 'and Duncan asked me to deal with the police, what was I meant to do – refuse? And after all that, what do I get but a bollocking from Alice!'

'All right, all right, keep your hair on. It's just Alice being Alice, you know how she is.'

'Incredibly, unbelievably rude.'

'Needs a good screw, as usual.' Ben threw out such remarks all the time, the more outrageous the better. They were made largely for effect, but also because for him there was more than a grain of truth in such primitive beliefs.

'You don't understand,' Simon cried, 'it's *me* she's got it in for. You should have seen her. It was hideous.'

'Perhaps it's you she wants to shag.' This thought caused him such amusement that he laughed loudly and suddenly.

'*Oh, for God's sake!*'

Simon's explosion of fury was so violent that it startled both of them. Ben thrust out a quieting hand. 'Look, calm down, will you? Calm down. It was only Alice. She's a pain, everyone knows that.' Then, dropping his head and looking at the floor, he muttered grudgingly, 'Listen, I do appreciate everything you've done. Really. I'm very grateful.'

Simon thought: And well may you look guilty, you shit. You should be bloody ashamed of yourself.

Ben looked at his watch. 'Hell – I'm late. Are we done? Anything else?'

'One thing,' Simon said. 'There was a call yesterday from Terry Devlin.'

'Oh yeah?'

'He seemed to know an awful lot about Catherine – about her condition, I mean.'

Ben was checking the time on the wall clock over the nursing station.

'Medical information,' Simon persisted. 'Stuff he could only have got from someone here.'

'Aha.' He was determined not to pay attention.

'*Ben*, are you listening? Someone's been talking out of turn, passing on confidential information.'

Ben was combing his fingers through his hair and pulling his shirt collar into shape. 'Well, it wasn't any of *us*, was it?' He was looking around for some shiny surface in which to check his reflection.

'Well, if it was any of the staff we should make a strong complaint.'

'I'll look into it.' It was the tone Ben used to humour people when he wanted them off his back.

'Aren't you bothered? I mean, it's none of his damned business.'

'Mmm?'

'But why would he want it—'

Ben gave the sudden explosive sigh of someone who is being sorely tried. 'Simon – for God's sake, because he's a control freak. Because he's got this thing about the family. Because he can't let go.'

When Simon still didn't get it Ben took a long-suffering breath and spelled it out as if for an idiot. 'Because he's soft – in – the – head.' He raised his eyebrows, he lifted a palm in the pose of someone awaiting a sign of comprehension. 'About – *Cath*.'

'You mean . . .'

'He had a thing for Cath's ma, Lizzie. Now he's transferred it to Cath. Call it continuity.'

'Oh.'

'Sort of sick really.'

'But I thought he pulled a fast one over the Langleys' house in Ireland.'

'He did. But then, that's always been his way of showing affection – to shaft his friends. Though it has to be said that Duncan was easy meat. Bit off more than he could chew . . .'

In the flow of people along the corridors Simon became aware of a familiar figure heading towards them and signalled a warning to Ben.

'. . . Out of his league on every front, silly old fool. Always been clueless when it comes to—' Catching the signal, Ben turned and, without a break in his flow, said easily to Duncan, 'Hey ho, Dunc. We were just sorting a few things out. So . . . I'm off to Fortnum's now to get some goodies for Cath. Cheer her up. Bit of champagne and caviar.'

'Good idea,' said Duncan, taking it literally. 'Can't do any harm, can it? Just a spoonful.'

Clapping Duncan on the arm, Ben gave a delighted chuckle, and for an instant he was the old Ben, the hard-living, hard-playing rogue with the appetite for life. 'No harm at all!'

As Duncan watched his son-in-law stride off, his lip trembled, he seemed to control his feelings with difficulty. 'What a thing for the poor chap. Married less than a year! Just setting out on the road of life. What a start! And being so bloody *good* about it. Determined to do his best for Cathy, you know. Going to pull out all the stops. Makes one feel very *moved*, you know. Very proud.' His voice reverberated with such honeyed, almost theatrical emotion that Simon couldn't help thinking that on some typically ill-judged level Duncan was rather enjoying the drama surrounding his daughter.

'How is Catherine?'

'Mmm?' Duncan turned and looked at Simon with

faint surprise as if registering his presence for the first time. 'Oh, coming along. Coming along. The doctors are doing a marvellous job. Under the best chap in London, you know, the very best. I made sure of that.'

Selective amnesia was a peculiar talent of Duncan's and his memory was never more uneven, it seemed, than when Simon had done him a favour. Not only had Simon been the person to suggest they should check out the consultant, but at Duncan's request he had also been the one to make the necessary enquiries.

'The operation yesterday – was it a success?'

'Oh, absolutely!' Duncan said expansively. 'Went very smoothly. Of course, it'll be quite a while before she's back on her feet. You know – lots of physiotherapy, lots of rest.'

Back on her feet. Could it be true? Everything Simon had heard told him it was unlikely, yet this didn't stop a small bubble of hope from rising irrepressibly to the surface of his mind. 'So . . . is that what they're saying, that she's going to be all right?'

'Oh – in time! In time! You know.'

Simon's hopes subsided. He should have remembered that making the right noises was part of Duncan's stock in trade, like his easy charm and air of patrician authority. For this reason it was never easy to get a fix on Duncan, never easy to tell what, if any, of his utterances were true.

'And how about her memory, Duncan?' he asked solicitously. 'Has it come back at all?'

'Memory?'

'The attack – does she remember anything?'

'Good God, haven't asked her!'

'It's just that I told the police that she couldn't remember anything, and it's on that basis that they're staying away.'

Duncan looked blank.

'You did ask me to deal with the police, if you remember.'

'Did I? Well, there we are. But now that things are quieter . . .'

'You did ask me to see the police, Duncan. Very definitely. And I'd be grateful if you could tell Alice, so that she doesn't go around saying that I—'

They were interrupted by an apologetic Sister Jones, pausing in a rapid flight up the corridor to confirm some arrangement with Duncan. Instantly Duncan produced his ready smile, his twinkling gaze, his attentive manner. With his fine even features, his high forehead and greying hair combed back to reveal a widow's peak, his lean stooped figure clad in a well-cut summer suit and clubbish tie, he had the distinguished air of the international boardroom, the embassy or the judge's chambers. By background, you would guess county and a well-trodden path through public school and Oxbridge. The truth, Simon knew, was somewhat closer to the Eastbourne suburbs, an independent day school and a short stint at some non-accredited college in America. From his father Duncan had inherited a love of horseflesh, though like his father it was invariably the laggardly and lame that attracted his money, and barely a month went by that Duncan didn't fret about his salary, his shares and the scandalous cost of living.

As Sister Jones hurried away, Duncan assumed an industrious expression. 'Before you go, Jardine – about

Ben. I'm worried . . . He needs to have some of the load taken off his shoulders, you know.'

'When you say *load*, Duncan?' It always got Simon's back up when Duncan called him by his last name, like some sort of hired hand.

'His workload,' Duncan declared as if this should have been self-evident. 'The thing is, while Ben's got so much on his plate – taking care of Catherine, dealing with the doctors – he won't have the time to run the business as he'd like. Simply not possible.' He spoke in the sonorous tone he used for board meetings, the inflated voice of authority and experience. 'And if I may say so, he shouldn't have to dash around the place like he did yesterday.' He shook his head reproachfully. 'Something *you* could have done, surely, Jardine. Not too much to ask, to step in and do the smaller trips.'

'He wasn't actually on RNP business yesterday, Duncan.'

Duncan frowned, as though Simon were making a rather shoddy attempt to deflect the argument. 'Difficult for you to deal with the core business on your own, of course – I do understand that. But I was thinking that if you liaised with Ben on a day-to-day basis, took instructions on the main decisions, then you might be able to keep things ticking over until Ben can get his eye on the ball again. I know it's a hell of a gap to fill—'

Simon said stiffly, 'I'm filling most of the gaps already, Duncan.'

'But you don't speak Polish.'

'I speak enough.'

'But you don't speak it *fluently*,' he argued triumphantly. 'And then there are all Ben's *contacts*. No,

no—' He shook his head decisively. 'You couldn't be
expected . . . not on your own . . . The thing is, what I
wanted to say was that if things threaten to go belly up
in any way, I know this fellow who might be able to
step in. Excellent chap. Bit of a linguist. Excellent
contacts—'

Simon snapped, 'I think I can handle things on my
own, Duncan.'

'Oh? Well, if you're sure,' he said doubtfully.

'Just like I handled *your* little crisis.'

Duncan didn't like to be reminded that his business
had been in need of rescue. 'Hardly did it on your own,
old chap,' he corrected him pedantically. 'A team effort.
That's all I was suggesting—' Reading Simon's
expression, he broke off with a look of mild injury.
'Never doubted you would do your best, er – Simon. It
was just a suggestion, that's all. Just trying to help. Just
trying to do the right thing by Ben.'

It was typical of Duncan to back off suddenly, to
justify himself with an air of baffled innocence, but it
didn't wash with Simon who had no time for insincerity
of this or any other kind.

'So – Alice,' Simon said resolutely. 'You'll tell her I
was acting on your instructions?'

'The thing is, I know you meant well, Simon – no
doubt about that – but it was a bit much, you know.
Going in and bothering Catherine like that.'

'I didn't *bother* her.'

'She was upset.'

'She was upset because of what has happened to her,
Duncan. Not because of *me*.'

'You didn't have to tell her. It was up to us, her
family.'

'I'm sorry, she asked me what happened and I told her. Very gently. Incredibly gently. What was I going to do – pretend she'd been in a car accident?' Simon was unable to prevent his voice from breaking slightly as he added, 'I think the world of Catherine. I would never do anything to harm her.'

'Oh well, there we are, there we are,' Duncan muttered, with a glance around the hall. 'But, look, Simon, the thing is, Ben and I will be able to handle everything from now on. So, er – you know.'

'I don't think I do know.'

'No longer necessary for you to deal with the police. And, er, while we appreciate your concern – your support – well, we're fine here too.' He angled his elegant head, waiting for a sign from Simon that he had understood. Forced by Simon's silence to elaborate, he said, 'No visitors except family, you see.'

'I see,' Simon said tightly. 'When she's a little better then?'

Duncan made the sort of gesture that could have meant anything, but which Simon recognised from long experience to be a rejection. From equally long experience, Simon carried off his departure with a composure and style that even Duncan with his fastidious eye for the social niceties couldn't have faulted. It wasn't until Simon reached the street that he allowed his humiliation and anger full rein. After all he'd done! After all the work he'd put in! Duncan and Alice had the nerve to treat him this way, like some paid hand! Had the nerve, he thought with a steadier passion, to think they could manage without him. Well, he thought grimly, time would teach them otherwise.

He continued to quiver with repressed indignation as

he drove home to Chelsea to drop the car off. It was only in the cab on his way to the office in Marylebone that his deeper disquiet about Wilson's words worked its way to the surface once more, and he again brooded unhappily on the 'overtones', the 'articles' that had been found next to Catherine. He racked his imagination as to what this something could be, his mind flitted across horrors and obscenities culled from films and books, and each image distressed and frightened him more than the last. He thought with a swell of emotion: I must stay close to her, I must protect her. And the thought of the months of guardianship ahead filled him with quiet joy.

Reaching the office, he got through his own work and much of Ben's as well, and some of the secretary's too because she was off sick. He worked quickly and conscientiously because it was not in his nature to do anything sloppily, but at some point in that long day a thought came to him and kept returning until it took on the solidity of a decision. He would give Ben and the business three months before leaving; he would not abandon either until they were functioning properly again. *He* at least understood the meaning of loyalty. He searched his compendious memory for the apt quotation and located it with satisfaction. *I'll prove more true than those that have more cunning to be strange.*

It was nine when he finally locked up. He took a cab to a fashionable media bar in Soho and drank two Manhattans before going on to a club he knew well, where the pleasures were certain and the price well within his budget.

Chapter Four

————

IN THE afternoons Catherine slept fitfully; a way of passing time or of postponing it. The interventions and routines of medical rounds were over, the physiotherapist gone, the family not expected nor encouraged until after five. She lay, eyes closed, absorbing the sounds of the city: the swish of tyres in the monsoon wet, the suppressed throb of the hot dry days, the rumbling of a stationary bus in the build-up to the rush hour. With these sounds came dreamy half-realised images of umbrellas and scorching sunshine and pallid faces on the number 19 of her student days. A life passing her by.

Her sense of detachment was reinforced by listening at a remove, with one ear only, for while her right ear had become attuned to the world beyond the window, the other explored an obscure inner world, a new-found universe in which reverberations and echoes moved secretively through layers of silence. The bones of her left ear had been damaged in the fall. Oddly, or perhaps not oddly at all, she concentrated her resentment and irritation on this one deadened ear, which of all her injuries seemed openly offensive.

Sleep, when it came, was uneasy, filled less with nightmares than a deep extended anxiety. Sometimes when she was disturbed by one of the staff she woke to find another more particular image imprinted on her mind, of an amorphous shadow blotting out the light, of seeing herself running, running, though never quite fast enough, so that she felt the heat of his hand inches from her shoulder. This scene repeated endlessly with different variations, darkness, light, doors, corridors. An anxiety dream. Or a reality dream.

'Catherine?'

She woke with a beat of alarm.

'Sorry to disturb you.' It was one of the black nurses, a woman with a rich mellifluous voice.

It was a moment before Catherine regained her bearings. Late afternoon. Hot and airless. Her last day before being moved.

'There's two police,' the nurse said. 'They want to know if they can talk to you. One is named Wilson. He says you know him.'

'Yes,' she said. 'I'll see them.' *And get the whole business over and done with*.

She asked the nurse to bring her a face-wipe, comb and mirror and to give her a few minutes before letting them in. Since losing most rights over her body, tidiness had become excessively important to her.

She did not realise that Wilson had entered the room until she felt the gaze of his button eyes. Behind him came the broad smiling face of Denise Cox. When Wilson made for Catherine's deaf side it was Denise who called him back with a diplomatic 'Boss?' and signalled him round to the other side of the bed.

'Right,' said Wilson, backtracking.

Denise was the victim liaison officer, a big-boned big-busted woman of about Catherine's age with cropped bleached hair, startlingly blue eyes and a soft confiding voice.

'So,' Denise said, 'off on your travels tomorrow.'

'Out of jail,' Catherine said. 'Into prison.'

Denise chuckled. 'They say prison's an improvement. Still running a florist's shop, I see.'

The flowers had kept coming, many from names she didn't recognise, people she and Ben must have met at the races or weekends away, others from distant friends of the family, or, on Ben's side, émigrés and ancient Polish countesses. 'Don't know half of them,' she said. 'Don't know how they heard.'

'Catherine, it was in the newspaper.'

This startled her. 'Why?'

'You've appeared on television. It made a story.'

'I don't want to be a *story*. Why was it a story?'

Denise used her reassuring voice. 'It was just a small piece. Nothing since.'

Wilson moved forward. 'We have no particular developments to report on your case as yet. But we still have several avenues to pursue. Three detectives are on the case this week.'

Catherine said, 'You're putting in a lot of work.'

'And will continue to do so,' he replied, adding one of his rather forced smiles.

He had no idea of how little she expected from him. She had no wish to know anything about her attacker, no wish to discover any details of his doubtless miserable life. While he remained an abstraction he remained safely in the past, like an encounter with lightning or a tornado, something which, though catastrophic at the time, would never touch her again.

'There's one thing we're having difficulty with,'

Wilson said in his rather high voice, 'and that's the list of stolen property. Is your husband away? Abroad perhaps?'

'No.'

'Oh?' He looked a little puzzled. 'I see ... He promised us a comprehensive list of missing items some time ago, but we can't seem to make contact. We've left numerous messages.'

Automatically coming to Ben's defence, Catherine said, 'He's always very busy. He works very hard.'

'But he's in London? He's been in to see you.'

'Oh yes.'

Wilson's mouth twitched. 'Could you ask him to get in touch? It would be most helpful.' Lifting his head, drawing himself up as if to indicate the start of the real business, he said, 'WPC Cox informs me that you have something to tell us.'

'I have very little to tell you,' Catherine informed him. 'I hope she explained.'

At Wilson's shoulder Denise nodded in confirmation. Wilson made a concessionary gesture. 'You've remembered something at any rate.'

Catherine persisted, 'Nothing useful, really.'

'All the same, we'll take it down as a statement and ask you to sign it, if that's all right.' He half turned to Denise, as if to remind himself of the right procedure for hospital cases. 'Yes – so long as you're up to it. You will stop me if it's too much?'

Catherine told herself, *Soon it will be over and done with*.

Denise produced a pad and sat down near the foot of the bed, so that all Catherine could see of her was the crown of brilliant yellow hair.

Wilson remained standing, hands in pockets, affecting an unhurried air that was belied by the restlessness in his eyes. 'If we could just get the matter of these calls out of the way. For the record. You say they were wrong numbers, not nuisance calls as such?'

'That's right. I'm sorry you were told otherwise.'

'How could you be sure they were wrong numbers?'

'A man asked for someone I'd never heard of.'

'He asked for the same person every time?'

'The other times he just rang off when he realised he was still getting the wrong number.'

'So in fact – forgive me – but you had no way of knowing it *was* the same caller?'

She explained slowly, 'But I do, I did. The other calls came regularly after that first call. And once I got the last call details.'

'Last call details?'

'The number. Off the 'last call' thingummy . . . function. It was the same number both times, not one I knew.'

'Did you make a note of the number?'

'No.'

'It wouldn't be stored on your mobile?'

'No. It only keeps the last – I think – ten calls.'

Wilson accepted this with no sign of disappointment. 'Do you remember if it was a London or country number? Or a mobile?'

'Really, it's so long ago. But . . . London, I think.'

'And how many calls did you get in all?'

She didn't try to suppress the flutter of exasperation in her voice. 'Oh – five? Six?'

'And all on your mobile?'

'Yes.'

'Spread over what length of time?'

'Look, I really can't remember.'

'But somewhere around Christmas?'

'I suppose so, yes.'

Wilson appeared to absorb this slowly. 'I'm not clear, then, why you told Emma Russell that you'd been having nuisance calls since November.'

'Emma was there when I got one of these calls. She got the wrong end of the stick. That's all.'

'She sounded very sure.'

'She always does.'

'Ah.'

And still Wilson seemed reluctant to let it go. Did he actively disbelieve her? Or did he think she'd forgotten to mention something whose significance only he could recognise?

'The television series you did, Catherine – it came out last autumn, didn't it? Did you get any calls as a result?'

'From possible clients, yes.'

'Is there a list?'

'It'll be on my desk at home somewhere.'

'Could someone find it for us, do you think?'

'I'll ask Ben. But, really, they were just ordinary people – people with gardens.'

'That may well be so, but we need to check all the same.' He moved on at last. 'Now the evening of the burglary . . . Why don't you take it at your own pace. In your own time.'

It was hard to get started. She looked up at the ceiling and tried to fix on the fragments of memory that had been coming back to her mysteriously and haphazardly, like snapshots arranged out of order.

'I remember the journey home from France,' she said. 'I remember the airport, and picking up the car and arriving at the house. I remember finding we had been burgled and hearing the sounds of a fight and running upstairs. Then this . . . shape rushed at me out of the darkness. I'm afraid that's all, from that time anyway. Later . . . I remember someone being there. I remember someone saying that help was on its way.' Catherine pulled a face. 'There you are. I warned you that it wasn't very much.'

Wilson nodded again, sombrely. 'Could I ask about the trip to France?' he asked in his rather nasal voice. 'This was a holiday?'

'A short break, yes.'

'You were away how long?'

'Three . . . four days.'

'You were planning to stay longer though?'

'Yes . . . Ben had to come back a couple of days early, and in the end I decided to come back with him.'

'Who knew about your plans?'

'What?' She had to think about this. 'My father . . .' She corrected herself uncertainly, 'No . . . I don't think I told him in fact. I don't think I told anyone. Not that I remember anyway.'

'The people you were staying with in France,' he prompted.

'Oh yes – them.'

'And your husband, he was coming back for a meeting, I believe?'

'He was going to America for a meeting the next day.'

'Ah, so his business associates in America would have known. Anyone in England?'

She sighed. 'You would have to ask him.'

Wilson made a show of absorbing this suggestion, and Catherine wondered if he was rather slow or rather pedantic or both.

'Could I ask about when you got to the house?' he said. 'It was your husband who unlocked the door, was it?'

'Yes.'

'And went in first?'

'Oh yes. I was still in the car, I was going to park it. I only waited till I was sure he was in the house.'

'And he got in all right?'

'Eventually.' This picture was strangely clear. 'He had a bit of trouble. That's why I waited. The key . . . it took him several tries. He even looked to see if he was using the right key. He had to sort of swing on the lock before he could get in. Then he turned and waved to show he was in.'

'And how long was it before you parked and got back to the house?'

'Oh – five minutes? There were no parking places. I had to go into the next street.'

'When you got back?'

'I knew something was wrong immediately. The house was dark. And I heard a strange sound. I called out.'

'What did you hear?'

'A shout,' she answered with reasonable confidence. 'Ben . . . shouting.'

'Do you remember what he was saying?'

'Saying?' Such detail was beyond her. 'No . . . I can't remember. No . . .'

'You say the house was dark. Were there no lights at all?'

Reluctantly, she dug deeper into her memory. 'There was one on, I think. Maybe two. But across the hall.'

'In other rooms?'

She closed her eyes for a moment, better to see the night. 'Yes.'

'Can you remember which?'

'The sitting room, I think. And the kitchen. Or it may have been . . . No, the kitchen. Down the passage. Yes, I remember that.'

'No light in the hall?'

She thought about this. 'No.'

'You didn't try to turn the hall light on?'

She was slow to speak because her answer was going to sound odd, even to herself. 'I don't think I did, no.'

'The kitchen and sitting-room lights,' Wilson continued, 'they hadn't been left on while you were away?'

Again she couldn't think why he should want such detail; again she answered obediently. 'The sitting room has a light on a time switch. A small lamp. I think it may just have been that one light, yes. But the kitchen – we never leave a light on in there, never.'

Wilson shifted his weight and attempted an expression of encouragement. 'Please – do go on again. From the moment you heard the sound and realised something was wrong.'

A pause while she searched through her memory so that she could be sure to stick to the steadier images, to what was reasonably certain, and stay clear of the less reliable visions that flickered uncertainly at the edges of her memory, like unfocused photographs. 'Yes . . .' she resumed with an effort. 'I heard Ben shouting upstairs. I called, but he only shouted again, so I ran upstairs.'

'And you don't remember what he was shouting?'

'No.' But this was Wilson's trick, of course, to make her slow the action that was spooling through her head, to wind the film back and replay it if she could. Following his unspoken command, she took herself back to the door of the house once again, she stood at the foot of the stairs. After a long while she murmured, 'He said something like "Get out, you bastard" or "What the hell are you doing, you bastard?" Something along those lines.'

As Ben's voice came back to her, she heard the rage in it, the roar of aggression; behind this, like an echo, she heard herself screaming at him, she felt the fear stir in her stomach like a reflex.

After a time Wilson prompted, 'Did you hear another voice at this stage?'

'Another? I don't think so.' Wanting to be clear, she added, 'What I mean is, I only remember Ben's voice. At that time. Yes . . .' She held up the remnant of memory as if to a strong light. 'Yes,' she confirmed. 'Only his.' But even as she said this another sound resonated faintly on the periphery of her mind, a sound that seemed to strike a lower and colder note. Another voice? Or Ben speaking in a different tone? Or was her imagination simply building on Wilson's suggestion? She excavated the moment more deeply and it seemed to her that the sound resonated again.

'Perhaps you should ask him that yourself,' she suggested again.

'Yes, but it always helps to have a story from two different witnesses,' Wilson explained in a speech he had obviously made dozens of times before. 'It's amazing what comes out. Things that the other person didn't notice. Or simply forgot.' He gave a brief professional smile. 'You're doing fine, Catherine. How're you feeling? Up to going on?'

Taking her silence as tacit agreement, he took her forward. 'So – you went upstairs?'

She returned to the scene with reluctance. 'It was dark up there. On the landing. I stopped. I reached across to the light switch and then . . . I wasn't sure if it was the best thing to do, to put the light on. Half of me . . .' She found herself on the brink of saying *wanted to hide*, and realised that it was true, that her sense of danger had been very strong. 'I wasn't sure what to do. I remember shouting Ben's name. Over and over again. I thought he might be hurt, I thought – well, I thought terrible things were happening.'

'There was noise?'

'Oh yes. Incredible noise. Crashing. Breaking. It sounded as though the place was being wrecked,' she whispered.

'But no voices?'

'No,' she decided, and immediately paused to examine the possibility again. 'No – only my own. I think I was yelling.'

'And where was this noise coming from?'

'The spare room. Which is our study.'

'And you couldn't see anything?'

'No. No, I couldn't see anything until . . .' Her breath locked high in her chest.

From the end of the bed Denise's head popped up, her eyebrows raised in silent enquiry.

'Take your time,' Wilson said quietly.

The rushing shadow had jumped into dark focus and, with it, the fear. Catherine took two long pulls of air. 'It all happened very quickly. I don't remember much. Just . . . this figure coming from nowhere. Suddenly. *Suddenly*. Rushing at me. And—' Another recollection came to her so unexpectedly that her first instinct was to distrust it, yet almost immediately it took on the shape and rigidity of memory. 'I forgot,' she added dutifully, 'there was this silence. Just before he came for me. This . . . long silence.'

Why had she stopped shouting? Why hadn't she called Ben's name one more time? If the thief had realised she was there, he might not have reacted so violently. Might not have attacked her. But even as she agonised over this she remembered the grip of that dreadful intense silence and knew that she had been incapable of breaking it.

'That's all I remember,' she said, though that wasn't quite true. In some fraction of time before the shadowy figure struck her she remembered a shrill unfamiliar sound, which was the sound of her own scream.

Wilson nodded slowly. 'You can't describe this man in any way?'

'No. It was so dark. He was just a – shape. Rushing. Very quickly.'

'Was he carrying anything? Holding anything? A weapon?'

She thought about this for some time. 'I . . . just don't know.'

Wilson turned away to say something to Denise, which she didn't hear. When he swung back his eyes fixed thoughtfully on Catherine's again. 'And later? After the accident?'

'Later,' she murmured. 'Well, I don't remember much, of course. A couple of small things, that's all.' She measured each word, to be sure of getting it right, but also to give substance to the little she did have to say. 'I remember being on the floor. It was like . . . coming round from an anaesthetic. I felt sick, totally disorientated. I knew . . . it was bad. I thought . . .' What she had thought was that she was going to die. Dimly, through the shock and injury, she had thought: So this is how it feels to die. 'The things I remember – they're pretty hazy.'

The door sounded and someone came into the room. Wilson turned sharply, there was a muttered exchange and whoever it was left again.

Wilson bent forward over the bed. 'You were saying?'

'Just two things. I'm not sure which came first.'

'That's all right.'

'In one there were blinding lights. Well . . . lights anyway. Perhaps they just seemed bright. I knew I was on the floor. And I knew there was someone there. Beside me. Kneeling or . . . I can't tell you who . . . or anything about them . . . I only know this person was there. It could have been an ambulance man, couldn't it?' she asked, wanting the reassurance of the obvious. 'Or whoever called the ambulance?'

Wilson nodded vaguely. 'Anything else you remember from this time?'

He already knew the answer, of course; Denise would have relayed it to him three days ago, when Catherine had told her.

'I remember something close to my face.'

'What sort of thing?'

'Something . . . softish. Fabric.'

'Now when you say close to your face – I'd like to be clear – do you mean it was being held over your face?'

'Not over, no,' she replied firmly. 'No, I was on my left side . . . well, my head was over to the left anyway. And this soft stuff was just . . . I don't know, against my face. Not pressed into it, just . . . against my face.'

'Touching your nose?'

'Well . . . yes.'

'And mouth?'

She knew where this was leading and she wanted to put him straight. 'Touching my mouth, but not pushed against it.'

'So there was no pressure as such?'

'You mean,' she said, 'was this person trying to suffocate me?'

Wilson's button eyes did not waver. 'I just want to be clear.'

Catherine exhaled slowly. 'There was no pressure.'

'Anything else you recall?'

With a final effort of memory, she stared at the blank screen of the ceiling and summoned the kneeling figure once again. This time, however, the effect was to blur the existing picture. How had she known this person was there? How had she known he was kneeling? Had this person spoken, or was it just the later one? Had there been two people at all, or had she doubled up one in a trick of memory? Before everything became irretrievably confused, she said, 'That's all I can tell you.'

'And the second occasion?'

'I think it was later, though I can't be sure. There was a voice. A man's voice. Calling my name.'

Denise's head tilted upwards. Wilson waited, motionless.

'I was still on the floor. In the same place – well, I assume so anyway. He said my name and something like, "They're on their way."'

'When you say he called you by your name . . .?'

'Catherine.'

'You're sure?'

'Yes.'

'And he said "They're on their way"?'

'Something like that. And "You're going to be all right." He said that several times.'

Another phrase came to her, something like *rest easy* or *lie easy*. But she might have lifted that from a film.

'Did you recognise the voice?'

'I don't think so.'

'Do you think you'd recognise this voice if you heard it again?'

She thought about this for a long time. 'I can't say,' she answered finally.

'Anything else you remember?'

'No, I . . . No.'

Wilson turned away and, bending down out of sight, said something to Denise in a low voice. Catherine heard a rustling and he straightened up again. 'Would you look at these items, Catherine, and tell me if you recognise them?'

'What are they?'

'If you could just tell me if you've seen them before. This is the first.'

He held up a transparent plastic bag bearing a white rectangular label marked with some sort of code number.

Inside was a small amount of lacy fabric that had once been white but was now stained and grubby. She reached up a hand to bring the bag closer.

'What are they – panties?'

'Yes.'

She felt a descent into cold. She whispered, 'Are you saying . . . they're *mine*?' Her mind raced on, making connections that filled her with foreboding.

Denise shot to her feet. Catherine stared at her helplessly. 'No, no,' Denise said. 'No, you were fully dressed when you were found.'

'Ah!'

'I swear,' Denise reassured her again. 'It wasn't like that.'

Catherine gave a short nervous laugh. 'For a moment there I thought I'd suffered a fate worse than death.' And then she laughed again, even more strangely, because the real joke was that, given the choice between sexual and neurological violation, she would have taken rape any day.

'Can I have a better look?' she asked.

Wilson had clearly allowed for this possibility because he produced plastic gloves and slipped them on before lifting the panties out of the plastic by one corner and holding them up.

The panties were not soiled with dirt, she saw now, but with what looked like dried blood, lots of it, covering almost every part of the fabric.

Wilson said, 'Take as long as you like.'

The panties were bikini style made from ersatz satin with lace trim at the leg, the sort that were sold everywhere. 'I don't think they're mine,' she said eventually. 'But I can't be sure.'

'You have some like these?'

'Sort of . . . but I think the lace was different. I can't be sure. Sorry.'

Wilson pushed out his lower lip in disappointment or resignation.

Catherine had to ask, 'The blood – is it mine?'

Wilson hesitated as he put the panties carefully back in the bag and re-sealed it. 'I'd rather not answer that just at the moment, if you don't mind.'

He reached down again towards his feet and produced another transparent bag. Inside was a length of skimpy diaphanous fabric, probably silk, in aqua green, also stained with blood, but not so extensively, just a series of blotches.

'No,' she said without hesitation. 'I've never seen it before.'

'You're absolutely certain?'

'It's a scarf, isn't it?' When Wilson nodded, she confirmed, 'No, definitely not mine.'

Wilson seemed neither surprised nor disappointed.

'Where did you find them, these things?'

He took his time before saying, 'At the scene. Thank you,' he added quickly, as if to curtail any further questions. 'You've been very helpful.'

'I don't think so,' she said. 'I don't think I've helped at all.'

She had come to look forward to the evenings. The family usually left by eight, and by nine the corridors were falling quiet as the last visitors to the surrounding wards drifted away. After Sister's rounds the night staff would come to check her mattress and lines and collar, and if they weren't too busy would chat for a while. When she was low she liked to talk to the Filipinos because they were practical and without sentiment, they did not share the universal reverence for the brave front; they believed in God striking you down and yours not to reason why and shifting for yourself by all the means at your disposal. When she was in a lighter mood she'd hope for an Irish nurse and some talk of men and parties and pubs. They could be offhand, even abrupt, these women from Limerick and Donegal, with their cutting tongues and acid wit, but she liked that too, because they expected nothing in return.

By ten there was silence over the floor apart from the click of an occasional door and the murmur of the traffic beyond the window. Then, with Walkman and headphones on, adjusted for mono listening, eyes closed, she would put on some baroque music and take a walk on strong striding legs into a garden. Sometimes it would be a garden from the past, one she'd seen through to completion, but more often than not she would walk her way through her current commission, a traditional country-house garden in Gloucestershire.

Her journey to the garden could be unpredictable. Sometimes it was like trying to cling to a fast escaping dream in the moment after you wake up; she scarcely made it to the gate before she found herself slipping back into reality and having to begin the journey all over again. Sometimes she never made it at all, and then the night seemed long.

Tonight, however, aided and abetted by two long swigs of brandy – extremely medicinal – and some

Scarlatti cantatas the journey was a doddle, just a quick flight, and she went straight to the large walled garden at one side of the Gloucestershire house. This was the part of the garden she saw most clearly. Once the derelict fruit cages and cold frames were removed, it would make a perfect ornamental garden, half vegetable, half flower garden; with secluded arbours and long vistas that drew you forward to the next turning, the next composition. There would be geometric beds containing decorative vegetables, purple- and silver-leaved, such as chard and artichoke, interspersed with red-leaved and exotic salads. In the centre there would be a fountain encircled by festooned plum trees, and against the walls espaliers of apple and pear and peach, while around the perimeter the wide flower and shrub borders would be themed by colour. Naturally there would be a white border – she was famous for her white borders – also a blue one, a pinky-mauve one, and what she called a 'Spanish' border, containing the passionate crimsons and inky-blues that went so well together: blood and death in the arena. She would bring in plenty of autumn and winter interest too, with winter honeysuckle and viburnums and early camellias.

The garden would be divided into seven areas, each with its own geometry. In the salad area there would be squares formed by the wider paths and edged in box. Within the squares, however, she had yet to decide between running the paths diagonally to make triangular beds, or at right angles to make smaller squares, or in two concentric circles intersecting a cross, in the style of a Celtic labyrinth.

In the real world someone touched her arm.

She opened her eyes with a start to see Ben. She pulled off the earphones. 'You gave me a shock.'

'A shock?' he cooed with sham sympathy. 'Thought you were awake, Moggy. They said you were.'

Catherine didn't have to catch the wine on his breathy kiss to realise that he was on his way back from dinner: his voice rang with affability, his eyes were heavy-lidded, his smile was addressed to the world at large.

'How's my girl, then? How's my Moggy?'

For the first week Catherine had not known how to answer this question, but now she said, 'Fine.'

'What, here on your lonesome?' Ben looked around with a show of surprise. 'I thought Alice was going to be here. Where's Alice?'

'She went ages ago. She had a date.'

'Not a *date* date?' He gave a mock leer.

'She didn't say.'

He hovered indecisively, as though in the absence of other people he might only stay a minute. She knew he found it easier when the family were there, or Emma, who was the only friend Catherine allowed to visit her, because then the burden of conversation was shared, the tone light-hearted. Whenever they were alone, his manner became rather forced, his talk wild and rambling, and then she had to remind herself how hard it must be for him, for all the family: the strain of seeing her stretched out like a piece of medical meat; the fear of mentioning the p-for-paralysis word; the need to put on a cheerful front.

'Good dinner?' she asked.

'Oh, you know, the usual blow out. That's what they always want.'

It had been a business do, Catherine remembered. Some Poles in London for a couple of days.

'A surprise for you!' Lifting his briefcase onto the bed, he pulled out a small package and brandished it aloft, like a conjurer producing his best trick.

Another present. She said, 'I wish you wouldn't.'

'What do you mean, *wish I wouldn't*?' The lightness of his voice didn't conceal the note of rebuke. 'Open it!' He thrust it into her hands.

The wrapping was well sealed and it took her a moment to find a way in. Pulling the paper off at last, she held up a miniature television designed to fit into the palm of one hand. She couldn't imagine when she would use it. 'Thanks.'

Her tone must have sounded less than enthusiastic because he made an expression of offence that was half-serious. '*Thanks?* But you haven't even looked at it yet. Turn it on – see what a great picture it's got.' When she failed to find the switch he plucked it from her grasp and fiddled with the controls. 'See?' He held it close above her face.

'It's amazing.'

Like a boy with a new toy, he showed her every channel and button, looking to her expectantly for suitable expressions of wonderment and appreciation. She realised he'd had more than just a glass or two of wine when he swayed gently and put out a hand to steady himself, though he managed to fuse it into one seamless movement that to anyone else would have appeared deliberate.

Putting the television to one side at last, he declared, 'It's for when everyone's driving you nuts!'

'All the time, you mean?'

He liked it when she showed the right spirit. 'All the time,' he echoed with a warm chuckle of approval. 'Absolutely!'

She felt a burst of love for him, for his quirky smile, his mischievous eyes, for the marvellous familiarity of him, and the novelty too, because however hard she tried her memory could never quite do him justice. Close behind this came a plunge of anxiety, which brought her up with a hard jolt. Would they ever survive this? Could any marriage survive this?

She asked, 'How's work?'

A lazy shrug. 'Got a lot of catching up to do. Sort out some nonsenses.'

'Nothing serious?'

'No, no.'

'Simon can't do it for you?'

'Ha! I wish!' Still in expansive mood, he asked, 'So, my darling Moggy, how are things?' Neither of them could remember how or why he had come to call her Moggy – they weren't cat lovers – but somehow the name had stuck.

She didn't attempt to list the various indignities of her day, nor describe the auditory tests that had showed almost no hearing in her damaged ear; like her moments of panic, anxiety and dread, these were things she had learnt not to talk about. 'Emma packed for me.'

Faint puzzlement flickered over his face and she knew that for a moment he'd forgotten she was being moved to the spinal unit the next day. 'Oh, right,' he said airily. This was Ben's way, to ignore the more unsettling things in life and concentrate on the positive. It was one of the things that had drawn Catherine to him, this belief that life could be lived in a permanent state of confidence and enthusiasm.

'There's an awful lot of champagne left over,' she mentioned. 'Could you take it home?'

'What, haven't we drunk it all? Hell! We'll soon put that right when you get to the new place! Lots of people coming to see you, Cath. They're all queuing up.'

'I don't want to see anyone. Please, Ben, tell them to stay away. Will you? *Please.*'

'Might cheer you up, you know.'

The thought of small talk appalled her, but what appalled her most of all was the thought of their curiosity and pity. 'No. Absolutely not. I would really hate it.'

'But they love you, darling heart. They want to come and dish out all the gossip. Give you the latest.' Catching her expression, he shook his head reprovingly and his voice took on a mildly exasperated edge. 'Mad to cut yourself off, Moggy. Got to have a bit of light relief sometimes, you know!'

When she didn't reply his eyes drooped, he gave a slight shrug and, reaching for a chair, pulled it up to the bed.

'Can't see you down there,' she reminded him as he sank down onto it with a sigh.

'No?' he murmured lazily. He stood up again and, having shifted indecisively once or twice, perched on the edge of the bed, which had long been established as the only place where she could see anyone properly.

'Now, what have I got to tell you?' he said abruptly, coming alive to the need for news. 'Yes! Got a call from

Sam Blake. You know – Sam and Livvy? Want us to go and stay with them in Barbados next Christmas. Bit of a wild child in his City days, of course, old Sam. Sailed close to the wind, so they say, but one hell of an operator, no doubt about that. Running an investment company now. On his way to a second bloody fortune, jammy bastard! But a fantastic place they've got in Barbados, apparently. *Her* family has pots of moolah, of course—'

Catherine found herself listening but not listening. This was the trick, she had learnt: to disconnect herself from such moments, from such conversations, from Ben's life, from her own too, though quite what her life involved now she couldn't have said. The only world she could focus on was small and contained: this room, this bed, this body, and the unit they were transferring her to in the morning. If she listened too closely to what Ben was saying it was like touching some terrible heat, the pain made her pull away.

Finally, when the word 'Barbados' filtered through yet again, she could bear it no longer and interrupted him in a voice that was too loud and too sharp. 'I forgot,' she said, 'the police were here.'

'Oh.' His smile had a glassy veneer. 'Wilson?'

'And the WPC.'

'The blonde job with the big boobs?'

'Well, it was the same one as before, anyway.' She heard the note of criticism in her voice and thought: This is no way to go, I'm sounding difficult. 'Yes, the blonde job. They said they'd been trying to get in touch with you.'

He rolled his eyes. 'For God's sake, I called them! Yesterday? Monday? They're never there. Hopeless!

What did they want, anyway? Let me guess,' he jeered languidly, 'to tell us they've found *nothing*.'

'More or less.'

'I knew it. And they came and bothered you just to tell you that? Sorry, darling, I should have got hold of them, shouldn't I? Should have told them to get lost. Forgive me?' He rolled towards her with an endearing boyish smile. 'Poor Moggy. Poor darling.' His voice had a bleary sentimental note. He squeezed her hand, then after a moment's hesitation reached out a second time and, still not entirely at ease with the role of bedside companion, laid his hand rather awkwardly in hers. He asked, 'What did they say? They've given up on the stupid phantom caller, I hope.'

'Yes. There's no way of tracing the calls.'

'Of course there isn't! And it wasn't anybody who had anything to do with anything – you said so yourself.'

'That's right,' she murmured.

'That's exactly what I told Simon! He should never have made such a big thing about it with the police. Never have encouraged Emma to make all those ridiculous statements!' With a final press of her hand he withdrew his own and in the process of settling himself more comfortably on the edge of the bed turned away slightly so that his face was partly in shadow.

She said, 'Wilson wanted a statement.'

'But I've given him a statement.'

'No, from me.'

He turned down his mouth in an expression of mystification. 'But why? To say what?'

'Just what I remember.'

'But, darling, you don't remember anything.'

'I remember going into the house.'

He shook his head firmly. 'No, no, you said you didn't—'

'But I do now. I remember now.'

His eyes narrowed almost to the point of invisibility, she sensed a sudden alertness in him. 'Since when?'

'Oh, I don't know. Things have been coming back to me in bits and pieces.'

'But are you sure?' he asked easily. 'It couldn't be' – he rotated a finger next to his temple, signalling brain problems – 'you've got a bit mixed up?'

'No, I remember moving into the driving seat to go and park, I remember you taking the cases up to the door.'

'You didn't say anything.' It was an accusation.

'It didn't seem terribly important.'

'Didn't seem important!' he jeered, flashing cold shark eyes at her.

She realised her mistake. It was like pressing a button, this route to Ben's insecurities. He couldn't bear the thought of being excluded in any way, of having even the smallest item of information kept from him. His mother had walked out when he was twelve and no one had given him a word of explanation, not then, and not later, certainly not his mother herself, who'd gone to America and barely been in contact since. He'd been brought up by a profligate and largely absent father who, among his other notable acts, had twice forgotten to pick Ben up from school at the end of term, and had once left him to find his own way back from France after taking up an invitation to go and stay with a minor *principessa* on Lake Como. Not surprisingly, Ben hated to feel he wasn't being told the full facts, or, worse still, that decisions were being made behind his back.

'Sorry,' Catherine said. 'I didn't realise I'd remembered anything very significant until the police asked me.'

Ben forced enthusiasm into a voice that was still cool with injury. 'So! Memory all coming back! That brain of yours! All there! All working! That's great!' Then, thinking this through, he leant towards her with an unfocused look of concern. 'Haven't remembered anything *upsetting* though, have you, my darling?'

'No.'

'Nothing about that *man*?'

'No,' she lied again.

He straightened up. 'Good! Can't have you upsetting yourself!'

This was the official family line, she had realised some days ago. Everything must be done to make sure she did not get upset, though this strategy rather awkwardly ruled out discussion of the immediate past and indefinite future.

She said reminiscently, 'But tell me – I can't quite remember – when you were at the door, trying to get in, you called something back to me. Something about the lock. Something . . .' She gave up. 'What was it?'

He was cautious suddenly, or slow, or distracted. 'What? Oh, I said the lock felt strange. Stiff.'

'Ah,' she breathed. It came back to her now. 'Yes . . . And the lights – I'm not going mad, am I? You didn't put any on, except for a couple at the back of the house.'

Ben drew his head back with a frown. 'No, darling, where on earth did you get that from? No, I put the hall light on, then when I realised the alarm wasn't set I went off on a hunt – saw the mess in the living room – did a complete round. No, I turned on every light in the place! Of course I did!' He shook his head firmly. 'But, Moggy darling, why go into all this now? What's the point?'

'I want to get a picture, I want to get it clear in my head, so that I can forget about it. That's all.'

He shrugged as though he was being persuaded against his better judgement.

She continued, 'What about when you went upstairs? Did you leave the hall light on?'

'Of course! And I put the landing light on, and then – well, I would have put the study light on, but the bastard was waiting for me, wasn't he?'

'I thought it was dark when I came in.'

He scoffed, 'No, darling. Now I know you've got it all mixed up!'

'Oh . . . well, then.'

'For God's sake, the lights were definitely on!' he insisted as if she had argued against him. 'Is that what you told the police, that the place was dark?'

'I said I thought the only lights were in the kitchen and the sitting room. But I must have got it wrong.'

'Totally!' He shook his head firmly. 'That's going to be great, isn't it? You saying it was dark, and me saying it was lit up like a Christmas tree. Ha!' He was annoyed certainly, but also rather amused, as if the idea of being an unreliable witness rather appealed to him.

'Sorry.'

He brushed it aside with a lift of one hand.

'One last thing.'

His attention was fading fast.

'Upstairs – when I got upstairs – someone was shouting. Yelling. It was you, wasn't it?'

'I should think so,' he said without hesitation. 'Well, I was bloody furious, wasn't I?' His eyes gleamed briefly.

'Did the man speak?'

'Mmm?' He had heard all right, but either he was thinking about it or he didn't know the answer. 'What a question, Moggy.'

He would have left it there if she hadn't pressed him. 'Did he say anything?'

Realising some effort of concentration was expected of him, Ben screwed up his eyes, he pushed out his lip, he exhaled slowly before shaking his head. 'Can't remember now. All lost in the mists.'

She was silent.

'Is that it?' He looked tired, or possibly the worse for alcohol.

'I think so.'

'Got your *picture*?'

'What?'

'You wanted a picture, you said. To get it clear in your head.'

'Yes, got my picture.'

'Good!' He lumbered to his feet. 'So, what time would you like me here in the morning?'

'Ten, if you wouldn't mind. I'm rather nervous.'

'Nervous? Why *nervous*, Moggy?'

'The thought of being moved.' She was aware that in showing this loss of nerve she was failing to show the kind of doughty spirit expected of her.

'Hey!' He pressed his palm tenderly to the side of her face. 'Not to worry. There's my girl!'

He bent down to kiss her and rest his cheek against hers, and she closed her eyes, better to draw in the warmth of him, the scent of him, the texture of his skin. She felt a rush of memory, an amalgam of the hundreds of nights they had spent together. In a surge of feeling, she put a hand around his head to bring his face still closer to hers, but just as her fingers tightened against the thick silky hair he pulled away.

'I miss you,' she whispered. Saying this was like breaching a dam, just a trickle for the moment but one sudden move and there'd be a torrent. The urge to give way to it was very strong. Her throat swelled, she felt all the pressure of her grief and self-pity. Yet something warned her against expressions of anguish. Partly, she had an irrational fear of voicing her terrors, as if this alone could give them the dread solidity of fact. More practically, she feared Ben's revulsion and dismay. Having no use for displays of emotion himself, he looked on them with mistrust and embarrassment.

In the end she said simply, 'Miss you so much.'

'Miss you too,' Ben said breezily. Then, clearly feeling that something else was expected of him, he added in a suggestive growl, 'Won't be long now!'

She managed to maintain her expression until he had gone, and then she began to weep, slowly at first, a trickle of hot silent tears that slipped coolly into her ears and hair. When these failed to take the edge off things, she cried with a sense of anger. Finally she remembered the brandy bottle. Reaching for it, she managed to knock it to the floor and had to call the nurse.

The bell was answered by an Irish girl named Kathleen: 'But you can call me Kate'.

'There's a bottle of brandy on the floor.'

She laughed. 'A nightcap, is it?'

'Have one yourself.'

'Trying to get me fired!' She found the bottle and, pushing a straw into the neck, held it to Catherine's mouth. If she noticed Catherine's undried tears she didn't mention them. When one sip stretched to four she exclaimed in mock disapproval, 'Steady on!'

'I'm leaving tomorrow.'

'So you are.'

'I'm frightened.'

'No need, I'm sure. They'll look after you better there. They'll be able to give you a lot more time than we can.' Capping the brandy bottle she put it back in the locker. 'Anything else I can do for you?'

'Give me another drink?'

'You're a devil! As bad as a Paddy.'

Catherine didn't want to be left alone quite yet. 'There're some letters on the locker,' she said. 'Would you read them to me?'

'Only one I can see.' She moved chocolates and tissues and paraphernalia. 'No, only one.'

'Well, that one, then.'

She saw Kate baulk at the length of it, five pages or so, but, perching on the edge of the bed, she began to read without complaint.

'*Dear Catherine, I hope you're continuing to make progress and that the flowers arrived safely. The roses were the last from the climbers on the west wall, which have blossomed so profusely though alas so briefly. I do not of course know their name – my ignorance would be laughable if it were not so shameful. However, I'm taking myself in hand, so far as common names go at least – I think it would be unrealistic to aspire to Latin at my age when I've still trouble enough with the spelling of the English language. A Mrs Kent is coming to tell me what's what. She is said to be an expert on gardens hereabouts (she's done quite a few gardens in Wicklow)—'*

'Wicklow!'

'Careful – my mam was a Wicklow girl.'

'Wicklow's got poncy gardens.'

'Poncy?' Kate laughed. '*Poncy.* Now there's a word!' Still laughing, she went back to the letter. 'Where are we? Ah yes, Mrs Kent . . . *I'm hoping she can tell me what's here and what Mick should or shouldn't be doing to keep everything in fine shape. I have a suspicion that Mick has done damage again – the shrubs down by the stream are looking hacked about and forlorn. But of course it's hard for me to say anything from a position of horticultural iliteracy.*' Kate looked up with a quick smile. 'He's misspelt illiteracy. *Now is the time to come clean and admit that the rhododendrons met with an unfortunate accident last year. Someone said that they were a menace and strangling the trees, so I told Mick to deal with them. The result, I'm afraid to say, was nothing short of slaughter. Mick got a bulldozer, although it may have been a JCB – I found it too painful to ask which particular weapon of mass destruction he had been let loose on. Not only did he uproot the rhododendrons around the trees to the north of the house (the ones I meant him to deal with) but also managed to lay waste to those on either side of the drive. I have not yet recovered from the shock of seeing the devastation, my stomach is still somewhere out by the gates, where it dropped through the bottom of my boots, but it taught me that Mick was not be trusted with shrubs and, apart from those down by the stream, I have curbed his worst impulses to slash at vegetation with a blunt instrument.'*

'For heaven's sake. Why does he write? Why does he bother?'

'What's that?'

'I wish I knew what he was after.'

'Why would he be after anything?'

'He has to be.'

'Are we stopping or are we going on?' She examined Catherine's face. 'Shall I just whisk through the rest? *So when Mrs Kent comes I will ask her what she recommends for the drive, whether to replant rhodies or to try some other shrubs. Aware of my responsibilities to Morne, I am determined to go cautiously and to obtain advice from every possible quarter. Of course I would dispense with all such opinions if I thought there was a chance of you coming and advising us on how to restore the gardens to their proper glory. I know that you must be thinking only of recovery at present, but once you see your way clear you would only have to give the smallest indication that you might consider it and I would keep all other ideas on hold. There is nothing more precious to me than the thought of restoring Morne to its former glory, as your mamma would have wished it to be, for as you know I hold her memory most dear.'*

'Really!'

'The idea doesn't appeal?'

'What idea?'

'The garden.'

'I'd rather die.'

'Sounds a nice job.'

'That's my home he's talking about. He stole it after my mother died. Got hold of the mortgage. Forced my father out. Everything's a deal. Everything's an opportunity to make a killing.' She remembered the expression her father used. 'He'd as soon sell his grandmother.'

'Ah,' Kate said heavily. 'I see. It couldn't be that he's got a conscience about it? Trying to make amends.'

'I doubt it.'

'A guilty conscience can strike us all,' Kate offered solemnly before returning once again to the letter. '*I am safer with trees – or should I say that trees are safer with me? I have been doing serious homework in the last couple of years and have discovered what you will know already, that there are some remarkable trees at Morne – the Irish yews around the hollow, surely older than the house itself, the oak on the south lawn, which Old Patrick from the village estimates to be 300 years old (do you think this is possible?), and the beeches, which seem to reach beyond the sky, but which I am told may go any day in a storm because they have shallow roots. It is a terrible thought, that they may go, so I have had some new beeches planted, ones of good size, already some twenty feet high, so that there will be some equally majestic trees in fifty years or so.*'

'That's enough, thanks.'

'There's only a few more lines. Just' – she scanned the page – 'news of Maeve, who's been unwell but is now recovering—'

'Chuck it in the bin.'

'Why don't I just put it on the side here?'

'I want it in the bin. If I could move from this bloody bed I would put it in the bin.'

'The bin it is, then.'

Despite the brandy, it took Catherine a long time to get to sleep, and then it was to dream all night, or so it seemed. She revisited the scenes she had described to Wilson, re-enacting them time and again, but with variations and additions that might or might not have been borrowed from other times and other dreams. In the morning two images remained intact. In one, which was recognisably a nightmare, she was in a dark place, making her way towards a series of rooms with half-open doors that radiated brilliant light. The floor was littered with what she took to be debris, but which turned out to be the heavy glutinous leaves of some vigorous plant whose tendrils wrapped themselves tighter and tighter around her legs, pulling her slowly to the floor. When she was completely immobilised something soft brushed against her face and clung to her nose and mouth and eyes, threatening to rob her of air. She would have fought the soft thing off but she couldn't move her arms. Someone who was Alice and then not Alice was somewhere close by, weeping and wailing softly.

In the other scene she replayed her arrival from France. She ran upstairs as before but, instead of stopping on the landing as she had described to Wilson, she ran on into the room where Ben and the man were fighting and found herself caught up in the struggle, though mysteriously unaffected by it. It was dark, but this didn't prevent her from seeing a weapon in the man's hand, a long baton that she identified as a baseball bat. In the instant she saw it, she realised that the man had finished with Ben, or perhaps Ben wasn't there any more, and was coming for her so fast that she didn't have time to raise her arms and ward off the blows. In the next instant she was back on the landing and the man was looming over her. As she cowered before him she saw the bat raised above his head, ready to strike.

In the morning the image of the baseball bat stayed with her and she decided to ask Ben if he thought the man might have used it in the attack. While she was about it she would also tell Ben what for some reason she'd failed to tell him the night before, about the blood-stained panties and scarf the police had asked her to identify.

In the event she mentioned neither. Ben arrived late, just behind the ambulance men, and by the time they had the chance to talk she'd realised that the baseball bat was probably a trick of her mind. Ben had always kept a baseball bat under the bed in case of intruders and, by association, her subconscious had in all likelihood transposed it into the dream.

She decided against mention of the blood-stained clothing for a very different reason, because despite police reassurances to the contrary Ben might believe she had been sexually assaulted, and that was one burden he didn't need.

Chapter Five

TERRY WAITED impatiently while Fergal arranged his long limbs untidily in the chair opposite, arms at every angle, legs skewed out to one side, like an abandoned marionette. Settled at last, he began to speak in a soft unhurried voice. 'I am giving you the dry bones of the situation as *they* see it. You follow me? No interpretation, no perspective. This is the official version, pure and simple.'

Terry could only nod.

'In essence, they have no suspects and no prospect of any suspects.'

'They're still thinking in terms of a straight burglary?'

Fergal hesitated, which wasn't like him at all. 'I'll come to that in a moment, if I may. It would be simpler if we could leave the questions till the end.'

Suitably corrected, Terry slid his elbows onto the desk and propped his chin on clenched fists. Thereafter he did not shift his gaze, did not move, as if to will Fergal forward by the intensity of his attention.

'The forensic people have found nothing obvious in the house,' Fergal began again, his accent belonging more than ever to some uncharted point midway across the Irish Sea. 'No known fingerprints, nothing of that nature. Signs of forced entry on the front door, but a neat professional job, a drill on the mortice, a pick on the latch. As for the alarm . . . Here, I have to say, my contact was short on information.' From his time-worn expression of forbearance he might have been a lecturer again, in receipt of a sloppy essay. 'He could not say if the alarm was linked to a security company, so we do not know if an automatic alarm call was sent, nor for that matter if one was received. All he could tell me was that the neighbours do not remember hearing an alarm bell ringing. Not of course that this means a great deal. False alarms are two a penny in that part of London.'

Terry remembered that Fergal had lived in London during his Cintel years, and perhaps at other less accountable times.

'However, if the exterior bell did indeed sound, it would have switched itself off after fifteen minutes. That is the law – no more than fifteen minutes. The ambulance people did not report hearing an alarm ringing when they arrived, nor was an alarm audible on the call to the emergency services, which suggests that if the alarm was triggered it occurred more than fifteen minutes before Catherine was . . . *discovered*. It's equally possible, of course, that the alarm was never set.'

By an effort of will, Terry remained silent. He tried to see this information through a police investigator's eyes, tried to find a pattern that would steer a thinking mind in the right direction.

Fergal twisted around in his seat. Any movement for Fergal was a performance: limbs drawn in, tall frame realigned, arms and legs uncoiled haphazardly. He turned his eyes to the thin Dublin sun, revealing the punishment of fifty-five troubled years, a poor diet and sixty a day, only recently abandoned. His sad intelligent face was long and thin, with a nose to match and a flop of lank greying hair. His skin was criss-crossed with deep lines, his eyelids heavy and drooping at the corners, while his forehead was set into a perpetual frown, as if to warn strangers away.

When he began to speak again, there was a rare tension about him which filled Terry with foreboding.

'The place was ransacked. *Their* word. I'm trying to obtain details. To find out whether every room had been searched, every cupboard, whether papers were rifled, or clothing, or everything. At any rate, things were stolen, though they don't yet have a complete list of what is missing. It seems that Ben Galitza has been somewhat difficult to pin down on that score. However, so far as they can tell it was mainly light stuff. Jewellery, ornaments, some silver. There was a small strong-box containing a few hundred pounds in cash, which was forced open.'

'Just cash?'

'That is what has been reported to the police.'

'Yes, yes,' Terry gasped apologetically.

'They're not sure what sort of weapon was used to attack Ben Galitza. Some sort of cosh, they think. They haven't found anything resembling a weapon, at any rate not in the house, not in the surrounding gardens.' Fergal's voice took on an abstracted tone. 'They are no nearer to discovering who made the ambulance call either. The ambulance crew didn't get a proper look at the man and he wasn't seen leaving.'

'Presumably, though, they would recognise him again if they saw him.'

'I have no information on that.'

Terry drew in a sharp breath. 'All right, but was anyone else seen leaving?'

'No reports of anyone, no.'

'Go on.'

Fergal fixed his sombre gaze on a point just below Terry's line of sight, and Terry knew that the bad news, whatever it might be, was very close.

'So, we have a burglary, we have a professional break-in. However, the police have reason to think that there was more to it than that. They think the intruder might have selected the Galitzas' home purposely, that he might have wanted to . . . get close to Catherine.' Fergal's eyes met Terry's alarmed gaze and continued stolidly, 'There had been calls for some months, silent calls to her mobile telephone, which cannot be traced. Also' – the hesitation again – 'certain *items* were discovered with Catherine. Close to Catherine.' He proceeded yet more slowly, weighing each word. 'There was a pair of panties . . . found under her head—'

'Her *own*, you mean?'

'Possibly. But not the ones she was wearing at the time. Her clothing was intact. No, the police are thinking that these panties might have been acquired from upstairs. Part of the burglar's haul, if you like.'

Terry repeated incredulously, 'His *haul* . . .?'

'We have an unbalanced person here,' Fergal informed him sternly. 'Someone who has broken in with the intention of thieving – no doubt about that – but also of getting some vicarious thrill from being near Catherine, from acquiring her underclothing. Are you with me now?'

It was several seconds before Terry managed a feeble nod.

'It was one of the ambulance crew who noticed these panties under her head. He pushed them aside when he fitted the collar to her neck and the police picked them up later. If you can imagine her lying on the hall floor with her head over to one side, to the left, then the panties were found between her ear and the floor. The thought is that these panties were placed against her ear to staunch the bleeding.' He held up an index finger as if to admonish himself. 'I should have mentioned that she was bleeding from her ear when they found her. I didn't mention that, did I? No . . . Well, she was bleeding quite profusely. Subsequently, tests have established that this blood on the panties was indeed Catherine's.'

'So it could simply have been someone trying to stop the bleeding?' Terry argued hopefully. 'Nothing sinister at all?'

'It *could* have been, yes.' But his tone suggested a very different tale and Terry prepared himself for whatever was still to come.

Fergal's expression darkened. 'Later on, when she arrived at the hospital, a scarf was found. A lady's silk scarf.' He looked down, his voice grew flat and urgent. 'It was found bundled up inside her skirt. Between her legs. This scarf had more blood on it.'

Terry stared at Fergal, groping for understanding. 'You mean she was *attacked*?'

'There was no evidence of that, no. There was no obvious source for the blood, you see . . . in that place. Besides which – most significantly – the blood was not Catherine's.'

Again Terry was floundering. 'Not Catherine's?' he repeated stupidly. 'But . . . You mean . . .' Fear lurched in his stomach.

'The blood was old. It belonged to a woman. They are thinking that it might have come from another victim of this attacker.'

It was all too much for Terry. Shuddering, he pushed himself back in his chair and pressed his hands over his face. 'Jesus, Jesus.' Among the conflicting thoughts that collided and jostled in his mind, one terrifying notion came roaring to the fore. Dropping his hands, he began urgently, 'Have they considered the possibility that—'

'No, we are not having random thoughts on this. This is the police, remember? They only know what they know. For the moment it has occurred to them to check the scarf, to find out if it belongs to Catherine. It does not. And if they have not already done so, they will check the DNA on the scarf against the national DNA data bank. They will check known offenders, discover who might have been in the area without an alibi. Then . . .' He lifted his shoulders, he spread his hands.

'But where will it lead, Fergal? That's the thing. Where will it end?'

He blew out his cheeks. 'At a guess? I would say that it will go nowhere. That in a month or so when they have failed to find a suspect they will wind the investigation down.'

Terry asked unhappily, 'And what will we do when that happens?'

Fergal's steady gaze contained a warning. 'We will do nothing.'

Terry wrestled with this idea, and finally submitted with a long sigh. 'If we must.'

With a last cautionary frown, Fergal pulled a small notebook from his breast pocket and flicked through it. 'So . . . the rest. Nothing more on Ben Galitza. He's generally regarded as a bit of an operator, but good for his debts. A big spender, but not thought to have any serious money worries. Seen as on the up and up, destined for bigger and better things, though likely to sail close to the wind with the regulations, tax laws, etcetera. Some people regard him as a one-man band – seem to be unaware of the partnership with Simon Jardine. Others say it's the link with Jardine that's the key to Galitza's success, Jardine being the money man, the steadying influence.' He looked up. 'That's about it. Unless you want a deeper look.'

Again Terry was uncertain. 'What about surveillance?'

'That all depends on what you are expecting – or hoping – to find.'

'I don't really know.'

'I think that rather answers your question then. Surveillance is very expensive and if you're not sure what you're after, then you could be talking weeks and weeks.'

Terry was already nodding rapidly. 'You're right. Forget it.'

Fergal produced a sheet of paper and slid it across the desk. 'The address of the spinal unit. I don't yet have the room number.' He looked at his watch, keen to get away. He had an invalid mother in a nursing home somewhere near Malahide whom he came back to visit once a fortnight.

Terry indicated one last question. 'I'm using Cintel for a job in Warsaw. Their man there is called Malinowski – do you know him? Is he all right?'

If Fergal was curious about Terry's interest in Poland he gave no sign. 'In my day Malinowski was a freelance,' he said. 'Mixed Cintel work with journalism. But solid, I'd say. Yes, solid.'

After he had gone, Terry went and stood at the window that overlooked the Liffey, his habitual retreat in times of crisis or distraction. The sky was dark with unshed rain, the water had taken on a benign silvery sheen, and on O'Connell Bridge two garishly painted tourist coaches were caught in the traffic. His eye strayed to the south bank and the top storey of The Kavanagh. Built from the shell of a former bank headquarters – appropriately the bank he himself used – the project had consumed his life for over two years. He had been obsessed by the determination to get it finished on schedule. In the event it had opened only two weeks late, which was no mean achievement in boomtime Dublin. But already the struggle seemed remote, the obsession curious and the duty he now owed the place oppressive, like a marriage after the passion has died.

Restlessly he went back to his desk and scooped up the Cintel report. He went through it once again, but found nothing he hadn't gleaned at the first two readings. Ben Galitza had been involved in protracted negotiations to buy some generators but the deal had collapsed for no apparent reason. One of the leading Warsaw-based speculators claimed to have been cheated over the lost deal but, coincidentally or not, he was locked in a power struggle with a rival for control of two vodka distilleries. Was this struggle connected? Who had ownership of the generators, or actively controlled them? Were they still for sale, or had they gone to another buyer?

Terry drafted a fax to Malinowski. He began with three questions: *Where are the generators? If they've been sold, who bought them? If not sold, why were they withdrawn from sale?* He knew there was something else he should ask but uncharacteristically it took him some minutes before he pinned it down and added a fourth question. *Has Galitza got involved in some other deal?* And still he wasn't ready to hand it to Bridget for transmission. There was something more, something obvious, which hovered stubbornly out of reach. He nursed several ideas and rejected them before it finally came to him. He grunted with satisfaction. He extended the last question to: *Has Galitza got involved in some other totally separate deal? Or has he done a secret back-door deal for the generators?*

For lunch he stayed at his desk and had a chicken salad with oil-free dressing and a glass of mineral water: part of a new regime to smarten up his waistline and his life. To the same end, he phoned Dinah and apologised for not having been in touch. She was sweet and understanding as ever; from her tone he might have dropped out of her life for two days rather than two weeks. He felt humbled by her seemingly endless capacity for forgiveness, and perhaps rather daunted by it too, though he quickly rejected this thought as negative and unworthy. No, he was lucky to have her, and it was high time he realised it. She would be good for him, he was mad not to grab her while he still had the chance. Feeling a little happier at this thought, he invited her down to Morne for Saturday evening with the understanding that she would stay on until Sunday night.

In the afternoon he chaired two meetings whose proceedings he first hurried along mercilessly then virtually ignored, so that no one was certain that the decisions he'd forced through with such despatch would survive the week.

It was a Thursday and, though Terry had decided to take a long weekend starting at four, he was still in his office at ten past, journeying back and forth through Fergal's report in his mind, one minute tormented by the possibility that he had missed something, the next racked by the possibility that he had not.

Finally he snatched up the phone and called Bridget in. 'Three years ago when I had dealings with Ben Galitza he had a girlfriend called Rebecca Child,' he told her. 'We all went to the Curragh together.'

'I remember. It was the Derby,' Bridget confirmed.

'I need to speak to her. Can we find her number?'

'Do we have an address?'

'London, I would think.'

Bridget pursed her mouth. She liked a challenge but only when she thought she could pull it off.

Terry said, 'I think she married.'

Bridget lifted one eyebrow. 'Well, that narrows the field.'

'There might be something in a British newspaper. If I remember, she married into a prominent Jewish family.'

*

Terry took the slow road to Morne because the main road would be busy and he liked the idea of driving Maeve in a leisurely fashion, with the radio on and Conn's broad head blocking the rear-view mirror, just like a regular family. The rain that had been threatening all day finally came on at six but obligingly fell all at once, so that by the time they were entering the Slaney valley the clouds were evaporating fast and shafts of golden light were brushing the slopes of the Wicklow Mountains.

Maeve sat quietly for most of the journey, only stirring to change the radio station or take her homeo-pathic hay fever remedy and blow her nose, but as they approached Morne he noticed that her hands were clenched against her legs and she seemed to be holding her breath. 'Dadda?' she whispered as he glanced across at her. 'Have you thought about . . .'

But her soft words were lost under the music. Hastily he reached forward to turn the radio off. 'Say again, my darling.'

She hesitated, as though she had suddenly thought better of the idea, and he laid an encouraging hand over hers. 'Have I thought . . .?' he prompted.

She took a deep breath. 'Have you thought about . . . who might have done this thing to Catherine?'

Now what in heaven is all this about? he wondered. What on this earth is going through her head? Deliber-ately choosing to take the question at face value, he said, 'It'll be a habitual thief. Young, probably on drugs, undoubtedly from a deprived background. In fact, your average criminal.'

'You don't think . . . it was someone who was trying to harm her?'

'What? You mean, *intentionally*?' He swept this idea aside with a sharp exclamation. 'No, I don't! No! Goodness! Why would anyone want to do that?'

'Or Ben?'

'What do you mean *Ben*?'

'Setting out to harm Ben but ending up hurting Catherine instead.'

'No, my darling! There's nothing to give an inkling of a thing like that. Goodness!' His laughter sounded unnatural. 'No, it was this fella barging his way out, that's all! In a panic at being discovered. A thief who found someone in his way!'

Maeve was frowning.

'No,' he hastened to reassure her again, 'it was a truly terrible thing to happen, of course it was! But it was an accident, my darling girl. Just an accident. Now, don't go thinking anything else. Don't go worrying yourself.'

She looked down at her lap, she flexed her hands. He sensed some deep reservation.

'There's no doubt about it, my darling. Cross my heart.'

Her eyes came up to his face.

He declared again, with a false laugh, 'Cross my heart!'

He was aware of her watching him for some time before she nodded, just the once, very slowly.

He cried brightly, 'Now, look – we're almost here!' They were entering the lane that twisted up through pastureland and tall hedgerows towards the groves of oak and beech that concealed Morne from the east. 'Just look at this summer! Just look at the trees! Have you ever seen them so heavy and so green!' He laughed with a joy that was only a little forced. 'I do so love this place! I do so love it here!'

'I loved Creagh,' Meave said in the voice of a child. 'Why didn't we stay at Creagh? Mamma had made it so fine.'

He kept a judicious silence. Creagh was the small house in an unprepossessing Dublin suburb that he and his late wife had bought in the first years of his success and subsequently built on to a couple of times with less than satisfactory results, before giving up on the place and moving to Foxrock. If Maeve felt a sense of loss he felt sure it was not for the house itself but for her mamma, who had died of a thrombosis when Maeve was thirteen, and for the difficult motherless years of her adolescence.

'Creagh was a good house,' he said at last. 'It did us well, no doubt about that. But you just wait until Morne's finished. Wait until the garden's planted and the decorating's done. It will be the finest place you ever saw.'

'Oh, Dadda,' she said with a weary shake of her head, 'but you'll never finish it, will you?'

This accusation took him aback. 'Good heavens, of course I will!'

'You've hardly started as it is.'

'The roof is insulated. And the windows all repaired.'

Maeve continued to shake her head. 'You'll never finish.'

He was still smarting at this curious and unwarranted remark when they turned in through the latticed iron gates of Morne.

With the demise of the rhododendrons the narrow winding drive had lost much of its capacity to tantalise and enthral; the house was now clearly visible over the inglorious tangle of roots and stumps. Yet, for Terry, it remained a stirring sight. Architecturally the house was nothing exceptional, indeed many would judge it excessively plain compared to the other landed houses in the neighbourhood. It was a two-storey oblong, two windows either side of the front door and five above, with a grey pebble-dash exterior and grey slate roof, and at the back, a small wing, two-up two-down, while across a cobbled courtyard were a number of dark outhouses and stabling for four horses. For Terry, the excessive simplicity of the frontage was redeemed by the long sash windows that reached almost to the ground, and the pillared portico that guarded the glass-panelled door, and the flowering creepers that adorned the grey façade, the whole given life and grandeur by the frame of splendid trees, yew and cedar to the left, oak and beech to the right. The house had four bedrooms, including one in the wing, and two ancient bathrooms with large-bore plumbing that rattled and sang, and a kitchen that had been poorly modernised in the sixties. It was a modest house for a rich man, but grand enough for him.

Would he ever finish doing it up? Did he want to? Had Maeve touched on some unexpected truth? Standing in front of the house, he surveyed the unkempt garden, the nettles footing the courtyard wall, the brambles fanning out from behind the outhouses, the weeds peeping through the gravel on the drive, and tried to picture the place as it would be once he'd got to grips with it, and though he couldn't quite visualise the flowers and shrubs that might come to be planted, he had no trouble in seeing the garden as an ordered place with neat beds and clipped hedges and smooth grass. It would happen in good time, once there was a plan.

'We'll see!' he said to the garden in general. 'We'll see what Mrs Kent says!'

Inside, the house had a musty unused smell, and he was the first to admit that the paintwork was shabby, the walls peeling in odd corners, and one of the kitchen units was losing its door. But he'd held back on repainting, just as he'd held back on the curtains and carpets, until he'd decided how to tackle the house as a whole. This was reasonable surely? This didn't imply a lack of will? The Langleys had left nothing behind, not a curtain, not a scrap of carpet, not a working light bulb. Having to start from scratch in this way it would have been easy to employ someone like Dinah, to give the place a 'look', but while he wasn't bothered by the tarting and titivating being visited on the Dublin house in the name of interior design, he baulked at the thought of imposing such ideas here, where such luxury and artificiality would be an affront. He wanted everything in the house to look natural and – the word came to him – timeless, and when he saw a way to achieve this, it would be done. If that was a sorry motive, he was guilty as charged.

So for the moment rugs covered odd sections of the floorboards, while the windows relied on shutters or cheap curtains. For furniture he'd bought a few antiques through a dealer employed on one of his hotels, he'd picked up an old pine table and chairs for the dining room from a shop in Cheltenham, and had chosen two new sofas and easy chairs to stand in the long living room which ran the depth of the house. The sofas and chairs weren't right, he knew that. For one thing, they looked too modern; for another, they all matched, something you never saw in old houses. But, as with everything else, he wasn't in a mind to do anything about them quite yet.

He might have been slow with the decorations, but he was quick to maintain the fabric, and while Maeve went to the kitchen to unpack the food he made a round of the place, inspecting stone, brick, pointing, slates, gutters, paths; anything that might be in need of the odd spot of repair.

This was an old routine; it had been his job as a kid, to fix everything at Morne. It had started when he was thirteen and Lizzie, alone for much of the time with one baby and another on the way, had needed someone to clear the snow. He'd resisted going, he'd found every excuse – these were Anglos after all, and Mr Langley the worst sort – but he'd needed the money and it was only the once, he'd told himself, on account of the snow. Ten years later he was still turning up almost every Saturday, even after he'd established his own building company, and started the first of his pizza restaurants.

It had been Lizzie he'd kept coming back for, of course. Her talk, her reading, her encouragement, her joy in friendship, which, he understood much later, was underscored by the strains of her marriage. It was she who'd bribed Terry to go to school, who'd cajoled him to do his homework, who'd declared him capable of conquering the world, and at some level he must have believed her because here he was, somewhere near the top of the muck heap. Why had she chosen to have faith in him? Why had she bothered? She used to say it was the challenge, but really it was the goodness of her quiet and unassuming heart.

Nowadays the study was the one room at Morne where he felt a little less like a visitor. It was a small west-facing room in the back extension, looking on to the terrace and lawn, with the avenue of yews beyond, and pasture and woodland in the distance.

Two years ago when he'd first acquired the house, he'd installed a desk, a chair and a couple of side tables in here with the idea of making it his workroom, a study in the strict sense of the word. Then, finding that he was spending much of his time here, he'd had the chimney reopened and added armchairs on either side of the fireplace. In no time a television and books had followed and, though the room was cramped and the desk squeezed into one corner, it was at least a cosy space that he could call his own.

Now he opened a window to let in the evening air and poured himself a stiff Jameson's while he picked up the messages that Bridget had left on his answering service. Her voice hummed with satisfaction when she announced that she had found a phone number for Rebecca Child, whose married name was Wiseman.

Terry settled himself at his desk and took several more sips of whiskey before dialling the number in London.

It rang for some time before an answering machine picked up with an announcement delivered by a cool female voice that he did not immediately recognise as Rebecca's. He was just about to put the phone down with the idea of calling later when the tape was interrupted by a sharp 'Hello?'

'Is this Rebecca Wiseman?'

'It is.'

'This is Terry Devlin.'

'Well, well!' she laughed. 'Hello, Mr Terry Devlin. Where are you – Ireland?'

'I am.'

'*Pity!* Otherwise I'd say let's meet for a drink!' The merriment in her voice, the slight blur to her words, made him suspect that she had started the party without him. 'Now how are you, Terry?'

'I'm not complaining. And how are you, Rebecca?'

'Ahh.' The sound drew out into a lingering lament. 'Married on the rebound, repenting in the lawyer's office. I'm getting a divorce.'

He tried to think how long it had been since she married. Two years? 'I'm really sorry to hear that.'

'I told myself I was doing the sensible thing, Terry, getting married. I told myself we had everything in common. Background, religion, interests. There was only one problem.'

'You didn't love him?'

'No passion either. And at the end of the day, there's got to be love or passion. If you don't fancy someone, you can't pretend. At least I can't.'

'No sticking it out?'

'I wish. But we can't all be good Catholics, Terry, not like you lot. For me, it's a case of one life, one chance. I want another shot at it. All or nothing.'

'Well . . . I wish you the best of luck.'

'Not free yourself?' There was a raunchy note to her voice.

He laughed. 'More trouble than I'm worth.'

'It was Ben,' she said in a voice suddenly drained of humour. 'If he hadn't dumped me quite so massively . . . I wanted to show him, you know? I wanted him to realise I could find someone else, snap of the fingers, no problem at all. Oh—' She pulled up short. 'You've heard about his wife?'

'I've heard.'

'Terrible.'

'Yes.'

'I only met her the once, you know.'

'Yes.'

He needed no reminding of that day; it was emblazoned on his memory perhaps even more vividly than on Rebecca's. It was the day of the Irish Derby, the day that Ben had met Catherine for the first time, and Rebecca had lost him. And, God save his soul, it had been Terry who'd introduced them.

'In fact it was Ben I was calling about,' Terry admitted.

'Ben? Oh for God's sake, Terry – I haven't seen him since we bust up.'

'Ah. I thought maybe . . . You're not in touch with anyone who knows him?'

'Hardly,' she scoffed. 'I made our friends choose when we split up – him or me. There was no fence-sitting, not the way I felt about things. No, if I hear about Ben at all nowadays – which I try not to – it's third-hand.'

'Ah. In that case . . .'

'Why're you asking, Terry? Come clean!'

'I just wondered how things were with Ben, that's all. What he was up to.'

'What – work? Money?'

'An overall picture – anything, everything. Money. Work. Life.'

'Life . . .? *Oh*.' It was a knowing sound. 'You mean, is he playing away?'

'I suppose that too, yes.'

'Shit, Terry, you're asking me what men like Ben get up to when their wives are unwell? Like I'm an expert or something?' She guffawed at the thought. 'But you still haven't told me – why the interest? He hasn't gone and got himself on the wrong side of you again, has he?'

'Something like that.'

'Well, *well*! You'd think he'd have learnt the first time round. You'd think he'd know it was mad to tangle with *you*, Terry! But then he was never too bright about that sort of thing, was he? Look, I wish I could help . . .' He could almost picture her lifting her shoulders in one of her more expansive gestures.

'Well . . . if you hear anything.'

'*If I hear!* You're a funny one. But I'll say yes to dinner when you're next in London.'

'I'll call you.'

'Promise?'

'It's a certainty, Rebecca.'

Ringing off, he poured himself another whiskey and saw again the day three years ago when he'd invited Ben and Rebecca to the Derby. Strange the details that had stayed in his mind: the stillness of the air, the sunshine falling on the women's hats, the pretty blue dress Maeve had been wearing. He remembered think-ing what a fine couple Ben and Rebecca made, how well suited they seemed, how much he liked her. Over lunch, mellow with champagne, he remembered feeling something close to contentment, with his business going well, and Maeve by his side, a picture at seventeen and not a care in the world.

After the second race the four of them had decided to wander down to the paddock. Had it been his idea? It hardly mattered now. There was quite a crowd below the stand, Terry took the lead as they eased their way through the mob. He paused to greet one or two people, turned to wave to someone in the distance and swung back to find Duncan and Catherine standing in his path. It was the first time he'd seen Catherine since the episode with the letter more than a year before. Time had done nothing to protect him from the lurch of mortification he felt at the sight of her. Somehow he managed a smile, a greeting; he bent to kiss her cheek. By some miracle of social programming he remembered to introduce everyone, and without muffing their names either. Ben and Catherine shook hands, said all the mundane things that people say when they are meeting for the first time on a beautiful day at the races. For Terry, the awkwardness seemed to have passed. The two parties moved on, the day sparkled, Terry felt a little easier in his mind. There was nothing to suggest that anything momentous had happened, nothing to suggest that Ben and Catherine's meeting was in any way significant, yet in those few minutes the world had shifted for all of them: by such insignificant events is one's whole future determined. Terry often wondered what direction their lives would have taken if he hadn't invited Ben and Rebecca to the Curragh that day, if instead of going to the paddock the four of them had chosen to visit one of the many boxes to which he had an invitation. But thoughts of that sort were a whip for one's own back, and there was no sense in meting out more punishment.

It was the next evening near midnight, when the whiskey was roaring and chasing through his veins, that Terry began a new letter. *Morne,* he wrote carefully at the top, and *Friday* because he couldn't remember the date. *Dear Catherine, I hope you will not mind me dropping you a line in your new place, but I thought I should report on the visit of the celebrated Mrs Kent. First, may I say that I hope your new place is to your liking and that the staff are looking after you well. If the food is half good and the other inhabitants do not speak unless spoken to I always think one is in with a chance . . .*

So, Morne received a visit from the illustrious Mrs Kent . . . I have to say that things did not get off to the best of starts when Conn took exception to her. Under normal circumstances Conn is not a partial dog – he would as soon lick an intruder's face as bite him – but for some reason he took against Mrs Kent. Perhaps it was her voice – commanding, I think, would be a fair description – perhaps she had the scent of a Rottweiler on her – we will never know – but he bared every one of his rickety teeth and shivered and shook and generally carried on alarmingly until I hauled him back into the house and locked him up.

This counted against me with Mrs K, along, so it appeared, with much else. She is a forceful personage, not so very old in years (forty?) but mature in manner, who carries her knowledge like an encyclopaedia. I went to the bottom of the class because I knew no plant names, had not rooted out the Russian vine that is growing through one of the yews, and had failed to realise that half the fruit trees had canker – or would it be fungus? As for the shrubs that bore the marks of Mick's blunt machete, she said that it didn't terribly matter since they should never have been planted there in the first place (the soil?). She said it was a pity the garden had fallen into such neglect, since some of the best things would be difficult to save. Like what? I asked. Like the avenue and the lavender garden and the rose arches, she said. It was then I began to wonder if we were going to see eye to eye, Mrs K and I. I love the lavender garden, you see. And the avenue, for that matter. And even the rose arches, though I'll admit that they're a little thin and scrawny. Be that as it may, after much tutting and sucking in of breath and looking at the angle of the sun (another black mark – I could not fix on south, let alone east or west), she decided she might, on reflection, advise on a grand plan. She began to describe a few possibilities, but I couldn't take them in – I think I was still smarting from the accusation of neglect (your mamma loved the place a bit wild, didn't she? and I'm sure she was right). However, I've said yes to an outline plan and a few drawings, and we'll see where we go from there.

He read this through in despair. What would she make of this nonsense? He thought of tearing it up and starting again, but after pouring himself another whiskey he fell asleep in the armchair, to be awoken several hours later, cold and stiff-necked, by the sound of his own snoring. The next morning he signed the letter without reading it through, and posted it in the village before he had the chance to think better of it.

Chapter Six

———

THE MATCH flared in the darkness, illuminating Julie Basing's plump face. Holding the hand-rolled smoke like a peashooter, she lit it with a short puff quickly followed by a second lingering drag. 'Hey,' she murmured contentedly, 'truly vicious.' She held it out to Catherine.

Catherine hesitated before taking it. This hesitation was as much a part of the nightly ritual as her acceptance. Inhaling, she felt her head swim almost immediately. 'Help.'

'Dunno what you been missin' till you get good stuff.'

Catherine passed it back. 'A bit strong for me.'

They sat side by side in a corner of the unit garden, on the farthest loop of the farthest path. From behind them, the lights of the wing cast a feeble glimmer. The night was warm and still. Above the horizon, the sky was tinted a hazy orange from the town, but high over their heads one or two stars were showing through, faint pinpricks in the velvety dome. Catherine watched the steady unblinking dot of a satellite moving mesmerically across the sky towards the mass of nearby trees, which stood like giant sentries, tall and silent and heavy, bowed down by the last heat of the long sum-

mer. Even before the first trees began to turn, it seemed
to her that she could smell mouldering leaves and
woodsmoke.

'I used to love autumn,' she said.

'Nah,' scoffed Julie, 'summer, Spain and sangria for
me.'

'In autumn you can plan for the next season.
Move plants that aren't thriving. Make good your
mistakes.'

'No sortin' my mistakes,' laughed Julie, who at
twenty-five had two children by different fathers and
no man to support her. 'You know, this stuff is *truly*
great. Why don' I roll you a couple of joints for
tomorrow?'

For an instant Catherine was tempted.

'Or you gonna stay ratted all weekend?'

Catherine gave an ironic laugh. 'Why not?'

'Shove some vodka in an Evian bottle, then you can
take nips mornin' and afternoon.'

'There'll be champagne, I expect.'

Julie was unimpressed. '*And?*'

'My sister's doing the food so . . . smoked salmon, I
should think.' At the thought of the party Catherine felt
a fresh stab of apprehension and, against routine and
instinct, accepted a second smoke. She took a deep pull,
savouring the workings of the drug, the languor, the
sense of lightness, most of all the blunting of anxiety,
which was like a small but perfect miracle.

Julie leant across and tapped her arm. 'Hey, it'll be
okay.'

'I told Ben I didn't want a party.' Catherine saw
again his closed expression, the distracted smile, the
narrow unresponsive eyes.

'Look at it this way, it's your birthday, and they're just tryin' to make you happy.'

'They'll fuss, I know they will. I'm dreading it.'

'I did, didn' I, first time back.'

'But you knew what to expect.'

'You're kiddin'. Me nan ran about like a strangled chicken, pushin' food at me. Me dad, he kept talkin' to me brother about the Cup, 'cos then he didn' have to look at me an' the big bad wheelchair. And me mum, she just went and cried her eyes out in the kitchen.' Julie had been riding pillion on her boyfriend's motorbike when they'd collided with a lorry and she'd been thrown thirty foot onto a low wall.

Catherine said, 'At least they didn't give you a party.'

'Yeah, well – they're all gonna say the wrong thing. Right? They're gonna treat you like a child. Right? They're gonna say' – she put on a Knightsbridge accent – 'We think you're so marvellous! We think you're so brave! They can' help it. They dunno no better. Just sink another dose o' champagne, get wasted, have a laugh.'

Julie's creed was simple. You made the most of everything life had to offer and ignored the rest. While this approach left out too much, it perfectly suited her own stubborn nature and the philosophy of the spinal unit, which was pragmatic and upbeat. As if in echo of this, a distant shout of laughter floated across the garden on the torpid air, followed by a ripple of good-natured jeers.

On her arrival, Catherine had been quietly appalled by the quasi-military camaraderie, the blind devotion to sports and team games, the institutional humour. For some weeks she had resisted the pressure to join in everything from quiz nights to group discussions and counselling sessions, where, against all instinct, you were expected to offer up your most private and painful thoughts to strangers. Yet before long she too had succumbed, as all but the most stubborn must succumb, because in the end it was a relief to fight on only one front at a time, to be carried along by the routine, the sense of shared experience, the knowledge that, for what was probably the last time in your life, no explanations were due. She had responded to the atmosphere of, if not mutual support, then mutual resistance, a unifying scorn for the preconceptions and mawkish sympathies of the outside world, and learnt to joke loudly and laugh falsely at a great many things that by most standards were not very funny.

Her family had greeted this flippant mood with transparent relief and renewed attempts to get her back into the swing, as they liked to call it. The birthday party was one of their more obvious tactics. They seemed to believe that social contact, no matter how superficial, was like good medicine, hard to take at first, but immensely beneficial in the long run.

'Ben comin' to get you?' Julie asked. 'He could chat up that boot-faced bint across the corridor again, then we might get a few more laughs.'

'He's coming at nine.'

'Been away again, has he?'

'Just very busy.'

'He works like crazy, don' he? Least you got that. A bloke who brings home the bread.'

Catherine murmured, 'I'm not so sure.' She said it softly but not so softly that Julie couldn't hear.

The pale disc of Julie's face turned and peered at her in the darkness. 'Not sure, how?'

It was a while before Catherine answered. 'I'm not sure if I've got the bloke, and I'm not sure if we've got any money.'

Julie drew in a long thoughtful breath. 'Ooops. You think he's playin' away?'

Catherine chose her words carefully, and each still felt like a small betrayal. 'I think there are things we need to talk about that we don't talk about.'

'Yeah, well, men never talk, do they, not unless they've got a gun to their heads.' She glanced around again and said in a tone of friendliness, 'Wanna talk about it now?'

'Not much to say really,' she lied.

'Talked to the shrink?'

'He says that Ben's showing the classic symptoms of survivor guilt. Or rather, double survivor guilt, because he didn't manage to protect me, and because it was me and not him who was severely injured. Something like that.'

'What's that got to do with playin' around, for Chris'sake?' Julie declared in a combative tone.

'Ah, well – how did he put it?' Catherine went through the motions of recalling the psychiatrist's argument, though she remembered it perfectly well. 'Dr Fellowes said that when a man's failed in his most basic role as protector it leaves him feeling unworthy and emasculated. And that if he feels bad enough he may go and do things that are out of character.'

'Oh, p-l-ease!' Julie gave a hearty groan. 'So they feel guilty, these men, so it's okay for them to go and fool around. I tell you, if it was a woman they'd say she was a load of rubbish. Shit, Cath – what I mean is that men get all the breaks. *That's* what I mean. So . . . ol' Shrinko – what's he suggest, then? Therapy?'

'He says I should make it clear to Ben that I don't hold him responsible in any way. That I still respect and esteem him.'

'Yeah, well – so? That's what men want all the time, innit? Respect and no bother.'

Sometimes in her bleaker moments Catherine remembered how Ben seemed to avoid contact with her new body. Occasionally, when she really wanted to torture herself, she thought he was actively repulsed by it. But then, as the group discussions had taught her, there was no state of paranoia from which the newly disabled were immune.

'That Shrinko,' Julie muttered, 'he's a case, if you ask me.'

Catherine said, 'He doesn't rate my own guilt much.'

'What's wrong with it, then? Not good enough, or what?'

Catherine began slowly, trying to make sense of it all over again. 'Ben and I had a terrible row in France. Our first really serious row. I felt it was hanging over us – I *still* feel it's hanging over us. I keep thinking that if it hadn't been for the stupid row the accident would never have happened.'

'What?' Julie gave an exaggerated sigh of disbelief. 'Now, *how* in God's heaven do you work *that* one out?'

'I was going to stay on in France while Ben went to America, but at the last minute I came back with him. Because of the row. You know – trying to make amends, hating the thought of parting badly. But all I managed to do was stir it up again. We had another tiff on the way in from the airport. So stupid – about something so unbelievably trivial—'

'Like what?'

'Oh, about whether these friends we'd been staying with had taken offence at this nickname Ben had given their child.'

'What name d'he call it?'

'Raucous.'

'And was it?'

'Well, yes, it was, but then all small children make a racket, don't they? The point was, it became an issue. So ridiculous! It just made everything worse again. And I just can't get it out of my head that if we hadn't been arguing then Ben would never have stormed up and tried to fight it out with the intruder. He would have called the police or got a neighbour or . . . well, *something* else.'

'Wan' my opinion? Sounds like a load of complete bollocks to me. Men fight. It's in the blood. Can' help it. Every bloke I've ever known has been a fighter, and I'm not just talking push and shove either. It's in their terosterone, or whatever you call it.' She took a second equally unsuccessful stab at it. 'Trerosterone? Anyway – second bloody nature.'

'But he was angry. He was tense. He wasn't thinking straight. If he'd been thinking straight . . .'

'So this makes it *your* fault? Give us a break, Cath! You did *nothin'* that no woman ain' done through history – you had a barny with your old man. What was the big row about the first time, anyway? What was the big tangle about in France?'

Music came on somewhere, a tinny jangle that pulsated across the darkened garden. 'Oh,' she sighed, 'money.'

'Well, that wouldn' be a first either, would it? Men spend, women mend.'

'It was awful. I've never seen him so angry.'

'They never like bein' told they're not safe with money, do they? Can' take it. Never have, never will.' Julie performed her nightly ritual, pinching off the burnt end of the joint and stashing the tiny stub in her tobacco tin. Then, matter-of-factly: 'So now you think you're broke? Broke, like no Caribbean this year? Or broke, like no rent money?'

An aircraft flew so high above that it might have been at the same altitude as the satellite, on the very edges of space. Catherine looked up and thought of the intense phone conversations that took Ben out into the garden for up to half an hour on end when he came to visit, the way he prowled up and down and gesticulated as he talked, and the tension in his face when he returned. She could think of nothing that could put that sort of fear into him but money. 'I don't know. Could be no rent money.'

'You can earn, then,' said Julie sweepingly. 'Go an' do yer gardens.'

'No money in gardens. No real money.'

'Skip away to Ireland, then. That Terry keeps askin' you to do his garden, don' he? An' he's hyper-rich. Sting him for a deadly sum, why don' you? What've you gotta lose?'

This was a subject they had covered several times before. Julie, who was far more sentimental than she liked to pretend, had fallen for the dubious charms of Terry's weekly epistles to the glories of dogs, gardens and rural life, which she stole as soon as Catherine had discarded them.

'I've told you,' Catherine repeated, 'I'll never go to Morne while Terry Devlin's there.'

'But his letters – he's tryin' to be friendly.'

'Ah, but why? That's what you always have to ask – why.'

'Goodness of his heart? Tryin' to make amends for what he did to yer dad?'

'I think not.' She spoke in a tone of great certainty, but in truth she still couldn't make up her mind about the letters, which arrived with unerring regularity every Tuesday and which she had come to read with rather more enjoyment than she liked to admit. Was Terry really trying to say sorry? Or was he completing the reversal of fortunes by taking a paternalistic and patronising interest in her welfare?

'Well, he can' be *all* bad, not if he's stinkin' rich,' Julie declared with her own unanswerable logic. 'Play him at his own game, I say. Take the job. Get him to lay on the private plane, the cars, the whole bit. Make it champagne all the way. Take the money and—' Julie broke off abruptly and turned her head to some distant sound that Catherine had missed. 'Someone callin' for you, Cath.' Swivelling her chair, she added waspishly, 'Well, well, if it isn't your secret admirer.'

Catherine turned herself around and saw a man silhouetted against the french windows. Even before he began to walk towards them she recognised Simon's lean upright figure and stifled a guilty sense of dismay.

Julie said in a low voice, 'Mr Dark Horse.'

'What?'

'Hidden depths. But murky, I'd say.'

'He's been a good friend,' Catherine hissed reprovingly before calling out, 'Hello, Simon.'

'I'm off then,' sang Julie and pushed herself rapidly away.

As Simon stooped to kiss Catherine on the cheek she caught the scent of his aftershave, which still managed to take her by surprise because it was so spicy.

'How are you, Catherine?'

As always he had brought flowers; as always they were white, exotic and almost certainly expensive.

'Thank you,' she said. 'How lovely.'

'And . . . this.' He thrust a slim volume into her hand and said in a breathless excited tone, 'I managed to find a copy!'

She couldn't think what it was, and in the dark it was impossible to read the title. 'Thank you.'

'It's a new edition. They've taken out some of the minor works and added a few more in the name of revisionism. But it's still got the best ones.'

She realised it was a book of poetry he'd talked about, and she in an unthinking moment had said she'd love to read it. 'That's very kind.'

'I hope you don't mind me turning up out of the blue, without letting you know,' he said in his soft deferential voice.

'Not at all.'

It was almost nine and a Friday. Unless he was abroad Simon usually came on Sundays first thing in the morning and on Wednesdays in the evening. Before leaving he would punctiliously arrange the day and time for his next visit.

'So . . .' Catherine stalled immediately. For no reason she could ever identify conversation with Simon did not flow easily. 'Why this unexpected surprise?'

'Have you spoken to Ben today?' he asked.

'No. But then he's picking me up at nine tomorrow. I'm going home for the weekend.'

'Of course. I forgot.'

Simon was not someone to forget anything, however small, and this, along with his unexpected appearance, made her ask, 'Nothing wrong?'

'No, no. I was just passing.' The attempt at casualness didn't come off. 'And . . . well, I've got a bit of news.'

'Good news, I hope.'

'Shall we go inside?'

'Simon! You're making me nervous.'

'Nothing bad, really. It'd be nice to sit somewhere, that's all. Shall I . . .?' He was offering to push her along the path.

They went to a corner of the smoking room, an airless box of a room in the style of an airport lounge with rows of chairs along the walls and bright overhead lights and coffee tables patterned with rings and cigarette burns. The place was empty except for a couple of girls puffing greedily under an anti-smoking poster.

Simon moved a chair round, positioning it at a precise angle to her wheelchair before sitting on the edge and leaning forward with his elbows on his knees. As always he was smartly dressed, wearing a light grey Italian suit with a deep blue shirt and silk tie. His dark hair was sleek and newly combed, his small rimless spectacles flawlessly polished, his tapered hands exceptionally white and soft-looking. She had long since guessed that he spent time grooming himself in the Gents before coming in search of her.

'Well?' she prompted lightly.

'First, how are you?' he asked, his eyes fixed hungrily on her face. 'How's the physio going?'

'Oh, I've finally understood how one can be driven to kill. The physios are deaf to shouts of pain.'

He examined her face carefully to gauge her mood before deciding to smile. 'But . . . progress?'

'It's better than sitting on my bum all day.'

Catherine had been lucky, her spinal cord was only partially severed. On a good day, which meant a day when the physios managed to goad her sufficiently, Catherine could manage one or two uncertain steps on callipers and crutches, rolling along like a caricature of a peg-legged sailor. The physios had promised that with 'just' a few more weeks' work she'd be able to manoeuvre herself quite a distance, still with callipers and crutches of course, and on surfaces that were hard and level. For uneven surfaces however, pavements, shops, the outside world in general, wheels would have to remain what they termed the 'chosen' form of transport, at least for the moment. Either from ignorance or tact, no one had suggested how she was going to get around gardens yet.

'And the new callipers?' Simon asked conscientiously. As always he forgot nothing.

He listened to her report with a loyal smile, and she remembered how strained his smile had been when he'd started visiting her almost three months ago, how his cheek used to flutter so violently that he would turn away to hide it, and how very wearing she had found him in those days, with his overwhelming attentiveness, his intense desire to please. At some point, thank heaven, he must have puzzled over the tension he seemed to engender in her and finally understood that he must pull back a little, he must have realised that even the best-intentioned concern must have its limits, because as the weeks had passed he'd moderated his attention, or at least concealed it. He'd learnt to laugh with something like spontaneity, to give the appearance of being at ease, he'd learnt not to scrutinise her every move, though nothing, it seemed, could ever quite dislodge the watchfulness from his dark steady eyes. It was as though he felt the need to remain constantly alert to the dangers of misunderstanding or misjudgement.

At first she could only get him to talk about his social life, the films and plays he'd seen, the charity dos he'd attended. He took peculiar pride in these activities, he talked about the famous names he'd met, as though this proved his credentials as a gregarious member of a racy crowd, which only made her suspect that he was rather lonely, an impression borne out by his mention of numerous girlfriends, but no one in particular.

Having exhausted his social life the conversation would often flag, and once, when the silence had stretched out longer than normal and Catherine was feeling unusually irritable, she'd turned to the subject she had been warned to avoid. She asked him about his background.

The effect had been unexpected. It was as though he'd been waiting for her question, had even prepared for it. With a slow nod and a glimmer of anticipation, he'd proceeded with solemnity to tell her that his paternal grandparents had been German Jewish immigrants, who'd settled in Manchester before the war. Simon's father had been the youngest of their six children. Simon had lost contact with him years ago, but believed he was running a business up north somewhere. Simon's mother was living with a sister who ran a clothes shop in Chigwell. His mother had grown up in Ilford in Essex, the daughter of a trade union official. She had gone to the Royal Ballet School on a scholarship and become a star of the Ballet Rambert – a fact Simon recounted with immense pride – until she gave up the touring life to have Simon, her only child. She and Simon's father had split up when Simon was four – acrimoniously, Catherine gathered – and Simon had lived with his mother in a small flat in Islington – 'not the smart end' – until he won a place at the City of London School, when they had moved out to a flat in Manor Park. Reading between the lines, Catherine guessed that the move to Manor Park had been forced on them by lack of money, and that for Simon's mother life as a jobbing dance teacher had been an unwelcome comedown.

In a further show of confidence, unprompted but not, she felt, unrehearsed, Simon had told her with a kind of offhand bravado that did not sit easily on him that he'd been unhappy at school, unhappy at university and only started to enjoy life when he'd qualified and begun to make money. 'I realised money was the way out,' he'd declared. '*The greatest of evils and the worst of crimes is poverty.*' He'd laughed, though she'd sensed that for him it wasn't much of a joke.

Over the weeks, Simon continued to volunteer more particles of his history like precious gifts, given willingly but also with some anxiety as to how they would be received and safeguarded. She couldn't imagine why he was so sensitive about his past. It couldn't be his origins, not in an era when it was entirely fashionable to have poor immigrant grandparents, nor his schooling, which had taken him to Cambridge and a law degree. His parents, then? If so, Catherine guessed it was his mother, whose life story seemed to have stopped some ten years ago when she'd gone to live with the sister in Chigwell. Though Simon clearly loved and admired his mother, he never talked about her in the present tense, nor explained how she passed her time, except to say 'quietly'. Catherine imagined Alzheimer's or mental illness.

This, then, was the uncertain basis of their unlikely relationship: medical updates, social reports and occasional confidences. She would have hesitated to call it a friendship, she wasn't even sure why she'd let the visits drift on week after week. Possibly because he made few demands on her, possibly because for all his awkwardness she felt oddly comfortable with him. If she'd stopped to wonder why he should want to come and see her quite so often, she would have put it down to his nature, which would always search out some cause to which he could offer his rather dutiful brand of devotion.

Only once had he unnerved her. 'Do you believe in fate?' he'd asked one evening. 'I don't mean in the Buddhist sense. Rather the coincidental sense. The belief that coincidence signals and determines our destinies.'

'That depends on the kind of coincidence. Nice ones, yes. Nasty ones, it's all a horrible plot.'

'I mean certain ... *bonds*. Certain connections.

You don't think they're significant? That they indicate a predisposition for two people to meet?' He was strangely agitated, his voice breathy and rushed, his mouth jerking slightly as he talked.

'It all seems like chance to me, how people meet.'

'But take *us*! You don't realise, there's no way you could know – there's a bond between *us*!'

'There is?'

'I've never told you before!' He almost lost his nerve then. He said with a false laugh, 'You're going to think it's stupid.'

'Try me.'

As so often before, she felt that it took an enormous effort of faith for him to voice his more private thoughts. 'My family,' he said at last with a gasp. 'When they came over from Germany – well, their name was Gartenbauer!' He watched eagerly for her reaction.

Catherine got half way there. 'Garden. Garden-*something*.'

'Garden builder!'

'Oh.' Now she was beginning to see. 'You mean – like me.'

He nodded happily, with a wide almost ecstatic grin. 'Both of us – garden builders!'

'But you became Jardine?' she asked, more to move the conversation along than from any real curiosity.

'Oh, my grandfather was all for anglicising the name to Garden, but my grandmother thought something French-sounding would be more distinguished.'

'Coming from Germany, was your grandfather interned during the war?'

She had startled him completely. 'Yes,' he whispered, and again the strange ecstasy came over his face. 'Yes . . . You knew.'

'I guessed.'

'That's what I mean – you're intuitive.'

'I wish,' she said, making light of it. 'Most of the time my intuition is precisely nil.'

'But there's intuition between *us*, isn't there? That's what I mean – a bond. Garden builders!'

She smiled and looked away.

'I can't talk to anyone like I talk to you, Catherine.' When she looked back, his eyes were hard and bright and needy.

'What about girlfriends? Isn't there someone special?'

A defensiveness came over his face. 'No one special, no.'

'One day, though.'

'I don't know. I think my standards are too high.'

'Ah, women don't suit pedestals. Too easy to topple off. I come off mine almost instantly. With Ben I think it was the third time we met when he found me picking some rough bits off my feet.'

With that, the strange intense moment had passed.

Watching him now, though, she saw the same tension in him, like a charge of electricity.

'So, what's this news?' she asked.

He sat upright and fixed her with his dark damp eyes. 'I wouldn't bother you with this, not tonight, but I wanted you to hear it from me before you heard it from – anyone else. I couldn't bear it if you thought the wrong thing, Catherine. I really couldn't bear it.'

It was the hint of supplication in his voice that

always jarred slightly, the invitation to be liked. She smiled quickly to reassure him.

'You see, I wouldn't want you to hear anything that wasn't entirely . . . *accurate*.'

She urged him forward again with a nod.

'The thing is . . . with enormous regret . . . I've made the decision to leave RNP. The fact is that Ben and I have ceased to pull in the same direction. In fact, it's been wrong for a long time. It's got to the stage where we'd be better off on our own. I'm deeply sorry, Catherine. Believe me.'

He had spoken in the hushed tones of someone imparting momentous news, and Catherine found herself replying with equal gravity. 'I'm sure Ben will be very sorry to lose you.'

The dark eyes did not leave hers. 'Obviously, if there had been any way of avoiding it, I would have moved heaven and earth. You know that. *Heaven and earth*, Catherine.'

'These things happen.'

'It wasn't lack of trying.'

'No, I understand.'

'Really?' His anxious gaze searched her face, looking for confirmation or reassurance. 'And I'd like you to know that it was no split-second decision. It's been obvious to me for a long time that it couldn't be made to work. But of course I wasn't going to do anything while Ben couldn't get away, while he was needed here with *you*.' His voice trembled slightly, his expression softened, as though the very mention of her was enough to move him. 'But now that he's back at work, now he's travelling again, I feel that I have no choice, I can't leave it any longer.'

'It's good of you to have waited. I'm sure Ben's very grateful.'

'Good of me?' He recoiled fastidiously at the suggestion. 'It wasn't a question of good. It was the *right* thing to do, Catherine, from every point of view. The *right* thing.'

She thought what a strange unfathomable person he was, so racked by the proprieties of life. There were moments when she felt in awe of his old-fashioned rectitude.

'But now,' he stated with a break in his voice, 'the time has finally come. I do hope you understand, Catherine. Believe me, if there'd been any other way . . .'

'You must do what you must do, Simon.'

He gave his odd breathy laugh, which seemed to jump out of his throat at the most incongruous moments. 'I have to say Ben's pretty angry about it.'

'He probably needs time to get used to the idea.'

'I'd like to think so, Catherine, I really would, but he's saying that I'm in breach of our agreement, that I'm not leaving him enough time to find someone else. But that's absolutely not true. I'm following the terms of our agreement to the letter. I want you to know that, Catherine. You have my word.' He examined her face again, searching for whatever it was he feared to find there. 'He's also accused me of leaving him in the lurch. He says I couldn't have chosen a worse time.'

'There's a lot on?'

'Nothing unusual. No, what he's complaining about is money. Saying we've got no money. But it's simply not true!' he argued vehemently. 'Completely the opposite! Catherine – I've been working flat out for the last four months to get us out of the woods, and now we're there. We're actually there. He's talking nonsense.'

'When you say *there* . . .?'

'Oh, the extra loans have been paid off, the extra overdrafts we took out in March. And we've enough left over to make up our back pay.'

Catherine prompted cautiously, 'But there was a bad patch?'

'Yes, but way back in the winter. *Now* . . . well, we haven't made a packet this financial year, but we haven't done badly either. I don't know what he's on about, Catherine, I really don't.'

'I see,' she said, though all that she saw was that Ben's worries must lie outside the business.

'What caused the glitch in the winter?' she asked after a while. 'Ben never really explained it to me.'

'Ah.' Simon exhaled heavily. 'It was the deal with Polska CMC. Twenty generators. A million quid each. We spent months setting it up and then it just . . . evaporated.' His voice rose at the memory. 'We never knew why. I tried to find out what had happened, I did everything I could to resurrect it, but it'd gone stone cold.' He gave a slow shrug, a lift of the shoulders, an upturn of both hands. 'We put everything into it. The set-up costs were huge, we lost a packet. It's taken all this time to claw our way back. Finally got there with the Bahrain contract. I tell you, Catherine, I've been eating, sleeping, *breathing* the goddam Bahrain contract. But now, at long last, we're there. By the skin of our teeth, I have to say. But we've made it.' He added in renewed indignation, 'And now Ben's saying I'm leaving at a bad time.'

There was nothing she could say to this.

'It's really not fair, Catherine.'

Was he really expecting her to take his side against Ben's? She said non-committally, 'I'll be sorry if you and Ben part on bad terms.'

He leant forward again, his moist eyes glowing with a passionate light. He reached out to touch her hand and she noticed that his own was rigid and trembling slightly. 'I couldn't bear it if you thought I was abandoning Ben at a bad time.'

It was at moments like this that Catherine remembered why she could find Simon rather trying. She gave a minute shrug.

'I rate loyalty above everything, Catherine. If you abandon your friends – well, it's all meaningless, isn't it?'

She nodded in the hope that he would drop the matter, but Simon was not someone to leave a subject before he had made his point.

He said, 'You do understand that I've tried to do everything possible to avoid this?'

She replied with heavy emphasis, 'I do understand, Simon.'

'Really?'

She held up both hands. 'Really!'

'It was just that—'

She shook with sudden anger. 'You don't have to go on! Please don't go on!'

He pulled back sharply as if she had struck him and looked quickly down at the floor, but not before she had seen the dart of injury in his face.

She sighed inwardly. This was the way with Simon, to push too far and then be astonished by the reaction. She muttered, 'I'm tired. It's been a long day.'

His face tightened with remorse. 'Of course. I wasn't thinking. Of course. How stupid. It's late. I should never have . . .'

They both took a moment to recover.

Catherine said, 'I'm sorry. I'm glad you came to tell me. You've been such a good friend . . .'

'No, my fault. My fault entirely.' He offered a soft unhappy smile.

Letting the last of her anger go, she touched his arm briefly and declared brightly, 'Well, then – pastures new for you and Ben!'

He said, 'There's one other bit of news.'

When he hesitated, when his cheek fluttered and jerked, she thought he was still smarting from her rebuke. Nothing in his manner prepared her for what he was about to say.

'The police are questioning someone.'

She stared at him.

'Since yesterday. That's why I asked if Ben had called. I thought he might have told you.'

And still she couldn't speak.

'But, Catherine, he's not the guy. He's just someone who's got caught with some of your property. They'll do him for receiving.'

'Receiving?' she echoed stupidly, as if she were unfamiliar with the term.

'He had a piece of your jewellery on him.'

Catherine had never thought that any of the stolen property would turn up, had never allowed herself to imagine seeing it again. 'What sort of jewellery?'

'A brooch, I think.'

She had only ever owned one brooch, a sunburst in malachite and amber given to her by her mother. She had kept it in her jewellery box in a chest of drawers in the bedroom.

'Who is he, this man?'

'Oh . . .' Simon made a dismissive gesture. 'The police gave minimal details. Mediterranean appearance, aged twenty-eight, I think.'

'And . . . is he known for this sort of thing?'

'They didn't say. But, Catherine,' Simon insisted in his most solicitous tone, 'I really wouldn't worry about it.'

But I do, she thought. This man had handled her mother's brooch, this man had touched her life and brought the burglary back into focus.

Simon leant forward and rested a hand on her forearm, then after the tiniest hesitation and a quick upward glance, shifted it onto her hand. The coolness of his touch belied the faint dampness on his forehead. 'I'll keep a watch on everything, Catherine. I'll make sure there's nothing for you to worry about. Really – you mustn't give this man another thought.'

She did, though. She thought about him for the rest of the evening and between disturbing dreams and when she woke early the next morning to face her twenty-ninth birthday.

Chapter Seven

———

'NEARLY THERE,' Emma cried rousingly. She was perched in the back of the car, sitting forward with her elbows resting on the two front seats, her head at Catherine's shoulder, a cigarette brandished aloft, within an inch of Ben's head.

Ben drove silently, with concentration. Catherine stared steadfastly ahead. They were passing along Holland Park Avenue, through air hazy with dust and fumes and heat that had gone on too long. On Campden Hill a chestnut drooped in the moistureless air, its outer leaves shrivelled like brown paper, in declaration of an early autumn.

For no apparent reason Emma squeezed Catherine's shoulder.

'We did tell you Jamie and Sue were coming, didn't we, darling? We couldn't leave them out – they just insisted on coming. Wanted to pop in for a quick drink, but in the end – well, we felt we couldn't *not* invite them to lunch. Could we, Ben? But we're still only ten. Oh – maybe it's twelve. Is it twelve?' This addressed to Ben. 'Anyway, darling, it's still nice and small, like you wanted.' Making a futile attempt to blow smoke backwards over her shoulder, she cried, 'But you must tell us exactly what *you* want to do, Cath. Just tell us!

We'll kick them all out at two thirty sharp if you need to lie down and rest. Quickest lunch in history. Honestly, darling – the *lot*! You must just tell us.'

They turned into Ladbroke Grove and, cresting Notting Hill, sped down the other side before turning east and crossing the fruit-and-vegetable end of the Portobello Road, which was thronged with stalls and shoppers and bands of shuffling tourists.

'God. Bloody Saturday,' Ben sighed. 'Bloody parking.'

'I found a space in All Saints Road last week,' Emma responded. 'The far end.'

And still Catherine looked ahead. Last Saturday Ben had not come to see her, neither had Emma. Ben, she remembered, had been tied up with a meeting.

'I can go and park the car, if you like,' Emma volunteered.

'Sure,' Ben murmured.

Nearing Westbourne Park, they made the last turn into the street of small stuccoed villas. Catherine registered the bunch of brilliantly coloured balloons attached to someone's front door and dimly attributed them to some kids' party. It was only when they got closer and she picked out the house that she said in cold anger, 'Could you remove them, please?'

Ben slowed the car and double-parked outside. There was a pause in which no one moved.

Catherine stated quietly, 'I'll wait here until the balloons have gone.'

Emma scrambled for her door. 'I'll do it.' She ran up the short path and began to pick at the ties holding the balloons to the door knocker.

Ben offered a rueful expression. '*Not* my idea.' He

looked her full in the face, and in the harsh sunlight she
noticed that his eyes had grown a web of small lines at
the corners, an unhealthy puffiness beneath, and whites
that were red from lack of sleep or strain, or both.

She said, 'You look so tired. Have you been overdoing it?'

He gave a short smile and ran his fingers lightly over
her hand. 'No more than usual, Moggy. Just a bit
hectic, that's all.'

'The business?'

He made a soothing gesture, a slow weave of his
hand from side to side, to suggest that he didn't want
to bother her with such things.

'You must tell me.'

'Oh, just a small glitch.'

'Is it Simon leaving the partnership? He told me last
night.'

'God, no!' he exclaimed derisively. 'No – that's a
blessing! He's been a complete pain. A real old woman.
No – it's not Simon!'

'Then . . .? Tell me.'

He seemed to come to a decision. Taking her hand,
he lifted it solemnly to his mouth and kissed it.
'Nothing I can't manage if you're there to help me
through, Moggy. Nothing we can't battle together.'

'But what is it? A deal? A contract?'

He flinched slightly and offered a brave tortured
smile. 'Sort of.'

It was a show of defencelessness so uncharacteristic
of him that it filled her with alarm. In the same instant
it came to her that this had been the reason for the
barrier between them. There was no estrangement, it
had all been in her head, it was just this bad deal, they

were going to be all right. At this realisation something
overturned inside her, she felt a wrench of love and
longing. 'What is it, darling? You know I'll do anything
to help.'

He gave his same forlorn smile. 'Later. We'll talk
about it later. As soon as we get a quiet moment.'

'Whatever it is, I wish you'd told me before. Why
didn't you tell me?'

He grimaced and gestured impossibility. 'Couldn't,
could I?'

'But if you can't tell *me* . . .'

'Didn't want to worry you, Moggy.'

She shook her head gently. 'Oh, Ben. Far better to
know . . .'

He would have climbed out then if she hadn't
reached across and touched his arm. 'We'll get rid of
everyone as soon as we can, won't we, darling? Be on
our own? So we can talk. I feel we never have the
chance to talk.'

Reaching for the door again, he said, 'Sure.'

Like a child, she called after him, 'Promise?'

'Promise.'

While he retrieved the wheelchair from the back,
Catherine watched Emma remove the last of the balloons from the door and take them inside. She had
loved this house from the moment she and Ben had first
seen it. It was narrow and red and gothic, a garish
interloper in a sedate low-built terrace of stucco and
grey brick. Built in 1896 for the pastor of the Methodist
chapel that had once stood in the adjacent street, the
house wasn't much bigger than its humble two-up two-
down neighbours, yet it dominated the street by the
stridency of its red brick, the height of its leaded

windows and the precipitous barge-boarded gable end that rose above the smooth line of slate roofs like the prow of a ship. Seeing it again after all these months, a number of images spooled through Catherine's mind: of the rain-soaked day she and Ben had moved in; of the weekend she had planted the tubs with early geraniums, now parched and bent; of a day just before the wedding when she had stood opposite the house and thought: *This is where I will live as a wife – a wife!*

Darker images crowded in from another time, only to vanish as Ben wrenched the door open and reached in to lift her out. He had set up the wheelchair as close as possible to the door, in the gap between two parked cars. Since the road was heavily cambered, the gap between the parked cars not all it might be and this was a piece of choreography they had never tried before, she arrived in the wheelchair at an odd angle with one hip in the air and without her cushion, and with the brake off so that the chair began to roll backwards towards the gutter. In the process of lunging out to grab the chair, Ben lost his balance and, teetering precariously on one foot, almost fell across her, only saving himself by twisting his body round in an awkward jerky motion and throwing his other foot to the ground. For an uncertain moment he hung all his weight on the chair arm. The chair rocked, jolted back, trembled, and was finally still. Ben, pinioned against a Jeep, pushed himself upright, panting hard.

Catherine had long since forced herself to find irony in such situations. She gave a raucous bray of laughter. 'Fuckin' Ada!' she yelped in mimicry of Julie. 'Almost a gonner!'

Ben glared at her in shock and what might have been

rage, his skin white, his lips drawn back against his teeth.

'Hey, it's okay,' she said placatingly. 'It's okay.' This was what she always failed to take into account – how even the smallest humiliation cut him to the quick.

Still breathing furiously, Ben squeezed rapidly between the chair and the Jeep and hauled her backwards onto the pavement. As he spun the wheelchair round to face the house Catherine murmured again, 'It's okay,' and reached over her shoulder to touch his hand, but either he'd removed it from the handle or she didn't reach far enough because she couldn't seem to make contact.

A cry and Alice hurried from the house. 'Sorry – on the phone!' She stooped to give Catherine a small hug, a show of affection that by Alice's standards was decidedly effusive. 'Happy birthday!' she cried.

'You look fantastic,' Catherine said.

A small smile of satisfaction twitched at Alice's mouth, she bowed her head in acknowledgement. 'Why, thank you.'

Until now Catherine hadn't appreciated quite how much weight Alice had lost. She was dressed in clothes she wouldn't have dreamt of wearing a few months ago, a skimpy top and tight trousers that emphasised the shape and curves of her new figure. She must have lost two stone, maybe more. Her hair was different too, newly cut and subtly highlighted with hints of amber. Her make-up, rather haphazard in the past, was dramatic and flawlessly applied, as though she'd been taking lessons from a professional. Overall, the effect was of transformation.

Catherine said, 'You're still eating now and again, I hope.'

'In restaurants,' Alice replied archly. 'Still got half a stone to go, though.'

'Don't overdo it.'

'No danger of that,' she declared drily. 'Never too thin, never too rich.'

'You're having a good time, then?'

Out of old instinct Alice bristled slightly – she had always resented family enquiries into her social life – before submitting with an expression of magnanimity. 'Mmm,' she smiled. 'A *great* time, actually.'

As Alice caught some signal from Ben and stepped back to let the wheelchair pass, Catherine thought: She's feeling good about herself. She's probably got a man. She's going to be happy after all.

Ahead, Emma was standing on the threshold, one hand resting on the open door, a broad smile on her face, and now Catherine was overtaken by a more disturbing thought, that Emma was welcoming her into her own home.

Inside, there were rapid discussions about cars, parking and luggage. People hurried about and dispersed, and for a moment Catherine was left alone in the hall.

Flowers stood on the side table, and, propped against the vase, a batch of brightly coloured envelopes, addressed to her. On the wall beyond, a new picture had appeared, a pen-and-ink drawing of a mediaeval street that might have been Prague or Warsaw. In the far corner the work to widen the loo door was evident in the bare patched-in plasterwork and primed but unpainted woodwork. The sixteenth-century blanket chest from Morne that used to stand tucked into the bend of the stairs had been shifted around at right angles until it stuck out beyond the newel post into the hall. It didn't fit in that position, it looked all wrong, but she supposed it had been put there to spare her feelings. According to whoever worked these things out, it was the front edge of the chest that had broken her back, although, in one of the more interesting ironies, it had also in all probability saved her life by breaking her fall and preventing her skull from meeting the stone floor at full force.

Finally she looked up the stairs, which rose with two turns to the short stretch of railed landing at the top. There was no sign of her fall. The weak rail had been replaced, the splintered banisters repaired. Directly below, the stone was smooth and unblemished. A little closer, however, she noticed a faint mark on one of the flags, a large irregular splodge the colour of tea. Blood? Or an old mark she hadn't noticed before? A memory tugged at her, she looked back towards the still-open door, and, in a faded image like sepia, she saw herself lying here at this spot, her cheek pressed against the flagstone, looking along the distance of the grey surface, out through the door towards the street.

'Champagne? Coffee?' Alice asked brightly, bending forward with her hands propped on her knees. 'Loo? Wash and brush up?'

Catherine usually asked people not to bend over her in the same way they bent over prams and pushchairs because, subconsciously or otherwise, they were apt to speak to her in the same over-precise over-loud tones they used for small children.

'Or guided tour?' Alice continued, like an energetic scout mistress.

'Guided tour?'

'Your new bedroom.'

'I think I can manage that myself, thank you.'

Catherine must have spoken more sharply than she meant to because Alice stiffened and shot upright. 'Of course. I'll leave you to it.'

Catherine hesitated at the door of what in the house's clerical days would have been the front parlour, but which from the first day of their occupancy she and Ben had agreed could only be a dining room. North-facing, noisy and dusty from the street, starved of sun except for a few fragile rays that slanted in on midsummer evenings, it had become a room for late dinners and candlelight, with its dark polished floorboards, rich terracotta walls, large splashy paintings and matt black woodwork and fireplace.

There had been alterations since her accident, but Ben's description had been sketchy and as she wheeled herself in she still wasn't sure what to expect.

The table and chairs had gone into storage. In their place was a bed, a bedside table with phone, and a television on a trolley. The black woodwork had been painted white – hastily by the look of the finish – the floorboards had been covered by a fitted carpet in deep parchment – laid recently from the amount of fluff – while the windows had been hung with muslin day curtains. But it was the bed that drew Catherine's unhappy gaze. It was what the English have the nerve to call a small double, but which by any reasonable standards cannot hold two people in harmony unless they sleep facing the same direction and turn in unison. Catherine told herself that this bed had been chosen because its head fitted neatly against the only available wall space while leaving room for the bedside table on one side and wheelchair access on the other. She told herself that nothing bigger would have been practical, since the window took up much of the second wall, the fireplace the next, the double doors to the sitting room the fourth. Yet even as she tried to persuade herself of this, she saw again the white melamine bedside table, the ugly utilitarian trolley, and, what she hadn't noticed before, tucked away behind the television, a cantilevered table on castors for taking meals in bed, and it came to her in a burst of humiliation that the place had been fitted out for an invalid.

Her mood did not improve when she realised that the rich terracotta walls that had seemed so atmospheric for suppers with wine and candlelight were going to look saturnine and claustrophobic in the cold light of morning, and – if worse were needed – Alice's voice suddenly rang through from the sitting room, each word audible, and she realised that the double doors were going to provide almost no barrier to sound.

In the hall Ben was calling her name. Sweeping in, he cried, 'There you are! Well, what do you think?' Stationing himself in front of the fireplace he surveyed the room as an estate agent might inspect a property that with just a little more attention might yet come up to scratch. 'Not too bad, is it? What do you think about the walls? Could do with a different colour perhaps.' He cast her a hasty smile, which to Catherine in her new mood seemed evasive. 'What do you think? Cream? White? Or maybe some sort of wallpaper? God, I'm hopeless on these things,' he added with the perverse masculine pride that men take in their deficiencies at renovations. 'What do you think, Moggy?'

In the instant before she answered, it occurred to her that she could do this gently, with tact, she could put it in such a way that he would come to understand her slowly and with less chance of taking offence; it occurred to her that only moments ago everything had been mending between them and this might set them back; but it was too late, her anger was too fierce, it carried her forward in a red-hot sea and she said bitterly, 'I hate it!'

'Well, that's what I'm saying – it can be changed—'

'No,' she cut in sharply, 'the *room*. I hate the entire room! Everything about it. Everything! I don't want to stay here – I don't want to be in here at all! I want to sleep upstairs.'

Ben's eyes darkened, his mouth curved downwards. 'But Moggy . . .' He gestured helplessness. 'How?'

'You could carry me!'

'You mean, just for tonight?' The lightness in his voice betrayed a premature relief.

'No, I mean, always,' she snapped, trembling.

He took a long laboured breath.

'Why not?' she cried, hating the petulance in her voice.

'Well, I could carry you up *sometimes*, of course I could.' Appearing to realise how grudging this must sound, he repeated with more enthusiasm, 'Of *course* I could! But what if I wasn't here? You'd be stuck.'

'What about a stairlift? I don't see why there can't be a stairlift!'

'I told you, Moggy,' he explained in a tone of great patience, 'it'd be a complicated business. All the bends, the landings . . . And if we decide to move – well!' He threw up a hand as if the argument were self-evident.

Her heart gave a tight thump. 'But we're not moving. We decided.' She heard her voice rise. 'I thought we'd decided. Hadn't we?' When he still didn't answer, she demanded unsteadily, 'Hadn't we, Ben?'

He muttered testily, 'Sure.'

'Well, then.' She forced a note of reason into her voice. 'You do see, darling, don't you, it'll be hopeless if I can't get upstairs.'

'Stairlifts are expensive, Cath.'

'Well, how expensive?'

'A lot.'

'But how much exactly?'

He dropped his gaze and his jaw tightened.

As the silence drew out, her throat seized, her eyes burnt hotly. 'You said you were getting a quote.'

He didn't like being caught out. His gaze sharpened, his lips compressed. 'There was no point. It was going to be something like six or seven thousand, and the fact is, Cath' – he tipped her an unhappy glance – 'I can't manage that sort of money right now.'

She stared at him. 'You mean . . . that's the reason?'

'Yup.'

'Money?' she asked stupidly, as if he hadn't made the situation perfectly clear.

'If I'd had anything to spare, Moggy, *anything* . . .' He gestured the whole world.

'But I thought . . . Simon said you'd managed to claw back the money, to pay off the overdrafts. He said you were back to where you were before this thing in Poland—'

Ben's anger was very sudden. He held up a splayed hand that trembled visibly, he said in a furious voice, 'This is nothing to do with Simon! How dare he try and interfere! Christ!'

'He didn't. I mean, he just told me that RNP was back on its feet. That's all. Nothing else.'

'He knows nothing about anything!' Ben cut a swathe through the air. 'Nothing!'

She slumped a little in her seat. 'Okay, okay . . .'

For a moment he stood still, locked into his anger. She called his name. When he didn't reply she called a second time and held out a conciliatory hand.

He turned at last and, seeing her hand, came and crouched beside the wheelchair. Wrapping his hand around hers, he smiled with a touch of the old tenderness. 'The thing is, Moggy . . .' He sighed as if he hardly knew how to go on. 'I would have preferred to talk about all this later when we've got more time but since it's come up . . . You don't mind?'

'Don't mind?'

'Talking about this now?'

'No, no,' she said eagerly.

'The thing is,' he said, 'I'm not just a bit short.'

'You mean . . .?'

He hated having to spell it out. He said sharply, 'I'm broke!'

She felt a pull of dread. 'When you say broke . . .?'

'Spectacularly. Incredibly. Completely.'

She gripped his hand more tightly. 'Tell me. How much?'

He gave an odd snort and muttered under his breath something that could have been, 'Bled dry.'

Her bad ear seemed to ring with the effort of trying to hear him. 'Did you say bled dry?'

He held up a hand as if to withdraw the remark, then, rising from his haunches, swung round and sat down on the bed, his elbows on his knees, his hands clasped tightly in front of him. Behind the faint smile that was his mask against all eventualities, his face was pitted with anxiety.

'Got into this agreement,' he said at last. 'Can't get out of it. Got to pay. No choice.' He shook his head slowly from side to side as if he still couldn't believe he had got himself into such a mess.

'How much do you owe?'

'Ah, there we are. It's a nice round two hundred thousand.' He gave a broken laugh. 'No half measures, Moggy!'

There was a long silence broken only by the sound of Emma calling to Alice in the next room, asking about a bowl for the olives.

Catherine was very still, as if this might help her to absorb what he was saying. She must have been holding her breath because she had to exhale suddenly and take a gulp of air. 'God.' And still she couldn't take it in. 'God,' she gasped again. Eventually she managed to say, 'It can't be put off, this debt?'

'No.'

'It can't be – renegotiated?'

He gave a small shake of his head, and there was a glint of brilliance in his eyes.

'But the overdraft – the one you paid off after the

Poland thing – can't you go back and rearrange it? Can't you—'

His fury reared up as rapidly as before. The blood rushed into his face, he shook slightly. 'I told you – Simon doesn't know what the hell he's talking about. Overdrafts! For God's sake! Stupid bloody idiot!'

'Can't it – I don't know – be paid in instalments?' She hadn't spoken particularly loudly but Ben flicked his eyes towards the double doors and shot her a furious warning. Catherine closed her eyes for a moment. 'What about instalments?' she repeated in a whisper.

Still in the grip of his indignation, he said tightly, 'No.'

The front door banged, a phone started ringing, voices sounded dimly in the hall. Catherine thought she recognised her father's laugh.

She said, 'But surely they'd agree to—'

'*No!*' he insisted with a small shudder. Then, almost by way of apology, he said bleakly, 'It's already in instalments, you see.'

She felt the blankness come over her that was her protection against bad news. 'You mean . . . there's more to pay?'

'Been paid.'

She went on asking questions mechanically, unemotionally, like an investigator who must collect the facts. 'There've been other instalments?'

He made another attempt at black humour. 'Ah – just a few! Three, actually.'

'Three,' she echoed dully. 'And this one . . .?'

'Is the last.'

'The earlier payments, were they . . .?' Seeing the answer in his face, she turned it into a statement. 'They were for the same amount.'

He held her gaze: it wasn't a denial.

Out in the street a child gave a sudden wail and a father's voice called out wearily.

Some part of her was in free fall, she had to hold herself steady. 'The money so far, how did you raise it? Where did it come from?'

'Oh, here and there.'

'Here and—!' She pulled herself up short. 'Tell me – where?'

'I don't know. Cash. Loans. Overdrafts. Anything I could get my hands on.'

Her calmness finally deserted her. 'But so *much*, Ben! Six hundred thousand! How was it possible to borrow so *much*?'

'Never mind *how* I borrowed it,' he said ominously. 'The point is, I did it. I've managed to pay off three quarters of the bloody debt. Something to be congratulated on, I would have thought!'

There was a pause like darkness.

'But it'll have to be repaid, won't it? How will we ever repay it, Ben? So *much*.'

'Oh, it'll only take a couple of years, maybe less,' he said dismissively. 'I've turned over far more than that before now. I can do it again.'

She was finally reduced to a bewildered silence. He'd never mentioned this sort of money before. He'd always told her that cash was tight.

'In the meantime, I've got to find this last bloody payment,' he said. 'And that's the problem, you see. Run out of people to lend it to me.' He gave a grim chuckle. 'Not much to be said at the end of the day, is there, Moggy? I've really fucked up this time.'

Knowing how proud he was, realising how much this admission must have cost him, she avoided anything that might be taken as a reproach and said carefully, 'There must be something. What about going bankrupt? All sorts of people go bankrupt. In fact, rich people seem to do it all the time.'

'Not an option.'

'But it's not such a dreadful thing nowadays,' she argued lightly. 'It's almost—'

'Just can't.'

She left this alone for the moment. 'All right. So what happens if you don't pay? They can only sue you, surely. And in the time it takes to get to court we might have found some money—'

'No.'

'I don't see why you can't stall them. There must be a way.'

He reverted to a flippant tone. 'Ah, well, you see they're threatening to *tell*. Have me locked up.'

'Locked up? How do you mean locked up?' She laughed nervously.

He threw her an irritated glance, as if she were being exceptionally dense.

There was a rap on the door. Even as her father called her name, she cried, 'Later!' in a fierce voice. She heard his steps shuffle a little before moving away.

She turned back to Ben. 'You mean that they could get you into trouble?'

'They think so.'

'Who *are* these people? How can they threaten you like this?'

He gave a defiant shrug. 'Just people who have come across something that – how shall I put it? – could be misinterpreted. They reckon I owe them some money and now they want it back. And if I don't give it to them, they'll drop me into what you might describe as deep shit.' He spread both hands, he tilted his head to one side: the storyteller reaching the end of his tale.

She stared at him blankly.

'For God's sake, don't get all disapproving on me, Moggy. I didn't do anything very terrible. Really! Lots of people have done the same. It's just that – well, technically speaking, it wasn't quite . . .' He sucked in his breath.

'Legal?'

He rolled his eyes a little roguishly, like a schoolboy who has been caught out in a misdemeanour but, given half a chance, would commit the same offence all over again.

'What you're saying is that these people are *blackmailing* you?'

He turned this idea over in his mind and agreed without rancour, 'If you like.'

'But who are they, for God's sake? What sort of people?'

'Oh . . .' He brushed this aside. 'Doesn't matter.'

'Doesn't matter?' she whispered incredulously.

In one of his rapid switches of mood, he shot her a look of sudden resentment. 'It's complicated!' he snapped. Scrambling to his feet, he paced restlessly off across the room.

She bit back her thoughts with difficulty. 'So what's to be done?' she said.

He came and stood before her, his arms hanging

limply at his sides, back in the role of the lost boy. He made a show of hunting through the possibilities, but she knew what was coming, she knew there was only one option.

In the end it was easier to say it for him. 'The house,' she murmured.

His gaze, the small regretful outward turn of his hands, gave her his answer.

A knock at the door again. Alice's voice said, 'Catherine? Ben? The police are here to see you.'

Ben's head jerked up. He muttered, 'Christ.' Meeting Catherine's eyes, he gave a nervy laugh. 'Thought we'd seen the last of them.'

Chapter Eight

———

'I HAVE to notify you,' Denise began formally, 'that last night we charged a man in relation to your case. The charges are aggravated burglary and grievous bodily harm.'

There was a moment of complete stillness. At some level, far removed from this news, Catherine took in the changes to the living room, the way the sofas had been pressed back against the walls, the arrival of a table lamp she'd never seen before and didn't like, with a tall entwined-metal base and a Japanese crushed-paper shade.

Ben, perched on a chair arm beside her, broke the silence with a sharp explosive hiss, a sound of disgust or dismay. 'Christ!' he muttered weakly.

Catherine was simply lost. 'I thought it was just my brooch. You'd found someone with the brooch.'

Denise's reply was deflected by Ben's insistent: 'Who is this guy?'

'His name is Jan Pavlik, commonly known as Johnny Pavlik.'

'*Pavlik?*' Seemingly unaware that this had sounded like a trumpet of recognition, it was a moment before Ben answered Catherine's searching gaze with a brusque indignant shrug. 'Strange sort of name,' he argued irritably.

Denise said, 'He came from the Czech Republic originally.'

'Don't tell me,' Ben scoffed, 'an illegal immigrant down on his luck.'

'He's an illegal immigrant, yes.'

'Ha!' Ben exclaimed, half surprised at the accuracy of his own prediction. 'How did I guess? And what else can we surmise?' he demanded sarcastically. 'Seeking asylum? Fiddling the welfare system?'

Quietly ignoring this outburst, Denise looked to Catherine for questions. But Catherine had no questions and no curiosity. The impulse to keep her distance was very strong. It was a matter of self-preservation born out of fear, not of Pavlik directly, but of her own feelings towards him: the fear that she might grow to feel something as exhausting and worthless as hate. Even allowing his name to imprint on her memory was like a small descent.

She would have left Ben to talk to Denise then, but something held her back and she realised she had a question after all.

'Has he done this sort of thing before?' she asked.

'Not as far as we know.'

'He's never attacked anyone?'

'Not that we're aware of.'

'No stalking or anything like that?'

'No.'

Ben interrupted in a tone of aggrievement, 'You never said you'd got a suspect.'

'We thought we just had someone for receiving. Then our investigations led us to realise that we had our man.'

'When did you realise?'

'Two days ago.'

'Two *days*,' he echoed accusingly.

'There was no point in saying anything until we were sure.'

Ben let this go with a sharp frown before asking in a more reasonable tone, 'How long's this Pavlik been over here then?'

'He's lived in London for approximately five years.'

'Age?'

'Twenty-eight.'

'Drifter?'

'No. He had regular work.'

'What sort of work?'

'As a waiter.'

'A *waiter*? Where?'

'Various places,' Denise said, clearly not wanting to be drawn.

'Into drugs?'

'Not that we know of.'

'But theft and robbery and crime, presumably.'

A faint frown sprang over Denise's broad forehead. 'He has no form.'

'But he's not going to be a beginner, is he?'

Denise didn't attempt to answer this.

Again Catherine decided to leave; again something held her back.

Ben asked almost crossly, 'Are you sure you've got the right guy?'

'We feel confident that we have enough evidence to support the charges, yes. We feel confident that the CPS will take the case to court.'

'But what evidence have you got?'

'It's forensic. That's all I can tell you at this stage.'

'You mean fingerprints, DNA, that sort of thing?'

'Well . . .' Denise struggled on that one. 'Loosely . . . yes.'

'And what does this guy say? Does he admit anything?'

'He's denying it, basically.'

'Don't tell me – he was at home with his girlfriend that night.'

'It may well be something along those lines, yes.'

'He's got a lawyer, I suppose.'

'Everyone's allowed a lawyer.'

'But one who knows all the tricks.'

'Most of them know all the tricks, I'm afraid.'

In the small pause that followed, Catherine asked quietly, 'So he was found with my mother's brooch?'

'Yes.'

The thought of avaricious hands on the unassuming amber brooch that her mother had given her at the end of her life was repellent. 'It was worth nothing to him,' she said. 'Not to anyone in fact. Twenty pounds, if that.'

Denise made a sympathetic face. 'You'll get it back after the trial.'

'I won't ever have to see this man, will I?' Catherine said. 'I won't have to go to court?'

'That'll be up to the lawyers to decide, Catherine. Not in our hands.'

Catherine looked away towards the small courtyard garden that she had rebuilt in the early spring, with York stone, raised beds along three walls, and a wall fountain. When she and Ben had left for France the first climbers and perennials had been coming into flower, the garden was showing what Catherine liked to call the first flush of promise. Since then, however, either the watering system hadn't been working properly or Ben had inadvertently turned it off, because many of the plants were missing presumed dead while the remainder were showing all the symptoms of drought and neglect.

'I'm rather cold,' she said. 'I think I'll go and get a cardigan.'

But before she could move, Ben cried, 'I'll go!' as though he'd been itching for just such an opportunity. He was on his feet and out of the door before she had the chance to tell him where to look.

Denise sat forward. 'I know how hard it is to face the business of court and giving evidence, Catherine. But if you do have to attend, I'll be there to see you through. If you like, we can go and look around the court in advance, work out where everyone'll be sitting, what'll happen when you arrive.'

Even before Denise had finished, Catherine had decided she would resist all but the most powerful arguments to give evidence. There was nothing she could say that Ben couldn't say better. He would make a good witness, clear and concise. What was almost as important, it would give him a role. The shrink's words reverberated in her head. *Try to make him feel protective of you.*

Denise added, 'It's hard to face an attacker, but most crime victims find it a lot harder when the offender never gets apprehended, when they have to live with the fact he's still out there, a threat to someone else.'

Catherine thought: Well, if most victims are like that,

then I'm the odd one out, aren't I? She said, 'How long before the trial?'

'Hard to say. But months rather than weeks.'

'And until then? He'll be in jail?'

Denise faltered momentarily. 'Could be given bail. Depends on the sort of lawyer he has and the magistrate on the day. The CPS may well oppose bail, but when it's a first offence they don't always win that argument, I'm afraid. I'd be lying if I said they did.' She added hastily, 'If we thought he was likely to be a threat we'd give you protection, Catherine.'

'But you don't think he will be?'

'Nothing to suggest it. DS Wilson and the lads have been through his room. Nothing to show he was a stalker. Nothing to show he'd ever heard of you. So they're pretty confident it was a random attack.'

The dark shadow flickered across Catherine's memory, she saw the advancing figure, the arm swinging rapidly upwards to come down with all its force, and a powerful but unwelcome thought sprang into her mind: He was waiting for me. He meant to come for me. This thought had come to her before a couple of times – if she was honest, maybe a dozen times – but she'd always rejected it, as she rejected it again now, because it was based on nothing more than fear, the irrational rangings of an overcharged imagination.

Denise stood up. 'Well . . .'

Dutifully, Catherine said, 'Thanks for everything. Will you tell the rest of the team that we're very grateful?'

'Sure.' She hesitated in the doorway. 'Nothing else you want to tell me, Catherine?'

'What do you mean?'

'Anything else you remember? Any thoughts?'

'No,' Catherine said warily. 'Why?'

'The phone calls. There's nothing more you can remember about them?'

Catherine maintained her expression. 'There *is* nothing to remember.'

Denise gave a sudden smile. 'Fine. Sorry to have interrupted your birthday, Catherine.'

'Denise?'

She stopped in the doorway.

'The calls weren't from this man. I promise you that.'

Denise greeted this statement with a quick nod. 'Of course.'

Duncan must have shown her out because soon after the front door sounded he put a tentative head into the room and, eyes lighting up, greeted Catherine as he had always greeted her, with a show of joy and unconcealed pride. Like an Italian father, he stood with his arms outstretched, his head at an angle, his face creased into an emotionally charged smile. He bent to kiss her. When he pulled back, his lower lip was trembling slightly. 'Darling girl! The happiest birthday in the whole world to my darling girl! And to be home. At last. *Home.*' He took a rapturous breath, his expression see-sawed between elation and other more lachrymose emotions. Abruptly, he cried, 'Champagne!' and threw a hand into the air, as if to summon a wine waiter. He beamed conspiratorially. 'Nothing less than bubbly will do, eh?'

This rallying cry had reverberated throughout Catherine's childhood, for her father had never needed much of an excuse for a celebration. He loved the ritual of champagne, the weighing of the bottle in his hands, the appraisal of the label – though as Catherine had got older the labels had got brasher and less worthy of reverence – the extracting of the cork, and the pouring of the first glasses. He was never happier than when he was master of ceremonies, setting the whole household into motion, as he did now, calling out to Emma for glasses, to an absent Ben for the ice bucket, to Alice for general unspecified assistance.

Catherine laid a hand on his sleeve. 'I need to find my cardigan, Pa. I think it's in the front room. Would you take me through?'

'Of course, darling!' He went about the task with all the gallantry of the military man he was frequently taken to be, opening the door with a flourish, skirting back round the wheelchair to push her carefully through into the hall, and executing a neat turn into the terracotta hospital room. Diligently, he asked where the cardigan might be.

'Pa?'

'Darling girl.'

'I was wondering . . . I'm a bit short of money.'

He threw out a hand: a problem easily solved. 'Got plenty! Just been to the cash machine. How much do you need, darling? Thirty? Fifty?'

'No, Pa.' All sort of thoughts went through her mind, of his generosity in small things, of his lifelong difficulties with larger sums, of his old age, not so far away. 'No, it's more – capital. Ben and I find we're rather in debt. It's all been a bit much recently, with all the extra expenses. I was wondering if you could manage a loan. Just for a year or so. Until we can pay you back.'

'Darling girl, you know I'd give you the earth . . .' His eyes travelled the floor. 'The earth.'

'Whatever you could manage, Pa.'

His mouth moved soundlessly, he made a hesitant gesture. 'Would five thousand be any good? I might be able to stretch to six.'

Somewhere, in a foolish and optimistic part of her brain, she'd hoped the restructuring of the wine business might have changed things, that he might have managed to put something substantial in the bank, but history and experience should have taught her otherwise. She mustered a grateful smile. 'That's very kind, Pa.'

He brightened. 'Just wish I could manage more, darling, but you know how it is . . . first the recession, then the pound, then these blasted day-trippers bringing wine in by the van-load. Company's struggling a bit. But it'll help, will it, the odd five thousand?'

'Yes.'

'You're sure?'

'Thank you, Pa. In fact, we might not even need it at the end of the day. But it's nice to know it's there.'

'Darling girl – *anything*!' He creased up his face into the endearing smile she knew so well.

Seeking reassurance where she could find it, she asked, 'You're all right for money generally, are you, Pa?'

'Me? Oh *yes*, darling. It's never easy, of course, managing to do everything one wants to do in this life. But I'm perfectly content. Got to count one's blessings.'

'No debts hanging over you? No mortgage?'

'No, no,' he cried resoundingly. 'Not a thing.'

He lived in a flat on the southern borders of Belgravia, in what the pedantic might describe as Pimlico. The place was overlooked and dark, the rooms poky, but it was handy for evenings spent at his club in Pall Mall, or as the spare man at dinner parties, for which he was in great demand.

'That business with Terry Devlin, it's all over and done with, is it?'

His face darkened a little. 'Thank *God*. Horrid little man.'

'What happened exactly, Pa?'

He viewed the question with faint disapproval. 'Darling . . . best forgotten, believe me.'

'I'd like to know.'

His expression slowly shifted through one of suspicion to profound alarm. 'You're not thinking of—? You wouldn't—? You don't need money *that* badly, darling girl?'

In attempting to shrug it off, she heard herself laugh falsely. 'No, no. I was just curious, that's all.'

'For a dreadful moment . . .' Grimacing, he relaxed again.

'You always said he'd cheated you. I wanted to know how, that's all.'

'How?' he repeated, looking unsettled again. 'Darling, very briefly – very simply – he called in the debt when I couldn't pay it, when he *knew* I couldn't pay it. Insisted on taking Morne. What could I do? How could I save it? Had to let it go. Broke my heart, as you know. Poor Mummy – I felt I'd failed her, that I'd betrayed her last wishes, to leave it to you and Alice. To sell if you wished!' He held up a hand as if to deny suggestions to the contrary. 'Oh yes, you could always have sold it – she was quite clear about that. But it was to be *your* decision after I'd gone.' His voice shook. 'But what could I do? He had the deeds of the house as security and when I couldn't pay he made me sign them over to him. It wasn't in the spirit of the agreement. Wasn't cricket. But then, what could you expect? That's how he's got where he is today, isn't it? By never missing a trick. By taking every advantage, and to hell with who gets hammered along the way.'

He turned his old soldier's face to the window, stoic in defeat. 'And after all we did for him,' he mused sadly. 'You would have thought, wouldn't you?'

He patted her arm, he smiled his most uplifting smile. 'Enough of unpleasant things. It's your birthday! We're celebrating! Now where's this cardigan?'

The search for her overnight bag was carried out with a brisk efficiency that took him round the room and out into the hall, where she heard him calling for Ben and Alice.

Alone, Catherine was soon oppressed by the dark musty room and the mockery of the narrow bed, and soon followed her father out into the hall to find that he had vanished. Hearing clattering from the back extension, she looked down the passage and saw Alice silhouetted against the kitchen window, chopping with a vigour that would have done credit to a commis chef. Energy was not something one readily associated with Alice, and again Catherine thought: She's happy. She must have found a man. On the heels of these thoughts came the worry that Alice would set her hopes too high too quickly, that her uncertainties would drive her to smother the poor fellow with unreasonable demands. Alice had long professed a disdain for men, mainly because over the years she had thrown herself at a whole series of unsuitable and unwinnable men who, in rejecting her, had reconfirmed her views both of the male sex and, fatally, of her own unworthiness. Catherine only hoped that the new figure marked a new confidence, that she would break through the ceiling of distrust and discover some self-belief.

From another part of the house came more elusive sounds. Turning her head to catch them, she traced hushed voices to the upstairs landing. Wheeling herself across the hall into the angle of the stairs she craned her head up and saw through the banisters Emma's back and, barely visible beyond, the top of Ben's head. Emma said something in a soft murmur. Ben responded in a voice pitched equally low. Catherine was about to call up when Ben moved forward and touched Emma's shoulder. It seemed to Catherine that what followed was relayed to her at two speeds, that each move was enacted both rapidly and in slow motion. Ben dropped his hand from Emma's shoulder and, looping both arms around her, pulled her close and leant his head against hers. It might have been Catherine's imagination but it seemed to her that his eyes were closed, as if with strong emotion. Emma, meanwhile, had raised her arms to embrace him around the waist. They stood locked together for what seemed a long time but was probably only seconds. As they began to pull apart, Catherine pushed herself swiftly away out of sight.

It was barely twelve when Duncan poured out the champagne and the family raised their glasses to toast her birthday. Catherine drank the first glass quickly and accepted a second in the full knowledge that, this early in the day, it would make her rapidly and irretrievably drunk.

Alice proclaimed, as though from the battlements, 'They will be gone in five minutes!' and described an enormous arc through the air as if to direct a cavalry charge towards the front door. 'Even if I have to *throw* them into the street with my bare hands.'

Catherine announced, 'I need a man.'

Alice grinned delightedly. 'Don't we all!'

'Preferably strong and sober.'

'Oh, *too much*!' she chortled.

'To get me upstairs.'

'Upstairs? Right – *upstairs*! No sooner said.' Alice waved an imaginary wand. 'Who would you like? Ben? Hugh? Charlie?'

'So many men to choose from!' For no particular reason, Catherine found this thought terribly funny and grinned ludicrously.

Alice's smile faded. She crouched at her side. 'You all right, Cath?'

'I'm *fine*.' This was far from the truth, since Catherine was not only several glasses the wrong side of happy but for the past four hours had been neglecting her bodily chores, the hated tasks, large and small, that averted pressure sores and bladder infections and spasms, sins and omissions for which she would doubtless pay dearly. Already she felt the prickle of sickly heat in her face, a trickle of cooler sweat against her shirt. 'Just need to go upstairs.'

Alice hovered uncertainly before murmuring, 'I'll get Ben.'

'No – Hugh.'

Hugh, an accomplished horseman when he wasn't being a lawyer, was fit and strong and picked Catherine up as if she were a bundle of rags. He grinned leerily down at her. 'I think you're wonderful,' he said, breathing wine and smoked salmon over her.

She laughed a little. 'Why, thank you.'

'We all think you're wonderful.'

Catherine turned her head sharply away so that he shouldn't see the scorn in her face, and asked Alice to fold the wheelchair and bring it upstairs.

As soon as she was safely ensconced on the upper landing, she whispered to Hugh in a tone of complicity, 'If anyone asks, could you tell them I'm sleeping?'

'Certainly!'

Beckoning him closer, she whispered, 'Unless you'd like to join me?'

He laughed too loud and too long, he couldn't quite conceal the look of embarrassment that crossed his face and when he retreated down the stairs his chuckle had the phoney ring of a stage comedian's.

While Alice went down to fetch her bags from the terracotta room, Catherine wheeled herself into the main bedroom and found not the untidiness and scattering of unwashed shirts she had been expecting but order and a neatly made bed. Before she had time to wonder if Ben had found a cleaning lady, the sweat started from her forehead, she shivered with cold or fever and pushed herself hastily towards the bathroom. Some weeks ago, when the stairlift had first come up for discussion, Ben had measured the upstairs doorways and pronounced them adequate, but his measurements must have been out somewhere because the bathroom door proved to be a tight squeeze, and she had to grasp the doorframe and drag herself through, scraping the wheels against the woodwork in the process. Sponging her face with cold water, she didn't feel much cooler. She closed her eyes but reopened them as her head spun and her stomach tightened with the nauseous acidity that comes from too much champagne and too little food. If she wasn't careful she was going to have a vicious hangover. It was too late to make herself sick, the only thing was water and antacid.

The medicine cabinet was out of reach on the wall and she had to wait for Alice to come back to find aspirin and Resolve. As Alice rummaged through the stock of medicines something on the upper shelf caught Catherine's eye. Light-headed with fever or alcohol or both, it was a moment before she understood what it was. Among the antibiotics and home remedies was a bottle of perfume. Pale amber in smooth glass. Gold top. Not her own.

When Catherine emerged from the bathroom five minutes later, Alice was waiting for her, smiling brightly.

'Anything else, Cath?' she asked, following her into the bedroom.

'A new head?'

'Did you have that much?'

'However much, it was too much.' Catherine waved a hand towards the wardrobes. '*Some* time you're going to have to go through my clothes for me, Ally. Sort 'em out. Chuck 'em out. Everything tight or vaguely tight. Ruthless. To hell with how much it cost.' Realising this was presuming rather a lot, she remembered her manners. 'If you wouldn't mind.'

Alice gave a stiff smile, her eyes shone with a fierce indecipherable light. 'You can't wear them?'

'Too hard to get on and off. Not likely to fit either. My world has gone pear-shaped in more than one sense of the word – words, excuse me. Everything has rather *settled*, you see, around my bum.'

The bed was a low one and Catherine eyed it wearily. 'Now, if I get onto this bloody bed, will I ever get off it again? More to the point, do I care?'

Alice's face had taken on an increasingly appalled expression.

Wondering dimly if she had caused offence, too muddled to work out what it might have been, Catherine held out an appeasing hand, her second of the day. Stepping forward to grasp it, Alice seemed to keep coming, to be falling towards the wheelchair, and instinctively Catherine flinched, pulled her head away, before she understood that the arms which reached out to envelop her roughly, the cheek that bumped awkwardly against hers, were proffered with intense emotion.

'Oh Cath,' Alice cried in a ragged voice, 'any time you need me. Any time at all.'

Catherine felt the absolute stillness, the freezing of sensation, that was her defence against pity. The sympathy she'd received today had brought home to her with dismal clarity the depressingly pessimistic view that the able-bodied held of disability. This, they were implying with their relentless compassion, is the end of life as you knew it, the end of almost everything that made it worthwhile, the end of all you had hoped to enjoy in the future, the end of beauty and physical attraction and – their first thought, though they would vigorously deny it – the end of a fulfilling sex life. To them she was now indistinguishable from her condition: paralysed Catherine, wheelchair Catherine, poor sad tragic Catherine. *She used to have it all, you know.* Each pitying smile, each hand laid tenderly on her shoulder, each compassionate hug was like a slap in the face. *We think you're wonderful* actually translated as *You are nothing now, except in terms of the heroic role we have chosen to bestow on you.* They would not be denied their right to pity her; they insisted on it, because then they could face themselves in the mirror with a small glow of self-congratulation.

And now her sister: Alice who knew better than most the indignity of finding herself an object of pity.

Catherine thought: The drink's making me bitter.

After Alice had helped her onto the bed, Catherine said, 'I'll be fine now, thanks.' But as Alice left the room Catherine called her back. 'Last thing. Would you look under the bed for me?'

Alice made a comical frown. 'Under the bed? What am I looking for?'

'A baseball bat.'

Dropping to her knees, Alice made a thorough search. 'Nothing here, Cath.'

'You're sure?'

Alice crawled round to the end of the bed and looked from there. 'Nothing.' She got breathlessly to her feet and laughed, 'What's it for – bit of self-defence?' She started and gave a sharp groan of horror, knuckle pressed histrionically to her mouth. 'Sorry, Cath, I didn't mean to . . . Oh, God, *God* – of course! You're worried about being here on your own! Is that what it is? Do you want me to stay? I'm happy to stay!'

Catherine wasn't quite ready for Alice in this protective role and spoke a little more sharply than she'd intended. 'Don't be ridiculous. It's nothing like that.'

'Sure?'

'Sure. Now, go away,' she growled. 'And leave me to rest. Everyone's so bloody keen on me *resting*. Well, tell them I'm bloody *resting* like a good girl, will you?'

When she'd gone, Catherine turned herself onto her side and, with her arm stretched across Ben's half of the bed, as though in her dreams she might find him there, fell into the leaden sleep of alcohol and extreme tiredness.

She woke groggily to full darkness and the rocking of the mattress as Ben sat down heavily on the edge of the bed at her back.

'Didn't realise you were up here, Moggy.' His voice was thick and unreadable. 'Thought you were resting downstairs. Why on earth did you come up here?'

She turned onto her back. 'It was too noisy downstairs.' Reaching for his hand, she added, 'And I wanted to be here, in our own bed.'

The light from the landing was too faint for her to see his face but she had the impression that his expression had hardened. She heard him exhale, a long slow breath. His hand was loose in hers.

She asked, 'Has everyone gone?'

'Except Emma. She's cooking supper. Pasta, I think. Do you want to come down? I can't say I'm entirely happy about carrying you, Moggy, not down those stairs, not when I've had a drink or two. But if we go slowly, I suppose . . .'

'I promise not to fall.' If Ben thought she was making a poor attempt at humour he didn't say so.

For a fraction of a second their conversation about the debts had seemed to belong to another time and place, but now it came crowding back through the steady beat of her headache, like an emotional hangover.

'How are you doing?' she asked.

'What?'

'Not worrying too much about the money?'

'Of course I'm worrying about the money,' he said testily.

'We never finished talking. The house – I'm not clear,' she said with dull dread. 'Are we going to have to sell it?'

'Sell it? God, no.'

'There's another way then?'

'A second mortgage. It's all arranged.'

'All arranged?'

'I've got the papers downstairs.'

Something inside her smarted a little at the realisation that he had arranged the whole thing and gathered the paperwork without telling her.

He said, 'We can get Emma to witness our signatures.'

'You mean, tonight?'

'Well, she's here. Might as well make the most of it.'

'Can't we leave it till tomorrow, darling?'

'But Moggy, she's *here*,' he repeated doggedly. 'And nothing's going to be different tomorrow.'

'I'd rather leave it, if you don't—'

He shot to his feet. 'You're not listening, Moggy!' His voice was pitched dangerously low. 'Nothing's going to be different tomorrow! And I need to be sure I'm getting this money – otherwise I might as well go and slit my bloody throat!'

'I'd just like to feel we'd talked it through properly, that's all. To be sure it's the best way.'

His voice rose suddenly. 'I *am* sure! And I'm telling you there *isn't* any other way!'

She'd only seen him this angry once before, during their big row in France. Among their friends he was known for being imperturbable, a reputation that perfectly suited his view of himself as a person who conducted his life on his own terms. It hurt her to see him like this because she knew how much he hated it.

When she finally spoke again it was soothingly. 'Darling, I didn't mean to suggest you hadn't looked into it properly . . . of course I didn't. It's just – I'd like to know how big this mortgage is going to be. And what happens if we can't keep up the payments.' He was very still and she couldn't make out his expression in the darkness. 'Could we lose everything? That's what I want to know. Because I've no other money, nothing at all—'

'Ah, so that's it!'

They had got onto dangerous ground. He didn't like to be reminded that it was Catherine's money that had paid for the deposit on the house.

'Couldn't we buy a tiny flat?' she asked. 'Have some security at least, and use the spare cash from this place—'

'Christ! No time! No time!'

On old ground one is destined to take the same turnings, and she heard herself say, 'I just think of Mummy. It was all the money she ever had. Everything she'd worked so hard to keep—' She had been about to say *to keep safe*.

'So it's *your* money now, is it?'

'Of course not. It's ours, of course it is. I'm just worried about what'll happen if we lose it.'

'We'll rent, we'll save for another place – God, I don't know! All I know is that if I don't get this cash together I'm bloody sunk! And now you're talking as if we had a whole bundle of options. Well, I'm telling you – there are no options!' He paced the room, he came to a halt in the light of the doorway and clasped a hand to his forehead in a final gesture of exasperation.

Catherine felt the future close in on her, dark and cold.

Appearing to calm himself with an effort, Ben came back and sank onto the bed with a long and heartfelt sigh. 'Oh Moggy . . .' He bent over and rested his cheek against hers. 'If there was any other way . . . We'll be all right, once we're through this. Promise you. We'll be fine.'

But she had lost the simple capacity for optimism. Before the accident, she might have looked on the prospect of hard times as a challenge, a fine test of commitment and loyalty, but now it frightened her. Now, she had special needs, not the least of which was security.

'Hey,' Ben murmured into her ear. Pulling back, he placed his palm against her cheek.

Heart heavy, she heard herself say, 'You can count on me.'

'I knew you wouldn't let me down. I knew it.' He kissed her briefly before scrambling to his feet again. 'Supper? Do you want to come down?'

'I'm not sure I can eat anything.'

'I'll call Emma up, then. I'll go and get the papers. We'll get it all over and done with.'

'Ben?'

He paused in the door.

'What happened to the baseball bat?'

A short pause in which the atmosphere seemed to sharpen. 'Good God,' he exclaimed, 'I don't know. Why do you ask?'

'I thought it might have been used in the attack.'

'*What?*' He gave a small incredulous laugh.

'I thought I was imagining things, and then I wasn't so sure, and now – well, it's gone.'

He moved back to the side of the bed. 'Moggy, you've been having bad dreams. I moved it ages ago.'

'Moved it? Where to?'

'Hell, I don't know,' he said airily. 'Somewhere out of the way. The cupboard under the stairs, I think. Or the study. Maybe the study.'

'Why?'

'Why?' he echoed as if the question were absurd. 'Because it was too dangerous to leave under the bed. They always say intruders grab a weapon and use it against you, don't they? Thought it'd be safer.'

'You don't think that this man' – she couldn't bring herself to say his name – 'could have found it, then?'

'No!' he scoffed dismissively. 'I moved it ages ago!'

'And it's still there, wherever you put it?'

He rolled his eyes and shook his head and completed the show of disbelief with a heavy sigh. 'I'll go and get it if you like!'

'Oh, don't bother now . . .'

'No, no!' he said with a weary half laugh. 'Never let

it be said.' He was already on his way out of the room. She heard a cupboard door being opened in the study, followed by a clattering, then the sound of his feet thudding down the stairs, followed by faint rattling in the hall. He must have run up the stairs much more quietly than he had gone down because the next thing she realised he was striding back into the room, holding the baseball bat up like a trophy. In a juxtaposition of light and dark, time and memory, she saw the attacker freeze-framed, as if lit by a flashbulb, the weapon high in his hand. The image vanished as quickly as it had come.

'There,' Ben declared, offering the bat up to her.

'God. I was so sure . . .'

'Think you had a few too many, Moggy. You were certainly well away down there! But you're feeling better now, eh? Slept it off?'

'I wasn't feeling well.'

'I'm not surprised,' he said in the same knowing tone.

Swinging the bat lightly in one hand he strode out of the room, leaving the door open. She saw him hesitate and, with the faintest glance back in her direction, take a right turn into the bathroom. A minute later the lavatory flushed, the plumbing hissed as the cold tap was run, and it may have been her imagination, it may have been a trick of an overwrought mind, but she thought she heard the click of the bathroom cabinet.

She saw him cross the landing and head downstairs. Within a couple of minutes, he was back with the documents in his hand. Emma appeared shortly afterwards, wiping her hands on an apron. She would have chattered, but Ben cut her short, and she made a comical face over his shoulder, a schoolgirl rebuked for talking in class.

'Shall I sit you up a little, Moggy?' Ben asked.

He fed the documents to her one by one, then took them to Emma and stood over her while she witnessed them, alert for any misaligned word.

'There!' he said, smiling. 'How about some supper, then?'

Catherine repeated, 'Not for me.'

Ben hurried off with the documents while Emma helped Catherine into the wheelchair for a trip to the bathroom. Once inside, Catherine ran the tap to disguise any noise and levered open the medicine cabinet with the lavatory brush. The bottle of perfume had gone.

Seeing her back to bed, Emma waved conspiratorially and whispered that she'd be back soon.

It seemed a long time before she returned. By then Catherine's brain felt heavy, there was a clamminess on her skin like the beginnings of fever.

Emma drew up a chair and began to chat. As she illuminated some comment with a sweep of one hand Catherine found herself trying to catch her scent, and thought: This way misery lies. Even as she tried to banish the idea from her mind, she interrupted Emma with, 'What's that perfume you're wearing?'

'Perfume?' She had to consider for a moment. 'Help. It's Givenchy, I think. Yes – Givenchy. Why, darling? Do you like it? Shall I buy you some? Let me buy you some. An extra birthday presie.' With a flick of her hair she leant forward excitedly. 'Thought we might go to Harvey Nicks when you're next home, eh?' She rolled her eyes, she lifted both shoulders, she hugged her fists together like a small child. Breaking off only to light a cigarette, she hurried on. 'Starting on the first floor – where *else*. Then on to raid the cashmeres – what do you think? Yeah? Then a boozy lunch on the top floor. Then' – she thrust her head forward, she gave a wild grin – 'a facial? Haircut? God, we could spend the *earth*!' Her smile died slowly, overtaken by a look of concern. 'You okay, Cath? You look so tired. Do you want to me to go away and let you sleep?'

'Tell me something first.'

'Of course!'

'Ben . . . has he been okay?'

Emma hesitated, as if to make sure she'd understood her correctly. 'Ben? You mean – recently? Generally? I think he's been fine. I mean, working hard. *Terribly* hard. No one ever gets to see him. And worried about you, of course. Fretting about getting the house adapted, getting the things you need. It's all he ever talks about, you know – how he wants to get everything right for you. How he wants to care for you.' At this, two thoughts sprang unbidden into Catherine's mind, that a caring role was not one that Ben would have chosen in a dozen lifetimes, and that even in the most dedicated of carers a sense of obligation didn't always sit easily with love and desire. Emma cast around for any last ideas before declaring firmly, 'But otherwise – no, *fine*.' She added tentatively, 'Why?'

'No one gets to see him, you say?'

'Absolutely not. Hasn't made a single party since I can't think when. Not the Hamilton wedding, not even Dunny's birthday, and you know how he adores Dunny. Oh – he *did* get to Jack's do – you know, his annual bash. Had a great time, the life and soul of the party.'

This was what Catherine always failed to allow for – Ben's skill at concealment, his ability to put on a front, especially for his friends, who doted on his irreverent sense of fun. In times of stress, there's a certain comfort to be gained from clichés, and now she heard herself ask, 'If there was something I should know, you would be the first to tell me, wouldn't you, Emms?'

Emma made a gesture of bewilderment, an arc of her cigarette. 'Something you should know? What *do* you mean, darling?'

'You know that old saying about the wife being the last to know.'

Emma's mouth dropped open, she rounded her eyes in a show of astonishment and incredulity. '*Darling . . .*' She was momentarily speechless. She gave a short nervous laugh. 'No . . . I've heard nothing like that. Really, darling. Nothing at all!' She took a deep breath, as if getting over the shock. 'Where on earth did you get that idea?'

Catherine closed her eyes. 'Nowhere, I expect.'

'No, Cath, *really*,' Emma argued again. 'Haven't heard a thing. And you know how everyone is with the gossip. They can't wait!'

'Tired now,' Catherine murmured. 'Leave the door open, would you? And the light?'

'Of course, darling.' She stood up and paused uncertainly before creeping out of the room.

Long after she'd gone, Catherine heard laughter downstairs and felt the worm of doubt turn once again in her stomach. After another fifteen minutes or so, the front door sounded and the house was quiet.

She dozed and waited, but it was an hour before she heard a stair creak and watched Ben steal into view. Seeing that she was awake, his body sagged into a stance of disapproval, he came into the room with a shake of his head. 'Thought you'd be asleep, Moggy. You must get your sleep, you know! Look, I'm going to work for a while, make a few calls to Singapore. Bound to finish late, so I'll crash downstairs. Don't want to disturb you.' When she didn't reply, he busied himself pulling the curtains more closely together and fetching water she didn't need. 'Now are you all right? Got everything you want?' He cast a critical eye over the room before turning the bedside light off. 'Night, Moggy.'

His kiss was dry and firm.

'Don't sleep downstairs,' she said, hating the note of entreaty in her voice. 'I don't care how late it is.'

A minute hesitation, like death. 'Of course,' he said lightly. 'If that's what you want, Moggy.'

It was three when he crept into the room and slid into the far side of the bed. When she shifted herself close to his back and reached an arm around his waist he squeezed her hand briefly and murmured good night. A few minutes later his breathing had settled into the slow steady rhythm of sleep.

She was woken at seven by a dull pain in her kidneys and the scorch of fever on her skin. She was alone in the bed and when she called out there was no reply. It was eight before she heard him moving around downstairs and managed to make him hear her. When the doctor came he measured her fever at over thirty-nine and, after dosing her with antibiotics, recommended she go straight back to the unit for specialised treatment.

Chapter Nine

———

SIMON ORDERED the cab to stop a prudent fifty yards from the magistrates' court and walked the rest of the way at a pace that was neither so leisurely nor so hurried that it would attract attention. He observed the people loitering outside the entrance in the skirring wind: a slick youth with a loosened tie, shouting into a mobile phone; a group of slovenly women with rounded shoulders and sour mouths, sucking on cigarettes. From the opposite direction a couple of lawyers appeared, striding along in the rapid ostentatious manner of the professional, briefcases clutched like proof of office.

Beyond the metal detector and security check, in the halls and passageways, were more families and defendants in various postures of anxiety or hostility. Again, Simon's quick glance took them in; again, no face was familiar. The daily list showed that Pavlik was fourth in Court 2. Simon slipped into the public gallery and sat in the back of the two rows.

The building was solid Edwardian but the courtroom had been refurbished in pale wood and day-bright lighting. The public gallery was not as he had imagined, on a higher level and set well back, but down on the floor of the court, separated from it by a tall screen of wood and glass. The bench was just to the left, giving the public a close and unexpurgated view of the law, personified this morning at one minute past ten thirty by a rotund stipendiary magistrate with a dyspeptic frown. To the right was the dock, with, at the rear, steps leading up from the basement cells. Finding his first choice of seat rather exposed, Simon moved back to a seat hidden by the corner of the screen.

The first case was a remand for assault and took a bare five minutes. The second was a drug-dealing offence that had been held over for pre-sentence reports. Reams of paper had been produced by probation officers, social workers and psychiatrists. The magistrate asked questions and the probation officer spoke. Simon counted the professionals involved, calculated their time and costs and thought savagely: No wonder the system's in a state of collapse. All this to administer justice to a hopeless youth who will take the first opportunity to reoffend because it wasn't his fault he was addicted to heroin and cocaine and had to undertake the arduous chore of dealing to pay for his habit. Nothing was anyone's fault any more, not by the time the social workers and pseudo-psychologists had pleaded their liberal rubbish. It made him furious just to listen to it.

The drug dealer was given six months and the third case called, a bag-snatcher seeking bail. Some noisy relatives lumbered into the gallery. A woman with a heavy cold and a filthy handkerchief sneezed her way out. Simon paid no attention when the door sounded again. It was only when an expanse of cream trouser suit appeared at his side and a hand touched his arm that he jerked his head up. Even then, it was a full second before he comprehended that the lipsticked smile, the short hair, the polished make-up belonged to Alice.

He gasped an unintelligible greeting.

Before he could think of anything to say, she squeezed past him into the row and sat down. 'I haven't missed anything, have I?'

He tried unsuccessfully to push the astonishment out of his face. 'I didn't know you were coming.'

'Wanted to see what he looked like,' she whispered. 'Wanted to be able to report to Cath.' She seemed chatty, even friendly, but, deciding not to take any chances, Simon gave the smallest of nods before turning his attention back to the proceedings.

Alice put her mouth to his ear. 'She's been ill, did you know?'

'Yes, I heard.'

'A kidney infection. But they caught it in time. She's better now.'

He made an expression of relief and felt her gaze linger on his face long after he had looked away again.

In his shock at her arrival, he realised that he had forgotten a simple and terrifying fact. It came to him now with a spring of cold sweat that her presence could ruin everything. Usually his mind was a clear one, he could see his way through most problems, but sometimes when he met a situation he had failed to foresee a strange panic would overtake him. He felt it now, a sort of mental gridlock in which his only lucid thought was that he was unable to think.

'What's going to happen today, then?' Her mouth was so close to his ear that he could feel her breath.

'He'll be remanded again, probably for a month.'

'Oh.' She sounded disappointed.

'And he's likely to apply for bail.'

'But he won't get it, will he?'

'It's more than possible.'

'*What?* And let him go and terrorise other women? How can they allow that?'

'They get more rights than their victims, I'm afraid.' The panic had eased a little, his mind was beginning to clear. He needed to explain his presence. Steeling himself to meet her gaze, he whispered, 'This charge was a surprise – they thought he was just handling stolen property, didn't they? So I thought I'd better come and see what was happening. Let Ben know, keep the family in the picture. I didn't realise you were coming, otherwise I'd have left it to you—' In danger of gabbling, he broke off abruptly.

If she thought his argument less than convincing, she made no sign. 'Oh, it's good of you to come,' she declared without hesitation. 'And good of you to be such a support to Catherine. She won't let anyone else visit her, you know. Apart from Emma, of course. It really worries us.'

'Oh, it's a pleasure to see her. An honour.' Immediately, he wished this rephrased. It had sounded too abject.

Again, mystifyingly, Alice seemed entirely pleased with him. Dropping her head a little, she cast him an upward glance and said, with a brief bite of her lower lip, 'I'm sorry I was so defensive before.'

Her soft voice, her smile, flustered him. He couldn't make out if this friendliness was a trick or a game, if she would suddenly turn on him. Her face seemed very close. He could see every detail of the make-up around her eyes, so cleverly applied, of her glossy pink lips, her hair, which had been cut in a short bouncy style. He felt the tension come into his cheek. 'That's all right.'

'I was just overreacting. You know – shock.'

He made an ambiguous gesture, he smiled blandly: nothing that could be taken as a judgement. Seizing the opportunity to forestall difficulties later, he said quickly, 'In case you think I'm rude, I'm going to have to dash immediately after the case.'

'Oh?' Her quick eyes appraised him openly. 'Perhaps we could meet later? After work?'

He couldn't make out why she was suggesting this. Did she want to compare notes? Discuss Pavlik?

The puzzlement must have shown in his face because she whispered, 'Just a drink.'

His cheek gave a jerk that almost caused his left eye to close, like some ghastly wink, and he lowered his head furiously. 'I might be late at the office. I'm not sure when I'll finish.'

'Why don't we make contact later?' She reached into her bag and gave him a card, then, producing pen and paper, waited for him to scribble his mobile phone number down. 'I'm free from about seven,' she smiled.

There was sudden movement in the court and his panic resurfaced, he felt the heat rise into his face. The bag-snatcher, having got bail, was strutting out of the court with a smirk on his face, followed by a lawyer with an armful of papers. The usher called Pavlik's name and the warder disappeared down the steps to the cells. There was a pause in which there was no movement save for the clerk's pen as she wrote up her notes. Simon shrank back a little as the warder reappeared, followed at last by Pavlik.

It seemed to Simon that everything in his mind and

body tautened as he watched Pavlik saunter up the last few steps and take his place in the dock. He appeared relaxed to the point of unconcern; he didn't look around the court, didn't look towards the gallery, but kept his eyes on the bench. Simon tried to read his expression, to guess at his state of mind, but his face was devoid of emotion. He might have been up for a parking offence.

'Is that him?' hissed Alice.

Without removing his eyes from Pavlik Simon gave a sharp peremptory nod. Pavlik was short, something like five four or five, but, standing next to a warder who must have been well over six foot, he looked positively stunted. However, his broad, well-shaped shoulders, his thick neck, revealed the body of a man who kept in shape. He was wearing a light blue shirt, well-pressed, no tie, and dark blue chinos. His black hair was newly washed and very shiny. Simon thought: So much for the deprivations of jail.

Alice leant close again. 'He's not what I expected!'

But Simon had transferred his gaze to the lawyers' tables, where a new face had appeared, a short rather moth-eaten man with an unhealthy pallor, collar-length white hair and pebble glasses, wearing an ancient pin-striped suit purchased in slimmer days. When the usher announced, 'Number four on your list, sir, represented by Mr Gresham,' he stood up and nodded to the bench and made an application for bail. The woman from the CPS objected on the grounds that the charge was a serious one, that the police had not had time to make full inquiries as to suitability for bail and, last but not least, the accused was an illegal immigrant who would have every possible reason to abscond. The pinstriped suit lumbered to his feet again and stated that, though Pavlik had entered the country illegally, he had in fact applied for political asylum. Since the members of his family who remained in the Czech Republic were suffering considerable persecution as gypsies, he had every reason to believe his application would be successful. He had been in this country for five years during which time he had never been in trouble with the law in any shape or form, had held down a steady job as a waiter for four years, had been resident in the same area for two years. Given bail, he had every intention of resuming his normal life, residing in his home and, if his job was still open, returning to his work. Furthermore, surety could be provided if necessary.

The magistrate commented crossly, 'It would have to be a substantial surety.'

'Yes, sir, that would be no problem.'

'Who's offering surety?'

'A friend of my client who has every faith in him.'

'And who is this friend?'

'Mr David Frankel, a retired solicitor.'

The magistrate looked over his spectacles. 'Mr Frankel is offering this surety in a personal capacity?'

'He is indeed, sir.'

'Is he here today?'

'No, sir, but I have authorisation.'

'How long has he known your client?'

The pinstriped suit referred to his notes. 'Two years.'

'Is he fully aware of all the circumstances? Not least that your client is an illegal immigrant?'

'He is, sir.'

Behind the magistrate's perpetual scowl, it was clear

he was softening. 'Does Mr Frankel live close to your client? Will he keep in regular contact?'

'Mr Frankel lives in Hendon, sir. My client lives in West Kilburn, not so far away. And yes, Mr Frankel will be in regular contact.'

'And where would your client live while on bail?'

The pinstripe read out an address. 'It's the room he's been renting for the past six months.'

The magistrate considered. 'This is a serious charge. The accused is an illegal immigrant. I must ask for surety of fifteen thousand pounds. Is Mr Frankel prepared to stand surety for that amount?'

'He is, sir.'

The magistrate gave a small sigh. 'In that case ... unless the CPS has other grounds for refusing bail?' The woman from the CPS bobbed up and shook her head. 'Bail is granted on a recognisance of fifteen thousand pounds and on condition that the accused reports to his local police station once a day and lives and sleeps at his address. Does he have a passport to surrender?'

'Sir, his only passport is a Czech passport, which is out of date.'

'And they're letting him out?' hissed Alice. 'I don't believe it!'

Simon cupped a hand to his ear, so as not to miss anything.

'Do you fully understand the conditions, Mr Pavlik?' the magistrate asked.

'I understand.' The words were strongly spoken.

'And you must report back to this court on the date that will be notified to you. Any failure to follow the conditions of the bail or to appear when notified and you will find yourself charged with a separate offence and go straight to prison. Is that clear?'

'It is, sir.'

The pinstriped suit ambled across to the clerk to lodge the surety while a warder directed Pavlik back towards the cells. Pavlik appeared to argue, or at least to question this, and the warder paused to explain something to him before Pavlik acquiesced with a nod and made his way down the stairs.

Retrieving his bag from the floor, Simon got hastily to his feet. 'That's it,' he said.

Alice exclaimed, 'You mean, he's out? He's free?'

Simon was already on his way to the door. 'He will be shortly.'

'That's outrageous!' She hurried after him into the hall.

Halting, Simon held out a hand to make it clear that he had to hurry away.

Tilting her head to one side, she said, 'But where are you going? Why don't we share a cab?'

'I've got an appointment out in the sticks.' In a moment of inspiration, he added something approaching the truth. 'But I thought I'd try and find out one or two things about Pavlik first.'

Before she had the chance to say anything else he lifted a hand in farewell and walked briskly over to the gaolers' window to confirm that Pavlik was being returned to Brixton for release. Looking back, he saw the pinstriped suit emerge from court and shamble arthritically across the hall in the direction of the main doors.

Back on plan, Simon thought exultantly. Nothing

amiss, nothing to give him away. Only his own stilted movements and the sweat like rain inside his shirt.

He thought of Catherine, as he often did in times of stress or rapture, and this steadied him.

It'll be fine, he spoke to her. *Leave it all to me.*

An hour later he sat in the back of a parked minicab in a quiet road in Brixton.

'How long we wait?' The driver was Turkish or Lebanese. His eyes in the mirror were black as treacle.

'As long as we have to.'

'One hour? Two hour?'

'I'm paying, aren't I? I told you, I don't know.'

They were parked in a small residential road with a view back across Brixton Hill to Jebb Avenue and the barriers to the prison.

Simon had already slipped off his suit jacket and tie and, folding them carefully, had lodged them in his bag with his shoes. Over his shirt he had put on a casual zip-up jacket and on his feet a pair of trainers. Ready on the seat beside him was a baseball cap and in his pocket some dark glasses, a weekly travel card, and cash in varying denominations should he need to take another cab and pay it off hurriedly. Finally, he had attached a strap to his bag so that he'd be able to carry it over his shoulder, just like a tourist, a student, or a waiter on his way to the evening shift. If nothing else, he owed himself the satisfaction of having prepared fully. He ran through the details again in his mind, but could think of nothing he'd forgotten.

While he watched the comings and goings from the

prison, he made calls on his mobile, marking each one off on the card that he had prepared the previous night. After an hour he was able to tick off the last call – a deal he was setting up in Argentina – and to place the card in the inner pocket of his jacket, where it lodged with such gratifying exactitude.

As two o'clock came and the time dragged on, he allowed himself to daydream gently of Catherine. In so far as such a thing was possible, he tried to ration his thoughts of her. When he'd discovered she was ill and not seeing visitors, he'd sent her a card and some Belgian chocolates from Fortnum & Mason because he thought she would appreciate something a little frivolous for a change. He imagined her face on receiving them, he saw her smiling a little as she read the card. He was amazingly sure of this smile, just as he was sure that she spoke warmly of him to other people. She was a steadfast person, Catherine, she would never speak unkindly behind his back. When he thought of the way their friendship had grown over the months, the warmth and devotion she had shown him, he felt a piercing sense of pride. If they could continue as they were, he would be more than happy, though when he allowed his daydreams full rein he couldn't help imagining the two of them living in a beautiful flat together, an airy modern place, high up with lots of natural light and a large terrace with a roof garden and a view, so that when he was away Catherine could look out over the city and tend her plants. At other times this vision was transposed to the country, to an eighteenth-century house, possibly a barn conversion, with an abundant garden and wonderful antiques. In both of these homes he could see each room, the decor, the colours, the china they ate off, the food they served, the lunch parties, the quiet dinners *à deux*. These images were so perfect, so richly formed that the contemplation of them caused him an exquisite suffering. He didn't need to be told that he was feeling the terrible joy of the unattainable.

The sight of the tall white-sided prison transport coming up Brixton Hill and slowing to turn into Jebb Avenue jolted him back to life. He checked the time: barely three. This could be the one: only the magistrates' courts disgorged their prisoners this early.

Adding another hour to the driver's time, he calculated the fare and paid, with the firm instruction that the driver was to wait the full time. In the unlikely event of Pavlik having transport, Simon didn't want to be left standing by the kerb. Pulling on the cap and sunglasses, stringing the bag over his shoulder, he climbed out and, crossing the main road, waited at a point where he could see along Jebb Avenue to the side of the prison but, with just two steps back, could move rapidly out of view.

After ten minutes, a youth clutching a brown-paper bag stepped out of the wicket gate. Five minutes later came an old man, puffing on a cigarette. Then, after another ten minutes, Pavlik. From the way he strode up Jebb Avenue he was not expecting transport.

With a lurch of excitement, Simon began to walk away from the prison in the wrong direction for town. When he glanced back, Pavlik had turned into the main road, heading north. Doubling back, Simon followed at a distance. Obligingly, Pavlik was wearing a bright blue jacket, which, with his dark hair and distinctive build, made him stand out like a beacon. Once, he paused for no apparent reason and looked round. Simon had to force himself to keep walking naturally, but it seemed Pavlik was only checking the route advertised on an approaching bus because, once it got close enough to read, he lost interest and resumed his earlier pace.

On reaching the bottom of Brixton Hill, he made for the underground. Closing up, Simon was four treads behind him on the escalator. A train drew out as they came onto the platform. For a time they were the only people waiting. Simon sauntered up to a chocolate dispensing machine and, hunting for some coins, selected an Aero bar. Other people dribbled onto the platform. Glancing back, he saw Pavlik waiting patiently, staring at the advertising hoarding on the other side of the track, apparently unaware that he was being followed.

When a train drew in, Simon got into the next-door carriage and kept an eye on Pavlik through the glass windows of the communicating doors. At Green Park, Pavlik got off and transferred to the Piccadilly Line. Again Simon took the precaution of getting into the next carriage, but as this train was far more crowded he didn't attempt to keep Pavlik in view but stuck his head out of the open doors at each stop. He didn't have to wait long; the bright blue jacket emerged at Leicester Square.

The walk up through Chinatown was rather pleasant in the weak sunshine. Simon began to relax a little. This whole business was proving far easier than he'd expected, although, as he hastily reminded himself, this was due not to any skill on his part but to Pavlik's total lack of suspicion.

Pavlik crossed Shaftesbury Avenue into Dean Street

and, just when Simon was wondering where he might be heading, he disappeared into a pub on the corner of Old Compton Street. A stiff drink after a week in the clink; Simon didn't blame him. Simon rounded the opposite corner and leant a shoulder against the plate-glass window of a pasta restaurant that offered a view of the pub door across a table of gobbling tourists.

Pavlik didn't drink for long – he must have kept it to a quick double – before he was on his way out again, and coming straight for Simon. Simon hastened off ahead of him down Old Compton Street and walked briskly into a sandwich bar. After Pavlik had passed, he came out again and followed him round the next corner into Frith Street. Pavlik slowed up now, going at a pace that was almost thoughtful, before stopping and smoothing his hair in the reflection of a glass shopfront. Apparently satisfied, he went a few more paces and stepped in through a door. Getting closer, Simon saw an old-fashioned Italian restaurant with pot plants and straw-clad Chianti bottles in the window. La Rondine.

The workplace, presumably. Would the management have kept his job open for him? If Gresham was to be believed, Pavlik had been in the same job for four years, a veritable old-timer in the flighty world of Soho. But Simon suspected that a few months would be more like it, and plenty of moonlighting after hours. Did illegal immigrants pay taxes? Presumably not. Asylum seekers got benefits, though. A beneficiary of the black economy twice over, then.

It was almost five and nearing the start of the evening shift. Simon was beginning to think he had an exceedingly long wait in front of him when Pavlik reappeared, heading back the way he had come. Turning hastily away, Simon found himself standing next to two slack-mouthed men, staring into a dark cavernous doorway lit by garish photographs advertising the bloated breasts and brassy attentions available in the basement beneath.

Following again at a safe distance, he had to hurry to match Pavlik's pace as he turned west along Old Compton Street and down into Shaftesbury Avenue. He was walking so much faster now that Simon almost lost him in the crowds near Piccadilly Circus, only picking him up as he bought an *Evening Standard* at the top of the subway steps. Three minutes later Simon was safely ensconced in the next-door carriage to Pavlik on a Bakerloo Line train, heading north. It was no surprise when Pavlik got off at Queen's Park, on the northern edge of West Kilburn.

As Simon followed him into the maze of residential roads that must surely mark the end of the trail, his exhilaration was overtaken by doubt. What next? Where was this really leading?

Pavlik stopped at a Pakistani corner shop, emerging a few minutes later with a full carrier bag. Simon judged his distance carefully now, staying far enough back not to be noticeable but not so far that he couldn't identify the house once Pavlik finally got home.

In the event, he needn't have worried. When Pavlik turned in through a black metal gate in a long street of identical two-storey villas he didn't disappear immediately but paused for several moments in the porch, giving Simon plenty of time to mark the precise doorway. Striding briskly past a minute later, Simon noted the brass number on the door, and a single bell. He'd been expecting two or three bells, denoting rooms or flatlets, but unless they had been placed somewhere unusual and he had missed them, the place had all the appearance of a single house. Was Pavlik a lodger then? Or a guest?

The road was called, in improbable imitation of grander places, Fifth Avenue, and when Simon examined the A–Z later he saw that it was indeed one of six.

His luck continued when, immediately on reaching the Harrow Road, a free cab appeared, going his way. Safely inside, speeding along against the flow of rush-hour traffic, he allowed himself some small sense of achievement. At least he'd established that Pavlik was intending to live at the address he'd given to the court. Now, at the slightest sign of trouble, Simon would know where to come. What he might do once he got there was, of course, an entirely different matter. He took refuge in the solemn promise he'd made in his heart to Catherine. *I'll make sure no one ever harms you again.*

There was only one aspect of the day that did not slot neatly away in his orderly mind. The house in Fifth Avenue had looked too prosperous to take in lodgers. The fresh paintwork, polished brass house number, new plantation-style shutters in the upstairs windows, fancy window boxes and plant tubs spoke of money to spare. As he realised too late that the cab was heading for Lancaster Gate and the bottleneck across the park, an answer presented itself. Pavlik was athletic and good-looking, one to stand out in a crowd. He might have a lover, a luster after firm flesh who kept him in style in Fifth Avenue.

The tailback across the park started at Lancaster Gate; it would be a long crawl. He retrieved his mobile phone from his document bag and switched it on.

Before he had the chance to pick up his messages, however, it rang. He had forgotten about Alice until her voice sang, 'How are you doing? Ready for that drink yet?'

Gripped by a mild euphoria, he agreed immediately and with an enthusiasm that surprised him. An hour later, having been home to shower and change, he found himself back in Soho, walking into the Atlantic Bar. Alice was waiting at the long curved counter, perched on a stool. She smiled when she saw him. Her appearance took him aback. She had changed out of the cream trouser suit into a black dress that was low-cut and flimsy. Since her figure was by any standards full, it was a dress that displayed its contents rather too conspicuously. When she took a breath her breasts bulged over the rim of the dress, and he took care to keep his eyes firmly above her neck.

She was drinking something bright green called a Japanese Slipper, and, though he usually stuck to white wine, he allowed himself a rare impulse and joined her. She asked what he'd managed to find out about Pavlik and didn't seem surprised or concerned when he reported a lack of success. Then, duty apparently done, she chattered about her life, which seemed to consist of a long succession of parties, dinners, and country week-ends. She dismissed her work in an estate agent's as boring, while the parties were spoken of with excite-ment, as though she regarded a packed social life as the only real mark of success. Once again, Simon wondered why she should bother with him, why she had gone to all this trouble to meet him for a drink. He didn't doubt there was a purpose behind it all. At one point, he turned the conversation towards Catherine in case this should provide a cue, but she didn't pick up on it.

'So,' she said with a soft smile, 'what about you? Busy?'

While he talked of Bahrain and Argentina she listened attentively, with bright eyes that never left his face. He had the feeling he was being minutely appraised, and that so far, against all odds, he appeared to be passing muster. Under the searchlight of her gaze he ordered another round of the green drink – a concoction of vodka, lime and something he'd never heard of – and, trying to enter into the spirit of this strange encounter, offered a breezy smile.

Alice said something that was lost in the general din. He bent closer. Whether it was the misguided smile that had encouraged her or she'd been planning to ask him all along, she said in her low musical voice, 'You don't have a significant other, do you?'

'Not significant, no.'

'I didn't think so,' she said mysteriously. 'Why not?' She tilted her head, she leant forward a little, and her bosom came towards him like – he remembered reading such a description in a book somewhere – a blancmange about to slide off its dish.

He said, 'Too busy, too much work, no talent for commitment.'

'Ah . . . commitment.' She smiled with mock wistfulness. 'What about non-significant others?'

'Oh, we all have those, don't we?'

'Do we?' she said, clearly relishing the idea. Then, with a cat-like smile, a narrowing of her eyes: 'So you're not looking for a significant other?'

'Not particularly, no.'

'Don't want to be tied down?'

'Something like that.'

'Quite right!'

She seemed pleased by his response. She flashed her eyes at him over her drink. It occurred to him that in other circumstances, with anyone but Alice, he might have suspected that he was being flirted with. He found this thought sufficiently alarming to change the subject. 'You know that I'm leaving RNP, that Ben and I are going our separate ways?'

Smiling dreamily, eyes still fastened teasingly on his, she came to this subject slowly. 'Mmm?' When he'd repeated the question, she said, 'I'd heard, yes.' Then, seriously: 'I'm not surprised.'

'Oh?'

'Well, Ben's a difficult sod, isn't he?'

Simon made a show of considering this idea as if it were entirely new to him. 'Yes, I suppose he is.'

'You know, I always used to envy Cath,' she said unexpectedly. 'When we were kids. And later. You know. Looks. Could eat all day long without putting on weight. Never had spots. And there I was . . . *well*!' She rolled her eyes self-deprecatingly.

Feeling some response was expected of him, Simon framed a frown of denial.

Misreading this, she declared defensively, 'Oh, don't get me wrong, I didn't actually *mind*. God, no! Quite the opposite.' She attempted a laugh. 'It quite suited me, you see. I could just get on with my life, do my own thing, and no one was any the wiser. Got away with far more than Cath. God, yes! Pa was always eagle-eyed where she was concerned, wanting to know where she'd been, what she'd been up to. But me . . .' Her eyes slid away, as though she'd said more than she'd intended to. 'So – when Cath got Ben, we all thought she'd found herself the best, just like we'd always thought she would. Got the golden man, the pick of the bunch.' She gave a small shrug, she said enigmatically, 'But now . . . well, I rather think she's got her work cut out for her, don't you?'

Simon found himself arguing Ben's case. 'Whatever else, he's doing his best for Catherine.'

'Do you think so?' The disdain in her voice left no doubt as to her opinion. 'It depends what you consider his *best*.'

'What are you trying to say?'

She paused, she eyed him thoughtfully. 'I don't think he's behaving very well. I think he's doing the dirty on her.'

'Oh? And why do you think that?'

She raised an eyebrow. 'I *could* tell you it was just a feeling. I *could* tell you I'm just a clever judge of character.'

'But?'

'*But*,' she said with a heavy sigh, 'I know he's seeing someone else.'

Simon stared at his drink. He felt sick with sudden excitement, as if in one accelerated action Catherine had found out and the way was open for him to step in. 'Ouch,' he murmured, to give himself more time. Then, with a look of suitable concern, he asked, 'Who's the woman?'

'That I don't know.'

He couldn't make out if she was holding out on him. 'But you know there's someone?'

'Oh yes. It was when I went round early one morning to collect something for Cath. I heard someone moving around upstairs. Ben tried to make a clatter, to hide it. But I heard all right – there was definitely someone up there.'

'It couldn't have been – I don't know – someone else? A friend?'

She let her head fall to one side, she rounded her eyes in a knowing expression of doubt.

'No,' he conceded. 'Just ships in the night, then? A one nighter?'

She shook her head. 'She'd left her car keys on the hall table. Think about it.' She raised a forefinger. 'It's only a regular routine that makes a woman do that.'

'You didn't recognise the keys?'

'No.'

His euphoria had quite gone. He'd lost all taste for the gaudy green cocktail. The clamour of the bar seemed to rise around him, unacceptably loud. 'It wouldn't be the first time,' he said casually.

Alice stared at him, as if to be sure of his meaning. 'Since they've been married, you mean?'

He gave a light shrug.

'Who was it?'

'I couldn't say.'

'But there was someone?'

He met her eyes, and it was a confirmation.

'The bastard,' she said.

She was thinking of pressing him further, but he made a show of looking at his watch. 'Sorry, I've got to go.'

He caught the flash of disappointment under the

forced smile. 'Oh, I was hoping to lure you off to supper,' she said.

'It's work. Can't escape. But another time.'

'Definitely?' She was still looking at him with something like suspicion, and it struck him that he must tread carefully with her.

'Definitely. In fact, next week? Tuesday?'

'Tuesday.' Brightening a little, she smiled lazily. 'I must let you go, then.' When she leant forward it was for a traditional meeting of cheeks, a token pouting of the lips. But then, as he straightened up, she reached up and, framing his face in her hands, neatly guided his mouth down to hers and kissed him full on the lips. Her mouth was slightly open and it seemed to him that the taste of her stayed with him for hours afterwards.

Chapter Ten

————

'No PERSONAL mail, no,' said Bridget's voice in Dublin. 'And none at Foxrock either.'

Sitting alone in the hotel suite, the phone tight against his ear, Terry stared unseeing at the gauze curtains stirring in the sluggish air, and thought: Well, what did I expect, for heaven's sake? With half an ear to Bridget as she ran through the arrangements for his return to Dublin, he finally accepted what had been obvious from the start: Catherine would never reply. It had been ridiculous to think she would.

When Bridget had rung off he went to the window and, parting the swathes of fabric, watched the dusk creep up from the Mayfair streets into a crystalline sky. Hoping for a response had been foolish, though perhaps not so foolish as the belief that friendly words and weekly letters could overcome the resentments of the past. It was the arrogance of success, of course, to assume that everything could be fixed, that nothing, not even grievances, could resist the forces of determination and money. And what had he been out to achieve anyway? Forgiveness? Peace of mind? Just salves to his own conscience, he noted severely, surely one of the more shameful forms of vanity.

No, there would be no letter from Catherine, and he

would write no more to her either. He should have learnt his lesson the first time and realised that the written word did not serve him well so far as Catherine was concerned. The letter he'd written her during the summer of Lizzie's illness was incised painfully on his memory. He had never understood how he had come to misjudge the situation so badly, but misjudge it he had. There was no undoing it then, and there was no undoing it now. He would have liked his thoughts of that time to be filled entirely with recollections of Lizzie, to remember the many moments of laughter and celebration that had overlaid the recognition of her slow deterioration. But the choice of memories was another thing that willpower alone couldn't provide.

When Lizzie had started treatment, he'd managed to visit her most Saturdays and the occasional mid-week evening. Later, he'd rented a house a mile or so away from Morne and taken short weekends. Finally, at Maeve's instigation – she said he needed a rest – he'd taken a whole month's holiday, an event unheard of before or since, though holiday was a relative term for him, six hours a day on the phone instead of sixteen, and three meetings a week instead of twenty.

At first he saw Catherine only occasionally when she flew in from England, where she was studying under some famous garden designer. He noticed in passing her freshness and exuberance, apparently undulled by four years in London, and her looks, which had settled on her well, which to his mind meant unaffectedly. If he was aware of feeling, it was the great and clear affection he felt for Lizzie. If he'd been asked to describe his heart, he would have said it was full.

In July, a week into his so-called holiday, Catherine

came for a two-week stay which extended indefinitely, and they began to walk together. She was a fast walker; he, for reasons his doctor could have spelt out, less so. Eventually, however, they found a pace, and the walks became a regular fixture of the afternoons while Lizzie was sleeping, and some of the early mornings too. Catherine told him about her life in London and the people she'd met and the gardens she was working on, and he felt he was listening to two people, the single girl enjoying the big city, and the working woman who viewed the world with more detachment. On some of their more adventurous expeditions, they began to talk of all the other things that two people discuss on long walks: wars and governments and the nature of progress; ambition and friendship and love. She was an optimist, he a realist; she was what she liked to term a benevolent atheist, he a more-or-less practising Catholic; and so, coming from opposing philosophies, they agreed on many things.

At other times, he teased her as he'd teased her when she was a child, and she rose enthusiastically to the well-remembered challenge, answering as she used to answer, with nonsense and wild exaggeration. Then, towards the end of each walk they would quietly revert to the subject that generally began and ended their outings, the matter of Lizzie's wellbeing and how to improve it. If their relationship felt comfortable he told himself it was because it had both boundaries and purpose; if he felt an affinity for her, it sprang from the ties of familiarity and time, and their mutual determination to support Lizzie through the weeks of her treatment.

Which moment changed everything? Which of them

had got it wrong? Apparently it was him, though for the life of him he still couldn't work out how. He'd deconstructed and re-examined the succession of events time and again, but still couldn't see how he'd misread the situation quite so thoroughly.

The first moment that stuck in his mind came on an early morning walk over the black hill to the north of Morne. They'd left Lizzie looking better than for some days, and Catherine was in a buoyant mood. They were talking about holidays and going abroad, and the relative merits of Paris and Rome, which they'd both visited, when Catherine paused abruptly and for no apparent reason turned to him and declared, straight-faced, 'I've been thinking – most women would do far better to go for older men, you know.'

This was a way of hers, to throw a provocative statement into the air and see how it would fall.

'And why is that?' he asked mildly.

'Because then they wouldn't run out of things to talk about on holiday.'

'Is that a danger with younger men?'

She gave a theatrical sigh, all breath and affectation. 'God, yes! The only thing they can talk about is sport. Oh, and bad jokes – why do they love bad jokes?'

'Don't be too hard on them.'

She walked on, pretending exasperation. 'No, they're worse than useless. Older men would suit us all much better. They've been to places, done things. They know what they want, they're much more relaxed with women.'

'Older men would certainly warm to an idea like that with no trouble at all. But how much older are we talking about here?'

She hadn't thought about this of course. Shrugging, she lobbed a figure up at random. 'Ten years? Fifteen?'

'Careful, at that rate you might consign a bright young thing to a decrepit old man like me.'

'Terry!' She touched his arm and grinned at him. 'You're not old! How old are you?'

'I need notice of that question.' He pretended to work it out. 'If Buddy Holly died in fifty-nine, then . . . I'm thirty-six.'

'Just a child.' She walked on for a while before stopping just as abruptly. 'Will you marry again?'

'Oh, for heaven's sake.' He wasn't quite ready for that question. 'Who can say?'

'Of course you will! You'd be a catch.'

He snorted, 'I think that's very much a matter of opinion.'

'Well, *I* think you'd be a catch.'

'Just goes to show your ideas about men are fatally misguided. Who'd want a workaholic heading for a heart attack?'

'Sounds perfect to me.' Then she'd leant across and kissed him lightly on the cheek. 'Seriously, I'm beginning to see you in an entirely new light. Careful!'

She was joking of course, it was a moment of light flirtation, gone in a trice, though not so light that it didn't add a small frisson to their next conversation, a frisson that might nevertheless have remained entirely harmless if a short while later, in an incident emblazoned just as strongly on his memory, she hadn't looped her arm through his and said, 'I love it here, Terry. Ireland will always be my home. I'm not sure I'll ever feel really comfortable in England.'

'Come back, then. Money galore in Ireland now –

there must be plenty of people who want their gardens uprooted.'

'Oh, it's not the work – there'd be plenty of work – it's the life here. Or rather, it's the social life.' She chuckled, 'By which I suppose I mean the men! Or rather, the *lack* of them. Too many good Catholic boys, Terry.'

'Religion's never stopped a man yet.'

She pulled a face of doubt. 'It's Madonnas or whores here.'

'You mean there's something in between?'

'Ha, ha.'

'So – if there was the right man, you'd stay.'

The laughter left her face, she considered this seriously. 'Yes,' she declared at last, as though the realisation had surprised her. 'Yes, do you know, I think I would.' Then, in a lightning switch, she cast him a mischievous look and said, 'I'd stay for someone like you.' He thought she was joking again, she was certainly laughing as she said it, but then she muddied the waters all over again by pushing herself up on her toes and kissing him full on the lips, a kiss that was not so brief that it could be judged an assertion of friendship, yet not quite so long that it constituted a firm declaration of interest either. He was tantalised and baffled in equal measure until he reminded himself that it was a strange intense time for them all, that under the strain of worrying and caring for her mother it was natural for Catherine to look for light relief in games of love and desire. He told himself this, but deep down the idea of loving her was just there, waiting to leap heartlessly to the surface.

She phoned with the dinner invitation the next day.

Looking back now, he could see that this was the point at which perspective and judgement began to desert him. At the time, though, it was easy to convince himself that the invitation was Catherine's idea, that as the one person who had Duncan's ear she'd persuaded her father that the time had finally come to treat Terry as one of the family. He saw it as a sign of her growing affection for him.

From this distance, the extent of his self-delusion cut him sharply. And when he really wanted to give himself a hard time, he let himself believe that the real reason for the summons had nothing to do with friendship or acceptance, and everything to do with Duncan's need for money, and that this had been as plain as the nose on his face, if only he'd chosen to see.

During the summer Duncan had been away a lot on business, which, as Terry well knew, meant buying mediocre wine expensively in France and wondering why he was then unable to shift it at a profit in Dublin. On the few occasions the two men had bumped into each other at Morne, Duncan had looked at Terry with his customary vague smile, delivered the equivocal greeting at which he was so adept, the muttered, 'Oh . . . Terry, I didn't know you were here', and, wearing a vacant expression, departed for another end of the house. So when, after twenty-odd years in which dinner invitations had been conspicuous by their absence, Terry suddenly found himself on Lizzie's right, very much the honoured guest, he took it as a sea change. The fatted calf was on the table, the silver was out, a half-decent claret filled his glass. Duncan was at his most gracious and urbane, the complete host, the practised raconteur, the all-round bon vivant. Lizzie, with echoes of her old self, sparkled with pleasure at having so many of her loved ones at the same table and stayed up until almost ten, which was late for her. Catherine was quieter than usual, distracted or thoughtful, though Terry in his half-unhinged state managed to translate this into a beguiling serenity. At a quarter past ten Catherine announced she was going upstairs to make sure Lizzie was all right. He had no doubt this was precisely what she had done, yet when he raked over this part of the evening later he couldn't help wondering if it was entirely by chance that he was left alone with Duncan.

Not that he was in the least surprised when Duncan brought up the subject of money; over the previous six or seven years it had become something of an annual event for Duncan to be in need of 'the odd loan'. Terry braced himself, however, because on the last occasion, just eight months before, Duncan had asked for quite a bit more than before. In the early years it had been two or three thousand, but suddenly it had jumped to twelve, and Terry hadn't yet been rich enough for long enough that every penny wasn't still precious to him. He'd had to remind himself that this was a duty, like giving to his own family, and that normal consider-ations didn't apply. There were always going to be certain people in your life, related by blood or circum-stance, who only had to look at money for it to vanish. His brother was one, his uncle another. Giving to them was a matter of obligation, you didn't quibble, you wrote it off and never dwelt on it again.

'And what can you offer by way of security?' he'd

asked Duncan on the occasion of the twelve thousand because they always went through the pretence of putting the loans on a business footing.

'I thought, the sporting rights for a couple of years?'

Since the oak wood had long since been cut down and the wood pigeon departed – there was no question of snipe – Terry had supposed he was talking about the fishing, though by the time the local poachers had finished with the brown trout that didn't add up to more than a couple of minnows. But he'd accepted because honour, however transparent, had to be satisfied.

This time, Duncan began in his customary way, with some bleak observations about the business climate, before announcing that he was experiencing a few 'ongoing difficulties', which were forcing him to reconsider his entire position, lock, stock and barrel. Not to beat about the bush, would Terry be interested in a business proposition? This, of course, was beating around every bush in sight, but Terry managed to hold his tongue while Duncan meandered back and forth, skirting the issue with a skill that would have done credit to a Cold War diplomat, before coming in at an oblique angle, with what might or might not have been a firm clue as to what he was after.

'So . . . I was thinking of going for a total restructuring,' he said.

'Your business finances, this is?'

Duncan made the gesture of a negotiator who didn't care to be drawn too soon, a hand twisted one way then the other. 'Well . . . could be a bit of both.'

'How much did you have in mind?'

Duncan gave a deprecating chuckle, as if the idea of

stating anything so bald as the precise sum he had in mind would be far too crass at this stage in the proceedings. 'Well . . .' He had the lazy insipid smile of a man who'd learnt at an early stage that an easy manner and ready charm could get you a surprisingly long way in life.

Without warning, Terry reached some limit of his patience. Leaning an elbow on the table, unfolding a hand towards Duncan, he demanded firmly, 'Now, what are we talking here, Duncan? Cash? A lot of cash? Because if we are, I think we might have a difficulty. You see, I'm not interested in the wine business. I've no wish to buy into it, I've no wish to have a stake in it. And I don't believe there's anything else we can usefully discuss in terms of a deal. There's really nothing I want to buy. So you see . . . there's a difficulty, Duncan.'

Duncan made a show of taking this in good part, because according to the dictates of his simple philosophy one kept smiling through thick and thin. He reminded Terry of a dog that keeps trying to please, even when it's down. 'Of course, of course. I wouldn't expect you to be interested in anything you didn't want. Lord, no!'

Terry raised an eyebrow, awaiting enlightenment.

'No, no . . .' insisted Duncan. 'I was thinking you might be interested in Morne.'

There was a pause that for Terry was nothing less than electric.

'Obviously, not immediately . . . with things as they are . . .' Duncan struck the brave sorrowful note of the loving husband who can only wait and hope. 'When Lizzie's better.' This was delivered in hushed tones.

'You mean . . .' And Terry could hardly say it. 'You want to sell Morne?'

'Sadly, it's the only sensible option. Business conditions are too difficult here. Far better in England. People actually *appreciate* wine there.'

Terry was groping for understanding. 'But you don't want to sell quite yet?'

'I was thinking of delayed completion.'

Which meant the money now, and the house handed over at his convenience.

'But, forgive me – isn't the house going to be Catherine's and Alice's? For some reason I had the idea that Lizzie was going to pass it on to the girls.'

Behind the bland eyes there was a shadow of annoyance. 'No, no – never the intention. Lizzie and I were always going to sell in the fullness of time. Go and live abroad. No, no – it's been settled for ages.'

'I see,' Terry murmured, though he didn't see at all. In twenty years of conversations with Lizzie he'd never heard the slightest suggestion of living abroad; quite the opposite. 'And you're sure this is the only option?'

Duncan went through the charade of considering this. 'I think it's the most realistic.'

Which meant, thought Terry, his debts have got completely out of hand. 'And . . . if I were unable to buy?'

'Oh, then I'd put it on the open market. Lots of Germans buying around here. Plenty of interest. No, I just thought with your ties to the area it might just suit you. A place to keep for your retirement, perhaps.' He spun a hand, plucking possibilities out of the air. 'A holiday home. A long-term investment.'

And still Terry couldn't quite take it in. 'So . . . one way or another, you're determined to sell?'

A gentle sigh. 'Sadly.'

'But you'd prefer to stay a while—'

'Until Lizzie's better.'

'Until she's better.' Terry felt the need to spell everything out in great detail. 'Which of course you couldn't do if you were to sell to a German?'

Duncan tilted his elegant head while he pondered this for a while, as though the thought hadn't quite occurred to him in this form before. 'That's right,' he agreed with a solemn nod. 'It would be – disruptive.'

Terry thought: So here we have it, this is the deal. He was to buy time for Lizzie, he was to provide for her happiness by letting her stay in the house that she loved for as long as she lived. He was to pay for this privilege, undoubtedly through the nose, and be content to wait for possession until such time as Duncan decided to move out.

It was the solution of Solomon, and Terry could only bow to Duncan's masterly reading of his character. At the same time he was pursued by a deep unease. 'What about Catherine and Alice?' he asked. 'How do they feel? Not to mention Lizzie.'

'Oh, they're not to know. *Mustn't* know,' Duncan cried with a pale laugh. 'It would upset them dreadfully. Not a good time to think of *change*, you know.'

'But . . . the girls do realise they're not to get the house.'

'They've known it for a long time. There's never been any question.'

'Nevertheless, wouldn't it be best to mention this business to them?'

'Best? I think *not*, Terry. Not for them, not for me. Not for any of us.'

'If you say so,' he agreed reluctantly. 'A private arrangement, then.'

Duncan was thrilled that Terry should finally grasp the essence of the scheme. He tapped his arm. 'That's it!'

'But Lizzie will have to sign the contract. She'll have to see it.'

'No, no – she won't need to be bothered with the contents, she won't need to be told what it's about,' said Duncan in the certain tone of a man who knows what's best for his wife, and again Terry's stomach tightened unhappily. Later, he assuaged his unease with the reminder that Duncan would have sold the house anyway, and doing it this way Lizzie would at least remain in ignorance of it.

Thereafter, the details were, in a sense, academic. It was a question of establishing how much Duncan needed immediately, on signature of contract, a sum that probably equated to his current debts and then some, and how much he wanted when the deeds were handed over, an indicator of how much he thought he'd need in the next year. Thereafter Terry offered yearly instalments, or a lump sum on vacant possession, or a combination of both up to the sum agreed. For form's sake he beat Duncan down on the total price, but by the time he shook on the deal he reckoned it was costing him sixty to seventy per cent more than Morne was worth at the fanciest possible market price.

This transaction did nothing for his peace of mind. He didn't want Morne, he felt uncomfortable at the idea of buying it behind Lizzie and Catherine's back, and, so far as the money was concerned, he didn't trust Duncan not to come back for more. And underlying all this anxiety, lapping just beneath the surface of his consciousness, were his tumultuous feelings for Catherine.

A couple of days later, he brought Maeve over to Morne for a picnic in the walled garden. Alice was there, and some neighbours and cousins. With all the comings and goings there was no chance to speak to Catherine alone, but when she glanced his way and smiled it seemed to him that there was a very private and particular message in her gaze. Imagination? Wishful thinking? The longings of a lonely man?

Early the following morning he arrived at Morne for their customary walk, but it was raining too hard and they stayed in the kitchen instead. Catherine was drained after tending to Lizzie in the night. Her eyes looked enormous and empty in the flat white light. After a while, though, she began to emerge from her tiredness, even to tease him a little, which always cheered her up, and when he suggested an expedition to Castledermot later for a spot of supper she agreed immediately.

The evening had stayed with him as a series of conversations interwoven by a long unspoken dialogue. He saw her face animated, sad, thoughtful, but most of all he saw her eyes, which seemed to contain but one simple message. As the evening wore on – could he have been so wrong? – it seemed to him that the two of them were gathered up in a growing and unequivocal understanding.

Two days later, in a state of agonised hope, he sent the letter. An invitation to go to Donegal for the weekend, but also, clearly spelt out between the lines, a man asking a woman if she wouldn't like to take things further, the nearest a man could get in such undemonstrative times to a declaration. He signed it 'with greatest love'.

The letter was written on perfectly ordinary paper, cream if he remembered correctly, but for all its apparent fragility it might have been written in stone.

Promptly at six thirty the desk rang up to announce Fergal. Wherever Fergal's natural habitat might be, it was clearly not the fin-de-siècle opulence of Claridge's Hotel. In his faded baggy-kneed trousers, his crumpled linen jacket with the drooping hem, his recalcitrant hair, he reminded Terry of a rather shambolic priest entering a lady's boudoir. As if to reinforce this impression, Fergal looked around him with curiosity and faint disapproval.

Settling himself as best he could in a cabriole-legged chair with roseate padded upholstery, Fergal swivelled his eyes, as if to encompass the whole building. 'Not thinking of buying this one, then?'

'Not just at the moment, Fergal.' Terry offered him a drink, which he declined with a spread of his hand.

'How's Maeve?'

'She's truly fine. She's off now with Dinah, buying up Bond Street and Knightsbridge and probably the rest of London as well.'

'She's well recovered, then?'

'Almost there, I do believe.' Terry sat down opposite. 'So?' he prompted fretfully.

Reaching into a sagging pocket, Fergal pulled out his notebook and flipped it open. But either he didn't need reminding of what it said or he hadn't written anything down anyway, because he closed it again and spoke from memory. 'Pavlik,' he stated solemnly, his shaggy eyebrows knotted together in what might have been weariness. 'Bail application successful. Fifteen thousand pounds surety. Required to report once a day to the local police station.'

'So. As expected, more or less. The lawyer—' He gestured a lapse of memory.

'Gresham.'

'Gresham. Any good?'

'Wily enough, I'd say.'

'The question is, will Pavlik keep to the bail terms? Or will he try to do a skip?'

'Hard to say. He has no passport, no papers to speak of, except for a forged national insurance card. He doesn't have too many alternatives, really.'

'He might get frightened into it.'

Fergal gave a laconic shrug. 'Thus far he's shown every indication of resuming his life, returning to his haunts. On release from Brixton he made his way to the restaurant where he works, presumably to tell them he is back in circulation, then on to West Kilburn, to the address given to the court. It's a house owned by a Mr Christopher Addleston. It seems Mr Addleston deals in antiques when he's out of work as an actor, which is much of the time.'

'So. That's it for the moment, is it?' Terry brought his hands down decisively on the chair arms in a move that invited agreement.

'Not quite. There are two complications,' said Fergal in a brogue that was suddenly very Irish indeed. 'Firstly, I was not the only person following Pavlik home.'

Terry felt a beat of alarm. 'What do you mean?' he asked, though he had heard him perfectly well the first time.

'There were three of us along the way. A bit of a procession, you might say.'

'Who was this other person?'

'I don't know. Sadly I wasn't able to follow him once he left Pavlik's because he managed to find the only free cab on the whole of the Harrow Road. I'm fairly sure he was an amateur, though. Certainly not police, and not a private eye. Though he took a lot of trouble, I'll say that for him. He was in the public gallery when Pavlik came up at the magistrate's. Wearing a smart suit, designer-style, young professional. Then when I spotted him outside Brixton he was in casual clothes, wearing a cap, dark glasses. But it was the same fella all right, no doubt about that. Early thirties, five ten or eleven, darkish hair, pale complexion.'

Sitting high in his chair, back board-straight, Terry made a wide gesture of incomprehension that was also an appeal. 'I don't understand. Who could it be, for heaven's sake?'

'There's one thing. He was joined in the public gallery of the court by a woman he knew, also young, also smartly dressed. I'm guessing here, but I don't think he was expecting her. I would say he was startled to see her. They talked a lot – well, whispered. Then, after Pavlik's appearance, they left the gallery together and parted in the hall.'

'And she? What did she look like?'

'Darkish hair. Medium height. What you might call – I think the term is – statuesque.'

'A big girl?' He was thinking of Alice.

'Oh, no. Trim, but curvaceous.'

'Black hair, you say?'

'No, somewhere between red and mid-brown. That rich glossy colour that catches every kind of light,' said Fergal, turning poetical. 'The colour, you might say, of mahogany.'

'And the style?'

'The style? Ah . . .' Fergal's vocabulary failed him here. He put a hand to the side of his head and made a corkscrew gesture that might have denoted Medusan locks. 'Short,' he offered feebly. 'In layers, I suppose.'

None of this fitted Alice. 'For God's sake, Fergal!' he cried in annoyance. Jumping up, he strode across the room and stopped by a window. 'What have we here? What's going on?'

'What we have here is someone who wanted to make sure Pavlik got home safe and sound,' said Fergal mildly. 'Or . . .'

Terry strode back and stood over him. '*Or?*'

'Possibly someone who wished to harm him.'

Terry almost laughed. 'And if someone did wish to harm him?'

For a moment they stared at each other in mutual incomprehension.

Terry shrugged. 'I meant, would we terribly care, for God's sake?'

Fergal looked mildly disappointed in him, as though he had betrayed a singular lack of judgement. 'I don't think it would be terribly useful.'

Terry gave a heavy sigh. 'I suppose not,' he agreed glumly and headed for the drinks tray. Having returned from a weekend at Longchamps in which he seemed to have passed precious few moments without a glass in his hand, he had been determined to abstain, at least for a few days, but now he poured himself a large Scotch. 'So what are you suggesting?' he added darkly. 'That we *protect* him?'

Fergal let this remark pass in silence.

Pacing back to his chair, perching on the edge of his seat, Terry declared, 'It may be that these people are going to try to make him talk, Fergal! It may be that they're after information. One way or another, we should *know*.'

'Ah. That brings me to the other thing.' Fergal paused to add weight to his words. 'Apparently he *did* talk to the police. Briefly. When he realised the seriousness of the accusations. Before Gresham got to him and told him to shut up.'

'Jesus!' Terry gasped. As the full implications sank in, he cried more fiercely, '*Jesus!* And what did he say?'

'He said that he'd been put up to the burglary, but denied absolutely the assault. Said he wasn't even there when it took place.'

Terry stared at him furiously. 'Put up to it? But he didn't say who by?'

'No. He just said he'd been hired to go in and burgle the place.'

'Curse it! Why didn't we know this before, for God's sake? Why weren't we told?'

'My contact isn't on the case himself. He can only get so much information at one time.'

'We should have paid him more then, shouldn't we!'

Fergal didn't deign to answer such madness, but continued in his calm voice, 'Pavlik said he broke in during the early hours of that Sunday morning, a good sixteen hours *before* the assault.'

Terry exclaimed, 'Hah!'

'Later he withdrew his comment about being put up to it. Refused to say a word. Just stuck to the story about breaking in well before the Galitzas arrived home.'

'Anything to back his story?'

'Pavlik said he spent Sunday evening with two acquaintances in a pub. But the police haven't been able to find them.'

'Not looking especially hard, I don't imagine,' Terry declared scathingly. 'But he knew these men, he knew their names?'

'Apparently so, yes.'

'Can we get them?'

'At a price.'

'Well, then!' Terry pushed himself restlessly to his feet once more. 'Well!' He paced to the far side of the room and back again. And still he couldn't remain in one spot; he turned, offered first one profile to Fergal, then the other. 'Only one thing for it, isn't there?'

'Find him his alibi?'

Terry jabbed a finger at Fergal. 'Get it in black and white, watertight, no possibility for error! Yes – find him his alibi!'

'It might take some extra men.'

Terry made a sweeping gesture. 'Whatever it takes.' His mind returned to the other disturbing element in the story. 'Just so long as these other people don't get to Pavlik first. We must find out who they are, Fergal.'

'Without more to go on . . .'

'Get whatever you need.'

'It's not a question of more men,' Fergal pointed out patiently. 'It's a question of there being nowhere to start.'

'There has to be!'

Fergal didn't answer but fixed his attention on a spot some three feet in front of his chair, in the depths of the Aubousson-style carpet.

'Well, do what you can,' Terry offered weakly, which was the best he could do by way of apology. He knocked back his drink, and, telling himself it had done him good, immediately went and poured himself another. 'Curse be to hell,' he muttered under his breath. 'Curse be to hell and back!'

Fergal waited until this small storm had passed before murmuring, 'I've made a few more enquiries about Ben Galitza, but failed to turn up anything new.'

'Nor me!' Terry exclaimed hotly, and for an instant it looked as though the storm would blow up again, worse than before. 'And not for want of trying, that's for sure! I have these facts, I have a *mountain* of facts, but much good they've done me. There's no sense in any of it, Fergal. No sense at all. It's like a play going on in the theatre next door – someone understands what's going on, but it certainly isn't me!'

'If I can help . . .'

He levelled his glass at Fergal. 'You can have a drink for a start.'

Fergal was not fond of Scotch, but took the drink and sipped at it dutifully because it was easier to go along with Terry in this mood.

Terry sat down again, and hunched forward with a

weary sigh. 'Right . . . this is the story. You will not be surprised to hear that it is a tale of money, greed and what should have been large profits,' he began, in the manner of a fable or a parody. 'It is also a tale of promises, broken and unbroken. The story takes us across many frontiers and many banking systems. We start in Poland, which is famous for its electrical cable and generator industries. We have a valuable consignment of generators that have been built for some hospitals in Germany. However, the order is cancelled – a contractual dispute over specifications. The person put in charge of finding a new buyer for these generators is a fixer called, let us say, Mr X. Mr X puts feelers out. In no time there is a firm bite. It all looks good. The price is fair. There's a middleman or two who wants his introduction fee, but then that's the way business is done over there. Mr X makes checks on these people he is intending to do business with. They are British, though reassuringly they speak Polish. He discovers they are known in Poland and some other countries in the old Eastern Bloc. They have done business in Hungary, the Czech Republic, Slovenia. They have a reputation for driving a hard bargain, but once terms are agreed they meet their contracts, they deliver on time, everything is done by the book. So, here we have it . . . it's all looking good for a deal that is going to be worth roughly fifty million US.'

'Has Mr X ever done such deals before?' Fergal asked quietly.

'Nothing like this. But he has a reputation for being nobody's fool. Canny. He's been wheeling and dealing locally for years.' Draining his glass, it seemed to Terry that he could see Mr X, that Mr X was large and pasty-faced, with bullet eyes and unfortunate manners. 'Then,' he resumed rapidly, 'for no apparent reason, the deal goes up in smoke. The middlemen don't get their money. Naturally, they are put out, but they offer their services again, they offer to find another buyer. However, Mr X is not interested. He says he is unable to sell the generators after all, that a decision has been taken by a higher authority – he hints at a government department – and the machines are off the market. End of story, we would believe. But some time later one of the middlemen hears on reliable authority that the generators have been shipped out of the country. Sent, he is told, to Gdansk. But where did they go from Gdansk?'

Recognising a narrative pause when he heard one, Fergal waited mutely.

'Cintel's best efforts were required here,' Terry commented. 'It took time . . . but they discovered that the ship carrying the generators was bound for Mexico, Colombia and Venezuela. In the meantime, back in Warsaw, Mr X has bought a BMW, he is renovating his house, he has sent his daughter to America for a couple of years. He says she's gone to be an au pair, but in fact she's attending an expensive college, and is able to accompany her richest classmates to Aspen on skiing trips.'

He pulled in a sharp breath, he shook his head; this was the end of his story. He rotated a hand towards Fergal. 'First thoughts, off the top of your head.'

Taking a long slow breath, Fergal went through the motions of setting his mind to this conundrum, his eyes narrowed as if against a fierce light, his mouth puckered in concentration, while Terry waited impatiently, alert to any change of expression.

'Clearly, Mr X or his masters struck a better deal,' intoned Fergal at last. 'But you have to ask why, having scented the improved deal, Mr X didn't go back to the first buyers to see if they would be prepared to better their price. In effect, to have an auction. Perhaps the second price was so much better there was no point.'

'But why would it be?' Terry demanded. 'Why offer a crazy price?'

Fergal circled a hand loosely to show that he was entering the realms of guesswork. 'It could be that Mr X was providing a service for the buyers, something quite separate from the provision of the generators. Who can say? Perhaps he was close to someone in the government who could put another far more lucrative contract their way, perhaps he could bribe an official to allow something in or out of the country . . .' The circling hand became more agitated. 'There's an endless list of possibilities. But in broad terms – there was more to the deal than meets the eye.'

'Okay,' Terry agreed. 'Another question. Who got rich out of this?'

Fergal regarded him with caution, suspecting, rightly, that this was a trick question. 'Everyone but the first unsuccessful buyers?'

'You would think so, yes.'

'The first buyers *did* get rich, then?'

'No.'

Tiring of this game, Fergal waited.

'No,' murmured Terry. 'They didn't get rich. They got very short of money indeed.'

'Ah.'

Sounds came from the next room, the chatter of Maeve and Dinah returning from their shopping trip.

'But one of them was *expecting* to get rich, Fergal. One of them was expecting to get very rich indeed.'

With a shake of his head, a setting of his mouth, Fergal unwound himself from the chair and got to his feet. He could offer no more opinions without additional information.

'Will you give my warmest regards to Maeve?' he asked as he left. 'And tell her that I've found her that book. She'll know the one I mean.'

Terry promised, but in the hurry to get changed and off to the theatre before curtain up it slipped his mind.

Rebecca made a fine entrance, with her firm stride, her head high, her strong austere beauty set off by the whiteness of her skin and the severity of her black suit.

'Well!' Terry declared as he got up to kiss her. 'Time has treated you well.' It was true. She had slimmed down and she had developed a style that managed to look both simple and sophisticated. Her dark hair was straight and loose around her shoulders and closer to auburn than he remembered. She wore little make-up, but with her bold eyes and clear skin she didn't need to.

She cast him an appraising glance. 'You're looking affluent.'

'You're a cruel woman, Rebecca.'

She laughed. 'I meant just that – affluent.'

'What you meant was that I'd put on weight.'

'It doesn't matter in a man.'

'Ah, but how I wish that were true.'

She ordered a salad but refused wine. He had invited her to the Connaught because it was quiet and the tables were well spaced, and because it was she who had contacted him and he didn't think she would have done so unless she had something to say.

To begin with, however, she made him tell her all about his business, his horses, and his life, though for her life was just another word for love life. He did his best to avoid answering that one. 'Oh, you know,' he said equivocally when she pressed him.

'No, I don't!'

There was curiosity in her persistence, but also, behind her brittle smile, a wistfulness. In the end she wore him down and he admitted, 'Well, there is someone, yes. A companion.'

'Ouch! What a word – *companion*. That says it all, Terry. God! *Companion*. That's *awful*. Is she married or something?'

'No.'

'*Companion*. You're not in love with her then,' she accused.

Finding some sort of consolation in honesty, he said, 'I don't know.'

'Don't know, won't know,' Rebecca remarked cryptically. 'In love with someone else?'

He laughed mildly at this. 'No.'

'Hoping to be in love with someone else?'

'I'm not a dreamer, Rebecca.'

She feigned horror. 'We're all dreamers, Terry.'

But he wasn't having it. 'I've got most things I want, I work hard, I have a good life. And the things I can't have I don't think about.'

'Wish I could say the same,' she said wryly. She told him about the changes in her life, the sale of the marital home in Hampstead, the new flat she had bought off Eaton Square, the progress of her divorce, which was going smoothly, she said, only because they'd refused to fight over money. 'But then neither of us need to,' she said matter-of-factly. 'My father died a couple of years ago.'

'I'm sorry.' He couldn't remember where the family money had come from, but he knew there was plenty of it.

'So here I am, rich and single, God help me.' She cast her eyes heavenward. 'Looking for Mr Right.'

'He'll come along.'

She shook her head at his naivety. 'Nah! I'm a difficult woman to please, Terry. I'll never be happy with a lawyer, doctor, all-round regular guy who wants me to stay at home like a good girl. I like my own life too much. I like my own *way* too much,' she declared regretfully. 'Used to getting what I want.'

'A bit hard on yourself.'

'Just honest.' She pushed her food around her plate. 'That's why Ben and I were so well suited.' She left this thought hanging in the air for a moment before looking up at him and giving the tiniest shrug. 'We were both coming from the same place. We both wanted the same things.'

'I wouldn't have put you and Ben in quite the same category so far as ambition went.'

'Oh, I wouldn't be so sure, Terry. I'm fairly determined when I want to be.' She gave an ironic smile that didn't entirely hide the self-disdain beneath. 'I often think back to that weekend in Ireland, you know,' she said reminiscently. 'The day at the Curragh. We were having such a good time.' She meant: before Catherine came along, before she lost Ben. 'And that other weekend we had with you, when you took us to the west coast. Though I have to say I did feel a bit – I suppose – *guilty*.'

'You, Rebecca? Why?'

'I knew what Ben was up to behind the scenes.'

'Oh, did you now?' said Terry calmly. 'And what was Ben up to?'

'Oh, trying it on,' she said with a chuckle. 'Financing that Mick what's-his-name to buy that hotel for a song, and then selling it straight on to you at a big profit.'

'It was still a good buy, mind.'

'But you pulled out.'

'Yes, I pulled out.'

She tilted her head, inviting explanations.

'I don't like people being untruthful – people who're meant to be on my side, at any rate.'

'Ben was furious.'

'Was he now? And why should that be?' Terry asked facetiously, though not without the small hope, albeit remote, of gaining some insight into Ben's character, which had long been a mystery to him.

'Oh, you'd blocked him, that's what you'd done. And he didn't think he'd done anything to deserve it. He didn't think he'd done anything wrong certainly. By his reckoning you'd encouraged him to set the whole thing up and then left him in the lurch. Ben's always been very good at seeing things from his own – well, *individual* – point of view.' She shook her head indulgently. 'He's never forgiven you.'

'One of his more curious decisions. Like not marrying you.'

Having shuffled her salad to one side of the plate, Rebecca finally gave up on it. 'You're quite wrong,' she said firmly. 'It would have been a disaster to marry me. He couldn't have stomached a wife with money, you see. He needed to be the one earning, the one wearing the financial trousers. Oh, Catherine could play around with her gardens, but it wasn't serious money, was it? No, from that point of view Catherine was perfect. Minor gentry down on their luck. Class without cash. Perfect!'

Terry had never had any pretensions to psychological insight; instinct had served him well enough over the years. He could only listen to this judgement with quiet dismay.

Rebecca said, 'There's another side to that coin, of course. A man who likes to feel in charge of his life, who's dead set on making his own way – he's not too good when things start going wrong.'

This speech made Terry wary in a way he couldn't quite identify.

'Don't get me wrong,' Rebecca added. 'I don't mean he'd get difficult or – *nasty*. No, rather that he's the sort to fall apart. Quite a pussycat really.'

He understood suddenly; she had made it obvious in so many ways. 'You've seen him recently?'

She met his eyes with a spark of acknowledgement.

Terry felt his stomach tighten unpleasantly. 'In what capacity? If I may ask?'

She reached into her handbag and pulled out a packet of cigarettes. 'I'm meant to have given up,' she murmured. 'But it's these or the weight.' Coming to the question in her own time, she said, 'Shoulder to cry on.'

'I see,' he said stiffly. 'And what does Ben have to cry about?'

'Plenty, actually.'

'Tell me, do.'

The scorn must have been strong in his voice because she looked at him sharply and hesitated. 'He's got money troubles,' she said cautiously.

'I can't say I'm entirely surprised.'

'Oh?'

'Always biting off more than he can chew.'

'But he's always been successful in the past, Terry. Always done well.'

'So these troubles are exceptional?'

'Absolutely! It's something totally unforeseen. Something desperately unfair, Terry. I wish I could tell you just how unfair. The thing is' – her dark eyes widened soulfully – 'I was going to ask if you might be able to manage some help . . .'

'For Ben? I rather think you've come to the wrong place, Rebecca.'

She leant closer and said earnestly, 'I know Ben hasn't done you any favours, Terry. I know he's been . . . less than clever in his dealings with you. But at heart he's not bad, he's just thoughtless.' Reading his expression, seeing she wasn't going to make progress on that tack, she withdrew the argument with an uplifted palm, a splay of her fingers. 'Listen . . .' She dropped her voice. 'Can I tell you something in absolute confidence? Will you promise not to tell anyone?'

'I'd rather not be entrusted with secrets that shouldn't be mine to keep, Rebecca.'

She gave a small sigh of frustration, then, after what appeared to be an intense inner debate, decided to trust him anyway. 'He's been blackmailed,' she said abruptly.

Terry did not alter his expression.

'I don't know the details, but it's something – *bad*. He's completely broke. Desperate for money. I thought maybe . . .' Taking a plunge, she said baldly, 'I thought you might want to help him because of . . . the situation. Because of Catherine. I'd lend them money myself, but my father knew me too well, I'm afraid. It's all tied up in trusts.'

Terry sipped his wine and suppressed the urge to knock back the rest of the glass in one. 'Blackmailers don't go away. They keep coming back. He should go to the police.'

'He can't.'

'Can't?' he enquired carefully. 'Or won't?'

'Can't.' She leant across and touched his arm. 'But look – this is the last payment. Definitely. If he can just get through this . . .'

'But, Rebecca, there's never a last payment.'

'Oh, but there is! The blackmailer said right at the outset that he only wanted half a million.'

'Only half a million?' Terry repeated caustically. 'That is a large amount of money by anyone's standards.'

'That was the amount that . . . was in dispute. I can't say any more.' By the sudden doubt in her face, she looked as though she had already said too much.

He folded his napkin and called for the bill. 'Rebecca, I'm not the person to ask. I'm sorry.'

She attempted a thin smile. 'Damn.'

'And, Rebecca?'

'Mmm?' She was hardly listening.

'Don't do anything you will later regret.'

Her eyes flashed defensively. 'Meaning?'

'Catherine needs her husband.'

'Hey,' she said with a lightness that didn't conceal her indignation, 'you don't have to tell me. I know that one thousand per cent. No, you've got me wrong if you think I've got ambitions in that direction, Terry. Believe me, once bitten! I wouldn't want Ben on a platter, not if he were free, single and on my doorstep. Besides which,' she argued more fiercely still, 'he won't ever leave her. He's determined to stay. Through thick and thin.' She shook her head firmly. 'No, Terry, you've got him wrong if you think he'd ever give up on her.'

Terry bowed to her judgement, though nothing could dislodge his impression that the lady had protested too much.

Dear Terry, Forgive me for not having replied before but I've received so many letters – something like four hundred, many from people I've never met – that I'm only just beginning to get to grips with them all. Catherine had started other letters the same way, which gave the words a sense of neutrality, but now she must thank him, and that required more careful thought. Eventually she wrote: *Thanks for writing so regularly, and thanks for the flowers from Morne, which were an extraordinary reminder.* He could read into that what he may. She went on: *Concerning the garden, I can't say that Mrs Kent's ideas are right or wrong, I can only say it all depends on what sort of a garden you want. Gardens do change and metamorphose. I think it's a mistake to try to keep them exactly the same. However, from what you describe of Mrs Kent's ideas, it sounds as though she's trying to create an English garden rather than an Irish one. While this might suit some places I suspect it would be wrong for Morne, where the strength of the garden has always been its relative lack of structure and the way it merges so perfectly into the surrounding countryside.*

Catherine paused, feeling cold and a little faint. The infection had left her exhausted. Even now, the pen shook slightly in her hand.

I will be glad to draw up some ideas for you, if you would still like me to. The best thing would be for me to produce some outline plans from memory, then if you approve them to draw up more detailed plans. If you want to take things further, I could arrange for the preparation of the site, the building of paths and struc-tures as appropriate, the purchase and planting of trees and plants, plus follow-up care for the first season if this is required.

My fee for outline plans would be . . . She wondered how much she could get away with and put down a figure that was three times her usual charge. She did the same for the other options. If he agreed to all three options she would also get a commission on the plants, which could bring the job in at well over ten thousand. She told herself that he could afford it.

If this is acceptable I could send you some outline ideas in a couple of months when I'm back at my desk.

She finished it *Yours, with thanks,* and added at the bottom *Perhaps you could reply to the above address in the first instance.*

Rather formal. Decidedly cool. Entirely reasonable.

She folded it and stuck it in the envelope before she had the urge to redraft it.

They'd given her a side room while she recuperated, and she took the opportunity to sleep through the afternoon. She was woken by Julie.

'Visitor,' she announced.

'Who?'

'Female and young.'

'But who?'

'Foreign-sounding name. Maeve?'

When Catherine eventually got herself to the front hall, she didn't immediately recognise the pale figure in black sitting in the waiting area. It was only as the woman stood up and stepped forward that Catherine realised with a slight shock that it was indeed Maeve.

'I hardly recognised you!' she declared.

'I've done a bad thing,' Maeve confessed, standing with her hands clasped, palms up, her elbows pinched in to her waist, like a supplicant. 'I've come unannounced. And that was wrong of me.'

Catherine reached out to grip her hand. 'There aren't many people I'm glad to see, but you're one of them.'

It was a blustery day with spitting rain but after a week in a stuffy sickroom Catherine was desperate for air, so they went outside and sat in a sheltered corner of the garden, by beds of thriving weeds and wilting roses whose petals were torn aloft by the scurrying wind.

'Are you warm enough?' Catherine asked.

'Me? Oh yes. And you?' Maeve was wearing a loose black jacket over a long black skirt and a woollen scarf wrapped several times around her neck, but no amount of clothing could disguise her obvious frailty. Her face was pinched, her hands thin and bony, there was not an ounce of flesh on her.

'Your father told me you'd been ill,' Catherine said.

'Oh.' She shook her head gently, as if the subject were hardly worthy of discussion. 'I'm on the mend now.'

'What was wrong?'

Maeve addressed this question hesitantly. 'It began with an infection, which turned into septicaemia. I was in intensive care for a week. And then just when I was getting over that I had a bad reaction to one of the drugs and went into a form of shock. So I managed to give everyone a second fright. And since then – well, it's been slow.' She spoke solemnly and unemotionally, her eyes lowered a little, her body so still that she might have been a figure in a painting, with her pale skin, her dark eyes, her hair held back in a band. Only the loose strands at her forehead provided movement as they were pulled to and fro by the wind. 'Anyway, I'm all right now,' she said.

'And what about the nursing? Are you still studying for that?' Asking this, Catherine remembered the shy chubby girl with rounded cheeks and a sweet smile in the garden at Morne, talking about her plans to study at a London teaching hospital.

'I'm switching to nursery nursing. I'm starting at a college in Dublin soon.'

'How lovely.'

'I'll be happier with children. It takes a special sort of dedication to care for the sick.'

'I'm sure you'll make a fine nursery nurse.'

Maeve glanced away, and once again Catherine was struck by the changes in her, the fragility of her body and the gravity of her expression. 'I'm so glad you came,' she said.

'Oh, I've wanted to for a long time, but it's only now . . . I'm on a trip with Dadda, you see. We've just come from Paris.'

'How nice.'

'Oh, I'd rather stay at home. I'm not a one for the race meetings or the restaurants or the shopping. But it pleases him to take me, so now and again I go along.'

'Your father – he's been writing to me every week.'

'Yes . . . he said.'

'I'm just in the process of replying. Will you tell him?'

'I'll tell him.'

'It's been hard to get round to letters.'

'I'm sure it has,' she replied in the same solemn manner.

'And the garden at Morne, tell him I'll be accepting his offer to redesign it—' Catching Maeve's look of astonishment, she paused. 'You didn't know?'

Maeve stared hastily down at her hands, frowning fiercely. 'I had no idea. I can't imagine why he should expect you to . . . why he should ask such a thing.'

'I gather he has doubts about Mrs Kent.'

Maeve was still breathing rapidly. 'Yes. Mrs Kent.'

There was a long pause in which Maeve continued to stare at her hands. Then, with an obvious effort to pick up the conversation again, she asked, 'And you, Catherine? How are things with you?'

'Things? Oh, they're as well as can be expected.'

'Will you get better?' she asked simply.

'If you mean, will I get back to how I was before, the answer's no.' Maeve watched her with rapt attention as she explained the limitations on her mobility,

the walking on smooth surfaces, the crutches and callipers. 'But there we are. There are worse things. I might
be quadriplegic, I might be dead. It's all a question of
how you look at it. The usual thing – cup half empty,
cup half full.'

'And how much longer will you be here?'

'Oh, out quite soon now. Got to get back to work!'

Maeve continued to gaze at her for a long while after
she'd finished speaking. Then, seeming to come to a
decision, she reached slowly into her handbag and
pulled out an envelope. 'Catherine . . . Here are the
keys to my flat. I want you to have them in case you
should ever need them.'

Catherine was bemused. 'Maeve, I . . .'

'It's just off Regent's Park. The address is in there
with the keys. Dadda wants me to keep the place but I
won't use it again, I know I won't. I'd like you to feel
you can use it any time you want to, any time at all.
For as long as you need it. I want you to know there's
somewhere safe for you, somewhere that no one will
. . . *bother* you.'

'Maeve, I . . . it's very kind of you, but I really don't
think I'll ever need it . . .'

'Oh, it's got a lift,' Maeve said hastily, as if this
might clinch the argument. 'And nice wide doors. And
the toilet's got space beside it – I checked everything
very carefully with the spinal injuries people.'

'But . . .'

Before she could think of anything to say Maeve
leant forward and, folding Catherine's hands around
the envelope, laid her own hands over the top. '*Please*
– it would make me so happy to feel that you knew it
was there.'

'But I have my home. With Ben.'

'Yes, of course. But it would make me happy.'

'I can't imagine I'd ever . . .'

'No. But still.'

Catherine gave in then, because it was easier to do so. 'Thank you,' she shrugged.

Maeve stood up. 'I have to go now. But I'm so very glad to have seen you, Catherine. You are in my thoughts and prayers always.'

When Maeve bent down to kiss her on the cheek, Catherine was reminded of a bird, her touch was so light.

Ten minutes later Emma came into sight, battling against the wind on the far side of the rose garden. Spotting Catherine, she altered course towards her with a quick wave. 'God, darling, it's wild out here! Aren't you dying? Listen – you'll never guess who *I've* just met.' Her eyes flashed.

'A girl called Maeve?'

'No, her daddy. The famous Terry. We've been chatting!'

Catherine stared at her.

'He was waiting in the hall. We had a long talk. He may be a villain, Cath, but I have to say he's rather good company.' When Catherine didn't speak, Emma added inconsequentially, 'He had a horse at Long-champs that lost by a head.' Then, not so inconsequentially. 'He's charming and he's rich. I tell you, a girl could be tempted!' With a shake of her head, she laughed at herself before pushing Catherine back through the gale.

Chapter Eleven

THE CAB from the airport jolted along as far as South Kensington where it had a small but ill-tempered altercation with a white Transit van and Simon abandoned it to walk the last half mile. To add to his woes there was a vicious wind, an advanced blast of midwinter, which cut through his thin raincoat and chilled his jetlagged bones, still somewhere on Argentinian time. '... *the wind's like a whetted knife* ...'

He lived in a thirties block at the Brompton Road end of Draycott Avenue. Seen through weary eyes in the early darkness, the box-like flat seemed arid and cheerless. He'd rented it as a temporary measure some eighteen months ago but, without the time or single-mindedness to find a place of his own, had stayed put. It was like a hotel room, just a place for marking time. The furnishings were bland and characterless, the style international-chintz, with skirted sofas and easy chairs in a floral design which, with relentless regard for uniformity, matched the curtains and tie-backs. In a fruitless attempt to stamp his mark on the place he'd bought some modern pictures, but they'd looked wrong under the low ceilings and had stayed where he'd left them, propped against a wall in the bedroom. The bathroom was tiny, the shower inadequate, the lighting execrable and the heating uncontrollable. Come what may, he had determined to buy a place of his own in January and move in immediately, onto bare boards if necessary.

The answering machine was showing eight messages, but he didn't attempt to listen to them until he'd taken a bath. He lay in water as hot as he could take for ten minutes, then went straight into a cold shower and felt the jetlag lift a little. He dressed for an evening that would take him to a drinks party, maybe a quick dinner if the company looked promising, and an early night.

He poured himself a glass of white wine before flipping on the answering machine, hoping, but not really daring to hope, that there'd be something from Catherine, who was now back at home. He'd called her from Argentina, but the first time her mobile had been switched off and he'd had to leave a message; the second time, irritatingly, Ben had answered, though Simon had deliberately not used the house line. Then this morning he'd called from the baggage hall at Heathrow to find her phone switched off again.

The tape spewed out its messages. There were two invitations to supper parties at flats shared by chaotic girls in Wandsworth and Battersea, neither of which tempted him, and another from a rather impressive girl he'd met at Cheltenham and never imagined hearing from again, which he would definitely accept. But his spirits, having lifted sharply at this, sank onto a more troubled plain as the next message brought Alice's low lingering voice into the room, wanting to know if he was back and whether he was free the next evening. Alice remained a puzzle to him. He'd taken her out to dinner twice and gone along with her to parties on another two evenings. After the second dinner she'd come for him in the cab with a voracious kiss, mouth open, breasts thrust hard against him, no possible doubt as to what she'd had in mind, and he'd had to plead an incipient cold to be sure of getting home intact and alone. Then at a party the next week Alice had been all over another man in full sight of him and everyone else. She seemed to live in a permanent frenzy, trying to do everything, go everywhere and, it would seem, have every man who happened her way. Sometimes he wondered if she was on drugs; at other times he thought she was trying to make up for time lost to her excess weight, now almost vanished. More recently, it had occurred to him with the abruptness of the obvious that her excesses might have rather more to do with Catherine, that, however terrible Catherine's accident, it had in a strange way allowed Alice to break free from cruel comparisons. What he couldn't work out, and what caused him suspicion, was where he was meant to fit into all this.

If he expected the last two messages to bring more welcome invitations he was soon disappointed. The next voice, which opened with a combative, 'Hello? If you're there, could you answer, please?' froze him gently, like an icy hand on his shoulder. Even before the voice announced itself as his aunt Betty he knew what was coming. 'It's no good, I'm at the end of my tether. I don't know what to do with her. She'll have to be admitted, Simon. I'm sorry, it's more than I can take. Could you please call *immediately*. This time I mean it! I'm at my wits' end. I have no life, I have no peace . . .' The voice broke into a sob. He saw the little house in Chigwell, with the garish purple-pink wallpaper, wriggly stripes above and stippling below a livid purple frieze, frilly curtains at the mock-leaded windows, cheap knick-knacks and dolls on the sills: straw-hatted Spaniards astride donkeys, flamenco dancers tossing their shawls. He saw the bedroom upstairs into which his mother barricaded herself on her days of fury, the multitude of ethnic-Indian cushions spilling off the bed, vying with the clutter of clothes and magazines and suitcases for floor space, for her revolt against tidiness was another gleeful source of conflict with her sister. He saw her in the darkness, lying slumped on the bed, head bent awkwardly against the wall, with the television on full blast and vodka, cigarettes and the cat for company.

He didn't have to imagine her language because it came blasting into the room with the next message. 'Simon? Come and get me – *now!* Do you hear me? Right *now*!' She was half choking, half sobbing with rage. 'You have *no* idea what it's like in this dead-end hell-hole. I'll go mad – *mad* – if I have to stay a moment longer. *Where are you, for God's sake?* You little bastard! You *shit*! Come and get me out of this *fucking – awful – place*! Do you hear me?' What he heard was the ominous hiss of her breath as she filled her lungs for the long agonised wail of fury and thwarted will that he knew so well, a moan that to his ears had come to sound like an animal's. Rasping for breath, she ranted incoherently for a while, the phone seemingly forgotten as she was caught up in a fever of grievances. Then came the sly wheedling tone of entreaty. 'Darling, darling, are you there? Are you? My darling boy, my baby, come and take your mum away. Come . . . If you only knew how vicious and cruel she is to me. *Vicious*.

She's always hated me – always, *always*! Oh, she always seems so *sweet*! Butter wouldn't melt. Little miss fucking *perfect*. But darling, you've no idea – she *tortures* me, she makes my life a *misery*. She won't even let me go *out*. She locks me in, the bitch, and I can't get out! She takes my *money*. I've nothing – *nothing*. Darling, darling . . . come and take me away. Please, darling. Please, please, please . . . *please*. Your mumsy needs you . . . Your mumsy loves you more than anything in the whole world . . .'

The earlier she started on the vodka, the fiercer her voice became, though the screaming and tears were always the same whatever time she started. He lowered the volume and watched the tape turning and turning while he dialled the house. It was still turning when Betty answered.

'She's broken the bedroom window,' Betty said without preamble. 'I was almost hoping she'd jump out.'

'What about the doctor?'

'He won't see her. He says if she won't take her antidepressants then there's nothing he can do. There's nothing I can do either, Simon. I've had it. She smashed the mirror yesterday.' He heard the niggardly note in her voice, the sound of someone counting the cost of the disruption. 'She's up there now, music on to wake the dead and the neighbours complaining. I tell you, I've had it this time!'

'I'll come tomorrow.'

'*Tomorrow!* I can't last till tomorrow. *Tonight*, Simon.'

And so he found himself looking in on the drinks party for a brief half hour before driving out through the unlovely regions of Leyton and Wanstead to Chigwell. He heard the music as he parked the car, and he heard her jeering at the world as he climbed the stairs. He called to her as he pushed his way past the makeshift barricade but she pretended not to hear him, nor to see him when he turned on the lamp, throwing her hands up over her head as if to repel him. It took him half an hour to calm her, to still the stream of invective and rage, and then she wept with great heaving sobs and clung to him, her fingers clawing at his arm, her tears and snot leaving trails down his shirt. Her unwashed hair smelt of filth and cigarette smoke and self-loathing. And all the time he tried to keep in his mind the image of her dancing the leading role in *Daphnis and Chloe*, the black and white shot of the impossibly high arabesque that he kept on the chest of drawers in his bedroom, because then he could almost forgive her.

These 'bouts', as they had all come to call them, followed a routine, and there was no departing from the tyranny of the progression, no short cuts to be expected or hoped for. The tears followed the rage; and after the tears came the slurred ramble of complaint and denunciation. To anyone else, the jumble of protest would have been incomprehensible, but he knew the script so well that it was like shorthand to him, he could extrapolate a sentence from a single word. Why was everyone against her? Why had she been abandoned? What had she done to deserve it? First the Company had turned against her, plotted to get her out, and after all she'd done for them, staying on through thick and thin, bad times and good. Who else had gone on stage sick, who else had danced time and again through the pain of injuries? And how had they thanked her? By kicking her in the teeth. Everyone was

against her. Everyone. Men – all bloody bastards,
Simon's father worst of all. Ditching her for that common tart, sloping away like a rat, making her beg for
the money he owed her. Just out for what he could get,
an easy time, burning money on booze and prostitutes,
the worst sort, coming back with their stink on him. A
bloody bastard, just like the rest of them . . .

The whining lament of self-pity followed the familiar
path, winding back and forth through endless repetitions, illogicalities and lost endings, until finally the
last stage was reached, the vengeful semi-comatose
silence, the ugly glare of distrust that followed him
blearily around the room as he tried to impose some
sort of order on the dump that was the floor.

Then, at long last, she slept.

By the time he'd bathed her face and hands and put
her to bed and gone down to have his ear bashed by
Betty for the best part of an hour over a bottle of wine,
it was almost midnight. To get away at all he had to
promise that he'd book another stint at a clinic, though
they both knew it would change nothing because his
mother's paranoia would always triumph over any
shaky resolve to stop drinking.

The road back to town was clear, but that didn't
stop it seeming to go on for ever, and by the time he
found a parking space near the flat he was more than
ready for his solitary bed.

He viewed the message light on the answering
machine with suspicion, fearing it might be Betty again,
or worse still, his mother, re-energised by her own
resentment, but the voice that floated into the room
sent his heart thudding with joy.

'Simon?' Catherine murmured faintly. 'Oh . . .'

His joy stalled as she gasped in a tone of panic or distress, 'Look . . . if you're not back too late, would you . . . could you . . . call . . . please . . . I'm on my own, and . . .' A gasp. 'If you could call.'

Christ, what a time to have left his mobile off! Tonight of all nights! What a bloody idiot! He cried aloud, 'God! God!' But it was also a cry of happiness and exhilaration because she needed him.

In his haste to dial the house he got it wrong and had to tap the number out again. As it began to ring he noticed the time was almost one. When it kept ringing without reply he wondered if she'd switched the phone off in her bedroom, if she'd simply gone to sleep, or . . . He tried her mobile. This too rang unanswered until the automatic message service picked up.

He grabbed his keys and raced for the car. Stealing across one set of red lights, openly jumping another, he reached Notting Hill in exactly thirteen minutes and, double-parking outside the darkened house, ran to the door and pressed long and hard on the bell before shouting her name through the letter box. He pressed his ear to the flap but heard nothing. There were no lights showing, not so much as a glimmer. He was about to beat on the door when he picked up a faint sound and, putting his ear back to the letter box, heard her call his name.

'Yes, it's me!' he called back, with a leap of elation. 'It's Simon! Are you all right?'

The rattle of a chain, the turn of one deadlock then another, and the door opened a fraction. In his haste to get in he crashed the door against her wheelchair.

'Wait,' she cried.

He retreated momentarily before opening the door

more carefully to find she had moved herself well back.
He went forward and squatted at her side. The hall was
very dark except for a strip of street lighting that slanted
across her mouth.

'Catherine, are you all right? What is it?'

Her mouth moved but it was a moment before she
managed to whisper, 'I'm all right.'

'What's happened? What is it?'

'Shut the door. Please.'

Pushing the door to, he found the light switch and
they both blinked in the sudden glare.

Crouching again, he took her hand. 'What is it?'

She took a steadying breath. 'There was someone
there.'

'Outside?'

'Yes.'

'Who was it?'

'I don't know.'

'Did he come to the door? Did he threaten you?'

She shook her head.

'Did he try to get in?'

'No. No . . . he was just *there*.'

'Well, you're all right now,' he assured her. 'You're
safe. Nothing can happen now. Nothing!'

She nodded with more certainty, as though she was
just beginning to believe it might be true. 'Thank you
for coming,' she said forlornly.

'Oh, Catherine!' His throat seized up, he shivered
with emotion. Reaching forward, he put his arms round
her and pulled her into an embrace that was necessarily
a little awkward because of the chair but none the less
sublime because, after a short pause, she brought her
hands up to his back and returned the embrace. He

continued to soothe her. 'It's okay, it's okay.' And all the time he wanted to shout with joy because he was holding her and she needed him.

Eventually he sat back on his heels and suggested a cup of tea, and smiled a little at the banality of it. He wheeled her into the kitchen and put the kettle on. She was still very dazed. Only when some life had come into her face did he finally ask with great gentleness, 'So . . . tell me exactly what happened.'

'It was probably nothing,' she said resolutely, as though she might somehow convince herself of this. 'Probably just a drunk.' Despite the time, she was still fully dressed, and he realised she'd intended to sit up all night alone in the dark.

'You saw him, though?'

'Yes.'

'Where?'

'Over the road.'

'What was he doing?'

She hesitated. 'Standing.'

He made a show of absorbing this thoughtfully. 'Watching the house, you mean?'

'I thought so . . .' Screwing up her face, she seemed to lose all confidence in her own judgement.

Before she could change her mind altogether, he moved her firmly forward. 'How long was he there?'

'I don't know . . . half an hour? Maybe longer.'

'And what time was this?'

But either she hadn't heard or her mind was somewhere else because she shook her head and frowned more deeply. 'What happened was . . . I've had this feeling . . . since Ben's been away . . .' A final hesitation and she got it out. 'I think someone's been following

me.' She glanced at him as though she half expected to
be disbelieved.

'Ben's *away*?'

'In Warsaw.'

Simon thought: How could he leave her? How could
he do it? He asked, 'This person – this man – when did
you first see him?'

'It was three days ago, when I went shopping. Emma
was with me. I thought I was imagining things. It was
only by chance . . . I just happened to notice this man
in the supermarket, and then again when we went to
lunch.'

'What did he look like?'

'That's the thing,' she admitted unhappily, 'I didn't
really get a look at him.'

'But you think it was the same man?'

'He was wearing this . . . hat.' She sketched a circle
in the air over her head. 'More of a cap, really. Blue,
faded, sort of cotton.'

'And you saw him twice on the same day?'

'Yes.'

'Any other day?'

She clamped her lips together as if to prevent herself
from saying anything too hasty. 'I don't know,' she
whispered. 'Sometimes I'm absolutely convinced there's
someone there and then – well, I think I'm just being
hysterical. The truth is, I'm not sure about any of it any
more.'

He put a hand on her shoulder and she tilted her
head over as though she might rest it against his arm.
She said bleakly, 'It's quite difficult . . . being here on
my own.'

'I bet it is.' Saying this, he thought with fresh fury:

Typical of Ben to leave her alone. Typical of his thoughtlessness.

'It's the practical things,' she said, 'it's not being able to go and check the windows easily. Not being able to get upstairs if I hear something. I thought I'd be all right about that, but I'm not.'

She'd been back from the unit exactly three weeks. 'Of course you're not all right about these things,' he cried, kneeling at her side. 'Nobody would be. There should be someone here with you all the time. You shouldn't be alone.'

'My carer comes in twice a day.'

'But that's the day.'

She clasped a hand over her eyes.

'It's all right,' he said, laying his fingers lightly on her arm. 'You're safe now.'

'It's not just that, it's . . .'

He waited uncertainly. Eventually he asked, 'There's something else?'

She bit her lip.

'Do you want to talk about it?'

'Can't.'

He waited again before saying firmly, 'Well, try to forget about everything now. Just think about getting some sleep. Listen, why I don't I stay downstairs tonight?' Realising that this might be where she herself slept, he added swiftly, 'Or wherever you think I'd make the best guard dog.' He made a feeble joke of it. 'Across the front doormat?'

Her hand came away from her face. 'I couldn't ask you to . . . I couldn't . . .' But her relief was transparent. 'I phoned Daddy, you see, but I forgot he'd gone to France. And Emma – she was out. And . . .' She fixed him with her extraordinary oval eyes. 'You really wouldn't mind?'

'It'd be an honour,' he said solemnly, feeling a sharp thrill of responsibility and pride. His offer was rewarded by a soft murmur of thanks and the vestige of a smile.

'We'll leave everything else till tomorrow. Sort it all out then. The police and so on.'

'The police?'

'We have to tell them about this man, Catherine.'

She looked unhappy again. 'But I'm not sure. I'm not sure it was the same man.'

'We should at least give them a description.'

'But what would I say?'

'Well, the man last night, for example – was he tall, medium, short?'

She was already shaking her head. 'It was so dark . . .'

'What about the man in the blue cap – what sort of height was he?'

She thought about this for some time. 'It's no good . . . I just don't remember. So you see – what could I tell them?'

'Well, one way and another, you can't stay here alone, that's for sure.'

'I suppose not.'

'I really don't think it's safe to stay here. I really don't!'

But she closed her eyes, beyond discussion. She wanted to sleep upstairs so he carried her there. She was light in his arms. When her hair brushed his cheek it was soft and sweet-smelling, and he drew in its scent as though it might purify him of that other hair in

Chigwell. He set up the wheelchair for her and turned on a couple of lights, then, taking the bedding she gave him, bade her a rather formal goodnight.

He took keys and went to re-park the car, calling up to tell her when he left and when he returned. He checked the locks twice, rattling them loudly so she should hear the sound and be reassured. He called a last goodnight, softly, and felt a thrill when she responded. The sofa was comfortable enough, but it was an hour before he slept, and then his night was broken by racing thoughts and anguished dreams. He didn't sleep deeply until very late, and then woke sluggishly long after he'd meant to, at eight.

He washed as best he could at the basin in the downstairs cloakroom before going into the hall and listening for Catherine. Hearing a muffled sound, he called up to her.

'In the study,' she replied.

The study was a converted bedroom with a small red sofa, a slatted wooden blind at the window, and two desks set against adjoining walls, Ben's minimal chrome, Catherine's a battered Victorian antique. In the corner was a round table laden with boxes, books and, perched on the top, one of the hats from Ben's collection of exotic headwear, an embroidered cap, Indian or Tibetan. The walls were decorated with Ben's school photographs and holiday snaps, but most of all with the hats, everything from solar topees and helmets to fedoras and deerstalkers, with, in pride of place, a Foreign Legion kepi, complete with neck flap.

He noted the evidence of Ben's struggle with the intruder, the deep gouge down one side of the Victorian desk, the splintered worktop, still unrepaired, while a new chair had appeared in place of the one reduced to matchwood. He knew that many of the pictures had new glass in them because he had collected them up himself and taken them to the framers in the first days after the incident.

Catherine was bent over her desk, sorting through a large pile of papers. 'Oh, I'm glad you're here,' she said in a strange intense voice, hardly glancing at him. 'Could you reach something for me, please?' Indicating a shelf above her head, she directed him to a ring file that was marked 'Clients Corr'. The moment he handed it to her she started leafing through it avidly, snapping the pages across.

He waited uncertainly, casting an eye over Ben's desk, which was also covered in a chaotic pile of papers. 'Would you like tea or coffee?' he asked after a time.

And still she was immersed in her search. 'It's here somewhere . . . I just can't remember which . . .'

'Can I help?'

'I'm looking for a letter.'

'Who from?'

'I don't know. But it would have been somewhere around November, December. Though it might have been an order . . . God, yes,' she sighed, 'it could have been an order.'

'What am I looking for?'

'What? Oh, a phone number pencilled on the top of something.'

It was hard to know where to start but he began a desultory shuffle through the letters and bills on the desk.

'No,' Catherine announced, riffling quickly through

the file once again. 'It's not here. Could you reach me
the suppliers file, please?'

When she'd started on this file he resumed his search
of the desk and couldn't help noticing that there were
quite a number of bills in red, as well as a last notice
from the electricity company and a threatening letter
from the council.

Catherine gave a soft gasp. 'Here it is,' she
whispered.

He looked over her shoulder and saw a letter from a
garden furniture company. Across the top was a number scribbled in pencil. Now that she'd found it, however, all the energy seemed to drain out of her, and she
stared at it gloomily.

Simon pulled up a chair and waited in silence.

'It takes me hours to get up stairs on my own,' she
said. 'On my bum. And then of course once I'm here
I'm lost without my sticks or the wheelchair. So I
haven't really had the chance to look before now. And
perhaps . . . I've been putting it off.'

She looked at him directly at last. Her eyes were dull
with tiredness and he guessed she hadn't slept much
either. 'This,' she said, lifting the sheet of paper up like
an exhibit, 'is what the police wanted to know about.
This is the number of the nuisance caller.' She dropped
the paper onto the desk from the tips of her fingers as
though it were faintly unclean and began to recount
grimly, 'One night when I was up here doing the
accounts there was a call. I knew who it was straight
away because the calls were always the same. Silence
but with that strong feeling there was someone there.
And quite often, breathing . . . I can't really describe it.

It was only later that I realised the call had come through on the ordinary phone, not the mobile. They'd always come through on the mobile before. It was just chance that no one else rang up in the meantime. So I dialled 1471, thinking I'd get one of those 'number not available' messages. But no – this was what I got.'

He reached for the letter and saw a central London number with an exchange that he didn't recognise. 'Did you try the number?'

She propped her head on her hand and closed her eyes for a long moment. 'No,' she murmured. 'No . . . I thought about it but then I decided I didn't terribly want to find out who was at the other end.' She said heavily, 'I was pretty sure it was a woman, you see.' She cast him a defiant look that told him it shouldn't be too difficult to work out the rest. Then, slowly: 'But now I do want to know. I want to know who it is.'

In the silence that followed he groped for the appropriate thing to say, and could think of nothing. It would have been equally false to protest disbelief at the idea of Ben's infidelity as to sympathise. He felt his eye twitch and rubbed a hand over his forehead to forestall it. Then a memory came back to him in a rush. 'But wasn't it a *man*? I thought you said it was a man?'

'That's what I *said*, yes. I didn't want them delving into our private life.'

'But that's what you told Emma.'

'Oh, she got it wrong initially – she always gets things wrong – and then I didn't bother to put her right. By that time, I'd realised, you see. And I didn't want anyone to know.'

'You're sure it was a woman?'

'Oh, yes.'

He looked down at the scribbled figures. 'Would you like me to give the number a try?'

'Would you?' In her gaze there was a gleam of fear, but also determination.

He reached across the desk for the phone and, pausing to rehearse some sort of speech, tapped in the number.

It rang, and continued to ring. After a full minute, he raised his eyebrows and she signalled for him to give up.

'Oh, well,' she said.

'Do you want me to find out who the number belongs to?'

'Can you do that?'

'I'll find a way.'

She thought about it, then shot him a grateful look. 'If you would.'

He stood up. 'Now, how about some breakfast?' he suggested busily, starting to plan all the other things he would do for her this morning, revelling in his new role as her carer.

She didn't seem to have heard. She was gazing past him in an unfocused way, fixed on some distant thought. 'I'm leaving,' she murmured softly.

He echoed, 'Leaving?'

'Leaving here. Going to live somewhere else for a while.'

'I have to say I think that's very sensible. You can't stay here alone.'

'What?' She frowned at him as if he had missed the point. 'No, I want to live on my own for a while. Somewhere else. I want to leave Ben.' She looked away to the window.

He sat down again, slowly. 'Because of this woman?'

She said in the same dreamlike murmur, 'I knew he wasn't going to be the easiest man to live with. I knew that I was going to have to be the one to make it work.' She paused and for a time he thought she wasn't going to go on. 'It wasn't that he wasn't keen to try – he was. Still is, in a way. He loves the idea of marriage. That's the trouble, really – he idealises it, he sees it as something separate, which it isn't – it's just a relationship with a label. You still have to get through all the day-to-day things. He didn't want to see the difficulties, he didn't want to think of it as anything but perfect, special, sort of apart.' She took a long breath. For an instant she focused on him before resuming her scrutiny of the window. 'I knew he'd be away a lot. I knew he'd look at other women. I knew that eventually the practicalities of marriage would wear him down and he'd feel disappointed in it and that he'd be unfaithful. What I didn't expect was for it to happen quite so quickly. I thought it would take years and years, a couple of children, boredom, the usual things. And then I imagined I'd probably take a deep breath and decide to live with it, pretend it wasn't happening, do what the smart women do, rise above it. In one way, I knew it was bad to be thinking like that, right at the start of our marriage, but I told myself it was realistic, it was practical, it was the price of loving someone . . . *complicated*. What I hadn't allowed for was . . .' She trailed off. She grew so still that she might have been in a trance. 'What I hadn't allowed for', she said at last with an effort, 'was to find that I was no longer loved. I think almost anything's bearable if you feel you're loved. Oh, he does all the practical things, he's there for me, he declares he'll never leave me, but it's like a mantra, something he keeps repeating to make himself believe it. It's like a grim act of faith for him, a penance. The truth is . . .' She swallowed suddenly, a tremor of emotion filled her eyes. 'The truth is he doesn't love me any more. Not as I am now, anyway. This new person wasn't part of the deal. This new person is too . . . *different*.' She gave a smile that shocked him, it was so bitter. 'Oh, his intentions are good, he tries to love me. But the fact is he can't.' She inhaled sharply. 'And that's all there is to it.'

Simon could hardly breathe for the ache in his heart. Never had he felt such tenderness, such a wish to protect and defend another human being.

Catherine absent-mindedly touched the papers on the desk. 'Just to add to everything else, we're broke. Not just a little broke either – horrendously terrifyingly broke. Normally . . . well, I'd stay and see it through. I'd wait till we'd sorted ourselves out. But' – the fire leapt into her face – 'he's been spending money on this or another *person*. That's what really hurts! That's what I can't take! We've remortgaged the house, we've risked everything – and he's been taking some woman to expensive restaurants.' Grabbing a piece of paper off the desk, she brandished it furiously. 'One of those bloody places in the food guide with Michelin stars, for God's sake! Two hundred and fifty fucking quid!'

Simon concealed an uneasy shiver. His admiration was threatened by dismay. It offended him to see Catherine in such a state of anger. Her dignity had seemed unshakeable, her courage fierce enough to withstand anything; it unsettled him to see her stripped of the very qualities that had always set her apart.

'So . . . I'm leaving today,' she announced in an uneven voice.

'But where will you go?'

'A friend's place.'

'Emma's?'

'No. Somewhere else. Somewhere secret.'

Immediately he saw a hidden place that only the two of them would know about, a place of clandestine visits and secret phone calls, where he would care for her. His spirits soared again, and he said passionately, 'Somewhere you'll be safe.'

'Yes.'

'Somewhere no one can follow you.'

'Somewhere Ben can't find me and talk me into coming back,' she said. 'I know myself too well, you see. I'd weaken. And I mustn't do that. I must have time on my own. I must have time to think. And to work again. I must have my work. It's hopeless here!' She was getting upset again. 'I can't get to my desk unless Ben's here to carry me up or I spend hours bumming my way up on my own. And I hate it downstairs, I hate it! I can't work down there!'

Again he was disconcerted by her fretfulness, which was somehow unworthy of her.

'So where is this place?' he asked.

'Oh . . . in the middle of town.'

'Is it suitable? Will you be able to manage there?'

'I'll manage,' she said with a touch of bravado.

'When do you want to go? I'll drive you.'

'No, no. You've done enough. No . . . And I've so much to sort out before I leave.' She grimaced at the pile of papers.

'Let me do that,' he said. 'Sort it all out.'

'Thanks, but it's all bills. Though God only knows how I'm going to pay them.'

'That's what I mean. I'll do it.'

She looked slightly shocked at the idea; money was an intimacy too far. 'No. Thanks, but no.'

He didn't argue. 'I'll wait downstairs then. Until you're ready to leave.'

She avoided his eye. 'Emma's going to take me,' she blurted. 'It's best that no one knows where I'm going.'

His heart lurched painfully. The familiar coldness came over him. 'I wouldn't tell anyone,' he said stiffly. 'I wouldn't dream of it.'

'No, of course you wouldn't. But I couldn't have you knowing and not Ben – it wouldn't be right.'

'Well, Emma's not going to keep the secret long, is she?' He tried to suppress the peevishness in his voice. 'Ben'll soon wheedle it out of her.'

This hadn't occurred to her. 'Do you think so?'

'Absolutely. When Ben sets his mind to something he doesn't give up. And Emma's not the most reliable of people. I wouldn't tell anyone, if I were you. You'll be on the mobile, won't you? Everyone'll be able to reach you, everyone'll be able to talk to you. No – if I were you I wouldn't tell a soul. Then you can be absolutely sure of your peace and quiet.'

'Yes, I . . .' She was full of doubt.

'I'll take you,' he said in a tone that didn't allow for argument.

'I'll tell Denise Cox where I'm going,' she decided finally. 'And I'll tell Daddy. I must tell Daddy.'

'Of course.' He stood up. 'I'll wait till you're ready to come down then.'

She looked at him contritely. 'I've upset you.'

'No, not at all.' His denial was too hasty; it rang with desperation.

'You've been so kind to me, Simon. The best possible friend.'

'It's an honour.' He managed a thin smile.

'Perhaps . . .' She indicated the papers. 'If you *would* sort a few things out . . .'

It was a peace offering. 'Of course. Why don't I put things into piles, ready for you to look through?'

'That would be lovely.' She squeezed his hand. 'You really are very good to me.'

It confused him that she should blow hot and cold in this way; it brought echoes of anguished times. But he forgave her because he'd taught himself that forgiveness was the most dignified way.

He brought up some coffee and, while Catherine went to the bedroom to collect some clothes, he began on the paperwork. The bills made by far the largest pile. A quick tally brought the damage to five thousand pounds or so, and that was just what lay on Catherine's desk. Listening for Catherine, he crossed the room and took a quick look at the scatter of papers on Ben's desk. There were documents relating to mortgages and cashed-in insurance policies, lawyers' and building society letters, but only two bills. One was from Ben's accountant, who Simon knew from the occasional work he'd done for RNP, the other from a law firm Simon had never heard of, for 'Fees as agreed'. Leaving these alone, he went back to the household bills and, coming to a decision, rolled them up and put them in his breast pocket.

By the time Catherine came back he'd filed some of the redundant stuff, had put the papers without an obvious home into a tray, leaving just a handful of letters on the desk top.

'But where are the bills?' she asked immediately.

'I've got them. I'll pay them. You can repay me when things improve.' He held up a hand to forestall argument. 'It's no big deal. I've got the cash, I wasn't planning to use it for anything.'

She cried, 'No!'

'The money's just sitting there.' He laughed it off. 'That's the advantage of no wife, no children, no mortgage – I've nothing to spend it on.'

She was torn, she began to argue, she fought one way and the other before giving in with a small sigh of resignation. 'I'll pay you back within a month,' she insisted. 'I've got this commission, a large garden. Starting in a couple of days. I'll pay you back as soon as I get the money. Oh, how I hate all this bloody debt! It's so destructive.'

'But fixable,' he said.

He asked her about the garden commission when they were loaded and in the car.

'It's in Ireland,' she told him.

'Great! Just come up, has it?'

'It's only been confirmed recently.'

'Near your old home?'

'Pretty near, yes,' she said.

'You're going there?'

'I'm flying on Thursday.'

'Can I help with transport?'

'No. It's all being arranged, thank you.'

He wondered how she was going to manage. He also wondered why she hadn't mentioned the job before.

Following her directions, he made for the Marylebone

Road and turned into a small street tucked in behind one of the Nash terraces on Regent's Park. The flat was in a mansion block with a wheelchair ramp, a porter and a lift. Number twenty was on the top floor with a view over the roofs of the Nash terrace to the treetops beyond. A quick tour revealed a sitting room, two bedrooms, a bathroom, and a kitchen with a table and four chairs. The place had the look of a pied-à-terre, well done up but rarely used. There were no photographs on show, no mementoes or waiting mail.

'Who does it belong to?' Simon asked.

'Oh . . . a childhood friend.'

'It's a nice place.'

Catherine stayed in the hall, looking rather lost, as though the enormity of her decision was only just sinking in.

Simon moved the bags into the larger bedroom and taking a closer look at the bathroom saw that it had a special shower for disabled people, one with low doors and a swing-out seat. 'Your friend's disabled as well, is she?' he called to Catherine.

She wheeled herself in and stared at the shower with bemusement. 'No.'

They were both silent for a moment.

'Well,' he murmured, 'it seems you were well and truly expected then.'

The note was attached to the fridge with a magnet. *Dear Catherine, Please feel you can stay here as long as you like – the place would only be empty and likely to stay that way for at least a year. The porter can bring in deliveries, and there's a nice man next door in Flat 19 who is the best possible neighbour and can be called on in emergencies. There's a car company (details on*

*the attached card) who will take you wherever you
want to go. The car service is my present to you, with
love and affection, M.*

Catherine shook her head when he gave it to her to
read. 'So incredibly kind.'

On his way to the car to collect more of Catherine's
belongings, Simon knocked on the porter's door, which
was opened by a wizened man in a uniformed jacket
with the top two buttons unfastened.

'I'm just moving Mrs Galitza into number twenty,'
Simon said conversationally.

'Ah yes?' The porter smiled, showing stained uneven
teeth. 'That'll be your car out at the front then, will it?'
he said in the accent of a stage Irishman.

'That's right.'

'Would you be wanting a hand?' He walked lightly
ahead on the bowed spindly legs of an ex-jockey,
leaving the reek of stale cigarettes and stout in his wake.
'Have to watch the wardens round here. Sharp as they
come.'

'I bet.'

'But I'll keep an eye,' he promised as he lifted some
books out of the boot.

'Mrs Galitza's not sure how long she's staying.'

'No, that's right.'

'She might need help now and then.'

'Oh, and I'll be glad to give it to her.'

'Your name?'

'Doyle.'

'The owner's being very kind, to offer the flat.'

'Indeed. Indeed.'

'I feel stupid – I've forgotten the owner's name.'

Doyle gave a fleeting smile, as if to commiserate on

the state of his memory, before turning away and carrying the books into the building.

In the lift, Simon prompted him again.

'Oh, I couldn't be sure about the names,' Doyle stated breezily. 'Most flats here are company owned. People come and go. Come and go.'

'So which company owns number twenty?'

Doyle affected an air of deep thought. 'Now wait a moment,' he mused, 'maybe it's an agency that deals with it. Yes, indeed, I believe it might be an agency, and I'm not sure I have the name.' His eyes held steady on the floor of the lift cage, and Simon finally understood that such information was not going to be made available to him.

Emerging from the lift, they passed an open door, the entrance to Flat 19, and went on down the corridor to find the door to Flat 20 also open, and a tall man leaning against the doorjamb, talking to Catherine.

The man turned and Simon felt himself appraised by a pair of hooded grey eyes set in a long lugubrious face.

'You are?' Simon asked challengingly.

'From next door,' the man explained softly. 'Just saying hello.' He could have been any age from fifty onwards, with a lanky frame, unkempt greying hair and the baggy uniform of an intellectual, shapeless trousers and brown corduroy jacket.

Since he showed no sign of introducing himself, Simon asked his name.

'Latimer,' he said before rooting around in his breast pocket for a card, which he handed to Catherine. 'Anything you need, just phone me. That's my mobile number. I'm never far away. I'm glad to do any shopping, errands ... I'm usually back and forth several times a day, so don't hesitate to ask.'

Catherine gave him an open smile, which advertised an immediate liking for her neighbour.

Pricked by doubts he couldn't name and envies he knew too well, Simon voiced caution as soon as they were alone. 'It might be wise to keep to yourself.'

'But he's just a neighbour!'

'I wish I lived next door to you. I wish I could watch over you.'

She gave a long patient sigh. 'Oh, Simon.' But words failed her and with an attempt at a smile she went to unpack her books.

Chapter Twelve

—————

TO APPROACH Morne was to leave the world by stages. First, the small turning off the main road at the signpost bearing the single place name, then, half a mile along a worn and uncertain road, the village. Few tourists ventured this way, and, as the jokers used to have it, those that came were only lost for the way out again, yet coming into the familiar straggle of houses Catherine saw that a bright new craft shop promoting linen and replica Celtic jewellery had been set up in what had been Reilly's drapery store, while at the far end of the narrow road that passed for a main street Paddy O'Donnell's pub, which had long sported mouldering wood for its door and window frames, had acquired a fresh coat of vivid green paint. Otherwise little had changed. Catherine was old enough to be glad of this, because she liked the place just as it was, and young enough to be sorry, because people her age still had to go elsewhere for work, albeit in these prosperous times no further than Dublin.

Beyond the village a gap in the high bank marked an unsigned turning onto a single-track road that wound up through hedgerows towards the brow of the hill and the gates of Morne: the stretch known simply as 'the lane'.

From the moment she'd left the flat, Catherine had experienced the sensation of being effortlessly conveyed. In London, she'd used the car service that Maeve had arranged, in Dublin Bridget had met her at the arrivals gate, accompanied by Pat, the driver, and escorted her to the Mercedes that stood at the kerb, guarded by another man, never identified, who immediately disappeared. On leaving the airport, Bridget had used her mobile phone to report to a nameless presence, who could only be Terry, that they were safely on their way. Bridget had then gone through the day's itinerary: the expected time of arrival, the lunch arrangements, the departure time, the check-in for the return flight. Nothing had been left to chance, and on this, Catherine's first solo expedition, she wasn't quite so brave or so proud that she wasn't glad of the assistance.

As the journey progressed Catherine found herself thinking: So this is money, this is how it feels. It was not after all a matter of ostentation, though there was an element of that in the Mercedes, but of seamless arrangements, of having people to check and double-check each detail to ensure that everything ran smoothly; people, moreover, who took their cue from those they served, who answered questions when asked, who chatted a little when prompted, but otherwise kept a measured silence.

The lane looked completely different, and this almost succeeded in unnerving her. The hedgerows had been trimmed so savagely that the branches, once tall and overhanging, had been reduced to woody stumps, which let a cold white light flood the road. For a crazy moment Catherine wondered if Terry's gardener hadn't been let loose here too, perhaps had blighted the entire neighbourhood. At the last bend, she prepared herself to see the house over a wasteland of uprooted shrubs, even – it was too terrible to imagine – completely denuded of its cover, whole trees or thickets gone. But when the gates came into view all the trees were standing, and when they turned up the drive it was between wide plantings of lusty new rhododendrons, most over two metres high, leaves shiny with nursery-nourished health and heavy with buds, and hardly a glimpse of the house until the very last turn.

The house looked both strange and utterly familiar, a place she might have left three years ago or yesterday. It was a moment before she understood that nothing had changed since the final months of her father's occupation, when times had been difficult and gardeners unreliable.

Fragments from Terry's letters came back to her, snippets that talked of wild tanglewoods and rampaging roses and unpruned trees and creepers with trumpet-like flowers unknown to the reference books. Never for a moment had she taken him seriously: she had thought it pure exaggeration, designed to amuse. Though the rhododendrons might have been slain, she had pictured the rest of the place in ruthless order, new gravel on the drive, fresh paint on the windows and all plant life firmly under control. Yet here was the past held still and magnified, the gravel thin and dusted with weeds, the strange mossy stain still clinging obdurately to the foot of the front wall like verdigris, climbers taking light from windows, lichen patterning the roof, and the tulip-shaped yew still sporting a ruff of nettles.

As Pat brought the wheelchair round from the back, a black dog ran up to the car, barking benevolently. It was a mongrel with one crooked leg and a rolling gait that reminded Catherine irresistibly of her own rather singular walk. 'Hello, Conn.'

Whether by chance or design, Terry didn't appear until she was in her chair, footrests set up, and ready to move. He came striding round the side of the house, dressed for the garden in ancient grass-stained trousers, a baggy sweater and a battered tweed hat. To complete the picture, he carried a pair of secateurs in one hand, and she couldn't help thinking that he had chosen both wardrobe and props very deliberately, to strike a casual note no doubt, but also to put her in mind of the days when he had carried out general maintenance for the Langley family at two pounds an hour.

She had rehearsed a pleasant but neutral tone. 'Pruning?'

'A desperate and futile attempt to bestow order on the roses.'

The hand he offered was large and warm, which reinforced her impression of a big man grown even bigger and more bear-like.

'There's coffee freshly made,' he said.

'And then if we could get straight to work? There's a lot to get through.'

'Of course.' He inclined his head, as if bowing to her professionalism, before flicking the briefest of glances over her head, a signal, it appeared, for Pat to begin pushing her towards the door while Terry went ahead.

On the few occasions when Catherine had bothered to imagine what Terry might have done to the interior of Morne, she had pictured rooms furnished in the country style peddled by department stores, largely floral, largely insipid, and largely bogus. Then, on reflection, she'd decided that Terry would have brought in one of the more esoteric designers, someone widely acknowledged to have seriously good taste, which she knew from her own experience of working for the newly rich was the quality they coveted most keenly, and that the resultant style would be somewhat austere, the rooms painted from head to toe in soft white or palest cream to offset a collection of spectacularly beautiful and expensive antiques. Nothing in her imaginings had prepared her for the sight that met her astonished gaze. Bare floorboards, a scattering of unattractive rugs, skimpy ill-fitting curtains, peeling paint in familiar if faded colours, walls with the ghostly outlines of the long-departed pictures she had known so well. In the dining room, camp chairs around a trestle table, and, visible through the drawing-room door, a strange modern sofa and what might have been a matching chair, looking shipwrecked amid plain walls and bare boards.

'I haven't done too much to the place,' Terry said vaguely.

Catherine could only think he was attempting irony.

'Would you care to freshen up?' he asked rather formally.

In another orchestrated move, the two men disappeared and Bridget stepped forward to offer help, which Catherine accepted as far as the cloakroom door. This room at least was furnished in recognisably country style, with a clutter of fishing rods, waterproofs, battered tweed hats and boots in every state of decrepitude.

When she emerged, Terry was waiting in the hall alone. He had taken off his hat, and she saw that his hair was receding and had begun to grey, and that it wasn't only his face that had grown rounder, but his waistline too. Again, she was reminded of a bear, though his eyes, which were grey-blue and steady, belonged to an altogether more watchful animal.

He smiled. 'Where would you like to start?'

She said crisply, 'If we could look at the plans somewhere?'

He directed her to the dining room where coffee was laid out on the trestle table: cafetière, cups, milk, cream, two kinds of sugar. 'Unless you'd prefer tea?'

She would have preferred tea, but she said coffee would be fine because she didn't want to delay things. While Terry poured, she caught fresh glimpses of the past: a faint damp-stain high on the wall in the shape of a seahorse, an area of chipped paint on the door-frame, the smudge of fingermarks around the light-switch, dilapidations that had gone unnoticed in the last years of her parents' occupation, but which, like the absent pictures and dispersed furniture, were a source of sharp nostalgia.

As Terry put the coffee tray to one side and sat down, she took the graphics from her folder and began to spread them out over the table. 'These are computer simulations of the garden from various vantage points,' she began in a rush, 'and at different intervals, after a year, two years, five years, and showing the different layouts and options, which I've kept to three, though of course they can be mixed and matched a bit if that's what you want.' She glanced up to find Terry watching her steadily and thoughtfully, with little sign of having absorbed what she was saying. 'Obviously these are very approximate,' she pressed on. 'They can only give you a rough idea, and the effect very much depends on the maturity of the trees and shrubs that you decide to plant.' As she went through the visuals in detail and explained the various options at some length, she became increasingly aware of his inattention. 'Are you clear so far?' she demanded briskly.

'I believe so.'

She decided to test him. 'So how do you feel about the woodland? Which option do you think you'd prefer?'

A gleam of understanding lit his face, as though he had read and appreciated her motives. 'I think I'd prefer to have the largest possible area of woodland,' he said, with a show of great seriousness. 'Either side of the glen and all the way down to the meadow and right along to the bridge. Complete with glades, as you suggest, and some coppicing to the north, to attract the birds. That was your second option, I believe, wasn't it?' He didn't pause to relish his moment of triumph. 'And I'd prefer wholly indigenous trees, or – how did you put it? – trees that have been growing here for at least a thousand years. *Almost* indigenous. Like most of the Irish, you might say. And four species sounds plenty to me. Oak, elm, hazel and . . . yew, was it? Yes, I think that will look very fine. And if it's fifty years to maturity – well, I grudgingly accept the risk of not being around to see them in their full glory.'

She should have realised that, even with minimal concentration, he would have an effortless grasp of content and detail.

'Only one thing . . .' He lifted a hand and rotated it in a gesture of unexpected grace. 'I don't think I can resist one item from your list of exotic species. A handkerchief tree. The name appeals to me. The idea appeals to me. I believe I've seen a picture of one. Would that be allowed?'

If he was being facetious, he hid it well.

'It's not a question of anything not being allowed,' she said. 'You can have whatever tree you like, wherever you like, so long as the soil's right. A handkerchief tree would probably be best on the edge of the lawn, in the rough grass, as a focal point.'

'In solitary splendour?'

'I would think so, yes.'

'When does it produce all those handkerchiefs?'

'May or thereabouts.'

'So . . . I should hold back on all my tears till springtime, then.' He said it lightly, but not so lightly that there wasn't a reflectiveness in his tone, and it struck her that for all his money and success life hadn't gone entirely his way.

She said, 'This woodland . . . You do realise the size of the undertaking?'

He bowed his head again and smiled. 'You've explained it very clearly.'

'It'll take some time to cost it accurately, but if you want semi-mature trees we're talking tens of thousands.'

He gave a considered shrug.

'You want to go ahead, then?'

'I believe so.'

'But why?' The instant the question was out, she wished it unsaid. She felt the heat come into her face.

He paused to make sure he had understood her. 'You mean, why bother?'

'I meant . . . I didn't realise you had such a feeling for trees.'

This explanation didn't fool him for a moment, but he answered it all the same, albeit wryly. 'Ireland has so little woodland, does it not? It's a small investment for the future. A gesture if you like. We'll all be moving on soon enough, won't we, but the trees, they'll still be here. My small piece of immortality.' He smiled broadly to show he didn't really take thoughts of immortality too seriously. 'Not much else one can leave behind. Besides, I was always sad that the old woods went.'

He was talking about the oak wood that had been felled before she was born in what must have been one of her father's first acts on marrying into the family and taking over the house. While she was growing up, this event had never been mentioned at Morne, except by unwitting neighbours, who'd soon found it a poor subject for conversation. She supposed it had been done for the money.

'You might say the woods here gave me some of my happiest memories,' Terry said. She'd forgotten his smile, the way it lifted one side of his mouth before spreading up into his eyes.

'The poaching, you mean?'

He drew in a soft breath of mock offence. 'Vermin control.'

'Ah.' She began to fold up the plans. 'Done from the goodness of your heart, then?'

'The pigeon were terrible. The rabbits worse.'

'And that was it, was it?'

Pretending seriousness, he made a show of searching his memory. 'I believe so.'

'Mummy said you used to take the brown trout.'

'I might have glimpsed them in passing, but they

were too quick for me,' he said ruefully. 'Never could master the tickle.'

'She said you used nets.'

'No, no, that was Paddy O'Brien!' he said firmly. 'He was a devil for the nets and the explosives. Your mamma always had that wrong,' he said fondly. 'For all the years I knew her, she had that wrong.'

Rather briskly, Catherine put the visuals back in their folder.

Taking his cue, Terry straightened up and placed both hands flat on the table. 'The garden,' he said, 'would you want to have a look around straight away or after lunch?'

She chose to go straight away. This contingency, like everything else, had been planned for. A golf buggy had appeared at the front of the house, as if by magic.

'Is this yours?' she asked disapprovingly, hating the thought that he had bought it specially.

'I borrowed it from a golf club over by Carlow,' he said immediately. 'The alternative was the quad, but I wasn't sure if it was your sort of thing.'

He was right, she couldn't have ridden pillion, not without her arms locked precariously around the driver's waist. At the same time, she viewed the buggy with resentment because it was everything that was safe and dull. 'A quad is just my sort of thing actually,' she declared childishly. 'But not very practical when I'm working and taking notes.'

Pat lifted her out of her chair into the buggy and wrapped a rug around her legs against a gathering wind. She thought again: The detail, the detail. And wondered yet again why Terry should go to all this trouble, what he could possibly want from her. In the next instant she persuaded herself that it really didn't matter. When the fee was large and you needed the money, explanations were something of a luxury.

'We've had a go at the worst of it,' Terry said cryptically as they set off around the side of the house onto the grass. 'Tidied things up a bit.'

'From what you described, it sounded like Sleeping Beauty's castle.'

'Ah, but we fought the worst of the brambles off the house. We hacked them back.'

As they emerged onto the lawn she saw beds with only a mild sprinkling of weeds and hedges with the barest stubble of new growth. 'Looks fine,' she commented.

'Wait till you see the shrubbery,' Terry said, rolling his eyes in mock despair.

'The machete?'

'Believe me, that would have been merciful.'

'And you've managed to restrain him since, your gardener?'

'We've had him chained hand and foot, worse than a felon.'

Led by the dog, zigzagging rapidly ahead, the buggy trundled across the lawn to the long walk, where she saw real work to be done on the avenue of yews, deadwood to be cut out, and tops to be tapered to let the light down. At the far end of the walk, framed by the long promenade of yews, was the ancient arbour encased in a tangle of rose stems, also in need of pruning, and when they reached the opening half way along the avenue, she saw that the wrought-iron gate was badly overgrown. Making the calculations that came automatically to her, she reckoned it would take a good gardener seven or eight weeks to get the remedial work done, and that was before any preparation for spring planting.

At the arbour, Terry turned the buggy onto the narrow grass path that led into the area of scrub known as the wilderness, and stopped. Before them, the ground sloped away through coarse grass and bracken, rowan and young hazel to the lip of the small gorge, which sheltered, deep in its cleft, the concealed stream. Further down the glen was the bridge, also hidden from this point, and visible on the far side, the wild-flower meadow with its autumn cover, a sea of tall silvery grasses that rippled and shivered in the wind.

'It will be a derry,' Terry announced as he surveyed the wilderness. 'I think I'm right in saying that means oak grove in old Irish, aren't I? When you think of all the smaller places, the crofts and the like, which are called something-or-another-derry you realise what the country must have looked like in the olden times.'

She was aware of him gazing at her again. 'So . . .' he murmured softly, as though passing from one thought to another.

She glanced at him expectantly, and was surprised to see him drop his eyes in what in any other man could have been a momentary shyness.

He indicated the wilderness. 'Will it be possible to grow wild flowers under the trees?' he asked, like a diligent pupil.

'While the trees are young, you'll be able to grow them almost everywhere. Later, well . . . there're one or

two species that tolerate shade. But in the glades –
that'll be the wonderful thing about the glades, walking
out of the trees into a sea of wild flowers.'

When she looked back at him he seemed distracted.

'Thank you again for sending the wild flowers,' she
said, wanting to get this out of the way. 'They were . . .'
She hesitated and settled on, 'different'.

'They probably didn't keep too long.'

'No, but that didn't matter.'

'You didn't mind then, that I sent them?'

'Mind? No. No, I . . . they were lovely.'

He seemed relieved. 'I'd wondered maybe . . .' But
with a sudden smile he left this thought aside and said
brightly, 'Now, tell me something, Catherine – if it were
up to you, how would you choose to do this garden?
Here in the wilderness, for example, would you make a
woodland of it?'

'I couldn't say. It's not my garden. That's the whole
point – it's an individual thing.'

'But it used to be your garden.'

'Never *mine*,' she protested. 'My family's. My
mother's.'

'All right,' he conceded easily. 'So if it were yours
now, at this moment, what would you do with it?'

'You're asking the impossible . . . It all depends on
how one feels about a place, how one sees it. I don't
live here any more, I couldn't have a view on that.'

He made a face of disappointment. 'So I can't have
the benefit of your opinion?'

'You told me what you were looking for in a garden.
I must go by that.'

He searched his memory. 'What did I say exactly?'

'You said . . . natural, tranquil, wooded.'

'Ah. I might have been concocting a thing or two there,' he said in the manner of the confessional. 'I don't think I really knew what I wanted. In truth, I'm still not too sure. Most of the time, I don't feel like a proprietor at all, you see. More like a caretaker who happened along.'

Her anger caught her unawares. 'We're all care-takers, aren't we?' Shuddering inwardly at the banality, she added, 'But you got the place. You acquired it.'

'Well . . . I ended up with it at any rate.'

'*Ended up with it?* You sound as though you didn't want it!' she retorted. Before he could answer she said with a pretence of indifference, 'But that's none of my business. And nothing to do with the garden. Which is what we're here to discuss, isn't it?'

There was a taut pause.

Terry said in a low voice, 'I think lunch will be ready and waiting. If you need to see anything else, perhaps we might do it later.'

He reversed the buggy back onto the main walk, and they returned to the house in a silence that she might have broken if she could have thought of anything pleasant to say.

The house was warm, the trestle table had been laid for two. Catherine could hear Bridget and another woman in the kitchen, chattering softly. Terry brought in soup and warm bread, and some wine. It was good wine, and Catherine decided she'd have at least two glasses, which was one more than the doctor had deemed healthy for her kidneys, or it might have been her liver, it suited her to forget which.

The skirmish still turning in her mind, Catherine maintained a deliberate coolness as they began to eat, but if Terry noticed or minded he gave no sign. He talked companionably about the latest neighbourhood gossip, the scandals and mishaps, 'though I've only half an ear to what's *really* going on.'

She'd forgotten quite how easy and unassuming his manner was, how his blend of banter and attentiveness made you feel you were the one person in the world he wanted to talk to. She'd forgotten how effectively he used this approach to draw you into a sense of friendship and intimacy, and how easy it was to believe in it. There had been a time in the long summer of her mother's illness when she'd been beguiled by this, when she'd come to look forward to their walks and their rambling absurd intense conversations, had even – it made her shudder now – begun to think of him with great fondness. But – thank God – she had found him out in time.

She accepted a third glass of wine even before he brought the main course.

'It was good to see Maeve at the unit that day,' she said. 'But you were there too. You should have come in and said hello.'

'I thought best not,' he said pleasantly. 'I thought one of us was probably enough.'

'How's she enjoying the nursery nursing? The new college?'

'A success, it seems.'

'And her health?'

'Oh, stronger, you know. Better by the day.'

'She was very ill, she said.'

'She nearly died.'

'Septicaemia.'

Lowering his fork, he said sharply, 'It was the incompetence of the doctors.'

'They didn't spot it in time?'

'Too busy banking their fees. I'd like to sue them to kingdom come, I'd like to see every last one of them struck off.' The quietness of his voice did not disguise the enmity beneath, and it seemed to Catherine that this gave the lie to the quiet charm that had gone before, that here at last was the vengeful man who did not take kindly to being thwarted. Then, as if to turn this impression on its head, he gave a long and heartfelt sigh. 'I'd do it if I believed for a moment that it could make up for the suffering Maeve has been through. But sometimes at the end of the day it's wiser to think about your future, your health, and whether you want something like that hanging over you, poisoning your life, for years and years to come. If you can't forgive, you can at least try to forget and put it behind you. This is Maeve's view. And it is mine.' He looked at her in a strange way, as though he wanted to say more, before changing the subject abruptly. 'But now, what about you, Catherine? How are you getting on?'

'Me?' She was immediately on her guard. 'Oh, well enough. I can't run like I used to, of course.'

Far from being embarrassed, he seemed to understand her need for bad jokes. 'But you're managing all right?'

'Oh yes.'

'It must be a matter of the practicalities, of a hundred small annoyances.'

'I've never tried counting them, but yes, the annoyances. And other people.'

He grasped her meaning immediately. 'Ah, they try too hard, do they? Kind to a fault?'

'They gush. They talk as though I were a child. That, or they look above me, past me, through me. I become invisible.'

'It could have advantages, being invisible . . . But perhaps not that many.'

'Not that many.'

'But you have your family, your friends.'

She said evasively, 'I have all I need.'

'And the house, it's been adapted? You're managing there?'

This answered the question that had been on her mind for some days: whether Terry knew she was living in the flat, whether Maeve had kept her promise of secrecy. 'The house . . . is not ideal,' she admitted. She hadn't intended to tell him about the difficulties of living in a two-storey house without a stairlift but he was a patient and attentive listener, and perhaps she'd got to the stage where she needed to tell somebody, but she found herself going through it at some length, finishing on a note of exasperation. In case this had given away too much, she added, 'Of course, we'd have put in a stairlift if we were sure about keeping the house. But we're still thinking about moving. We haven't made up our minds yet.'

'But what happens when Ben's away – you're not on your own there, are you?'

She stiffened. 'Occasionally.'

A long pause in which he fiddled with a spoon and seemed noticeably ill at ease. Several times he seemed on the point of speaking before he finally asked, 'And the trial of this man?'

'It starts next week.'

'Are you going to have to appear yourself?'

'No.'

'But still a strain, I imagine.'

'Only if I let it be.'

'You have plenty of support?'

He had asked it with such open concern that she answered this too. 'Yes. The police are very good.'

'Support's very important,' he muttered vaguely.

Another silence during which Terry laced and unlaced his fingers several times. 'Ben's still in partnership with Mr Jardine, is he?' he asked eventually.

She queried the subject with a frown.

'I was just curious,' he said.

'Actually, no,' she answered cautiously. 'Simon decided to go his own way.'

'I see. Since when?'

'Oh, quite recently.'

'Ah. But it was a mutual thing, was it?'

'Completely.'

And with that, the strange stilted questions came to an end.

There was a pudding, but she couldn't eat it. There was more wine, which she could manage very well. Over coffee, he asked about her work, but aware that the wine was in danger of making her garrulous she got him to talk about his work instead.

'Oh, it reached the stage last year where I had no life of my own, working insane hours, so I decided to pull back a little, to give myself a bit more time to stand and stare, to travel a bit.'

'With Maeve?'

'Ah, when I can. No, usually with Dinah, my lady friend.'

This took Catherine completely by surprise, it was an effort to keep the astonishment out of her face, though the moment she stopped to think about it she realised that Terry would never have stayed unattached for long. In Dublin circles – in any circles – he was probably seen as a great catch. No, what had caught her out was the passage of time. In her mind he was still the rather solitary man from five years ago, the widower of under two years with the touching devotion to her mother. Also, and unforgivably, he was the arrogant self-made man who'd managed to equate love with power, and had the nerve to suggest a relationship with her at the very moment when he was in the process of defrauding her father.

'So,' she said carefully, 'this spare time – will you be spending it at Morne?'

'I'm always trying to come more often.'

'How often do you get here at the moment?'

'Ah. Not as often as I'd like,' he said a touch sheepishly.

'Weekends?' she persisted.

'Once a month, if I'm lucky. Bit of a waste, really.'

It could have been the wine, it could have been the reminders of the past, but the resentment welled up in her again. 'Yet you were so anxious to get hold of this place.'

He paused. 'I wouldn't say anxious exactly.'

'Well, you didn't miss the opportunity.'

'I never saw it as an opportunity, Catherine.'

'It was a favour, then?' She hated the sarcasm in her voice.

'No,' he said with dignity, 'not that, either.'

And still she wouldn't let go. 'So Morne just fell into your lap.'

His eyes darkened, he gazed at her with something like disappointment. 'I didn't seek to come here, Catherine.'

She shook her head at him in mute anger.

Slowly, with the air of someone undergoing an ordeal he would rather avoid, Terry slid his elbows onto the table and made a cage of his fingers, before saying in a considered tone, 'I never wanted this house, Catherine. In fact, I've never known what to do with it. I'd sell it tomorrow if I felt it was the right thing to do.'

'But you took over the mortgage, you . . . foreclosed on it – or whatever it is. You were bound to end up with the place.'

Again, he chose his words carefully. 'I only did what I was asked to do.'

'You're suggesting Daddy *wanted* to give up the house?'

'It wasn't quite as simple as that, Catherine.'

'So how complicated was it? Either my father wanted to stay or he didn't.'

'Perhaps you should ask him.'

'I already have.'

He dropped his eyes, he sat back in his seat with a small gesture of submission, and said quietly, 'Then you must take that as your answer, mustn't you?'

The dependency clinic stood in the grounds of a private hospital serving the commuter belts of Kent and East Sussex. It was the cheapest Simon had been able to find,

which wasn't saying a great deal because all the private
clinics were daylight robbery. But National Health
places were impossible to find unless the addict was
prepared to wait months. So far as his mother was
concerned no amount of waiting would ever make the
time right, of course, but the six weeks would at least
offer a respite for Betty. And for me, he thought. Most
of all for me.

Following accepted practice, his mother was to share
a room; following normal routine, she informed the
nurse that this would be out of the question. The
inevitable scene ensued. First the imperious *froideur*,
the grand inspection of the premises and the announcement that it wouldn't do, as though she'd booked
the Ritz and been shown a seedy B & B; then the
reasoned argument, delivered in a sweet voice of injured
innocence.

Some token tears followed, then, when these proved
futile, came the venom, delivered with skill and preci-
sion because she knew exactly what she was doing
when she was sober.

'I only have to look at him to feel sick,' she told the
staff. 'Because he's just like his father – a two-faced
shit.'

The lexicon varied but the substance always
remained the same. When he finally got her into the
room and unpacked, she sat on the bed like a martyr,
face set, mouth pulled down, eyes drooping, talking of
suicide. He remonstrated, as he always did, but she
wouldn't be denied her outpouring of bitterness, her
chance to visit her anger on him in the name of his
father.

The next stage brought a familiar turmoil, a surge of

heat and tension, like the spiking of an old wound. She told him things about his father that no mother should ever tell a son, things that as a child he'd barely understood except to know that they were hurtful and loathsome and must surely be his fault, things that as he'd grown older he'd heard with growing confusion and despair, and something else dark and shameful which he dare not name.

He listened as he always listened, silently, obediently, feeling the heat and disgust which had long ago become indistinguishable to him, until they reached the last stage, the long process of pacifying her, of repeating the reassurances and promises of devotion that she'd heard a hundred times before, but still demanded of him feverishly, like a liturgy from an abandoned religion.

He returned to London with a sense of deep fatigue and nagging dread, knowing it was only a matter of time before she threatened to walk out, wondering as always how many phone calls and blandishments it would take to dissuade her.

His mood didn't improve when he realised he was going to be late for his meeting with Wilson. Nearing town, it began spotting with rain. By the time he parked in Notting Hill it was bucketing down. He jogged into the police station exactly forty-five minutes late. Fortunately Wilson hadn't gone out. While he waited for him to come down to the lobby, Simon ran a comb quickly through his dripping hair and dried his spectacles with a handkerchief.

'Mr Jardine! Brought the weather with you, I see.' In keeping with his little quip, Wilson seemed lively, almost cheerful: the clear-up rate improved perhaps, or no murders this week. 'How's Catherine?' he asked.

'Fine, thank you.'

Wilson took him through the pass door. 'She did better than expected, I gather. Earned herself early release.'

'She said she couldn't take more of the physio's sadism. That and the quiz nights.'

Wilson gave the obligatory laugh, then, finding a vacant interview room, waved Simon to a seat. 'So, what can I do for you?' he demanded crisply.

'I just wanted to catch up really. I've been away—'

'Argentina, you said?' Sitting on the other side of the table, he made a show of racking his brains. 'Pampas? Or have I got that completely wrong?'

There seemed no limit to his bonhomie today. Simon replied pleasantly, 'I only got as far as Buenos Aires.'

'Ah. No pampas then.'

'Not a lot.' Hoping this had exhausted the travel talk, Simon ventured, 'There were a couple of things I wanted to ask, if that's all right.'

Wilson gestured him on with a flip of his hand, as if he'd be the last person to hold things up.

'This is a bit difficult,' Simon began with a suitably awkward laugh. 'I don't want Catherine to think I'm going behind her back. It's just that ... well, she happened to mention that she'd come across the number of that nuisance caller. She made a note of it late one night, thought she'd lost it, then found it again a couple of days ago.'

Wilson made a face of great puzzlement. 'But the calls came through on her mobile telephone. There was no easy way to trace them.'

'That's right. But this time the call came through on the house line, and she used 1471 to get the number.'

Wilson tightened his lips. 'But this call – it was silent, like the rest?'

'As I understand it.'

'So it could have been someone else altogether?'

'Possibly,' Simon conceded rapidly. 'But Catherine thought not. She thought it was the same person.'

'Though the person didn't speak?'

'That's right.'

They exchanged a complicit smile, as if to say: this is the way women are, intuitive, beyond simple logic.

'And we're not talking wrong numbers any more?'

Simon chose to answer this with a diplomatic shrug.

'I never thought we were,' Wilson remarked heavily. 'Not for a second.'

Under Wilson's unwavering gaze, Simon reached into his wallet for the slip of paper he'd prepared and handed it over. Wilson laid the number on the table without looking at it. 'I'll get it checked this afternoon.'

'You'll let me know, obviously? Rather than Catherine? So she's not bothered.'

When Wilson's eyes narrowed Simon thought for a moment he'd gone too far. But apparently it was just Wilson's way, to consider all requests with circumspection, because the next moment he nodded unconcernedly and lifted his eyebrows, ready for the other item on the agenda.

'Yes . . . Again, I'm going a bit behind Catherine's back.' Simon frowned to show that even the mildest subterfuge was distasteful to him. 'She didn't want to tell you in case it was nothing, in case it caused unnecessary fuss, but I thought you should know. The thing is, Catherine had the idea that someone might be following her earlier this week.'

Wilson's look of polite interest sharpened into something more terrier-like. 'Did she get a look at this person?'

'No. Not enough to give a description anyway. It happened twice. She *thinks* it happened twice. The first time, she was out shopping and saw this man in a blue cap twice within the space of an hour. Sort of loitering nearby. Then on Tuesday night there was someone standing opposite the house for quite a while. But she couldn't say if it was the same man.'

'A blue cap? Loitering?' Wilson asked in a flat tone of disappointment. 'That was it?' Then, without waiting for an answer: 'And the man outside the house – she only saw him the once?'

'Apparently.'

'Did he appear to be watching the house? Or just hanging about?'

'It was very dark.' Simon made a regretful face.

'Height? Age? Weight? Ethnic group?' Wilson rattled the questions off without expectation of anything useful by way of reply.

'Nothing.'

'And no similar incidents since?'

'No, but then she's moved into this flat for the time being, and it's quite a long way from the house.'

'Ah yes, WPC Cox did inform me.'

'I encouraged her to go. While her husband's away.'

'Good idea,' Wilson muttered vaguely.

'It was just to be on the safe side.'

Coming to a decision, Wilson said, 'Yes, best thing all round, because I regret to say we won't be able to follow up on these incidents. Without a description to go on, without any certainty that she was being followed . . .' He gestured sympathy. 'Perhaps she's just a bit nervous, what with the trial coming up. A bit jumpy with her husband being away.'

'You don't think it could have been Pavlik?'

'Pavlik? Not likely.'

'Why?'

'Never been a stalker. No reason to start now. No motive to try to intimidate Catherine. She can't identify him as her assailant.'

'He's been keeping to his bail conditions?'

'He must be reporting daily to his local nick, otherwise we'd have heard soon enough.'

'And the other conditions?'

'We assume everything's all right unless we hear to the contrary.'

Simon wanted to say: Well, he wasn't bloody working at La Rondine last night for a start, and the house in Fifth Avenue was deserted till at least three in the morning, so I don't know how you can sit there and assume anything at all.

'We did check things out at the beginning,' Wilson volunteered smoothly. 'Visited his landlord.' He added with what might have been a sneer, 'Though landlord is not the word some might choose.'

Simon was silent.

'Protector,' Wilson threw into the air. 'Admirer. An older man with – what shall we say? – charming manners and a voice to match.' He made a knowing face.

'Gay, you mean?'

'It would seem so, yes.'

'But . . .' In a theatrical gesture of incomprehension, Simon touched his fingertips to his temples. 'I thought

. . . You mentioned sexual overtones . . . in the attack. You talked about a possible stalker.'

'That's right.'

'But if Pavlik's gay, then surely . . .?'

With the manner of someone only too glad to enlighten others, Wilson said, 'I'm no psychologist, Mr Jardine, but from what the experts tell me Pavlik wouldn't be the first homosexual to have violently mixed feelings about women. Apparently some of them adore and worship women from afar, but once they get close, then something called – I think I'm right – *heterophobia* kicks in. All mixed up with Oedipus-type feelings. Revulsion, revenge. Getting back at mother and women in general for all the imaginary wrongs they've suffered. Confused sexual feelings. I've explained it badly, but it's something like that.'

'What about these *objects* that were found? The ones that made you think he was psychotic?'

'Yes . . .' Wilson grunted. 'But in the end they may not feature much in the trial.'

'Why not?'

Wilson hesitated. 'There's a question mark over whether the CPS will be able to make much use of them. There's no way of linking the items to Pavlik, you see. Nothing forensic.'

'And what were these items?'

'Some lace panties. A lady's scarf.'

Simon frowned. 'Catherine's?'

Wilson shook his head.

'They were found near her?'

'The panties under her head, soaked with her own blood. The scarf . . . tucked up her skirt. With blood on it, but not hers.'

Simon's heart gave a cold thump. He felt a blend of revulsion and curiosity. He looked away and took a long breath, to give himself time. 'And you think these items were put there by Pavlik?'

'We think he carried them around with him, ready for a moment like this. A collector, you might say. An enthusiast for deviant little items. Probably graduated from thieving off washing lines.'

And still Simon couldn't make any sense of this information.

Wilson peered at him. 'You all right?'

'Yes, I'm just . . . shocked.'

'Catherine didn't tell you then?'

Simon's throat swelled, his voice choked slightly as he said, 'No, she never mentioned it.'

'Well, I'm sure she just wanted to put it out of her mind.'

Sensing that Wilson was about to call a halt, Simon asked hastily, 'But tell me, why can't this be used against him?'

'Oh, it'll be used, but the CPS won't go strong on it. If Pavlik had been a known stalker, a known collector of women's underwear, if there'd been forensic evidence . . . When Pavlik agreed to a body sample we thought we'd get him on some DNA traces, something on the scarf at least, but' – he pursed his mouth – 'no such luck.'

Simon said with a light laugh, 'So what evidence *do* you have against Pavlik?'

'Oh, we can prove he was in the house. We can prove he was upstairs in the second bedroom. We've got four different strands of fibre plus some specks of very unusual paint. Then, what else . . .?' He checked his memory. 'We've got a witness who'll say Pavlik boasted about breaking and entering. And of course he was caught trying to flog the jewellery.'

'That's going to be enough, is it?'

Wilson gave the mirthless chuckle of someone who'd seen too many prosecutions turn to dust. 'Mr Jardine, you're a lawyer. You know how it is. There're no certainties in this game. It only takes a smart barrister. It only takes a jury who're easily swayed. I wish I could promise you that Pavlik's going to be put away. But I can't. According to the defence disclosures, two men are going to swear they spent the whole of that Sunday evening with Pavlik.'

Simon made a show of absorbing this. 'And will it stand up, this alibi?'

'Who knows?' Wilson exclaimed contemptuously. 'Pavlik's got a very sharp legal team. Presumably they wouldn't be fielding these two witnesses unless they thought it might be of benefit to them. As I say, I can't give you any guarantees.'

A sliver of fear slid into Simon's stomach. 'A sharp legal team? What do you mean?'

'The CPS people know them. Top firm of solicitors. Top QC.'

'Top firm?' he said incredulously. 'What, this man Gresham?'

Wilson offered this up to his memory. 'No, no – he's changed them all. No, the solicitor's something else like . . . Blake? Black? And the QC, one of those that comes at ten thousand a day.'

Feeling slightly sick, Simon continued to hold very still. 'A totally new team?'

'No expense spared.'

'But how can Pavlik afford people like that?'

'Mr Jardine, I don't think we have to look very far to work out who's paying, do we?' Wilson said in the tone of a schoolmaster explaining the basics to a dim pupil. 'Pavlik lives with an older man. An older man with a bit of money.' He shrugged to suggest that this settled the argument, and, pushing back his chair, got briskly to his feet.

Simon moved slowly, with a sense of being weighed down. 'So he might get off? You're saying there's a good chance he'll get off?'

'I'm saying that I can't give you any assurances, Mr Jardine. That's all. But it wouldn't be fair to anyone to promise he's going to be put away.'

Chapter Thirteen

———

THE PLANE was late leaving and late arriving. By the
time the car reached Regent's Park Catherine was in
that state of exhaustion and muddle-headedness that
comes from a long day punctuated by wine and ranging
emotions, otherwise she wouldn't have turned down
the driver's offer to escort her up to the door of the flat,
wouldn't have assured him when they reached the lift
that she'd be able to manage the rest of the way on her
own.

The lift rose smoothly, the doors opened all right,
but when she wheeled herself out it was to see strange
numbers on the doors of the flats because she was one
floor too low. Then, as if her patience needed further
testing, on recalling the lift and reaching the door of
number twenty, it was to wrench the keys from her bag
with clumsy fingers and see them fly from her hand and
fall to the floor, where they hit the polished wooden
strip beside the runner and slid into a deep corner, the
one place she couldn't reach from the chair.

Early on in this long game of adjustment and transformation, she'd learnt either to laugh at such mishaps,
as she'd laughed at her birthday skirmish with the
escaping wheelchair and the gutter, or more often to
rage, for which she'd acquired a voluptuous repertoire

of short sharp swear words; but never, if she could help it, to get upset, not because she was in the least stoic, far from it, but because tears infuriated her far more than whatever had caused them. Nothing was worth the sense of defeat, certainly not anything so measly as a set of keys, because one thing was certain, there were going to be plenty more lost keys and annoyances to come. Tonight, however, she had little energy for exasperation, and certainly none for laughter, and resorted to a muttered commentary that took her back along the passage to a radiator casing, where she removed the armrest from the wheelchair and, hanging onto the top of the casing, swung herself out and down to the floor. Doing a bummer, as it was known in the trade, was like sex, best practised in private. Sliding herself along the floor on her backside, she reached the keys and dropped them in her lap, turned herself round and shuffled back to the flat door. Resting against the jamb for a few moments, she addressed an indifferent world like some bag lady in a shop doorway. 'Well, you've got this far at least. Well done! Well done! Got *something* half right . . .'

The answering voice seemed to spring out of the darkness. 'Are you all right, Catherine?'

With a gasp, she looked up to see her neighbour from Flat 19. 'God!' she cried with a nervous laugh. 'You gave me a shock!'

He made a penitent face. 'I apologise. I didn't mean to startle you. How can I help?' he enquired solicitously. 'Shall I bring your wheelchair over?'

'Thank you . . .' She couldn't think how he'd crept up on her. She hadn't heard his door open, hadn't heard him approach. As he padded off to fetch the wheelchair she looked at his feet, wondering if he'd be barefoot, and saw battered suede shoes with crêpe soles.

Parking the wheelchair at her side, he waited with a grave expression on his long face.

'Thank you, Mr Latimer.'

'Please – call me Fergal.'

'Fergal. You really did give me a bit of a fright there.'

'My apologies.'

'I didn't hear you come out.'

'I was looking for the cat. One has to go stealthily to have a chance of catching him.'

'A cat? I haven't seen a cat.'

'A tortoiseshell called Bertie. He's Maeve's cat really. And a bit of an escape artist. Likes to roam the corridors unsupervised at night.'

She said, 'Rather like me, you mean?' and held up her arms to be lifted. 'If you wouldn't mind?'

He picked her up and sat her in the chair and, unprompted, slotted the armrest back in place as though he were a master of wheelchair assembly. He unlocked the door for her and reached inside to switch on the lights before returning to the corridor to collect her briefcase. 'Now, can I get you anything? Tea? Coffee? A kettle for a hot-water bottle? Something a little stronger?'

There was an accent she hadn't caught before. Matching it to his name she said in a tone of mild accusation, 'You're Irish.'

He dipped his head in acknowledgement.

'But I've just been to Ireland today,' she said. 'I've just come back.'

'Ah. Is that so?' The comment was polite but incurious. 'It must have been a very long day for you.'

'Yes.' Voicing it, she felt a fresh wave of weariness.

'Can I make you a drink?'

There was a steadfastness about Fergal, a calm unhurried quality that made her surrender herself to his care without question. 'Tea would be lovely.'

While Fergal padded around in the kitchen, filling a kettle, she retrieved her mobile from the hall table where she'd left it that morning and dialled in for her messages, which, according to the robotic voice, totalled six. As expected, there was the daily call from her father, dutiful questions first, asking how she was managing, did she need anything, his tone fervent and anxious, then – his voice warming instantly – a list of treats she might like to consider: a glass of champagne at the American Bar, a trip to the theatre, a dozen oysters at Bentley's. She had no interest in such outings, she had told him so more than once, but there was no deterring him because for Duncan life without treats was a life unlived.

There were messages from Emma and Alice, both sounding hurt, both wanting to know where the hell was she and what she meant by hiding herself away like this. The similarity of the phrasing made her suspect they had been agreeing tactics.

Then Ben.

Her heart tightened at the sound of his voice, which seemed very close for Poland.

'Catherine? Where are you?' he began coldly. 'What the hell's going on? What does this note mean – gone away? Gone away *where*, for God's sake?'

She realised then: he was home. Her stomach lurched, she felt she could hardly breathe.

'Are you feeling all right? Has something happened?

I mean, this note – it sounds like you've bloody *left home*. No address, no nothing. What the hell does it mean? It sounds like . . .' There was a sharp hiss. 'Christ! I do wish someone would bloody tell me what the hell's going on. I couldn't get any sense out of your father. Nothing that didn't scare the shit out of me anyway. Talked about you being somewhere and he couldn't say *where*. What the hell did he mean? Pissed, I suppose. Your father, I mean.' A rapid sigh. 'Well, I'm *here* anyway. I'm *back*. I got an early plane. *Specially.*' Another sigh. 'And *if* it's not too much to ask I'd like to know where you are and when you'll be back!' The message ended abruptly.

The next message also brought Ben's voice, but calmer.

'Moggy, sorry if I was . . . angry. It was just a hell of a shock. You know – getting back to find this strange note and an empty house. Darling, where are you? Please call me. I'm so worried. This note sounds so . . .' His voice broke. 'Moggy, I love you. I'll be worried sick until you call. Christ, this note frightens me. You will call? *Please.*'

Fergal appeared with the tea. Wordlessly, he put it beside her and, in the absence of chairs in the tiny hall, wedged his lanky frame into the corner and looked away into a distance of his own making.

The final call was – inevitably – from Simon. Her keeper, her guardian, who yesterday had taken it on himself to phone four times and drop by in the evening with some food she hadn't asked for and didn't need. Hearing his voice she prepared herself for the diligent questions, the request to phone him, his hope of seeing her the next day. Tonight, however, his voice took her by surprise, it was so taut, so urgent. 'It's really very important that you call me, Catherine. However late you get in. You must call me straight away. Please, it's extremely important! And, Catherine, I know this sounds strange – I can't explain – but trust me, please – don't speak to *anyone* until you've spoken to me. No one at all.' He made a sound of frustration. 'Really, Catherine – *no one*. And – it's nothing to be worried about – but don't open your door to anyone, will you? *No one*. Not even . . . Just no one!'

'I guessed at milk no sugar,' Fergal said as she switched off the phone.

'Thank you.'

'Is there anything else I can get you?' His voice was very soft.

She shook her head. 'Where do you come from, Fergal?'

'Dublin.'

'You go back sometimes?'

'Now and again.'

'You have family there?'

But a part of her had ceased to listen, and sensing this he soon fell quiet again. She was thinking: Who should I call? Ben? Simon? Neither of them? Arguments with Ben demanded energy and agility, and she was short of both tonight. Even when she was feeling reasonably sharp-witted he could usually outmanoeuvre her. He had a way of leaving an argument just as she was getting to grips with it, and launching off into another, with no backtracking permitted. And she knew how it would be this time. He would take the high moral ground: the injured party, hurt and bewildered, innocent of all charges, declaring devotion. The expensive dinner would be business or an old friend. The double room at the country house hotel would be booked for a Pole and his girlfriend who hadn't turned up. If that didn't work he would cajole, charm, bully, plead with her, and then start from the beginning all over again. He wouldn't stop – wouldn't allow her to ring off – until he'd extracted a promise to return to him. The prospect of such determination might have touched her if she hadn't suspected it was driven as much by anxiety as love, for though Ben was desperate to do his duty, by far the sharpest and least ambiguous emotion in his soul was the fear of losing control.

Fergal, at ease with silence, waited quietly in his corner perch, his gaze fixed on some inner world.

Catherine said, 'How peaceful it is here.'

'For the centre of London.' He produced the closest thing she had seen to a smile. 'Now, you're sure there's nothing more I can get for you?'

You could get me a hard heart, thought Catherine. You could get me a heart that could shut Ben's message out of my mind and let me go to sleep without guilt. 'No, thanks.'

'In that case . . .' He straightened up slowly. Standing, he resembled a tall stork-like bird, with his long loose limbs and his shoulders raised high around his ears, an impression reinforced by the enquiring tilt at which he held his head. 'I'll wish you a good night. Oh!' He thrust a hand into his pocket and pulled out a card. 'I gave you my mobile number before. But for the night perhaps you should have the number next door. Just in case.' He placed it on the table beside her before making for the door. 'You're going to be all right now?'

'Fine, thanks. Good night.'

'Take care, Catherine.'

This time she heard the door of his flat sound as he closed it behind him. She heard a fainter click, which might have been an internal door opening, and then the soft rush of a communal pipe somewhere between the walls. The tea cooled in her hand. At some point she must have put it down, but she had no recollection of it. Her memory was caught elsewhere, in a place she couldn't name.

Take care, Catherine.

It's the tiredness, she decided. It must be the tiredness because it makes no sense.

You're going to be all right now.

She tried to capture the precise sound, word, intonation that had jogged the dark corner of her memory.

Catherine . . . You're all right, Catherine. You're going to be all right.

It was the softness of his voice, it was his choice of words. It meant nothing, couldn't mean anything unless . . . Thoughts seized in her mind, caught on improbabilities, rushed off again, stopped and stalled.

At some point her eyes fell to the card on the table beside her. There seemed no order to events after that; they might have happened all at once or minutes apart. She looked at the number and it meant nothing and everything. Like his voice it belonged to another time, another place. She closed her mind to it; she opened her reason to it: she knew, but refused to know that she had seen it before.

The entry-phone buzzer sounded, and that also seemed to come from another world. She held still as if this might deny the sound, but it buzzed again, and she thought dimly: Simon.

But it was her father's voice that spoke her name. Then: 'Let me in, darling.'

She pressed the door-release and waited for him calmly, with a sense of disconnection. Whatever had happened here, whatever she had begun to grasp in these few minutes were like secrets, to be hidden away until another time.

Before opening the flat door, she folded the card and slipped it deep into her pocket.

At the sight of her, Duncan gave a show of immense relief, a clutching of both hands together, a heavenward roll of his eyes. 'Thank the Lord you're safe, darling! I can't tell you how worried we've been!'

As he opened his arms and stooped to embrace her she saw over his shoulder the dark figure of Simon, caught in the shadows between the passage and the doorway. Her father straightened up and stood aside with a glance towards Simon, who came slowly forward into the light.

'Thank God,' Simon said forcefully, his mouth working with suppressed emotion. 'Thank God.'

'For heaven's sake,' Catherine sighed with sharp impatience. 'What is it?'

Her father gestured towards Simon.

'Well?' she demanded.

'The nuisance caller,' Simon announced gravely. 'I'm sorry to have to tell you, Catherine' – he lowered his voice to a confidential murmur – 'but the phone number belongs to the flat next door.'

There was a pause in which she held his gaze. 'Yes,' she said very deliberately, 'I know.'

Simon blinked at her. 'The flat next door to *here*, I mean.'

'Yes.'

He frowned at her, before saying, in the manner of a further announcement, 'We've told the police.'

'*What?*'

'They would have come anyway,' he argued defensively.

'Oh, why did you have to do that? I wish you hadn't done that!'

'But they traced the number for us. And Denise Cox knows you're living here – they'd have worked it out for themselves.'

'You shouldn't have gone behind my back, Simon. You should have asked me first!'

Simon appeared to shudder, his cheek danced furiously, for an instant his eyes were very dark.

Duncan touched Simon's arm to gesture him to one side, and said to Catherine, 'But darling heart, these calls, this place—'

'It isn't something for the police, Pa.'

'My dear girl, listen . . . I'm sorry to have to tell you . . . it may come as a bit of a shock . . .' He half crouched to bring himself down to her level. 'Darling, darling . . .' His expression suggested he would do anything to spare her such news. 'The thing is, both this flat and the one next door are owned by this company,' he began unhappily. 'And the thing is, darling girl, the company is controlled by – I wish I didn't have to tell you this' – he made a gesture as if to berate the gods – 'well, dear heart, they're both owned by Terry Devlin.' He paused mournfully, waiting for some sign that she had understood. 'This one *and* the one next door,' he repeated for clarity. Glancing to Simon as if for help, he resumed unhappily, 'You see . . . this Latimer and his nasty calls – the thing is, darling girl, I'm afraid to say it was all a vile way of trying to get at Ben through you.' He took her hand, his face creased with mortification. 'I'm so terribly sorry, darling.'

'Get at Ben?' she echoed.

'I'm afraid so.'

'But why?'

'I know it's hard to take it all in,' Duncan said, ignoring her question. 'I know you thought that nice daughter of Devlin's was just being kind. I know, I *know* how *painful* and *beastly* it must be to realise just how badly you've been taken in—'

'For God's sake, Pa,' she protested. 'This is crazy! This is madness! Why would Terry want to get at Ben?' She looked from her father to Simon and back again.

Duncan's eyes slid away helplessly. 'Darling girl . . .' He patted her hand abruptly and straightened up. 'Best if Ben explains it all, I think. Definitely best. He can tell you.'

'I can tell you,' Simon cut in, his face animated by a strange excitement. 'It's all about money.'

Duncan shot him a reproving glance. 'I don't think it's for *you* to talk about this, Jardine. This is something for Ben!'

Simon said directly to Catherine, 'It's very simple. Ben owes Devlin money, and Devlin wants it back.'

Duncan said rather pompously, 'Can we *please* leave this to Ben. He'll be here any minute.'

Catherine stared at her father. 'You've told Ben I'm here?'

'I know I promised, darling, but I thought it best . . . in all the circumstances . . . The thing is, darling girl, he's absolutely frantic. Frantic! I can't tell you! And he can explain everything, you see. Much better than me, better than either of us!' His gaze flittered everywhere but to her face; he was ill at ease with explanations of betrayal. 'And we thought, since it's not safe for you here, that you'd want to go home, you see. We thought he should come and take you home . . .' Hoping the worst was over, he ventured to look her in the eye, armed with his most defenceless smile.

She said, 'I understand, Pa,' because there was nothing else to say.

He beamed, his entire face dissolved into an expression of relief. 'For the best, darling!'

But she wasn't ready to forgive the summoning of the police, and Simon must have read this in her face because he said in a voice that quivered with self-justification, 'It was out of my hands. Ben's making an official complaint. He wants Latimer arrested. There was nothing I could do.'

She shook her head obdurately.

Simon's face was very white. 'I would have done anything, *anything* . . .' But the words blocked in his throat, he seemed almost dazed, and with a strange gasp he turned on his heel and left.

Every night, work-day or weekend, Soho was the same nowadays, crowds of secretaries and traders up from their East End strongholds, armed with bulging pay packets and raucous laughter, spilling out of the pubs to block the pavements, even in late November. Stepping past them, forced out into the street itself, Simon thought: To the coarse and loud-mouthed, the modern world. Only La Rondine retained the flavour of a gentler era. The post-theatre diners were few and soberly dressed and, keen to catch the last trains back to the garden suburbs, were all gone by midnight. From the other side of the street Simon watched the illuminated sign of the swallow fall dark and a waiter hastily relay the last table with white cloth and crimson napkins.

On arriving, he'd made a close pass of the frontage and spotted Pavlik in full waiterly stride, swerving rapidly between tables with a cluster of stemmed glasses high in one hand. The sight of him had produced a shiver of relief or terror, he didn't care to identify which, while the knife in his pocket might have been molten steel, it seemed to sear his hand so badly.

When Pavlik emerged, Simon prepared himself to match a fast pace. But Pavlik seemed tired tonight, he stepped out slowly. He shrugged his leather jacket higher onto his shoulders before ambling off through the crowds, hands thrust into his pockets, head low. He turned into Old Compton Street, apparently making for Piccadilly and the tube, only to take the next right into Dean Street, which was not the direction for home at all. When Simon rounded the corner it was to see him on the opposite pavement, slowing up to turn into an entrance with a smoked glass door and no sign to say what sort of a place it was.

Simon gave it five minutes and pushed open the glass door to a reception area, a long passage dimly lit by downlighters and the throb of bass music rising from the basement. Guarding the entrance were two men at a desk, clones with shaved heads, heavy moustaches, earrings, black leather jackets copiously adorned with studs; a clear and unambiguous indication, if any were needed, of the style and tone of the establishment beneath.

It was a membership club, no ID, no questions asked, a year's subscription in advance. Simon retreated to the street in a state of jittery frustration. This was all he needed, Pavlik on the pull. Two minutes, two hours: he might be all bloody night. Even then he might appear with a ghastly pick-up, or someone eager to take him home, though from the look of the place it wasn't for tender hearts. Simon decided to give it an hour, and took up his cold vigil in an office doorway, which smelt of disinfectant and rotting vegetables.

Watching the comings and goings at the smoked glass door, he tried to make out if the club's clients stayed for long, but it was impossible to tell because they all began to look the same to him, like soldiers in an outlandish inter-galactic army, with their uniform black jackets and convict hair and strutting steps.

One fifteen; and the hopelessness crept up on him in a tide of loss and yearning. He'd blown it. This would achieve nothing; Pavlik would walk free from court and have his revenge; Catherine would hate him for ever. He slumped a little in the doorway, counting off the regrets and lost opportunities, pondering the unfairness of a life half lived.

Pavlik emerged just after one thirty. He was alone. He came out fast, heading south at a stride just short of a run, quickly vanishing into Old Compton Street. In his haste to follow, Simon ran across the street, dodged between some dawdlers on the corner and promptly cannoned into two men on the far side, one of whom declared comically to his vanishing back, 'Excuse *me*!' Simon sped on and saw Pavlik disappearing round a bend ahead, at the same frantic pace.

Simon caught him again in Brewer Street, going west. Following a few yards behind, he almost had heart failure when Pavlik glanced back over his shoulder. But either he didn't see him, or he was looking for something else entirely, because he hurried on in the same way as before, without looking back again.

Within sight of Regent Street, with no warning at all, Pavlik suddenly broke into a sprint, flat out, arms pumping, head back, and jumping a barrier wove through a line of oncoming traffic to disappear behind a stationary bus on the far side of the street.

Simon ground to an unsteady halt, panting hard, and watched Pavlik take his seat on the N36 bus as it drew away, going north.

The first cabbie he tried had left his adventurous spirit with his sense of humour, in another life, and drove off with a sour grimace. The second driver laughed, game for anything that broke the routine, even if it was a predictable succession of stops and starts along Oxford Street and up the Edgware Road, towards Paddington and the north-west.

When the bus reached the Harrow Road, Simon told the cabbie to overtake and drop him just short of Fifth Avenue.

He walked fast and chose a spot opposite the house in the shadows of an overhanging shrub. Pavlik's lover didn't seem to be at home: there were no lights on, not even a porch light, and the ground-floor curtains were undrawn. He waited impatiently, the sweat cold on his back, the blood hammering in his ears, the knife sharp and unwieldy and terrifying as he fingered it in his pocket. How hard did you have to push it in? And where? Just under the ribs? The neck? God, God, he wanted to be sick. He had the shakes. His guts churned hotly, threatening action.

How much longer? *Where are you, you shit?*

Just when he thought he might have made a ludicrous misjudgement, that Pavlik might have turned around and gone in a different direction, he saw in the steady beam of a street lamp the squat athletic figure walking unhurriedly up the road, head low, eyes on the pavement, no scent of danger.

Simon slipped his spectacles into his pocket and waited for Pavlik to turn in through the gate, then, blood running high, nerves thrumming, he began to run lightly across the road. At the point where he adjusted his stride to leap onto the opposite pavement he still believed he might reach him undetected. In the moment when he landed awkwardly and one foot brushed roughly against the paving stone, he knew that he wouldn't, and then the blood sang in his ears, he felt the blind lust of pursuit. As he covered the last two yards, he watched Pavlik twist around defensively.

The sight of Pavlik's half-raised hands sent a shot of doubt into Simon's heart and in an action he hadn't planned and certainly didn't have time to think through he cranked his left forearm back to take a swipe across Pavlik's head or neck, while keeping the knife low in his right hand, ready to thrust upwards.

He had caught Pavlik by surprise, but not so much by surprise that his reflexes weren't working perfectly. He ducked to one side and twisted away so that Simon's left fist glanced ineffectually off the top of his head, and when Simon thrust the knife up he found air and then something hard: brick or stone, the blade bounced off it all the same. Pavlik must have seen the blade, or heard it, because he caught Simon's wrist and chopped down hard on it with such force that the knife might have been blown from Simon's hand, it left his grasp so quickly.

For some reason Pavlik let go of Simon's wrist, perhaps to swing at him, but Simon was too fast for him. Driven by panic or fury, he grabbed the front of Pavlik's jacket in both hands and, bunching it up under his jaw, jammed his head hard against the door. The sound of Pavlik's howl seemed to fill the whole street.

Simon yelled into his face, 'You shit!'

Pavlik fell silent, or maybe he couldn't breathe. His eyes bulged, the whites gleaming in the dull light, his lips were drawn back over his teeth. He gave a sharp hiss, a sound of contempt or fear.

'You're a dead man, you bastard,' Simon roared, voice juddering, 'unless you tell me – who the hell's bought you? Who's paying you?'

Pavlik gasped something that Simon didn't hear.

'Come on, *come on*! Who's bought you, you fucker? *Who's bought you?*'

Pavlik stared down his nose at him, and Simon caught the stench of alcohol on his breath. 'Talk crazy,' he hissed.

'Who the hell is it? Galitza? Devlin? *Give me the name, you shit!*'

Even before Pavlik's face contorted and swelled, even before Simon heard the long intake of breath and felt the sturdy arms coming up against his chest, he felt the panic of the weaker man. As Pavlik shoved him forcefully away, Simon saw the hurried jab coming and managed to duck it by a hair's breadth. He got in one feeble upward blow to Pavlik's side – it was like hitting stone – before he realised that Pavlik was cranking his fist back for something far more serious. In an effort to forestall him, Simon lunged for a neck-lock that didn't come off though it succeeded in throwing Pavlik off-balance and disabling the blow. Reaching out blindly, Simon grabbed desperately for clothing, flesh, anything and finally got some sort of a grip on an arm. They wrestled fiercely, toppling a dustbin, and almost fell before regaining their feet. Simon tried for the neck-lock again, but Pavlik had his balance this time, rooted and square to the ground, and pushed Simon's arm aside as if it were matchwood. An instant later Simon felt an explosion against his ribs, a hammer-blow that doubled him over in a jackknife and drove the air from his lungs in an agonised rush. The second fist caught the side of his head, a cracking blow that sent him sprawling to the ground, grating his face over concrete or stone. He rolled over – he was somewhere in the doorway – and came up in a crouch, gasping. From the corner of his eye he saw Pavlik turning to run for it, and felt a fresh surge of anger. Scrambling after him, his empty lungs fighting for air that wouldn't come, Simon made a dive for him. He managed to grab one leg at knee level and for a ludicrous moment they were caught in a grotesque pavement ballet, one man hopping and kicking, the other hanging on grimly. Then Pavlik twisted round and swung a fist onto the side of Simon's head, precisely where he'd struck it before, and Simon yelped as the pain shot through his brain like fire. He had the impression of passing out, though he remembered rolling onto his back and shouting after Pavlik, 'I'll kill you!'

He heard savage sobs and realised they were his own. He curled up on his side and, cradling his head with his arm, vomited until the nausea faded.

Eventually, he staggered to his feet and, groaning aloud, made his uncertain way to the Harrow Road. The first two cabs sailed past, the drivers' eyes carefully averted, and it was only by stepping out in front of the next that he got it to stop at all. Even then, he had to persuade the cabbie that he'd been mugged, and no, he wouldn't bleed all over his precious interior, and yes, he still had enough money for the sodding fare.

At Draycott Avenue he thrust a note at the cabbie and waited doggedly for every penny of his change, no bloody tip, before stumbling towards the entrance. As he fumbled for his key he heard a woman call his name and, disorientated, looked around open-mouthed.

'Simon!'

He stared stupidly at Alice.

'*God!*' she cried, getting a proper look at him. She helped him into the lobby. 'What the hell happened to you?'

He looked down and saw that his suit and shirt were covered in blood.

Up in the flat she bathed and disinfected his face where it had scraped along the stonework, and put ice to the lump on his head, and prodded his ribs gently to see if they were broken.

'The party was so boring. I was hoping you'd liven things up a bit,' she said, laughing at the absurdity of it all.

He told her he'd been mugged, but didn't want to bother with the police.

They had a large brandy each, his washed down with two painkillers, before she put him to bed. He was glad when she slid in next to him. He wanted sympathy, he wanted the proximity of a warm body, most of all he wanted to obliterate his fear in the transitory joy of sex.

'Let's get some sleep now, Moggy. It's very late.' Ben reached for the bedside lamp.

'I still don't understand.'

Abandoning the lamp switch, Ben took a long breath of ill-concealed dismay and, rolling back, dropping his arm heavily onto his stomach, turned his head on the pillow to look at her. 'What is it you don't understand, Moggy? God knows, I've tried to explain. I've told you twice – *three* times – there *is* no other woman. The bloody hotel room was for that stupid oaf Casimir and his ghastly blonde totty. I took Rebecca out to lunch – *once*. The last of the big spenders. Guilty as charged. That's it!'

'It's not that. I've got all that,' Catherine said quietly, though there were things she had chosen not to mention, like the perfume in the bathroom cabinet, and what had or hadn't passed between him and Emma. 'It's this business with Terry Devlin,' she said slowly. 'I don't understand why . . . I thought you'd fallen out years ago. I thought you hated him. I thought you were never going to do business with him again.'

'God alone knows, so did I!' he agreed lavishly. 'Last thing I wanted! But a deal's a deal. If it looks like a good one, you have to go with it, even if it means supping with the devil. Or you *think* you have to go with it,' he added with a grunt of regret.

'So you ended up owing him all this money?'

'Darling love,' he said heavily. 'It wasn't quite as simple as that. It was a business thing.'

Softening her voice, she persevered, 'I need to understand. Please tell me.'

He became so still, his eyes so vacant, that he might have been lost to the conversation altogether. 'Okay,' he said at last, coming to a decision. 'Basically . . . Terry advanced some money against the prospect of this deal in Poland. That's all there was to it really. The deal was going to take a year or so to complete. Maybe longer. He knew that, there was never any question of a fixed time.'

'This deal . . . what was it for?'

Another pause, a slight shrug. 'A hotel.'

'I didn't think RNP went in for that sort of thing.'

He gave her a narrow look. 'It doesn't. This was a one-off. Nothing to do with RNP.'

She absorbed this with surprise before struggling on. 'And something went wrong?'

'It appears so. *I* thought we had an agreement. The terms were perfectly reasonable. He agreed to them quickly enough anyway! But then . . . then he went and decided he wanted to – *foreclose*.'

'And he threatened you?'

'Let's just say he wasn't going to be put off.'

'He was going to use this . . . bad thing against you?'

'Yeah,' he mused distractedly. 'Yeah.'

'You're saying that Terry was the blackmailer?'

'I'm saying that Terry knows how to get his way when he wants it badly enough.'

There was a part of Ben that had always taken refuge in abstruseness, and she was too tired to press him further. 'It's all over now, though, is it?' she asked. 'He's got his money back?'

'Mmm?' Again, a vagueness came over him. Again, it was a moment before he answered. 'Oh yeah. I've kept my part of the bargain all right.'

'And . . . the nuisance calls?'

'Oh, bully-boy stuff. Latimer's his errand boy.'

'But why *me*? Coming through on *my* phone?'

He said, shame-faced, 'I got them, too, Moggy. Calls.'

She stared at him and pushed herself up on one elbow to see his face more clearly. 'You never told me that.'

'Didn't want to worry you.' His brusqueness had given way to a sort of misery.

'But . . .' She bowed her head for a moment while she caught her breath. 'Is there anything else you haven't told me?'

He shook his head and putting a hand on her shoulder caressed it softly. 'It's been a dreadful time, Moggy. Not being able to tell you the half of it.'

'But it would have been far, far better if you'd told me. Far better.'

'Not too late now?'

And still she hung her head.

'Moggy – I'm sorry. I'm really sorry.'

She looked up to find him smiling contritely, the child asking for forgiveness. When this didn't produce

an effect he breathed, 'Oh, Moggy . . .' He touched her
hair and his eyes took on the liquid glint that in the
dim days of uncomplicated happiness had so often
formed a prelude to love-making.

He guided her head back to the pillow and they lay
side by side, faces inches apart, caught in the stillness of
the night and in the awareness of each other. It was
astonishing to have forgotten the force of this stillness,
the slow deepening of sensation, the closeness that was
all the more potent because their bodies were not quite
touching. But forgotten it she had, partly from a need
to protect herself from the ache of rejection, partly
because no amount of remembering could ever do
justice to it. She had wanted this moment for so long,
had fixed her hopes on it so unquestioningly, that now
. . . As he murmured the endearments that were the first
waymarks along the familiar path, she felt something
stall inside her, she was caught up by a huge emptiness.
Her body responded with a host of old and new
sensations, some mechanical, some lost for ever, some
that would need to be reinterpreted or re-learned. But
her mind was somewhere else, floating in a sea of loss
that had no name.

Chapter Fourteen

CATHERINE WAS ready and waiting by the front door in her long coat and scarf when she heard the car halt in the road outside and the sound of brisk footsteps on the pavement. Reaching up to slip the latch, she saw in the early gloom the face of Mike, the driver who'd taken her to the airport for the flight to Dublin. He held the door open for her as she levered herself upright and made her way out, then, following her directions, locked up and slid the keys into her pocket.

It was four o'clock and already pitch dark. There was a cold snapping wind, a hint of snow. Her breath vaporised and was sucked away into the murky swirl of the streetlights.

Mike helped her off the pavement; she wasn't yet so confident with crutches that she could swing them forward from one level to another and be absolutely sure her legs would follow. He saw her into the car, understanding immediately how this must be done. She thought how they all followed a type, these people who worked for Terry Devlin, willing, efficient and taciturn.

Before setting off, Mike passed her an evening newspaper, and she thought at first that he meant her to read something about the trial, but when she searched the news pages it was to find nothing but blizzards in

the east, snowstorms in the north and the doom mer-
chants blaming the early winter on global warming. She
flicked through the paper once again, but if there was
anything about the case it must have been very small.
At the start of the trial the papers had carried reports
of the prosecution's opening case under extravagant
headlines, the most restrained of which was 'Burglar
accused of throwing TV girl from landing'. Reading
these accounts – all with a sensational slant, all containing errors of fact – she'd had the impression of reading
about a fictional character loosely connected to herself
by name and – when they got it right – by age, a person
who'd been constructed from a series of stereotypical
images to form a more digestible version of herself.
Redrawn in this way, she had become 'beautiful', her
career as a 'popular presenter' had been 'blossoming',
she was newly married to a 'dynamic entrepreneur',
and of course she was 'paralysed'. It was like viewing
herself through the wrong end of a telescope: she saw a
person who was diminished and indistinct.

At the mansion block, Doyle must have been looking
out for them because the moment they drew up he came
scuttling out like a crab, head tucked down, shoulders
hunched against the wind, to open her door. She replied
to his greeting absent-mindedly, because her attention
had been caught by the sight of Fergal emerging from
the entrance.

'How are you, Catherine?' he said, coming forward
to help her up the steps.

'They haven't locked you away then, Fergal?'

He cast her a small admonitory frown, as though it
were inappropriate to make light of such things. In the

lobby he said rather formally, 'I'm glad you telephoned. Had you been trying for long?'

'For two or three days, off and on. In the rush I lost your mobile number.'

'I was away in Dublin, seeing my mother.'

'The police – they've finished with you then, have they?'

'I believe so.'

'What did you tell them?'

'I told them that it was a mistake.'

'And what sort of a mistake, may I ask?'

He didn't reply until the lift had arrived. 'I told them,' he said in a considered voice, 'that it was a private matter.'

She held her tongue with difficulty. Once in the lift, however, she asked firmly, 'And the man following me?'

'I know nothing of anyone following you, Catherine.'

'No?' She would have argued with him, because in recent weeks she had learnt to question all facts offered to her by way of explanation, but something held her back. She realised, with mild surprise, that it was a belief in his honesty. 'Oh, well,' she sighed, 'I was never sure there was anyone anyway.'

The lift stopped, the door opened, Fergal held a hand over the sensor to stop it from closing again. His lugubrious face took on an expression of great solemnity and some discomfort. 'I have to tell you though, Catherine, that there was someone watching over you in the night. The man outside your house – I can only offer my sincere apologies that the fool should have alarmed you and caused you distress.' With this speech, Fergal himself became almost agitated. 'He was meant to stay in the car, to keep his distance. He disobeyed his instructions. He was dismissed immediately.'

There was a long moment in which Catherine couldn't speak, except to breathe in a tone of incredulity, 'My God.'

The silence was broken by a sharp buzz as someone tried to summon the lift. Fergal stepped out and, restraining the door once more, helped Catherine onto the landing. The door closed with an impatient whir.

'Terry asked you to set it up, did he?' Catherine asked with iron calmness. 'This – *watch*?'

'Yes.'

'How long has it been going on?'

'It was simply for those few days. While you were on your own in the house.'

'You *knew* I was on my own? But how did you—' She broke off as the answer came to her. Ben had gone to Poland; he must have gone with Terry's knowledge, perhaps even his blessing, to sort out this business of theirs, or to raise money, or . . . But she had tired of trying to understand the crazy world of Ben's dealings. 'But why put a man outside?' she asked. Then, as her anger began to goad her more fiercely, she repeated with indignation, '*Why?*'

'To watch over you. Nothing more, Catherine.'

'But the reason, Fergal. Why should you want to do that? What am I saying? I mean, of course, why should *Terry* want to do that? To spy on me?'

'Never to spy, Catherine. Never that.' Fergal spoke with the sadness of misunderstanding. 'It was merely to make sure you came to no harm.'

'But who would want to harm me? Tell me! Do you know of someone who wants to harm me? *Do* you, Fergal?' All pretence of calm left her then, and she exclaimed bitterly, 'Why, oh why do I feel that I'm the last to be told anything! Why do I feel that I'm being treated like a child! Or worse – like a *nothing*, a *nobody*!'

Fergal said placatingly, 'I myself am not aware of any particular person who wishes to harm you, Catherine.'

'But Terry knows of someone perhaps? Is that it? *Is* it?' She snorted, 'But I suppose you would have to get his permission to answer that!' With this retort, she turned perilously fast, maintaining her balance only by a panicky jolting move of one crutch, and started her unwieldy progress towards the flat.

Reaching the bend in the passage, she saw Maeve standing in the open doorway of number twenty, so still that Catherine felt sure she must have been there for some time and heard her spat with Fergal. Maeve came forward tentatively, hands out as if to embrace Catherine, before losing her nerve and coming to a sudden halt with her hands clasped tightly together. 'Come in,' she whispered at the floor, before leading the way.

Catherine glanced back, but there was no sign of Fergal. Watching, presumably, and waiting.

An elderly tortoiseshell trotted determinedly into the flat just ahead of Catherine. Maeve shooed him into the kitchen with a brief awkward smile before gesturing Catherine towards the sitting room.

'Oh, Catherine, how I've been dreading this moment,' she said, taking Catherine's coat. 'And how I've wished to talk to you for so long.'

Once Catherine was settled in an armchair, Maeve seemed to lose what small amount of confidence she might have had. Wringing her hands, she cast around in desperation. 'Oh, there's tea,' she said breathlessly. 'I made some tea. Will you?' As she pointed jerkily towards a nearby table Catherine saw that her hand was trembling.

'Thank you,' Catherine said formally.

Maeve went to the side table and moved to pick up the teapot, then the milk, then the teapot again, before appearing to forget why she was there. As her hand paused indecisively in midair, the rest of her also seemed to be in imminent danger of stalling. She swayed slightly and gasped.

'Why don't you sit down?' Catherine suggested. 'We could have tea later.'

Blinking rapidly, Maeve half turned and, taking this in at last, gave a dazed nod. It was another few seconds before she managed to unlock her limbs and manoeuvre herself to a chair.

'Are you all right?'

She whispered, 'Yes, I ... Forgive me. I ... stupid ...'

Appearing to remember some instruction she had been given for just such an occasion, she closed her eyes and took a long slow breath, holding on to it for several seconds before exhaling at the same measured rate. She did this twice before opening her eyes again. 'I forget to breathe,' she gasped. 'Then I breathe too much. Hyper-ventilation. It makes me feel faint.'

With her transparent skin she looked even paler than in the rose garden, and, if anything, thinner, though this may have been the effect of her clothes, a black ribbed sweater that clung to her body and a long straight skirt through which her hip bones protruded in sharp crescents. Without make-up, her wide-set eyes appeared to float in her face, adding to her air of distraction.

Pressing a hand to her chest, appearing to recover a little, she managed to say, 'The trial – Fergal said the verdict's due any minute.'

'They thought today. But now it'll be tomorrow. Probably.'

Maeve absorbed this slowly. 'Aha. And you yourself, Catherine,' she asked in her soft whispering voice, 'did you have to go to the court and appear?'

Suppressing her impatience, Catherine answered mildly, 'They didn't need me there. Or rather, I told them I wasn't going, so they had no choice but to manage without me. They had Ben, of course. He gave evidence.'

Again Maeve pondered this for some time, and again Catherine had to curb her restlessness.

'And what's going to happen at the trial?' Maeve asked in the same halting voice. 'Will he be sent to prison?'

'Will he be sent to prison?' Catherine repeated vaguely, as though she hadn't given this much thought. 'I think, all in all, from what people tell me, reading between the lines – probably not.'

'Oh . . . *Oh*! I'm so very sorry.'

'It doesn't bother me.'

Maeve searched Catherine's face in open bewilderment. 'You don't mind?'

'I mind, yes. But I'm not going to let it rule my life.'

'But, Catherine, I don't understand – why won't he go to prison?'

'He has an alibi. Apparently it's rather a good one.'

'Oh. But is that enough? How can that be enough?'

Catherine shrugged.

'What a pity no one saw him!' she declared with sudden passion.

Catherine said drily, 'Quite.'

With a surge of colour, Maeve stared hastily at the floor and became stranded once more in a world where she could neither breathe nor speak.

Catherine prompted firmly, 'So . . . this flat, Maeve – it isn't yours?'

Maeve looked startled by the question, but also relieved.

'No,' she agreed meekly, 'This flat is Dadda's. Mine's next door. I mean – it used to be mine, when I was here.'

'And you phoned from there?'

She whispered, 'Sometimes, yes.'

'Why me, Maeve? Why not Ben? It was Ben you wanted, wasn't it?'

'I never meant you any harm, Catherine,' she moaned wretchedly. 'Never. Please believe me. *Please*.'

'But you've been' – she chose one of the more delicate expressions – '*seeing* Ben?'

'I wish— I didn't mean to— I . . .' Maeve's face contorted, her eyes gleamed with tears.

'When did it start?'

Her gaze fixed pleadingly on Catherine. 'Oh, it was all over before your marriage. I swear. I *swear*!'

Catherine kept very still.

'That was one thing I could not have done. Not that! Never! No – once you were married! I promise! For the rest . . .' She bowed her head. 'I cannot justify anything to you. Not a single thing. What I did was wicked, utterly wicked. When I think back now, I can't believe that I could have behaved in that way, telling myself I was doing no harm, knowing full well that I was doing dreadful harm to everybody, to the Lord, to myself, to . . . *you*. I can only say that I seemed to lose all power over myself, that I couldn't seem to stop myself, or to fight my way free. It's not enough to say that though, is it? You can always stop yourself if you try hard enough! I just couldn't – *couldn't* – stop.' She sank forward, caging her eyes with rigid fingers, until her forehead was virtually resting on her knees.

'And when did it finish?' Catherine asked in a voice that conceded nothing.

A gasp. 'That September.'

Maeve would have been nineteen then, which pushed Catherine towards the question: 'How long had it been going on?'

Maeve's reply was almost inaudible, and Catherine had to repeat it for confirmation. 'A year?' She thought: That would be about right. By then she and Ben had been together two years, long enough for him to welcome a little diversion before settling down to the serious business of marriage. And of course – the really irresistible attraction of such a diversion – with Terry Devlin's daughter.

'A year . . .' she murmured again. It was only with the greatest effort that she asked, 'And . . . how did it happen, Maeve? How did it start?'

Maeve lifted her head a little. 'It was me. I . . . called him.'

'Just like that?'

'He'd . . . said to call him. I knew no one in London. He said to call him for lunch and . . .'

'You'd seen him, though. Somewhere. Not long before.'

'At the races.'

Of course, Catherine thought. The races. Where it appeared that everyone in her life was doomed to meet and part. 'And how often did you see him?' she asked.

'Perhaps . . . once every two weeks.' Her head was going down again, her voice fading.

Catherine pondered the questions that sprang into a hurt and saddened mind. What did you do? Where did you go? When in the day did you meet? How many hours did you spend together? Did he say he cared for you? Did he promise to look after you?

Strangely – but perhaps not so strangely after all – she hoped Ben had been kind to her.

'What did you want when you phoned the house, Maeve? Why call?'

Maeve was crying, the tears dripping from her nose and cheeks unchecked. 'I just wanted him to *speak* to me,' she sobbed. 'To accept that I still existed, that he couldn't just pretend I wasn't *there* any more. I wanted to make him speak to me – that's all! Oh, it was a dreadful *madness*, Catherine – a dreadful *madness*. I couldn't think of anything else at all. Nothing, nothing! My studies, my friends – I did nothing, saw nobody for weeks and weeks. All I could think about was making him talk to me! Just talk to me.' She raised a hand as if to deflect an accusation. 'Oh, don't think for a moment

I had any other ideas! No, no, I knew he'd never want to see me again, not like that. No, I just wanted to . . . *talk*, to make him *realise* . . .' She struggled to express some other idea, but gave up with a gesture of hopelessness.

'And your illness?'

'Oh, I wanted to die,' she announced matter-of-factly. 'I rejoiced at the thought of dying. Lord forgive me, but I hoped and prayed for it. It was like a terrible darkness all around me, the wish to die. I couldn't see my way clear. I couldn't imagine the darkness going away. That's what happens when you're very ill – you can't see a way clear, you can't imagine it's ever going to end. I'd learnt about such things in college, I knew it was a terrible illness, depression, but you don't understand it when it's happening to you. The only thing you know is that the pain is unbearable. I realise now that I was in great need of treatment, that I was very, very ill – ill in my body and ill in my mind, that I needed the right drugs. I know that *now* . . .'

Catherine softened a little. It was impossible to feel angry in the face of such unhappiness. 'But you almost died, you said. You were seriously ill.'

'Yes,' she answered in a flat voice directed at her knees. 'I hadn't been eating, I'd lost weight, too much weight. And when I got ill, I didn't go to the doctor. I never thought . . . It didn't seem important, you know? It was only when I got a fever. Even then I didn't think to tell anyone. And the next thing I knew I was in the hospital.' She finished this speech as she had begun it, in the same measured delivery.

Catherine let the silence draw out before asking, 'And me, Maeve? Why did you make the calls to me?'

'I thought – I thought—' She started again. 'I was beyond reason, Catherine, beyond reason . . . I thought that we might meet, you and I, that we might talk . . . Oh, not that I was going to say anything to you. No, no – not a word. No, I simply thought that if we talked, then . . .' Her voice faded again in shame or disbelief. '. . . *I might just see him.*'

This brought a parallel memory to Catherine, of a time when she'd been young and impressionable and had formed a mercifully brief obsession for an older man she'd met at a polo match. He was beautiful and rich and amusing; in the short time before she realised he was also self-indulgent, lazy and unkind she'd waited in for his calls, caught up in a frenzy of hope.

She murmured, 'On the phone once, I heard you crying.'

'Oh, I didn't mean for that to happen,' Maeve protested. 'I always meant to speak to you, even if it was just to say hello, but I never could.' She directed a groan of scorn at herself. 'Of course I couldn't! It was part of the madness, to think I could talk to you as if nothing had happened. Lord help me!'

'But you spoke to Ben sometimes?'

'Yes.'

'And?' she asked with an attempt at lightness. 'What did he say?' She had to interrupt Maeve's whispered reply to ask her to speak up. 'My hearing,' she explained patiently, 'is not so good as it used to be.'

'He said he couldn't see me,' Maeve said in a voice that was barely more audible. 'He said it wouldn't be possible.'

'So you never saw him?'

'No.'

Catherine waited for the rest of it. It was a while coming, a minute or more, and arrived obliquely in a flurry of unconnected fragments and repetitions, told in the same rushed whisper, which she had to strain to hear. 'Oh, I understood,' Maeve began, apparently referring to Ben's refusal to see her. 'I knew it wasn't possible . . . I knew, but at the same time . . . I went to Mauritius, I went to Italy. But it was no good, I couldn't bear it. I only wanted to . . . It wasn't that I expected anything – no, no. But I had this terrible *need* to . . . This, this—' She made a gesture of frustration. 'It was as though I had no room for anything else in my head. I used to imagine so often, used to think about it all the time, day and night . . . I didn't *expect* anything, I just . . .' She lost her way altogether then. She pressed a palm to her forehead. When she picked up the threads again, it was with new resolve. 'I wanted my say,' she declared, with a sense of discovery. 'I wanted a proper end to it, a moment I could look back on and think: That was the end of it and I had my say. I wanted peace. That's all. Peace.' She added bleakly, 'Of course, there was nothing to be said. And no peace to be had. But that was how I felt at the time.'

She searched in her sleeve for a handkerchief and blew her nose. She was calmer now, and when she continued her story it was in a steadier voice, her eyes fixed on a point somewhere near the foot of Catherine's chair. 'I managed to speak to Ben just before you went to France. Of course he didn't want to speak to me, to see me, but I begged, I used every argument, I said it would just be for five minutes. He finally agreed. Just to keep me quiet, of course. But he agreed. He said he'd be back early from France, on the Sunday. He said you were staying on longer. He said he'd call me when he got in. I knew he wouldn't, of course. I knew he'd . . . well, I just knew he wouldn't. So I decided to wait for him.'

She wrapped her arms tightly around her waist, as though to ward off the cold, before pushing herself onwards. 'I arrived at the house in the morning and there was no one in. I went to a coffee place in Portobello, and came back again, then one of your neighbours kept looking at me, so I went and had some lunch and came back again. I don't know how many times I came back – four, five times? Then . . .' She stiffened, her voice rose. 'When it was getting dark I thought I saw a light in the house. I rang the bell and waited. And then—' She glanced uncertainly at Catherine. 'I looked up and I thought I saw the blind move. Oh, I tell you, I've gone through it in my mind time and again! *Time and again!* And I'm never sure if it really moved or it was a trick of the light or . . . You know how it is when you look up suddenly and it's almost dark and you're not sure what you've seen. But of course I was ready to convince myself that it was Ben. I thought he'd spotted me and was hiding from me, pretending he wasn't there. I pressed on the bell and kept pressing and pressing . . .' Unwrapping her arms from her waist, she immediately crossed them again over her thin chest and gripped her upper arms, as though for protection. 'I went and waited across the street. I was upset. I thought – Oh, I was in a dire state, Catherine. What can I tell you? Angry. Wretched. Crying my eyes out.'

Her voice had risen dangerously, her breath was coming in short gasps, and it was only by a visible effort that she slowed herself down. 'Then I realised I had to calm myself. It was no good being in a state like that. If it was him in there, I didn't want him to see me like that. Hysterical, pathetic. So I went to the pub round the corner and cleaned myself up and dried my face and had a glass of wine for some courage. It must have been about fifteen, twenty minutes before I got back. Then . . . well . . .' She made a small agonised gesture, a plea to be spared the last of the story.

But for Catherine the story was everything. She said implacably, 'You found the front door open?'

'Yes.'

Still Maeve hoped for a reprieve, and still Catherine wouldn't give it to her. 'Was it dark inside?'

'More . . . dim,' she replied with a droop of resignation. 'There was a light at the back somewhere. That's why I didn't see you to begin with. I stood in the doorway and called out. Not loudly, just a sort of hello. I called several times, then I plucked up courage to go in. And then . . .'

'You saw me.'

The tears had returned silently. 'It was like the most terrible nightmare in the world – to see you there. The blood – oh, the blood! It was like a black lake. I thought you were dead. I felt sure you were dead!' A shudder snatched at her body.

'But I wasn't.'

She closed her eyes at the memory of her relief.

'And then?'

'Then . . . oh, I wish I could tell you I did everything possible for you, everything I was trained to do! I wish I could say I went through all the right procedures! But my mind was in a state. I couldn't think. It was like a dream – I didn't feel I was there at all. I can't remember very much ... Everything was all mixed up. I was crying and carrying on. I felt it was all my fault, Catherine. I felt somehow I was to blame! And the blood – all I could see was the blood. There was so much of it! I was desperate to stop it. *Desperate*. I tried hankies ... I tried anything I could find. Eventually – I don't know how long it was – I began to come out of it, to wake up, to think about what I should do. Finally I went and turned on a light and felt your pulse. I knew I mustn't move you – at least I knew that! I knew I mustn't even straighten your head. But Catherine – I completely forgot to check your pupils and your breathing and your airways and to make sure you weren't choking. I completely forgot!' She cried in disgust, 'Why did I ever think I could make a nurse! It was madness to think I could ever be a nurse!'

Refolding the handkerchief in trembling fingers, she used it to rub the tears ferociously from her cheeks. 'Then Fergal arrived. He was everything that I was not. Practical and calm. He phoned for the ambulance. He did all the things I should have done – checked your airways, your breathing. He went upstairs and found Ben and checked on him as well. Fergal is one of those people – there is nothing he can't do.'

A growing listlessness crept over her. Her grip on her arms loosened, her hands dropped, she settled back in her chair and closed her eyes momentarily as her head sank against the cushion. 'Fergal told me to go and wait in the car. He said he'd deal with everything else. I wanted to stay, I was desperate to stay, but he made me go. He said it wouldn't do any good if I was still there when the ambulance arrived. He said it would only make things difficult for everyone. That's what I mean,' she said wonderingly, 'he thinks of everything.'

'But, Maeve, why was Fergal there in the first place? What brought him?'

'Why?' Maeve echoed as if this should have been obvious. 'Oh,' she breathed with a show of understanding, 'because of Dadda! Dadda had told him to keep an eye on me. To follow me, really. Fergal was there to watch over me.'

Another person to be watched over. But the deeper realisations came to Catherine in slow stages, first as small nudges of suspicion, then as lurches of shock and comprehension. 'Fergal was there all day?'

'Oh no, he didn't come until that minute. No, I fooled him into thinking I'd gone to the doctor and then out with a friend. No, it was only when I didn't come back . . .'

'But he knew where to come? He knew where to find you?'

She gave a single nod.

'He knew about Ben?'

Catherine missed her murmured reply, but then the answer was written in her expression.

'And your father – did he know too?'

She nodded again, miserably.

Catherine's heart squeezed coldly. 'When did he find out about you and Ben?'

Maeve's expression was full of pain. She didn't answer.

'When did he find out?' Catherine repeated with quiet insistence.

'When I was ill,' Maeve breathed.

'He knows the full story?'

Her frown said yes.

At this, a whole succession of possibilities cascaded into Catherine's mind, one building on another, each more disturbing than the one before. At each realisation she pricked with fresh anger and mortification. He had known! He had known all along! She pictured the scene at Morne, the tour of the garden, the lunch, and all she could think was: He looked at me and he knew! And when he wrote all those letters – he had known then too. The letters that had given her such secret pleasure, which she had looked forward to each week – this knowledge had infected every word. And in the midst of this long rocky storm of feeling, one thought wedged firmly in her mind. A father does not forgive the man who takes his daughter's innocence.

Catherine picked up her shoulder bag to leave. 'One thing, Maeve. The ambulance men found some panties under my head. They were yours, were they? You put them there to stop the bleeding?'

Maeve stared aghast. 'Panties . . . Did I . . .? Oh . . . Oh.' She flushed and dropped her head. 'Oh, I didn't realise. Oh . . .'

'There were yours?' Catherine persisted.

'Yes, I . . . always have some . . . in case . . . in my bag . . . in case of . . . you know . . . emergencies.'

Catherine assumed she meant emergencies of the feminine kind, and wondered at her fastidiousness. 'And the scarf, Maeve – whose blood was on it?'

'Scarf?' she repeated dully.

'It *was* yours, wasn't it?'

Again the confusion, the flush of what looked like shame.

'Whose blood was on it?' Catherine repeated.

'It was mine.'

'You'd hurt yourself?'

Her eyes slid away, her voice faded to a whisper.
'No . . . it was from before.'

Catherine waited silently.

'From . . . when I was bleeding and . . . he cared for
me.'

Catherine couldn't disguise the incredulity in her
voice. 'That was why you kept it?'

Maeve nodded silently, with a heartbreaking tenderness, which Catherine could only gaze at with a kind of
awe.

'I'll be going now,' she said to break the spell.

Maeve jumped to the front of her seat in renewed
agitation. 'Oh, Catherine – I'm so very sorry for everything! I feel it's all my fault. I feel I'm to blame for
everything!'

'Why? Don't be silly.'

'But if I'd got there sooner. If I'd stayed outside the
house and waited. I can't stop thinking, *If only, if only.*'

'There was nothing you could have done.'

'But I might have seen him! I might have stopped
him! I can't help going over it again and again. I can't
help thinking that I must have caused it to happen . . .
I can't explain. There was even a time when I
thought—' She started guiltily.

Catherine asked quietly, 'What was it you thought?'

Maeve gave a strange laugh. 'Oh, nothing!'

But her fresh open face was incapable of concealment, and Catherine read something there that made
her insist, 'Tell me.'

'Oh, it was just ... When I was in a state – a real state! – I thought – really, it's nonsensical' – she made a face of disbelief – 'I thought it was Dadda!'

Catherine held her expression. 'In what way?'

'Oh . . .' Again, Maeve tried to brush it aside. 'That he wanted to see Ben hurt. That he'd sent someone.'

'Does he do that? Send people?'

'Oh *no*! *No!*' In her horror, Maeve kept repeating this. '*No, no.* It was just *me*. I was imagining it! No, Dadda would never do a thing like that! No, never. It was just the madness in my head.'

The moment Catherine began to manoeuvre herself upright, Maeve leapt to her feet.

'Oh, Catherine, I'm so terribly sorry for everything.'

'Don't feel sorry about the accident,' Catherine insisted. 'You probably saved my life, you and Fergal. Someone else might have tried to move me and succeeded in finishing me off.'

'I didn't even check your airways,' Maeve sighed inconsolably. 'I didn't check your breathing. Oh, I'm no use, Catherine. No use to anyone!'

When Catherine kissed her cheek, she had the sense of kissing a forsaken child.

In the car Mike said, 'There was an item on the news, Mrs Galitza. I don't know if you've heard—'

'About the trial?'

'Yes, the man, he—'

'Not now, Mike, thank you.'

A surprised pause, before he said humbly, 'Right ho.'

She wasn't ready for more; not yet. There was only so much that could be absorbed at one time. She needed to catch her breath, to make sense of her emotions. Her heart was raging; her heart was icy. She felt calm; she felt wild with bitterness. She kept thinking: How could he? How could he betray me so deeply? And then, almost as passionately: How could he destroy Maeve? She had no idea what she felt for him any more. She loved him, she despised him; she yearned for him, she felt sick at the thought of him; he was achingly familiar to her, he was a stranger, unnerving and suspect. One minute she strived to forgive him, to make allowances for his troubled nature; the next she wanted to be rid of him for ever. She hated to give up, but she knew it was essential to give up sometimes if one was to hold on to some shred of self-respect.

And all the time the facts kept racketing around her head, stinging and tormenting her: the whole year that it had lasted, the very year that she and Ben had been planning their future together, gone house-hunting, found and bought; the subterfuge that Ben had exercised so flawlessly, the late meetings, some of which couldn't have been business meetings at all, the evenings when he'd reported on his day and must have reported lies; the declarations of love and devotion that had meant whatever had suited him at the time, nothing, something, everything.

But if the facts were hard to bear, the unknown was worse, because there was no stopping your thoughts then, the only limits were the limits of imagination, and just then it felt as though her imagination had no limits at all. She saw the two of them together, she saw Ben's foxy grin, she saw Maeve's childlike gaze, and for a while she let the images run on painfully, in the hope they might burn themselves out.

The car swept down from the overpass towards
Paddington: ten minutes to home. Ten minutes to prepare. One morning recently, Catherine had woken to a
vivid nightmare in which she'd been struggling in deep
water, her legs useless because they were dragged down
with weights. Lying there in half sleep, she'd thought
dramatically, with a surge of self-pity: That's how it is
for me – I'm drowning by degrees. I can't survive any
more! But in the full light of day she'd seen her situation
rather more prosaically. You could always survive, so
long as you took things slowly, with time to catch your
breath in between.

Well, she was getting her breath back now, and as
the car skirted the north side of Paddington Station, she
had the strength to say, 'Sorry, Mike – what was it you
heard on the radio?'

He met her eye in the mirror to check that he hadn't
misheard. 'There was an item about the trial of the
burglar, ma'am.'

'And what did they say?'

Again, the anxious glance in the mirror. 'Not guilty
of the GBH, ma'am. Guilty of something lesser.'

'Thank you, Mike.'

In the remaining minutes before reaching home she
had imposed some semblance of calm. She thought: I'm
getting as bad as Ben, all cover and pretence.

At the house, someone must have been looking out
for her because the front door swung open as Mike
helped her up onto the pavement.

It was Emma who ran out, crying, 'We've been
worried sick about you, Cath! Where've you been?'

'Is Ben here?'

'And your father. And Denise Cox. Where've you

been? I got here sharp at four and you weren't here! You gave me heart failure, Cath!'

'I left a note for Ben saying I was going out.'

'Well, no one told *me*!' In the frosty air Emma's breath plumed sharply, like steam. 'But come on in, darling – it's so *cold*.'

Denise and her father stood just inside the door, solicitously, like mourners at a funeral.

'I heard the news,' Catherine declared before she crossed the threshold.

'I'm sorry,' Denise said, stepping back to let her pass. 'Sometimes these things happen, and you never know what you could have done differently.'

'Darling heart,' her father cried, wrapping her in a tortured embrace, 'there's no damned justice! None at all!'

Catherine sat down to take off her coat, and remarked in the same brisk tone as before, 'I forgot to ask – is he out and walking free?'

'One year suspended,' Denise said. 'For the burglary. We lost the GBH on the alibi.'

'The damned alibi!' Duncan muttered furiously. 'The jury swallowed it hook, line and sinker. Believe anything, these people!'

'Emma?' Catherine called. 'I'd love some tea.'

Emma pulled the cigarette she was about to light hastily out of her mouth. 'Of course, darling,' she agreed effusively and hurried away.

Catherine laid a hand on her father's arm. 'Pa, would you get my wheelchair for me? I'm too tired to walk any more today.'

'Darling girl, of course!' Clutching her shoulder, he compressed his mouth in a grimace of unbearable pride.

'Walking! All this walking! I tell you!' He flung a look at Denise, inviting her to share a moment of celebration.

'Just explain it to me,' Catherine asked Denise once Duncan was out of earshot.

'He admitted burglary, but sixteen hours earlier. He said he'd broken in, taken the valuables. But that was it. He said he'd left the door open and unlatched, and anyone could have walked in off the street, and presumably did. When you arrived home at ten on the Sunday night, he had these two witnesses to swear that he was drinking with them in a pub in Soho. They were independent witnesses, that's what really swung it in Pavlik's favour. Neither knew him particularly well. No axe to grind. And definite about the date.' She made a face as if to say, what can one do? 'And the legal team – this top QC – they made it watertight.'

'I'm sure they did.'

A door slammed above and Ben came running down the stairs, wearing his harassed face. 'Christ, the phone – it hasn't stopped.' Twisting to a halt in front of Catherine, he adjusted his expression to one of grave concern. 'Denise has told you?' He looked to Denise for confirmation before crouching lightly at Catherine's feet. 'What a bummer, eh, darling? What an absolute bastard.' He took her hands in his and held them delicately, with a sort of reverence. 'Have to look on it as the closing of a chapter, I'm afraid. Have to look ahead to new and better things.'

Catherine always forgot how perfectly he could match his mood to the occasion. 'New and better things?' She laughed darkly and unnaturally.

A flicker of doubt crossed Ben's face before he too laughed, falsely. Duncan, appearing with the wheelchair, lifted his head enthusiastically to the sound. 'That's right, damnation to them all!'

Denise was pulling her coat on.

Catherine said jauntily, 'This is goodbye then!'

'The case will stay open, you know. For as long as it takes,' she said. 'We won't give up on it.' And promptly spoilt the effect by dropping her eyes.

After she'd gone, they sat in the sitting room to drink the tea that Emma had made and few wanted. Duncan opted for a stiff whisky.

'Sun safely over the yardarm, I think. Not drinking alone, am I? What about you, Ben?'

Ben flicked a thoughtful glance at Catherine. 'No, Duncan, not for the moment.'

'Emma?' Duncan asked with mock despair.

'No, I'm going to stick with tea,' Emma said, directing a complicit smile at Catherine, as if to show that she was prepared to stand by her even in the smallest things.

Securely ensconced in an armchair with his glass cradled to his chest, Duncan launched forth on the subject of juries and their deplorable gullibility, and – a favourite lament – the lack of education among the populace as a whole. Emma, on the other hand, was more inclined to put the jury's failure down to the modern practice of passing the buck, of ducking every type of responsibility that society asked of them, responsibility for themselves, their families, their health and welfare. Citizenly responsibilities came *way* down their list of priorities, in fact so close to rock bottom as made no difference. Now it was a who-cares-and-stuff-everybody-else society. Most people's aim was to get by with the minimum bother. The jury had found it easier to let Pavlik off than go through the mental effort of weighing up the evidence.

Duncan waved his glass airily and proclaimed that this proved his point precisely, it was the fault of appalling educational standards.

And all the while, Catherine gazed out into the black, dead garden and felt Ben watching her.

Finally, when Duncan and Emma had heartily agreed on the underhand tactics of the defence lawyers and the CPS's lamentable cross-examination of the alibi witnesses, who'd obviously been put up to it – you could tell by the shiftiness in their eyes – a silence fell. By chance, everyone looked at Catherine at the same moment.

'I want to thank you for your support,' she said, 'for everything you've done for me. But now I want you to go.'

Emma must have caught something in her tone because as she bent to kiss her goodbye she said, 'You all right, darling?'

'*Me?*' Catherine declared in a voice that was pitched too high. 'I'm fine!'

Duncan, shielded by good intentions, oblivious to the finer nuances of atmosphere, beamed happily at her. 'There's my girl! Leave you to a cosy evening, my darling. Just know that we all love you. In my case, to absolute bits!'

He planted a loud kiss on her cheek. As he drew back, Catherine saw a face on which life and love and loss had left no mark, and could only envy him.

'Well!' Ben said a little too brightly once he had seen them out. 'Would you like that drink now, Moggy?'

'You have one.'

Unable to gauge her mood, he eyed her warily. 'Don't want to drink alone.'

'I've gone on the wagon, so I'm no good to you.'

'Is there something wrong?' he asked solicitously. 'I mean, is it the trial or something else?' He sat down in the chair next to her and, sitting forward with his arms resting on his knees, offered a cautious smile.

The games that she might play. The traps that she might lay for him before delivering up the series of ugly little truths that would mark the point of no return. The temptation was there, part of her wanted the satisfaction of humiliating him, yet the victories would be cheap, the process antagonising, and at the end of the day she yearned for peace.

'It's over,' she said a little unsteadily. 'Between you and me. It's all finished. I know about Maeve. I know about the phone calls – everything. And I don't think there can be any going back, do you? So I'd like you to leave. I'd like you to move out.'

For a full five seconds he didn't move. His eyes stayed fixed on hers. She felt he was weighing up the various approaches he might take and finding them all wanting.

'Oh, Moggy, I'm so terribly sorry,' he cried at last, in a racked and hoarse voice, and she realised that he had decided on the full and frank approach, the placing of his head on the block. 'What can I say? It was unforgivable. I could tell you it was a last fling, I could say that I called a halt long before the wedding but she threatened to kill herself – I was terrified that she *would* kill herself – I could make a dozen different excuses, but—' He paused with a deep contrite sigh. 'In the end there are no excuses, are there? It was totally wrong.'

He dropped his head onto his hands, he gasped miserably. Raising his head again, he looked at her imploringly. 'Moggy, if I could undo it all I would. Believe me. I've never stopped loving you. Never! In fact, I know this sounds crazy' – in the tiny pause that followed she had the feeling that he was assessing just how crazy it might sound – 'but it was a way of proving to myself how *right* you were for me, how much I *truly* loved you. It was a sort of confirmation of everything we were aiming for, if that doesn't sound too insane. I loved you so much – *so much!* – but I still had this ridiculous fear of the commitment we were making. I mean, marriage is such a huge and daunting thing, isn't it? And I thought that a last fling, a last sort of *test*.' Again the glance, again the measurement of progress. She was careful to show nothing in her face, and this encouraged him to continue in the same vein. 'The crazy thing is that I knew straight away that it meant nothing – *nothing* – that it was just as I'd thought – you were everything to me, Moggy. *Everything.* But by then – well, she was being difficult, threatening to phone, come round, you name it. Basically to try and ruin our lives.' He slumped a little, he gave a long laboured breath. 'I was weak, Moggy. Utterly weak. I can only say I haven't stopped regretting it for a single moment ever since.'

'*You* were weak?'

He didn't like that. His eyes narrowed, his voice took on a note of self-justification. 'Look, I wanted to be kind to her, I tried my best to be kind to her, but it was the worst possible thing with someone like that. You've no idea – she kept phoning and saying she was going to take mouthfuls of tablets. She was wildly unstable, absolutely hysterical. Someone like that – you can't reason with them. You can't begin to deal with them.' But the conviction was fading from his voice. Standing up, he paced across the room and came back to stand over her, restless and fretful. Sitting down again, he declared in a tone of near despair, 'I don't want us to be finished, Moggy! I don't want it at all. I'd be lost without you. Completely lost. We make a great team, you and me! Admit it, Moggy – we're good together!'

He was waiting doggedly for an answer. She murmured, 'I used to think so, yes.'

Grasping at this, he tried his old winning smile, the roguish half-closed eyes: the handsome devilish son of a gun. 'Could be again, Moggy.' He ducked his head to catch her gaze. 'No reason why not! You and me. Hey,' he sang in the soft fluid tone he used to bring her round to his point of view.

Looking at him, she felt an immense distance. She thought: It's all a technique, it's all a game, it means nothing. And yet like an autonomic reflex part of her responded, an unbidden sway of the flesh and the heart.

He covered her hand with his. She looked down at it, she felt the warmth of it, and thought: But there can't be any going back.

She murmured, 'I'd like to know – on the night of the burglary, were you expecting to see Maeve?'

He pursed his mouth at having to go back to Maeve. '*See* her? Christ, no.'

'But you told her you would.'

'What? No, no, I just told her something – anything – to get her off the phone.'

'So you weren't expecting her?'

He pulled up his mouth in mystification. 'Christ, no! *Hardly*. Why would I be expecting her?'

'No, I . . . It was just something she said.'

He caressed her hand, as if to soften the mood again, and cast her a hopeful gaze. 'So, Moggy . . .' Lifting her hand, he bent and kissed it. His voice was low and tender again. 'Could be a team again, you and me. Hey? What do you say?'

Taking her silence as a sign of encouragement, he moved forward as if to embrace her, but she pulled her hand away very deliberately and said with a tremor of anger, 'There's been someone else though, hasn't there, Ben? Since Maeve. In fact – recently.'

He sank back onto the edge of his seat. 'What?' He glared at her defensively. 'For God's sake, where did you get that idea from?' Then, with a show of indignation: 'No, Moggy – absolutely not. That's a crazy idea.'

But she had startled him, she knew she had. As if to underline this, he repeated in a blustery tone, 'No, I'd like to know where you got that idea from. Was it that lunch with Rebecca? That stupid hotel room? I told you what that bloody hotel room was about – precisely *nothing*. Bloody Casimir and his blonde! There *was* no story. What more can I say?' His eyes flashed angrily.

'And the perfume in the bathroom?'

He held her gaze just a little too long, she saw the flicker of realisation. 'Perfume?' he responded, too late. 'I don't know anything about perfume. What perfume?' When she didn't say anything, he repeated angrily, '*What perfume?*'

'It doesn't matter.'

'Doesn't matter! You've accused me of something and now you won't even talk about it.'

'It's hard to talk when . . .' She took a steadying breath. 'When there've been so many lies. All that time you were seeing Maeve. The phone calls. Saying you were being blackmailed. Was there any blackmail?' she asked wearily. 'No,' she added immediately, 'don't bother to answer that. It's not important.'

'Christ! You think I'd make up something like that?' he retorted, taking the offensive. 'You think I'd *pretend* I was being taken to the financial cleaners! God, I may have done a few things – but not *that*!' Shooting angrily to his feet, he went across to the drinks tray to pour himself a whisky. Glass in hand, he leant back against the table and said sulkily, 'So that's it, is it? Just write the whole thing off. No thinking about it, talking it through, giving it time?'

'I don't think there's much point.'

He lifted one shoulder, he pushed out his lip in a Gallic gesture of indifference. When he drank, the gaze that met hers over the rim of his glass was blank and cold.

She said, 'I might have felt differently if . . .' Here were the most painful words of all. 'If I thought you still loved me.'

'But I've said so! I do!'

'I think you've tried very hard, but I think that it's all a terrible effort for you. The burglary, the attack . . . we've both changed. I know you find it hard to love me as I am now.'

'So you don't even believe me when I say I love you!'

'I suppose that's it, yes,' she agreed.

'Great!' he scoffed sarcastically. 'So everything's been

a lie, has it? All the good times. All the fun we've had together.'

'The fun's over, Ben.'

'Well, that sums it up, doesn't it. You don't want to know. You're not interested in even trying! You're giving up!'

'Yes.'

'And just when the going gets tough!'

She said reasonably, 'The going got difficult when you began seeing Maeve.' She suppressed the urge to say, *and this other woman.*

'The money – I mean the money. This is when I need your support.'

'You've had my support. You'll still have my support so far as the money goes.'

'Fat lot of good,' he mumbled.

They didn't look at each other. The silence stretched out and settled around them like darkness.

Abruptly, he tossed the rest of his drink back and slapped the glass down. 'I'm to leave then. Is that what you want?'

'I think it's best.'

'*Best? Best?* Who for, for God's sake? You don't know what you're doing, you really don't!' He had got himself into a strange fury that was almost like a panic. 'This is going to be the *end* for me. *And* for this house. The house'll have to go, you do realise that, don't you? Don't think we can keep it because we can't! It'll have to go!'

She shrugged.

'You don't seem to understand what I'm saying.'

'I do, it's got nothing to do with *us.*'

'It's got everything—' He broke off with a shudder of exasperation. 'You just don't understand!'

She looked away. 'Apparently not.'

He stalked to the door. 'Well, don't blame me, that's all,' he flung back reproachfully. 'Don't bloody say I haven't tried!'

She made herself a proper supper, no half measures. It was quite a performance, levering herself up to hook things out of the higher cupboards, hunting for pans that had been put away in strange places, but it was occupation, it was therapy, it was all the things that the unit encouraged. Occupational therapy, and get the hell on with life and, if that didn't do the trick, there was always the help line and the quiet voice of the sister—brother, trained in advice and anodyne sympathy.

Well, she wanted to get the hell on with life, which at this precise moment was pasta with tomato and basil sauce, salad with dressing, freshly made and no modifying the recipe. She opened a bottle of vintage burgundy, one Ben had been keeping for a special occasion, and, pouring a glass, holding it up as if in a toast, made herself a promise, that if she couldn't stick to the one glass she'd give up booze altogether, for at least a year, absolutely no cheating, even if everyone said she was miserable as sin.

She sat at the small table in the kitchen. Knife, fork, cheapskate napkin of kitchen paper. Meal in front of her, glass of wine: a small cause for celebration. She turned on the counter-top television and flicked through the channels. There was a programme she actually wanted to see. She thought: There! Not so very hard after all. Only her jittery stomach threatened trouble. The first mouthful went down, however, and stayed down, smoothed by the wine. Smoothed *enormously* by the wine, she thought as the doorbell rang, long and loud.

Her heart lurched and plummeted. He'd come back. He couldn't bear to stay away. Then she remembered with both relief and disappointment that he had his key, of course he still had his key: he had no reason to ring.

Her father, then. Or Emma.

She sat immobile, wishing the world away. The bell sounded again, and still she didn't move.

'Catherine?' The voice that came drifting down the passage was muffled, but unmistakably Simon's.

She wheeled herself to the door and, unfastening it, opened it just a short distance, to show that she was not at home to anyone, not even friends.

He loomed into the doorway, shoulders hunched high, face pale, looking frozen or worn out.

She said, 'Simon, it's not a very convenient time, I'm afraid.'

'Is Ben here?' he asked.

His eyes gleamed in the half light. She thought: He's come to sympathise about the verdict, he wants to wallow in it, chew over every detail.

'He's out, but . . .'

'I can come in then,' he said, gasping a little.

'Another day, Simon. I've just made supper and then I'm going straight to bed. I'm sorry.'

'But I must see you,' he said with a hint of desperation. He put a hand on the edge of the door as if to push his way in and she heard the rasping of his breath, as though he'd been running. 'Please, Catherine. *Please*.'

'Can't it wait?'

'*No*,' he cried urgently. 'There's something I have to tell you. Something very important!'

He seemed to stagger as he came in, like someone near exhaustion. When he turned to face her, she saw that his hair was awry and hanging damply over his forehead and his spectacles were spotted with moisture. As he struggled to speak she became aware of the breathlessness again.

'What *is* the matter, Simon?'

'I – I've got bad news.'

'What is it?' For a wild moment she thought: It's Ben. He's hurt.

'Pavlik,' he gasped. 'He left court and walked straight into the arms of Terry Devlin's people!' He seemed to think she should understand the implications of this because he waited in agitation for a reaction. When none came, he cried, 'Don't you see?'

Her stomach tightened. 'No.'

He began to gabble, 'His defence was bought and paid for by Devlin. *Devlin!* I knew there was somebody, I knew there had to be. Devlin went and found his alibi for him. The two men in the pub – well, the police couldn't find them, could they? Couldn't find them *anywhere*. But *Devlin* did. Just like that. Must have put them up to it, mustn't he? You see? Bought and paid for. And the legal team – the solicitor, the QC – all paid for by Devlin! All part of the deal! I tell you, he just walked straight into the arms of that man Latimer! They just – walked off together!'

'Slow down,' she begged, throwing up both hands.

Fresh damp had sprung onto his forehead, his cheek was jerking so violently that it brought up the corner of his mouth like a leer.

Beckoning him to follow, she led the way down the passage to the kitchen and pointed to a chair. 'Sit down.'

She fetched a glass and poured him some wine. 'Drink it,' she commanded, 'and start again, please. Slowly.'

He knocked back half the glass, and it seemed to steady him a little. His eyes hunted around the room before they finally settled somewhere on the table in front of her. Between the staccato statements, his gaze flicked up to hers. 'Devlin paid for Pavlik's defence. He found the witnesses, the ones that got him off the charge. Pavlik's there with them now, with Devlin's people. Bought and paid for.'

'Are you trying to say . . .' She paused to get it right. 'Are you saying that Terry Devlin hired Pavlik to come and break in?'

Simon gazed at her with a bitter expression, and nodded slowly and deliberately three or four times. 'He was after the papers. The papers in the strongbox. He wanted them. And he got them.'

'Papers,' she repeated dully.

Leaning forward, Simon spoke avidly, his eyes glinting behind the misted glasses. 'The papers that proved Ben was cheating him. That Ben had done a secret deal. That he was stealing all the profit. *And* . . .' His voice rose to a fierce note. 'The generators? From Warsaw? Ben took an extra ten million and shuffled it on to Bermuda and the Caymans for his clients in Colombia. It was dirty money, Catherine. *Dirty money.*' He shivered with disgust. 'The bank codes and transfer details were in the strongbox, and that's what he wanted, Devlin wanted the proof. And he got it! He got the proof!'

She felt oddly calm, as though all this were happening in another life. She looked away to the pinboard with the display of postcards and party snaps. She saw a clipping from the society pages of a *Tatler*-style freebie magazine, showing Ben and herself at a wedding. Mr and Mrs Ben Galitza, smiling confidently into the future.

'*Catherine?* Do you understand what I'm saying? It was Devlin. *Devlin.*'

'Yes,' she said, 'I understand.'

Her lack of reaction confounded him, he clutched at her hand, but she was in the past somewhere, thinking about Ben and Maeve.

When she finally focused on Simon again, it was to say, 'You look terrible. You mustn't take all this to heart, you know. It's not the end of the world.'

But he wouldn't have it, there was no consoling him.

'Go home,' she said. 'Get some sleep.'

'I don't want to leave you.'

'I'll be fine.'

'What time's Ben coming back?'

'He isn't coming back.'

He gasped slightly. 'Then . . . can I guard you again tonight, Catherine? Can I watch over you? It would make me so . . . *happy.*' He said the word gently, as though in the midst of all his distress he were trying it out for size and finding it perfect.

Chapter Fifteen

SHE WOKE to the sound of knocking, so faint it might have belonged to her dream. After a while it came again, a tentative brush of fingertips against wood. In the second or two before she answered, Catherine placed herself in time, and the previous day came back to her in a series of interlocking layers, each lit by a stark image: Maeve bent forward, weeping into her hands; Ben's eyes staring coldly at her over his drink; and Terry pondering his next move at the massive desk that her imagination had drawn for him silhouetted against a tall window. Truth and lies, but blurring now, and gaining distance. In one of those insights that seem so revelational in the waking hours but always fail to survive the light of day, she decided: The truth is not so important as the leaving of it behind.

She didn't give Simon any thought until she remembered the knock.

'I've brought up some breakfast,' he announced when she called out to him.

The bedside clock said eight; she was surprised at how long and how well she had slept. She ran a hand through her hair and, pulling herself up against the pillows, told him to come in.

His head came slowly round the door. 'How are you feeling, Catherine? Are you all right?'

'I'm fine.'

Encouraged by this, his shoulders appeared. 'Shall I bring the breakfast in now?'

'Why not?'

He put the tray on the bed and when he straightened up his face was empty of all expression. He said, 'All safe and sound.' It was a watchman's report.

'Thank you.'

'I found some cranberry juice – is that okay? And a croissant, and some toast.' He was like a zealous waiter running through a difficult order. 'I've made both tea and coffee. I'll drink whichever you don't want.'

There was butter and marmalade. The tray had a proper cloth, and a napkin lay folded on one side. She murmured, 'Spoilt.'

'Of course. What else?' His smile flickered uncertainly. He glanced around for a seat, only to change his mind and lean against the door frame, hands in pockets, in a casual pose that succeeded in making him look rather stiff. His clothes were slightly crumpled and his chin was dark with stubble, but his hair was damped down and neatly combed, his spectacles were polished. She had the feeling he'd been up for some hours.

'I'm sorry about last night,' he said in a thick voice. 'Coming out with everything in such a rush like that. I must have frightened you. I'm sorry. I wasn't thinking straight. The last thing I wanted was to frighten you.'

It occurred to her that if anyone had been frightened, it had been Simon, though incensed might have been a better word.

'It was just the shock – the complete disbelief,' he said, as if to confirm this.

'Of course.'

Straightening up, he moved restlessly towards her. 'And the powerlessness of seeing it happen under your very nose.'

'Forget it. Really. *I* have.'

But with Simon, forgetting was never an easy matter.

An evangelical light had come into his eyes, and when he began to talk it was in a rapid insistent voice that echoed the strange fury of the previous night. 'You see, I thought I'd hang around after the verdict. I just thought, *I wonder, I wonder*. It was just a hunch, that was all. Just a feeling that there might be something to see. Some *evidence*. But never, *never*, did I think that it'd be so absolutely *blatant*. Latimer was waiting for him right there at the door of the court – right there, Catherine! Went up and greeted him, then shook the barrister's hand. Congratulating him for a job well done, presumably. And Pavlik over the moon, of course. The bastard actually laughed. *Laughed.* Then they went off together, him and Latimer. Obviously all planned, all set up, because there was a car waiting. Driver, engine running, the lot. Just swept them away. Gone!'

She picked up the coffee and held it out to him. He came forward jerkily, and when he grasped the saucer, the cup rattled. Stilling it swiftly with one hand, he met her gaze and finally seemed to read the message there, that enough was enough, that for her it was too early in the day for all this, or perhaps too late for any day at all.

'Sorry,' he said solemnly. 'Here I am worrying you again. I didn't mean to. Absolutely not . . . *Sorry*.'

His concern touched her because it was so confused and earnest, but also because it was nice not to wake to an empty house. She hadn't been brought breakfast in bed since the early days with Ben.

'Take the coffee,' she said.

Settling self-consciously on the edge of the bed, he gave that odd disjointed laugh of his, the small gasp that came out of nowhere. 'No,' he smiled, trying to make himself come alive, 'what I really wanted to say – what I came up especially to say – was how about going away for the day? I wasn't planning to do very much work today anyway. Why don't we go somewhere? Give ourselves time away from the madding crowd! Go somewhere marvellous for lunch. The *Manoir*, perhaps. And a drive in the country. Perhaps to the coast. Or' – he took a stab at spontaneity – 'Paris! How about Paris?'

'It's a lovely thought, Simon, but I've so much to do. Money to earn for a start. Rather urgently, in fact.'

'But it's just one day, Catherine. The weather's cleared up a bit. It's much warmer than it looks. Please.' There was a feverishness in his pleading.

'It's tempting, it really is, but another time.'

'But tomorrow might never come,' he said with intense seriousness. 'We could go on postponing the important things for ever, Catherine – for *ever* – and wake up one day to find we'd done none of the things we really wanted to do!'

'Don't remind me,' she agreed lightly.

'*Please*, Catherine. It would be so perfect. The whole

day together. *Please*.' Then, with a drop of his head and a quick upward glance: 'I do have a slight ulterior motive.' He said it with the air of laying himself at her mercy, but also with a gleam of excitement.

'Oh yes?'

'There's a house. Just the other side of Oxford. I want you to come and look at it with me.'

She was slow on the uptake. 'What house? Why?'

'A place I want to buy.' His eyes were glittering now, he put his coffee cup hurriedly on the tray. 'A stunning Queen Anne house. Would you come and see it with me? Would you, Catherine? It looks perfect from the photographs. I haven't fixed a viewing, but if the agent can't arrange anything in time I thought we could see it from the outside, get an idea, ask if we can at least see the gardens. The gardens, Catherine – they look amazing. Though you mightn't think so, of course! You might think they're all wrong, that they need a lot of work. But there's a knot garden and a walled garden and a rose garden, and a lake and—'

'A lake! God, it sounds *enormous*.'

'No, no,' he retreated immediately. 'The lake's really quite small, I think. And the house – well, it's got eight bedrooms, so not too large. Then there're the outhouses and two cottages. And the grounds – fifteen acres in all.'

'And just the other side of Oxford? But, Simon, you're talking really serious money for a house like that. Two million at least.'

'Quite a bit, yes.'

She made a face of incredulity.

'Oh, I can manage it all right,' he said with a touchy modesty. 'I've been doing rather well on my own. More than well. Never seem to get round to spending it.' Then, hastily, as though fearing some loss of momentum: 'You'll tell me what you'd like changed, won't you, Catherine? In the house and the garden?'

Still absorbing the surprise of his new-found prosperity, she missed the reference to the house. 'Is this a commission then?' she teased mildly. 'Are you signing me on?'

'In a way,' he said enigmatically, and, looking away hastily, wouldn't be drawn further.

In the terrace off Eaton Square the morning light arrived early, reflected by the immaculate white stucco and sparkling windows. For the rich, even the winter dawn looms brighter.

In the car, Terry sat hunched in the back and thought longingly of home. In his mind even the overdressed house at Foxrock had taken on an emotional appeal out of all proportion to its real place in his affections. He found himself thinking with overt fondness of the heavy damasks and drapes and curlicues, of the Hollywood bathrooms and gilt taps, because it was there, in his memory at least, that he had lived simply with Maeve, and, God willing, hoped to live as simply again. He felt the overblown yearning of the exile stuck in an alien land by an interminable and futile war. With luck he should be back in Dublin by evening, yet each moment he had to stay in London was a moment too long, because his heart had gone out of the fight, and his soul too, and the duties that faced him this morning seemed irksome and repugnant. The campaign had gone on too long, the victory had been short and unsatisfactory. He was tired, but most of all he was tired of the struggle, which for him was tantamount to declaring a tiredness for life.

In the front of the car, Fergal murmured something to Mike then fell silent again, bowing his head contemplatively.

As eight came and went, Terry kept his eyes doggedly on the portico of number fifty-three, waiting for the swing of the black door. A succession of people emerged or gained admittance from the adjoining houses, City men and domestics and decorators, and the occasional well-dressed young woman, bolting off to work. And still Terry watched the one door, with patience, because he knew it was about to be repaid, but also with exasperation, because it was typical of Ben Galitza to make him wait.

It was ten past when Ben finally ambled out and paused on the top step. In the short unguarded moment before Fergal got out of the car and proclaimed their whereabouts, Ben's mouth was compressed sourly, he wore a troubled frown, and Terry found himself thinking: Good! I hope you're hurting!

At the sight of Fergal, a mask of indifference slipped over Ben's face. He sauntered over and got into the back of the car without meeting Terry's gaze, which was probably just as well because Terry wasn't attempting to hide anything in his expression just then.

'Charming,' Ben declared sarcastically, without preamble. 'But then you have absolutely no shame, have you, Terry? Your instincts automatically reduce you to the lowest of the low because it's all you know.'

Terry watched Mike close the car door behind him

and walk round the bonnet to join Fergal on the pavement.

'So, you've had me followed and now you think you've proved a point,' Ben continued caustically, addressing the windscreen. 'You're going to call in the guarantee and you're going to destroy my life, and I hope it brings you nothing but misery because you'll be wrong, you see. Not that you'll be interested in hearing anything to do with the *truth*, of course. *Oh no*, because you'll have your mind made up. Because you had your mind made up right from the beginning.' He gave a long sigh of disgust. '*Christ.*'

Terry was silent. His mind was on the call he'd made at seven thirty this morning to the third-floor flat high above them, and the sound of Rebecca's angry hiss as she exclaimed, 'Who the hell is this? Do you realise what time it is?' and then the startled pause as he'd asked for Ben, and – it might have been his imagination – the intake of breath as she'd recognised Terry's voice.

'You're such an arrogant sod, Terry!' Ben snapped, with a sudden display of fury that came from nowhere. 'You and your pathetic *terms*! I told you at the outset they were completely unworkable and bloody patronising and deeply offensive—'

'They were cheap at the price,' Terry interjected quietly.

'*Only* someone who thought he was God bloody Almighty would try to interfere in other people's lives the way *you* do,' Ben scoffed viciously. 'You think you can control everyone's lives the way you control your workers and your minions and your bloody empire and all the people who think you're God. Well, I've got news for you – there're a whole world of people who think you're a bloody dangerous officious sanctimonious tyrant and won't put up with it.' In his fury, he spluttered incoherently before delivering his final salvo. 'You should take your half-baked Catholic morals back to the bogs where they belong, and mind your own bloody business.'

And still Terry didn't speak. He was recalling their conversation at The Shelbourne all those months ago. He was remembering Ben's protestations of devotion to Catherine, of the absolute irrelevance of money in his conduct towards her, of how nothing that Terry could say or do would in any way influence him in what love and duty would have compelled him to do anyway, which was to stay firmly by her side. The very idea that he could be induced to stay was deeply insulting. Only someone who believed that people could be bought and sold would have suggested such a despicable thing. And all the time Terry had reminded himself that you might misjudge a man once, but only a fool did it a second time. This was the man who had set out to cheat him over a deal from which they both stood to make a fair profit, had exploited Maeve pitilessly while he was betraying Catherine, and for all he knew in those confused and tumultuous days was also the man who had brought about the whole catastrophe of Catherine's accident. This was the man who, despite his protestations, was going to accept Terry's terms because his outrage was grounded less on scruples than an aversion to having restrictions placed on his god-given freedom to do exactly as he pleased.

'So you haven't broken the terms then?' Terry enquired mildly. 'Is that what you're saying?'

'I'm saying you're going to believe what you choose to bloody believe, so what's the point.'

'Try me.'

With a harsh sigh of forbearance, Ben announced in the heavy contemptuous tones of someone who's wasting his breath, 'The situation *is* that the situation's out of my hands. Catherine's decided she needs some space for a while. She's asked me to move out, maybe for the short term, maybe for ever. So I *can't* take care of her because she doesn't *want* me to. So you see? The terms can't bloody apply, because she's made the decision to leave me, and that's all there is to it. And before you start thinking precisely what I can *see* you're thinking, it was nothing that I did, and nothing that I failed to do. She just wants to be on her own, it's *her* decision, and there's nothing I can do about it. Okay? Absolutely *nothing*. I've stood by her a thousand per cent, I've done everything I could possibly do to make her happy – everything I would have done *anyway*, I may add, without your bloody interference – but she wants out. All right? And I came here to Rebecca's because I had nowhere else to bloody go.' He rolled his eyes. 'Christ, the very fact that I'm having to *explain* this to you . . .'

Terry said nothing. He was wondering if this was what Catherine really wanted. If so, he secretly rejoiced for her.

'And if you don't bloody believe me – which you won't, of course – go and ask her yourself,' Ben muttered petulantly. 'Or ask the entire world – everyone'll know soon enough, I'm sure. Though of course they'll go and blame *me*. *Inevitably*. So much more convenient to cast me as the villain. I'm not crippled, I just tried to kill the bastard who attacked her. *No* allowing for the fact that it's Catherine who wants out, no allowing for the fact that it's Catherine who's broken—' He bit hard on his lip, as if to stifle his despair, before muttering scathingly, 'Oh, for God's sake, what do I care what you believe? Withdraw the bloody guarantee. I'm not going to beg. Do your bloody worst.'

Terry said with the same appearance of great calm, 'I didn't come about that, in fact.'

There was a pause while Ben turned to look at him for the first time. 'What do you mean? You had me bloody followed, for Christ's sake! You've caught me at Rebecca's. What else is this about if it's not that?'

'I've only had you followed since last night,' Terry remarked wearily. 'And only because I needed to know where to find you.'

And still Ben stared, though now his curiosity was tinged with resentment at the realisation that he had poured out his excuses and aired his humiliation for nothing. 'So what the hell *is* it about then? Why the hell go to all this trouble?'

Terry said unhurriedly, 'Rightly or wrongly, I took it on myself to find out who burgled your house and why, and I thought you might be interested to know what I've discovered. Oh, and I wanted to ask you a few questions. Yes,' he said carefully, as if correcting a lapse, 'to ask you to fill in the gaps.'

Ben's eyes were very sharp and very still. 'You *know*?'

'I took the precaution of buying Pavlik the best defence in town.'

'You *what*?'

Terry thrust up a quieting hand. 'And I found him his alibi – or rather, I located the witnesses who could attest to his alibi, the ones the police in all their diligence had failed to find – or failed to look for. It was true, you see. Pavlik was not there at the time of the attack. He was innocent of that charge. So ... in exchange for this service, Pavlik told me who had paid him to break in. And why. Well, more or less why. I think that's where you might be able to fill in some of the details.' Without waiting for an answer, Terry continued in a musing tone, 'Pavlik's *employer* – if that's the word – had already bought him a defence of sorts, but Pavlik didn't trust his employer one inch. He had the feeling that the defence lawyer he'd been given might be renowned more for his obscurity and incompetence than for his talent, and that he, Pavlik, might have been cast in the role of sacrificial lamb. He feared to tell the police the truth because he feared for his life, and he had no name for his employer anyway, no proper name, so he doubted very much that they would believe him. With good reason, I would suspect.'

Ben seemed overwhelmed or frozen, or both, so Terry continued, 'I will say straight away that I began these investigations with the idea that you yourself might have a very great deal to answer for. More, I mean, than you have to answer for already. I had the idea that you had meant to harm Catherine—'

'For God's sake!' Ben exclaimed, emerging from his daze with a jolt.

'Allow me to finish,' said Terry on a warning note. 'I thought you might have harmed her because you believed she was someone else – because you believed she was Maeve.'

The short but startled pause that followed was broken by Terry whose voice maintained an iron calm.

'You were expecting Maeve – or rather, you should have been expecting her if you had bothered to remember the arrangement you'd made. And, as I saw it, there she was, turning up at an inconvenient moment, a nuisance to you, an encumbrance' – his voice broke a little, it was all he could do to steady it – 'she'd become ill and bothersome, you wanted well rid of her, her sudden arrival was the last straw.'

'But I didn't—'

'That was how I *believed* it to be,' Terry interrupted, with his first show of impatience. 'That was how I saw it at the *beginning*. For a long time it was hard to make out what had happened because when Maeve returned she was wild with grief. Inconsolable. Because – you must have realised – it was she who discovered Catherine on the floor.'

Ben looked defensive. 'Oh.'

'At first I knew only what Maeve was able to tell me, and for a long time she could say very little. She was in a terrible state. Finding Catherine like that, thinking she was dead. And coming on top of her other griefs, which, as you will know better than anyone, were considerable and had been going on for some time.'

Ben dropped his head, though whether it was from anything as decent as shame it was impossible to tell.

There was another pause in which Ben turned to stare out of the window and Terry fought old battles with his own grief and anguish. The temptation to rage at Ben was very strong, he longed to beat his arrogant head against a wall and demand to know what had been going through his mind when he took Maeve's innocence and generosity and trampled on it so mercilessly, he wanted to ask what kind of man could take satisfaction from such destruction. But he made the supreme effort to restrain himself, partly because he strongly suspected that Ben's satisfaction had come precisely from the fact that Maeve was his daughter, and partly because at the end of the day there was no arguing with a man with only the slenderest grasp on decency and morality, there was no winning a quarrel in which painful revelations might come to light, only to haunt him cruelly for ever afterwards. It was almost more than he could bear, to stay quiet, but he told himself there was more to be gained by keeping a dignified silence.

'Then I heard that Pavlik had a story to tell,' Terry resumed after a moment. 'For a price. So I struck the deal, not because I especially wanted to nail *you* – though the Lord only knows, that would have given me the most enormous satisfaction – but because I wanted the truth for Catherine. I wanted her to know that it was your dealings that had brought it all about.'

Ben opened his mouth as if to protest, only to think better of it and draw in his lips tightly.

'Pavlik told us he'd been hired to break into the house so that his employer could remove or copy some papers. What were the papers, Galitza?'

Again Ben seemed on the point of arguing, again he decided against it. 'Details of financial transactions,' he replied in a flat sulky voice.

'What transactions?'

'Normal business transactions,' he said as if explaining the obvious to an ignoramus. 'Money coming in and going out again. Bank details and statements. Access codes. The *normal* things.'

Without warning, something overturned in Terry, his

stomach lurched, his anger flowed over him like a red-hot sea, his throat seized and it was all he could do not to shout. '*Details!*' he echoed in a voice that shook audibly. 'Come on, *come on*. What details? Of money laundering? Of the profits from the secret deal for the generators that you pulled off behind everyone's backs? *Come on*, let's have a little truth for a change! I know it comes hard to you, the truth, but humour me, let me have a little flavour of it! What was it about – money that you had forgotten to pass on? Money that you had forgotten to share? Money that was illegally obtained? Come now – let's have something like the unvarnished truth here!'

'All right, all right!' Ben replied savagely. 'It was money I was passing on for some customers. I didn't ask where it came from, I didn't ask where it was going, I only knew where it had to go when it left my hands, and that's where I sent it.' He added in a more reasonable tone, 'But I guess I upset some people along the way. There's a dealer in Warsaw, a middleman I've dealt with for years, someone who's got fingers in every pie – or so he likes to think. He got miffed when he realised I'd cut him out.'

'So it was him, is that what you're saying? It was him who sent the employer to come and reclaim the money?'

'Yup. He as good as told me he was coming after it.'

'What did he get for his burglary?' Terry demanded, not letting up for a moment. '*Precisely.*'

Ben didn't want to answer that one, he would have shrugged it off, but something in Terry's expression made him give in with bad grace. 'He managed to empty my bank account—'

'So he got all the pass-codes and access details!'

Ben didn't like being reminded of his stupidity. 'Yes!' he hissed sardonically.

'Foreign banks?'

'Bermuda, the Caymans.'

'But he wanted more?'

'He demanded the same again in lieu of his cut.'

'*Or else?* There has to be an *or else.*'

'Or a photocopy of the transaction details to the authorities.'

'So – stymied. Your profit gone, and then black-mailed to boot. That must have hurt. My Lord, that must have hurt!'

Not sure whether this was offered in a spirit of gloating or irony. Ben clenched his jaw furiously.

Terry continued in the same tone of jaunty sarcasm, 'This middleman must have felt as sore as a scalded cat to go to all that trouble. Polish Mafia, was he? Dabbling in drugs and all sorts, didn't like you muscling in – was that it? Still . . . to go to all that trouble. But then, I suppose the money alone was worth it. Your cut was – what? – a million dollars or so? And then the million in recompense. So, two million dollars. Well, yes, that would have gone a long way to making him feel better. It would make anyone feel better, would it not?'

'None of it excuses what was done to Catherine!' Ben cried bitterly, finding his voice again. 'Nothing I've done could ever justify *that* sort of thuggery!'

'No,' Terry agreed abruptly, calming down at last. 'No, nothing at all.'

He watched a pretty woman coming out of a house opposite, carrying a small child on one hip, its short legs straddling her waist. She had a large bag over her other shoulder, and a folded pushchair in her hand. Despite all the paraphernalia, she made her way down the steps with assurance and grace, and in some un-focused way Terry was reminded of Catherine. Except that Catherine would never know the simple pleasure of carrying her child on her hip and depositing it – crying now – into a pushchair.

'Did it never occur to you', Terry murmured, his eyes still on the woman, 'to try to get even with this man after what he'd done?'

'What – declare war against the Polish business community? This guy's still doing a whole bundle of legitimate deals. He's got influence. He'd make my name mud. I'd never be able to do a deal there again.'

'So you decided to take your medicine instead.' He added, with the slightest touch of irony, 'Like a man.'

Ben closed his eyes expressively.

The moment of revelation had almost come. Yet again Terry felt no sense of triumph, only emptiness. 'It never occurred to you to look closer to home?'

He got Ben's full attention then, the eyes swung round, alert, wary.

'You didn't think there was anyone here who might have felt entitled to that money?'

'Like?'

'Someone you'd cut out of a deal he was expecting to share in?'

'No.'

Ben might have cunning, he might be quick, but Terry always forgot to allow for the fact that he wasn't outstandingly bright. 'What about your company? Wasn't it expecting the benefit of your profits?'

'You mean . . .' Ben hesitated, he thought it through, he dismissed it with a laugh. 'Simon?'

Terry lifted his eyebrows.

'*Simon?*'

'Pavlik met him in a gay club, knew him as someone called Christian. It was a cash deal, the burglary. Half up front, half after the break in.'

Ben was already shaking his head with a superior knowing smile. 'Simon couldn't – wouldn't – he's incapable . . . No, no, for God's sake . . . We were – *are* – friends.' With each denial he was slowly but surely talking himself into the possibility. 'And a gay club? He's never been that way – I mean, not to *my* knowledge! And why would he want to – I've never cut him out of anything—' He stalled suddenly, his eyes flickered crossly, he became indignant. 'Christ, he did okay, we made money, he had nothing to complain about. I mean, he was my number two, for God's sake. I mean, we were partners, I gave him half of everything, of *course* I did, but I did all the *deals*, I had all the contacts, nothing would have happened without me. And then he goes and—' He made a dismissive exclamation, then in the next breath demanded coldly: 'You're *sure*?'

'Pavlik described him, we showed him a photograph.'

'But he only met him – the once, was it? – in a club! How could he be sure?'

Terry paused, embarrassed. 'According to Pavlik, they had a, er – transient relationship.'

Ben pulled back, startled. 'Jesus. *Jesus.*' His face slowly contorted as his fury grew. 'And Pavlik identified him from a photograph?'

'For sure.'

'That bastard! He cleaned me bloody out! Took everything! And had the brass nerve to— And after all we did together! God – what a two-faced— *God!*' He had flushed with anger, his handsome mouth was pinched and rigid. Then his expression clouded as fresh realisations and doubts came to him. Twisting round in his seat, he stared at Terry. 'He was the one who attacked me?' It took him a moment to absorb this. 'God, if I could . . .' He clenched his fists like a school-boy itching to get his own back. Again he turned to Terry and stared. 'And Catherine?' He couldn't bring himself to spell it out. 'He did *that* to Catherine? He . . .' Then, with confusion, 'But he *adores* her, he's always hanging around her, he's like her bloody shadow! He's like a lapdog!' And finally, in a murmur: 'The burglar alarm, he knew the code of course. It was the same as the office. Yes, yes . . . he knew the code.'

He was finally there. He understood it all.

Now that the unpleasant task was over, Terry was suddenly desperate to be away. The sense of revulsion rose in him like a panic, he felt he would suffocate if he stayed in the same space as Galitza for a second longer.

'I propose to tell the police this morning,' he announced, opening the window to a blast of cold air.

Ben raised his head to this. 'Hey, what about *me*? I don't want them bloody nosing about in my affairs. No, I think that would be an appalling idea!'

'I'll leave it twelve hours, then. That will give you time to settle on your story.'

'You *shit*.'

Ignoring this, beginning to feel more cheerful all of a

sudden, Terry asked, 'Where's Jardine now, do you know?'

'No idea.' Then he hissed bleakly, 'Spending my money, presumably.'

Heavy clouds swept low over the valley, driving veils of thin sleet up the ramp of fields into the exposed garden, agitating the animals in the topiary and swirling plumes of leaves up into the branches of the black-limbed beeches.

'Not much point in seeing more,' Catherine said.

'But it gives you an idea?'

'Oh yes.'

Simon turned the wheelchair round and pushed her back along the path through a brick arch into the relative sanctuary of the rose garden.

'It's beautifully maintained,' she called back over her shoulder.

'You like it?'

'I think it's a splendid garden.'

'You wouldn't want to change it?'

'Not in any major way. It'd be a waste of your money.'

He turned the chair round and tipped it backwards a little to pull it up some shallow steps. 'But it could be improved?' he asked.

'Oh, the planting could be improved, I'm sure, but you'd have to see it through an entire season before you'd know what you wanted to do.'

'So if I bought it now . . .?'

'You'd begin to have a good idea by May.'

They came round the side of the house onto the gravel sweep where the car was parked. 'Six months then,' he said.

'More or less.'

He opened the car door for her and held the chair steady while she transferred herself. He waited until she was settled then brought a rug round from the back to lay over her knees.

'Really, I'm fine,' she insisted, but he was already crouching down to wrap the rug around her legs.

'Just until the car warms up,' he said protectively, and cast her a diffident smile.

When he'd stowed the wheelchair he sat in the driver's seat with the door open and his feet on the gravel and changed his shoes, placing the dirty ones in a plastic bag, which he carried round to the boot. He then took off his waterproof jacket and, shaking the rain from it, folded it neatly and laid it with care on the back seat. Watching this, Catherine wondered how he was going to manage country life, in which mud, dirt and wet clothes had a way of sneaking into the best-defended homes. But then the whole day had been overlaid with an odd sense of unreality. Leaving shortly before ten, they had taken the slow road along the Thames through Henley and Cliveden, arriving at Bray at exactly twelve thirty – Simon had speeded up a little so they shouldn't be late – where they'd eaten a rich ornate lunch. Simon had talked a lot about lifestyle, the importance of getting it right, of the futility of working hard unless you had something worthwhile to come home to, how the bedrock of a good life was non-negotiable: strong values and a united family and unstinting loyalty and solid friends. The house, still unseen, appeared to be central to this vision, a pivot or a symbol, and the garden too, though by his own admission he'd never felt the need for one in the past. He'd rambled a bit, repeated himself a great deal, but there was no doubting his passion and sincerity, nor the sharp edge of desperation beneath, as though by focusing so closely on his dream, having earned the money to realise it, he knew it would slip from his grasp. He was suffused with a nervous jumpy energy that had the moods chasing over his face faster than she could follow them. Hope, despair, anxiety – she had never seen him in such turmoil. His cheek trembled almost continuously, he had developed a new habit of sucking in his lips, and now and again when he looked away it seemed to her that his eyes contained desolation.

Climbing into the car at last, Simon sat with his hands on the wheel and looked up at the façade. 'Well,' he said, 'what do you think?'

He had asked this several times during their tour of the house. She could only repeat, 'I think it's stunning.' She added on a cautionary note, 'Though I hate to think what they're asking for it.'

'It's a fair price.'

'You'll need to add a lot for the furnishings,' she warned him. 'And then there'll be the maintenance, of course. A full-time gardener, I'd have thought. And probably a housekeeper too.'

He said softly, 'Could you live here, Catherine?'

She was about to make some mundane reply when, glancing across at him, she found him watching her with a strange intensity, and paused. She was struck by the uncomfortable thought that he was serious. 'Me? I'd love to live in a beautiful place, of course I would.

But,' she added hastily, 'I think something smaller would suit me far better.'

And still his brilliant eyes remained fixed on her face. 'But . . . if you found yourself here . . . you could like it?'

Oh God, she thought, he's about to make a declaration. 'You can like all sorts of places, can't you?' she said in a tone that was deliberately offhand. 'It all depends on—' She was about to say, *on who you're with and whether you're happy*, but pulled herself up just in time, and said lightly, 'On where you happen to find yourself.' She ducked forward to look up at the sky. 'Could we get going now?' she asked breezily. 'It'll be dark soon. And I'd like to get home.'

'But Ben and you,' he said relentlessly, 'it's over, isn't it? He's gone? You're going to need someone to look after you.'

'I really can't discuss Ben.'

'But Catherine – wouldn't you be happy here?' His voice had risen, his breath was coming fast. 'We both like the same things. We could make it the most beautiful house in the world. Antiques and pictures, and people in for lunch. Not *all* the time of course! We could go abroad for some of the winter, we could travel. But this would be our home, we could make the garden the best garden for miles. Oh, God,' he groaned furiously, 'I'm making it sound as though it's all about *that*! It's not – what I mean is, what I've been saying very badly, is that I want to look after you, Catherine, take care of you. I want that more than anything in the world.'

'Simon, *please*.' She waved a hand inarticulately. 'Not now. This isn't the time. I'm sorry.' She exhaled slowly. 'If we could just go home.' She looked firmly ahead through the windscreen.

'Oh, I do realise it's rather soon,' he gasped in a voice of sudden reason. 'Of course I do. I realise you're still upset about Rebecca. That's natural . . .'

The name resounded darkly in her head. *Rebecca.*

'. . . You're bound to be. And I appreciate that you can't actually decide at the moment. That you can't make promises. I wouldn't expect you to.'

Rebecca. In the instant that she felt the first stab of anguish, she also understood that Rebecca was the obvious choice for Ben in a time of trouble. He would have wanted sympathy, familiarity and lack of complications, more or less in that order; he would have wanted someone who understood this instinctively, someone who knew him well, an old lover without expectations; or, with expectations and the shrewdness to hide them.

Ben and Rebecca. A story that she had interrupted.

She had missed much of what Simon had been saying. Now he was asking insistently, '*Catherine?* Will you? *Will you?*'

She looked at him helplessly, she made as if to touch his arm by way of apology. 'Have you known about Rebecca for long?' she asked.

He didn't want to talk about Rebecca, he frowned. 'I saw them together once. I was trying to catch Ben one morning and . . . I saw them.'

'At the house. She was at the house?'

He looked mildly abashed, as if he'd said too much, but not so abashed that he didn't nod in confirmation, before resuming with quiet insistence, 'Just say you'll think about it, Catherine.'

'Sorry?'

'Say you won't rule it out. That's all.' He gave a laugh that seemed to catch in his throat, there was a sheen of nervousness on his temple. 'We'd be so happy here, I know we would. Think – this garden with two garden makers!'

The attempt at light-heartedness only succeeded in striking a note of pathos, and again it seemed to her that his longing hid a deep pessimism, that he knew his chances were hopeless.

She began to recite the ritualistic words of rejection. 'Simon, I'm terribly flattered, and I'm terribly honoured, but I can't possibly begin to think about the future at the moment, not in any shape or form. I have no idea where my marriage is. I have no idea what I want myself.' Seeing his pain, she ploughed on, forcing an overt note of kindness into her voice, hating the string of platitudes. 'I like you, of course I do, I value your friendship, but I have to say that I've never thought of you as anything but a friend. And I can't say that's ever going to change. I just can't. I'm sorry.'

He turned his head sharply to look away through the windscreen. After a while he started the engine. 'I understand,' he said in a voice that was very controlled, but also very close to breaking. 'Thank you at least for being such a good friend.'

'No, no,' she said, far too quickly, 'I'm the one who's grateful to *you*.'

She thought: I got that wrong. No, she corrected herself, we both got it wrong. His timing couldn't have been worse, and he had sprung it on her: he hadn't thought it through at all. He hadn't taken account of the upheavals that had shaken her life over the last two days; or perhaps he had, and rushed at the opportunity. At this thought, her indignation grew, and she began to see his declaration as an intrusion, wildly insensitive and very unfair.

They drove for a long time in silence. Wearied by the tension, she took out her phone and announced in a light voice, 'Just going to pick up my messages.' In the dusk, his profile was severe. He didn't look towards her and he didn't speak.

She hadn't really expected a message from Ben, but she was miffed not to get one all the same. Instead, there was her father's standard message, complete with diversionary ideas – it was a trip to the races now, a lunch with friends. Then Emma's voice, diffident, loyal, a little troubled, possibly hurt, asking if she could do anything for her. In her mind, Catherine apologised: *I thought it was you, Emma, and I was wrong.* It seemed extraordinary now to believe Emma capable of such sustained and accomplished deceit, but a tortured imagination is a wild imagination, in which it's a short step from an embrace to a well-established affair.

After Emma came three or four business calls that she would play back later. Then Alice, in a panicky tone that made Catherine instantly alert.

'Cath, wherever you are, please call me straight away. I went round to the house, but you weren't there. I've got to speak to you. I'm at work. Usual number. But I'll leave my mobile on as well, just in case.' A pause, then, distractedly: 'Hope you're okay.' And urgently: 'Cath – straight away.'

Catherine ruled out a broken love affair; Alice had always been too proud to come to her with those. A family problem then? Pa running up debts and not telling anyone? Or Ben, going to Alice with some sob story about being thrown out? But even as she brought up Alice's name on the display and pressed the dial key, she discounted that one. Ben was frightened of Alice; he would rather choke than confide in her.

'Where are you?' Alice cried hastily.

'On a motorway, coming back from the country.'

'When will you be back?'

'An hour or so.'

'An *hour*?' A sigh of frustration.

'Why? What's happened?' She was thinking of Pa.

As if reading her mind, Alice declared brusquely, 'Oh, it's not Pa. Nothing like that. No, it's . . . to do with your burglary, Cath. Something you should know. Something that the *police* should know.' She was sounding slightly hysterical.

'Give me a clue.'

A hesitation, as if she couldn't make up her mind how much to say. 'It's about Simon,' she said eventually. 'Something really bad, Cath.'

Without thinking, Catherine glanced across at him. His eyes swivelled round and met hers briefly. In the instant before she looked away again, she saw a strange brilliance in his eyes.

'Tell me,' she said, selecting her most casual tone.

'But can you talk? Are you driving?'

'Hardly driving.'

'Oh no, of *course* not. *God*, no – stupid of me. No . . . But it might take a moment. Is it all right? Who're you with? Who's driving you?'

'A colleague.'

She made a nervous exclamation. 'God, I thought for a moment it might have been Simon.'

'So,' Catherine said lightly, 'what's the problem exactly?'

A pause while Alice chose her words, which she delivered with a kind of agonised excitement. 'You remember I went to the court that day when Pavlik first came up? The magistrates' court? And Simon was there too?'

'Aha.'

'Well, when the bail was arranged, they mentioned the name of this man who was going to guarantee the bail – or whatever the word is – and well, I hardly registered the name. I mean, it was no one I knew. I never thought to remember it. And I was so appalled at the fact Pavlik was getting bail that I just didn't pay much attention.'

'No.'

'Anyway, I just realised a couple of hours ago – well, in fact it was last week that I actually heard the name again, but it just didn't click until today, I just couldn't remember where I'd heard it before. You know how it is – you hear names, and you just don't connect them. It was only today that I finally realised it was the *same* guy. And even then I got Denise Cox to check the court records for the name of the man who put the money up. It took her all day to get the information. I couldn't say how urgent it was, of course, and I went almost *mad* waiting, but at last she came through with it, and it was the *same* guy, Cath.'

'The same as who?'

Alice slowed down a little as she said rather stiffly, 'The same as the man who left a message on Simon's machine. While I was there. Last week. In Simon's flat. His name's David Frankel. He's a solicitor. He's the same man. But, Cath, he talked like a *friend* in the message. First name stuff. Sort of, how are you, Simon, and can you phone me some time. But, Cath – why would Simon know him unless . . .? You see what I mean?' she cried on a rising note of fear. 'It's all wrong, isn't it?'

Catherine said calmly, 'I see what you mean, yes.'

'What should we do?'

Catherine said, 'I can't think just at the moment.' And it was true. Her mind had stalled, her thoughts were all over the place.

'But, Cath, if Simon was involved with this man, if they put up the bail, then—'

'I understand what you're saying. Let's talk about this later. I'll call you.'

As she rang off, Simon asked, with echoes of his old anxiety and attentiveness, 'Everything all right, Catherine?'

Reaching the house, he stopped the car with a slight jolt and gripped the top of the wheel, his shoulders hunched, his head bent forward, like some awful parody of a boy racer. 'I'm sorry if I frightened you,' he cried in a rush of anguish. 'It was the last thing I intended. The last thing in the world! I knew it wasn't the best moment, I knew it was a bit too soon. But I could just *see* us there, Catherine! I could see us in that house with all those beautiful rooms, and the garden, and the lake, and the country life. It's what I've always dreamt of, you see. Always. From when I was small, when we lived in a rat-hole flat with filthy windows and dirty carpets. That's what I dreamt of – a place like that!' His voice had risen emotionally, and dipped again. 'I knew it was hoping for a lot, of course, to think you'd want to share it with me. I knew the chances were a bit slim. I knew—' The words seized in his throat, he inhaled unevenly. 'But you've got to dream a bit, haven't you?' His nervous laugh emerged as a ragged gasp. 'You've got to go for things, otherwise what's the use? Got to believe it's going to happen.' He turned to her. 'Forgiven?' When she didn't reply he begged furiously, '*Please*, Catherine.'

'Sure,' she murmured. 'Forget it. It's not important. But I'd like to get into the house now, if you don't mind. I'm tired.'

Something in her voice must have alerted him because he stiffened and gave her a long searching look before climbing out of the car.

When he wheeled her up to the house, he seemed preoccupied, and it wasn't until they were inside that he spoke again. His words came as a statement delivered in a flat voice. 'You're not forgiving me then.'

'I told you – it's not important.'

He twisted his head, as if to catch her tone. 'There's something else,' he said tightly.

She began to pull off her coat and waved him firmly away when he tried to help. In the car, she'd decided to leave the business of Simon and Frankel to the police, she no longer trusted her judgement on matters involving explanations, excuses and lies. But now as she struggled ineffectually with the sleeves of her coat, her frustration got tangled up with a wider anger, and she said accusingly, 'I'm told that you know someone called David Frankel.'

Freeing herself from the last sleeve, she threw the

coat in the general direction of a chair and looked up to find him staring at her, white-faced, as if someone had struck him.

'Well?'

He seemed frozen. He might not have been breathing.

'David Frankel,' she repeated slowly as if addressing an idiot. 'You know him?'

A barely discernible nod.

'He was the man who put up the bail money.'

He closed his eyes tightly. He seemed to shrivel visibly, to retreat into his body in a dozen minute ways, his head to settle lower into his neck, his hands to shrink against his body, his shoulders to slump by infinitesimal degrees.

'Well?' she demanded in cold exasperation.

'Oh, Catherine . . .' he whispered faintly. He lowered his head.

'You're making me think bad things, Simon.' And now it was her own voice that was shaking. 'You're making me think you arranged Pavlik's defence. You're making me think he was working for you!'

He tried to speak, but only choked.

'For God's sake!' she cried contemptuously.

'Oh, Catherine!' It was an agonised wail, a great cry of despair. Suddenly he clamped his hands over his face, and she realised with astonishment that he'd begun to cry. He tried to say something, which she couldn't at first make out through the increasingly violent sobs. 'I never meant . . . Never, never, *never*!'

'For God's sake!' she snapped, in terror at what he might say.

He dropped his hands from his face and flung them

down by his sides, palms spread wide. With his bowed head and splayed hands, he was like a supplicant offering himself for retribution. And still he sobbed. The tears dripped off his nose, tracking down a long skein of mucus that dangled from the tip. Spikes of hair had fallen forward, masking his eyes. 'It was a *mistake*! A terrible, ghastly *mistake*!' The 'mistake' was drawn out in a long moan of misery. 'If you knew how I've tortured myself – how I've begged for it not to have happened! God, there hasn't been a *moment*, not a single moment that I haven't *begged* to be struck down, that I haven't longed for it to be me. If *I* could have been the one – I'd have given anything for it to have been me! Oh Catherine, if I could have brought you back, made you whole again – I'd have done anything – I'd have died a thousand deaths – a thousand million deaths. Believe me, Catherine, there hasn't been a moment – not a *second* that I haven't wished it undone – that I haven't *longed* for it not to have happened. I've dreamt so often of catching you as you fell, I've rushed to catch you—'

'It was Pavlik. You hired him. It was Pavlik who attacked me. Is that what you're saying? *Is that it, Simon?*'

He raised his head. His face was distorted and ugly with despair.

She read her answer, and one part of her was in immediate and fierce revolt against it, refused absolutely to accept it, did not want to admit to the message in his eyes, not now, not *ever*, while another part of her was sickened with revulsion and betrayal, was recoiling from the depth of his treachery, though even as the rage shook her, it began to ebb rapidly away.

Simon was gesticulating violently. 'Don't you see, don't you see, Catherine – I didn't realise it was *you*. I had no idea it was *you*. Don't you see . . .' His legs buckled slowly, for a moment he stood like someone who'd been shot and refuses to fall, until he finally sank forward onto his knees, which met the stone with a sharp crack. Like my head, she thought. My head would have sounded like that. *Crack!*

'I thought it was *her*, Catherine!' He held his arms up wide, like a priest. 'I thought it was the girl! I heard her ring, I saw her knocking! I saw the awful sick look on her face that they always get when they're around Ben. The disgusting foul look before they throw themselves at him, just like cheap common tarts! I've seen them time and again, getting that same sick disgusting look in their eyes.' With a whimper, he brought his hands down in a savage cutting motion, as if to haul himself back from some brink. 'I saw her there,' he began again in a shuddering voice. 'Knocking on the door, thinking he was there, desperate to get at him. And, Catherine, I realised he was betraying *you* just like he was betraying *me*! I thought: He's doing to Catherine what he's doing to me! And I felt sick, I felt disgusted, I wanted to kill him with my bare hands!'

He had begun to cry again, his cheek was dancing so violently that his face seemed permanently askew. 'He sold me out, Catherine. Betrayed me!' he sobbed in a voice of fresh despair. 'After all my *work*. After *everything* I'd put into that deal – heart, soul, energy, bloody *devotion* – and what did he do? He went and cut me out. Cheated me! Without a second thought, without a moment's hesitation! Because I was nothing to him, you

see. I was just a load of *shit*! Someone he could treat
like *dirt*! Just like he was treating you, Catherine. He
was going to have that girl, just like he'd had a thousand girls, and not care a shit! The fact that he was
married to *you*, to someone as fantastic and wonderful
as *you* – well, what would *he* care? He takes people
and uses them. Always has. Greedy, greedy – always
wanting more, more, more. Never enough money in the
world for him. Never enough women. And loyalty?
Christ, what a *joke*! Loyalty means fuck all to him. It's
just a *word*! He doesn't begin to know the meaning—'
He made the strange choking sound again and, clasping
his head in both hands, sucked in long gulps of air as if
he were suffocating.

'The girl,' Catherine said in a low voice, 'did you
mean to hurt her?'

His head came up slowly, he looked at her, aghast.
'God, no! *No!* She – *you* – took me totally by surprise!
I thought when Ben arrived that he was alone – I
thought he'd come back from France a day early without you. He was meant to be coming back the next day
on his own, Catherine! You were meant to be staying
on in France. That was what he told me! That was how
we left it and when I heard him come in, and I looked
down and saw him alone, it never *occurred* to me that
you were somewhere behind him. When he caught me
upstairs and we fought, I never thought for a second
there'd be anyone else!'

He dragged a hand across his eyes, rubbing them
viciously. 'It was a complete shock when I heard someone calling. I thought it had to be *her*, I thought it was
the *girl* come back, that they'd planned to meet. I only
meant to push her out of the way, to make sure she

didn't see me. But then . . . then I got angry, I wanted to *punish* her for being in your house, I wanted to *punish* her for behaving like a cheap . . .'

He trailed off, the energy went out of him, he sank back on his haunches and lowered his hands onto his knees. He whispered, 'But it was you.'

There was a long pause in which the only sound was the rasp of his breathing.

Finally she asked, 'And you blackmailed Ben?'

'I wanted my money,' he said dully. 'I wanted him to know what it was like to pay up. I'd got the proof of what he'd been up to. I used it to make sure I got my money.'

'You took what he owed you?'

'Double. Exactly double. He never worked that out! It never occurred to him that I could have done such a thing, you see.' He was still close enough to tears that he laughed easily. 'He thought—'

The doorbell made them both start a little. They exchanged glances, Catherine's bewildered, his afraid.

She moved towards the door. 'Who is it?' she called.

'Catherine, it's Fergal.'

She looked back towards Simon. He was still kneeling, his eyes fixed on the floor.

She opened the door a short way.

Fergal seemed immensely tall against the darkness. His expression was very stern. He said in a voice designed to carry, 'Just calling by to see you're all right, Catherine.'

She took a deep breath. 'I'm all right,' she said.

Flicking his eyes towards the road, Fergal added in a whisper, 'I've got Mike right here. We could have the police round in a jiff.'

From behind her, Simon said flatly, 'He knows, Catherine. He knows everything.'

As she moved back to let Fergal pass, Catherine pretended faint irritation. 'Watching over me again, were you, Fergal?'

'Oh no. Never,' he remonstrated gently. 'No, if you're to thank anyone, Catherine, it should be Mr Devlin.'

Chapter Sixteen

———

Foxrock, 21st February.

Dear Catherine, Forgive me for not having been able to meet up with you for so long. Christmas seemed to arrive in a terrible rush, and then as you know I was off to the US for the best part of two weeks, and then back to a situation here that has conspired to keep me chained to my desk ever since. But Fergal tells me that you've had a good offer on the house. I'm glad things have moved so fast. I hope that you'll find what you're looking for in the way of a new place very soon. A fresh start is a great thing.

Regarding the financial matters, the final account is now complete. Fergal will give you the details. He is in London from this Saturday evening and will phone you to arrange a time to call.

I hope Bridget has been able to provide you with all the necessary liaison over the garden – I'm afraid I haven't had the time or the mind to give it proper attention. But I have every hope of getting down to Morne to see the work begin. And if, as Bridget tells me, you will be coming over before then (to plan the excavations?), then we will definitely meet, though it may have to be in Dublin.

Maeve sends her fondest love. She is good and busy.
Your friend, as ever,
Terry

Built in sturdy post-modern style on the site of a
demolished church in Bayswater, the block was four
years old but looked older. The agent had extolled the
virtues of the stainless steel kitchens and bathrooms,
but Catherine had taken the flat not for the gleam of its
plumbing but for its position high on the fifth floor, its
south-west-facing terrace, and the reserved parking in
the basement garage below.

Arriving on this Sunday morning, letting some air in,
she also discovered that you could hear church bells
drifting from the direction of Hyde Park, and the faint
screech of shunting trains beyond Paddington Station.

While waiting for Fergal, she took measurements
and inspected the decorators' progress. The whole place
was to be white: a space intentionally blank. She would
impose some sort of mark with her antiques, her pictures, and the few bits of modern furniture she had yet
to choose. But possessions would be kept to a minimum. She had the instincts of an itinerant now; no
sooner camped than ready to move on. It was no
coincidence that the feeder road to the Westway was
barely fifty yards away.

It was just before eleven when Fergal rang the bell.

'I thought we were doomed to the phone for ever.'
Her smile didn't entirely hide the reproach beneath.

He pecked her cheek. 'Not for want of seeing you,
Catherine.'

She gave him a conducted tour, which took all of

two minutes. 'A tidy little place,' he commented, with the forced interest of a man who expects little of his surroundings.

They sat on two cheap plastic chairs belonging to the decorators. A slow rain speckled the windows.

'So, what's going on, Fergal? Why are you two rushing around like mad? You're bad enough, but *Terry* . . . We've talked twice, I think, since Christmas.'

'Oh, you know how he is, always saying he's going to ease up, and then he's away again, after another hotel, another enterprise.'

'It's not that he's gone off the idea of the garden then?'

'Oh no, it won't be that!' he declared without hesitation. 'No, it'll be the hours he's working, all God made and more. Which isn't to say he won't be keeping an eye. He always keeps an eye. You can be sure he's fully aware of the progress of the garden.'

'So what's this project, Fergal?'

Fergal took on the abstruse expression of someone whose lips are sealed. 'Empire building, you might say.'

Taking her shrug as a display of bewilderment, Fergal hastened to add, 'Oh, it's not for the money that he does it. Never the money. The house at Foxrock, it's not grand, you know, not by the standards of some in Dublin. No, he's a restless spirit, that's the truth of it. It's in his nature to look for the next challenge. Apart from the horses and the racing, there's little to occupy him, you see.'

'But Maeve, he's got Maeve.'

'Aha. But then he hasn't seen so very much of her since Christmas. She's found herself some new friends. Students like herself. They're always away somewhere

– walking the hills, or off to the films, or gone to the dancing. It's a great thing for her, the dancing.'

'So she's happy, Fergal?'

He made a speculative gesture. 'She will be, I believe. Yes, one day.'

Catherine had an image of Maeve in a group, dancing, and of Terry going back to an empty house.

'I was hoping to meet Terry at Morne this week,' she said. 'But of course it doesn't look as though he'll be free. When I ask Bridget what to do she just tells me to go ahead.'

'I would do that very thing then,' Fergal suggested calmly. 'Go ahead. Take it as a declaration of faith in your judgement.'

'Supposing he doesn't like the result?'

'You can tell him he should have paid more attention,' Fergal retorted uncompromisingly.

Despite Fergal's reassurances, Catherine couldn't quite rid herself of the idea that, having done his duty by everyone, Terry had moved on, that, subconsciously or otherwise, he was distancing himself from the past and everything associated with the period of Maeve's obsession. And, as Catherine hardly needed reminding, associations didn't come much stronger than herself.

Fergal cleared his throat in the manner of someone getting down to business. 'So . . . I have brought what Mr Devlin likes to call the final account.' He pulled a paper from his breast pocket and handed it to her. 'He wants to know if it meets with your approval.'

It was a list of six charities, with, against each one, the sum it had received by way of anonymous donation. Since drugs had seemed the most likely source of the money, it had been Catherine's idea that a large proportion of it went to addiction and rehabilitation projects. For the rest, she had left the decisions to Terry. The total came to over three-quarters of a million pounds.

'It looks fine,' she said.

'Mr Devlin also wanted to be sure that you had received everything that was owing to you. That nothing was outstanding.'

This was Fergal's way of asking if Ben had made over the house proceeds and signed the other papers relating to the separation settlement. 'My solicitor tells me it's all gone through,' she said.

'And the house sale?'

'Completion next week.'

'So, you're all set then?'

She had no real reason to disagree. Her work was picking up, she had financial security again, she had this place, and a modified car in the garage below. Everything she needed, and yet, and yet . . . she felt unsettled. She was alone and lonely, of course: that was part of it. But also, somewhere in the long process of drawing a line under the past, she'd developed a sense of unfinished business, of matters unresolved. Gradually, amid the legal discussions, the house clearance, the impending divorce, the shadow of an idea had begun to form on the edge of her mind.

She grasped at it now. 'There's something I've been wanting to ask you.'

He waited attentively.

Catherine began slowly, almost casually. 'It's just a small thing. I don't even know if you'll be able to tell me. About the accident . . . the attack.'

A slight wariness crept into his eyes.

'When you arrived that night, when you saw me there . . . you checked my pulse, my breathing. Presumably you checked on the bleeding too, to see where it was coming from.' She turned this into a question with a lift of her head.

Fergal's shaggy eyebrows drew into a frown. 'I did,' he said.

'And where was it coming from, the blood?'

'Your ear. Your left ear.'

'Aha,' she murmured, attempting to sound indifferent. 'And that was it? Nowhere else?'

'So far as I could tell.'

'And Maeve . . . she'd tried to mop up the blood?'

Fergal's eyes were very still, and she had the feeling he was way ahead of her. 'Apparently so.'

'A pair of panties, wasn't it?'

'I was not aware of what they were at the time. I thought – if I thought at all – that it was a handkerchief.'

Catherine made a show of absorbing this. 'And the scarf? Did you see the scarf?'

There was a taut silence. 'No,' he said.

Catherine shrugged lightly. 'But you knew she'd left a scarf?'

He hesitated. 'Not then. I was told later.'

'And you know where it was found?'

She wasn't sure if it was embarrassment that made him grow uncomfortable, or the confirmation of where this had been leading. 'I believe I heard a while later.'

She looked away to the window and the misty rooftops. 'When Maeve was ill,' she said in a low voice, 'was it just chance that she got septicaemia, Fergal? That she nearly died?'

She left it several seconds before looking back at him.

He was staring at her obdurately.

'Or was there a procedure that went wrong?'

'I couldn't answer that,' he growled, dropping his eyes.

She asked so quietly that it was almost a whisper, 'Was there an abortion, Fergal?'

He tightened his lips. 'I could not say.'

'Could not or must not?'

He didn't reply.

'I understand,' she murmured, turning her head to scrutinise the window once more. 'Suppose, though, that I simply asked you to indicate if I was wrong – nothing more. Just . . . if I was wrong.' She left this thought in the air for a moment while she transferred her gaze to her hands. 'The reason I ask, Fergal, is that I want to leave the whole thing behind. I hardly need tell you how important it is to me. But I'm still finding it difficult. Partly, I'm finding it difficult to understand why Maeve should have been so . . . persistent. But if you were to indicate to me that I wasn't wrong, then it would begin to make sense, you see. I would understand why she did what she did, why she came to the house that day. I would feel very much clearer.' In her mind, she added, *about Ben as well. And about Terry.* 'It would make it that much easier to put it all behind me.'

Unable to explain it any better, she finally brought her eyes up to his.

His frown had returned, deeper than ever, his eyes hunted across the floor as he wrestled with some inner debate. Finally, he seemed to come to a decision. His mournful eyes lifted to hers and he affirmed with a soft sigh, 'No, Catherine, you would not be wrong.'

She embraced him solemnly at the door. 'Tell Bridget I'll be coming to Morne on Thursday. If she could make the arrangements.'

The sky was still stormy from recent rain, but as the car left the village and turned up the lane the clouds seemed to break up a little, the air to brighten. Passing through the gates, climbing towards the house, the rhododendrons drooped and glistened, tattoos of rain dropped from overhanging branches, and the surface of the drive ran with a web of rivulets.

Catherine had expected a gardener's car, or the golf buggy, or both, but there were three jalopies and two vans outside the house, one with ladders, another with faded signwriting that said *Decorators*.

Though it had stopped raining, the driver insisted on holding an umbrella over her. He promised to return in three hours.

Inside the house there were dustsheets and ladders. The hall had been painted a soft cream, the drawing room was turning a slightly warmer shade of white. The floors had been sanded and sealed. The dining-room walls had been filled and rubbed down, and a sample of eggshell blue daubed across the furthest wall in a broad cross. A selection of curtain samples had been pinned to the shutters. Through the doorway to the kitchen, she glimpsed new units in pale wood and a gleaming hardwood floor.

The men were taking a smoking break in a corner of

the drawing room. 'Ah, if you're after Mick, he'll be
back directly,' one of them told her.

She waited in the dining room, sitting at the trestle
table, most of which had been taken over by paint pots
and rolls of lining paper. She tried to clear her mind for
the meeting with the landscaping contractors and tree
specialists, but all she could think was, *So he's going to
use the place after all*. She examined her emotions with
curiosity, and decided she was glad.

A vehicle approached the house with a soft hum and
drew up noisily on the gravel. A car door slammed,
footsteps sounded, the front door cannoned open and
crashed against the stop, and through the open doorway she saw Terry stride across the hall to peer into the
drawing room. Half way back across the hall he saw
her and hastened forward again.

She laughed as she called out his name.

He took both her hands in his and smiled. When he
kissed her, his cheek was smooth and she caught a scent
of aftershave.

He stood back and regarded her appraisingly, and
she noticed his eyes, which were clear and bright, and
very steady.

'You look well, Catherine.'

He seemed taller and to have lost a little weight,
though that may have been the effect of his suit, which
was dark and beautifully cut and undoubtedly expensive.

'I didn't think you were able to come!' she said.

'It's amazing what Bridget can do with the diary
when she really tries.'

He continued to survey her openly and fondly for
quite a while before turning to pull a chair up to the
table. As he sat down, he slipped the button of his

jacket and smoothed his tie, and it occurred to her that he spent most of his life in such well-made clothes, and that the image she'd held of him all these months, the rather self-conscious figure in the misguided gardening outfit, had been quite wrong.

She said, 'Your empire won't crumble while you're away then?'

He grinned. 'It's the vanity of self-made men to think that the ship will hit the rocks the moment their backs are turned.' He rotated a hand, and she remembered the unexpected grace of his gestures. 'I should have two hours at least before danger looms.'

'*That* long.' She turned down her mouth in mock rebuke.

'But I'll take as long as I need today, because it's not often I get the chance to see you, Catherine.'

'Entirely your fault, Terry.'

Beneath his smile, he was rueful as he said, 'Yes, my life is madness at the moment.'

She indicated the room. 'You didn't tell me you were doing the house.'

'Ah? Didn't I?' He affected a bafflement that was entirely unconvincing. 'It's just a quick coat of paint really, to make it presentable.'

'But the kitchen . . . the curtains and colours. You've got someone helping you? A designer?'

He gave her an odd look as though he wasn't entirely sure how to interpret this question. 'A designer? Yes, but no one I know,' he said with a quiet emphasis whose significance she could only guess at. 'Bridget organised someone.'

'And you're going to use the place? You're going to come regularly?'

'Ah, well . . . we'll see.' Abruptly, he changed the subject. 'Now, Catherine, I want to know – the final account? You were happy with it?'

'Oh, yes.'

'Good, because I can tell you, it's been the devil's own job giving away money that you do not own and cannot possibly account for, money that will get you into jail quicker than a raid on the Central Bank. My financial man's been red-eyed and drowned in sweat. Like someone handed a hot coal – trying desperately to pass the damn thing on without dropping it on his foot.' A gleam of mischief came into Terry's eyes, and she had the feeling he had secretly enjoyed the challenge.

'However it was done, it was worth it.'

'Indeed it was, Catherine. Indeed.' Risking the decorators' dust, he slid his elbows onto the table and rested his chin on his hands. 'I also thought it prudent to make some enquiries about our mutual acquaintance.' He added anxiously, 'If you should like to know, that is?'

'Sure.'

'It seems he's in Argentina. Buenos Aires. He's set up an import–export business there.'

She felt nothing at this news except, perhaps, a lack of surprise.

'I still say, Catherine – and this'll be the last time, I swear – I'll not say it again – that you were too generous to him.' He held up a hand as if to forestall her objections. 'I know, I know – he was more of a case for the doctors than the courts, but—'

'Terry, I think he would have killed himself. In fact, I know he would.'

He frowned, he came round to the idea reluctantly. 'Very well. I must accept your judgement on that.'

'And if anyone should have ended up in court, shouldn't it have been Ben?'

His expression clouded, he said with feeling, 'Indeed. And where is he, still . . .?'

'In Eaton Square, so far as I know. Oh, I don't mind, Terry. Why should I mind? Better Rebecca than some poor girl who'd take him seriously and get hurt.'

They fell into a thoughtful silence, broken when they both began to speak at the same instant, broke off, only to speak over each other once again.

'There are two things I—'

'There was something—'

He said immediately, 'No, after you,' and smiled his slow smile that started at one corner of his mouth and spread up into his eyes. She had forgotten how striking his eyes were, more blue than grey, and how unflinching.

She had to look down at her hands before she could find the courage to start. 'Before we discuss the garden, there are a couple of—'

'Oh, I've no need to discuss the garden,' he said quickly.

'What?'

'I'm here to see you. I'm not worried about the garden.'

'Oh,' she repeated uncertainly. 'But all these people are coming—'

'I'll wait. I'll wait for as long as necessary.'

She took a deep breath. 'There are two things I want to say to you before we go any further,' she began with strange formality. 'Firstly, that I owe you an apology.

About this house, how you came to own it. My father's never been terribly truthful about money. I've always known it, really. I just found it hard to accept at the time. Somehow, the loss of the house got bound up in Mummy's death. It was too much for me to accept that Pa had sold it under our feet just when Mummy was dying. I'm afraid I believed what he said – all the bad things he told us about you – because it suited me to. The alternative was too painful.' She looked up at him. 'I got some sort of admission out of Pa the other day. Not a lot – you can imagine – but enough to make me suspect that the truth was very different. I don't know what the arrangements were, but I'm sure they were very generous. As always. Whatever else, Terry, you are the most absurdly generous man I know. So . . . I want to apologise. I hope that you'll be able to forgive me.'

Matching the note of formality, he bowed his head in acceptance. When he looked up again he seemed pleased.

In her relief at having got this out of the way, she almost forgot the second matter. 'Oh yes!' she exclaimed. 'I loved your letters.'

She had caught him by surprise. 'I'm sorry?'

'I loved the letters you sent me. I read them all many times. I wanted you to know that they gave me enormous pleasure.'

'But they were a poor effort,' he argued. 'I'm no good at that sort of thing.'

'You're wrong. And in fact . . . I owe you another apology. For sending such an awful reply to that letter you sent me that summer—'

He interrupted sharply, 'No, no – too long ago,

Catherine. Best forgotten. Water under the bridge. No, no – an age away!'

But she could see he hadn't forgotten, she could see that the wound still smarted, and she felt an ache of regret and something else that was very like longing.

'I'm sorry, I . . .' But seeing the warning flash in his eyes, she said rapidly, 'What was it you wanted to say? I interrupted you.'

'I think – later,' he said.

It was an hour before the contractors left, an hour that Terry spent alone in the study. She found him hunched over his desk on the phone. At some point he had changed into casual clothes, more country than gardening, which suited him far better.

He mimed a greeting. While she waited for him to finish, she watched him and thought of the letter he had written her that summer. She couldn't recall the exact words he had used, but she remembered that they'd been good honest words, straight from the heart. It occurred to her – perhaps hadn't been far from her mind for a long time – that she had been foolish to turn him down.

'Now then!' he cried as he rang off. 'Time to wrap up!'

The quad stood in the stable yard. He lifted her on and got on behind her. They went slowly because she had to brace herself on the handlebars, and he had to keep one arm tight around her waist.

A short way up the hill, he turned the machine around so they could look back at the house. 'What I wanted to say was – it's yours,' he said. 'I always intended to give it to you.'

She leant to one side so she could look back at his face. 'The house?'

'The house.'

'But I don't want it, Terry!'

'I'm giving it to you anyway.'

'And I can't possibly accept it.'

He gave a sharp sigh. 'Now, why did I think you were going to say that? Unlimited loan then?'

'No.'

He looked down at her. 'Why not?'

'I wouldn't want to live here on my own. It wouldn't be practical for a start.'

He conceded this grudgingly. 'Will you come often then?'

'As often as I'm invited.'

This idea floated tantalisingly between them.

'You drive a hard bargain, Catherine. But I agree.'

Betrayal

For Andrew,
with love and gratitude

One

I WOKE WITH a terrible start, my heart crashing against my ribs, and fumbled for the burbling alarm. Sinking back on the pillow, I waited for my heart to quieten down and my brain to stop racketing. Dream fragments jostled disturbingly in my mind. Most were nightmarish, riddled with scenes where I was caught red-handed in some misdemeanour. Only one held any comfort, and for a moment I clung to the warm echo of a time long ago, a faded image of a remote bay and firelight, and, at the water's edge, the slim elusive figure of Sylvie.

Then, in the harsh dawn light, this, too, plunged into nightmare as it came to me with a fresh lurch of disbelief that Sylvie was dead, and that I would have to wake to this stark knowledge for the rest of my life.

My violent awakening hadn't disturbed Ginny. She lay on the far side of the bed, her thin arm reaching out across the pillows towards me, the eye-mask reducing her face to a ghostly triangle of mouth and chin. At some point in the night she had turned on the light and taken a pill. She had glanced towards me but I had feigned sleep. In the dark of the night I had felt too raw for conversation, too unsure of where

1

it might lead. Ginny hadn't been fooled, she'd known I was awake, but we'd both kept up the pretence.

I slid out of bed, sending a shower of papers to the floor: the amended buyout terms I had tried to read at one-thirty or whenever it was I had got to bed. Soundlessly, I put the pages into some sort of order and noticed that my hands were trembling. I showered and shaved, nicking the scar on my upper lip as I always did when I was tense or more than usually overtired. Some beads of watery blood dropped into the basin and I wiped them away with a tissue. I didn't have to look too closely into the mirror to know that the worries of the last few months were stamped all over my face.

I reached for a cord jacket, the sort of thing I generally wore for a day at Hartford, but, remembering the message I would be delivering to the people there, I changed it for a suit of sober grey worsted. I must have lost some weight because the waistband was slack and I had to search out a pair of braces.

I went down to make some three-spoon coffee to keep me awake on the journey. It was barely six-thirty but someone had already been into the house. The girl we contracted to do the flowers must have been to market early because through the open door to the laundry room I could see several large buckets crammed with fresh blooms standing amid spatterings of water. That meant we were having a party tonight. It also meant that, not for the first time, it had slipped my mind. The prospect of a houseful of chattering people filled me with dismay. I dimly

2

hoped it wasn't going to be a charity event, then at least I might know a few of them.

A soft conspiratorial knock sounded from the hall. I unbolted the door to find Julia, my assistant, poised tensely on the step.

In my jittery state I assumed bad news. 'What's happened?'

'Nothing's happened,' she said hastily.

'Then what are you doing here?' I asked, more in curiosity than annoyance.

She handed me a file. 'I thought you might want this.' She made a doubtful face that admitted to the thinness of the excuse.

I waved her in. 'A bit early for you, isn't it?'

She gave a short laugh, glad that I could still tease her. 'I *have* been up at dawn before, you know. Well – once.'

The file was one we both knew I didn't really need. I raised a questioning eyebrow.

'Today's *Times*,' she announced. Pulling the business section out of her bag, she found the page for me.

It was in the snippets column, the place where they put the news that isn't going to influence share prices. The source, whoever it was, had been meticulous with the facts. 'Buoyant' china and lighting manufacturer A. L. Cumberland, fresh from its takeover of – and it stung me to read it – 'debt-ridden' HartWell Glass, the family-owned crystal and tableware company, was putting HartWell's loss-making Hartford Crystal division up for grabs. Cumberland's chairman was quoted as saying that slow-moving crystal did not mesh well with Cumberland's dynamic mass-market product profile.

But it was the final paragraph that really needled. *After years of lacklustre sales and low investment, Hartford Crystal would seem ripe for absorption by brand leaders in the highly competitive export-dependent crystal market. An attempted management buyout led by HartWell's erstwhile joint managing director and major shareholder, Hugh Wellesley, is thought to be facing an uphill struggle.*

Julia remarked, 'A bitch, eh?'

'Yup,' I said bitterly.

'I thought you'd better see it.' Julia fought a losing battle against her indignation. 'You can't help noticing the timing!' she hissed. 'I had an idea something like this was coming, that's why I went and got the papers on the way over.'

If she meant to surprise me, she succeeded. 'You knew?'

'Well, I guessed. Don't ask how. You wouldn't approve.'

Not yet thirty, Julia was the best assistant I'd ever had, exceptionally shrewd and efficient, yet when she'd first arrived her attitude, openly cynical and opportunistic, had rather disturbed me. Now I took a more ambivalent view.

'You think it came from inside Cumberland?'

She gave me a heavy look. 'I *know* it did.'

She meant it had come from Howard who, until the takeover, had shared the managing directorship of HartWell with me. In the process of courting Cumberland and negotiating the takeover, Howard had managed to secure himself a seat on the Cumberland

4

board and a lucrative share option deal. For Howard there was no such thing as an old loyalty, and the moment he'd stepped over the Cumberland threshold six weeks ago he'd belonged to them, heart and soul.

'It could have come from a City guru,' I suggested.

'Sometimes, Hugh, I think you're too trusting for this world.'

I shook suddenly, the tensions welled up, I heard myself snap, 'And sometimes I think you're too damn sure of yourself!'

Her eyes rounded, she stared at me, eventually she stammered, 'Sorry. You're right. That was out of order.'

'It's just . . .' I pressed a hand to my head, I couldn't explain.

Julia was still looking astonished. I think she had been under the illusion that I never lost my temper.

Regaining some control, I gestured apology. 'It's just that I don't want to think about who might have done it. Not when it's too late to do anything about it.'

'No, of course . . .'

There was a short silence while we both recovered from our second angry words in the two years we had worked together. The first, I realised with dismay, had been only yesterday.

Finally Julia said in a muted voice, 'I know you said you wanted to drive yourself down to Hartford, but I've got a driver on standby just in case. I thought you'd be exhausted.'

'I'll drive myself.'

She gave it one more try. 'It's such a long way and he's just outside.'

But I wouldn't have been comfortable arriving at Hartford in a chauffeur-driven car, not when there was an axe hanging over the factory's future.

'No, but thanks anyway.' I took *The Times* and *Telegraph* from her and opened the door.

'Sorry I was out of line,' she repeated unhappily. 'I think you're right, it's altogether too early for me.'

'For all of us,' I smiled.

She hesitated. 'You're looking terribly tired.'

'I'll catch up on the weekend.'

'If there's any more I can do. To take some of the load . . .'

'I don't think so, but thanks anyway.'

She paused on the point of saying more, then, thinking better of it, declared, 'Good luck for today. I hope it goes well. You really deserve it!' In a gesture that was uncharacteristically demonstrative she reached out and grasped my hand in both of hers before striding off down the street.

In the kitchen I quickly leafed through the papers. I turned each page with an odd mixture of dread and hope, but there was nothing more about Sylvie. The initial report two days ago had been sparse: a woman's body had been recovered from the River Dart; it had been identified as that of Sylvie Mathieson. I wasn't sure what I expected now. Some details of how she had died perhaps; some idea of what the police were doing. But maybe there was simply nothing to report. Maybe the police had imposed a news blackout. The uncertainty did nothing for the anxiety that coiled and twisted in my belly.

I gulped the rest of my coffee and thrust the *Times*

article into my briefcase. Crossing the kitchen, I glimpsed the flowers again. I picked out a white fluffy bloom – it might have been a dahlia – and, not really sure what I meant by the gesture, carried it upstairs and propped it on the pillow next to Ginny. I took a sheet from the pad and scribbled 'Sorry'. I didn't know what I meant by that either. All I knew was that flowers and notes were thin substitutes for all the time we never had together.

Looking down at Ginny, I felt the familiar blend of bewilderment and guilt, mainly guilt. Things hadn't been right between us for such a long time, and I didn't really know why. But then my whole life seemed to have gone adrift, and I wasn't absolutely sure why that had happened either.

I changed my mind about the flower – too crass – and thrust it into the bin.

I was halfway down the stairs when Ginny's voice cried out, 'Hugh. *Hugh?*'

She was sitting up in bed, her mask pushed back over her head. 'What's the time?'

She looked so fragile that I felt a pull in my chest somewhere, a tug of emotion and regret.

'Sorry, I didn't mean to wake you—'

She focused on me. 'Where are you going?'

'Hartford.'

'Must you?'

'I've got a meeting.'

She seemed momentarily confused by this and I guessed she was still groggy from the sleeping pill or whatever it was she had taken in the night.

'You won't be late back?' she asked.

'I'll do my best.'

'You haven't forgotten tonight?'

'No.' But I couldn't maintain the pretence. 'What's the party for exactly?'

Usually Ginny would cast me a flicker of resentment at such lapses, as though I made a point of forgetting these things simply to belittle the importance of her work, but nothing showed on her face. Instead she said dully, 'It's for the premature baby unit, the fund-raising committee. I promised ages ago.'

'Am I essential?' Seeing her eyes widen in reproach, I added hurriedly, 'I'll try not to be too late. I'll do my best.' For all her shoulder-rubbing with the great and the good, for all her grace and poise, Ginny had never found it easy to face the world on her own. Even as I made my promise I knew with sinking heart that I'd be unlikely to keep it, and that by letting her down I would yet again be fulfilling her gloomy expectations of me.

Aware of the time, I moved towards the door.

'It's the last party,' Ginny said abruptly. 'No more after this.'

I turned back. I wasn't sure what to make of this statement, except that it was meant to be momentous in some way. 'No more?'

She gave a slow shake of the head and pressed her fingertips to the corners of her eyes. I tried to read the signs. Was I expected to question her, to listen to whatever social disappointments or imagined slights had led to this decision? If so, Ginny's timing was as unerring as ever; she always managed to choose a moment when I was rushing off to some meeting or so tired that I could barely think. Yet she could never understand how this, more than anything, doomed our conversations to failure before they had even started.

'I'm desperately late,' I ventured. 'Otherwise—'

I waited for the soft glance of injury she produced on these occasions, but her face was bare of emotion. She gave the faintest of nods, and my heart lifted as it always did when we avoided a tiff.

'I'll see you later,' she said, reaching up to pull the mask back over her eyes. 'Oh, and Hugh?'

Trying not to show the slightest impatience, I put my head back round the door.

'Take care, won't you?'

She said it with strange solemnity, and it struck me again how very thin she looked.

'Of course.'

'You're overdoing it at the moment.'

'Just until the buyout's over . . .'

Her eyes were unfocused, she was hardly listening. 'Well, take care anyway.'

Winding my way through the Chelsea streets, driving out through the suburbs, I did take care. The coffee and lack of sleep had made me light-headed and I didn't entirely trust my reactions. But as the well-worn road to Totnes unwound before me and my mind skittered over the myriad problems that lay ahead, my concentration began to waver. To keep alert, I turned on the radio and aimed the air vents at my face.

The *Times* article kept returning to haunt me. The

more I tried to persuade myself that it wouldn't diminish our chances of funding the buyout, the more damaging it seemed to become. And, when I really wanted to torture myself, which was quite often, I imagined Zircon, the venture capitalists who were backing our bid, having second thoughts and pulling out altogether.

Needing to take some action, however unproductive, I called Julia on the car phone and asked her to find a corporate PR adviser for us. Then I spent a fruitless twenty minutes trying to locate Pollinger, our contact at Zircon, but, despite mobiles, pagers and home numbers, he seemed to lead an elusive life.

In search of distraction, I switched on the radio again and, finding a discussion programme, raised the volume until the voices filled the car.

I was on the M5, somewhere past Taunton, when a blaring horn brought me to my senses with a jolt of adrenalin. A car was looming up in front of me. In the instant that I realised it was stationary I also knew that I couldn't possibly stop in time. I jerked the wheel to the left and braked hard and felt the car kick round as the rear wheels lost their grip. I must have twisted the wheel the other way because the car performed a snake-like manoeuvre and skidded again as it shot across the middle lane, narrowly missing the front of a large coach. The inside lane came at me in slow motion, any approaching traffic hidden by the bulk of the coach, but the lane must have been empty because the next moment the car was shuddering sideways across the hard shoulder and hitting the kerb with an almighty bang that almost lifted me off my seat.

The car rocked to a standstill, the engine stalled. All I could hear was the radio newscaster droning on. I sat motionless with my hands clutched to the wheel, the sweat cold against my ribs, until someone opened the door and asked me if I was all right.

I heard myself say I was okay. I must have sounded convincing because, after the man told me several times to stop driving like a bloody maniac, he slammed the door and walked back to the coach, which was parked some way ahead on the hard shoulder.

It was a long time before I could think about setting off again. I kept reliving the near-miss and the seconds preceding it, when the newscaster had spoken Sylvie's name. His cool detached voice kept running through my mind, like a tape being played over and over again, yet only two words really registered, and both felt like something driven against my heart. *Stabbed and bound.*

I got shakily out of the car and heaved the sparse contents of my stomach onto the grass verge. When I felt a bit better I walked round the car to look for signs of damage, but the wheels seemed all right, the tyres still had air. Not knowing what else I should check, I got back into the driver's seat and, after a last five minutes with my head back and my eyes closed, I started the engine.

I drove gingerly, half expecting knocking sounds or wobbles from the steering, but after a time I forgot to worry about the car and slowly accelerated to mid-lane speed, my mind miles away again, in a dark and distant place.

I arrived at Hartford half an hour late. Driving in through the gates, I tried to picture the factory through the eyes of potential investors. With its twenties architecture, drab brickwork and mean windows, the place had the air of old glories long faded, while its clusters of ventilation pipes and aluminium chimneys suggested spasmodic and piece-meal modernisation. Only the recently completed warehouse, a spare metal structure in cobalt blue, emitted anything approaching an up-to-date image. *Lacklustre sales . . . Low investment . . .* The newspaper's comments were ill-founded but they still pricked at me.

George Banes came out to meet me. The production director was a burly man, his large belly testing the fastenings on his shirt, with a thick head of hair that had been silvery grey for as long as I had known him, which was almost twenty years.

'Thought the traffic might delay you,' he commented, as we shook hands and made for the entrance, 'so I told the staff we'd meet at ten minutes to noon.'

'You explained that it was just an update?'

'I did. I said you wanted to keep them abreast of developments but that there was nothing definite at the moment.'

Even now, in my state of preoccupation, I couldn't walk through the doors of the factory without feeling a proprietorial thrill. I was too much my father's son, too deeply instilled with his old-style paternalistic

12

pride not to feel an attachment to the place that was decidedly emotional.

George took me into the office that had been my father's and would have been mine if Howard hadn't pressed for what he liked to call an integrated management structure, and insisted we put the management and sales of all three divisions under one roof at Slough.

The room was virtually unchanged since my father's retirement ten years ago. His wide oak desk stood in the same spot by the window, the ancient wooden in- and out-trays squatting on a worn leather surface that still bore the pattern of a hundred ink marks. When I was a small boy this room had seemed cavernous, and my father, behind the mass of his desk, an oddly distant figure. It was only when he finished his business and took me down to the factory floor and chatted in his easy soft-voiced manner that I had felt I knew him again.

George brought coffee and we sat down at the conference table.

'So it's all signed up with Zircon?' he demanded eagerly.

'It's signed.'

'No quibbles with the business plan?'

George and I had worked so hard on the business plan that we knew every word and financial projection by heart. 'No quibbles with the business plan,' I reassured him, and saw his eyes spark with satisfaction. 'But I tell you, George, whatever happened to them on the playing fields of Eton, it turned their hearts to stone.' I was thinking of the additional leverage the venture capitalists had demanded, and the personal guarantees covering the fifty per cent of my personal worth that was not already committed to the buyout. 'They've made financial pain into an art form.' I managed an ironic laugh.

'But they're behind us now, that's the important thing.'

'They still have their doubts about me, I think. Or rather the idea of me.'

'What? *Why?*'

'According to the City, family firms are breeding grounds for inefficiency and nepotism. And a family buyout – well!' I rolled my eyes. 'That's even more unhealthy. Incest.'

'But that's ridiculous! It's not like that here. Don't they realise that? We've always been a team, for God's sake! And, this buyout – well, we're all in it together, aren't we?'

We certainly were. George was putting fifty thousand cash into the buyout, and another fifty thousand against his house. So were Alan and John, the other Hartford directors. But that was how the venture capitalists liked it, to have the whole lot of us over a financial barrel.

I passed George the page from *The Times*. 'This may not help.'

George read the article and spluttered, 'What's this? Years of low investment? What are they damn well talking about! We've upgraded the batching plant, for God's sake. We've installed the stem-pulling machines—'

'It's nonsense, of course—'

14

'And lacklustre sales! They've stood up bloody well, considering. Apart from Packenhams.'

This was one of our worst blows, being de-listed by London's second largest department store.

George thrashed a hand against the paper. 'Who gives them this rubbish?'

But I didn't try to answer that.

George hadn't cooled down yet. 'It makes Hartford sound like some cottage industry filled with Luddites! As if we'd fought change tooth and nail!'

The irony wasn't lost on either of us. While Howard and I had been running the company it had hardly stopped changing. That was the whole trouble. We had moved too far, too fast, expanding rapidly into mass-market glass and chinaware just as trading conditions began to worsen. While my father was alive he hadn't liked much of what we had been doing but had never tried to interfere. I was glad he had died in February. It had saved him the anguish of seeing quite what a mess I had made of everything.

'At the end of the day it's only a newspaper story,' I said.

George, forcing himself back to his natural state of optimism, declared, 'Right! Right!' He laughed loudly and abruptly. 'We never thought it was going to be easy, did we?'

I laughed too, awkwardly. This deal was the hardest thing I had ever attempted. In the six weeks since the Cumberland takeover, I had been cut loose from the new parent company to run Hartford Crystal on a nil-salary basis, while simultaneously planning to buy it out. Raising the three million pounds of leverage from the banks, keeping all the financial and legal balls in the air, pulling together all the strands of what was an amazingly complex deal, was a Herculean task which, even on an eighteen-hour day, was stretching me to my limits. Much of the time I was suffused with a wild conviction that we would pull it off, and then I flew on adrenalin. At other times, faced by endless setbacks, I settled into something more mechanical, a mindless persistence fuelled by the determination to save what I had so foolishly jeopardised.

There was no mystery about my motives. For me this buyout was about restitution. My father had worked hard for twenty years to build up the company and pass it on to me in good shape, while I had worked hard for ten to achieve nothing more, it seemed, than to let it slip away and threaten the livelihoods of all the people who worked for us. I wanted it back, I wanted to show what I could do with it now that I was free of Howard and his remorseless drive for diversification. I wanted to make a success of it for my own sake, certainly, but more than that I wanted to feel I could look the employees in the eye again.

George and I talked our way through the monthly sales figures and were just starting on the cash flow analysis when a woman's voice sounded in the outer office. There was something about it, the suggestion of a lazy laugh, of dark overtones, that caught at my memory and chilled my heart.

'You all right?' George asked.

'Fine.' Reaching for my coffee, I promptly knocked

it over. Trying to retrieve the cup, I got that wrong too and sent it flying across the table.

I muttered 'Jesus!' Then as I picked the cup off the floor: 'What an idiot!' I gave a disbelieving laugh. But as soon as George had gone in search of a cloth I sat in silence, wondering what on earth was happening to me and whether this was just frayed nerves or a form of delayed shock. Whatever, the loss of control frightened me, and I was unnerved by the thought that it might happen again.

By the time George returned with a roll of kitchen paper, I was staring bleakly at the pool of coffee, trying to suppress visions of dark water and Sylvie's flesh, mutilated and cold.

'Do you want something to eat?' George asked when he had finished clearing up. 'A sandwich? Biscuits?'

'Thanks, no.'

He peered at me. 'You look as though you need something. If you don't mind my saying so.'

I shook my head and jumped to my feet. 'We'd better go.'

As we made our way towards the factory floor George's secretary hailed me from her office. 'Mr Hugh, a message from Dr Wellesley. He'll be free from twelve-thirty.'

'Hugh or Mr Wellesley,' I corrected her half-heartedly, having largely abandoned the hope that the long-serving staff would drop their archaic terms of address. 'My brother will be at home, will he?'

'Yes. And there was an enquiry from a Detective

Inspector Henderson. No details. Just could you call him?'

She gave me a slip of paper with a number. The area code was Exeter. 'Thank you.'

I glanced at the number again, then, stuffing it into my pocket, walked quickly away. George caught up and started singing the praises of some training scheme, but I was hardly listening. I was wondering what questions the police would ask me. I had no doubt it was Sylvie they wanted to talk to me about, it could hardly be anything else. We must have been seen together, on the pontoon perhaps, or the boat. Such things did not go unnoticed in a small community like Dittisham. Ever since Sylvie's death I had been telling myself that this summons would come, yet now it had materialised I felt oddly shaken.

We reached the batching plant and I managed to ask the warehousemen some sensible questions about the new forklift and the revised storage bay layout. The route George and I took through the factory had been laid down since the beginning of time. After a circuit of the storage bay which took us past pallets of silica, lead oxide, litharge and potassium, we inspected the computerised batch mixer, then, after a few minutes with the batch quality control staff, we went through to the heat of the blowing room.

The dull roar of the furnaces still stirred me in some atavistic way. The transmutation of. the dry amalgam into clear lava still seemed like some mysterious alchemy. The groups of schoolchildren and visitors who toured the factory on the overhead walkways lingered longest over the blowers as they ballooned and moulded the cooling lava into shape, or beside the cutters as they chased the designs into the glass, waiting in nervous delight for them to make an error and abandon the goblet, tumbler or bowl to the reprocessing bin with a crash of splintering glass. But for me the fascination had always lain here, in the unimaginable heat, in the impenetrable trembling magma that seemed incapable of any transformation, let alone the miraculous metamorphosis into a material both dense and transparent, both complex and flawless.

Bill, our senior master blower, raised his eyebrows in greeting. Many years ago when I had worked here in my university vacations, sweeping floors and wheeling bins, Bill had tried to teach me to blow the simplest shape. My best effort sat at home somewhere, a far-from-round object of uneven thickness with a trail of bubbles up one side.

The factory buzzer cut our tour short at the grinding and polishing area. Following George towards the canteen, the ideas for my speech, such as they were, seemed to scatter, and I wished I'd made more time to prepare.

As the staff gathered I greeted as many as I could by name. A few had been at Hartford for thirty years or more; some twenty; a good number for more than ten. There were two entire families – father, sons, daughters-in-law. We even had a grandmother and granddaughter on the payroll. A hundred and fifty employees in all, people whose lives were dependent on this factory, and – never had I needed less reminding – on my ability to restore its fortunes.

The moment came. George called for silence and I stepped forward, beset by strange emotions.

'As soon as the takeover was agreed I promised to keep you in touch with developments,' I began. 'I also promised you that we were going to do everything in our power to get this management buyout off the ground.' Voicing it, I felt a new weight of responsibility. 'Well, the good news is that we've reached agreement with some venture capital people called Zircon. They're going to put up about a quarter of the money. That still leaves a full half to be raised from the banks, and I won't pretend that it's proving to be easy, because it isn't. We're in the second round of talks with two banks, the Chartered and the West Country Mutual. We haven't been turned down yet. That's all I can tell you so far.'

I caught the eye of Madge, grader and glass washer, sitting solidly on a chair directly in front of me. She was glaring at me: a combative expression, an anxious one, or a combination of both.

'Now, when Cumberland took us over I warned you that sentiment would play no part in their calculations. And though they've given us first call on buying Hartford, we still have to match the best price on offer. I have to tell you that according to our latest information they're talking to Donington and maybe some other companies too.'

The feeling of disconnection hit me again. Without warning my brain did an abrupt shift, a sort of sideways jump, and I completely lost track. When I finally managed to speak, I stumbled, not sure if I was making sense. I heard myself say, 'Now we're very attractive . . .' A lone titter rose up, and, glancing uncertainly towards the sound, I grappled for the thread of my argument. 'Our name and reputation are the attractions,' I said at last. 'And of course our designs. But valuing a name and reputation is not the same as valuing a workforce.'

That had sounded all right, but my brain was functioning with agonising slowness. 'People like Donington have the capacity to produce the Hartford range at their own plants so, if they outbid us, well – you can imagine. This factory will almost certainly close.'

I was back on track at last, my mind free of whatever had constrained it. I thrust some optimism back into my voice. 'But we can make damned sure that doesn't happen! We can make sure that our bid is bigger and better than anyone else's!' I paused, trying unsuccessfully to gauge their mood, before plunging on. 'Now, we've already asked a lot from you, I know that. And you've responded one hundred per cent and that's the entire reason we've managed to keep going as long as we have. But the venture capital people want one more undertaking, and that's what I've come to ask you today. They want a formal undertaking that you'll agree to a two-year period of wage restraint.'

I explained how this would work, how their share options and profit-sharing schemes would remain unaffected. I told them that if it had been left to me I wouldn't have asked them for anything in writing, but venture capitalists were altogether more cautious animals.

I said a lot more of what I hoped were the right

things before halting with a sense of relief. My brain was clear, but my momentary disorientation had shaken me and I didn't want to risk it happening again. I had no intention of going on, I certainly didn't mean to get onto emotional ground, but my judgement was all over the place and, without any idea of where it might lead, I found myself saying forcibly, 'You know, some people believe tradition's a bad thing, that it's the enemy of change – the great modern god Change. But I believe that the traditions we've built up here really matter, that they actually *help* us to change in a productive way. We've been together so long that we think like a family, we take each other into account, we're not just out for ourselves and to hell with the next man . . .' I broke off, aware of how pretentious this must sound to people who, at the end of the day, just wanted a regular job like everyone else. 'What I mean is – I believe that this company is worth fighting for. And not just for what comes off the end of the production line. But for the way we do things here.'

A voice piped up, 'We certainly do it our way!' and there was a ripple of laughter followed by a call of 'You can say that again!' and a smattering of applause.

Buoyed up by their irreverence, I laughed with them before delivering a few last words.

When I stepped down my shirt was damp with sweat and I pulled at my collar to loosen it. Madge brought me a glass of water. 'No need to worry about us, Hugh.' After twenty-five years at Hartford she used my name with a disarming familiarity. 'We're the least of your troubles.'

'Madge . . . That's good to know.'

'We don't mind the wages, we don't mind being asked to do the overtime, what we *don't* like is being second best to cheap glass and tableware.'

'I never meant Hartford to be second best.'

'Got your head turned, didn't you?' Madge prided herself on her blunt speaking. 'Big ideas.'

I couldn't deny it and I didn't try.

Madge, who was a grandmother ten times over, gave me the sort of admonitory nod she probably reserved for her own middle-aged sons.

George and I lingered for a few minutes answering questions before walking back to the office.

'Good speech,' he exclaimed delightedly. 'Just what we needed.' He caught my expression. 'You weren't happy with it?'

I gestured inarticulately. 'Take no notice of me. Too much on my mind.'

'You really don't look well. I noticed the moment you arrived. Are you sure you won't have something to eat?'

'I'm all right.' I made a feeble attempt at humour. 'Just a nervous breakdown. Well – if I could ever find the time.' I looked at my watch and made for the door.

Before leaving, I found an empty office and phoned the Exeter number. Detective Inspector Henderson wasn't available but I spoke to a Detective Sergeant Jones who asked if I could call in during the afternoon.

23

'Will it take long?'

'Can't say, sir.'

'I have to be back in London by seven. I could give you half an hour at two-thirty. If you wanted longer we'd have to make it another day.'

'Very well, sir. We'll see you at two-thirty then.'

'Who should I ask for?'

'Anyone on Detective Inspector Henderson's team.'

I thought I knew where the police station was, but asked for directions just in case. It was only after I'd put the phone down that I realised that Sergeant Jones hadn't offered to tell me what the matter was about and I hadn't asked him.

George walked me to the car. 'They're right behind the buyout, you know,' he said. 'Everyone here, they'll back us all the way.'

Behind my smile, I was beset by doubts. Having worked so single-mindedly towards the buyout, having pursued it to the point of obsession, it had suddenly lost focus and significance, like some all-consuming passion that inexplicably falls flat. I told myself that my loss of momentum was due to exhaustion, to the punishing pace I had forced on myself in recent weeks. I kept telling myself this because I didn't want to think about my other problems and how they were eating into my confidence.

The road was clogged with the last of the summer caravans, there were roadworks in the town, and I didn't turn onto the Dartmouth road until almost a quarter to one. I drove as fast as I dared and probably faster than I should have. I had the idea that if I was forced to concentrate on my driving then I wouldn't have time to think.

It didn't work, of course. My thoughts simply became less controllable, popping up like muggers in the night. I kept thinking of the last time I had travelled this road, heading not for my brother's place, but for Dittisham and my old family home, standing empty on the dark river. It seemed incredible that I had driven along this road just five days ago, that I had travelled with longing still dragging at my heart, and that when I had arrived at the house and opened it up and drawn back the curtains and put on all the lights I had still half hoped that Sylvie would see my childish signal and come.

I turned off the road into David's drive with relief. I couldn't have faced Dittisham today.

Furze Lodge was an early-nineteenth-century rectory in the grand style, with eight bedrooms, a staff flat and stable block in grounds of five acres. Seeing the immaculate garden, the freshly painted doors and windows, I wondered how much the place cost David and Mary to run. It couldn't be less than fifty thousand a year, not with a live-in couple and at least two horses. When you added the school fees – they had a boy and a girl, both teenagers, both at expensive boarding schools – the charity events Mary hosted and the rest of their community commitments, their expenditure must have exceeded David's income as a GP by a very wide margin indeed. Like me, he had relied heavily on his HartWell dividends. Like me, I imagined he had been feeling the pinch.

I found David in the rather gloomy study which

doubled as a consulting room for his private patients. He sat behind his ancient kneehole desk in a charcoal pinstripe suit complete with waistcoat and watch chain, and when he looked up he eyed me over gold-rimmed half-moon spectacles, so completely the doctor that he had taken the image almost to the point of parody.

'You look terrible,' he remarked immediately.

'Thanks,' I said. 'I'm glad I'm not one of your patients or I might get depressed.'

'Have you seen anyone?'

'What? No. I'm fine.'

He was shuffling paper as he talked. 'You should see someone.'

'I'll be all right once this business is over. It's just frantic at the moment, that's all.'

'Are you sleeping?'

'Don't find the time.'

'What about those tablets I gave you? Have you been taking them?'

I vaguely remembered the tablets he was talking about, but couldn't think where I'd put them. 'Probably not.'

'They don't work unless you take them regularly.'

'What are they meant to do anyway?'

David pulled open a drawer, took out a bottle of pills and chucked them across to me. 'Don't forget this time.'

It was easier to put them into my pocket than to argue. Until this summer David had rarely showed much interest in my health, and I had never expected him to. David was two years older than me, we had been close as children, but since growing up we had never been too involved in each other's lives. If I'd ever stopped to consider our relationship, I suppose I would have described it as practical.

'How are things with you?' I asked automatically.

'Me?' he said in a tone of self-mockery. I noticed that his hair, once so dark, was greying rapidly at the temples and that his cheeks were criss-crossed with deepening lines, though these signs of age did little to detract from his patrician looks, which women found impressive enough to remark on. Like me, he seemed to have gone against the trend and kept his waistline. Unlike me, he had lost none of his hair.

'Oh, I survive,' he said with irony.

'The old loves playing up?' South Devon was retirement country, with a population that David had once described as ninety and skyrocketing.

'They get ill and fed up,' he said heavily. 'They want magic potions.'

Watching him tidy his desk it occurred to me that he, too, was a tired man, and that he was tired because he didn't enjoy his work. With his sharp brain and wide skills, he would have made a good consultant, but though he'd completed two years as a senior houseman he had failed the big surgical exams and never given them another shot. This had caused my father much grief, not because of the failure itself, but because David hadn't had the backbone to persevere. For my father, lack of effort was almost the greatest sin of all, and doubly so when you were blessed with inherited money. He believed that financial security gave you a duty not to depend on it, that it was almost immoral to rely on the sweat and tears of previous generations. It seemed to Pa that David had succumbed to the easy option, and he never quite got over it.

I looked nervously at my watch.

David stood up. 'I'll fetch Mary.'

But he made no move towards the door. Instead he glanced back at me and said in his cool professional voice, 'You heard about Sylvie Mathieson?'

'I did, yes. Awful.'

'She was stabbed apparently.'

'God,' I breathed.

'Dumped in the river.'

'They have no idea who—?'

'No.'

I wasn't sure I wanted more details, but I couldn't stop myself asking, 'Where did they find her?'

'On the first bend there, near the Anchor Stone. The body was caught against a rock. Dead less than a day, they think. Wrapped in plastic, tied up with rope.'

'God.'

David picked up a pen and examined the nib, then put it down again as if it had been guilty of distracting him. When he spoke again his tone was hedged with reservations, as though he were still debating the wisdom of mentioning the subject. 'She was all over the place, you know.'

I stared at him, my mouth suddenly dry. 'What do you mean?'

'Oh, the full bit,' he said airily. 'Lovers. Drugs.'

My stomach tightened. I felt an unreasonable anger. 'How do you know?'

'Oh . . .' His shrug implied contacts in the right places. 'One hears.'

I wanted to ask him why he was so quick to believe such rumours, but I pushed myself to my feet instead so that he couldn't read my face. 'She was always a free spirit,' I proclaimed. 'She always went her own way.'

I didn't have to look at him to know he was wearing a sceptical expression.

'Thought you'd better know, that's all.'

I turned. 'Me? Why?'

'Well, you were in love with her once, weren't you? ' He spoke in the curt voice he used to distance himself from anything that bordered on the emotional.

'Yes . . .' Why had I thought he meant anything else? 'Yes, I was. Yes.' And saying it, I had a fleeting memory of those distant feelings, so intense and innocent and full of hope. 'A long time ago.'

'Look—' David began irritably. But he broke off at the sound of footsteps in the hall.

Mary came in and her face lit up. 'Hugh!' she sang.

I went to kiss her cheek but, with the reproving tut of a mother hen, she pulled me into a generous hug. Standing back to inspect me, she cried, 'How *are* you?'

'I'm fine.'

She shook her head and rolled her eyes in mock exasperation. 'I don't know . . . Is it worth it? Just look at you!'

29

'Don't *you* start,' I protested. 'David's bad enough, giving me pills.'

'It's not pills you want, it's a rest! Isn't it, darling?' she flung at David. Turning back to me. 'You'll stay for lunch at least?'

'I've got to leave at two.'

'Hopeless!' she declared. 'Hopeless!' And her eyes flashed with their habitual amusement.

I said, 'I can always come back again if we don't get through it—'

'I meant, you have to eat! I'll go and fetch something now.' She threw a questioning look at David. 'Shall I?'

'Well, perhaps we can just get started . . .'

'Fine!' she said immediately. 'In a minute then!' She perched on the chair David had pulled up for her and fixed me with a bright stare. I had always liked Mary. She was a determined extrovert who believed that the secret of life was to laugh at whatever came your way. If her high spirits were sometimes a little relentless they hid a compassionate and generous personality, quick to leap to the aid of those in trouble. A solicitor who had given up her practice on marrying David, she did good works on the boards of hospices and children's homes, and was a prison visitor at Dartmoor.

She had a sturdy body with an angular face, ruddy cheeks, and eyebrows that seemed too dark and bold for her colouring, and her appearance wasn't enhanced by her practical tweed skirt, shapeless jumper and cropped hair. But if her looks were plain, they were thoroughly redeemed by her unwavering good nature.

She could not have been more different from Howard, either in appearance or personality, and sometimes I had to remind myself that they were brother and sister. Mary was so much a part of our family, both in spirit and fact, that I tended to forget she might sometimes have divided loyalties. When our two families had jointly and harmoniously controlled HartWell this had not been an issue. But if Mary had felt torn over the acrimonious falling out between Howard and me, she had been very discreet about it.

'We've looked through this buyout proposal thing,' David began, leaning back in his chair and pulling his spectacles off his nose in a practised gesture. 'I can't say we're a hundred per cent clear on *everything* . . .'

So I took them through it, item by item. The investment opportunity, the risks, the potential for significant capital gains. I told them what the new team had already achieved, what was left to get right. When I talked about the future, how we believed we could turn the company round in a few months, some of my old fire returned, I began to sound evangelical again.

Mary listened with partial attention, her sharp eyes on mine, a smile hovering at the corners of her mouth. When I had finished she looked meaningfully at David, and I guessed she was prompting him to ask some pre-arranged question.

'Yes . . .' murmured David, catching her eye.

'Suppose we put in, say, fifty thousand now, could we put in more later?'

I tried not to show my disappointment. Only last week David had been talking about a minimum of a hundred and fifty thousand. 'It would be difficult,' I said carefully. 'You see, there's only going to be so much equity and once the buyout's gone through, that's it, there won't be any more for sale.' I glanced from one to the other and wondered if they had actually decided on this reduced figure but didn't like to tell me.

Mary recognised my anxiety and gave me a sympathetic little grin.

David roused himself to murmur, 'After the last two years, the losses . . .'

'I know. And that's why I want you to come in with us, David. To make good your losses. The potential is there, we believe that very strongly.'

Engrossed in some inner deliberations, David narrowed his eyes and tapped his fingertips together.

Mary tried to catch his attention again but, failing, shrugged at me and said in a theatrical whisper, 'We wanted to ask – what about income? What income could we expect?'

'There would be no dividends until we got into profit.'

David picked up on that. 'And that could be years?'

'Hopefully a lot less.'

'*Hopefully*,' he repeated with a censorious look, as though he had succeeded in catching me out.

I started on our strategy then, how we intended to go out and sell ourselves hard on the Hartford name and quality. But catching the expression of boredom on David's face, an expression I knew so well – lids hooded, his dark winged eyebrows lifted outwards in a satanic arch – I cut it short.

'Listen—' I said forcefully, 'I'm putting everything I have into this. I wouldn't be doing it unless I believed *absolutely* that we could pull it off.'

Mary exclaimed in mock horror, 'Everything?'

'Certainly all the cash I have. And' – I gave a weak chuckle – 'quite a lot I don't. I'm borrowing as much as I can.' And far more than was safe or wise, though I didn't say that.

I tried not to think of how much I stood to lose if the buyout failed, and how much I had at risk if it succeeded. I tried to forget how very overextended I already was. Ginny and I had a lifestyle that didn't come cheap. We had second homes in Provence and Wiltshire, we had staff and cars, until last year we had bought good modern pictures, and we entertained on what could only be described as a grand scale. Even allowing for all this, the outpouring of cash was so relentless that I could never quite grasp where it went. Since last year when the HartWell dividends had plummeted and I had taken a voluntary reduction in salary, we had tried to cut back. Ginny had been in charge of the economies, but for some reason I could never understand her cuts seemed to make little impact on our bank balance, and whenever I thought of the future I felt an upsurge of panic.

Mary screwed up her face in an extravagant imitation of alarm. 'I hope you're not expecting us to do the same!'

'Of course not. I wouldn't want you to. You must only invest what you can afford.'

David drawled, 'And if the company goes down the plughole?'

'It won't.'

'But if it does?' he insisted with a tinge of impatience.

'Then the banks would get first call.'

'And we'd get—?'

'Nothing.'

He grimaced, *'Exactly!'*

I was aware of Mary watching me closely again. She gave a sudden chuckle. 'A bit of a gamble then!' She made it sound like a flutter on the horses.

David sat forward. 'We'll need time to think about it.'

'Of course.' I looked from one to the other. 'Though it would help enormously if you could give me some idea of how long you'll need.'

David pursed his lips. 'I don't know—' He shot a look at Mary. 'The weekend? Say, Tuesday?'

She shrugged her agreement.

'Tuesday then.'

It could have been worse. Suppressing the urge to press my case further, I mustered a grin.

In the short silence that followed, Mary jumped to her feet. 'I'll go and do that lunch!'

'I'm not sure I've got time, Mary.'

She wagged her finger at me. 'It's only a sandwich. Won't take a moment.' There was something brittle, almost peremptory, in her tone. She paused at the door. 'Have you told Hugh about Dittisham, David?'

'Ah . . . no.'

Mary caught my eye and, reverting to her more familiar role, made a face of jokey forbearance as she disappeared into the hall.

'The thing is, we might have a buyer,' David told me when she had gone. 'Someone who wants it pretty quick. We heard this morning. Prepared to pay the asking price.'

I felt a pinch of loss. Dittisham had been the home of our childhood, the place in which I had spent many untroubled years, the house in which our parents had lived all their married lives. Until our mother's death twenty years ago, it had stood at the very core of the family. Yet while the child in me hated to think of other people living there, the realist knew that, with Pa dead too, it had to go.

'When do these people want it?' I asked.

'In a month.'

'You'll let me know, will you? I'll need to clear some stuff out.'

'You can't clear it out now?'

'No chance.' Reminded as always of the time, I reached for my briefcase and jumped to my feet.

'Hugh—'

There was something about his tone, a warning note, which made me pause. He came round the desk and, half sitting on it, folded his arms. 'The thing is . . .' he said with a sigh of annoyance, 'the police have been asking about Sylvie.'

A small pull in my chest somewhere. 'Asking?'

'They came to see me yesterday.'

'You? Why you?'

35

David frowned as if I were being particularly dense. 'Because she was my patient.'

I must have let some of the surprise show in my face because he said, 'Didn't you realise?'

I gave a shrug. 'No . . . Well, I simply never thought about it. You didn't say . . .'

'Anyway, the point is' – and he hesitated as if he would rather have avoided the whole subject – 'they seem to think that Sylvie was on the boat a few weeks ago.'

I didn't need to ask which boat he meant. During the summer David and I had been keeping an eye on Pa's cruiser *Ellie Miller* while we decided what to do with her.

I made a show of puzzlement. I asked evenly, 'Why do they think that?'

'They didn't say. Listen, it's none of my business, but . . . Well, be careful of those cretins, won't you?'

'Careful?' But we both knew what he meant.

'If Sylvie was seen on the boat with you, they might make too much out of it. Assume you were, you know –' he flapped an impatient hand – 'together.'

'Did they say that?' I blurted.

'No, *no*. But you know how their minds work. One-track. In *my* experience, anyway.'

I had been so desperate to talk to someone about Sylvie for such a long time that I almost told him then. I wanted to explain the extraordinary hold she had always exercised over my imagination, and in telling him perhaps to explain it better to myself. I think I wanted to hear him say that he understood, that it could have been the same for him. Yet something held me back: an instinct for secrecy, a fear of being misunderstood, a doubt as to how he would receive such confidences. David had never been one for letting his feelings get the better of him; as far as I knew he had never lost his head over anything, far less a woman.

I said abruptly, 'They've already been in touch, actually.'

'The police? You've seen them?'

'Soon. In half an hour, in fact.'

'Oh!' He looked at his watch, reached back over his desk for his diary and flicked a page over. 'If you want me to come along, I *might* be able to swing it.'

'I don't think that'll be necessary.' But the fact that he'd suggested it planted a small seed of anxiety in my heart.

'Sure?'

'Sure.'

'All right,' he conceded immediately. 'But don't forget, Hugh – they have small brains. Strictly one-track.'

Two

THE DETECTIVE settled himself in his seat. 'Sorry to have kept you, sir.'

'I am rather pressed for time,' I remarked. 'Is this likely to take long?'

His look suggested that police business did not hurry for anyone, especially people who liked to think they had more important things to do.

Taking the cap off his pen, he began to write laboriously on a pro forma pad.

'E . . . S . . .' I said, reading my name upside down. 'After *Well*, it's E . . . S . . .'

'Ah . . .' He amended it to *Wellesley*. 'And your address?'

I gave it to him, complete with post code.

'That's central London, is it, sir?'

'Yes. Chelsea.'

'Now . . .' He fixed me with a bland stare. 'You were acquainted with Sylvie Mathieson, were you, Mr Wellesley?'

'Yes.'

'And did you know Sylvie well?' His use of her first name threw me a little, it made our conversation sound like some casual discussion about an old friend. But then the whole interview had an unexpectedly informal air, with the comfortable chairs, the open door, the chatter floating in from the passage and the way the interview had been allocated to neither Henderson nor Jones, but to this Detective Constable Reith, who, with his smooth unshadowed chin and clear complexion, looked far too young to be doing this or any other job.

'At one time I knew her well,' I said. 'We met – oh, fifteen or sixteen years ago. But I didn't see her for a long time after that, not until this summer in fact.'

'This summer. And did you see her often?'

I inhaled abruptly. 'No. She came to the boat once. No – twice.'

'The boat?'

'My father's cruising yacht. My father died recently. I was keeping an eye on the boat. Pumping it out, that sort of thing. She swam by one day.'

He blinked. 'Swam by?'

'Yes, swam up to the boat. We started talking. She came aboard for tea.' Tea: how quaint that sounded, redolent of afternoon and sunlight and respectability.

'Where did this happen?'

'At Dittisham. The boat's moored in front of my father's house.'

'And when was this?'

'It must have been—' I frowned with the effort of memory. 'June? Some time then.'

'And the other time Sylvie came to the boat, did she swim over on that occasion as well?' He was intrigued by the swimming, as if this marked Sylvie out as some kind of oddity.

'No, she was rowing a small dinghy. She was on her way to another boat.'

'And which boat was that?'

'Oh, I don't know its name. But it's an old-fashioned boat, thirty-five feet or so, a white cutter with a bowsprit. Moored a little further down river, past the ferry.'

'You saw her go to it, did you?'

'Well – I knew she was on her way to a boat. I assumed it was that one. I'd seen her on it before.'

'You'd seen Sylvie on it before?' he repeated stolidly.

'Yes.'

'And when was that?'

'She was with a group of people, they were going off somewhere. It must have been around... the beginning of July? Yes – the beginning of July.'

'Did you recognise the people she was with?'

'No.'

'You could point the boat out to us, though?'

'I *could* ...' I made no effort to conceal my reluctance. 'But I'd rather not. I don't come down here very often. I'm just on my way back to London now. It would be rather inconvenient. I'm extremely busy at the moment.'

'I mean – if necessary.'

'If necessary,' I conceded, trying not to sound openly uncooperative. 'But I'm sure the harbour master will be able to tell you straight away. There can't be many cutters with bowsprits moored the other side of the ferry.'

Reith nodded in an unfocused way. 'So, er ... apart

from these two visits, did you see Sylvie on any other occasions?'

'I saw her by the river once. We chatted for a minute.'

'And that was all? You saw her just the three times?'

'To talk to, yes.' And saying this I felt a sudden heat, a prickle of sweat against my shirt, and thought what a poor liar I would make if I had to do it on a grand scale.

'Did you know who she mixed with? Who her friends were?'

'No,' I said a little too hastily. Then, more matter-of-factly: 'The only time I saw her with anyone was when she was on the boat with that group. And once I saw her walking with someone. Well, I *think* it was Sylvie. She was a long way off.' How these tiny untruths seemed to slip effortlessly off my tongue. Yet I could hardly admit that I had watched her covertly through binoculars, like some pathetic Peeping Tom.

'It was a man she was with?'

'It looked like it, yes. Though he had long hair. Noticeably long, onto his shoulders or even longer.'

'And she didn't mention the names of any friends when she was in conversation with you?'

'No.'

Reith shuffled a piece of paper. 'Now, Mr Wellesley, where were you between noon on Saturday last, the thirtieth of September, and noon on Sunday, the following day?'

I thought I had maintained my expression but

41

perhaps he caught a hint of alarm in my eyes because he added coolly, 'A standard question, Mr Wellesley.'

As I met his unwavering gaze he suddenly didn't seem so young any more. 'Of course . . .' I cleared my throat. 'On Saturday I worked in my office in Hammersmith until mid-afternoon. I left at . . . it must have been about three. Then I drove straight down to Dittisham. I arrived at dusk – so, about seven-thirty, I suppose. I opened up the house—'

'What house are we talking about, sir?' He was making detailed notes now.

'My late father's house – Dittisham House. And then . . . I drove into Dartmouth to buy some food—'

A pause while he got it down. 'So, what time would that have been?'

I really had to get this right. 'Oh . . . eight-fifteen? Maybe a little after. Yes, about eight-thirty.'

'And where did you shop, sir?'

'Well, I went to the Co-op first, but it was closed, so I went to the Spar shop by the church. It was the only place I could find. That was open, I mean.'

'Which church is that, sir?'

'Which church?' I repeated, momentarily confounded by the pedantry of the question. 'I've no idea what it's called, if that's what you mean. But the one right down in the town, near the quay.'

I wondered if he was writing so slowly out of an overdeveloped sense of clerical diligence, or a perverse wish to delay me even longer. 'Then?' he asked at last.

'I went back to the house. My wife arrived shortly afterwards.'

42

'Your wife? And her name is—?'

'Virginia Wellesley.'

'Mrs Virginia Wellesley.' I watched him record it in block capitals. 'And she is of the same address?'

'I'm sorry?'

'London. She lives with you at—' He peered at his notes. 'Glebe Place?'

'Yes.'

The conversation had taken on a fantastic quality, both predictable and bizarre. The leisurely nature of the proceedings, the meandering questions, seemed grotesquely inappropriate to the terrible event that had brought us here.

'So at what time did you get back to the house and see your wife?'

I went through the motions of dredging my memory again. 'Well – nine or so.'

'And then?'

'We had some supper and went to bed.'

'And the next day?'

'Oh, wait a minute, I forgot . . . That evening my brother called in briefly, at about ten.'

'Your brother being?'

'David Wellesley. Dr Wellesley. He practises in Dartmouth.'

Reith held his pen awkwardly, knuckles bent like a child, and the nib laboured ever more slowly across the page. 'And the next day?'

'Help . . .' I rubbed my forehead. 'We must have got up at about eight and then we worked on the house and the boat. Clearing out cupboards and attics, that sort of thing.' Yet again I waited for his pen to catch up. 'Then in the evening we went back to London.'

'What time would that be, sir?'

'When we left? Oh – nine. Just after.'

He read laboriously through what he had written, then looked up and smiled his bleak professional smile. 'Thank you, sir.'

Even then I wasn't sure he had finished until he closed his notebook and got to his feet. I rose and shook his hand. 'I hope you find whoever did it,' I said. 'She was . . .' What was I trying to say? Why had I even started? '. . . a lovely person.'

'Was she, sir?' And his eyes slid away knowingly.

I drove fast again, often touching a hundred, sometimes exceeding it, stopping only to buy petrol and a mineral water. Julia called me on the car phone and gave me the messages in her cool staccato. The Chartered Bank had brought forward our next meeting to the following day at eleven-thirty, which I took as a wholly encouraging sign, but my satisfaction evaporated with the next message. Graham Moncrieff, the leader of our legal team, had called to say that he'd hit a problem with the Cumberland lawyers. It seemed Cumberland were backing out of their agreement to lease us the Hartford properties, and were suddenly insisting we buy the factory and warehousing outright.

For the second time that day I almost had an accident, straying out of my lane to earn a prolonged blast from a Range Rover.

Containing my anger and disbelief only with difficulty, slowing down to a sedate sixty, I told Julia to fix a meeting with Howard for some time the next day.

'You don't have any slots left.'

'Breakfast. Evening. Midnight, if necessary. But some time tomorrow, Julia.'

I asked her to save the rest of the messages and rang off. I needed time to calm down; I needed time to absorb the full implications of Cumberland's about-turn. If they forced this issue, if they made us purchase the factory, we would have to raise more money, another million at the very least. Just when we'd presented our final figures to the banks; just when we had the last of the money almost within our grasp. Cumberland weren't just moving the goalposts, they were taking them away altogether. Finding another million would be hard: we had tapped every source, we had called in every debt, we had milked every contact.

If this manoeuvre was designed to defeat us then it registered high on the scale of dirty tricks. But was it a manoeuvre? Did Cumberland want us to lose, or did they simply want to squeeze more cash out of us? Howard would know. Though whether he would be prepared to tell me was another matter.

This was the aspect of business I had always disliked and tried my best to avoid, the backbiting and chicanery, the breaking of trust, the pressing of every last advantage until your opponent bled. Howard regarded my scruples as a quaint but fatal flaw. He thought I was soft, and he was probably right. But I quite liked the idea of leaving the dignity of my opponents intact; if it was a flaw to dislike making enemies, then I possessed it in good measure.

I was going to be late. I almost called Julia to ask her to let Ginny know, but in recent weeks such second-hand messages had resulted in ruffled feelings. Ginny had accused me of finding excuses to avoid calling her. Realising that there was a small but undeniable grain of truth in this, feeling ashamed of it, I determined to call her myself.

'I've been held up,' I said as soon as she answered. I could hear voices in the background.

'Will you be very late?'

'Seven, I hope. Seven-thirty at the latest. If you don't mind me unwashed.'

'I don't mind if you don't.'

She sounded so subdued that I asked, 'Are you all right?'

'Feeling a bit rough. A touch of flu, I think.'

One of the voices in the background was male, a caterer or maintenance man. In the old days we would have joked about Ginny having a secret lover, but we didn't joke about that sort of thing any more.

I said, 'I'm sorry not to be there to help.'

'I'll manage.'

'You're sure you don't need a doctor?'

'No, no. I'll just go to bed as soon as everyone's gone.'

It was a quarter to eight by the time I finally turned into Glebe Place. The party was larger than I'd imagined. After a long hunt for a parking place – the garage was blocked, the adjacent streets tightly packed – I followed some guests into the house to find a wall of backs in every doorway and people spilling out of the drawing room into the conservatory.

A woman loomed up. 'Hello, Hugh! What a super party! You always give such super parties!'

Mouthing greetings, wearing my best smile, I moved through the room in search of Ginny. I finally spotted her by the fireplace, her back to me. She had done her hair a new way, or perhaps it was an old way that I'd forgotten, pulled severely back and held at her neck in a thick band, though this did nothing to diminish the brilliance of her hair, which was auburn and exceptionally glossy. She was wearing a plain black dress and when she turned I noticed that, apart from pearl earrings, she wore no jewellery. This didn't prevent her from looking exquisite; nothing could ever do that. She had a heart-shaped face with high cheekbones, a fine nose, and winged eyebrows that gave her an elfin quality.

She was smiling at someone. It was a smile I recognised, brittle and nervous.

'I'm here,' I announced unnecessarily. 'Everything okay?'

'The caterers got the food wrong.'

'Is it serious?'

'It's all doughy stuff. And spiced chicken. They forgot the smoked salmon parcels and the roulades!' She exhaled with a tiny shudder. 'Well, it's too late now, I suppose.' Her eyes, bright with illness or anxiety or both, darted constantly around the room. For a moment we stood silently amid the cacophonous swell, two castaways in a storm of our own making, then Ginny drifted away and I found myself talking to a City man about interest rates.

Slowly I succumbed to the rhythm of the party: enquiring after health and business, deflecting questions, spinning thin jokes, talking but not listening too well. The champagne made me tired and slow-witted, and I soon abandoned it for mineral water. Later someone made a speech about the premature baby unit and the need for funds and we all applauded.

A voice sighed at my elbow. 'Hello, you.' It was Caroline Adam, a friend of Ginny's and something high-powered in PR. She had wide red lips and tousled silvery blonde hair and was tall enough to look me straight in the eye. 'The man of the moment,' she declared.

'I am?'

'I call you two the golden couple. So beautiful, so clever, so – *everything*.'

I couldn't begin to respond to that, and didn't try.

'How are you in fact?' There was a slyness in her manner.

'Fine,' I said.

'And Ginny? She's looking a bit pale. I noticed straight away.'

'She thinks she might have flu.'

'Ah,' Caroline breathed, her heavy-lashed eyes fixed on mine. 'But you guys are okay?' Her smile did nothing to take the edge off the question.

A sickening thought struck me: that Ginny had confided in this woman, had spilled out the most painful details of our unhappiness. And fast on this thought came the idea that Ginny had talked about my visits to Dittisham, had even – a sinking thought – read something suspicious into them.

'Couldn't be better,' I said with terrible joviality.

Caroline searched my face, and I had the feeling that little escaped her voracious eyes. 'Glad to hear it,' she said at last. 'So many people falling by the wayside. Owing their last bootlace to Lloyd's. Jobless at fifty. Reduced to selling herbal remedies from their dining rooms. No wonder marriages creak under the strain. And we're all meant to be more caring!'

Had Ginny suspected something all this time? Had she thought I was having an affair? As the idea took hold, my spirits shrank at the prospect of the confrontations ahead.

'Though when it comes to caring,' Caroline was saying with a provocative smile, 'I think you poor beleaguered men have had a raw deal. I think us beastly women have pushed you too far, and you all need spoiling and cosseting again, just like in the bad old days.' She gave me a look that wasn't entirely frivolous.

The noise seemed to rise up around me, the drink sang in my brain, I had reached some limit that I barely recognised. With an indeterminate salute, I moved rapidly away and escaped into the garden. I knew I shouldn't let the Carolines of this world get to me. Mischief-making was a compulsion with her and if it hadn't been such a very long day I would have remembered that sooner. I would also have remembered that, whatever else Ginny had reproached me for, she had never hinted at infidelity.

Besides, our unhappiness had set in long before the summer, at some point in the long years since love had given way to bewilderment.

Standing there in the sulphurous darkness of the London night, the party a distant murmur, I tried to picture a time when things might be different, when the business would be back on its feet, when Ginny and I would be happy again, when in some miraculous way I would be free of worry and guilt. But the idea wouldn't form, it seemed too remote, and, taking a last breath of damp leafy air, I trudged back towards the house.

A few guests lingered remorselessly until nine-thirty, and we didn't close the door on the caterers until after ten.

'You go to bed,' I told Ginny. 'I'll finish down here.'

'I'm all right.' She sat on the edge of a chair by the fireplace. 'I don't think it's flu after all.'

'Are you sure?'

She gave a faint nod, her eyes doggedly on mine, and I realised she wanted to talk.

I poured myself a brandy, almost certainly the last thing I needed, and sat in the chair opposite. 'Well, that seemed to go all right, didn't it?' I said with forced brightness. 'I don't think anyone noticed the food.'

She sat like a governess, her arms held into her sides, her shoulders braced, austere and unyielding. 'How was your day?' she asked.

'Oh, you know . . .'

'No, I don't. Tell me.' And she fixed me with a look of strange intensity.

'Well . . . I told the Hartford staff what was happening. I saw David and Mary for lunch.'

'And what was it you told the staff?' she persisted solemnly.

'Oh, I gave them the latest news in all its glory!'

'Please, Hugh – I'd like to know.'

If I looked surprised it was because Ginny had never shown much interest in the details of the business. 'Sorry,' I said penitently. 'What did I tell them? Well . . . I made Cumberland sound pretty ogre-ish. I said they'd sell Hartford to the highest bidder, and, if it didn't happen to be us, then the staff faced almost certain redundancy. I said the future under a buyout would be pretty tough. But I think I made the bad times with us sound marginally more attractive than being out of work.'

She was listening intently, a small frown on her forehead, so I went on, explaining some of the risks involved in making our bid, and the hard work that lay ahead.

'But you believe in the buyout?' she said. 'It's what you want?'

'What I want?' I gave a shaky laugh. 'I think so! When I last did any rational thinking anyway.'

'There you go again,' she said, her voice rising.

'Where again?'

'Not answering me properly.'

'I'm sorry.' I heard the note of injury in my voice and suppressed it. 'Yes, it's what I want.' Articulating this gave my feelings new force. 'Yes. *Yes*. I can't just let it be written off. Not when it's got so much going for it. Oh, I know what you all think,' I said as if she represented the rest of my family. 'You think it's just the *tradition* or something, that I'm incapable of letting go. But it's not just that. It's the people at Hartford, and the place . . . I love it! I love everything to do with it!'

Ginny said gravely, 'So long as it's what you want.'

'Okay, and I want to be the person running it!' I conceded, as if this had been in dispute. 'I want to run it because I think I can do a better job than anyone else. With the right team beside me – and without crazy delusions of grandeur!' Just thinking about Howard stirred me to anger once more, and it was a moment before I took in what Ginny was saying.

' . . . I phoned the estate agent, threatened to take the house elsewhere unless they drummed up more interest in Melton. The man suggested some ads in the glossy magazines – which *we* pay for, of course. I agreed, but I told him he was on trial, that we'd give him six weeks at the most. Then . . .' Some thought distracted her, she blinked rapidly. 'Then . . . I asked the Murrays which agent they used for their place in France. Those local people are sharks, you know.'

Her calm acceptance caused me a flutter of remorse. 'I'm sorry it's come to this.'

She dismissed this with a slight lift of her shoulders. 'Too many houses anyway.'

'But you loved Melton.' And she had loved the house in Provence too. Her great passion was for decorating, her great talent for putting furniture and objects and colours together in fabulous combinations. She had made the houses into showcases, and their loss would be far more painful for her than for me. But at least we were talking about it. There had been a time when Ginny seemed to think that I wanted to sell the houses for some capricious reason of my own, out of perversity, or even, in her blacker moments, because I wanted to undermine her in some way. For a while I had hardly dared to ask how the agents were getting on.

I ventured another risky subject, the matter of the costly couple who ran Melton. 'The Kemps, have we managed to . . .?'

'Yes, yes. They left a week ago. I told you.'

'You did? Sorry.' Another apology, another small descent.

'Mrs Hoskins has agreed to go in three times a week.'

'Well done.'

'Will we have to sell this place as well?' she asked in a voice that was deliberately calm.

'No, of course not!' I made a poor stab at humour. 'No, I thought we'd go mad and keep at least one roof over our heads! The doorways along the Strand are a bit draughty. And you don't meet the same class of dosser, so they tell me . . . Old Etonians, Lloyd's bankrupts—'

'Please don't!' she exclaimed suddenly, and the tension stretched out between us. 'I do wish you'd just – *tell* me things! Sometimes you treat me like an idiot!'

'I *am* telling you,' I responded mildly. 'And I've never treated you like—'

'But if you're going to be at Hartford all the time, we can't live up here, can we?'

'In time we could certainly think about moving nearer, yes.'

She exhaled sharply with exasperation. 'Of course we'll have to. It's the only thing to do.'

I wasn't sure what to make of this Ginny, vibrating with the usual tensions, yet unexpectedly and miraculously focused.

'But we don't have to live at Dittisham, do we?' she demanded.

'No.'

'But you *were* thinking about it.'

It had been the briefest of suggestions, made soon after my father died, when I was still in a state of disbelief. The thought of losing both my father and the house where I had grown up had seemed too much to bear, and for a few weeks I'd nursed emotional ideas of restoring the place and using it for summer weekends. My imagination had cast a golden wash of nostalgia over the prospect; I had seen children in the garden again, and barbecues on the terrace, and Easter treasure hunts, and expeditions on the river. 'It was just a thought. But no, it's being sold. There was an offer today.'

'Ah.' And the relief showed in her face.

We both looked away into the unlit fire. The fake logs were so cleverly finished with ash and scorch marks that they were indistinguishable from the real thing; Ginny had seen them in America and ordered them specially. I felt her glance back at me, gathering herself to speak again.

'That girl – the one they found in the river – did you hear anything?'

I kept myself steady, I showed nothing in my face. I brought my eyes back to hers. 'Oh, David mentioned something. She was stabbed, apparently. Then dumped in the water.'

'They haven't got any idea who did it?'

'I don't think so.'

A pause. 'You might have told me, you know.'

'Told you what?'

'That it was *her*.' And Ginny's voice was charged with an emotion I couldn't read.

I didn't say anything.

'That she was the one you were in love with.'

I took a slow breath. 'It was a long time ago, Ginny.'

'But it *was* her?' And her voice trembled slightly.

'Yes.'

'The one you wanted to marry, but couldn't.'

'Who said that?'

She dropped her eyes briefly, as if caught in some subterfuge. 'Mary.'

'Well, I wouldn't believe everything Mary tells you,' I retorted, wondering what else Mary had said. Then, to soften my words: 'Honestly, darling . . .'

'I don't mind, it's not that,' she said, her voice high. 'I just wish you'd told me.'

'Really, it wasn't anything . . .'

'You did want to marry her though?'

There was a relentlessness in Ginny, an inability to let go, that reverberated through our arguments like the beat of a discordant drum. Hearing it now in her voice, knowing what was to come, I said hotly, 'It never got to that stage. There was never any

55

question . . .' She was waiting for me to elaborate. 'Sylvie was very young,' I explained unhappily. 'Only sixteen.'

Something in the way Ginny took this, the suggestion of a nod, made me think that she already knew, that Mary must have told her, and, fired by the drink and the endless day, I felt a surge of resentment against this exchange of notes.

Ginny took a moment to frame her next question. 'You saw her this summer?' And the coolness of her voice did nothing to disguise its tautness.

'Once or twice.'

'And she was' – the hesitation again, the careful choice of words – 'living in Dittisham?'

'I don't know. I didn't ask.'

'Mary said she was running a shop. Pottery or handicrafts . . .'

'Well, Mary would be the one to know.' I threw the last of the brandy down my throat and got up.

'Mary thought—'

I twisted away to hide my exasperation and despair. I was so exhausted, I had survived so much today, that I longed to shout out, to beg her to leave it alone and give me some peace.

'She thought the police would want to question everyone who was near the river on the weekend.'

Constrained by habit, or possibly futility, I made myself turn back and say, 'Yes, I expect she's right.'

'So they might want to question us?'

I gestured the possibility.

'And you? Because you used to know her?'

'Yes. Well, in fact—' I would have given anything

not to talk about it just then, but one bad moment was probably as good as another. 'They already have. Today.' And I thought: now we start the argument in earnest. Because I have failed to tell her immediately. Because she'll think I have something to hide.

But she was very still, her eyes fastened on my face. 'And?'

'Oh, it was just what you'd expect. They asked if I knew Sylvie. If I'd seen her this summer. It didn't take long. Mainly because I didn't have much to tell them.'

A progression of thoughts flickered over Ginny's face like shadows across a screen. 'There we are, then,' she exhaled finally.

It was a moment before I realised that there was to be no row after all, that she was going to leave the subject alone. With the relief came an extraordinary fatigue, like a coat of lead.

'I must get to bed.'

'Yes,' she declared. 'You've had it! So've I!' She swung away and walked towards the stairs without looking back.

Yet I didn't sleep immediately. And nor did Ginny. We lay on either side of the bed, facing away from each other, and I thought that this must be the lone-liest feeling in the world, to lie beside each other yet find ourselves unable to reach out, to have things to say yet find it impossible to speak. Also – and the thought travelled painfully out of the past – to remember how different it had been at the beginning, the closeness – and yes, the love – that we had once felt for each other, and to realise that, for some reason that neither of us understood, those times seemed to have slipped for ever beyond our grasp.

Later something made me wake. The wind, the distant pattering of rain. And close by, the sound of Ginny's breathing, coming in uneven jerks. A tiny gasp, then another. I rolled over and put my hand on her shoulder. She stiffened and held her breath. I moved to touch her cheek beneath the mask, to feel the tears I knew I would find there, but she pushed my hand away and said in a harsh voice, 'What is it? What's the matter?'

I had no answer, and in the end it was easier to say 'Nothing' and turn away.

It was just before seven-thirty as I pressed the security code into the keypad at the entrance of the HartWell offices in Slough. The panel shrieked at me and for a moment I thought Cumberland must have had the code changed, but I must have had the code wrong first time because at my second attempt the door buzzed its acceptance. I noticed that the heavy inner doors of solid glass emblazoned with the HartWell logo had not yet been replaced. That logo. Howard and I had argued about every detail of it – the style, the size, the colour, you name it. In those days we had thrived on argument, it had been the lifeblood of our partnership, a stimulus for problem solving and fresh ideas, a constant source of hilarity, and the only way we knew to keep our minds sharp in the face of our terrifying success. Well, success that had been terrifying for me anyway; Howard took it as his due.

In the early days of our expansion into mass-market glass and china we had measured success in terms of turnover and profit margins. But profit margins don't protect you from recession or cut-throat tactics by your competitors. And for Hartford, heavily dependent on exports, margins don't defend you against the dollar taking a nosedive from which it never recovers.

I looked into my old office. The large Hartford crystal vase dating from the fifties stood in its usual place on the side table, now bereft of flowers. The aerial photograph of the Hartford factory still hung on the wall next to the dusty outlines of the two pictures I had removed to my temporary office in Hammersmith: a photograph of my father greeting a young Prince of Wales at Hartford during a visit in the seventies; and a picture of me as a self-conscious eighteen-year-old, trying to blow crystal.

No amount of framed pictures or crystal vases could ever have made me feel comfortable in this hermetically sealed glasshouse. Slough may have been equidistant from Hartford and our factories to the north, and convenient for Heathrow, but for me, imbued with the hands-on philosophy of my father, the place was a bureaucratic no-man's land that had left me feeling dangerously out of touch.

I waited in Howard's outer office. One thing I had learnt to rely on in my years with Howard was that he would always be late for our meetings, and, knowing full well that today would be no exception, I determined to remain calm.

It was ten to eight when Howard made one of the

silent entrances at which he was so proficient. I looked up and there he was, filling the doorway. He was wearing a dark suit, expensively cut to disguise the weight which had settled evenly, and, despite his much-vaunted gym expeditions, it seemed permanently, over his broad frame. Crossing the room, he slid a hand elegantly down one lapel and unbuttoned his jacket with a flick of his thumb.

'Is it just us?' he asked in feigned surprise.

'Who else was there meant to be?'

'I thought – lawyers, accountants. No?' He affected this ironic air when he wanted to intimidate me.

'Don't talk rubbish.'

He attempted an ingenuous look, something he had never quite managed to master, and I noticed that his grey eyes were looking puffy, and his hair, normally immaculate, was unkempt around the collar, while his cheeks were beginning to develop an unhealthy mottled look. But then if my social life was full, Howard's was frenetic. Since his divorce four years before, he frequently featured in the glossy magazines that Ginny liked to read, pictured with a string of society women. When I had last chosen to listen, someone had told me that he was keen to marry the twice-divorced daughter of a landed duke.

He unlocked his office and led the way to his desk.

'This isn't to do with the buyout then?' he drawled, sinking into his high-backed leather chair.

'Of course it is!' I said tightly, avoiding the strategically low-seated guest chair opposite his desk and fetching a higher one from the conference area.

'And you really don't feel you want anyone else here?'

Recognising this as a no-win question, I ignored it and demanded, 'What's this problem about the leasing agreement for the Hartford properties?'

But he was still playing games. 'I need coffee,' he announced languidly, casting around as if this might cause a cup to appear out of nowhere.

I growled, 'Forget the coffee. I've only got fifteen minutes.'

Suddenly he laughed, a rich chuckle that rumbled on after he had stopped smiling. 'Hugh,' he scolded. 'Always in such a rush.'

'Too damned right!'

He regarded me with something approaching affection, though it could just as easily have been pity, and then, this show of indulgence having served its purpose, which was to wind me up, he got down to business.

'Is there a problem?' he murmured.

'You know damn well there is. It was agreed that we could *lease* all the properties from Cumberland. There was never any talk of buying!'

'Oh?' He affected puzzlement. 'Wasn't there? Are you sure you aren't thinking of the earlier discussions? At the first merger talks perhaps?'

I was never sure why Howard liked to call the takeover a merger. Because he had instigated the deal perhaps. Or because it boosted his view of his own standing on the main board. 'You know perfectly well which discussions I'm talking about, Howard,' I said, determined not to give him the satisfaction of seeing

61

me lose my temper. 'When the outline buyout terms were agreed. In August.'

Howard grimaced elegantly. 'I don't think anything was actually *decided*, Hugh.' He made a show of testing this recollection against his memory. 'No,' he murmured, 'I'm sure I'm right in saying Cumberland didn't commit itself to a leasing arrangement.'

'It was agreed in principle, Howard!'

'It was just one *option*, Hugh.'

'More than an option, Howard! A commitment!'

His face took on an expression of forbearance wearing thin. 'Whatever your recollection, Hugh, the situation is that Cumberland cannot possibly agree to a leasing agreement. In a buyout you expect the customer to *buy*. Cumberland doesn't want the Hartford properties left on its books. It wants to dispose of them. *Not* unreasonable in the circumstances.'

'Unreasonable if you've made a commitment.'

'Hugh – a commitment is something in writing, something agreed by one's lawyers.'

'For Cumberland, maybe.'

'Come – for anyone, surely.'

'So do I take it the matter's no longer open to negotiation?' I said stiffly.

'On the price?' he asked, deliberately choosing to misunderstand.

'On the option to lease!'

He sighed with a sort of paternal irritation. 'I thought I'd made it clear, Hugh. Didn't I make it clear?' He spread his hands questioningly. 'Leasing is not an option.'

Despite my intention to remain calm, I heard my

resentment break through. 'Cumberland are reneging, then? I just want to be quite clear.'

'Hugh, I strongly object to that. There's no question of reneging. How can there be when we never agreed anything?'

'You realise this could sabotage the entire buyout?'

'Oh?' He was suddenly a picture of imitation concern. 'Well, I'm very sorry to hear that, I really am. I know how hard you've been working on it.'

'Come on, don't tell me you didn't realise!' I said bitterly.

'Realise?' The shrug was hopelessly exaggerated. Such a bloody bad actor. But then overplaying the scene was all part of the satisfaction for him. 'How could I realise, Hugh?'

I shook my head, not trusting myself to speak.

'Surely the additional cash won't be that hard to find?'

He was fishing, he wanted to know just how far we had got with the banks, but I was damned if I was going to give him that sort of information. 'It's not the money, Howard, it's the timing, as you well know! The Cumberland board have had the outline agreement for six weeks – *six weeks* – and they suddenly decide on this *now*. That's as close to sabotage as you can get!'

'Well, I'm sorry but Cumberland can hardly be blamed if you've rushed things at *your* end, Hugh. The proposal had to be evaluated very carefully. You couldn't expect us to do it overnight. I'm sorry if you're going to have to go back and renegotiate with the banks, but that's hardly our problem, is it?'

Looking at him, a suspicion formed in my mind. It came to me that Howard himself had engineered this whole situation, that, for some reasons of his own, he wanted my bid to fail.

I stood up. I fully intended to leave with my pride intact, but my anger got the better of me. 'Sleeping all right, are you, Howard?'

'Oh, come on, Hugh,' he said with the injured air of someone fending off an unprovoked attack. 'That's always been your trouble, you know – taking things personally.'

'With you, I don't know any other way to take them.'

'Business is business, Hugh. You've never been able to grasp that, have you?'

The morning tailback began just beyond Heathrow. As I joined the haze of shuffling traffic, I thought back over the years of my partnership with Howard. Though I'd never harboured too many illusions about him, while I'd seen him instigate some pretty ruthless manoeuvres in his time, I'd always liked to think there were certain limits beyond which he wouldn't go, that the sixty years during which our two families had jointly owned and run HartWell counted for something – a remnant of loyalty, perhaps, a fragment of sympathy – and that he would draw the line at actively plotting against me.

I liked to think such fine noble thoughts because if I didn't I began to contemplate walking away from the whole miserable business and going to live a hermit's life in France. I'd had such thoughts before, in early summer when the full extent of the crisis at HartWell was becoming clear, when I realised that Howard had engineered the takeover behind my back, when I began to appreciate just how completely I had let the real control slip from my grasp. Then I was dogged by a sense of worthlessness and futility: my mid-life crisis. An absurdly frivolous term for the doubt that had taken to descending on me without warning, turning my thinking inside out, making me question things that at my age did not bear questioning. Despairing of the present, clutching at the past, harbouring visions of what might have been. Hungry for escape and solace; ripe for the idea of Sylvie.

Fumbling with the radio, I turned on the eight-thirty headlines, knowing that there would be nothing about Sylvie, yet needing to hear it for myself. An exercise in reassurance. Or paranoia.

The traffic did not ease and I reached the three-room office suite in Hammersmith five minutes before Julia and I were due to leave for the meeting with the Chartered Bank. I had rented this place as a temporary London base while we negotiated the buyout. It wasn't so much an office as a space from which I made calls and sent letters. All the meetings – and there were up to three a day – took place at the City offices of the various bankers, lawyers and accountants acting for us or for Cumberland. Very occasionally meetings were held at Hartford itself, four hours' drive to the south-west.

Before Julia could collar me, I phoned Moncrieff to check what I already knew, that we had no legal remedy against Cumberland for reneging on the leasing agreement. I followed this with a swift call to Pollinger at Zircon to alert him to the fact that we would be asking for more money. He warned me that unless I was prepared to give Zircon a bigger slice of the equity then the most I could expect from them would be a quarter of the extra million.

Julia put her head round the door. 'I know I shouldn't, but I couldn't help overhearing. That bastard!' I didn't need to ask who she was referring to. So far as Julia was concerned, Howard had rat status.

'It would have been a board decision, Julia.'

'Yes, but who proposed the idea?'

'No point in worrying about that now.'

'That's what you always say.' Instantly she made a disclaiming wave of the hand. 'Sorry. *Sorry*. What I meant was, *I* wouldn't be half as forgiving. You're too nice, that's your trouble.'

'It's nothing to do with being *nice*,' I grimaced, smarting at the compliment. 'It's a question of being realistic.'

Julia conceded this with a dubious face, and looked at her watch. 'We've got to go.'

'One more call,' I bargained.

My bank manager was a bland insubstantial character named Elliott. With the various personal loans I had been forced to negotiate, I had got to see quite a lot of him over the last two years. He did not sound surprised that I was asking for money again.

'This mortgage would be additional to your existing building society mortgage?'

'That's right.'

'Five hundred thousand is rather a large sum for a mortgage, Mr Wellesley. That sort of sum would usually come into the range of a business loan, subject to business rates.'

'But you'll consider it?'

'This would be in addition to the loan on the country property?'

'That's right.'

A pause. 'So on the Chelsea house, the new mortgage would take the loan up to ninety per cent of its value?'

'That would be on a conservative valuation. But – yes.'

'Well – I'll look into it,' he said cautiously. 'But, Mr Wellesley, are you quite sure you want to put your home at stake?'

'Yes.'

'You have considered what would happen if your business were to fail?'

'Yes,' I said testily.

'And your wife – she's happy with the arrangement?'

'I realise she'll have to agree to it,' I said. 'I'm aware of the law.'

'Very well. I'll come back to you as soon as I can.'

Julia appeared in the doorway wearing her we-really-have-to-leave face, but I held up a delaying hand and, when she had frowned her disapproval and disappeared, I called Ginny, only to get the answering machine. I told the tape I should be home by eight. It was only after I'd rung off that it occurred to me that Ginny might have flu after all and be lying ill in bed. She was prone to catch all the nastier bugs and to suffer them badly. Convalescence, with its inactivity, always depressed her, and it was then that I became acutely aware of how isolated she was without children. During the five or so years when we had actively discussed our childlessness and gone through various fertility investigations I had once or twice mentioned adoption, but she had brimmed with dark resentment at the idea, as though it were an admission of defeat or an allotment of blame, and I hadn't brought up the subject again. Now we never talked about children at all.

Julia came in briskly. 'We really have to go.' She tipped her head to one side and cast me a sharp glance. 'Are you okay?'

'Don't you start.'

'You look awful again.'

'What do you mean *again*?' I grabbed my briefcase and sprang to my feet. 'You're as bad as my old nanny. I'm fine.'

But I can't have sounded too convincing because as we headed for the door she demanded, 'When did you last eat?' Interpreting my silence correctly, she announced that she would get some sandwiches on the way.

Hurrying down the stairs I tried to concentrate on the crucial meeting ahead. I dreaded pitching to bankers, it was like reasoning with wet dough. They were malleable enough, you felt things were shaping up, but at the end of the day you were never quite sure what you had ended up with.

We emerged fast into the lobby. Through the doors

I could see Tony, the driver Julia regularly hired to take us into the City, standing at the bottom of the steps beside his Rover. Two men crossed in front of the Rover and came up the steps towards the entrance. I swung the door back for Julia just as the first of the visitors pushed through the opposite door. I registered a crumpled raincoat, sparse greying hair, a thin mouth in a fleshy face. The second man was younger, taller and fitter. I wasn't sure what it was about them – the white shirts, the well-worn clothes, their air of purpose – but, coloured by the events of the previous day, my imagination momentarily cast them as policemen.

I hurried on towards the car.

Tony had the rear door open and I was just about to duck in when a voice called, 'Mr Wellesley?'

I straightened up and looked round. Julia said sharply, 'Can I help you?' and turned to intercept the approaching men.

The one with grey hair ignored her and continued towards me with the rolling gait of someone with a hip problem. Digging into his breast pocket, he produced a card mounted in a leather case and, holding it up at eye level so there was no possibility of my missing it, announced himself as Detective Inspector Henderson.

'You are Mr Hugh William Wellesley?'

'Yes.'

'I'd like to ask you to accompany me to Exeter, sir, to help us with our inquiries into the death of Sylvie Mathieson.'

I felt a draining in my stomach. 'But yesterday – I saw your man Reith. I told him everything.'

'We'd be grateful for more details, sir,' he said in a flat voice. 'And a statement, if you don't mind.'

I spread my hands helplessly, I opened my mouth a couple of times to speak, I felt a sudden heat. 'I'll be glad to help in any way I can – of course,' I said at last. 'But I'm on my way to a vital meeting and I'm already late.' I glanced towards Julia as if for support and met her startled gaze.

'The matter is rather important, sir.'

Disbelief and mounting alarm made me exclaim, 'So is *this!* You don't understand, Inspector – I *have* to get to this meeting!'

Henderson pondered this with the air of someone who has heard a lot of excuses in his time, but my incredulity and panic must have made some sort of impression because after a show of consideration, he agreed to wait. I told him my meeting would take one and a half hours. We settled on two.

In accepting this, I realised with dismay that I had agreed to go all the way back to Exeter.

Three

W<small>E ARRIVED</small> in darkness and monsoon rain. The approaches to the police station were blocked by manoeuvring cars, and we were forced to scurry head down through the deluge to the shimmering entrance. Inside, Henderson shook the water from his collar and pressed his thin hair down to his scalp. Wiping my forehead, I glanced up and saw David.

I grinned weakly. I'd guessed he might be here, I knew Julia had called ahead, but the sight of his sardonic face still gave my spirits a lift. The long journey from London had done nothing for my peace of mind.

David had someone with him, a young thin-faced man with floppy blond hair and a cast in one eye. 'This is Charles Tingwall of Ruthven & Forbes,' David announced. 'He's here to look after your interests.'

I wasn't sure how I felt about this. To my impressionable mind, programmed by a hundred television dramas, hiring yourself a solicitor suggested you had something to hide. But in the next more considered moment, I realised that, irrespective of appearances, it was a sensible precaution that I would be foolish not to take.

Tingwall gave me a dry handshake and turned to Henderson.

'On what basis is Mr Wellesley here, Inspector?' The two men moved to one side, as if for negotiations. I could just hear the policeman recite, 'We are hoping Mr Wellesley can help us with our inquiries into the death of Sylvie Mathieson.'

Tingwall then asked: 'Is Mr Wellesley here as a witness, then, or a suspect?'

'As a witness.'

'In which case—'

I didn't hear any more as David said to me in a robust voice that seemed to carry across the reception area to the duty officer at the enquiry window, 'What did I tell you? Small brains.'

I frowned a protest at him.

Deliberately misreading my look, he added, 'Don't worry, Tingwall will get it sorted. He came highly recommended.' He added in a tone that was almost offhand, 'Have they said why you're here?'

'No.'

'Well . . . it has to be the lover scenario, doesn't it?'

'Oh thanks. *Thanks.*'

'What else could it be?' he said with a flicker of impatience. 'I told you – they've got one-track minds. Just remember, they're guessing. Don't let them rattle you. Just tell them where to get off.'

I wasn't so sure it would be that easy. I wasn't so sure I would feel quite so confident on this alien territory.

Tingwall and Henderson turned back.

'I'd like some time with Mr Wellesley,' Tingwall announced.

Henderson offered, 'Five minutes?'

'I'm sure Mr Wellesley could do with a sandwich and a wash and brush up.'

'Fifteen, then.'

'Twenty?' Tingwall raised an eyebrow at me. 'Mr Wellesley's come a very long way.'

Henderson yielded with a cursory nod before limping away.

For some reason this well-practised professional exchange did nothing to reassure me.

I said I wasn't hungry but Tingwall sent David off to buy sandwiches anyway and led me to a bench in a corner of the reception area, away from the lugubrious gaze of the duty officer.

'Now, Mr Wellesley,' Tingwall began in a hushed tone, 'I just want to be sure – they didn't arrest you?'

'Arrest me? *No.*'

'They didn't caution you?'

'No.'

'There was no mention of anything you may say being given in evidence?'

'No.'

'Fine.' He gave me a brief smile which was undermined by the cast in his left eye. 'And you haven't said anything to them already?'

'I gave them a statement yesterday.'

This was obviously the first he'd heard of it. 'And what did you tell them exactly?'

I gave him a rough summary, and found myself

wondering for the hundredth time where I might have slipped up.

'And you didn't say anything in the car on the way down?'

'What? No.' Apart from a couple of offers to stop at service areas, Henderson and his cohort Phipps had maintained a steadfast silence during the entire journey. If their intention had been to unnerve me, then they had partially succeeded.

'Have you anything to add to yesterday's statement?'

'No.'

'They haven't given you any idea of why they've asked you back?' Tingwall enquired cautiously.

I shrugged, 'No.'

'And you yourself can't think of any reason?'

'No.'

Tingwall tapped his fingers together pensively. 'Well, if they've got their wires crossed, I mean if they're completely on the wrong track, then you must say so.' He waited for a sign that I had understood this. Getting nothing back, he spelled it out again. 'If they have some notion that's completely wrong, then you must put them right.'

The thought of what they could have got wrong made me feel ill, but I managed a faint nod.

'Now, you should be aware of your rights—'

'My rights?' I protested. 'God – you make it sound as though I'm about to be charged or something.'

'I apologise. I didn't make myself clear. I meant your rights at interview.'

'I'm not sure that makes me feel a whole lot better.

The way everyone's going on I'm beginning to feel like a suspect.'

'The police do that to everyone, I'm afraid. It's their way.' He gave the unconvincing smile again. 'Now, you are here in an entirely voluntary capacity, to help them with their inquiries. As a result, nothing you say can be held against you. If, however, they suddenly decide to caution you, mid-interview or whatever, then I must warn you that everything will change.'

Far from bolstering my confidence, this conversation was eroding it fast. 'So you think I *am* a suspect?'

'Er – no, Mr Wellesley.' Tingwall chose his words with the care of someone picking his way over barbed wire. 'Not at all. At the same time . . .' He was struggling to get it right. '. . . they don't usually bring someone all this way unless they think, rightly or wrongly, that he or she has information of some kind.'

Even in my more optimistic moments I'd realised that the police wouldn't have sent their big guns to bring me all the way down here unless they believed I had something to tell them. But it was one thing to think it, and quite another to hear it from a professional.

'In that case,' I said, 'you'd better spell it out for me.'

Now that he was on firmer ground, Tingwall moved confidently into his stride. 'The important thing to remember is that you don't have to answer any questions you don't want to.'

My anxieties shot back to the surface. 'Won't that look bad?'

'It doesn't matter how it looks. If there are any areas that you feel are best left unanswered – for whatever reason – then you shouldn't answer them.'

'But it's not like that,' I murmured. 'I told them everything yesterday.'

'Fine. But bear it in mind, all the same,' Tingwall said.

I felt bound to ask, 'And if I don't want to answer? What do I say?'

'I leave that up to you,' he said with curious emphasis, as if there was an obvious conclusion to be drawn from this.

I didn't understand and said so.

'Well, let's put it this way . . .' His disconcerting squinty eyes seemed to focus somewhere on my left cheek. 'It's better to say you can't remember than to be vague or to change your mind. And if you're simply not sure of something, again, don't just take a stab at it, don't give a vague answer. Just say you can't remember. Keep it simple.'

I took a long breath. 'Okay.'

David came back with the sandwiches, but I still wasn't hungry and, leaving David with Tingwall, I asked the duty officer the way to the gents. The basins were smeared with dirt, one was missing its plug, and the taps were the type that switch themselves off after yielding a niggardly trickle. I splashed some water over my face and washed my hands. Drying my face with a paper towel, I told myself I felt refreshed.

When I got back to the reception area David was

pulling on his coat. 'I'm going over to the hospital. I'll come back later.'

'Don't feel you have to.'

'Well, it's hardly out of my way, is it?' he replied in the brusque tone he used to discourage further discussion.

I followed him outside and we stood under the dripping porch. 'I was thinking,' I said, 'if this gets out, if the press get hold of it . . . *Christ.*' The idea was enough to shake me.

'I've talked to Tingwall about that. He's dealing with it.'

'He is?'

'No guarantees, though. The press are always sniffing around. He can only try.'

I clamped my eyes shut in an attempt to close out images of the newspaper headlines. 'What a time to choose!'

David couldn't think what I was talking about.

'The buyout!'

'Oh.'

'The Chartered Bank is on the brink of committing itself. The thing's practically off the ground.'

'Well, that's good.' But his tone conveyed a lack of interest.

'Off the ground, subject to raising the rest of the money, I mean.'

I said this so that he wouldn't think I was taking his support for granted, but he interpreted it as an untimely attempt to push my case.

'Yes, well,' he said with visible irritation, 'Give us time, eh?'

'I didn't mean that.' But it was too complicated to put the matter right and reluctantly I let it pass.

David looked at his watch. He frequently gave this impression of needing to be somewhere else; it was one of his stratagems for keeping people, particularly difficult patients, at arm's length.

'Listen,' I said, 'Ginny doesn't know where I am. I thought it best, in case she worried – you know. But now . . . well, I'm not so sure. I'd hate her to hear about this from someone else.'

'Ah, she knows, in fact. I called and told her.'

'You did?' I should have been annoyed at such peremptory action, and part of me was, yet Ginny would have had to know sooner or later, and I was quite relieved that David had been the one to tell her. He could always be relied on to down-play a crisis, and his uncompromising brand of logic would have checked Ginny's tendency to overreaction.

As if to confirm this, he said, 'I told her not to come down. I said there was absolutely no point, that it was just a routine thing and she was best at home.'

'And she was happy about that?'

'Oh yes,' he said emphatically.

I said with a tremor of emotion, 'Thanks.'

With an offhand wave and a sharp twitch of the mouth in what might have been intended as a smile, he went out into the rain.

Tingwall announced our readiness and a uniformed officer let us through a security door and along a passage to a door marked Interview Room 2. This was a different room from the one where I'd talked to Reith. The floor was uncarpeted, the chairs hard and upright, and there was a tape recorder at one end of the table. The fluorescent lighting gave off a ghostly flicker, and there was a stale tang of cigarettes and heavily scented floor polish.

Tingwall and I sat on one side of the table, Henderson on the other, with Reith to his left. Phipps stood against the wall, by the door.

Henderson intoned some preliminaries in an expressionless voice, thanking me for my willingness to help them with their inquiries – as if he had offered me much option – explaining that he simply wished to establish one or two facts. His thin, lipless mouth was like a slit set at random amid the broad heavy features. He had the skin of a heavy smoker, porous and etched with webs of deep lines, and his eyes were hooded and droopy as a spaniel's. It was a spent and punished face, but not, I felt, a stupid one.

He repeated most of the questions that Reith had asked me the day before. How did I know Sylvie, when and where had I seen her in the last few months, what had happened when we met.

I took my answers slowly, matching them to the ones I had given Reith the day before, conscious of Henderson's washed-out eyes and his air of quiet watchfulness. As we progressed, part of me stood outside myself wondering what sort of an impression I was making, yet the more self-aware I became the more unnatural I sounded to my own ears and the more I felt I was exhibiting the body language of someone with something to hide.

'To summarise then,' Henderson said, 'the first time you saw Sylvie Mathieson this summer was when she swam to the boat and you had tea together for perhaps forty-five minutes?'

'Yes.'

'The second time she also came to the boat and you—'

'She didn't come on board,' I corrected him mildly. 'She just tapped on the hull.'

'So she remained in this other boat she came in, and you talked for ten minutes?'

'Yes.'

'And the third time you met on the quay?'

'We bumped into each other, yes.'

'And you talked for—?'

'Oh . . . two, three minutes. At the most.'

'So, it was just the three times then?'

I hated the way that repetition etched these details deeper and deeper into the stone of fact. 'I think so, yes.'

'You *think* so?'

'Well, as far as I remember.'

His eyes flickered to life. 'Your memory could be faulty then? Might it have been four times that you met, or five, or even more?'

'No. *No*. If it was more than three, then it wasn't much more. Four at the outside.' This was sounding terrible. I was beginning to appreciate Tingwall's warning about vague answers.

'Well, if it was four, on what other occasion did you meet her?'

'Look, I'm not sure I did meet her again. But if I did it was probably on the water. But really, I can't remember.'

I felt sure Henderson would pursue this, but for some reason he took on a distant look, and asked, 'You spent a lot of time on the water this summer, did you?'

'A few weekends, that's all.'

'Out sailing?'

'Only once. Mainly I was just doing the maintenance.'

Appearing distracted, Henderson dropped his eyes and gave a slight nod. When he looked up again his gaze had regained its watchfulness. 'How would you describe your relationship with Sylvie Mathieson?' he asked, and suddenly there was a charge in the air.

'Well – old friends, I suppose. Though we hadn't seen each other for many years.'

'Nothing more than that?'

So David was right: I was to be cast as Sylvie's secret lover. 'No,' I said.

'You weren't involved in a sexual relationship?'

I took a moment to answer. I wanted to strike the right note, somewhere between indignation and candour. 'No.'

'Just . . . er, *friends*?'

'That's right.'

His old man's eyes appraised me coldly. 'You had known each other in the past?'

I had already told him this. 'Yes.'

'When was it that you met exactly?'

'It must be . . .' I frowned with the effort of the mental arithmetic. 'Sixteen years ago.'

'And what was your relationship then?'

I didn't want to answer that, not with anything

that approached the truth anyway. The very thought of telling this leery grey-faced man with his pasted-down hair and tight collar what I had once felt for Sylvie made me bristle. Eventually I said, 'We used to go out together.'

'She was your girlfriend?'

'For a time, yes.'

'Was it a sexual relationship?'

My resentment rose in a hot wave. I threw a glance at Tingwall, who was already protesting, 'That can hardly be relevant to your present inquiries, Inspector.'

'We're talking about sixteen years ago,' Henderson said reasonably. 'Surely that's not a problem, Mr Wellesley?'

Before Tingwall could interject again, I said hotly, 'Well, it is, actually, because it's really none of your business.'

'You prefer not to answer the question then, Mr Wellesley?'

'That's right,' I said shakily.

There was a shift in the atmosphere then, a palpable hardening in their attitude towards me. I felt as though I had the word *suspect* tattooed across my forehead.

'May I ask how long this non-specific relationship lasted?' Henderson asked drily.

I thought about not answering that as well, but murmured grudgingly, 'A year and a half.'

'You were how old at the time, Mr Wellesley?'

I had no doubt he knew the answer to that, he just wanted to hear me say it. 'I was twenty-six.'

'And when you met Sylvie Mathieson she was fifteen years old?'

'Sixteen.'

'Er ... Not if it was sixteen years ago, Mr Wellesley.'

'I remembered her as sixteen – but you may be right.'

'I ask because I'm wondering if that's why there appears to be a difficulty over the question.' When I made no response he explained, 'If she was fifteen, a sexual relationship would of course have been illegal. If it would help, I can ask about your relationship after Miss Mathieson had turned sixteen. What was the nature of it then?'

Tingwall broke in angrily, 'I think we've established that this question can have no relevance to the present inquiry, and that my client is perfectly entitled not to answer it. He is here to help with your inquiries, Inspector, not to be grilled on his personal life.'

Henderson accepted this with a splaying of his thick fingers, a slight shrug of the shoulders, as if the approach, though doomed to failure, had been worth one last try.

'Well, let's move on then,' he said, sticking out his fleshy chin with something like relish. 'Perhaps we could go over your movements last weekend? In some detail.'

He wanted everything. What time I had left for work on the Saturday morning, what I had done in the office, who could vouch for the fact that I had left Hammersmith at about three.

'There was no one else there,' I explained. 'I was alone in the office.'

'No security staff?'

'At the main door, yes. But I don't know the weekend staff, and they don't know me. There are dozens of companies in the building. I just rent rooms there.'

'So no one saw you leave?'

'No.'

'And nothing to confirm the time you started your journey?'

I thought for a moment. 'No.'

'And you say it took you four and a half hours to reach Dittisham?'

'Well – a little less. I arrived between seven-fifteen and seven-thirty. But longer than usual, certainly. The traffic was terrible. There was a crash on the M4 near Swindon, a big tailback.'

'No one saw you arrive at Dittisham?'

'Not that I'm aware of, no. Someone in the village, maybe.'

'You came through the village?'

'It's the only way to the house.'

'What car were you driving?'

'My BMW.' A memory stirred. 'But I did stop for petrol.'

'Where was this?'

'I can never remember the name of the place. It's on the motorway somewhere this side of Bristol. But I'll have the receipt somewhere.'

A glimmer of something like disappointment showed in Henderson's face. 'So what time would this have been?'

'I don't know. About five-thirty, I suppose. Maybe even later. Six, possibly. The jam was terrible.'

Henderson leant back in his chair and eyed me thoughtfully before saying to Tingwall, 'Perhaps this receipt could be found?'

Tingwall played hard to get. 'I'll look into it,' he said.

Henderson brought his attention back to me. 'So you didn't see anyone when you arrived at Dittisham?'

I was finding this a strain and made no effort to hide it. 'No,' I sighed heavily.

'You went straight to your late father's house?'

'Yes.'

We established that on arriving I had done some fairly normal things like putting on lights, having a drink, taking a look around.

'And then?'

'I went into Dartmouth to buy some food.' Anticipating the next question, I added, 'It must have been about eight-thirty when I got to the Co-op and found it shut.'

'If I may interrupt,' Tingwall cut in smoothly. 'It couldn't have been any later than eight when Mr Wellesley arrived in town.'

There was a silence while we stared expectantly at Tingwall.

'My client's brother, Dr David Wellesley, left a meeting in the town just before eight and saw Mr Wellesley driving along Duke Street shortly afterwards.'

'Dr Wellesley is sure about that?' Henderson asked.

'Quite certain.'

'Was he alone?'

'Was who alone?' Tingwall asked, deliberately choosing to be obtuse.

'Doctor Wellesley.'

Tingwall pulled an expression of exaggerated surprise, as if he couldn't imagine the relevance of the question. 'I *believe* so, yes. I could check, of course. But, er, there's no doubt about the time and place.'

'And he can make a statement to that effect?'

'If *necessary*, of course.'

Henderson turned back to me with a fusion of disappointment and irritation written on his face. He had thought I was his man, and he didn't like the idea of getting it wrong.

'And your wife arrived at about nine?' he asked mechanically.

'Yes.'

'And you were together for the rest of the weekend?'

'Yes.'

'Very well, Mr Wellesley, that'll be all for the moment,' he said crisply, pushing his chair back. 'But I'd be grateful if this petrol receipt could be found,' he said to Tingwall. 'And I'd like Mr Wellesley to return in the morning to make a formal statement, if he would be agreeable. And I'd be grateful if Mrs Wellesley could make a short statement too.'

Catching my glance, Tingwall launched into negotiations over Ginny, asking if a statement was really necessary, and if so, whether she couldn't make it in London. Then they moved on to David's statement and whether that was really necessary either, but by that time I was hardly listening. I was adjusting to the idea that I seemed to be off the hook.

David slowed as we approached the entrance to Furze Lodge. 'Sure you won't change your mind?'

'No,' I said. 'Thanks anyway.'

'The children'll be doing their own thing. They won't bother you. I'm lucky if they talk to *me*.'

'It's not that. Really.'

David shrugged as he accelerated past the gates. 'There mightn't be any bedding at Dittisham, you know. Mary's been clearing things out.'

'I'll find something. Don't worry. I just need to crash out . . .' I explained lamely.

'Fine.'

For several minutes we continued in silence towards Dittisham, with only the hiss of the wipers and the swish of the wet tyres and the blurred beams of the headlights on the shining road ahead.

Since picking me up from the police station David had talked almost continuously, a dry monologue about tying up the last details of Pa's estate, about the children's progress at school; about anything except what had just happened. I was grateful not to have to talk, I needed time to regain my equilibrium, but now there was something I had to say. 'I'm not sure you did the right thing, you know – telling Tingwall that – but thanks anyway.'

He knew perfectly well what I was referring to but affected a lack of interest and understanding.

I said it for both of us: 'Telling Tingwall you saw me in town.' I had already broached this at the beginning of the journey, but he hadn't responded then either. 'But look, David, I don't want you to get yourself into a corner.'

'Don't be ridiculous!'

'You say that, but what happens if they find out? Who knows, I might have been seen somewhere else at eight, driving through Dittisham, something like that.'

'But you *did* go into town about then, didn't you?' And he threw me a look of complete innocence.

'David – it was more like eight-thirty.'

He tossed a hand in the air. 'A few minutes. So what?'

'Half an hour,' I argued unhappily.

He slowed to take the steep hill down through the village. 'I wouldn't worry about it.'

'Wouldn't it be best not to tie yourself to a definite time, though, just in case?'

'Really, Hugh.' He shook his head as if I were a total mystery to him.

A whorl of leaves spun across our path as we turned through the gates of Dittisham House. The security lights blinked on, the shrubs glinted darkly, we rounded the slight bend and the house rose up before us, its tall windows gaping blackly like empty eyes. This was the moment I had been dreading, the moment when the memories would pounce. And for an instant the images did rear up, of Sylvie leaning lazily against the french windows, the sunlight making a halo of her hair, and then, like turning the page of an album, a darker picture took its place, of Sylvie on the boat, shivering in my sweater, hair dripping wet, mouth poised provocatively in that laughing way of hers.

Then we parked, the wind shivered against the car and the images faded. I thought that if this was the worst it would get then I would survive it.

Something was different about the house but in the shadowy beams of the outside lights it took me a moment to work out what it was. The ceanothus that covered much of the stonework, forming a ledge for the upstairs windows and an arch for the porch, had come away from the wall and fallen, broken and shrivelled, onto the gravel in a forlorn heap of rotting leaves. Pa had only been dead a few months, yet already the place seemed to have acquired a long-abandoned air. For a moment I felt so woebegone that I considered going to stay at David's after all.

'Lucky to be getting the price for this place, you know,' David remarked. 'Not many houses fetching the full whack nowadays.'

'It's the water,' I suggested. 'People love the idea of water.'

David, having chosen to live inland, wasn't ready to admit to the drawing power of the river. 'Mmm,' he grunted dubiously. 'It's a good-sized house, remember. Not so many of those around.'

And not so many that were quite so pretty either. An early-nineteenth-century villa with an Edwardian extension, it had floor-length windows and on the river side two bays with a verandah supported by iron trellises. The garden fell in a succession of two terraces and a lawn to the river below.

'Drink?' I asked brightly.

David hesitated, and I realised how much I wanted him to accept.

'But if you can't . . .' I offered immediately. 'If you have to get back . . .'

'Well . . . Unless you're desperate?'

I was desperate to talk, but this wouldn't be what David had in mind. For him a couple of stiff drinks were a palliative against the trials of the day, not an excuse for unburdening the soul, an exercise he had always regarded with the greatest suspicion.

'No, I'm fine,' I said.

'You've got a key?'

'I left one in the porch, thanks.' I pushed open the door and the wind swooped into the car. I couldn't leave without saying, 'You were dead right, by the way.'

'Oh?'

The wind shook the door, threatening to slam it, and I pulled it shut again.

'About what the police had in mind. I was meant to be the jealous lover.'

David gave a derisive grunt. 'I told you, they're cretins.'

He restarted the engine and, still shaking his head, waited for me to get out.

'Look, when you said she had lovers—'

He made a face. 'Did I?'

'Yesterday. You said she was all over the place, that she had several lovers,' I persisted.

He shrugged dismissively. 'It was just gossip.'

'But this gossip – did it mention me?' I was still brooding over what had brought the police to my door.

'No, *no*.'

'Nobody even hinted . . .?'

'No! There was no mention of any names. It was nothing like that.'

'What about the chap with long hair, the one she went around with? Presumably the police are on to him?'

'God only knows. Really, I have no idea.'

'You'd think the police would be on to him.'

'Perhaps they are,' he said briskly.

But still I couldn't leave it alone. After the events of the last week I had to talk to someone. 'The thing is . . . well, I didn't quite tell them everything. You see, I did see something of Sylvie this summer. More than I said I did, anyway. She . . . I—'

'Look, I'd forget it, if I were you,' he cut in, his eyes alight with impatience or anger. 'I wouldn't discuss it with anyone.'

I felt like saying: Since when were you anyone? With an effort I stayed silent, but the reproach must have shown in my face because he made a grudging gesture of appeasement. 'Best to let things lie.'

'I wasn't actually planning on talking to a whole lot of people about it,' I protested.

'Not with anyone,' he repeated in the tone of a stern parent.

It's amazing how your family can undermine you, how in the space of a few words they can catch you unawares and demolish your confidence. What did David imagine I might be about to admit to? What did he think I knew? When we were young he had had a talent for putting me down, for ridiculing my efforts, and for an instant I felt echoes of old humiliations and childish resentments, the younger brother once more.

We said a stiff goodnight. Watching him drive off, I felt relieved to be alone.

The house was cold but once I had turned on some lights and put a match to the gas fire in Pa's study the gloom soon lifted. The good furniture had gone to the salerooms some weeks ago, but the heavy damask curtains still hung at the windows, the carpets and older rugs remained, Pa's battered kneehole desk still straddled one corner, and there was a comfortable chair to pull up to the fire.

The Scotch wasn't on the mantelpiece where I had last seen it and for an anxious moment I thought Mary or Mrs Perry, the cleaner, had removed it, but after a quick hunt I found it standing in solitary state in the cupboard where the family photo albums had always lived. There were no albums there now, and I assumed the family mementoes were accumulating at Furze Lodge with David and Mary.

I poured myself a hefty measure and took several large gulps before topping the glass up again. Until this summer I'd never been a great drinker – I'd never particularly liked the sensation of losing my wits – but tonight like a few other nights recently I wanted a small measure of oblivion.

The wind was racketing in the chimneys, the windows were humming and rattling to a frenetic rhythm and, outside, the rushing trees sounded as though they were about to storm the house.

The phone made me start. Imbued with the day's paranoia, I considered not answering it.

'There you are,' gasped Ginny when I finally picked up the receiver. 'How did it go?'

'Not an experience I'd like to repeat.'

'But it's over?'

I gave a pale laugh. 'I sincerely hope so.'

'They've finished with you?'

'It looks like it.'

She made a slight sound, an exhalation or a sigh. 'Well, thank God for that.' A pause, then: 'You're staying there?'

'I'll get a train back tomorrow.'

'When will you arrive?'

'In the afternoon some time. Not sure when.' I didn't say I had to go to Exeter first to make the statement.

A hesitation, then she said in a rush, 'Why did they want you back? What was it all about?'

'I've no idea.'

'But there must have been a reason,' she said, and there was an edge to her voice.

'They didn't say, Ginny. But they want you to make a statement, I'm afraid.'

'What do you mean?'

'It's a routine thing,' I said, playing it down. 'Establishing where everyone was. They just want to confirm that we met up at nine that night and left for London on Saturday evening.'

She didn't reply.

'Ginny?'

'When? When do I have to make this statement?'

'There's no hurry, I don't think. There's this lawyer Charles Tingwall who's arranging it for us. He's fixing it so you can do yours in London. It won't be very complicated.'

'And it's a routine thing, you say? They're asking everyone?'

'Well – people who were around,' I lied.

I could hear her breathing, always a sign that she was getting tense. 'I see.'

'I'll tell you more tomorrow. All right?'

Another pause, and I knew she was working up to something. 'But why did they want to see you? Please tell me. They must have given you a reason.'

'They didn't.'

'What did they ask you, then? What sort of questions?'

'Look, I'll tell you all about it tomorrow.'

'Will you?' I caught a note of accusation in her voice.

'Of course.'

'Of course,' she echoed in a tone of open scepticism.

'Sorry?'

'Nothing.'

'Ginny – they had it all wrong.'

'Did they?'

Suddenly I felt beleaguered. Where was the unconditional family support? First David, now Ginny.

Suppressing a dart of self-pity, I said, 'Tomorrow, Ginny. Let's talk about it tomorrow.'

Her voice broke slightly as she said a curt 'Fine', and I could picture the uncertainty and reproach in her face. I nearly called her back, I fully intended to, but, unable to face more questions, I poured myself another Scotch instead.

I took my drink to the window and stared out into the darkness. A light on the far side of the river blinked through the flickering branches, the wind whistled in the eaves. Draining my glass, I pulled at the bolts of the french windows and walked out into the blustering gale. Crossing the stone terrace to the steps, I felt my way down to the next level where sodden grass pulled at my shoes. A last flight of steps and I was descending the sloping lawn towards the water. The arches of the pergola rose dimly to one side, the bare branches of the fruit trees swished angrily near by, the deeper blackness of the summer-house loomed somewhere to the right. Misjudging the distance, I almost walked into the low wall that marked the river boundary.

The wind was barrelling down the deep cut of the river, pulling at my jacket, buffeting my ears, and it was much colder. The darkness was so thick that I couldn't make out the state of the tide, whether the water was high or there was a sea of mud, though I fancied I could hear the rip of the ebb close by. A sprinkling of lights gave height and form to the ridges and creeks of the opposite banks, while away to my right the lights of Dittisham and the ferry landing gave shape to the curve of the river. But the water itself was hidden, a secretive ribbon of ink coursing towards the sea.

Somewhere in front of me was *Ellie Miller*, lying to her mooring, her squat shape lost against the greater blackness of the night. No cabin lights showing now, no laughter echoing across the water, no lazy rippling of the tide in the warm summer air. Maybe it was the drink, maybe it was the tensions of the day, but I felt such a jumble of emotions that my eyelids pricked with fierce heat and I gasped for breath. Visions came: of water pressing into Sylvie's mouth and eyes, of her body bumping against the rocks, of unspeakable wounds in her flesh. The images were vivid yet curiously opaque, like my images of Sylvie as she had been in life. I saw her clearly: I saw her dimly. She was featureless and exhilarating and proud; she was distant and elusive and cold. She was open and devious; she was sensuous and cruel and base. I realised then that she would baffle me just as thoroughly in death as she had confused me in life.

I turned away and stumbled up the slope. Above the thrashing of the trees I heard a baleful cry. I stopped. It rose again, a chilling sound carried high on the wind. It seemed to come from the river, and in a moment of disorientation and fear my nightmare roared back to life and everything stalled inside me, my heart and breathing seized, and I was overcome by a sensation of imminent disaster.

The next whoop brought me bumping back to reality. It was a very human sound, very much in the present. Looking up the slope I saw a figure outlined against the french windows.

'There you are!' sang Mary as I climbed the last of the steps and entered the pool of light. Drawing me inside the house, she gave a theatrical shiver. 'Wow, it's wild out there!' Railing against the climate, she pulled the windows shut and drew the curtains. 'I've brought some sheets for you!' she declared heartily. 'And some breakfast. Can't have you camping! But how are you? I want to know how you are!'

I couldn't hide my feelings, perhaps I didn't try, because when she took a better look at me her face creased into a picture of concern. 'Oh, Hugh!' she sighed. 'That bad?'

'Just a bit tired and emotional.' I laughed to make it sound like a joke. I went in search of another glass. 'I'm awfully glad to see you.'

'You should have come and stayed with us, you twit. But I know – ' she added with a laugh and a flip of the wrist ' – the kids are home for the weekend! You're not the only one. They get too much for me sometimes. All those teenage moods. All that ghastly music – rock or rap or whatever it is.'

I fetched a chair from Pa's desk and offered her a whisky which she accepted with a show of conspiratorial glee, as though drinking was always a bit of a lark.

We sat on either side of the fire.

'So,' she grimaced sympathetically. 'What a beastly day for you.'

'Yes, as days go . . .' I sank back into my chair. 'Cumberland put another million quid on the price of the buyout. Just when we'd raised most of the money.'

'I hope that wasn't Howard's doing.'

'Oh . . . I wouldn't have thought so.'

Perhaps it was my hesitation, perhaps it was something in my tone, but Mary rolled her eyes and sighed, 'Oh, you don't have to hide it from me. Nothing surprises me about my brother. You know, I'll be glad when the buyout's over and our two families never work together again.' She tutted, 'But this extra money – will you be able to raise it?'

'I don't honestly know.'

'It's too bad, after all your efforts . . .' She watched me for a moment. 'Now what about the police? Were they horrible?' Her tone was feisty, like a warrior who at the slightest provocation would take up cudgels in my defence.

'It may seem crazy,' I said, 'but for a while back there I really thought they were going to lock me up.'

She wasn't sure how seriously she was meant to take this and her mouth jerked into an uncertain smile. 'Poor Hugh! How awful!'

'They seemed so *fixed* on me. That's what was so bloody terrifying.'

She looked fierce again. 'They gave you a bad time?'

'It felt like it, but then I haven't exactly got a lot of experience to measure it against. But you know the worst thing? It was not knowing why they'd called me in. Was my crime to have been seen with Sylvie? Christ, if that's a crime! Or did they think they had something else on me – you know, something they didn't tell me about? I suppose that's how they get people,' I laughed grimly. 'By making them think they know something damning about them.'

'Skunks!' Mary declared. 'It's just bullying, isn't it?' Taking a gulp of her drink, she eyed me over the rim of her glass. 'They didn't give you any idea then? What it was?'

I shook my head. 'With all these lovers she was meant to have, you'd have thought they'd have had plenty of other candidates to interview.'

Mary looked at me with open interest. 'She had lots of lovers?'

'According to David.'

'Really?' Her eyes flashed, she gave a sudden snort. 'Well, well! We all knew about the youth with the long hair – at least, we *assumed* he was the lover – but as for the rest . . . Mmm!' She widened her eyes in anticipation of disclosures to come. 'I must get David to tell me more.'

'He says he doesn't know any more. It was just a rumour.'

'A rumour. Ahh.' She looked away into the fire, then, trying to lift my mood: 'But they're satisfied now, the police?'

I considered this. 'You know something? I'm really not sure. I have this feeling that they'll come back.'

'Come back . . . But, Hugh, that's ridiculous – why should they?' Yet the question wasn't entirely rhetorical, there was curiosity behind it, and I realised that Mary, like the rest of my family, didn't seem to have ruled out the possibility that I had something to hide.

'I was going to ask *you* actually,' I said. 'Was I meant to be having an affair with Sylvie? Was the neighbourhood buzzing with it? If so I'd really like someone to tell me because I seem to be the last to know.'

'I've never heard anything.' But her tone was so hedged with reservations, her manner so strained, that I looked up sharply. Taking the opportunity with obvious relief, she said, 'Look, Hugh, I'd better tell you – it's just possible Mrs Perry may have told the police something.'

'Mrs *Perry*? But what?'

'That she saw your car outside Sylvie Mathieson's cottage. In fact . . . well' – she made a regretful face – 'we both did. I was driving her, you see. Her car had broken down, she hadn't been here for weeks, and the place was getting so dirty that I drove her here one day and picked her up again when she'd finished. And on the way back we saw your car . . .'

Something folded in me then, my defences evaporated, and all the accumulated tensions spilled out in a rush of dread. 'Oh God . . .'

Mary asked tentatively, 'You, er . . . didn't tell the police you'd been there?'

'No.' I clasped a hand over my eyes.

I heard her scramble to her feet. Crouching beside my chair, she gave me a rough comradely hug. 'Hugh, they can't make too much out of that.'

'No?' I exclaimed bitterly. 'They'll assume I've lied about everything, won't they?'

She sat back on her sturdy haunches. 'But an assumption? That's nothing, *nothing*.'

I looked into her strong irrepressible face, I saw the concern there, and the fierce loyalty, and I said,

100

'Mary . . . It wasn't the only thing I didn't tell them about.'

She said in a small voice, 'Oh dear.'

Neither of us spoke for a long moment, then she said almost gruffly, 'Do you want to tell me about it?'

Aware that I was taking a step whose consequences I hadn't begun to consider but not caring too much, I said weakly, 'It's a complete mess, Mary.'

'Hugh . . . don't be silly!' She grasped my shoulder and shook it, as if to imbue me with optimism. 'Wait . . .' Getting up, she replenished our glasses from the bottle on the mantel before pulling her chair closer and sitting down with a look of anxious concentration.

'I don't know where to start . . .'

But I did know. I knew exactly where I should start if I was going to make any sense of it. 'There was this dreadful week,' I began slowly. 'A nightmare week at the end of the most appalling month.' I paused. 'I think I cracked up a bit . . .' I thought about this. 'Yes – that was it, really. At the end of the day, Mary, I think I went off my head.'

Four

'DAVID CALLED it depression. He even prescribed me anti-depressants. Typical David! If only it'd been that simple. Pop the pills and lose your troubles! But it wasn't depression, you see. Not in the way he meant it anyway. It was sheer disbelief. Everything was going wrong and I couldn't seem to do anything to stop it. The business was in trouble and still sliding, the banks were moving in for their pound of flesh, and it suddenly hit me – I mean, quite suddenly, in the period of a day or so – that we were in real danger of losing the company. And then . . .' It was still mortifying to say it. 'Howard was going behind my back, setting up the takeover. It took me for ever to realise it. God, I was so slow! Good old Hugh – blind to the obvious!' My laugh sounded bitter to my ears.

'And then . . . things were difficult at home. Ginny thought – well, I don't know what she thought, that was half the trouble – but we started to disagree over nothing, everything. There was this awful *wall* between us. We couldn't seem to make contact. We seemed to wear each other down the whole time. And the money . . . She couldn't see how desperately we needed to cut down, she had this blind spot. She just . . .' But my words were stifled by the peculiar mixture of exasperation and guilt that Ginny always seemed to engender in me, and I returned to less confusing ground. 'You know the worst thing, though, about the company? The worst thing was knowing that it was my own stupidity, my own pig-headed bloody idiocy that had got us into trouble.'

'Come on – what about Howard?' Mary protested. 'It must have been his fault too.'

'Oh, Howard didn't know any better,' I exclaimed sweepingly. 'Howard was the ideas man, always had been, while my talent, such as it was, was for keeping us on the tracks financially. That was the theory anyway. But then I completely lost it! I let myself get seduced by ideas of easy money and limitless expansion. Pure conceit. I thought I knew best, you see! Prudence, restraint, all the things Pa had preached – well, they were just quaint and outdated, weren't they? Leverage was the name of the game. You borrowed up to the hilt, you traded right up to your limits.'

'But the board, the accountants,' Mary argued, 'they should have realised, surely?'

'They were under Howard's spell, just like the rest of us. And everything seemed to go so well at first, you see. Profits booming. Sales rocketing. Except for poor old Hartford, of course, which was left in the dumps.'

'So it all seemed hopeless?' she said, drawing me back to the story.

'Not immediately, no. For a long time I believed the situation could be salvaged. I worked like mad on the restructuring plan, I took a pay cut – half my salary. I really thought I could get it all together.'

'Then?'

'Then . . .' The memory caught me with fresh force. 'Then I realised what Howard was up to.'

I found out purely by chance. One day my driver was off sick and it was Howard's driver, Brian, who chauffeured me to our bankers for yet another fraught meeting on restructuring – a City euphemism for raising more money at heavy cost. I made some remark about the traffic and Brian launched into a stream of good-natured complaint about contraflows and road-works, and how it was getting increasingly difficult to outmanoeuvre them. Stafford last week had been a particular challenge, he told me, because an accident on the M6 had caused a ten-mile tailback.

I thought of reasons for Howard to go to Stafford, I came up with a few, all perfectly plausible, yet, even as I tried to talk myself into believing them, a single thought chimed insistently in my mind: that Cumberland had its headquarters in Stafford, along with three of its four factories.

Watching Brian in the rear-view mirror, I went through a show of searching my memory. 'Ah yes . . . that was Howard's meeting with – who was it?'

Brian was about to reply when his eyes jumped guiltily and there was an awkward pause before he mumbled something unconvincing about some lunch engagement Howard had had at a hotel whose name he couldn't recall. When he dropped me off he was still looking uneasy, and then I knew all I needed to know.

Over the years I had discovered that there were only two ways of approaching Howard on subjects he wasn't ready to discuss. One was to lift his mood with a joke; the other was to tackle him head-on, with something approaching aggression.

The next morning as soon as he was free I strode into his office and planted myself in front of his desk. I hadn't slept much the night before, my nerves were humming, and I could feel a pulse beating high in my head. Howard glanced up from some report and raised a lazy eyebrow.

'Tell me about Cumberland,' I said.

He sank back in his chair. He took his time. I could almost see his mind working. 'Cumberland?'

'You've had a meeting with them?'

'There's no need to get upset, Hugh,' he said smoothly. 'I was just opening out our options. The beginning of a contingency plan, if you like. Something to consider if the banks get threatening.'

A wild inarticulate anger rose over me, I had to clamp my lips together to stop them trembling. 'How could you?' I knew it was the wrong thing to say to Howard, for whom a moral stance was always a source of irritation, but I was beyond discretion.

'Look, it's no good taking an emotional line on this,' he intoned in his most infuriating way. 'That's been half our trouble, Hugh. No objectivity.'

I couldn't begin to work out what objectivity had to do with betrayal. I said unsteadily, 'Behind my *back*, Howard.'

'Don't be ridiculous!' he declared. 'It was just a preliminary chat to see how the ground lay. Nothing to get excited about. I was going to talk to you about it today. I mean, just *think* about it, Hugh,' he argued archly, 'I could hardly progress anything without you, could I?'

'And how *does* the ground lie, Howard?'

Reverting to old mannerisms, he gave a cat-like smile and dropped a half-wink in an expression that wouldn't have looked amiss on a used-car dealer. 'I tell you – they're rather hot for us! Oh, they're not letting on, of course, but they'd be mad not to progress the idea and they know it.'

'And what exactly is the idea, Howard? A takeover?'

He looked offended. 'God, no! A merger. A *merger*,' he repeated, as if I were incapable of taking it in first time. 'Integration of administration, distribution and sales. Big savings to be made, Hugh, big savings.'

'And where would Hartford fit into this?'

He tightened his lips and slowly shook his head as though I had conjured up this remark just to try him. 'Hartford is a great asset, Hugh. Nobody's going to throw it away, now are they?'

Staring at him, then, I wondered which of us had gone mad, whether he had always been like this or I was the one who had changed. It seemed incredible that we had ever worked happily together, or that I had ever trusted him.

But even then I hadn't really grasped the situation. 'No more clandestine meetings,' I warned him. 'No more going behind my back, Howard. No more going behind the board's back!'

The way his eyes slid away, the knowing look that drifted across his face told me the rest of the story.

'I *see*. How silly of me,' I said bitterly. 'You've been setting the scene for the board, have you?'

'Hugh, all this anger really doesn't help, you know. I do wish we could discuss this rationally.' He gave a small sigh and waited, as though a little sensible reflection would cause me to see the childishness of my ways.

'And your family?' I asked as levelly as possible.

'My family are all in favour of finding a happy conclusion.'

A suspicion leapt into my mind. 'And *my* family? Where do they stand?'

He spread his hands, the picture of baffled innocence. 'I wouldn't know. But presumably they're aware of how precarious the situation is? Presumably they've read the financial reports? I mean – I *presume*.'

He wanted me to see through him. He wanted me to think he'd already persuaded my family to vote for a takeover. He wanted me to think it, and, hating myself for being so easily manipulated, I did.

'Thanks for letting me know,' I said tightly.

Howard shook his head again and pulled himself indolently to his feet. He paused, running his hand down his tie as if to test its smoothness. 'Sometimes it's important to remember that there's no disgrace in making money, Hugh. No disgrace in cashing in one's hard-earned assets and reaping the rewards of success.'

107

'*Success?*' Sometimes Howard simply robbed me of speech.

'Success.' He lifted his head to the sound of it. 'You seem to have a problem with that, Hugh.'

'No, Howard, no. I don't have a problem with that.'

I stopped sleeping then. I spent hours staring into the darkness, burning with disbelief. The shock wasn't so much that Howard was prepared to sell the business out – he had absolutely no sentimentality where money was concerned – but that after all our years together he was prepared to treat me with such contempt.

In the next couple of days I embarked on a frantic damage limitation exercise. I phoned each of the board in turn, I threw together a paper listing the reasons a merger would be a bad idea, but of course Howard had been there ahead of me. He'd laid his ground very carefully. He'd already won them over.

'It was then I began to lose heart, Mary. Or to lose faith in myself, which probably amounted to the same thing. I began to question things I hadn't questioned in a long time. Wondering why on earth I'd been slaving away for most of my working life if it was to get stabbed in the back by my partner.'

Mary nodded ruefully at this. She never took exception to criticism of Howard; sometimes she actively endorsed it.

'I thought of all the years that had just vanished – just *gone*. I thought of the hours I'd worked, all the evenings and weekends I'd never got home, all the time I'd never found for Ginny . . .'

'She never seemed to mind too much.'

'Oh, she never complained. But it mattered. It mattered a lot. We were always in such a rush that in the end I think we simply forgot how to talk.' I grasped at a new realisation and floated it tentatively. 'Or we were frightened to talk. I think there may have been something of that too. We were frightened in case we had to face up to how . . . *wrong* things were. How very differently things had turned out from the way we'd expected.'

Mary leant forward and turned the fire down.

'And then . . . oh, it was everything, really. I began to think a lot about Pa. How much I missed the old devil – you know? And how little time I'd found for him towards the end.'

'Not your fault.'

'Oh, but I should have *made* time, Mary. You can always make time if you really try. I didn't try hard enough. I think I was ashamed. I didn't want to have to tell him how badly the business was doing. I didn't want to admit how everything he'd worked for was slipping away.' Halted by force of memory, I felt a fresh pull of affection and loss. The old man had maddened me sometimes, especially when I was a young man; he had been forceful and opinionated, he had been shamelessly paternalistic, particularly towards women, my mother included, but he had also been a spectacularly successful human being, full of warmth and feeling, and ingrained with a strong sense of duty and loyalty.

'So you were feeling pretty low?'

'Low? Yes – *low*. But you know something?'

Mary shook her head, and her sharp eyes did not leave my face.

'The idea of losing the business was terrible, of course it was, but I would have bounced back all right. I was stunned – yes, and angry, too – but it was more of a *reaction* than a state of mind. I hadn't really given up. I was just exhausted, utterly wiped out. All I needed, really, was some sleep and the chance to work things out. A bit of time, that was all.'

Mary read my expression and raised an eyebrow. 'But you didn't get it?'

'It wasn't Ginny's fault,' I insisted, betraying my guilts. 'People, fund-raising, parties . . . It was her whole life. I'd left her alone so much, what else did she have?'

Mary's face was still, deliberately so.

I continued to argue unhappily, 'What else did she have? No, whatever went wrong, Mary, it wasn't Ginny's fault.'

It was on the Friday at breakfast – the first breakfast we'd managed to have together in some time – that I realised what sort of a weekend lay ahead.

Ginny peered at me and exclaimed, 'Oh, such woe!'

I arranged my face into something more cheerful and mumbled about bankers giving us a hard time, and how life would be a lot easier without them.

When I picked up the newspaper she turned away to make the orange juice. The whir of the electric squeezer rose to a sudden shriek. 'This thing's playing up,' she tutted. 'I might buy us one of those shiny steel things. You know, the smart Italian jobs that look like cappuccino machines.'

She poured the juice into a glass and wiped her slender fingers on a cloth. She stood in profile, the glossy fall of her hair tucked behind one ear, her features unreadable, and for an instant she seemed like a stranger, someone I had always known yet hardly knew at all. I looked away abruptly because the idea frightened me so much.

She put the juice on the counter and, sliding onto the stool opposite, flicked her hair back from her forehead with a characteristic sweep of her hand. 'I thought I'd leave about ten, as soon as the fish man delivers,' she announced in the light rapid tones she used to discuss arrangements. 'You did order enough wine, didn't you, darling? It's soup then fish then duck, remember.'

It came back to me then that we were having one of our social weekends in Wiltshire. Ginny always went down to Melton early to make sure everything was ready. 'How many people?' I asked, trying not to think of the expense.

'Twelve. And Cook thinks the pudding could do with some dessert wine. Is that all right, darling? I mean, I would organise it, but . . .' She gave a tiny shrug. She took a strange pride in boasting that she knew absolutely nothing about wine, except whether it was any good or not, which she could establish at the first sip.

Weekends at Melton followed a pattern. We gave

a dinner party on the Friday or Saturday with never less than four courses produced by a hired cook we referred to as Cook, and served by the male half of our housekeeping couple masquerading as a butler. On the Saturday we went to some sporting event with our house guests – usually racing or polo – and on whichever evening we were not entertaining we dined at another large house. On Sunday nights, if no guests were staying on, I caught up with some of my paperwork before getting up at five-thirty to drive to London.

'You'll be sitting next to Lady Werner,' Ginny informed me. 'She's on lots of boards and welfare organisations. Limps a bit, injured herself hunting years ago, still very horsy. They've got lots in training, Derby-winners and things . . .'

I tried to speak, but Ginny was at full gallop.

'. . . But she's a trustee of the family charitable trust, you see, along with Sir Frank – they run it together – and they give big donations . . . well, the trust does. We might get as much as fifty thousand for three years running. And they're awfully nice really—'

'Ginny—!' It came out more harshly than I meant it to.

Her eyes widened, her mouth twitched. 'What?'

I was going to bring up the subject of our expenses, but I faltered. I wasn't sure I could face the inevitable upset. I could never work out if Ginny believed against all the evidence that she was cutting back, or whether she was simply incapable of doing so, but whenever I mentioned the subject she grew so prickly and defensive that reasonable discussion became virtually impossible.

'Nothing,' I said hastily. 'Anything else I need to do for the weekend?'

'Absolutely not,' she declared with the touchy pride of a born organiser. Then, eyeing me: 'What on earth's the matter?'

'Just desperately tired, that's all.'

'I can never understand why you have to do it all. Why can't some of these people take the work off your hands?'

But I didn't have the energy to explain. 'They just can't.'

When she realised I wasn't going to elaborate she tightened her mouth and went to fetch fresh coffee. Returning, she rested her small chin on her hands and blinked rapidly, a sure sign that she was nervous of whatever she was about to say. 'By the way,' she began with studied casualness, 'Eddie Maynard's going off to that shooting school for a weekend course. He wanted to know if you were interested in going with him, but I said you were far too busy—'

'Ginny,' I said with more patience than I was feeling, 'it's not a matter of being too busy. I'm simply not interested in shooting, and that's all there is to it.'

'But you used to be.'

'No, Ginny. I may have said once—'

'More than once.'

'Only as a sort of joke,' I protested.

'I see,' she said in a small voice, as if I had altered my story simply to make her look foolish.

She had clung to this ridiculous hope that I would

take up shooting for some time; why, I could never fathom. I loathed guns and it saddened me to see wild ducks hanging in people's game larders.

'Having a place in the country doesn't mean we have to do what country people do.' I realised too late how critical this sounded.

'It's not that!' she protested, breathing fast. 'You seem to think I want you to take it up for some . . . some . . .' She agitated her hand. 'For some *snobbish* reason! I just thought how lovely it'd be for you to have an interest down there, something that'd give you a bit of exercise and fresh air. And you make it sound . . .' She was gasping for air now, wheezing from low in her chest. I fetched her inhaler from the basket in the corner of the kitchen. Grabbing it, she pulled two squirts into her lungs.

I dropped an arm lightly round her shoulders. 'Darling, I didn't mean it like that.'

'Oh, yes you did,' she cried between gulps.

'I just like to relax at Melton, that's all.'

She fought to speak. Eventually, after an agonising pull on her lungs, she managed to gasp, 'You really think other people's opinions are important to me! It's so insulting!'

I dropped wearily onto the stool next to her.

'That's what you think, isn't it?' she demanded.

What I really thought came to me with the clarity that only unhappiness can bring: that it was in Ginny's nature to strive for perfection, that she couldn't bear any area of our lives to fall short of some far-reaching ideal, and that, by setting herself such high standards, she doomed both of us to constant struggle. With this insight came another, equally clear: that I was deeply weary of this self-imposed burden, that I would gladly leave it all behind.

'I think it'd be nice to slow down a bit,' I said.

She cast me a guarded look. 'Slow down . . .? In what way?'

'Try not to do quite so much.'

'You mean – my charity work?'

'Of course not, no! I meant, see friends less often. Have more evenings to ourselves.'

She was fighting for breath again. 'But we don't see people *that* often! And you've always said you loved seeing them! And now suddenly . . .! You're being very confusing, Hugh. And very unfair!'

'It's partly the expense,' I said, grasping the nettle. 'We have to cut back.'

She cast me a look of quiet injury, as if I had broken all the rules of fair argument. 'I know that,' she said stiffly.

'Any joy with the accounts?' I tried to hit a light note, absolutely free of reproach.

She gave a long rasping cough and reached for her inhaler again. 'I've had a look through the bills, if that's what you mean.'

'You can see, then, that we're way over budget.'

'But we never had a budget, darling! You talk about this budget as if it was something passed at a board meeting.' Her eyes were exceptionally bright, close to anger or tears. 'I never knew anything about this budget until you invented it! You seem to think I've been spending money like water! D'you think I don't check the bills? D'you think I don't get the best prices?

And I can't just cancel dinners arranged *months* ago. It's taken me a *year* to get the Werners to dinner, a whole year!'

'All I'm saying is that we really must cut back.'

'You make it sound as though it's my fault—'

'No, no,' I said hastily. 'Of course it's not your fault . . .'

'Provence was your idea!'

This was old ground. 'Yes.'

'And Melton.'

I let that one pass; it simply wasn't worth arguing about. 'Melton *has* to go as quickly as possible,' I said.

'D'you think I don't know that?' she cried. 'I've been on to the estate agent every day! *Every* day!'

I remembered other things, the redecorating of the drawing room here at Glebe Place that appeared to be going ahead though I thought we'd agreed to cancel it, and the housekeeper in Provence who was meant to have left last month but still seemed to be in place, and I got that sick clammy feeling I always got when I realised that our spending was still way out of control.

'I'm doing all I can!' Ginny declared, sparking with reproach. 'You make it sound as though I'm trying to make things worse or something!'

'Of course I don't think that. I just—' But a futility blocked my words.

Ginny's mouth was buttoned down in that expression of hurt and abandonment I knew so well, and, with a swoop of defeat, I reached for her hand. 'Sorry, sorry . . .' I wondered how many times we said sorry to each other in the course of an average tiff, and how little this immense weight of apology seemed to achieve.

'It's all right,' she said, with a glint of the uncertain humour she used to signal the end of our arguments. 'I'll cut down on the cat food and serve up leftovers and fire Consuela. And if all else fails I can always go on the streets.' She gave a brave little smile. 'Not past it yet.'

I took my cue. 'You can say that again. You'd make a fortune.'

As I put my arms round her I had the sensation of falling off the edge of my life and not being able to stop.

'Do you shoot?' asked Lady Werner.

'No, I'm afraid not.'

'Ride?'

'The last horse spotted my beginner's label at fifty yards and rubbed me off against a tree.'

Lady Werner had the generosity to laugh before turning to respond to the man on her right. It was a relief not to talk for a moment. I was finding conversation hard, partly because I'd drunk too much wine – I was making the most of the last of the good claret I'd laid down ten years ago – partly because my troubles kept blundering into the forefront of my mind, obstructing my words.

I stared dimly at the brilliant scene before me, at the banks of candles and flowers extending down the table, at the rich ruby glow of the wall hangings, at the blood-red and gold of the wine reflected off the crystal; I saw Ginny at the far end of the table, her marble complexion and fine-etched beauty perfectly framed by the vibrant colours around her. I watched her tilt her head towards Werner and listen with rapt attention, and I felt disconnected from the scene, like an imposter in some exotic spectacle.

When the party moved to the drawing room for coffee, I slipped away upstairs and sat in the quiet of the bathroom, gripping my head in my hands, staring unseeing at the carpet. When a return could be avoided no longer, I splashed cold water over my face and made my way back downstairs.

Fortunately Werner wasn't a demanding conversationalist. I only had to slip in the occasional nod or comment to keep him going for half an hour on the subject of art sponsorship. Harder to stomach was a lawyer called Hodgworth-Hill, whose smooth overbearing manner and open contempt for what he called the common herd began to grate on my overstretched nerves. I wondered why Ginny had asked him; I couldn't imagine he was involved in charity work. Listening to his gabble I felt a sudden upsurge of resentment. I had the suspicion he would be the last of the dinner guests to leave and I was right.

'But he's staying,' Ginny declared when I caught her in the hall. 'I told you! Come and play backgammon!' she urged with feverish gaiety. 'Come on! We'll set up two boards!'

She pulled at my hand but I mumbled an excuse about needing to go upstairs for a minute.

Her return to the drawing room was greeted with a cheer. I heard the bombastic tones of the lawyer, followed by shouts of raucous laughter and the clink of glasses, and something overturned inside me. I stood there in the hall, trying to make sense of my raging thoughts, aware that I had reached some terrifying crisis but not absolutely sure what it was about, let alone how to contain it. I only knew that I couldn't face another moment among these people, that I had to get away.

Once the urge to flee overtook me, it became a desperate compulsion. I didn't stop to think where I would go or how long I would stay away, I didn't pause to consider Ginny, I only knew I had to escape. I raced upstairs and, throwing my evening clothes on the floor, pulled on some old jeans and a sweater. Pausing only to scribble a note to Ginny, I blundered out to my car and careered off.

It was madness to drive. I was way over the drink-driving limit, but the stupidity of what I was doing was lost in my greater panic and the need to feel that I was, in some muddled way, regaining a degree of control over my life.

I set out blindly, yet there was never any question of where I would go. Dittisham was the one place I could be alone, the one place where I would have a chance to think.

There was little traffic, the motorway was like a wide black tunnel, I had the sensation of flying. Somehow I stayed awake, miraculously I didn't kill anyone. Arriving at Dittisham in the dead of night, I wandered from room to room. I couldn't get over how quiet it was. The hush was miraculous, an all-enveloping cocoon of calm. It seemed to me that I had never really noticed it before, that my mind had been closed to such things for a long time.

Exhaustion made me maudlin. I felt a sudden longing for the past, for the simplicity and focus of my early life. I thought of my father and how much he had meant to me. I grasped at the more elusive memories of my mother, dead for more than twenty years, and thought how little I had really known her.

Eventually I climbed the stairs and, hesitating outside the guest room Ginny and I had always used when we came to stay, passed on down the passage to the small room that had been mine as a boy. It was a storage room now, stacked with trunks and tea chests, but an old metal bed still stood in one corner, and, perched on a rickety table next to it, a lamp from my Indian travels, crowned by a parchment shade. Beneath the bed were my watercolours, hundreds of them, bundled into cardboard folders, relics of the years when I'd had the ambition to paint. It was many years since I had attempted any sort of picture.

Opening the window, I lay down on the hard mattress under an ancient blanket. There was hardly any wind, just a faint movement in the air, but it must have been wafting from the river because I could hear the faint lapping of water. Stupefied by the memories of a thousand untroubled nights, I slept like a child.

'Nothing gentle about the way David woke me, of course. Rattled the bed head. He wasn't too pleased with me.'

'Well, we hadn't had the best of nights,' Mary com-

120

mented drily. 'Ginny called at something like two, then again half an hour later, not to mention the calls the next morning. We told her you probably weren't answering the phone, but she wanted David to go and find you there and then, in the middle of the night.'

'I didn't hear the phone, I'm afraid.'

'Why should you?' For the first time it struck me that Mary actively disapproved of Ginny's permanent state of edgy anxiety.

'I didn't mean to worry Ginny.'

'David flatly refused, of course. To go out and look for you. Until the morning anyway.'

'I wasn't leaving her – it was nothing like that,' I said, seeking to justify myself further. 'I never stopped loving her . . .' But in saying this I was no longer sure what I meant by love, and whether it must always contain so much effort and pain. 'She worked so hard at everything, at making our lives . . . *full*.'

Mary studied her drink. 'But you had to get away,' she reminded me.

Defending Ginny was something of a reflex with me, but for once I let it pass. 'Yes, I had to get away.'

'We all need space from time to time.'

'Yes.'

But my response was too half-hearted for Mary. 'Nothing wrong in that,' she argued.

'No. You're right.'

She nodded firmly.

'So . . . There was poor David,' I said, finding my way back into the story. 'He made the mistake of asking me what the matter was – and got the lot. All my angst, yards of it. The business, Howard, Pa's death. And of course, me and Ginny . . . It just poured out, I'm afraid.'

'I hope he was sympathetic.'

'Well, you know how he is. Not his strongest suit. But on the whole – yes. Apart from the one subject that he really should have learnt to leave well alone by now. He kept on about fertility treatment and whether Ginny'd tried the latest method, whatever its name is. He'd sent us some information about it. He was convinced that not having children was at the root of our problems, and however much I told him that it wasn't an issue he just listened with that maddening all-knowing expression on his face. Sometimes I think he sees absolutely everything in medical terms, even relationships.'

Mary raised her eyebrows slightly at this, but made no comment. She never voiced any grumbles about her marriage, although among the family it had long been acknowledged that my brother wasn't the easiest of people to live with.

'Anyway, at the end of it all he declared that I was just depressed, and gave me some tablets. Typical David! Nothing that can't be fixed by getting dosed up! Oh, don't get me wrong – I didn't really expect any more. I mean, David has quite enough on his plate, doesn't he? People's troubles all day long. No, it was enough to have someone to talk to – that was all I needed really.'

I looked into the fire. 'But then, Mary, the strangest thing, the strangest thing . . .' I hunched forward as the memory gripped me. 'We went down to the river

– David wanted to look at the river wall or whatever it was that needed repairing – and I was rambling on about the past, about the summers we used to have, the golden times – I was still in a bit of a state, I can tell you – and, talking about those years, the best years, I thought of Sylvie. Nothing too surprising about that – we'd spent that long summer together, do you remember? The one when it was really scorching?'

'I remember.'

'But the thing was – just as she came into my mind, at the very instant I thought of her, I looked across the river and there she was! I thought I was dreaming. Well, I thought I was seeing things, actually. Then I thought it must be someone else who looked just like her. She was in a dinghy with a whole lot of other people, going up river. But that hair, the way she sat, her profile . . . David couldn't see the likeness, but for me it was blinding. I felt a great bolt of recognition and – well, I'm not sure what. Hope? Something like that. I couldn't get her out of my mind. I was overwhelmed . . . bewitched. I had the strangest feeling – this sounds mad – that everything would be all right if I could get to see her again, that she would be able to *save* me in some way. Crazy! *Crazy!* But you have to remember I wasn't thinking straight. I still hadn't had much sleep – what time did David come over that morning? Seven? Eight? So, four hours at the most. I wasn't sure what was real any more. I told myself my mind was playing tricks. But somewhere deep down there was this tiny irrational ray of hope that it *was* her. Part of me was desperate for some sort of escape, I suppose, and Sylvie represented something precious and beautiful. She was my Avalon; or the *idea* of her . . . I'd been so happy with her, you see. I'd felt so full of – *possibilities*. It was the only time in my life that I'd felt free.' The wind roared outside, the house creaked like an old ship. I looked up. 'I don't know – is this making any sense?'

She gave a slight nod, though her eyes seemed to have taken on a harsher, more judgmental light.

'By the time I went out to *Ellie Miller* that afternoon, I'd persuaded myself it was a hallucination. I'd slept a bit by then, I'd come down to earth with a bang, I was feeling bloody awful, in fact—'

'What were you doing on *Ellie*?'

'Oh, checking her over, pumping the bilges. David asked me to go out, to save him a trip. I was glad, actually. It gave me a reason to stay down. I couldn't have gone back to Melton. I couldn't have faced anybody just then.'

'No.'

'But Mary, I'd forgotten how utterly glorious the river could be. It was a perfect day, quiet, warm, no one about. It was so peaceful! So I stayed on board for a while, sitting there on the mooring, drinking Pa's whisky, thinking things through. Mentally, it was rather a toss-up between shooting myself and dying of sheer love of life. I was a bit emotional, to say the least.'

Sitting there on the boat I had remembered all the good times I'd had when I was young, the trips with

Pa on *Ellie Miller*, the passages up the coast, the expeditions ashore; the excitement of the night watches, the running jokes we'd enjoyed, the long companionable silences.

It was on one of these trips in my late teens that my father had confided in me about his early life, about his strained relationship with his own father, the lack of communication and affection, and how he had strived to succeed because he'd felt it was the only way to win his father's approval. He wanted it to be different for me. He wanted me to succeed for my own sake, and because I loved the business.

There had been a time when I'd resented his blithe assumption that I would follow him into the business. At seventeen I'd made up my mind to become a designer, which was the closest I could get to being an artist and still get paid. My father hadn't tried to talk me out of it exactly, but he'd got various family friends and godparents to point out some of the disadvantages. I hadn't improved my chances by failing to get in to the first two art colleges I'd tried. And when I was offered a place at Oxford to read languages, I began to recognise the inevitability of what lay ahead. My father was characteristically generous, sending me round the world in my gap year, funding all my travel in the vacations. After that I felt it would have been ungrateful not to give the business a try.

I hadn't regretted my choice, only my failure to make a success of it.

I missed my father. No one tells you how to grieve properly, how much pain to expect, how much guilt and anger, and whether it's normal to have long periods when you feel nothing at all. In the months since his death, my grief had seemed both inadequate and incomplete.

Going to the chart table, I lifted the lid and found his job list lying on the top of the charts where he had always kept it. I picked it up with gentle hands and laid it on the table. Seeing the elegant handwriting made shaky by age, the neat columns of jobs with all but three systematically crossed off, I wept for him at last.

'And then . . .' The picture burned brightly in my mind. 'Sylvie appeared. I heard this knocking on the hull and I went up on deck but I couldn't see anything. No boat, nothing. Then the knocking came again and I went to the stern and there she was in the water. Well, I couldn't believe my eyes. I just stared at her. Then she laughed at me, and, Mary, it was like a dream only *more* so. You see, she hadn't changed. She was just the same. It was as though . . . as though *nothing* had changed.'

My throat was dry, I coughed, and Mary passed me the last of her whisky.

Gulping it, I echoed, 'She was just the same.' I saw her standing in the cabin, with that dramatic colouring she had inherited from her French mother, the long black hair sticking wetly to her shoulders, and the white translucent skin touched with faint freckles; and I could only wonder again at the smoothness of her skin, the way it was completely untouched by

126

time, as if she'd skipped all the intervening years and lived no other life.

'I pulled her out of the water and she scolded me for letting her stand there and shiver. I just laughed because she was talking to me as if we'd last seen each other a few hours ago. That was her gift . . .' I reached for a thought I had never fully identified before. 'Her gift was for *intimacy*. She could make you feel you were the only person in the world, or at least the only person she really cared about. She made you feel that being with her was everything, that there couldn't be anything more important or more exciting. That suddenly everything was possible. And I needed that, Mary! I needed to feel . . . well, that I could have some sort of life away from all the pressure, the endless succession of disasters. That I could forget – for a while anyway – and be . . .' I gave an ironic gasp. 'Be *free*.'

I heard Sylvie's voice again, that extraordinary rich voice of hers that could communicate so many different, often contradictory, messages. She was sitting in the saloon, wrapped in the only towel I could find and an old waterproof jacket of Pa's, a whisky in her hand, with her head tilted to one side, chin tucked in or suddenly thrown up in that French way of hers. Only her gaze was unwavering, her almond eyes fixed on mine with a glittering absorption, as if no time had intervened and we had never stopped being soul-mates. She told me about her new life, the pottery shop in Dartmouth where she was working, the cottage she was renting just outside Dittisham. She loved it here, she told me. Her return was a spiritual thing, she needed to be in touch with elemental things, with water and wind and creativity. She was going to start sculpting. Near water she felt empowered, she could draw on wells of creativity, she felt supremely in touch with her body and her spiritual energies.

No one I knew talked in this way. Among my contemporaries this would have been dismissed as New Age psycho-babble, yet Sylvie imbued it with a sort of grandeur, and an earthiness too. There was an undercurrent of self-indulgence there, a strong hint of physicality and hedonism. But then even at fifteen Sylvie had exuded a powerful animal sensuality, a breathtaking sexual assurance, which, with her flamboyant defiance for convention, had produced an overwhelming effect on the rather staid young man I had been when we'd met.

The effect she had on me as we sat in the boat drinking whisky sixteen years later wasn't terribly different. I laughed too much and too quickly, I heard myself trying to impress and amuse her, I felt a ridiculous effervescent pleasure. With a sense of the miraculous, I felt myself come alive again.

When she got up to leave she rested the back of her hand against my face, and gave that little cat-grin of hers, all enchantment and promise.

Mary clasped her hands under her chin. 'Then?' She was urging me forward, and I realised how late it must be.

'Then?' I sighed. 'Well, I had to see her again. In

fact, I couldn't think of much else. It was a desperate thing – a sort of compulsion. I couldn't get her out of my mind. It was . . .' But the memory caught at me, and stalled my thoughts.

After a while Mary said softly, 'You had an affair?'

Distracted, I stared into the fire, I shook my head in lingering disbelief. 'For a long time nothing happened. I thought she was just wary of involvement, I thought it was her conscience. That she was bothered by me being married. Quite funny, really, in retrospect.' My smile emerged as a bleak grimace. 'By the time I realised she had no conscience whatsoever, it was too late. I was completely hooked. I'd completely lost my judgment. And she used that, she used *me*.' Saying it, I felt a fresh plunge of humiliation. 'She led me a complete dance. That's exactly what it was – a dance!'

Mary said something which I missed, and she had to repeat it. 'Did you see her last weekend?' Her voice had a sudden tension to it.

'No.' Then, as I absorbed the implications of what she had said, I stared at her. '*No*, Mary, I did not.'

Mary said rapidly, as if to get it over and done with, 'You weren't on the boat with her?'

'No.'

She cast me an odd look, as though something about this disturbed her.

'*Mary*.'

'I only meant that it wouldn't have looked too good if you had been,' she explained in a rush. 'That was all.'

'I did not see her last weekend,' I repeated forcefully.

She nodded but her eyes still held a spark of doubt.

'I hadn't seen her for two weeks!'

She held up a defensive hand. 'Hugh, I believe you. Really. *Really.*'

The ringing of the phone cut into the unhappy pause that followed.

It was Tingwall. 'Look,' he said, 'I didn't want to bother you so late, but I thought you'd better know that I've had a call from the press.'

'Christ. What did they want?'

'I think I've quashed any ideas they might have had. Told them you and your wife were just possible witnesses because you lived on the river. That sort of thing.'

'Did they buy it?'

'One can but hope.'

Five

GINNY APPEARED on the landing above, a wraith against the sunlit window. 'You're back,' she declared, sounding agitated. She touched an anxious hand to her uncombed hair, then to the fastening of her wrap. 'What's the time? I fell asleep.'

'It's about four. Are you all right?' And asking this, I wasn't sure what sort of response to expect. Even at the best of times I found it difficult to gauge Ginny's mood.

'It was flu after all,' she said matter-of-factly, 'but I think I'm over the worst of it now. And you? No more from the police?'

'No.'

'Well,' she breathed, 'that's something. And me? Do I still have to . . . ?'

'Tingwall's arranged for you to go to Chelsea police station on Monday, if that's all right. They'll only need a brief statement.'

She nodded solemnly.

Turning towards the bedroom, she paused for long enough to catch my eye and issue a silent but unequivocal plea. The moment of account was not to be delayed, I realised, and climbing the stairs I attempted to prepare myself for whatever was to come, wrath or recrimination.

She was smoothing the bed. 'I'm sorry about what I said on the phone,' she announced immediately, and there was a note of rehearsal in her voice. 'I didn't mean to be unhelpful.'

'No . . . I wasn't too helpful myself.'

'I just wanted to know what the police thought they were up to, that was all. I was worried.' She was on the point of saying more but, ducking her eyes, sat down abruptly at her dressing table and began to brush her hair with sharp strokes that made it crackle.

I asked, 'Do you want to talk about it now?'

She twisted round and said, 'Please,' as though we had plucked this subject out of the air.

I sat on the edge of the bed. 'Well . . . They knew Sylvie had dropped in to see me on the boat a couple of times. This was ages ago, June some time. I'd already told them that. And I'd told them I'd bumped into her by the ferry once. But for some reason – and I've no idea what – they came down on me like a ton of bricks. The full treatment.' I gave a shuddering laugh. 'They have this way of making you feel they're not going to believe a word you say. Scary. *Terrifying*. Anyway, they were extremely keen to know where I was when Sylvie was killed. Luckily, I could account for most of that Saturday – David saw me in Dartmouth hunting for food and then you arrived and then David popped in later . . . So, one way and another, there wasn't time for me to have been anywhere else.'

She absorbed this with stern concentration. 'And

you've no idea what it was that made them pick on you?'

I shook my head.

'But there was *something*?'

'Possibly – presumably . . .'

'And they didn't tell you what?'

'No.'

She gave an anxious laugh which hid none of her curiosity. 'But what reason could they have had for dragging you all the way down there again?'

'Ginny, I don't know.'

She searched my face for the lie, and I met her gaze as best I could.

She looked away. 'What else did they want to know?'

'Oh, you can imagine. How well I knew Sylvie, that sort of thing.'

'And they were happy with . . . what you said?'

I shrugged. 'They had to be, didn't they?'

She drew a ragged breath. 'How could they do it anyway – drag you off like that? Did they have the right?'

'I'm not sure, darling. But it would have looked strange if I'd refused, wouldn't it?'

She considered this. 'Yes, I suppose it would.' She twisted the hairbrush in her lap, her delicate features etched with unease. 'And you don't know what it was that made them want to see you again?'

'No.'

She made an attempt to smile. 'But you must have some idea.'

Here it was again, the inability to let go, the

constant chafing. 'I really don't know, Ginny. But they must have thought I was having an affair with Sylvie, mustn't they? If I was meant to have killed her I would hardly have done it without a reason, and that's the obvious one, isn't it?'

I could hear the sound of her breathing, the rasping that preceded an attack, and I wondered how long it would be before she reached for the inhaler.

'And you've no idea what made them think . . .?'

It wasn't a challenge this time, more a craving for reassurance. So I denied it again, because it was far too late to do anything else.

Conflicting emotions passed across Ginny's face, then with a jerky movement she put the hairbrush back in its place on the dressing table. 'Well, at least they've got it straight at last!' she said, striking a bright nervy note. 'We can begin to forget the whole wretched business.'

She was waiting for me to agree; she wanted to hear me say that I was putting everything to do with Sylvie behind me.

'Let's hope so.'

She shot me a sharp look.

'It's the press,' I explained. 'They seem to have heard about my visit to the police. And we all know what they're like. Given half a chance, they'll blow it up out of all proportion. That'd be all I need, with the buyout coming together.'

She was blinking rapidly, pulling hard on her lungs. 'But how did the press hear about it?'

'Who knows? These things get out, don't they?' And for no apparent reason I thought of Howard.

Her forehead wrinkled into a rare frown, and I noticed how strained she was looking, and how dark were the shadows around her eyes. 'What happened? Did they phone?'

'They called Tingwall. He seems to think he's palmed them off all right.'

She shook her head. 'It's not so easy to palm them off! They have a way of coming back. We should make a plan.'

Ginny's mother had been a famous beauty who'd led what in charitable terms might be described as an eventful life, with three husbands, numerous lovers, and an unwavering talent for attracting scandal. After a childhood in the spotlight, Ginny had good reason to consider herself something of an expert on the press.

'The thing is . . .' she murmured, thinking her way through it. 'You must be sure to speak to them if they call. Be completely open. Utterly polite and terribly nice. Even jokey. Mummy always said that you could get away with murder if you made the press laugh.' She looked at me with her great fluid eyes, the irony of what she had said completely lost on her, or calmly unacknowledged.

'I'm not sure I'm quite up to cracking jokes, Ginny.'

'Be jolly, then. Carefree. If they catch the slightest hint of panic around you, they'll be back for more, like jackals.'

This was what I always forgot, her astuteness, her talent for reading situations.

'It's terribly important to appear friendly,' she

stressed. 'You can be rather cool, you know. I've heard you with journalists. You can sound rather offhand.'

'Can I? I hadn't realised. Well, I'll do my best.' I picked up her inhaler from the bedside table and took it across to her.

'Tone makes all the difference . . .' But she could hardly say it, she was so short of breath.

She took the inhaler from my hand, drew on it greedily and gave two or three harsh coughs. From the gardens below came the sound of children playing and the wail of an electric lawn mower. I kept forgetting it was Saturday.

After a while I asked, 'All right?'

She nodded impatiently. She never liked to talk about her asthma. 'Oh, Julia came by with a stack of papers for you. I put them in the study.'

'Thanks.'

She twisted round on the stool and examined her face in the mirror. 'Will you have time for dinner?' Above the breathlessness her voice was still taut.

'Of course. I'll make time.'

'I thought we'd have something silly, like eggs and baked beans.' She reached for her face cream and I saw that her hand was trembling.

I felt a surge of remorse. 'Ginny—'

'It's all right!@' she declared, smearing the cream fiercely over her cheeks, 'I'm not going to ask if you had an affair! I assure you – I don't want to know!' Abandoning her face abruptly, she clamped her hands together on the surface of the table and stared down at them. She whispered, 'But I would like to know if you loved her.'

I stared at her dumbly in the glass.

'And don't lie, please,' she added, her voice rising sharply. 'I couldn't bear it.'

'I didn't love her,' I said.

She looked up and our eyes met in the mirror. I saw hope in her face, and wretchedness.

'I didn't love her,' I repeated.

She searched my expression, then, gasping, looked down and nodded rapidly.

'It was—'

'No! Don't say any more!' She fumbled for the cream again. 'Don't!'

I felt a familiar gust of helplessness and uncertainty. Did she mean it? Sometimes her most effusive denials turned out to be cries for reassurance which, despite the absence of firm clues, I was meant to decipher and assuage. I was still searching for the right thing to say when she glanced up and said briskly, 'I'll see you later then. You really don't mind eggs and baked beans?'

Relief made me smile stupidly. 'Can't think of anything better.'

She nodded again, and returned to her makeup.

I leant down and kissed the top of her head. When I looked up again she had averted her eyes.

With the paperwork was a note from Julia. 'I can't find that petrol receipt,' she wrote. 'I don't think you ever gave it to me. It's no great problem. I can get the details from MasterCard and/or the service

137

station, but I just thought I'd mention it, in case you had it lying around.'

I looked in the compartment of my wallet where I usually put receipts and credit card counterfoils before handing them over to Julia at the end of each week. The petrol receipt wasn't there, nor the credit card voucher. I remembered handing my card to the cashier at the service station, I remembered signing the slip, but the rest of the exchange, like the drive itself, was a blur. I had spent the journey trying not to think about Sylvie but thinking, in the end, of little else. All sorts of fantasies had crowded my brain: I imagined her waiting for me at Dittisham, I heard the phone ringing as I walked in, or if these were too much to hope for, I saw myself finding a note, telling me where to find her. They were desperate impossible fantasies, born of obsession. I knew full well that there would be no sign of her, that as usual she would be doing her best to avoid me, and that if I was to have any chance of seeing her I would have to go and search for her myself.

Nearing Dittisham I persuaded myself that I would be able to exercise some self-control, that I would have the strength of will to maintain some dignity and stay away from her, yet I knew perfectly well that I would go and look for her. I was incapable of stopping myself. The urge to see her was like a craving. I was consumed by the need to know what had gone wrong, why she had so brutally cut me out of her life. I was desperate to retrieve what she had so tantalisingly proffered and so abruptly snatched away; I wanted the euphoria again, the surge of long-forgotten emotions, the sensation of being completely and spectacularly alive. I knew our affair was over, yet I couldn't accept it. I needed to know if she'd intended to humiliate me, if she'd meant to set me up quite so effortlessly: I needed to know just how thoroughly I'd been deceived.

Approaching Dittisham, I went through a pantomime of normality. I avoided Sylvie's cottage and drove straight to the house. I forced myself to go inside and turn on the water heater, to pour myself a drink and sit by the window as if I intended to have a quiet evening. I even convinced myself that I would be satisfied by going upstairs to David's old bedroom and focusing my specially purchased binoculars on the stretch of river just beyond the ferry where the white yacht with the bowsprit lay at her mooring. But the stillness of the scene, the complete absence of life on board were both a torment and a challenge. It was then that I gave up all pretence of self-possession and drove off in search of her.

I had spent an hour on some amended cash flow projections when Ginny buzzed through to say that David was on the line.

'We're just on our way out,' he declared, ever swift to establish that his time was limited. 'Wanted to let you know what we've decided for the buyout. It'll be fifty thousand. Can't do more, I'm afraid.'

Overcoming my disappointment, I said, 'David – thank you.'

'The thing is, we've tied up quite a bit in this trust

for the children. And the terms of the trust – you know, we're simply not allowed to invest in anything risky.'

'I understand.'

'Well, there we are.'

'You won't regret it.'

'I should hope not!' And his tone wasn't entirely facetious.

'Thanks again for yesterday.'

'Mmm?' he murmured distractedly, and I could hear the sound of turning pages as his attention wandered.

'For coming to the police station.'

'Oh, that reminds me,' he drawled. 'Mary heard something on the lawyers' scandal-vine this morning – you know how she is for having her ear to the ground. She was going to call you. She didn't get a name,' he said, meandering towards the point, 'but she heard that someone got hauled in for questioning late last night.'

'But who? Does she know?'

'I told you, she didn't get the details,' he said in his busy voice, the one he used to presage the end of his conversations. 'But I told you it would be all right, didn't I?' David's confidence had a certain steamroller quality to it, a momentum that did not allow for dissent.

'Yes, I suppose—'

'Got to rush.'

'David, I can't thank you enough for putting your faith in the buyout—'

'Not a bit,' he cut in and, with a grunt that might have been a goodbye, he rang off.

I brooded for a long time, wondering who Henderson might have hauled in for questioning. The unprepossessing long-haired youth perhaps? The owner of the white cutter? Or another of this tribe of lovers that Sylvie was meant to have had?

She was all over the place. David's words still reverberated in my mind. I had always known that Sylvie lived by her own rules, that her addiction to the sensual took her beyond normal limits, but I had pushed the obvious consequences of this thought from my mind. During our affair I had not dared to face the idea that I was sharing her with someone else. I had been too frightened of the emotions that such a suspicion might unleash in me.

The wail of a siren sounded from the direction of the King's Road. Gazing out into the dark gardens, beyond the tracery of branches to the lights of the neighbouring houses, I felt immensely glad that it was all over, that I had recovered most of my sanity and equilibrium. I had not liked myself very much while I was in thrall to Sylvie, I had not enjoyed being in a state of misery and abject longing; most of all, I had disliked being at the mercy of emotions that were so intense, obsessive and ultimately demeaning.

The siren echoed in the distance. Returning to the present with a sense of relief, I pulled out a sheet of paper and set down the figures that were already written large in my head. A shortfall of a hundred thousand from David; one million more to be found on the total price tag of the company. Against this I might be able to raise five hundred thousand on this house and Zircon might come up with two hundred and fifty thousand. I didn't need to be an Einstein to see I was still short by three hundred and fifty thousand.

I didn't blame David for reducing his investment. The takeover had brought him some shares in Cumberland and a little cash, but the total was less than a third of what he could have expected a few years back if we'd sold HartWell at the height of its fortunes. And for all I knew he and Mary might need cash for other things: they might be planning early retirement, they could even be up to their ears in debt. David might have been my brother, but so far as his financial affairs went I hardly knew him at all.

Given enough sweat and tears, I could probably raise the extra money from the Chartered Bank, but I was loathe to go back to them cap in hand unless absolutely necessary. At best it would look as though George and I had failed to do our homework properly, at worst we would simply appear incompetent. Then there was the time element. Renegotiations could take weeks and I suspected that Cumberland would use the time to solicit a better offer from elsewhere and announce a tight cut-off date for final bids. When I really wanted to frighten myself I imagined that the juicy offer was already on the table and that Howard had planted his million-pound bombshell to raise the stakes, and, accidentally or otherwise, jeopardise our chances of success.

Three hundred and fifty thousand. It shouldn't be too hard to find, so long as nothing happened to rock the boat. I tried not to think of the press and the positive storm they could raise without uttering a single word of libel.

I scribbled a line through my calculations and threw them into the bin. I heard Ginny approaching to summon me to supper, and an absurd bubble of contentment rose up in me at the thought of baked beans at the kitchen table with my wife.

'Everything went into the wash.' Already Ginny's expression was taking on the defensive look she acquired whenever she thought she might have done the wrong thing. We were in the dressing room, standing in front of the open wardrobe.

'What about the beige cords?'

'They went to the cleaners.'

'And you didn't happen to notice anything in the pockets?'

'No.' She said it a little too quickly, and I guessed she hadn't looked. 'Was it something vital?' she asked.

I shrugged, 'Not really,' and began to get undressed.

'What was it?'

'Just a receipt.'

'What for?'

'Oh – petrol, that's all.'

'But you have to find it?'

She had sensed something. It was ridiculous not to tell her. 'The police want to have a look at it. To establish what time I was on the motorway last Saturday.'

This seemed to confuse her. 'On Saturday?' She half turned towards the wardrobe as though to start undressing, only to turn back with a frown. '*Saturday? And it's important, the time you got the petrol?'

'The police think so.' I threw my socks into the basket and reached for a robe. 'I told them I arrived at Dittisham shortly after seven, but they weren't inclined to believe me, not without some backup anyway. Not the most trusting of souls.'

'And it's *lost*, this receipt!'

'Oh, it doesn't matter. It's not essential.' I explained how the information could be tracked down through the credit card company.

But something was still disturbing her. 'What will it tell them, the receipt?'

'Tell them? That I was somewhere near Bristol at five-thirty that afternoon. Well, I *think* it was five-thirty, but I'm not so sure now. I wish I hadn't said five-thirty, in fact, in case I was wrong.'

'Could you be wrong?'

'Who knows? It wouldn't be the end of the world anyway.'

'You say that! But supposing it was earlier? Could it have been earlier?'

'Well, maybe half an hour or so – not a lot.'

She was looking appalled.

'Ginny!' I laughed, putting an arm around her shoulders. 'It's all right, really.'

But she wasn't so easily pacified. 'You *say* that . . .'

'I *know* it.'

She cried, 'You can't *know*.'

'You worry too much.' I drew her into an embrace

and rested my cheek against the richness of her hair. Her stiff body seemed to tremble in my arms, like a frail storm-tossed bird.

I began to rock her slightly and to murmur soft reassurances, as I had always done in times of stress or reconciliation. Her body did not yield.

I whispered, 'It's so good to be home, Ginny. You can't imagine.' I meant, good to be home with just the two of us and no hordes to be wined and dined, though I didn't say that.

Eventually I pulled back a little and, cupping a hand under her chin, leant down to kiss her.

She didn't retreat, but she didn't kiss me back either.

I didn't blame her, I didn't expect instant absolution, but I did need to know that forgiveness wasn't a total impossibility either.

'Ginny,' I whispered awkwardly. 'Darling ... if I caused you any grief then I'm—'

She gave a small cry and wrenched herself free. For a moment she agitated a hand at me, unable to speak. 'Not now,' she gulped, her eyes brimming. 'I can't deal with that *now*!' She turned and hurried into the bedroom.

'Ginny!'

But something prevented me from pursuing her, futility or weariness. Retreating to a hot bath, I stayed in it for a long time. I comforted myself with thoughts of a not-too-distant time when life would be more settled, when memories of this summer would have faded and Ginny and I would be established not too far from Hartford, in a country house that might look something like David's, with land and gardens and an interior with enough potential to stimulate Ginny's designer instincts, a time when we would have adjusted our lives to an altogether gentler pace and in some as yet unidentifiable way moved our relationship forward, into calmer waters.

It was after midnight when I finally went into the bedroom. The lights were off but I knew Ginny wasn't asleep. Going softly round to her side of the bed, I leant down and kissed her head.

Her eyes glittered up at me.

I said, 'Do you want me to sleep in the other room?'

'I'd prefer it if you didn't.'

My heart lifted. 'Then I'll stay.'

'I don't want to be alone.' It was a statement delivered without emotion.

I thought of all the weekends when I had left her to go down to Dittisham. 'No.'

'I don't think I could bear to be alone again.'

Was this the bargain then? A commitment to curtail my freedom?

I steeled myself to say, 'I'll never leave you alone again, I promise.'

'That would mean so much. If you could manage it.' There was no irony in her voice.

A little later, as I was beginning to doze off, she propped herself up on one elbow, and without switching on the light, shook a tablet from a bottle and washed it down with water. When she settled down again her foot touched my leg and she did not move it away.

*

It was a good twenty years since, as a fresh-faced graduate with more confidence than sense, I had undertaken my sales training under Ronald Simms and got my first inkling of what it was like at the sharp end of the business. Ronald Simms was a representative of the old school. He worked his patch to a hallowed schedule, he knew the names of the buyers' children and the ailments of their wives, he wore white shirts with starched collars which did permanent battle with his Adam's apple, and he called me Mr Hugh, just as he called my father Mr Richard.

Sitting in the lounge of the Churchill Hotel with the Packenhams buyer I was reminded of the time Ronald and I had been preparing to pitch a difficult sale. 'You remember what I told you?' he'd remarked. 'That with the Hartford name there's no such thing as a cold sale? Well, that doesn't stop some sales from being a bit chillier than others.'

This sale was definitely on the chilly side. Miss Stevens, who with her doll face and timid posture appeared a disconcerting twenty though she must have been a good eight to ten years older, had been the Packenhams china and glass buyer for two years, and was showing no chinks in her considerable armour. She had de-listed Hartford Crystal five months ago because we had given Harrods a better price, and since walking into the lounge and offering me her limp handshake she had made it plain that she wasn't about to relent.

'Miss Stevens, I can only say I'm horrified by what happened. I can assure you quite categorically that it's never been our policy to discriminate. I can only imagine it was an appalling error on the part of the sales people. The only thing I can do is to offer you my sincere apologies. And my personal guarantee that it will never happen again.'

Her unyielding look said: It's a little too late for that now.

'All I can tell you is that things are going to be different at Hartford once the buyout goes through. We're putting everything we have into it – financially, I mean, as well as blood, sweat and tears – and we wouldn't be doing that unless we believed one hundred per cent in the product. You see, we feel we have something really special in Hartford crystal. We feel—' I broke off as another of Ronald's maxims came back to rap me over the knuckles: Don't tell them what to think, tell them what's new. 'What's new,' I said, 'is that Hartford will be run by the people on the spot, the people who know the business backwards. And I can honestly say that we're going to make a damned sight better job of it.'

Behind Miss Stevens' spectacles something stirred, though it was hard to tell what sort of emotion it might be. 'It wouldn't be hard to make a better job of it,' she commented in her wispy voice.

'But, Miss Stevens, however successful we are – and we *are* going to be successful – none of it'll be any good if Hartford crystal isn't on sale in Packenhams—'

My mobile phone sent up a warble from my briefcase. 'I'm so sorry,' I said rapidly. 'Only my secretary has this number and she wouldn't call me unless it was extremely urgent.'

Miss Stevens looked at her watch as she reached for her coffee.

I snatched up the phone and growled, 'Yes?'

'*Sorry*,' Julia hissed, 'but there's a photographer snooping around outside the office and your wife just called to say there're a couple at Glebe Place too. Thought you ought to be warned.'

'Hell.'

Above the coffee cup Miss Stevens' eyes, enlarged by her lenses, watched me speculatively.

'Have they phoned, the press?'

'No.'

'Well, let me know if they do. And don't say a word to anyone about this, will you?'

'Of course not,' she said indignantly. 'Oh, and George called to say he thinks he can raise another forty-five thousand.'

I dropped the phone into my case. 'I'm so sorry about that. It was, umm . . . urgent.' For an instant I imagined that the photographers had followed me here, that they were waiting for me to leave the hotel. 'So . . . I was saying that . . .' I groped for my thread. 'Our plans . . . Yes, we're going to advertise in the colour supplements over the three weeks leading up to Christmas, and what we'd really like to do is mount a special spring promotion with Packenhams.' I brought out a folder and passed it across to her. 'It's all in here.'

Miss Stevens slid her cup onto the table and sat forward, preparing to leave.

'Look,' I said hastily, 'I very much want you to change your mind about us, Miss Stevens. I'm not sure how I can achieve that, but – well, I'm going to keep trying!'

'Mr Wellesley, I'll consider your proposals. That's all I can say.' Her little-girl voice reminded me more than ever of a shop girl fresh out of school. Standing up, she smoothed the skirt of her bad suit. She hesitated before announcing, 'My father risked our home for his business.'

I didn't say anything.

'He lost both the house and the business.'

'I'm sorry.'

'So were we.'

'Miss Stevens – we're not going to fail.'

She eyed me appraisingly. 'No,' she said, 'I don't suppose you are.' And in the moment before she turned away she gave me a look that wasn't entirely unsympathetic.

'They're standing right outside the door,' Ginny told me. Her voice faded and crackled in the earpiece as my cab swung along the Bayswater Road. '. . . Photographers and a reporter.'

'How many?'

'Three of them. I have to go out in a minute. But I know what I'm going to say to them.'

'Ginny . . .' I didn't want her to realise how appalled I was. 'Wouldn't it be better to say nothing?'

'Don't worry – it won't be much.'

I felt powerless. 'Well, be careful, for God's sake.'

'I will.' She sounded listless, or depressed; it was hard to tell with such a bad connection.

'How are you feeling?'

'Me? Umm . . .' She took her time. 'Oh, all right.'

'What about the doctor?'

'That's where I'm going, to see him.'

'Let me know what he says, won't you?'

'Yes.'

'Don't let him give you any old thing.'

'No.'

She had slept most of the day before. When she'd finally got up we had spent the time like two battle-weary warriors home from the fray. After the tensions of the previous night we'd kept a respectful distance, speaking little and with caution. Over an early supper we had discussed the sale of Melton and its contents, and I had drawn some comfort from the prosaicness of our conversation. Later we'd watched television in bed and as we'd fallen asleep Ginny had made no objection when I'd slid an arm loosely round her waist.

I said, 'You haven't been to the police station then?'

'I didn't feel well enough.'

'No, of course not. I left a message for Tingwall, to warn him you might not be up to it. He'll square it with the people at Exeter.'

'While you're on,' she said. 'The petrol receipt, have you . . .?'

'Julia's still chasing it. But it'll be fine, really.' A roaring came over the ether as though we were entering a tunnel. 'Take care,' I shouted. 'And do watch out for those people.' I had a vision of the photographers pushing their lenses into Ginny's face.

'Don't worry.' Her voice was breaking up badly, but I thought she said, 'I'm used to them, remember.'

Nearing the office I peered over the cabbie's shoulder, but there were no photographers outside the building and no one loitering in the entrance. I strode inside with an itchy feeling between my shoulder blades and a powerful urge to look behind me.

Julia told me the photographer had abandoned his vigil twenty minutes before.

'And it was definitely me he was looking for?' I asked, knowing the answer.

She put the messages in front of me and nodded. 'He tried to get information from the security man. Wanted to know if you'd been in today.'

I tried to shrug if off, I tried to tell myself that they would lose interest quickly enough, but all the time a small doom-laden voice wondered why they should come now, when the police had finished with me.

Julia waited for me to read the messages. 'Oh, that petrol receipt?' she said. 'I got the MasterCard details. It was the Gordano service station on the M5. Just past Bristol. And the time – you've no idea what I had to go through to get this, I had to bribe the station manager to sort through all his till rolls! Anyway, it was four-fifteen.'

I felt a pull of apprehension. 'Are you sure?'

'Yes.' But giving me the benefit of the doubt she hurried into her office and came back with her notebook. 'Here we are.' She showed me the entry. 'Four-fifteen.'

I'd been miles out then. I had told Henderson five-thirty to six. What on earth had made me say that? I realised that, far from leaving the office at three, I must have left long before, maybe as early as two. I had been in such a state of confusion that afternoon that anything was possible.

I could see now that it had been a mistake to commit myself to such a firm guess. Being half an hour out might have looked understandable, but a whole hour was going to seem careless. Yet it was the easiest thing in the world to make a mistake about the time. Well, I hoped that was how the police would view it anyway. Suddenly I needed reassurance. I was about to call Tingwall when Julia buzzed through to tell me Mary was on the line.

'Hang on,' called Mary the moment I greeted her. In the background I could hear the squawky voices of cartoon characters on the television, then, rising above the sound, Mary yelling good-naturedly to someone to turn the thing down.

'Henry's home with flu,' she complained cheerfully. 'If it's not one thing it's another. Listen, did you speak to David? Did he call you?'

'Yes. Look, I'm really very grateful for your support.'

'But it's only fifty thousand.'

'Whatever you feel comfortable with is fine with me.'

'Well, it's not fine with me,' she declared in the crisp authoritative tones she'd retained from her legal days. 'I'd like to put in some of my own money.'

'Mary, that's sweet of you, but I couldn't accept it.'

'Why not?'

'Because . . . I wouldn't feel happy.'

'Why wouldn't you feel happy? It's my money. Nothing to do with David. Oh, I'll tell him, if that's what you're worried about – though I very much hope it isn't!'

I knew Mary had money of her own; quite apart from the HartWell shares which she and Howard had inherited from their father, they had also been left antiques and silver and cash, though I'd never been clear on how much was involved, nor the extent to which Mary's capital had been merged with David's or tied up in the children's trusts.

She asked, 'How much do you need?'

I laughed, 'Mary, you don't want to ask!'

'I am asking!'

I laughed again. 'Okay . . . As of today we're still short by three hundred and five thousand. Assuming Cumberland agrees the valuation.'

'Can't manage all of that, but you can count me in for a hundred thousand.'

'*Mary.*'

'Actually on second thoughts I might not tell David. What do you think? No, no . . . I'll have to, won't I?' She sighed, an overblown sound made for effect. 'He won't like it, will he? You know how he is – caution, caution. Never backed a horse in his life.'

'Mary, I don't know what to say.'

'Don't say anything, then. Oh!' She gasped. 'One person who must never find out – Howard!'

'There's no risk of that, Mary. We're not exactly speaking.'

'You'll keep it totally anonymous? Just you, me and David?'

'Of course.'

'Well, there we are then!'

'Mary, you're amazing.'

'Since you mention it . . .' And she gave a gravelly laugh.

'You don't want time to think about it?'

'I've done my thinking. And my thinking says you're going to make me rich.'

'Mary, I'll certainly do my best.'

She gave a hum of amusement and we said goodbye.

I sat in a state of barely controlled elation, knowing that there was still some way to go, that I mustn't on any account think of celebrating, but feeling too optimistic and too starved of good fortune not to do so.

Julia came in and, catching my mood, demanded, 'The good news?'

'Only two hundred and five thousand to go!'

Julia thrust a fist into the air, and performed a curious shimmy with her hips.

Pushing thoughts of the press to the back of my mind, I rang Hartford to tell George, then spent the rest of the afternoon calculating the revised figures for Zircon, which Julia typed and sent off by special messenger, and arranging the necessary meetings for the rest of the week. There were three sets of documents to be finalised urgently: the company articles for the new firm, Hartford Crystal Ltd; the Shareholders' Agreement with Zircon; and the agreement for the new company to purchase the assets, trading names and working capital of the old Hartford Division. I wanted everything ready for signature before the end of the week, in case Howard pulled a fast one. It was an ambitious schedule, but not an impossible one.

At five, lifted by the satisfactions of the day, I said to Julia, 'You know something? I'm beginning to think we're making some progress.' I was too superstitious to talk about success.

'I keep telling you – the light at the end of the tunnel isn't always an approaching train.'

I had been trying Ginny all afternoon and getting the answering machine. Now the line was engaged. I hoped the doctor had given her some vitamins. It was a long time since I had seen her so low, though I hardly needed reminding that much of the responsibility for that lay at my door. I hated the idea of having made her unhappy, yet it seemed to me that unhappiness had been creeping up on us for a long time, and that without it I would almost certainly have resisted the final slide into betrayal.

There are a dozen ways to block out unhappiness. Ginny and I had chosen work, as much as we could fit into a single day, so that we never had time to question the purpose of it all.

I knew the structure of Ginny's days, where she went, who she saw; I knew about the committee meetings, the working lunches, the hours on the phone, the shopping; but I had never known if these activities were a real source of contentment to her. She had always taken her duties seriously, the duties of keeping house – the food on the table, the flowers and decorations, the supervision of the diary – and the duties of her charity work, which she undertook with immense conscientiousness; but did she feel a sense of achievement at the end of it all? She never expressed any views one way or the other. She seemed to distrust discussions of happiness, as though such scrutiny would tempt fate and undermine whatever joys she did possess.

I was packing my briefcase when Julia buzzed through to say that Tingwall was on the line.

'I was going to call you,' I said immediately, and started to tell him about the petrol receipt.

'Perhaps we can leave that for another time,' he interrupted. 'I have bad news, I'm afraid. The police want you to come in again, and this time it'll be as a suspect. They've served a number of search warrants on us.'

My heart thumped once against my chest. 'What do you mean?'

'They've obtained warrants to search Dittisham House, and the *Ellie Miller*, and to remove your car.'

The room seemed to sway, I felt the blood drain from my head. 'You're joking!' I could hardly get the words out. 'You're bloody joking!'

'They'll arrest you on suspicion as a formality. But please remember it's not the same as being charged.'

'Christ . . . *Christ* . . .' I found my way onto my chair. 'Why? *Why?*'

'They don't have to tell us, I'm afraid. And we have no way of finding out.'

'But there must be some reason!'

'In so far as the police have to show the magistrate good cause before he'll sign the warrants – yes, there must be. Magistrates do vary, of course, some let things through on a nod, but on the whole . . .'

My disbelief was overtaken by the painful realisation that, like it or not, I had to deal with this nightmare which had so suddenly and firmly attached itself to me. 'The boat, you say? And the car?'

'I've arranged for your brother to hand over the keys to Dittisham House and the boat. They've got your car.'

It took me a moment to grasp what he was saying. 'They've got it?'

'They're at your house. I said you'd surrender to them there. I thought you might find it more convenient.'

'They're there *now*?'

'Yes. And Mr Wellesley? I need hardly tell you not to say anything until you get to Exeter. I'll see you there.'

'Charles?'

'Yes?'

It hit me suddenly, the enormity of what lay ahead, and my throat swelled, I felt a surge of panic and self-pity. 'This whole thing is ridiculous!'

'I'm sure.'

'They're quite wrong.'

A slight pause. 'We'll sort it out.'

'They're wrong.' I heard the entreaty in my voice, and the desperation.

'Just remember not to say anything on the way down. All right?'

I blurted something to an astonished Julia before walking blindly down to the street and hailing a cab. The driver set off at a fair lick and as we sped towards Chelsea I had the sensation that everything in my life was moving too fast, like a film run at double speed. I tried to prepare myself for what was to come but my mind was all over the place, caught between despair, reason and a growing panic. Sporadically I tried to reach Ginny on the mobile but the line was always engaged.

I'd forgotten the photographers. As we entered Glebe Place I saw them clustered around the gate. Thrusting money at the cabbie, I walked through their clicking lenses, not looking at them but not hiding my head either.

Ginny must have been watching for me because she opened the door as I approached.

Phipps and Reith were standing behind her in the hall.

Ginny whispered, 'They have a warrant.'

Reith stepped forward and delivered in a dull monotone, 'Hugh William Wellesley, I am arresting you on suspicion of the murder of Sylvie Anne Mathieson—'

I began to shake my head.

'—You do not have to say anything. But it may harm your defence if you do not mention when questioned something which you later rely on in court. Anything you do say may be given in evidence. Do you understand?'

My brain responded, but it took a little longer for my lips to obey. 'I understand.'

Ginny said, 'I would like to accompany my husband to Devon. I hope that'll be acceptable.'

Reith exchanged a look with Phipps. 'If you wish, ma'am.'

'And my husband will need a few minutes to wash and collect a change of clothes.'

Reith looked uncertain, but he must have decided I wasn't suicide material because he nodded abruptly and stood back to let me pass.

Ginny followed me upstairs to the bedroom and closed the door rapidly. 'What have they found out?' she breathed.

'Do you think I know? Do you think they called and told me?' Hearing the childishness in my voice, I groaned, 'Sorry. *Sorry.*'

'Hugh – we've got to think this through.'

'There's nothing to think through! There's nothing we can do!' I was choking with frustration. 'This time it'll be all over the papers – you realise that? Over everything. Christ!'

Ginny gripped my forearm. 'Hugh – we must think!' she gasped. 'We must think!' And her voice was trembling. 'Listen – what did you tell the police? No, no,' she corrected herself with an impatient wave of both hands. 'No – what I mean is, was Sylvie ever in the car with you?'

I didn't understand what she was getting at. 'I think . . . once.' I went through the exercise of sifting my memory, though I knew perfectly well I wasn't mistaken. 'Yes. Once.'

'Did you tell the police that?'

I looked at Ginny and suddenly I began to understand. 'Oh God.'

'And the house? Did you say she'd been there?'

I shook my head miserably.

'Tell me what you did say, tell me!' And she was alive with a furious energy.

'It's not so much what I did say, it's what I didn't say. When they asked me when and where I'd seen her, I just didn't mention the house. Or the car.'

Ginny closed her eyes for a moment as if to absorb the full impact of what I was saying. 'And she *touched* things at the house?'

'What?'

'Doors. Glasses – I don't know, I don't know. *Things*.'

I saw Sylvie watching me over the rim of her glass, I saw her holding a cup of coffee. 'Yes, she touched things.'

There was a silence like darkness. Ginny took a sudden breath and seemed to speak by sheer force of will. 'They'll know then.'

I sat on the bed and leant forward with my head in my hands. 'Oh, Ginny . . . I'm so sorry. I'm so sorry.'

'No, no!' she cried. 'Listen!' She sat beside me and pulled my hands away from my face and shook my shoulder until I looked at her. 'I'll say that *I* invited her to the house.'

'What?'

She nodded sharply. 'I'll say you introduced us, and I saw her in the village and invited her for coffee. I'll say it was just at the end of August. I'll say you

were out on the boat, getting it ready for the weekend—'

'Ginny, *Ginny . . .*' My heart squeezed with gratitude, she meant so well. 'But darling, they'll want
exact dates, times. It simply wouldn't work. If – no,
when they found out you weren't there – it would
only make things worse.'

She clamped her lips together, she intertwined her
long nervous fingers, she gave a small ironic laugh.
'But I *was* there that weekend, you see.' She took a
breath halfway between a rasp and a sob. 'And I did
see her. I saw her at the house.'

I could only stare at her.

'I didn't go to Provence,' she explained. 'I drove
down to find you.'

I looked into her face, I saw the slight shame there,
and the hurt, and knew it was true. 'Oh, Ginny.'

She was straining to breathe but when I tried to
fetch her inhaler she grasped my arm and held me
back. 'I saw you go to the boat too. I saw you sailing
off. But Hugh, I wasn't the only one. Someone else
saw you go – someone at the inn – and they told
David, and David asked me if it had been me on
board, and I told him it was. I said it was me!' As if
to impress this on me, she shook my arm again. 'And
then Mary asked me as well, and I told her. I told her
it was me. So that's what we've got to stick to, Hugh,'
she urged through the labouring of her lungs, 'that's
what we must swear to! We must say that it was *me.*'

I felt an inner crumbling, a sudden loss of will.
The idea of committing myself to more lies was bad
enough, but to try and carry off such fragile deceits

seemed utterly futile. 'It's no good, Ginny. It's no good.'

'What do you mean?' And her grasp was very tight.

'They'll find out. Honestly, Ginny, it'll only make things worse.'

'No!' Her vehemence took me by surprise. '*No!* What are you thinking of! *What are you thinking of!*' She was trembling again.

'It'll be better to tell the truth. They'll find out anyway!' And the thought sent me into a new chasm of despair.

'You can't! You can't!' She knelt in front of me and clasped my face in her hands so that I was forced to look into the fierceness of her eyes. 'Think of *me*, Hugh! Think of *me!*'

The tears sparkled angrily in her eyes, she cried for breath. Hurriedly I fetched her inhaler. As she pulled the drug into her lungs her gaze didn't leave my face.

'Ginny, I'm sorry,' I said wearily. 'I'm so very sorry.'

'Don't be sorry,' she gasped angrily, 'be brave! Be *brave!* For me, Hugh. *Please*. Do it for *me!*'

Six

I'VE FORGOTTEN what excuse I found for going back to Dittisham that first time. To sort out attics, to do some work on the boat. It didn't matter, really, because Ginny soon got the message that I wanted to be on my own. Coming on top of my late-night flight from the house party, this did little to ease the tension between us. Ginny wanted explanations and reassurances which I could not give her, while I dreamed of solitude and peace of mind, longings which I dared not voice for fear of making things worse.

We were meant to be having dinner with some friends from New York on the Friday, and Sunday lunch with neighbours, but I said I couldn't face people, which was true, and suggested Ginny go without me, which I knew full well she would never do.

I had a conscience about that, but it got lost in the desperation to get away. That week I had been on a two-day whistle-stop to some of our major customers in France and Belgium, I had been fighting the banks tooth and claw on a daily basis to extend our loan arrangements, and at an acrimonious meeting the HartWell board had outvoted me and passed Howard's motion to open formal merger discussions with Cumberland. By Friday I was drained of small talk, I was incapable of putting on a front for other people and pretending that things were just fine. Things were far from fine, and I knew that the greatest crisis of all was in myself.

Sylvie had been drifting through my mind ever since the swimming incident two weeks before, yet I told myself I wasn't going back to Dittisham to see her. I told myself I was going back to Dittisham to sort myself out, which contained more than enough truth to placate my conscience.

I reached the house after midnight on Friday and slept through until six, which in those insomniac times was something of a record. Then, seized with the fierce energy that exhaustion brings, I drove into town and took the ferry to Kingswear and, parking up on the cliffs, walked the coastal path until my legs ached. On the way back I took a detour into Brixham and, finding a dingy cafe near the harbour, devoured a plate of limp bacon and crusty eggs, washed down with bitter tea.

On returning to the house I made a half-hearted attempt to sort through Pa's books, but restlessness soon had me wandering aimlessly from window to window and back again. Eventually I put the books to one side and walked down the garden to the edge of the water. Down river, beyond the ferry, I could see the old-fashioned cutter with the bowsprit that Sylvie'd told me she and her friends took out most weekends. This Saturday the boat floated at its moorings, devoid of life.

I sat on the bank, watching the tide creeping in

and the gulls squabbling in the sky above *Ellie Miller* and the scurrying ferry as it carried the hikers and holiday-makers across to Greenway. I stayed for almost an hour, finally trudging back up the hill when heavy clouds covered the sun. Approaching the house I heard the phone ringing, but something prevented me from hurrying to answer it and by the time I got inside it had stopped.

Still unable to settle, I went into town again and drove the streets until I found the pottery shop where Sylvie worked. It was a small place squeezed into a row of handicraft shops in a narrow street near the harbour. Brightly coloured pots and bowls lined the shelves that straddled the window. Through the open door I could make out a fiftyish woman in an ethnic dress sitting by the till, reading a newspaper. She seemed to be alone. I drove on to the supermarket, roaming desultorily among the shelves, buying whisky, milk and breakfast cereal, before ending up in a pub and passing an unsatisfactory twenty minutes with a beer and a solid meat pie.

As soon as I got back to the house I went upstairs to David's old room and looked down river.

The cutter had gone.

I felt a ridiculous sense of aggrievement, as if I had been unfairly excluded. I searched the house for binoculars and, finding none, strode down to the water's edge to take another look. There was no doubt: the cutter had gone, leaving a squat wooden dinghy at her mooring.

My resentment burned on childishly. When I made sense of this absurd emotion, I realised it was based on envy, a naive and sentimental longing to be part of Sylvie's adventure, to sail off to God knows where, as we had done in the languorous days of that endless summer long ago, to some quiet cove maybe, or France, or nowhere very much at all. I yearned for the simplicity of those days, when we were faced by nothing more challenging than a trick at the tiller or a change of sail. Most of all perhaps, I yearned for the love and laughter we had shared, and which seemed to have faded inexorably from my life.

I had told Ginny I would be back by the following evening but I found reasons to put off my departure. Sorting Pa's books took a lot longer than I'd thought – or I made sure it did – then I persuaded myself that I needed to get out to *Ellie Miller* and pump her bilges. In the soft summer afternoon I collected oars and rowlocks from the garage and walked through the village to the quay.

I found the dinghy underneath two others in a stack of tenders jostling for space on the end of the ferry pontoon. Setting out, I didn't take my usual route to *Ellie*, which was to run parallel to the mud flats until the river widened a little and I could cross where the current was weakest, but rowed straight into the ebbing tide which would carry me close by the cutter's mooring. When I reached the mooring, there was nothing to see, of course, just the buoy and a battered plywood dinghy with badly chipped gunwales and a gash down one side.

Ellie had quite a bit of water in her, so I guessed David hadn't been aboard for a while. Once I had pumped her dry I looked around for other jobs to do:

anything to delay my return. I pottered about for an hour or so, running the engine, doing odd bits of maintenance; and all the time I was keeping an eye out for the cutter's return.

Closing the engine compartment, on the point of packing up and going home, I looked out through the main hatch and saw the top of a mast in movement. I climbed up the companionway for a better view, and there was the white cutter, coming up to her mooring. I counted four people on board. Even at that distance Sylvie's slim figure was unmistakable.

It was then that I should have understood the nature of my secret hopes for Sylvie. My agitation should have warned me, and the unwarranted hostility I felt at the sight of the two men in the group, one of whom I immediately cast as Sylvie's lover.

The four were in a hurry to get ashore. If they had a mainsail cover they didn't put it on, and they forgot to tighten the halyards, let alone tie them off to the shrouds. As they pulled the dinghy alongside and started to load it, Sylvie stood in the cockpit, hands on hips, and I had the idea she was arguing with one of the men, a tall figure with bushy fair hair. The second man, a wiry figure with dark shoulder-length hair, got into the dinghy and took the bags handed down by the other woman.

I reached into the companionway for the binoculars. By the time I had focused on Sylvie, she had moved to the side deck. If she wasn't arguing with the fair-haired man then she was putting her message over pretty forcefully, weaving expansive gestures in the air, and I almost laughed to watch her, her body was so expressive. The fair-haired man seemed to make a point of turning his back on her before climbing down into the dinghy. Finally, after another exchange of words, Sylvie chucked a dismissive hand in the air and, with apparent bad grace, joined her companions in the dinghy.

Up until that moment I might still have held back, I might have persuaded myself to keep my distance, but as the fair-haired man rowed the dinghy towards the quay Sylvie twisted in her seat and, in a pose that would have looked utterly affected if it hadn't been so typical of her, thrust a hand into the water and, turning her head as if to watch the ripples, let her cheek fall against her shoulder.

Quite suddenly I felt sure she was looking at me. It was as though she had known from the beginning that I was there and had expressly engineered this scene for our benefit.

I lifted my hand and waved to her, and though I couldn't be absolutely sure it seemed to me that she returned my smile before turning back to her companions. This small inconsequential smile rapidly took on a mammoth significance in my mind. My pulse quickened, I felt a foolish excitement. It was then that I knew I must see her again.

By the time I reached the quay she and her friends had disappeared. I hurried back to the house and, sitting at Pa's desk, spent half an hour composing a note. I would love to see her again, I wrote; our meeting on the boat had been all too brief, I would be down the next weekend, would she be interested in going for a sail . . .

In my new mood of calculation I realised it would be better to meet on the boat where there was no danger of David or Mary walking in on us, where the exigencies of finding crew members often threw the unlikeliest of people together. Even then I recognised that any relationship I might have with Sylvie, however innocent, would need to be discreet. Sylvie carried her sexuality too blatantly for anyone to believe she was capable of anything so casual as friendship. Even at fifteen, her style, her indifference to opinion, had attracted misunderstanding and gossip.

I found an envelope and, sealing the note, drove into town and posted it through the pottery shop's door before heading back to London.

The week brought a succession of crisis meetings. Galvanised by inflammatory talk of imminent financial disaster from Howard the board voted to rush the takeover proposal straight to the shareholders, which was little more than a formality when half the shareholders sat on the board, and the rest were married or related to them.

Facing almost certain defeat, I functioned in a schizophrenic state of acceptance and despair. I threw myself at problems, as if by sheer force of effort I might find some miraculous solution to HartWell's difficulties. I rarely got home before ten and then it was only to work until late in the night. Conversations with Ginny seemed to be confined to the subjects of meals, transport and laundry.

I tried not to think about the weekend, yet the idea

of seeing Sylvie glittered quietly in the back of my mind like a distant beacon across a dark sea.

By Friday what I had discounted as unshakeable tiredness had turned into the first flutterings of fever. That didn't stop me from driving down to Dittisham, of course. I told Ginny I needed to work away from the telephone.

There was no message from Sylvie at the house, no answering note on the mat.

I had a bad night, sweating heavily and periodically kicking the covers off, only to wake cold and shivering a short time later. I came to at nine the next morning, my mouth parched and my forehead burning. I found some aspirin in a medicine cabinet and took a couple. Then I dragged a duvet and pillow down to Pa's study, and, pulling the sofa in front of the open windows, lay propped up against the arm so that I could see down the length of the garden to the river. Armed with a jug of water and a book, I dozed sporadically.

I woke to see a figure standing in the window. It was Sylvie.

You're ill, she said with a small sniff.

You don't sound very sympathetic, I smiled.

No, I'm not, she declared, because it means we won't be able to go sailing and the weather's perfect.

You would have come? It was the foolish question of an anxious lover.

She gave that laughing shrug of hers. Yes, why not?

I offered: I might be well enough by tomorrow.

But that prospect didn't seem to interest her.

I couldn't stop looking at her. I had forgotten the way her hair clouded out from her head and fell softly to her shoulders. I had forgotten the fullness of her lips and the way she pushed them forward whenever she finished speaking, so that every statement, however mundane, seemed to contain an invitation.

Next weekend, I said. Let's make it next weekend.

She lit a cigarette and sniffed again. Leaning back against the window frame, she gave me a sideways look, her almond eyes slanted like a cat's. Can we go to France? she said.

France? I repeated stupidly.

She was serious. She was waiting for my answer.

Well, I said hurriedly, it would be great, of course it would, but the boat's not really in commission. And I'm not sure I am, either. I mean, I haven't been sailing for a long time.

Her fluid lips had taken on a brooding look. It would be so nice, she said. And she gave the 'nice' an enticing quality.

My heart pulled with long-forgotten excitement. I knew I would agree. The thought of leaving my muddled life behind for a couple of days was irresistible.

I don't know, I said, putting up a last pretence of reluctance. I could ask the yard to look at the boat, I suppose. They could probably get her ready in time.

Her smile seemed to say: You see how easy it could be.

I hope you can navigate, I said, only half joking.

Sylvie frowned. Don't you have GPS?

It's installed, yes.

She flashed her eyes at me. Well, then.

I don't know how to work it, I admitted.

But *I* do, she said.

I shook my head and laughed. Can you organise the food? I asked.

She repeated with mock horror: Food? as though she never deigned to touch the stuff.

I laughed again because her ploy was so outrageously transparent and because I was soaring with a feverish elation.

Where would we go? I asked.

She drew on her cigarette and blew out a long plume of smoke. Cherbourg.

Cherbourg? I said. But it's always so crowded.

She looked away. Oh, there's a good restaurant there. And I want to buy some shoes.

Shoes!

She gave another sniff. Yes, shoes. And now it was her turn to laugh.

I tried not to remember how easy it was to get to Cherbourg but how very hard it was to sail back against the prevailing winds.

We could leave on Friday? she asked.

We'd have to, I said, to be sure of getting back on Sunday.

That's good, she said.

We wouldn't have very long in Cherbourg.

Who cares? It'll be wonderful! And she gave a low chuckle, a mischievous smile.

I looked at that smile and suddenly my desire for her expanded into something so intense that it seemed to grip my heart, to rob me of breath. But if in that moment my longing sharpened into something more passionate, it also darkened into something more possessive. Even then, before our affair had begun, I was haunted by the thought that she would leave me.

Tell me what you've been doing all these years, I asked her.

She waved her cigarette dismissively in the air.

I pressed her: No, really – where have you been? What have you been doing?

The past, she shrugged. It's over. There's nothing to tell.

Come on, Sylvie, I remonstrated lightly.

But she wouldn't tell me, not much anyway. All she would say was that there had been good times and bad times. She had travelled a bit – she tilted an upturned hand towards what might have been far-off places – then she had lived in Paris, then the Midi. Then . . . She shrugged. Really, she said, the past is past. The important thing is that I'm here and I'm going to do my sculpture and I feel so happy and free. She repeated: So happy and free! And languidly, in a gesture that contained an element of self-parody, she laughingly raised her arms as if to embrace the sun.

I had no reason to think that this lazy extravagant rapture was anything but an expression of genuine pleasure. I did not glimpse the determination in her eyes, nor the singlemindedness.

She turned back to me. You look bad, she said.

Thanks for your encouragement, I laughed.

Isn't anyone looking after you? she asked in mock surprise.

No one knows I'm here.

She came closer and peered at me. Have you taken anything? she said. I have this herbal stuff that cleanses the bloodstream.

Anything that does things for my bloodstream must be good, I said.

Shall I bring some food, too?

I thought you refused to have anything to do with food.

Ha, ha, she said. But you're sick, aren't you?

And that's different?

That means I'll take pity on you. She poured me a glass of water as if to prove it. Coughing suddenly, she pulled out a handkerchief and blew her nose.

You don't sound so good yourself, I said.

She brushed this thought aside with a flip of one hand.

Will you eat with me? I asked.

Her lips formed an arch of uncertainty, her shoulders rose slightly, not so much a shrug as a granting of possibilities. What would you like to eat? she asked.

I'm not too hungry at the moment.

But you will be later. She was already moving towards the windows.

Will I?

Oh, I think so, she said, and there was a subtle but deliberate duality in her voice that made me laugh again.

Grinning back, she fluttered her fingers in farewell and was gone.

When will you be back? I called after her, suspecting, quite rightly, that I would get no reply.

I dozed again, but fitfully. My sleep was disturbed by a recurring dream in which I was waiting endlessly for Sylvie aboard *Ellie Miller*, only to look up and see her on the white cutter, sailing away with her friends. In the way of such dreams I opened my mouth to yell to her but no sound came.

The telephone woke me and took me unsteadily across to the desk. It was Ginny, wanting to know if I was all right. I told her I had flu and would be heading back at around noon the next day. If I hadn't been feeling so rough I would have remembered that mention of flu was bound to be a mistake. Ginny would fret, she would urge me to hire a driver to take me home, and, though she wouldn't mean to, she would be unable to leave the subject alone and then, despite my best intentions, I would become brusque and impatient until, finally, we both retreated, bruised and hurt.

But you can't drive with flu, she said.

I'll be all right by tomorrow.

But have you still got a temperature?

No, it's gone. I'm sure it's gone.

But Hugh, you mustn't even *think* of driving while you've got a fever.

I really do think it's gone.

But you must be very weak.

Honestly, darling—

A movement caught my eye and I looked round to see Sylvie moving silently into the room with a bag of shopping under one arm.

176

She put a finger against her lips, making conspirators of us both, and I felt a lurch of guilty excitement.

Really, I'll be fine, I said to Ginny as I watched Sylvie disappear in the direction of the kitchen. If not, I'll catch a train.

Promise?

Feeling a twinge of remorse, I said: I promise. And it didn't make me feel any better to know that remorse alone wouldn't stop me from going to France with Sylvie the next weekend.

Ashamed of my capacity for duplicity but unable, it seemed, to suppress it, I did not interrupt Ginny's repeated expressions of concern, I took time to reassure her. Yet the moment I had put the phone down I pushed thoughts of loyalty and conscience to the back of my mind and hurried towards the kitchen, my heart beating absurdly.

Sylvie was standing by the kettle, waiting for it to boil.

It tastes disgusting, she said.

What does?

What I'm going to give you.

I creased my nose. I'm not very brave, I said.

I think you talk nonsense. And she used that tone of intimacy again, the one that suggested we might still be lovers.

Do I have to? I said.

Things that are good for you are always hard to swallow.

Always? I said, assuming a roguish expression. Oh, I do hope not!

I thought I was so witty, I thought I was so dazzling. But that was the effect she had on me; she made me feel attractive and clever again, and in restoring my self-esteem gave me a new sense of my own possibilities.

I inspected the meal she had brought. A tin of soup, a tin of sardines, a few tomatoes, a couple of bread rolls, two apples.

A banquet, I said facetiously.

She lit a cigarette and held it between thumb and forefinger, like a screen gangster. I didn't have any money, she said.

You should have told me!

She smiled her cat-smile. Why? Would you have given me some?

I cast my eyes heavenwards in mock despair.

Are you nice and rich? she asked, and, being Sylvie, it was a direct question.

Rich is a relative word, I said. But I've got enough to take us to France at any rate, and give us a good meal when we get there.

She considered this with the pretence of gravity, and gave a characteristic sniff. Well, it's a start, she said. And she tilted me an expression of mock disdain.

A start? I said, thrilling to this game of words. A start of what? A start to where?

But she turned away as the kettle boiled and, pouring some hot water into a mug, stirred in some grey powder. She lifted the potion to her nose and pulled down her mouth in a show of disgust before handing it to me.

That bad? I said.

Let's see just how brave you are, she said, and her eyes issued all sorts of challenges.

The liquid was far too hot and, putting the mug to one side, I held her gaze for a long moment before stepping into the space that separated us and, reaching slowly up, rested the back of my hand against the softness of her cheek. Her eyes, which seemed at a distance to be almost black, glittered with a fierce amber light, and when I began to move the back of my fingers against her skin her lids drooped in bliss, like a basking cat.

I ran my palm down her hair and onto her neck and she let her head fall back as if to open herself up to me.

It was she who heard the sound first. She straightened her head and her eyes flashed a warning. Then I heard it too, the crunch of a car on the gravel.

I made a face and, leaving Sylvie where she was, crossed to the hall window to see David getting out of his car. I went back to alert Sylvie, but there was no sign of her in the kitchen and it wasn't until I had looked into the study and the garden that I realised she had vanished.

David wasn't too thrilled to see me, especially when I told him I'd been ill, because then he felt duty-bound to do doctorly things like taking my temperature and pulse. If he thought it strange that I should have come down on my own without telling him or Mary, then he didn't comment on it. He had come to check the house and didn't stay long. As soon as he had gone I went out into the garden and called Sylvie's name but, though I waited hopefully, she did not return.

I called the boat yard first thing on Monday morning and they promised to go and inspect *Ellie Miller* within the hour. I should have remembered that for boat yards time is an elastic concept. When I chased them up on Wednesday they'd only just decided that *Ellie*'s fastenings looked a bit dodgy around the stem and she'd need to come out of the water for a week while they fixed them. I questioned the need for such drastic work, but I was only making noises to vent my disappointment. I had learnt enough from my father to know that fastenings were serious, and that you didn't put to sea if they weren't in good shape.

I sat through two interminable meetings that afternoon. Whenever the discussion flagged, my mind strayed to ways of salvaging the weekend. It would be difficult to stay at Dittisham – David dropped in at odd times to check the house and Mary was still clearing the attics – and I had the feeling that Sylvie's cottage wouldn't be suitable either, though I didn't care to think too closely about why that should be. A hotel then? A weekend abroad? There would be a risk of discovery but, overruling my last shreds of judgment, I persuaded myself that it would be too small to worry about.

As soon as I had the chance I found a private phone and, my stomach tight, my palms damp, I called the pottery shop. A strange female answered and, overtaken by some guilty reflex, I put the phone down without speaking. Calming myself, I called again and asked for Sylvie, to be told that she wasn't in and might not be in again until Friday. The woman wouldn't give me Sylvie's number but offered to take mine and pass it on. I didn't leave my name, I just said it was about the weekend and gave the number of my direct line at the office.

But I couldn't leave it there, it was all too indefinite, so I sent a letter by express delivery to the pottery shop with a note asking the shop to forward it urgently. In the letter I explained to Sylvie about the problems with the boat and suggested, with all the subtlety of a determined man, that a quiet weekend at a guide-recommended hotel on the northern edge of Dartmoor might be quite fun. Or else – trying to pre-empt Sylvie's disdain for the mundane and predictable – a couple of days in Nice or Madrid. I asked her to ring me at the office as soon as possible, or, if all else failed, I would meet her at Dittisham on Friday at six.

She didn't ring. I tried calling the pottery shop but it was always the same woman and I kept putting the phone down. On Friday I skipped a midday meeting and drove down early in a state of jittery anxiety.

I went past the pottery shop but it was closed. I opened up the house and waited until past six but she did not come. I poured myself a whisky and forced myself to wait for another half hour before climbing the stairs to David's old room and going to the window.

I had to brace myself to look down river because part of me dreaded what I might see. The cutter was not at her mooring.

I topped up my whisky and forced myself to wait for another two hours. At ten, despite the evidence of the absent cutter, I went looking for her. I knew the pottery shop would be just as empty as before, but that didn't stop me from driving past and peering into the darkened interior.

On the way back I examined every cottage I passed, as if their lights might provide some clue as to which was Sylvie's. Several had cars outside, but I didn't know if she had a car, let alone what make it might be.

I parked near the bottom of the village and went into the pub overlooking the ferry. As I made my way through the crowd to the bar I recognised some men from the boat yard, and with them an assistant harbour master named Horrocks who had known my father well. They were a jovial loquacious bunch, flushed with beer, and, after I'd bought them a drink, it didn't take long to bring the conversation round to the white cutter. Oh, that lot! they cackled derisively. The hippies and weirdos! The boat was called *Samphire*, they informed me, and her owner was a dropout by the name of Hayden who had once been a professional skipper on a massive private yacht in the Med and now lived up Totnes way with no apparent means of support.

She's a pretty boat, I said to explain my interest.

Pretty on board too! cracked one of the lads. All the boys got long hair!

I asked if they cruised far. The same wag reckoned they went just as far as they needed to go out of sight of the shore and start one of their sex and drugs parties. With drunken relish he told me that earlier in the summer they'd been spotted in a quiet bay prancing around the deck naked or as near as dammit.

They went to Alderney a lot, Horrocks the assistant harbour master told me more soberly, but this weekend he happened to know they were headed for Barfleur. That was the destination they'd filed with the customs anyway, though he doubted they'd make it back in a hurry with a westerly gale forecast.

I slept badly, waking regularly through the night. At first light I went to the window in David's room and looked down the river. Driving rain blotted out the dawn and it was another half an hour before I could be certain that the cutter hadn't yet returned to her mooring.

I closed up the house and drove back to London. I don't remember what reason I gave Ginny for coming home sooner than I'd planned, something about the weather being so dreadful that I couldn't work on the boat. Having received my decision to spend yet another weekend at Dittisham with a burst of exasperation, she greeted my unexpected return in stony silence.

Haunted though I was by Sylvie, I wasn't yet so obsessed that I could abandon Ginny for a third weekend running, and we spent a quiet two days at Melton, with only a drinks party and a casual supper with neighbours to be survived. I don't know whether Ginny had decided tenderness was her best tactic or had recognised that beneath my moods and preoccupations lay a bedrock of despair, but she treated me with cautious affection and sudden eruptions of bleak humour. When we made love I thought of Sylvie and had the decency to feel ashamed.

I might have kept away from Dittisham for another weekend, maybe a lot longer, if Sylvie hadn't called. She came through on my direct line and, in typical Sylvie fashion, did not give her name or even say hello, but announced herself with a question.

Is the boat ready? she asked.

It was a moment before I could speak. What happened to you? I said at last.

What do you mean? she said with breezy innocence.

You know what I mean, I said sternly. When we were meant to be going to France.

But the boat wasn't ready. You said it wasn't ready.

Yes, but I'd made other plans for us, if you remember. I was expecting you. You could at least have let me know. I heard the peevishness in my voice and tried to suppress it.

Oh, but it wouldn't have been any fun going somewhere else, she said. It's so lovely to sail. I love to sail.

You seem to get plenty of sailing on *Samphire*.

She gave a dreamy murmuring laugh, and I couldn't tell if she had missed the reproof in my remark or had merely chosen to ignore it.

She asked: So is the boat ready? Can we go?

It's not that easy, I said. And saying this I remembered how true this was, how Ginny had arranged something for the weekend and I would have to lie to her if I was to get away.

Ahh, Sylvie said. It was a long lingering sound, a sigh but also a signal of dwindling interest.

I have other plans, I explained. But it was a feeble attempt at resistance; I had been prepared to forgive her the moment I heard her voice.

So we can't go?

I made more doubtful noises to bolster the remnants of my pride, then caved in. It might be possible, I said.

Possible?

Possible.

You don't sound very keen.

It's not that. I *am* keen. But after last time how can I be sure you'll turn up?

Oh, I'll be there, Munchkin.

The nickname caught me unawares and bowled me back to the past, to a time when her promises had contained untold possibilities and our greatest intimacy had sprung from the exchange of our most secret thoughts.

We'd have to leave by six, I said.

Sure, she said. And I had the idea she was wearing her cat-smile.

Give me your address and number, I said, in case there're any problems.

Will there be problems?

No, but I must be able to get hold of you, just in case.

She hummed a little, as though considering the merits of my request, then informed me lazily that she lived at Blackwell Cottage up Farrars Lane. She could never remember the phone number, she said –

a statement I tried not to greet with scepticism – and took three shots at it before deciding that she probably had it right.

Where shall we meet? I asked.

I don't know. The end of the pontoon, by the dinghies?

No, I said quickly, thinking of who might see us.

Oh, Hugh, she sang teasingly, you haven't changed, have you? All right, pick me up from *Samphire* then.

Is that all right?

Sure, she said.

I said: If you don't turn up, I'll kill you.

She laughed, as though I had made a really witty joke.

Don't forget the food, I said, but she had already rung off.

A doggedness overtook my thinking then, a sort of tunnel vision that left out the more uncomfortable truths. My life was in danger of going off the rails; I knew in my heart that an affair was the very last thing likely to put it back on track, yet I couldn't let go. I clung to the idea of Sylvie as a drowning man clings to a lifeline. I found justifications. I told myself that Sylvie had been the great unrealised love of my life, that she had belonged to a golden future which had been unfairly denied me, and therefore, by some circuitous logic, that I had the right to reclaim her. I persuaded myself that, after stoically enduring the strains of my marriage, I deserved something more exhilarating and undemanding. And the final time-worn excuse: Sylvie's world in no way impinged on mine, Ginny would never find out, no harm would be done. I told myself all this, and sometimes I even managed to believe it.

I didn't like myself very much when I lied to Ginny again, but that didn't stop me from carrying it off effectively. I managed to look her in the eye when I told her I wanted to go sailing at the weekend. Only when she offered to join me did I feel a touch of conscience. Knowing how much she disliked boats, I realised that this suggestion had cost her some effort. But guilt made me unkind, I told her bluntly that I preferred to go on my own.

Ginny flinched slightly. But why alone? she asked.

I need time to think, I said.

But can't I help?

You help a lot, I said. You really do. I just need time away from everything.

It was that Melton weekend, she declared. Something happened then, didn't it? Why can't you tell me what it was?

It wasn't anything in particular.

But you ran out of the house without a word! You just disappeared!

All those people, I said in a fit of honesty. I had nothing to say to them.

So I shouldn't have invited them?

I'm not saying that, I said wearily. It was probably me.

But you didn't like them?

To lie or risk the truth? I said at last: Not all of them, no.

She began to breathe hard, her face took on a cornered look. She said: So it was my fault, then.

I closed my eyes briefly before saying: Ginny, it's not a question of fault. The how and why isn't important, don't you see?

But she didn't see. She gave me a long wounded gaze before tightening her mouth and leaving the room. I found her crying in the kitchen and, like two actors doomed to repeat our lines in a long-running drama, we began our habitual progression through apprehension and reassurance, doubt and comfort. While Ginny demanded to know where she had gone wrong, I repeated the well-used phrases that would eventually restore us to a rocky equilibrium. It seemed to me that we succeeded in reaching an uneasy reconciliation not because either of us was ever truly consoled by what the other had said, but because the prospect of the alternative was too terrible for either of us to contemplate.

I promised to make more of an effort with her friends, I promised us more time together, but I would not give way on the matter of the weekend, and the next day Ginny announced stiffly that she would go and stay at Melton on her own. I felt remorse, but mainly I felt relief.

I ordered a hamper from Fortnum's and supplemented it with some basics from the Dittisham village shop when I got down on Friday afternoon. I tried not to look at the weather, but it was impossible to miss the flailing of the trees and the angry cat's paws on the water. I persuaded myself that the gusts couldn't be stronger than force five, but when I went

188

to pick up an almanac from the chandlery they told me there was a gale warning out.

The first spatterings of rain freckled the water as I rowed out to *Ellie* and by the time I had unloaded the stores and got the boat ready for sea it was hammering down. When I set out for *Samphire* at ten to six the outlines of the cutter were barely visible through the murk.

I waited in *Samphire*'s cockpit, getting increasingly damp and anxious. Sylvie finally appeared at six-thirty, a crouched figure in yellow waterproofs emerging from curtains of rain. I called a bright greeting but she did not reply. Leaving her dinghy tied to the cutter, we went on in mine.

Fabulous weather! I exclaimed wryly. Would you believe it?

But she did not speak until we stood dripping in *Ellie*'s saloon.

I suppose this means we won't be going, she said.

It doesn't look like it, I said and told her about the gale warning.

Her eyes narrowed, she gave a very French display of displeasure, a hiss, a flash of her eyes, and a clamping of her hands to her upper arms, as though to contain her annoyance.

Think about it this way, I said in my most cheering and, I hoped, beguiling manner, the view here is better than Cherbourg and the chef's willing if not able. We have wine. We have food. Even – I made a triumphant gesture – candles!

She did not begin to relent until we were on our second glass of wine. In my mood of insecurity I tried too hard to amuse her, I spoke too loudly, I rattled around the galley like some television chef, stirring extravagantly, making bad jokes, dispensing wine with wild sweeps of the arm. Against logic I felt I was responsible for her discontent and must lift her out of it. But then I was still running blind; I wouldn't have recognised reality if it had come and knocked me on the head. It was a long time before I understood that it was not me who was the main attraction, but France.

We ate, we opened a second bottle of wine. Sylvie emerged slowly from her preoccupations. For a time she sat motionless in her seat, barely listening to what I was saying, then, thrusting an elbow onto the table, she rested her cheek on her hand and watched me with amused detachment. She went to the loo and when she came back she seemed to have made up her mind to enchant me again.

She began to talk lazily, tantalisingly, leading the conversation off in great meandering loops or changing direction abruptly, delighting in her ability to catch me out in small inconsistencies, scolding me now and again in that teasing manner of hers; and once again I had this exhilarating idea that I was the only person in the world for her, that, deep down, there had never been anyone else.

She sneezed, I thought she had a cold, but when I fussed over her she laughed at me fondly and reached across the table to touch my face.

The energy left her as rapidly as it had come. She fell into a dreamy silence, her glass tilted in her hand. I moved onto the seat beside her, my heart racing high in my chest, my nerves taut with hope. Removing her glass to the safety of the table, I touched her hair and kissed her gently on the lips before pulling back, constrained by uncertainty.

She smiled her animal-smile, her eyes narrowed and she came towards me with her head arched back and her lips open.

I rushed at her then, all finesse cast aside. I pushed my mouth onto hers, I grabbed for her breast, it was all I could do not to rip at her clothes.

She flicked her tongue against mine, she gave a low sensuous moan, and it seemed to me that I had never wanted anyone or anything so much in my life.

At first the change was almost imperceptible. Her mouth slackened a little, she became heavier in my arms. Then, quite suddenly, her responses died away altogether and she sank limply against the back of the seat. I stared at her in disbelief. I called her name. She stirred once and laughed softly, then fell into an impenetrable sleep. I shook her, I shouted, but there was no rousing her.

I railed at her, at the wind, at the whole damn world, at myself; by turns I became philosophical and angry and maudlin. Eventually I grew tired. I stretched her out on the bunk and covered her with a sleeping bag, and lay down on the opposite side of the saloon.

I must have slept that night but it didn't seem like it. The gale racketed until dawn. I lay listening to the whine of the halyards and the thrumming of the mast and the fierce slap of the water against the hull, and I felt the night would never end.

The sun was high when I woke. I saw the empty wine bottles, and beyond them, the empty bunk.

She had taken the dinghy.

It was half an hour before I managed to hitch a lift from a passing boat and get ashore. I drove directly to Farrars Lane. Blackwell Cottage was set back from the road behind an overgrown garden. It was a tiny run-down place with mean windows, peeling grey paint and a rusting transit van standing inside the gates on a patch of weedy gravel.

I beat on the door. The silence reached out derisively, and I hammered again, my fist keeping time with the pounding of my heart.

A sound; a door opening or closing. Unhurried steps approached across an uncarpeted floor, the latch clicked and the door opened an inch or two to reveal a man's eye and dark uncombed hair falling across an unshaven chin. The face pulled back. I pushed the door open and stepped into a tiny hall with dark paint, cramped stairs and the smell of damp.

I shouted at the receding back of the long-haired man: Where's Sylvie?

He kept going up the narrow passageway, and I shouted again.

I'm here, Sylvie said. She appeared from the dark front room. I was just coming to find you, she said.

I didn't trust myself to speak.

She lifted a shoulder, she spread a palm. She said again: I was just coming to find you.

Who the hell's he? I jerked my head up the passage.

Joe? He's an old friend. That's all, she said, reading my mind only too well.

Oh yes? I heard the infantile sarcasm in my voice.

Yes, she insisted laughingly. I've known him for ever. She reached up and passed a comforting hand down my cheek, and I shuddered under her touch.

She seemed completely unaffected by the night's alcohol. Her eyes were clear and bright, her skin had a translucent sheen. Her loveliness stood out in stark contrast to the dinginess of the cottage.

Shall we go? she said, and she led the way down the path.

We got into the car and still I couldn't speak.

I had to come and collect something, she explained. I thought I'd get back to the boat before you woke.

Well, you didn't, I said. And there was a choke in my voice.

She put a hand on my knee. Poor Munchkin, she said. Her lips formed the shape of a kiss, her hand moved on my leg, and there was nothing in either gesture that was not completely deliberate. She said: Let's go to the house.

She could have suggested an alleyway and I would have agreed. From that moment on my anger and my lust became inextricably entangled and I never managed to separate them again.

We drove to the house in silence. Once inside we stood slightly apart, weighing each other up as though for combat, then Sylvie took my hand and pulled me upstairs and into David's old room.

I stood before her, not moving, not speaking. Perhaps she liked that, perhaps that made it into a game for her, because she smiled to herself before reaching forward and sliding her hand under my shirt.

Her eyes were very black as her hands travelled over my chest and up my back and then down, down over my bum to curl inwards around the back of my thighs.

I didn't respond immediately, I didn't want her to see how deeply engulfed I was. When I finally touched her it was to grasp her shoulders, but in my attempt to keep some control I must have gripped her more tightly than I realised because she flinched slightly and shivered.

I held my grip. Her lips opened, she gave a harsh sigh, a challenge or a capitulation. I realised with a blend of fascination and exultation that there were no barriers for her, that in her greed for experiences she set no bounds, and the realisation was an incitement to a more terrifying desire. In that moment I was finally lost.

We just made it to the bed. It was over in minutes. Later we made love in the study on the sofa with the lights on.

During the night she disappeared, leaving no word. Her telephone didn't answer. This was the pattern of things to come, the pattern of uncertainty and torment that Sylvie practised on me so effortlessly.

It was not long after this, in late July, that Cumberland agreed in principle to the buyout. Leaving Howard and the lawyers to negotiate the finer points of the takeover, I spent much of the next two weeks at Hartford, drawing up a business plan. George offered to put me up, but I always found excuses to stay at Dittisham.

Sometimes Sylvie would announce that she couldn't see me; she never felt she had to give a reason and she laughed at me when I demanded one. And when she did agree to meet me she would often be late or, worst of all, simply fail to turn up. Then, sick at heart, dismayed at my own weakness, I would look for her at the cottage or the shop, I would train my newly purchased binoculars on *Samphire*, I would walk through the village to the quay. Many times I would swear to finish with her, yet I continued to search for her with the same ghastly masochistic craving.

When I finally tracked her down I would question her pathetically, my humiliation mingled with undiminished longing. Finding me in this mood she would regard me with pity, and when I reached for her would pull away impatiently and leave without explanation. In those moments I began to understand how people could kill each other.

When she did let me make love to her – just twice in those two weeks – it was on the promise of making the long-delayed trip to France. I still didn't get it, of course; I was still too dazzled to understand the significance of France.

I couldn't get away over the following two weekends – a family wedding, then a batch of buyout meetings – but I slipped down midweek a couple of times. By then I had lost all restraint, and all caution too. I took risks, I left cryptic phone messages with long-haired Joe – calling myself M, my token to discretion – and once I took Sylvie out to dinner at a restaurant in the country where we could easily have bumped into people I knew. She laid down her terms at that dinner, she said she didn't want to carry on unless we could get away to France. In my blindness I was flattered, I thought she wanted to relive our old adventures, to escape the madding crowd and be alone with me, and, desperate for my moment of happiness, I heard myself promise faithfully to take her to France the next weekend.

By tradition Ginny and I always left for a ten-day break in Provence on the Friday of the August bank holiday weekend, but at two days' notice I told Ginny I couldn't go. I said I had too much work at Hartford, that she should go on her own for a day or so to prod the estate agents into action and inspect the house. If she had put up a fierce argument, if she had challenged me about an affair, my conscience might have got the better of me, but she didn't, and with an adulterer's logic I took her acceptance as some kind of permission.

I couldn't get down to Dittisham until midnight on the Friday. Sylvie was waiting for me at the house. It was too late to go out to the boat that night, so we picnicked in the study by the french windows. The anticipation was like a drug. My head was light, my pulse racing. We made love on the sofa with the curtains undrawn.

As Sylvie moved over my body I thought I heard a sound outside but, lost to the sensations of the moment, I quickly pushed the idea from my mind.

Seven

HENDERSON PREPARED unhurriedly, arranging his papers, checking the recorder, ignoring me.

Tingwall poured me a cup of water and murmured, 'Okay?'

I nodded, trying to suppress my nerves. 'We'll get a break at some point?'

'Oh yes, I'll make sure we do.'

'I don't want my wife sitting there for hours.'

'Don't worry, we won't go on all night.'

It was the same interview room as before. Reith was sitting a foot or so back from the table, to Henderson's left. Phipps was propping up the wall by the door. The air was hot and stale as though the room had just been vacated by another team in pursuit of a sweating quarry. For an instant I wondered what the air was like in prison, whether it was like this or worse, whether it stank of sweat and urine and drugs, and fear whispered in my stomach.

The tape recorder was switched on. Henderson intoned some preliminaries, informing me the interview was being recorded and that I could take a copy of the tape away with me if I so wished. He then logged the time, the place, and identified each person in the room.

He slid his heavy forearms onto the table and raised his gloomy eyes to mine. 'Mr Wellesley, could you please take us through your movements on Saturday, the thirtieth of September?'

'I got the time of the petrol wrong,' I announced straight away. 'It was earlier than I thought. Four-fifteen.'

'And where did you buy this petrol?'

'At the Gordano service station.'

'And that's on the M5?'

'Yes, just this side of Bristol.'

'Four-fifteen . . . So what time did you leave London?'

'It must have been nearer two-thirty. Maybe even two.'

'In your previous statement you stated that it was three o'clock.'

'I was working hard that day. I was under a lot of pressure. I didn't notice the time.'

'And what time did you arrive in Dittisham?'

'At about quarter past seven.'

'So it took you three hours to get from just past Bristol to Dittisham?'

'Yes.'

'Though the traffic jam you mentioned in your previous statement was *before* Bristol, *before* you stopped for petrol?'

'The traffic was heavy everywhere. It was a Saturday.'

'But three hours, Mr Wellesley?' He tilted his ponderous head. 'Even if the traffic was heavy it would be extremely unusual to take that long, surely?'

198

I shrugged. 'Well, that's how long it took.'

'These timings seem rather uncertain in your mind, Mr Wellesley.'

'No. I've got them right now.'

'How can you be sure when you arrived in Dittisham?'

'I noticed the time because I needed to buy some food and I realised the village shop would be closed.'

'Yet you can't account for this unusually long journey time?'

'No. Yes. I mean – I can only tell you what happened.'

'Indeed,' he said, and the scepticism showed in his voice.

He looked down briefly. 'What time did you arrange to meet Sylvie Mathieson that day?'

My mouth dried slightly. 'I had no arrangement to meet her.'

'Come now. You had an arrangement to meet her early that evening, didn't you?'

'No, I did not.'

'You had an arrangement to meet her on your father's boat, the *Ellie Miller*?'

'I had no arrangement to meet her that day.'

'Not that day?' He affected a look of curiosity. 'Another day then?'

'No.'

'You met Sylvie on the boat regularly, didn't you, Mr Wellesley?'

I glared at him. I didn't reply.

'I repeat, you met her on the boat regularly?'

'I told you – I met her there twice.'

199

'You also went to her home, didn't you? To Blackwell Cottage?'

I realised, then, that his information could only have come from Joe. Long-haired, spaced-out Joe.

'You went to her home more than once?'

I shook my head.

'Could you speak out, please, Mr Wellesley?'

'I've told you how often I saw her.' I was fighting for time. I was trying to work out if Joe would be able to identify me after a brief glimpse through a crack in a door and a slightly longer look in darkness when he was stoned out of his mind. I was also trying to decide whether drug addicts were likely to be regarded as reliable witnesses.

'The question I'm putting to you, Mr Wellesley, is whether you met her regularly?'

'I had no arrangement to meet her that day,' I repeated doggedly, not answering the question.

'But what about all the other times?' Henderson said, still asking it.

'I told you how often I met her.'

'Three or four times?'

'Yes.'

'But that was all lies, wasn't it, Mr Wellesley? You saw her much more often than that, didn't you?'

'I did not meet her on that Saturday.' It was the only tactic I could think of, to repeat the point like a liturgy.

'You're not answering my question, Mr Wellesley. You met Sylvie Mathieson on a regular basis, didn't you?'

'I did not meet her on a regular basis.'

'You're denying it then?'

I thought of Ginny, of what she had asked of me, and he got his direct answer at last. 'Yes.'

Henderson turned down his rat-trap mouth and moved on. 'You went on a trip to France on the boat, didn't you? At the end of August?'

'Yes.'

'You went with Sylvie Mathieson?'

'No. I went with my wife.'

Henderson raised his brows slightly at that. 'You went with your wife?'

'Yes.'

'Are you sure about that?'

'It's hardly something I'd be mistaken about.'

His mouth compressed into a sharp line, he fixed me with his droopy eyes. 'Presumably not.' He addressed himself to Tingwall. 'Would Mrs Wellesley be prepared to make a statement to this effect?'

Tingwall gave me the briefest glance. 'Er, I would have to confer, obviously, but I imagine there will be no difficulty.'

Returning to me, Henderson murmured, 'But you did go on a trip with Sylvie Mathieson at some point, didn't you, Mr Wellesley?'

'No.'

'What – no trip at all?'

'No.'

'Never mind France. Anywhere . . . Up the river?'

I exhaled harshly. 'No.'

Henderson tapped his stubby fingers twice on the table. 'What about there in the harbour then? You spent time with Sylvie Mathieson on the boat there, didn't you?'

'Just the once, as I told you. And the time she rowed over and talked to me from a boat.'

'Perhaps you'd care to reconsider your answer, Mr Wellesley. You see, there are witnesses who will say they saw Sylvie Mathieson on the' – he referred to his notes – '*Ellie Miller* more than once or twice. They'll say they saw her there several times.'

'I've already told you she came to the boat just twice.'

'And you don't want to add to that statement?'

'No.'

'But there *were* other times, weren't there, Mr Wellesley?'

'I've told you.'

'And what about these witnesses, the ones who saw Sylvie visiting you on the boat?'

'I have no idea.'

'Come now, Mr Wellesley, we know you saw her regularly. Why not tell us about it?'

This was his method then, a kind of verbal bullying. The technique was transparent enough, yet I could see how it might wear people down, how they might tell him what he wanted to hear just to win some respite. I wondered if he realised that in most respects I was already won over, that I hardly needed any wearing down, that if it hadn't been for my solemn promise to Ginny and the dire interpretation I felt sure he would put on any admissions I might make, I would have told him the truth about the affair half an hour ago. An affair was nothing, after all, compared to murder. This thing had gone on too long and become too frightening for considerations of pride.

'There's nothing more to tell.'

Henderson appraised me with open interest, trying to gauge whether I was mad or simply stupid.

'What about Saturday, the thirtieth of September? You met Sylvie Mathieson there on the boat, didn't you?'

'I've told you – no.'

'You met her because you were having an affair with her, didn't you?'

I made no answer.

'You met her in the same way that you'd met her many times before, but this time you had an argument which got out of hand and you killed her.'

Everything had been leading up to this statement, yet the baldness of it still took me aback.

'That's not true.'

'Perhaps you didn't mean to kill her. Perhaps it was just a moment of anger.'

'Listen—' I tried to maintain a reasonable tone. 'I did not see her that day. I did not arrange to meet her. And I certainly did not kill her. And no matter how many times you ask these questions, no matter how often you suggest these – *things* – nothing's ever going to change that.' I added emotionally: 'Because it simply isn't true.'

Reith exchanged a knowing glance with Phipps. Only Henderson's expression did not alter.

'It isn't true,' I repeated, lifting my hands helplessly.

203

My words fell unheeded into the silence.

Henderson sighed, 'Let's go back to Saturday, the thirtieth of September, shall we?'

I looked at Tingwall but his absorbed expression gave me no guidance.

We went over it again in minute detail, the unusually long journey, the period that Henderson referred to as unaccounted time, the rest of the weekend. We went back over how well I had known Sylvie, the two visits to the boat, the conversations. We continued in this way for an hour or more. I made no slips, I had learnt my story too well by then, yet the air seemed to grow steadily closer, the lights harsher, and I was glad when Tingwall asked for a break.

Henderson agreed calmly, 'Very well.' He went through the signing off procedure for the benefit of the tape, then switched off the machine. 'Oh, and Mr Tingwall? We would like Mr Wellesley's fingerprints, if that's acceptable.'

Tingwall's squint intensified. 'This would be for elimination purposes, would it?'

Henderson conceded with a faint shrug. 'If you like.'

Tingwall asked for a moment to confer and took me into the corridor. 'Listen,' he whispered, 'if we refuse I have the feeling they'll just slap a charge on you, and then the prints'll be compulsory anyway. So it might be best to agree. It seems to me that the longer we put off a charge, the better.'

I nodded meekly and we went back into the room.

'Mr Wellesley will be happy to comply,' Tingwall announced.

'I believe Mrs Wellesley's downstairs, is that correct?'

Tingwall confirmed it.

'I trust she'll also be agreeable to providing prints?'

'Is this necessary?' I demanded.

Studiously ignoring me, Henderson looked to Tingwall for a reply.

Henderson's attitude suddenly infuriated me. 'I'm asking,' I said, 'if this is really necessary.'

Tingwall began to speak but I hushed him with a splayed hand.

When Henderson finally addressed me it was grudgingly, as though he was granting me an unnecessary indulgence. 'To conduct an elimination process,' he intoned, 'we have to have the prints of everyone who had access.'

'That's an awful lot of people,' I retorted, though I didn't know what access he was talking about. 'My whole family for a start!'

Tingwall cut in smoothly, 'Will an hour be all right, Inspector? Mr Wellesley will need something to eat before everything closes for the night. And I will need time to confer.'

Henderson looked at his watch. 'Fingerprints in fifteen minutes? And we'll continue the interview in the morning at nine.'

Tingwall nodded, and drew me aside. 'It'll be a night in the cells, I'm afraid. But I'll bring in a sandwich, otherwise you'll get nothing till breakfast.'

'How long do I have to stay here?'

'They can hold you twenty-four hours without charge. Thirty-six with the superintendent's say-so.'

'I didn't mean to get angry,' I said.

He raised an eyebrow.

'Will it count against me?'

Tingwall caught my bleak attempt at humour. 'Listen – compared to most of his customers you're a saint.'

I waited in the stuffy interview room with a yawning Phipps until Tingwall reappeared.

'Mrs Wellesley has agreed to the fingerprinting,' he said when Phipps had left. 'She asked for you to be present. And I said I thought that could be arranged.' There was admiration in his voice, and deference; it seemed that Tingwall had been rather taken by Ginny.

'Listen,' I said, 'am I going mad or . . . If there were drugs in Sylvie's body then why aren't the police looking into that side of things? Why aren't they chasing those connections?'

Tingwall's eyes took on a wary light. 'Drugs? Were there drugs?'

'That's what my brother said. He'd heard from somewhere – the hospital, some doctors. And if she was into drugs there must have been dealers, drug addicts . . . Perhaps she was in debt to them. Perhaps . . . I don't know – but something.'

Tingwall mulled on this. 'It would certainly seem like an area worth investigating,' he said cautiously.

'So why are they ignoring it?'

'We don't know they are. They could well be looking into it.'

'Oh yes?' I said heavily. 'Well, it doesn't seem that way to me. It seems to me that they've made up their minds.'

'It's not easy to tell the police what to do, Hugh. They don't always like it. But I'll try.' He didn't look too hopeful.

Phipps came to lead us to the fingerprinting room. Ginny was already there, sitting apart from the waiting officers. When she saw me she rose hurriedly and kissed me. Standing in that dreary room with her classy Joseph suit and her long slender legs and her curtain of shining hair, she looked like a vision visited on a wasteland.

'All right?' she whispered, and there was no mistaking the question in her eyes.

'All right,' I said, and my look told her what she wanted to know, that I had kept my promise and stuck to our story.

She clutched my arm in a gesture of encouragement and complicity.

We stood at the desk side by side like a couple in a register office. When Ginny offered up her hand to the sergeant I saw that she was trembling. As the sergeant rolled the first of her fingers across the paper she gave a shudder that travelled the length of her body. When the last print was taken she exhaled suddenly and, wiping the ink from her fingers, turned and gave me an anxious lopsided smile. Looking at her then I couldn't imagine why I had ever thought I didn't love her.

In the morning they let me out of the cell to wash and shave. I turned down the large fried breakfast and settled for dark tea and dry toast. Tingwall appeared at nine, looking very young with his smooth scrubbed skin and bright expression.

He told me the interview had been postponed and no new time fixed.

'Is that good or bad?'

'Impossible to say.'

'So I could be here all day?'

'Yes.'

I didn't ask about the press, because I knew that if there wasn't anything in the papers today, there would be tomorrow, and I wasn't ready to face up to the consequences of that quite yet.

'They've asked for your wife to make her statement this morning so I've arranged it for eleven. Your sister-in-law is driving her in.'

'Will I be able to see her?'

He made an apologetic face. 'Probably not.'

Ginny had stayed the night at Furze Lodge. David and Mary would have been kind and attentive, but probably rather overwhelming too, and I suspected that she would be feeling the strain.

After Tingwall left I asked for pen and paper, which the duty officers let me have, and, in an attempt at normality, I balanced the paper on my knee and tried to work on some marketing plans. But the gesture was hopeless, I simply couldn't concentrate, and after a while I lay on the bunk staring at the ceiling, wondering how people could survive this for days on end. At noon a plate of fish and chips arrived with a gluey pudding and more strong tea. At one Tingwall came to tell me that Ginny had made her statement without a hitch and the whole thing had been completed in just over an hour.

'She did very well,' Tingwall remarked with an odd embarrassed smile, as though he were especially proud of her. 'They haven't said anything about you,' he added. 'No interview time set.'

'Is that good or bad?'

'Can't say. They may be waiting for something.'

The afternoon was endless. By three I was pacing the cell, by five I was asking for Tingwall. It came to me then that, unnerving though imprisonment may be, it is not the lack of freedom which most undermines you, it is the sudden powerlessness, the sheer inability to communicate.

They finally called me at nine. We took our places in the interview room like seasoned players. At first Henderson did not diverge from his routine. He retrod the same ground, I carefully repeated my answers. The new question was an hour coming. We were going through the weekend of Sylvie's death when Henderson said: 'On the Sunday you were away from your wife for some of the time, is that right?'

I wondered exactly what Ginny had told them. 'There were lots of chores to be done that weekend,' I said. 'We split the tasks between us. Mostly I was in the house, and yes – for some of the time my wife was doing other jobs.'

'She was away on the boat for two hours?'

'I can't remember how long she was there, but yes, she went to the boat.'

'You asked her to go there?'

'No. No, it was ... There were certain jobs that only I could do – sorting through trunks, papers, that sort of thing. It was simply the way it worked out, that she should go to the boat.'

'What was she doing on the boat exactly?'

'Oh ... Cleaning it out, taking things off. Preparing the boat to be laid up.'

'Laid up?'

'Hauled out of the water and put ashore for the winter.'

'She always did that job, did she?'

'No, it was my father who did that sort of thing. It was his boat. He always looked after it.'

'So why should your wife go and do the job? How would she know what to do?'

I understood now. I had sent Ginny to the boat as a ploy to get her out of the house and win time to cover up my crime of the previous night. Or perhaps they weren't absolutely sure when Sylvie had been killed. Perhaps they thought I had done it on the Sunday morning and calmly proceeded to carry her body down to the river in full view of the walkers and rowers and weekend sailors, and dumped her in the river.

'My wife knew the boat well. She used to sail on it when we were first married. She knew what had to be done – clearing out the galley, taking off the bedding – that kind of thing.'

'That was what you asked her to do, was it? The galley and the bedding?'

'I told you – we didn't go into detail. I left it up to her. She's very good at all that.'

Henderson pondered this. 'And while she was away you . . .?'

'I went through a trunkful of old letters.'

'You didn't see anyone?'

'Well – no. I was up in the attic.'

'No one came to the house?'

'Not that I know of. I probably wouldn't have heard the doorbell.'

Henderson watched me tensely. 'And what time did your wife return?'

'About one? No – twelve-thirty.'

'And then what happened?'

'We had lunch. As my wife will have told you.'

He was still for a moment, then in a display of disappointment or resignation he fanned out his fleshy fingers and flexed his shoulders before moving back to old ground.

And that was the turning point, though I didn't realise it immediately. Henderson went through the motions for another half hour or so, but his voice took on a weary tone, he looked at his watch from time to time, and Tingwall, reading the signs, began to push for an end to the proceedings. Like barrow boys, they began to negotiate. Taking me aside, Tingwall asked me if as a concession I might be willing to stay in the area for a couple of days.

'Do I have to?'

'No. But it might persuade them not to apply for a custody extension.'

And so I agreed because by that time I would have done almost anything to get out of there.

It wasn't until I walked into the reception area and

saw Ginny that I allowed myself anything approaching relief.

She gasped when she saw me. 'Thank God,' she kept saying. 'Thank God.' And she began to cry, half laughing as she did so.

'It may not be over,' I said.

She searched my face, she absorbed this slowly. 'Well, let's cross that bridge when we come to it.'

It was almost midnight when the taxi dropped us at Furze Lodge. David opened the door.

'You shouldn't have waited up,' I said.

'What the hell,' he said airily, and kissed Ginny on both cheeks.

'I'm rather tired,' Ginny announced in a subdued voice. 'I think I'll go straight to bed.'

I offered to bring her up a hot drink. At first she said not to bother, but perhaps she understood that in my inept inarticulate way I was trying to show my gratitude to her, because she changed her mind and said if there was a camomile tea she'd love one, otherwise anything would do.

I followed David into the kitchen and watched him hunt vaguely through a couple of cupboards. 'We're not really into herbal stuff,' he declared apologetically. Eventually he found a lone sachet of peppermint tea.

'Well?' he demanded as he filled the kettle and plumped it on the Aga.

'Well . . . they've let me out, but they think I did it.'

'Think or know?'

'Actually,' I protested stiffly, 'there's nothing to know.'

'I meant,' he retorted with a flash of impatience, 'what evidence do they have?'

'They're not saying.'

Shaking his head, he disappeared and came back almost immediately with a bottle of Scotch and two glasses.

'David, you said that Sylvie was into drugs—'

He slung the glasses onto the counter between us. 'Did I?'

'Yes. You said so the other day. You said she was into all sorts of stuff.'

He slopped some whisky into the glasses and pulled his mouth down into an expression of denial. 'I don't think so.'

'For Christ's sake, David!' He had done this when we were younger, made some bold statement only to disclaim it later and somehow shift the blame for the misunderstanding onto me.

Under my furious gaze he made a grudging concession with a lift of one shoulder, and waved an ambiguous hand. 'It was a rumour, that was all. Hospital gossip. You know – the police pathologist drops a hint. Or it might have been a forensic technician. But it's not too reliable that sort of thing. Believe me.'

'But she was your patient.'

'Ha!' My naivety brought a hint of bitter amusement to his face. 'You think patients tell their doctors everything? You think they tell them about their secret drinking and their forty fags a day and their extra-curricular pills?' He lifted his eyes expressively.

'Sylvie only came to see me a couple of times and the subject of whether she was on drugs didn't *exactly* come up.'

'What about the people she mixed with?'

He took a swig of his drink. 'Haven't a clue.'

'There was that deadbeat with the long hair.'

'Which one?' he exclaimed sardonically, as if his surgery was beset by long-haired deadbeats.

'Joe something.'

'Doesn't ring a bell.'

'And someone called Hayden.'

He shook his head. 'Not one of mine. Well – so far as I know.'

'She used to go sailing on Hayden's boat. That's what they said at the boat yard, anyway.'

'And he's a druggy, is that it?'

'Someone must have been.' I dragged my hands wearily down my face. 'Oh, I don't know, I don't bloody know, David. It's all such a bloody nightmare.'

'Well,' he said laconically, 'it's not worth panicking about, is it? They can't get you for something you didn't do, can they?'

'I hope not,' I said fervently. 'But sometimes . . .'

'For what it's worth,' he continued in the same brisk tone, 'we'll do what we can. You know – support and all that.'

After such a day my emotions were running close to the surface and when I thanked him my eyes misted over, the words caught in my throat.

Looking alarmed at this display, David said sharply, 'I gather they want our fingerprints.'

'Yes,' I said, pulling myself together. 'For elimination purposes – that's what they call it. Tingwall can explain it better than me. Apparently you don't have to agree, but if you don't they could insist.'

David gave a shrug suggesting that it was no skin off his nose, then turned away to deal with the boiling kettle.

'The family contacted me,' he said over his shoulder.

'Family?'

'Sylvie's brother. Jean-something. Jean-Paul.'

A memory flickered, an image of a self-absorbed guitar-playing youth who had appeared once or twice during that distant summer. 'God . . . I'd forgotten.'

'An *academic* of some sort. Bristol.'

'What did he want?'

David poured hot water into a mug. 'Oh, where to go for the burial arrangements, that kind of thing.'

I hadn't thought about her family. I hadn't thought about the funeral. 'When will all that be?'

David dunked the bag of mint tea uncertainly into the mug, then lifted it out and, creasing his brows in faint annoyance, dropped it in again. 'Oh, not for quite a time, I wouldn't think.' He added casually: 'He wanted to know how to get in touch with you.'

'*Me?*' The thought disturbed me profoundly. 'Why?'

'Not sure. Old time's sake maybe.' And I couldn't tell if he meant this ironically. 'Anyway I talked him out of it.'

'He didn't realise that I was the prime suspect, then?' I said with a lurch of self-pity.

'Probably not, no.'

This was the way of the future, I realised. In my new state of social unacceptability I would have to rely on my family to shield me from unsuitable encounters, and my lawyers to protect me from the worst intrusions of the press.

David yawned and rubbed his eyes savagely with his forefingers.

'Sorry,' I said immediately. 'I'm keeping you up.'

'No, if you want to talk . . .' He stood there doing his best to look approachable, but it was not something that came easily to him, and it showed in the restlessness of his eyes and the wariness of his manner. As boys we had told each other everything, we had been accomplices in many a misdemeanour and covered for each other steadfastly, yet in our early teens David had abruptly distanced himself from me and the world in general, and in the muddle of adolescence I had never been sure why.

'Thanks for the offer,' I said, 'but I'm exhausted.'

He nodded with what might have been relief and, turning off the lights, led the way upstairs.

I carried the tea in to Ginny as she lay reading a magazine in bed and, placing it on the table beside her, kissed her on the forehead. She smiled a loyal smile, and it came to me that, if I was to be locked away, this would be the worst deprivation of all, the loss of such moments of quiet domesticity.

After a restless night I woke early to a clear sky and scents of autumn. I lay in bed and remembered waking to a morning like this not so long ago and thinking how lucky I was to be alive. That must have been before the cash flow crisis, before David told me that Pa had cancer.

Ginny had taken some pills and was still asleep. I got up quietly and, making myself some coffee, carried it out into the freshness of the garden. My shoes darkened as I wandered across the dew-laden grass. Above me the leaves of the oaks were saffron, lemon and gold, and on the far side of the croquet lawn a maple blazed. Somewhere a lone bird was calling. It was best not to consider the beauty of it all; that way lay depression and despair.

A sound made me turn and there, in a reprise of our meeting at Dittisham House, was Mary, waving hard. She closed the door behind her and came striding towards me in her Barbour jacket, knee-length skirt and gumboots, her round face cracked into a smile.

'I meant to stay awake last night,' she declared indignantly as soon as she had kissed me. 'I told David to give me a shout the moment you arrived! Honestly!' With a flick of the hand, she gestured the futility of such expectations. 'But listen – how are you?'

'How am I?' I considered this with a mournful laugh. 'Oh, for public consumption, I'm fine. You know – full of righteous indignation and protesting my innocence from the rooftops. But in reality . . . Quite frankly, Mary, when I'm not feeling choked I'm scared stiff.'

'They've found out, have they, about you and Sylvie?'

I lifted my shoulders. 'God only knows. They're not saying.'

'And what have *you* told *them?*'

'Nothing.'

'Nothing,' she repeated thoughtfully, as though she wasn't entirely convinced of the wisdom of this but didn't like to mention it.

'Well, what am I going to tell them, Mary?' I argued with sudden heat. 'That as it happens they're dead on track, that I've lied through my teeth, that I had a wild affair with Sylvie, that I had every reason to kill her—'

'*Every* reason?' she interrupted with a small embarrassed laugh.

In telling her, I realised that I was testing the story against a time when I might have to deliver it on a larger stage. 'Well, she'd dropped me, hadn't she? Finished the whole thing. Just – without warning. For no reason at all. She wouldn't say why. In fact, she wouldn't communicate at all. She deliberately avoided me. Just . . . cut me out! She was brilliant at that,' I added wryly, 'at shutting people out.'

'*Oh*,' Mary murmured, her face puckered with concern. 'Oh. I hadn't realised.'

'Oh, I knew it was no good!' I declared. 'I knew the whole thing was hopeless! I realised she wasn't the same person. I realised she'd changed out of all recognition. In many ways she was utterly *un*likeable. But still, but *still* . . . I couldn't *stop* myself, you see. I just couldn't.'

Mary absorbed this with the faraway look of someone attempting to imagine a passion completely outside her own experience. 'Poor old thing,' she said at last. 'How awful for you!'

We strolled towards the croquet lawn.

'When was this?' Mary asked.

'Oh—' I muttered vaguely. 'At the end of August.'

A pause. 'You mean – when you sailed to France?'

'Thereabouts.'

'Aha.' And she drew the sound out until it took on a wealth of meaning. 'I realised it must have been Sylvie on the boat with you.'

I halted.

'Ginny's always hated sailing so much.'

'God. Does anyone else . . . David . . .?'

'I don't think so.'

'The thing is . . . we're saying it was Ginny. We're telling the police we went to France together. Ginny's absolutely determined. She's making a statement about it. You won't . . .' I gestured feebly. 'I mean . . . not to anyone?'

Mary fixed me with her most fiery look. 'If you weren't in such a state, I'd take that as a bloomin' insult!'

'Sorry. *Sorry*, Mary. Sometimes I get paranoid.'

She shook her head fondly and we continued our walk.

'Hate to mention it and all that,' she said after a while, 'but Ginny wasn't anywhere else when she was meant to be sailing with you, was she? I mean, nowhere *obvious*.'

'No.'

Whether she was simply being tactful or had

deduced that Ginny had come secretly to Dittisham, she didn't ask me to elaborate on this curious answer.

I hesitated, knowing I was about to test Mary's patience yet further. 'I'm going to be paranoid again,' I announced. 'But I've got to ask – you haven't told David anything at all, have you? About me and Sylvie?'

'Don't be ridiculous!' She threw her head back and gave a sharp laugh, half amusement, half scorn. 'He wouldn't listen anyway!'

We had reached a bench set on a small rise overlooking the croquet lawn. Pulling a scarf out of her pocket, Mary began to sweep the dew from the seat with broad strokes.

'Oh, it's not that he isn't *concerned*', she assured me. 'It's just that he doesn't like to hear about anything even faintly disturbing. Never has done. He's the original ostrich when it comes to problems and crises. Just blanks them all out. That's why he should never have been a GP – can't deal with the patients. And that's why I've brought up the children almost single-handed. Oh, don't think I'm bleating!' she added breezily, beating the last drops from the wood with whip-like flicks of the scarf end. 'Because I'm not. It's just the way he is. I don't *mind*. Having stuck with his foibles for all these years, I'm certainly not about to give up on him now!' She gave another bray-like laugh and, sitting down and crossing her muscular legs, patted the seat next to her.

'What happens now?' she asked in the bracing tones of a pragmatist.

'Oh, more questioning, I suppose.' I sank disconsolately onto the seat. 'But I want Tingwall to press them on what *else* they're doing. On why they haven't bothered to look into the rest of Sylvie's life. Like her drug connections for a start.'

Mary threw me a glance. 'She was involved with drugs?'

'One way and another.'

'Blimey!' she exhaled noisily with a kind of baffled admiration, as though other people's lives never failed to amaze her. 'She told you, did she?'

'Me?' I gave an ironic laugh. 'Hardly. But then if I'd been in my right mind she wouldn't have had to. It was staring me in the face. She had a runny nose half the time. And she'd be morose one minute and go off to the loo and, hey presto, when she came back she'd be full of life again.'

'And you're saying the police haven't realised this?'

'No,' I conceded. 'I suppose they must have done. I mean, if David knew . . .'

'David knew?'

'Some rumour on the medical grapevine.'

'Ah.'

'But the police don't seem interested in following it up – finding out about her pals, where she got the stuff from, that sort of thing.'

Mary, picking her way cautiously through alien territory, ventured, 'You mean she might have been mixing with dealers and other dubious specimens?'

I chucked the dregs of my coffee onto the grass. 'That's exactly what I mean.'

In the silence a light aircraft droned overhead and we both looked up at it.

I said in a rush, 'She worked for them.' I got it out quickly before I had second thoughts.

Still following the plane, Mary took her time. 'She worked for the dealers?'

'The trips she took on *Samphire*. They were all about drugs.'

Mary turned to examine my face. 'They had them on board?'

'They picked them up in France. I don't know exactly what sort of stuff it was, but it was hard stuff. Powder of some sort.'

Mary waited silently while I found the words to tell the rest of the miserable tale.

'Sylvie fell out with her chums,' I began. 'Well, I guess she did because suddenly *Samphire* went to sea without her or didn't go to sea at all. *So . . .*' I spread my hands derisively. 'Alternative plan. Set up in business on your own. Find a mug with a boat, preferably someone who's pretty naive and malleable—'

'Oh, Hugh.'

'—Use him to get you to France.'

'Oh no.'

'—Collect your package, allow your dewy-eyed lover to stand you an expensive meal before getting him to sail you back. Then leave him to carry the can.'

Mary looked alarmed. 'You mean you got *caught*?'

The memory gripped me and I shuddered. 'So nearly, Mary. So nearly.

*

As *Ellie Miller* crept out from under the lee of the land and caught the first uncertain gusts of wind, I felt the elation of someone who had forgotten the extraordinary illusion of freedom you get at sea, the sense of leaving the world behind.

I went about the boat, trimming sheets, tightening halyards, entering the log, and relived the exhilaration of my boyhood trips, when my father had expected no crew member to stop until all the tasks were done, when no sail was considered trimmed until it had passed his beneficent scrutiny, when, at twenty, I was first entrusted with the job of navigator. The pride I had felt, and the fear of failure, and the satisfaction when the destination was made.

The wind was westerly and fresh. It was *Ellie*'s weather, a steady force five on the quarter, downhill all the way. As the old girl gathered pace she groaned and creaked in grumpy contentment, like a grandmother exercising her stiffened joints. Water hissed and surged along the hull, the crockery rattled in the galley, somewhere wood moved complainingly against wood. Hearing such long-forgotten sounds, feeling the movement of the boat under my feet, it seemed to me that, in abandoning sailing for all these years, I had left something important behind, a part of my past, a part of myself.

Sylvie sat in the cockpit for an hour or so, chatting desultorily, before going below to sleep. After lunch, I dozed for a couple of hours while she kept watch. When I came back on deck she was in one of her more ebullient moods. She told me a little more about her life in France, though not so much that I could piece many facts together. There had been a house in the Midi, with, it seemed, several people in residence, though she wouldn't be drawn on their relationship to each other. Lovers, husbands, wives; it was all very vague. Had it been a happy time? I asked. Oh, happy enough, she said. Then she turned her almond eyes on mine and said in that low sonorous voice of hers: But not happy like we were happy, Munchkin.

That was all it took, one small remark, and my heart squeezed with foolish joy, and, for a short time at least, the doubts that constantly lurked at the edges of my feelings for Sylvie faded away. In a moment of euphoria all my romantic notions of undying love came rushing back, I thought in ludicrously grandiose terms of the great wheels of fate that had brought Sylvie and me together again. For a short while, until the unease returned, I was besotted again.

As dusk fell and we sighted the beams of the Casquets and Cap de la Hague, the breeze stiffened and *Ellie* picked up her skirts and rushed headlong for land at a galloping six and a half knots. We tied up in the marina at half past midnight. The strange thing was that, though I had nurtured visions of sleeping beside Sylvie in some quiet harbour ever since our affair had begun, something made me retreat. I still wanted her terribly, but it was an ugly craving that drove me to make love to her that night, an urge to possess her at all costs, almost an act of retribution for the helplessness she engendered in me, and once I had left her body, once she had curved against me ready for sleep, something about the intimacy of the position and its implications of domesticity unsettled me and after a few minutes I crept away to a bunk in the saloon.

I woke to find Sylvie on her way out to buy croissants and bread. There was a tautness about her that morning, a barely concealed impatience, and no sooner had she returned than she announced she wanted to go out again.

The shoe shops open? I grinned.

She shrugged: And other things.

I asked if it could wait half an hour while we had our coffee.

You don't have to come, she said, and behind the empty smile there was a dark cold look in her eye.

But I want to, I said lightly, trying to dispel the tension.

She sat still for a minute or two, then climbed up the companionway. I thought she was waiting for me in the cockpit, I didn't hear her step onto the pontoon, but, light-footed as she was, she must have gone immediately, because by the time I had taken a last gulp of scorching coffee and gone up to find her she had vanished. Suppressing a fury, I locked the boat up and walked briskly towards the town.

Approaching the shopping area I saw her distinctive figure a long way ahead, turning a corner into a side street. I accelerated to a jog then a steady run but on reaching the corner she had disappeared. It was a street of small family shops: a brilliantly lit *boucherie*, a musty *librairie*, a *boulangerie* with a queue snaking out onto the pavement, then – I congratulated myself – a shoe shop. The window was plastered with sale signs so it wasn't until I went inside that I realised she wasn't there.

My resentment flared again, I felt a surge of anticipation. For the first time I imagined hurting her, taking her arm and squeezing it until she yelped.

At the end of the street was an open market set in a small square. The place was crowded, the stalls tightly packed, but I saw her almost immediately. At first I thought she was eyeing the baubles on a trinket stall, but then she turned to the young man beside her and spoke to him, and I realised with a jolt that they seemed to know each other.

Stupefied, I watched as they walked purposefully towards a narrow lane radiating off the square to the south. Following at a distance I saw them pause halfway down and turn into a doorway. For ten minutes I waited a few yards away, my imagination ballooning uncontrollably, my temper simmering. I was on the point of beating on the door when she calmly reappeared, alone.

I stepped forward so that she could not fail to see me.

She showed no surprise. Rather she gave a vague sign of recognition, as if she'd half expected to find me there, like someone who, having been kind to a stray dog, can't shake the animal off. She walked past me without breaking her stride so that I was forced to catch up with her. This small act was typical of her insensitivity, one of the many small humiliations that she perpetrated quite thoughtlessly and indiscriminately in pursuit of her own interests.

I grabbed her arm and spun her round. How dare you waltz off like that, I hissed.

I thought you'd be bored. I had this errand to do.

Errand? I crowed sarcastically. What, meeting someone?

She shook her head in exasperation or dismissal, and then I did something I had never done in my life before – I hurt a woman. Living out my violent imagining, I gripped her arm until she went white and winced with pain.

Don't ever treat me like that again! I shouted before walking blindly away.

I had lunch alone, going over and over the affair in my mind, wondering how one person could push me to such terrifying extremes of emotion. I had always considered myself a mild man, someone who kept his reason under pressure, yet when I had gripped her arm I had been shaking with rage. It frightened me to have lost control so completely; it terrified me to think it might happen again.

When I returned to the boat Sylvie was sitting on the foredeck reading a book. Ignoring her I went below. She followed and, coming up behind me, circled her arms round my waist and laid her head against my back.

Don't be cross, she sighed. We were having such a good time.

But you just walked off!

I wasn't going to be long. Please, Munchkin, life is too short.

How do I know you won't do it again?

I won't, I promise.

I cross-examined her about the man at the stall, I demanded to know what they'd been doing together in the flat or whatever the place was. He was just a friend of a friend, she said, someone who worked in the market; she'd simply been collecting something from him, a favour for the mutual friend.

I gave up then, because no answer would ever satisfy me nor quell my darker suspicions.

And I forgave her. I forgave her because I wanted the pain and humiliation to end. And because the dreadful sick longing was still dragging at my heart.

Just don't do it again, I said weakly.

Later we went to an expensive restaurant and had a mediocre seafood dinner which took over an hour to arrive. We had agreed to start the return trip immediately after the meal, though that didn't stop me from drinking far too much, and it was more by luck than judgment that we bumped only one boat as we manoeuvred out of the berth.

The wind was dead on the nose, force four or five. After half an hour bucketing about in a nasty chop I returned my dinner to the ocean and, leaving much of the helming to Sylvie, spent a miserable night between the cockpit and the guardrails, retching on an empty stomach.

Dawn brought little improvement. The wind rose to a stiff six or seven and showed no signs of backing. In her day *Ellie* had been a tough old girl, but with all the talk of fastenings and planking I didn't dare drive her too hard. By midday we had made good a paltry thirty-five miles and I was beginning to despair of ever getting home. Seeing my exhaustion, ignoring my half-hearted resistance, Sylvie took a long watch in the morning and again in the afternoon, leaving me to curl up on a sodden bunk and, oblivious to the drip of a persistent deck leak, catch some sleep. I loved Sylvie then, I loved her toughness and her resilience and the fearless face she turned to the wind, a wild child in a wild sea.

At six the wind finally backed, and we began to make up some time, but it was still four in the morning before we turned up the path of the Kingswear light. Motoring past the Blackstone, Sylvie handed me a brandy and I drank it in one.

Any lingering anger I might have felt about the Cherbourg episode was lost in the euphoric camaraderie one always feels at the end of a hard trip and my gratitude to Sylvie for being such a game crew. We had another brandy and she blew an alcoholic kiss against my mouth, and I felt ridiculously happy again.

We rounded the Kingswear bend in that strange time before the true dawn, when the shadows seem to play tricks, when shapes form and instantly dissolve again. Glancing towards the fishermen's quay beside the station, I saw a large motor launch against the piles, and in my imagination it seemed to me that men were standing on the deck.

As we continued up river, Sylvie kept looking astern and when I asked her if she would go below and find the searchlight she didn't respond. Instead she made a hiss of intense irritation. *Shit! Merde!* she cried angrily. They're coming! Hurry! Hurry!

I looked behind and saw nothing. What the hell do you mean? I demanded.

But she would only growl: Hurry! And when I didn't react she grabbed for the throttle and pushed it as far forward as it would go.

For Christ's sake! I argued, trying not to succumb to the atmosphere of panic. As we charged through the lines of moorings, I kept glancing over my shoulder and finally I saw what Sylvie had seen: some way astern, against the myriad illuminations of the town, the steaming lights of a motor vessel were moving, coming our way and gaining steadily. When I looked ahead again Sylvie had gone below. Controlling my fury with difficulty, I kept shouting at her, asking what the hell was going on.

When she finally reappeared she was almost naked. In the ruby glow of the compass light I saw brief underclothes and a dark band around her waist. Touching the band I felt the smoothness of heavy parcel tape which she appeared to have wound around herself several times. I couldn't work out what the tape was for until she turned to clamber onto the side deck and I saw the bulging packet held to the small of her back. I reached out and prodded the packet: under the plastic it was soft, like flour or sugar.

I kept shouting: What the hell, Sylvie? But it was more of a cry of disbelief than anything else. Even I could no longer ignore an interpretation of events which sickened my stomach and deadened my heart.

I went on yelling at her above the engine noise but she didn't answer. She was too busy working out where we were along the river, how far from Ditti-sham and where she might be able to climb ashore if she swam for it now, and balancing these factors against the speed of the approaching customs launch.

Above the throb of the engine Sylvie shouted: I wasn't on board, you understand? Not on any of the trip! You went alone! Stick to it or we'll both be in trouble!

Then she clambered over the rails and lunged headfirst into the darkness. Her dive made hardly a ripple. I kept looking back but I didn't see her surface. It was part of her luck, or possibly her judgment, but just a few seconds later the customs boat's powerful searchlight sprang on and bathed *Ellie* in a blaze of blinding light.

I slowed down, I let the launch catch up and come alongside. I answered their challenge. Name of vessel? Where from? Home port? I hesitated over 'How many aboard?' before replying with an uneasy heart: One.

The launch towed *Ellie* to a mooring and two officers came aboard. They went through the ship's papers and my passport. They did not seem surprised that I was alone. They asked me if I had notified them of the boat's departure for France. When I admitted that I had failed to do so they asked me if I realised I had broken the law. I did now, I said. I explained that I had not sailed for some years, that I was out of touch, but all the time I was waiting wretchedly for the moment when they would search the boat and find Sylvie's handbag and passport and all the other signs that there had been someone else on board.

In the end their search was pretty cursory, just a rummage through the lockers and bilges, a hand thrust into the sail bags. They took no notice of the fact that some of the clothes were female. Wherever Sylvie had hidden her handbag she had made a good job of it.

Maybe it was the reference to having lived on the river for many years or the mention of a doctor brother having charge of the boat, but they let me off with no more than a stern caution.

I took *Ellie* up river to her mooring in a state of blank exhaustion. I found Sylvie's handbag in a side pocket of her holdall. It contained hairbrush, lip salve and moisturiser. No passport, no money, no identification. I realised she must have put them in the bundle so artfully strapped to her back. Clever Sylvie. Sly Sylvie. Not missing a trick. Never missing a trick, even with me.

Once ashore I drove straight to the cottage. I told myself that I needed to be sure that Sylvie had survived her swim, but the truth was far uglier and less altruistic. My anger was cold and bleak, I wanted to have it out with her, I wanted to know if my deepest suspicions were correct and she had been using me all along. I wanted to hear it from her mouth.

I walked into the cottage without knocking. There was no one in the lower rooms. Taking the dingy stairs two at a time, I peered into a back bedroom so strewn with clothes and junk that the floor was virtually invisible. Approaching the front room, I heard a slight sound from inside and, heart hammering, hesitated for a second before thrusting it open.

Some dense material must have been fixed over the window because the small room was very dark except for two candles burning either side of a large bed which filled virtually half the available space. Sylvie lay propped up on the pillows, entirely naked and uncovered, like something from a Botticelli. Beside her was the dark hairy figure of Joe, equally naked, like something from a horror film. Sylvie turned her head towards me with immense slowness as though it were very heavy, and creased up her eyes with the effort of focusing. Joe was on another planet altogether, blowing out his lips and chuckling wildly to himself like a bin case.

Sylvie, focusing at last, gave a warm smile and a low laugh. Come and join us, she said.

Joe's manic giggles followed me down to the car and fed my nightmares for weeks to come. In one dream I watched Sylvie dive into the water with a lead weight tied to her back. When I realised she was drowning I did nothing to save her.

Eight

I WOKE beside Ginny in the airy yellow guest room at Furze Lodge and wondered, as I had wondered on each of the previous two mornings, if this would be the day when I would be summoned again. Sometimes I saw the delay as a sign that, despite their investigation of houses, boats and cars, the police had found nothing against me and would soon be forced to admit their mistake. At other less confident moments I saw the delay in more sinister terms. I imagined that somehow or another they had assembled a few miserable scraps of evidence against me and were simply waiting for the right moment to return.

The uncertainty lurked in my gut, I couldn't eat, I slept badly, yet on this morning, as each morning before it, I got into a company car and drove to Hartford as if life were perfectly normal.

I had told George and the others about my arrest, I had made no bones about being under suspicion. I had even managed to make a thin joke about the possibility of being arrested again. They may have noticed how shaken I was, they may even have suspected that so far as my relationship with Sylvie was concerned there was unlikely to be smoke without fire, but on the face of it they refused to take the idea seriously and studiously avoided the subject, as if the outcome of the investigations was so much a foregone conclusion that it required no comment. And so, in the midst of my personal emergency, we continued to work flat out towards the buyout, due for completion in two weeks' time. George was pursuing another fifty thousand, Alan thought he'd identified an investor good for a hundred thousand, we were near agreement with the staff on the wage and productivity agreement, and later in the day the Chartered Bank people were arriving for their crucial tour of the factory.

There was no need to make any sort of announcement about my arrest to the Hartford staff. With forensic people all over Dittisham House and *Ellie* beneath plastic sheeting at the boat yard under a twenty-four-hour police guard, with divers searching the river bed around *Ellie*'s mooring, the news might as well have been broadcast in ten languages on all four channels. The local rag could also have saved itself its rather coy report about an unnamed man being arrested and released on police bail, and printed my name two inches high.

The staff did not mean to make life uncomfortable for me. They smiled to my face and did not stare at me until my back was turned, but their curiosity was so palpable that whenever I went down to the factory floor I felt like an exhibit in a zoo, and it wasn't long before I found excuses to stay away.

Evenings at Furze Lodge had developed their own tensions. While David retreated into his habitual mood of preoccupation, Mary compensated with a bracing show of family solidarity. Her constant flow of chatter gave conversations a certain momentum, it was impossible to distrust her good intentions, yet after a couple of days the verbal onslaught began to wear family affections thin. There was a brittleness in Mary's manner, a determination in her cheerfulness that didn't allow for weakness or doubt, and for me, in my questionable state of confidence, this approach left out too much.

I don't know what I'd expected from Ginny – not a great deal in the way of understanding perhaps – but I had misjudged her. By sheer force of will she managed to impose a rigid dignity on herself, a kind of all-encompassing calm, and, knowing what this must have cost her, knowing how alien it was to her anxious jittery nature, I was doubly grateful. It was as though she had taken a decision to rule herself out of the equation, to suppress her own feelings and concentrate all her efforts on me. When under this new guise she offered small gestures of support, when her thin fingers reached for my hand and grasped it, I was terribly moved.

On the Wednesday evening as we sat in the kitchen after David and Mary had gone to bed I said, 'I wouldn't be able to survive this without you.'

She shot me a look which contained a flash of uncertainty. 'We'll get through it,' she said.

'Once this is over everything'll be different. I promise.'

Her eyelids began to beat. 'Will it?'

'I'll cut down on work, we'll spend more time together.'

'Oh Hugh.' Shaking her head, she said without rancour, 'You'll always work too hard. You won't change.'

'But I want to change. I don't want to go on in the same way. What's it achieved, all this work?'

'It's made you happy.'

'Has it? Once, maybe. But I keep thinking of what it's done to us. It hasn't made *us* happy, has it?' I really wanted to know. 'Has it?'

She said in a wary voice, 'I thought we *were* happy. At least I always felt happy when you were happy.' She stood up abruptly and took the coffee cups to the sink. 'And when you weren't happy any more . . .' She hesitated before saying with sudden anguish, 'Then I didn't know what to do.'

'You should have said something.'

'Should I? But, darling, what would I have said? It seemed to me that everything I did was wrong, that you were determined to . . . move away from me.' She shook her head to deter me from denying it. 'No, it's true, you know it's true.'

'I never blamed you for anything. I just felt – *besieged*.'

She came back to the table. 'I would have done anything to help. Anything. I felt so useless. Worthless. I felt you didn't need me any more.'

'Ginny – it was never a question of not needing you any more. I just . . . lost my way.' But my avowals were beginning to sound contrived even to my own

237

ears, and I fell back on a more certain truth. 'Well, I need you now, that's for sure.'

She smiled ruefully at that, and when we went to bed we held each other for a long time.

Ginny's mood of containment held until Thursday when Tingwall told us that the police wanted her back in Exeter for a further statement. Then, despite her attempts at calm, she showed some of her old nerves.

'It must be the trip to France,' she gasped.

'Why?'

'They didn't ask me very much about it before. Only dates, things like that. They must want more detail.'

We were sitting side by side on the bed in our room at Furze Lodge, the only place where we could be certain of being alone.

'It'll be all right, won't it?' she asked. 'So long as we stick to what we said. That's the important thing, isn't it?'

The desperation of her plea did little to reassure me, not only because it reminded me of how thin our story about France was and how easily the police would see through it, but because it made me suspect that, however much she denied it, Ginny believed I had a lot more than France to hide.

'That's the thing, isn't it?' she repeated, seeking some reassurance of her own. 'To stick to it?'

'I suppose so.'

'You don't sound very sure.'

'Ginny – I'm *not* sure,' I admitted straight away. 'Oh, I know saying we were together seemed like the best thing to do at the time,' I argued cautiously. 'I'm not blaming you, darling, but I can't help thinking how bad it'll look if the truth comes out.'

'How would it come out?'

'I don't know. But it has to be a possibility, doesn't it?'

'You were seen in France?'

'No. Well – not that I'm aware of anyway. Though we had dinner at that restaurant in Cherbourg, the one all the British go to, and you know how it is, there's always someone, isn't there? And then when we set out we rowed out from the pontoon in full view of the village—' I halted, remembering that Ginny herself had seen us, that Ginny had been on the shore somewhere, watching secretly, and an avalanche of unhappy thoughts followed as I wondered how long she had been there and what else she had seen that weekend. I closed my eyes involuntarily at the memory of Sylvie and me on the sofa at Dittisham House, in full view of the uncurtained windows.

'Even if no one saw Sylvie, there's still . . .' I hesitated, weighing up the wisdom of delivering such a belated and unwelcome truth. 'The thing is . . . on the way back from France, coming up the river that night, the customs came and boarded us. Well, not *us*. Sylvie wasn't there. She'd disappeared, swum for it. There was just me. But the point is, I told them I was alone. They could *see* I was alone. And now we've told the police you were on board. If they compare notes with the customs how do we explain you not being there? Why would I have wanted to hide *you*?'

Ginny looked down at her hands and I could hear

239

her breath catching in her lungs. She didn't speak for some time. Finally she raised her eyes towards the window and announced in a tight voice, 'We have to stick to what we said.'

'Yes,' I murmured, though it was more to convince myself than anything else.

Ginny had started to overbreathe and, in an effort to regain control, she tightened her mouth to slow her intake of air before blowing out with a slight hiss, like a smoker exhaling a long plume of smoke.

'Could you take me through it?' she said between breaths. 'What you told them? I want to be sure of getting it right.'

I thought back to the interview room and Henderson and the long stream of questions. 'All I said was that it was you who'd come to France with me, not Sylvie. I didn't give them any details, though. They didn't ask for any.'

'But I must have them, mustn't I?' she pointed out. 'In case they ask.'

So I told her what time we had left the river, and how perfect the weather had been on the way over and how quickly we had reached Cherbourg. I described the market place and the restaurant and the dinner, and the long hard slog back across the Channel. If the police challenged her about the customs raid, I suggested she tell them that she had been in a hurry to get ashore and had asked me to drop her at a jetty in the town where she could find a cab. As an explanation it didn't make a lot of sense, but it was all I could think of.

Ginny absorbed this with a fierce concentration,

chewing on her lip, nodding from time to time like an earnest student.

'And the last weekend, when she died, can we go over that again, just in case?' Her voice faltered and she disowned this display of weakness with a brief grimace.

'I simply told them what happened. How I got down to Dittisham at about seven-fifteen—'

'I meant—' She wheeled a hand. 'What did *we* do? What did you tell them about *us*?'

Here was the focused Ginny, the one who always caught me off-balance. 'Of course . . .' I made another effort of memory. 'I just told them what we did. I said you arrived at about nine, that we had a basic supper.'

'Was I expected?'

'They didn't ask me that. But . . . I certainly didn't say you weren't.' I remembered the sound of the front door opening and the sight of Ginny appearing in the doorway, and how I had stood there in blank surprise.

'Why had we travelled down separately?'

'They didn't ask that either.'

She ventured, 'I could have been held up in London, doing some homework for a committee meeting, couldn't I? What do you think?' she asked anxiously. 'Will that do?'

I laid my hand on hers. 'I'm sure that'll be fine.'

She didn't withdraw her hand exactly, but she didn't welcome the distraction either, and I took my hand away again. I said, 'They didn't ask any of this before?'

'No, it was just times and events, nothing else. Did I say I was arriving at nine or . . .?' She was thinking the thing through as she went along. 'Or hadn't we said a time?'

'We needn't have said a time.'

'The evening then . . . I'd told you I'd be getting down some time in the evening,' she recited before leading herself resolutely on. 'And after that?'

'Oh, I said we had supper. I didn't give them many details – nothing about what we ate or anything like that – then I said David popped in at about ten and stayed a few minutes. Then we went to bed at about eleven-thirty. It *was* about then, wasn't it? Then they asked about Sunday. I was vague about when we had breakfast – I thought about nine – then I said we spent the rest of the day going through the house and the boat.'

'Going through them, that's what you said?'

'Yes . . . Clearing everything out of the house before it was sold. Sorting through the attics, that kind of thing.'

'And the boat?'

'I said we were getting *Ellie* ready to be laid up. They weren't sure what laid up meant,' I added, recalling Henderson's pedantic query. 'I had to explain. They seemed interested in the fact that it was you who'd gone to the boat while I'd stayed in the house.'

'Yes?' she urged.

'I explained that I was busy with Pa's papers, that it was left to you to do the other jobs. I said I didn't tell you to go to the boat, that it just sort of worked out that way.'

'And? What else?'

'That was all.'

'Those were your exact words?'

'I think so. But darling,' I said gently, 'I don't think we have to match our stories word for word. In fact, it'll sound really odd if we do.'

She gave me the look she reserved for my less intelligent statements. 'I do realise that,' she said with a show of patience. 'But I still needed to know.'

'Sorry,' I said, wondering how she put up with me. '*Sorry.*'

'What about the rest of the weekend?'

'I told them we had lunch at about one. That we worked on through the afternoon and left for London at about nine.'

She was waiting expectantly again.

'That was it,' I said.

She looked thoughtful, then, reasserting her new-found composure, said, 'I just wanted to be clear.' Some doubt must have remained on my face because she added, 'I'm frightened of saying the wrong thing, that's all.'

She didn't speak during the drive to Exeter. She looked intently at the road ahead, and I had the feeling that she was going over the story again in her mind.

To avoid any chance encounters with the press we'd arranged to meet Tingwall at a hotel on the outskirts of town before he took Ginny on to the police station.

As Tingwall came across the lobby I searched his face for a hint of developments, but he was too busy

243

giving Ginny a mushy dumbstruck stare to be sending out those sorts of signals.

'What's the news?' I asked, bidding for his attention.

He dragged his gaze towards me. 'News?' he echoed. 'Oh, nothing, I'm afraid. And nothing on the car or the house, either. No saying when they'll be finished with them.'

'What about getting back to London?' I sighed. 'I've had to miss a couple of important meetings.'

'If you can hang on a bit longer. Say, till the weekend.'

'And if something comes up and I have to leave?'

'Let me know. *Please*. Just let me know.'

Before I could say more, Ginny touched my arm, as if to remind me of why we were here.

'All right?' I murmured to her profile as we walked out to the car park but, keyed up for the ordeal ahead, she didn't reply. Tingwall sped ahead and opened the door of his car for her and waited solicitously while she got in. He closed the door like a chauffeur, softly, with only the faintest click. I saw him smile to her as he got in beside her.

I stood and watched them drive off but she didn't look back.

Beginning a potentially long wait, I sat in the car and prepared to make some calls. I hadn't shouted my troubles from the rooftops, I certainly hadn't mentioned them to the people at Zircon or the banks, and Julia had been careful to put the postponed meetings down to general scheduling problems. A small paragraph announcing 'an arrest' had appeared in two of the national dailies that morning, but either the police had been laudably reticent or some legal principle prevented the press from saying too much because neither report had mentioned my name. I had been hoping my anonymity would last but the moment I got through to Pollinger at Zircon I knew my period of grace was over.

The tone of his greeting warned me before he said crisply: 'Hear you've had a spot of bother.'

'This police inquiry, you mean?' I said casually. 'I was interviewed, yes – the victim was someone I'd known years ago – but that was it.'

'I heard, *arrested*.'

I didn't try to deny it. 'The police overreacted a bit, to put it mildly. But they let me go straight away without charge.'

'All sorted then, is it?'

'Yes,' I lied.

'Not good for the buyout.'

'I'm aware of that.'

'This sort of rumour needs to be knocked firmly on the head, Wellesley, otherwise it could keep doing the rounds. Get fixed in people's minds.'

I wasn't sure I knew how to go about killing any sort of rumour, let alone one this salacious. 'How did you hear?'

'Me?' Pollinger had gone into the City straight from Winchester; he wasn't used to being asked to reveal his sources. 'Look, all I can tell you is that if the story isn't all over the place by now, it soon will be.'

'What do you think, then? A press release?'

'A bit of a sledgehammer, old chap. A letter to your backers might be a bit more politic.'

Pollinger was right about the news travelling fast. Julia confirmed it as soon as I spoke to her. Most of Cumberland knew, she told me, and at least two of their lawyers, and possibly the Chartered Bank, though she couldn't be absolutely sure about the bank, short of asking them outright. Oh, she added caustically, Howard had called, asking if it was true that I had been charged with murder. She had taken the liberty of telling him that, if his spies couldn't do any better than that, he should think about taking them off his payroll. She hoped that was all right.

It was a strange feeling sitting there in a car park on the outskirts of Exeter, knowing that my life was being picked over in a dozen offices up and down the country. I could imagine how thrilled the banks were at the prospect of loaning their money to someone who looked as though he might be charged with murder at any moment. And I could see Howard hastily diving into his damage limitation mode, rapidly distancing himself from me and the buyout, and casting it about that, in all the years we had worked together, he'd always had his doubts about my stability.

I asked Julia to draft a fax to Zircon and the banks, explaining the situation and setting their minds at rest. I didn't have the heart, or the nerve, to make any more calls after that. I sat listlessly in the car, watching the traffic go by and thinking of Ginny. I pictured her in the stuffy interview room, sitting straight-backed on the worn chair, meeting

Henderson's cool gaze as she told him about the cup of coffee she was meant to have had with Sylvie at Dittisham House. I saw Henderson searching her face as she described bumping into Sylvie in the village and inviting her over. I heard him ask her what she and Sylvie had talked about. Then – the tactic was so obvious that I winced at not having thought of it and warned her – I heard him trying to catch her out, asking her what Sylvie was wearing, whether she'd been driving a car, and if so what sort of car it had been. I pictured Ginny pale and tense in the face of this crisis, yet, oddly, I didn't hear her falter. Though I replayed the scene several times, though I built up Henderson into some kind of super-sleuth, Ginny's aura of composure remained unassailable in my mind.

My confidence wavered only when I thought of the places where the police might have found Sylvie's fingerprints – in David's old room, on the bed post – and how hard it would be to explain their presence after a single coffee session. But you could go mad thinking things like that. You could go mad wishing for the hundredth time that you hadn't lied about something so mundane as an extra-marital affair.

I closed my eyes. I must have dozed for quite a time because it was dark when the sound of the passenger door woke me.

'How was it?' I asked Ginny as she climbed in.

She sank into the seat and shook her head. 'I'm so tired,' she sighed. 'I'm so tired. Can we just go back, please?'

As I drove I kept glancing across at her. She had

her head pressed against the headrest and her eyes closed. After a minute or two she said, 'I'm not sure. How it went.' And there was something in her voice that sounded a small warning in my mind.

'The weekend in France?'

'He didn't ask about that.' Each word seemed an enormous effort for her.

'Nothing at all?'

'No.' Her voice was so faint I could barely pick it up.

'And having Sylvie in for coffee?'

'No.'

'What – *nothing*?'

'Oh, I told him,' she murmured. 'I told him, but he didn't want that.'

'What did he want then?'

She didn't speak for so long that I began to think she hadn't heard. 'He wanted to know how often I'd been at Dittisham.'

I tried to read her profile in the reflection of the lights. 'What did you say?'

'I said . . . I said I hadn't been down very often. Just three times. He . . .' Another pause. 'He wanted dates. I told him I'd need my diary, that I'd have to let him know. But it wasn't that he really wanted . . .'

'What was it then?'

She dropped her head forward and her hair fell across her cheek. 'That last weekend,' she whispered. 'He wanted to know all about that last weekend.'

'What, the times or . . .?'

With great weariness she lifted her head again and looked ahead. 'Sunday. Mainly the Sunday.'

'What about the Sunday?' I had to force my attention back to the road.

'Everything.' She echoed bitterly: 'Everything.'

'But what about it?' I repeated doggedly.

She didn't reply.

'*Ginny* . . .'

'The boat. It was the boat.'

I had a bad feeling then, a sick foreboding. When I next glanced across, Ginny had half turned her face towards me, her expression hidden in the darkness.

'They know she was killed on the boat.'

My stomach lurched, I had a strong sense of unreality. I looked for a place to stop and there was nowhere. Finally I saw a farm gateway and lurched to a halt across it. '*They said that?* They said she was killed on *Ellie*?'

'They didn't have to say. It was obvious.'

'What do you mean?' I cried.

'Everything they asked . . . Everything.' Her voice was harsh, close to desperation or tears. 'Wanted to know who'd been on board . . . Why I'd gone out there on the Sunday . . . Whose idea it was . . . Why I'd scrubbed the floor . . . Had I noticed any marks or' – she could hardly say it – 'stains. *Stains*. They didn't have to say, did they? They *know*. They know she was killed on the boat.'

'That's ridiculous!' I argued. 'You must have got it wrong! You must have!'

She shook her head, and kept shaking it.

'But Ginny, that's crazy! How can they . . . How can they . . . Christ! It's ridiculous! You *must* have got it wrong!' I babbled on like this for a moment or two until I drifted to a forlorn halt and, leaning my fore-head against the wheel, closed my eyes. 'Christ.' And this time it was an expression of dread.

I heard the squirt of Ginny's inhaler. She gave a couple of deep coughs before whispering in a raw voice, 'Let's get home.'

The two men from the Chartered Bank were in their mid-forties, wearing almost identical grey suits, and with the untroubled faintly jocular air of employees of large organisations who have never known what it's like to risk their own money or have their careers seriously on the line.

They liked the glass blowers best. They stood back and shook their heads in self-conscious admiration before venturing forward for a closer look. They asked the standard questions. How did the team of blowers manage to produce the correct shape and thickness each and every time, how did they prevent bubbles from getting into the walls of the glass, and how long did they work before taking a break.

They peered dutifully at the cutters manipulating the blanks against the cutting wheels, they inspected the packing room, and then George and I led them back to the front hall to present each of them with a gift set of six wine goblets and a decanter, which they could safely take home without having to mention it on their tax returns.

We smiled as we escorted them out to their car and shook hands. They smiled back. None of this smiling fooled anyone. No final commitment had been made, no date had been fixed for signing the loan agreement. The two executives would only say that they were returning to the bank for 'final consultations' and would let us know within three days. It was inconceivable that these final consultations would not involve discussion of my fax, transmitted the previous day to all our backers. Julia had written the text. While avoiding blatant untruths, she had managed to suggest that rumours of my arrest were little more than pernicious gossip, put about by those with a vested interest in seeing the buyout fail. When she first read it out to me I'd told her that this was incendiary talk, that allegations of conspiracy could easily backfire, but with so many distractions I was no match for Julia at her most persuasive, and the fax went out more or less as she had drafted it.

George and I waved the car off and strolled back. It was a lovely autumn day, bright and clear with a slight bite to the air. The factory looked almost handsome in the afternoon sunlight, its dingy bricks tinged with a rosy hue, the ventilation pipes gleaming like the funnels of a steamship. The main doors had been given a hasty coat of blue paint for the bankers' visit while the flower troughs on either side were newly planted in scarlet and white. The old place looked like a middle-aged girl tarted up for a new lover.

'I'm sorry if I lose it for us,' I said.

'What do you mean?' But he knew exactly what I meant.

'This trouble of mine – it could be more of a liability than we realised.'

'Nonsense.' He gave me a glare that was both a denial and an acknowledgment.

'Look at it from their point of view.' I tipped my head in the direction of our recently departed guests. 'Would you commit two million plus to someone who might be locked away for life?'

'But you're not going to be locked away.'

'They don't know that though, do they?'

'You're beginning to sound like Howard, for God's sake!'

Realising his gaffe, he gave an exaggerated grimace.

'What's Howard been saying?'

'Hugh . . .' He made a gesture as if to suggest we forget the whole thing, then almost as quickly lifted a resigned hand to concede the uselessness of trying. 'Oh, he's been bleating on.'

'Saying?'

'Talking some tripe about assurances. Saying Cumberland requires assurances.'

'Oh, yes?' I laughed grimly. 'What kind of assurances?'

'That we're in a position to continue with the buyout. That sort of stuff.'

'Or else? What was the "or else"?'

'Hugh, he was just making noises. You know him.'

'What was it, George?'

'Oh, he talked some stuff about having to consider the best interests of the shareholders.'

'He wants to break our agreement?'

'He didn't say that.'

'But that was what he meant.'

'You know the way Howard is – it was just talk.'

I didn't believe for a moment that it was just talk. Howard would have seized any excuse to block our bid and prevent me from making a success of Hartford. He couldn't bear the thought of my showing what could be done with the company when he wasn't around to interfere in it.

The era of extended lunches and early weekends might have died with the eighties, but at four on a Friday afternoon it was still hard to find a lawyer at his desk. Moncrieff's assistant told me that he was at a meeting out of town, while the rest of the legal team were tied up elsewhere and weren't due back in the office until Monday. I called Julia and asked her to reach Moncrieff at home that evening and set up a meeting for the next day.

'And if he can't do Saturday?'

'Sunday, then. And I want a meeting with Howard and the Cumberland people on Monday.'

'Something's happened?' Julia asked.

'Not if I can help it.'

With the decision to leave for London hot in my mind, I stuffed my papers into my briefcase and, amid memories of happier departures, unhooked my coat from the ancient coat stand that had stood sentry since my father's day, and hurried out into the passage.

The traffic was slow. I tried to call ahead to Furze Lodge to warn Ginny to start packing, but the line was engaged. I also tried to contact Tingwall, but I wasn't too sorry when the receptionist said he wouldn't be back that day. It gave me the excuse not to tell him what I was doing until later, when it would be too late for him to try and talk me out of it.

Mary appeared at the door as I drew up.

'How were the bankers?' she called brightly.

'Oh, grey suits. Vapid. Banker-ish.'

'What did they come up with?'

We went into the house. 'Not a lot. Nothing so risky as a commitment anyway. Mary – we'll be leaving tonight. I want to thank you for everything. For putting up with us all this time.'

Surprise passed over her face, then doubt, and finally a sudden effusive delight. 'They've said you can go?'

'No, but I'm going anyway.'

Her expression fell away. 'But do you have to go tonight? You couldn't leave it till morning?' She was trying to tell me something. 'It's Ginny,' she admitted at last.

Instinctively I glanced towards the stairs. 'What's the matter with her?'

'Nothing serious. David's given her something.'

'She's ill?'

Mary raised an eyebrow and gave me a look that contained a trace of disapproval. 'She hasn't been eating. She's been spending most of the day in bed. David thinks it's stress.'

Bemused, I cast back over the last few days. I hadn't noticed Ginny failing to eat, not when we'd been together in the evenings anyway. And days in bed – nobody had mentioned anything about that to me, certainly not Ginny. None of this prevented me from feeling an immediate responsibility; where Ginny was concerned my guilt had no end.

'If that's the case, all the more reason to get home,' I told Mary as I made for the stairs.

Ginny was lying propped up in bed, her eyes closed, a magazine open on her lap. As I came in she twisted her head on the pillow and, murmuring a hasty greeting, sat up on one elbow.

I came round the bed and said, 'I thought we'd go back to London.'

She asked no questions. She simply said, 'Are we leaving now?'

'If you're up to it.'

She nodded and rubbed her eyes before throwing back the covers and getting up.

'Mary says you haven't been eating.'

She made a dismissive gesture. 'Mary doesn't know everything.' She went into the bathroom and began running some water.

'You are happy to go back tonight?' I called. 'You would tell me if you weren't?'

She reappeared. 'Whatever you want.' But she spoke carelessly, and I wondered what sort of tablets David had given her, whether they were addling her brain.

'We'll have a holiday once this is over,' I said lightly. 'Somewhere wonderful, like Barbados.'

She lifted her head and considered this. 'That would be nice,' she said and went back into the bathroom.

Following uncertainly, I found her in front of the mirror, smoothing the skin beneath her eyes. Still staring at her reflection, she dropped her hands and asked contemplatively, 'Do you love me? I mean, just a little?'

I made a sound that came out all wrong, an exclamation that was almost a snort. 'Of course I do. More than a little, Ginny. A *lot*!'

'I couldn't bear it if you didn't love me at all. If you hated me.'

I came up behind her and put my arms around her. 'Ginny, I love you very much. I couldn't have managed anything without you.'

'I've got things wrong a lot of the time, haven't I?'

'Nonsense!'

'Oh, I have. I know I have. Things haven't worked out the way you'd hoped, have they? Our life has been – *different*. But if I've tried too hard – oh, you don't have to say anything, I know I've tried too hard – it was only because I loved you.'

'Ginny!' The snort again, as though I couldn't think of what to say. 'You mustn't blame yourself for anything! You've been wonderful. Everything I could have asked for.'

'Not everything,' she corrected me gravely, frowning at her hands. 'Not everything . . .' Her eyes found mine again. 'But it hasn't been so terrible either, has it? Not so bad?'

I turned her towards me and hugged her. When I drew back I gave a shaky smile. 'I do love you.'

'I'm just sorry,' she breathed. 'Sorry . . .' And she might have been apologising for the entire world.

'Let's go home,' I said.

We packed steadily. Ginny finished before me and

went and stood at the window, looking out into the dusk.

From the front of the house came the distant crunch of wheels on gravel. Something about the sound made me glance up. Ginny had heard it too. She stared at me, her face blanched of colour. For an instant neither of us moved, then I strode out onto the landing and across to a front window that looked down onto the drive.

Two cars, several uniforms, Henderson getting out.

The scene lurched, my stomach jolted, and I had the sensation of losing my balance. I made my way blindly back to the bedroom.

'It's them! It's the police, for Christ's sake!' Fury had me charging rapidly towards the stairs, ready for blood or battle.

'Hugh!'

But I didn't stop and I didn't look back. The doorbell rang through the house. At the bottom of the stairs I met Mary coming from the kitchen.

'Shall I call the solicitors?' she offered in a worried voice.

I shook my head as I went to the front door and wrenched it open.

Henderson stood before me with Phipps and Reith, and in the rearguard four uniformed officers, two of them women.

Henderson gave me a lugubrious nod. 'Mr Wellesley. Perhaps we could come in?'

'Just get on with it, Inspector,' I said, my throat tight with indignation. 'Just say what you've got to say! But I warn you, you'd better be exceedingly sure of your ground.' I could feel myself trembling, and there was a heat in my face.

Henderson hesitated and looked past me into the hall.

'Just get on with it!'

His gaze fastened itself on a point over my left shoulder.

With a half-glance I saw Ginny moving up beside me.

'Mrs Wellesley,' Henderson said, and it sounded more like a statement than a greeting. His eyes still fixed on her, he turned to face her more fully and for some wild unaccountable reason I suddenly realised what was coming, and even as he opened his mouth, I cried, 'No—'

'Mrs Virginia Wellesley, I'm arresting you on suspicion of the murder of Sylvie Mathieson—'

'No!'

'You do not have to say anything. But it may harm your defence—'

'Don't be bloody ridiculous!' I protested. 'This is absolutely crazy!' Phipps moved forward and placed his body halfway between mine and Henderson's, forcing me to step back.

'. . . something which you later rely on in court . . .'

I stared at Ginny. She was very still, her eyes lowered.

'. . . Anything you do say may be given in evidence.'

'This is mad! *Mad!*'

But Henderson's voice was grinding on. Then, reaching the end of his chant, he was asking Ginny if she understood and she was giving the shadow of a nod. Then everyone was in motion. The policewomen were coming forward and beginning to usher Ginny outside, the detectives were moving out toward the cars. Only Henderson remained.

'For Christ's sake!' I cried furiously.

Henderson said to me, 'Perhaps you'd like to pack up a few things for your wife, Mr Wellesley. Or . . .' he glanced towards Mary '. . . whoever.'

But I could only repeat, 'You're mad! She knows nothing! She wasn't anywhere near the river!'

'Mr Wellesley, we'll be leaving shortly. I do recommend you pack a few things for your wife.'

But my brain was bursting, I couldn't hear.

Mary's voice said, 'I'll go.'

Henderson began to turn away but I grabbed his arm. 'Just tell me,' I pleaded. 'Just *tell* me – *why*? What has she done? What could she possibly have done?'

Henderson made a doubtful face, then, taking a quick glance over his shoulder as if to make sure no one was within earshot, said in a low murmur, 'There is a substantial case to answer, Mr Wellesley.'

'Like what?' I gasped.

He spread his hands, gesturing impossibilities. 'I'm sorry.'

'Like *what*?'

But he had turned away. Unable to grasp the full enormity of what was happening, or unwilling to, I followed him numbly to the car where Ginny was already sitting between the two female officers. I was about to call to her when Mary's voice came from behind: 'Which one, Hugh? Which case? *Hugh?*'

Turning, it took me a moment to understand that she was referring to our suitcases which she had brought down from our room. I fetched Ginny's case and handed it to a constable.

Engines were being started. I remembered Ginny's inhaler. I just had time to race up and fetch her hand-bag and hand it in through the car window before the final door slammed and the cars sped away.

Watching the last car disappear into the lane I felt Mary's arm around me, and realised that the angry gasps I could hear were the sounds of my own despair.

Nine

'WHAT REALLY worries me,' I said, hearing the emotion that was never far from my voice, 'is that she won't survive in that place. It'll make her ill. I mean, worse than she is already. The dirt, the conditions, the filthy sanitary arrangements. No *lavatories*, for God's sake. It'll kill her. Just kill her.'

'I appreciate your concerns, Hugh,' Tingwall ventured gently. 'But I did make full representations. I sent in the doctor's letter. I checked with the medical staff and they're fully aware of her condition. She's under permanent supervision.' He added in a transparent attempt at cheerfulness, 'And she seemed okay when I last saw her. She said her room was all right. She said they were looking after her.'

The fact that Ginny had talked to Tingwall when, on both of my visits, she had hardly spoken a word to me shouldn't have bothered me quite as much as it did, yet I couldn't shake off the feeling that she was excluding me on purpose. 'We have to get her out of there,' I insisted unreasonably.

'We'll do our best, Hugh.'

We had only just begun our meeting yet already I was facing the wall of helplessness that seemed to dominate all my recent discussions with Tingwall.

'I'm sure you'll try your best but, if you don't mind my saying so, it seems to me that precious little progress is actually being made.'

Tingwall frowned at the surface of his desk. 'Hugh, I realise that the whole thing must be very difficult for you. I realise how anxious you are. However, we're faced with these procedures, and we have to follow them, with no guarantee of the outcome.'

I held up a hand. 'Hang on. What are you saying exactly? Are you saying' – and my voice hit a warning note – 'that we might not get bail?'

'I'm not saying that, Hugh, not at all. But bail is very much the exception in a case like this. We'll have to show good cause, we'll have to argue it carefully.'

'So?' I made a gesture of bafflement. 'If anyone has good cause it must be Ginny, surely.'

'We can certainly set out a case—'

'What about getting a QC? Surely we should have a QC on this?'

'We can certainly approach Counsel—'

'Charles – let's just hire the best man there is. Tomorrow. The *best*.' I was steamrollering him, I knew I was, but the law, with its nonchalance and mind-bending complexities, was testing my patience.

We were sitting in Tingwall's office, a tall room at the front of a converted Georgian house on a noisy road near the centre of Exeter. This was my third visit in a week; my third visit since Ginny had been formally charged late on Saturday night; a week in which I had seen her brought to court and remanded in custody, in which I had twice made desperate ineffectual attempts at conversation in the bleak visiting room at the prison near Bristol; a week in which I had gone through every shade of disbelief and despair, during which I had attempted to apply logic and reason and emotion to what had happened and found nothing but incomprehension and dread. My thoughts went round and round and came out nowhere. My nights were riddled with nightmares and sudden panics. Confusion and doubt had wrenched my anchors away; I drifted back and forth on the tide of my uncertainties, ready to believe anything and nothing, to fight on and give in, to challenge everything and question nothing.

'I'm not saying we won't get bail,' Tingwall was saying. 'Not by any means. But I don't want to raise your hopes too far either.'

'But what could be the problem?' I asked, trying to hit a conciliatory note. 'What reason could they have for refusing?'

Tingwall interlaced his bony fingers. 'Obviously there's no suggestion that Ginny—' He caught my glance. 'You don't mind? She asked me to call her that.'

'No. Of course.'

'There's no suggestion that she's about to abscond or reoffend – that's hardly an issue. But with a murder charge the magistrates are bound to consider other factors, like the medical report.'

'Well, that'll be devastating, surely. She's already had two bad attacks. What more do they want? Her asthma's triggered by stress and dirt and damp.'

Tingwall gave a slow nod, like a bow. 'We'll certainly cite that, yes. I've already written to Ginny's

263

specialist asking for a letter. But the court will also have the psychiatric assessment to consider—'

'Psychiatric assessment?' I was instantly defensive. Every time I thought I was getting to grips with the procedures something like this turned up, another bolt from the blue.

'I did mention it,' Tingwall pointed out delicately. He waited for some sign from me before continuing, 'In serious cases they always ask for a psychiatric assessment, partly to establish whether the accused is mentally capable of facing charges—'

'Sane, you mean?'

'Yes.'

I couldn't bear the euphemisms that crept in, the fine obfuscating language. 'If you could keep it simple . . . ?'

Tingwall took this reprimand on the chin, with a quick frown of contrition. 'Also,' he continued, 'to assess whether the accused is likely to be a danger to him or herself.'

'Suicide?' I laughed dismissively. 'Ginny wouldn't do that. Not unless she's forced to stay in that place at any rate.'

'Maybe not.' Tingwall felt his way carefully forward. 'But, Hugh, I have to tell you that our man Robertson—' He peered at me. 'You remember, I said it was important to get our own assessment?'

'He's a psychiatrist?' In my shock I could remember none of this.

'Yes. He saw Ginny on Wednesday, and' – he made a regretful face – 'I'm afraid his findings aren't as unequivocal as I would have wished.'

Suddenly I was full of pain. 'He's saying she's unbalanced?'

'What he says is, he feels he cannot vouch entirely for Ginny's state of mind. Not at the moment, anyway.'

'But who is this Robertson?' I demanded, looking for an escape. 'Is he the best person? Do we want a second opinion?'

'He was recommended. But we could consider getting someone else in, yes. But before making a final decision I think we should be guided by Counsel.'

We had completed another circle. 'What are we waiting for then?' I asked. 'Why haven't we got a QC?'

'The best QCs are very busy, Hugh. I'm making enquiries, I'm trying to find out which of the top names are available. It's not always easy to get the person you want.'

I pushed myself to my feet and took my frustration to the window. 'Okay,' I said, descending into sudden weariness. 'So how long is all this going to take?'

'The bail application? I think we should hold it for another week. It'll give us time to prepare really thoroughly, to get this second medical opinion, if that's what we decide.'

Outside, the good burghers of Exeter meandered along the pavements, going about their errands, wearing their own troubles on their faces. I wondered how many had read about Ginny's appearance in court and what they had made of it, whether they had skimmed the item or picked over it with avid curiosity. Whether they, too, had decided she must be slightly off her head. Picturing Ginny's life being raked over in this way was almost more than I could bear. Yet I knew full well that the news coverage so far was as nothing to what would come if the case went to trial.

I turned back. 'This psychiatric assessment – it's standard, is it?'

Tingwall gave me an odd indecipherable look. 'We *could* have refused it.'

I was incredulous. 'Then why the hell didn't we? Why didn't we—' A notion lodged in my head; it seemed so obvious that I couldn't think why it hadn't come to me before. 'How many murder cases have you handled before this, Charles?'

Tingwall inclined his head to acknowledge the fairness of the question. 'Perhaps I could answer that by mentioning that, contrary to what many people think, murder's a fairly rare crime, and this region must have one of the lowest murder rates in the country. And most of the murders that do occur are domestic or fairly straightforward or both, by which I mean there's usually very little doubt as to who was responsible. It's more a question of why, and whether it was self-defence, and so on. There are very few – extremely few – cases in which the facts are . . .' he chose his words '. . . rather more open to interpretation. So, to answer your question, this firm has handled three murders in the last eighteen months, which is a lot by local standards, in fact two more than any other firm in Exeter. Now if Ginny feels she would like to go to people with more expertise, then I would understand completely, and I would do my best to hand the case on to another firm in good order, if that was what she so wished. As for the psychiatric assessment . . . I can only say that I thought it was for the best.'

I dropped back into my chair and regarded Tingwall's thin intense face. 'What's your opinion?' I asked drily. 'Do you think Ginny would do better elsewhere?'

Tingwall pondered this with his habitual diligence. 'Some of the big London firms would certainly have greater experience in this type of case. Against that, a local firm has the advantage of local knowledge, and of being on the spot, with experience of the local courts. A big city firm might have more immediate access to the right experts, to specialist knowledge, but a small country firm, if it does its homework properly, wouldn't let that be a problem. If at first you can't find the right expert,' he recited with a forefinger in the air, 'then you keep looking until you track him down.' He grew solemn again before cocking me a half-smile. 'Being a small outfit, we might also try harder.'

Despite his youth and relative inexperience, despite the gaffe over the psychiatric assessment, my first instinct was to stay with Tingwall. Yet this was Ginny's future we were talking about. Getting this decision right was probably the most important thing I could ever do for her. Before putting the matter to Ginny I decided to check it out with some lawyer friends in London. I said, 'I'll have to speak to my wife.'

'Of course. It's for her to decide.' He gave a

diffident smile. 'Perhaps I should say ... if she decided to entrust me with the case I would give it my very best shot. Everything I had.'

'I'll tell her that.'

A slight softening had come over Tingwall's face, a shadow of his fascination for Ginny, grown distant now, and sadder.

'You're visiting her tomorrow morning?' he asked, resuming a suitable briskness. 'Give her my best regards, would you? And tell her I'll see her before court on Monday.' Behind him the calf-bound legal tomes marched brashly along the shelves, at his elbow a stack of files teetered precariously, and I wondered how many other cases he had on the go.

'What'll happen on Monday exactly?'

'Not a lot. The Crown Prosecution Service will ask for a further remand, and I will ask that it be set for a week, and the magistrates will agree. And that's it.'

'We don't question anything?'

'The evidence, you mean? Not at this stage, no.'

'When, then?'

Tingwall's narrow eyes flicked away briefly, he pursed his lips. 'It's highly unlikely we would want to challenge anything before the trial. Though that can't be decided, finally, until we see the prosecution's evidence.'

I said with disgust, 'And the trial's eight months away.'

'It could be six.'

'And there's no chance of getting the case stopped before then?'

Tingwall was looking uneasy, as he always did

when I talked in this way. 'I think we have to face the fact that it's very unlikely.'

My frustration resurfaced. 'It all sounds so *negative*.'

Tingwall considered this with detachment. 'I would hope – realistic.'

I pulled my hands down my face and let my anger go. I knew I shouldn't take my disappointment out on Tingwall, yet a part of me needed to challenge the frightening mood of inevitability which seemed to have attached itself to Ginny's case.

'You think the evidence is that strong?' I hadn't meant to ask this; I wasn't sure that I was ready to hear the answer.

'As laid out by the police,' Tingwall stated cautiously, 'as specified by them, the evidence would seem sufficient to take the case to trial.'

So far I had avoided discussion of the evidence. There are things that aren't that easy to face. But now, finally, I braced myself to confront the facts, partly to test Tingwall's knowledge against my own, but also – there was no denying it – to feed my own hunger for understanding, to embellish the reel of film that kept running through my head with images and colour.

'Tell me what they have,' I asked calmly. 'As you understand it. The evidence so far.'

Tingwall shot me a questioning glance, then stood up. 'Of course. Coffee?' He went to a side table and, pouring two cups from a Thermos jug, brought them over. He pulled up a chair and, setting it at an angle to mine, sat on the edge of the seat, hunched forward with his arms resting on his knees, and began to speak in the gentle measured tones of a storyteller.

'I asked the police for a summary of their main evidence immediately after Ginny was charged. And it was the same as the evidence listed in court on Monday. Now it's possible they may be holding something back on the principle that you don't give away any more than you have to at this stage of the proceedings, but I doubt it. In a case like this I think they'd produce everything they had, just to be sure. So . . .' He clasped his hands together. 'The first thing they stated was that several traces of the victim's blood had been found on the floor of the *Ellie Miller*, thus establishing the boat as the scene of the crime. Now this was a categorical statement, based on forensic evidence, so we can assume that they have run DNA tests and so on. Then . . .' He paused to take a sip of coffee and gather his thoughts. 'Then they said that Ginny's fingerprint had been found in a bloodstain on the boat, and that this blood was also the victim's.'

I had meant to keep quiet, but I said, 'This forensic stuff, it's cut and dried, is it?'

'Usually, yes. In the case of DNA, particularly so.' He was like a cat on a precarious ledge, choosing the safest place to step. 'With other forensic evidence, it can sometimes be . . . open to interpretation. Often it's a matter of the individual expert's opinion – and opinions can differ. Very occasionally they differ considerably. What we can do, of course, is hire our own expert to examine whatever evidence it is and run his own tests. If his findings give us a chance of challenging the prosecution's expert, then – well, obviously we'd pursue that avenue rigorously, get a third opinion and so on. The first step – and I think I mentioned this to you the other day – is to get a pathologist to carry out a post-mortem for us. I've made enquiries and Dr James Bagnall could do it next week. He's the best man, quite famous now. If the police pathologist has missed anything, he'll find it. And his opinion would count for a great deal. He's done a lot of murders – all the ones you read about.'

And now this one: another to be read about.

'I'll go ahead then, shall I?' Tingwall asked. 'With Dr Bagnall?'

'Yes,' I said, trying not to think of Sylvie's body and what would happen to it under Bagnall's knife. 'I interrupted you. On the evidence.'

Tingwall's disconcerting gaze flicked up to me, before fixing itself on the floor some five or six feet in front of him. 'Next . . . The police are saying that they have a witness who saw Ginny rowing out to the boat on the *Saturday* afternoon, when she says she was only just starting out from London. Now identification evidence is always soft evidence, and if this was the only thing the prosecution had to go on we'd certainly consider challenging it at an early stage.'

But it was not the only evidence, and he moved quickly on. 'Finally, they cited Ginny's own statement, that she went to *Ellie Miller* the next day, the Sunday, and scrubbed the boat clean. The inference being that she was removing blood and so on.'

In the silence that followed I replayed that Sunday

morning in my mind, as I had replayed it so many times in the last week. I saw Ginny in jeans and a loose top, packing a plastic bucket with cleaning materials to take out to the boat. I held her face close to my mind's eye and searched her expression for signs of trauma and despair, I recalled snippets of our dialogue and scanned the casually uttered words for intimations of disaster, yet I found nothing, no hint at all. Casting Ginny in an innocent role, I saw someone keen to participate in the boat-orientated life at Dittisham from which I had excluded her for so long that summer, eager to muck in and show me what she could contribute, and, in so doing, make a go of our marriage again: Ginny the peacemaker, fraught with nothing more sinister than anxiety. Then I cast her as someone frighteningly different, a person I scarcely recognised, someone calculating and vindictive, cold and methodical, someone who was capable not only of committing such a terrible act, but of behaving as if it had never happened, and in this incarnation her mild agitation that morning finally took on a guilty significance.

Tingwall murmured, 'Of course we must wait for the prosecution to serve their statements on us before we can be absolutely sure of what we're up against, and that won't be for some weeks yet.'

'But at the moment it looks pretty bad?' I said, staring straight into his crooked eyes.

'I wouldn't use a word like bad, Hugh. But there's certainly a serious case to answer.'

This judgment, though I had been expecting it, was like a band tightening around my heart.

I braced myself to ask, 'What's the worst that can happen?'

'The worst?' He jerked his head back slightly, as though recoiling from an unpleasant task. 'I really . . . That's something for the QC to advise.'

I persevered, 'If she was found guilty?'

He said with great reluctance, 'For murder, it's a mandatory life sentence. But Hugh, there are bound to be mitigating circumstances, the chance of a lesser charge—'

'Bound to be?'

'Of course! Ginny's case is never going to fall into the same category as a cold-blooded gang murderer. There are so many ways to play this, Hugh. She could plead guilty to manslaughter on the grounds of diminished responsibility, for example. She could say she was under such intolerable strain that she lost her head. She could say she was severely provoked and reacted in an instant of madness. Or she might have been suffering severe clinical depression. There are so many ways to approach this, Hugh. So many ways to win a jury's understanding.'

'And for manslaughter?'

He was not enjoying this game. He blew out his lips. 'It varies so much, I couldn't give you a figure. It all depends on the circumstances and the judge. Anything from a few years to fifteen, eighteen, with half off for good behaviour. It's such a wide range.'

Significantly less than life, at any rate. For some reason I fastened on to the idea of seven years as a time which seemed survivable, a time which, long though it was, had a foreseeable end. I imagined visiting Ginny in prison year after year, the two of us getting older, nearing fifty before we could start our lives again, in France perhaps, or Italy. Survivable.

A lorry shuddered past in the street outside, filling the room with a low rumble.

'So manslaughter might be the best bet?' I said, groping for reassurance.

'We'll have to wait for Counsel's recommendations, and he won't be able to put anything to Ginny until he has everything in front of him, until he has her story.'

Ginny's story. The great unknown. Part of me longed to hear it, the other part lived in dread of what it might contain. 'She hasn't said anything to you?'

'No. And I haven't pressed her. The only thing I would like to know fairly soon, though, is whether anyone can vouch for her whereabouts on that Saturday afternoon. In my experience alibi witnesses are best caught early, before their memories fade. But she hasn't really been in any state to consider that, so I'll ask her again on Monday.'

'An alibi witness?' I said doubtfully. 'You think that's likely?'

He looked rather disappointed in me, as if I had failed to grasp an essential point. 'What *I* think is neither here nor there,' he stated. 'At this stage we must rule out nothing at all. It would be a terrible mistake to overlook the smallest thing that might help the defence. A case must never be lost for lack of trying.'

He did not remove his energetic gaze from my face

until he was sure I had understood the importance of what he was saying, and in that moment I felt an upsurge of confidence in him, and, with this, a small easing of the burden.

'No stone unturned,' I said.

We got to our feet.

'Not a pebble either.' He endorsed this with a diffident smile. 'You mustn't believe there's nothing that can be done, Hugh. It's very rare that nothing can be done.'

But just then it seemed to me that Ginny's situation was almost hopeless.

A horn tooted and I looked round to see my car move off a yellow line and sweep in to the kerb beside me. Julia lowered the window and one glimpse of her expression told me that there had been no call from Cumberland.

'Want to drive?' she asked.

I shook my head and went round to the passenger side.

'So, no reprieve?' I asked, getting in.

She cast me a scathing glance. 'Was there ever likely to be? All this talk of asking the board to reconsider at the eleventh hour was just Howard playing off both sides against the middle. There was never a chance!'

It was over then. At some point that morning the Cumberland board had formally accepted a bid from another company, a glass manufacturer called Donington. In their explanatory fax to the Hartford team, sent at six last evening after rumours had been circulating all day, the board had cited their responsibility to serve the best interests of the shareholders, a duty they felt would be best fulfilled by accepting the Donington bid.

So it was over, for me at least. Late last night George had talked about fighting the Cumberland board, about writing to every Cumberland shareholder to put the facts before them, to call an extraordinary general meeting and persuade them to oppose the Donington bid and back our own; he had talked about unleashing every trick in the book, using the media, the politicians, all the spoiling tactics we could think of. He talked fiercely, he made a lot of sense, but in my heart I knew my own fight was over. I was ready to let Hartford go, I was no longer bothered by the idea of Howard beating me. In the shadow of Ginny's catastrophe my own battles seemed rather insignificant. The only thing that still had the power to upset me was the thought of Hartford closing, of the people who would never work there again, and the death of the furnaces.

Julia drove along the one-way system, muttering at the lack of road signs, until I pointed her towards the Totnes road.

'George has told everyone, has he?' I asked.

'He will have by now. He warned them yesterday, so they'd be ready for it. And while we're on the subject of staff,' Julia added firmly, 'I'll stay on for as long as you want me, a day or a month, and no redundancy required, thank you very much. I've got another job lined up for when I leave.'

'I wish I could keep you on.'

'That's all right.'

'Won't be able to afford you.'

'That's what my boyfriends say.'

I hadn't faced the money situation yet. Now that the buyout had failed I would have to meet the expenses of the bid, for which I had made myself personally liable – the fees of the venture capitalists, accountants and lawyers – a sum I didn't care to add up quite yet but which would certainly run a long way into six figures. And then, most important of all, I would need to put plenty aside for Ginny's defence, on which no expense was to be spared.

'When did it finally come back?' I said, indicating the car.

'Wednesday.'

I looked for traces of the police examination. Fingerprint powder or whatever they used, but the dashboard was clean and there was nothing to be seen on the doors.

'Mary told me they've finished with Dittisham House as well,' Julia added, 'though it's too late to save the sale, apparently. The people got fed up with waiting.'

Or they didn't like the notoriety that was fast attaching itself to the house, though neither of us remarked on that.

'Mary wanted to know if you were intending to stay the night with them.'

I hadn't got that far. All week I had been choosing a place to sleep almost at random, sometimes driving miles back to London after seeing Tingwall, sometimes travelling the forty minutes to Melton after seeing Ginny at the prison, or one day – it must have been Wednesday – just shutting myself away in Glebe Place, drinking and sleeping, occasionally crying my eyes out, until, waking at two in the morning, I had driven through the night to Dittisham and, going down to the quay, sat on a wall watching the dawn come up. When it was light I had gone to the boat yard and through the fence looked at the draped outline of *Ellie* on the hard standing, and briefly wept again.

I hadn't stayed with Mary and David since the weekend. I hadn't been avoiding them exactly, but at the same time I wasn't ready to discuss the details of Ginny's case with anyone but Tingwall. Julia understood this intuitively, as did David, who, though he had called several times, had been careful to restrict himself to practical matters. Mary was unlikely to be so easily rebuffed, however. When we'd spoken on the phone she'd kept asking the sort of questions that I wasn't ready to answer. While I still valued our friendship, while it had seemed natural to confide in her on the subject of Sylvie, Ginny was an entirely different matter, and, for the moment at least, Mary's curiosity had caused me to pull up my drawbridge.

'I'll decide later,' I said.

'Mary said she could leave supper out for you if you were late. That reminds me.' Julia reached behind her seat and handed me a sandwich. 'It's compulsory,' she said.

I didn't argue. I'd been eating spasmodically, if at

all, and I knew that if I was to be any good to Ginny I had to start pulling myself together.

We reached Hartford under a darkening sky and spitting rain, which cast a gloom over the factory windows and leached the colour from the flowers around the entrance.

Heather, the receptionist, raised puffy eyes and dabbed at them with a handkerchief. 'Oh, Mr Wellesley, I'm so sorry,' she cried, pulling a tragic face.

'I'm very sorry too, Heather.' And for a confusing instant I wondered if we were talking about Hartford or Ginny.

George, Alan and John were waiting in Pa's old office. We shook hands with more than usual energy, the closest we could safely get to emotion.

George declared with a defiant upward thrust of one fist: 'We may have lost the battle, Hugh, but we haven't lost the war! They had the nerve to tell us Donington's bid was worth more than ours? Well, it's not! They're taking some of it in Donington shares – aiming for another merger or whatever – and the market value of the shares is ten pence down on the paper value. I've been on to the lawyers. They say it's good enough for an extraordinary general meeting. We can still get 'em, Hugh! We can still win!' And he gave an excited cry that seemed to intensify the flush of his florid cheeks.

Because I couldn't think of what else to say, I murmured, 'You've been busy then.'

We clustered around the table, ready to sit down. There was a pause while Alan and John looked towards George, waiting for him to make some sort of announcement.

'Yes, uhh . . .' George frowned. 'All of us would like to express our sadness at what has happened to your wife, Hugh. And we'd like you to know that if there's anything we can do you only have to call on us. Anything at all.'

'Thank you.'

'I'd like to second that,' said Alan.

John added a brisk, 'Me too.'

'Thank you. I can only say that . . .' It was hard to compose even these few words. 'I appreciate your thoughts. And if my family problems tipped Cumberland's decision against us, then I regret that very much. For you and for everyone else at Hartford.'

George made an exclamation of denial and Alan followed fast with: 'Listen – Cumberland were out to make our lives difficult from the start, weren't they?'

'Howard was, you mean,' George chipped in. 'One way or another.'

Alan urged, 'Don't blame yourself, Hugh. It was always going to be a battle.'

They were saying what they thought I wanted to hear, but I knew, as they must have known, that the publicity over Ginny, the terrible nature of the crime, and the knowledge that, with all my problems and preoccupations, I couldn't possibly sustain any practical involvement in Hartford, must have counted heavily against us.

There was a slight pause, a moment of mutual sympathy and unease, before we left the subject behind.

Even as we were settling in our seats, George launched his plan of attack. 'The first step,' he said blithely, 'is to get this EGM off the ground. All we need is the backing of ten per cent of the equity. What with your holding, Hugh and your brother's—'

'George—'

Perhaps he knew what was coming, because he frowned at my interruption.

'Are you sure you still have Zircon and the banks behind you?'

I had used 'you' not 'we' and 'us', but if he realised I was excluding myself from this process he didn't comment on it.

'I was coming round to that,' he said rapidly. 'I realise only too well that we'll have to sell them the idea of hanging on. But if we're going to get this EGM off the ground at all, we have to move fast.'

'I think you might have to move fast on the banks too,' I said in my most diplomatic tone. 'I think they'll already have gone cold on you, and the news of the Donington bid will finish them off. I think there's no time to lose.'

This was met by an exchange of glances between George and Alan.

George said, 'In fact, we were hoping you might tackle the banks. We thought it would come best from you.'

'Don't be ridiculous. It would come worst from me. They won't want to know about me.'

'Why not?'

Was this a mistaken show of loyalty or could he really not see the problem? 'George, quite apart from my personal credibility, they'll know I can't possibly have my eye on the ball any more. They'll know I can't possibly give it a hundred per cent, and they'll be dead right.'

'We realise it won't be easy for you, Hugh. We realise your time will be limited. But we've discussed it – and, Hugh, we don't think we can do it without you.'

'I think you could do it without me very well.'

George ignored this. 'You talk the banks' language.'

How to make him realise it was all over? 'I'm out, George.'

'We'll do the rest, all the legwork, all the nitty-gritty. We'll take everything off your back. Just the banks, Hugh,' George pleaded. 'Please – just give it a try.'

I had forgotten how stubborn George could be, and how this quality, so valuable in a production director, could seem less attractive from the receiving end. 'My heart simply wouldn't be in it,' I said, trying to spell it out for him.

'That's the way you feel now, Hugh. And we all understand that. But give it a while. Give it a few days, give it a week.'

'No time,' I argued again. 'I wouldn't have the time.'

'Maybe not just at the moment. But in the future, maybe you'll have more time than you think. Maybe you'll be glad of a project.'

Unexpectedly, this hit a chord. In the months ahead I had been planning to spend my time supporting Ginny, meeting lawyers, doing everything I could.

But now that some of the shock had worn off I could see that I had perhaps been idealising my role, or at least oversimplifying it. Once Ginny got bail she might not want me under her feet the whole time, and I might be glad of some distraction; both of us might be desperate for a semblance of normal life.

Seeing the chink in my armour, George played his last card. 'We owe it to our people, Hugh,' he said in a blatant appeal to my conscience. 'Otherwise they'll be on the scrapheap, claiming benefits, having their skills go to waste. Surely we owe them one last go.'

'I might do more damage than good. With the banks.'

'We'll risk it.'

'Don't say I didn't warn you.'

They were waiting.

'I'll *think* about it,' I sighed, realising that this was as good as a promise and that, somehow or another, I had managed to manoeuvre myself into a corner.

I dropped Julia at the station and drove on to Dartmouth to see David. His surgery, a utilitarian single-storey building which he shared with his two partners, was set on a precipitous slope above the harbour with views across to Kingswear and the marina. Among the sea of yacht masts I found myself looking for the sleek outlines of the customs launch and wondering if the customs men had known of Sylvie's activities before our trip to France. In the next moment I pushed the thought impatiently aside. What did it matter now? It was finished. Sylvie would never be coming back. Except, it seemed, to destroy my life.

The surgery had been refurbished since my last visit. The waiting area had acquired pale wooden chairs with padded seats, potted plants and framed prints, and, on one wall, an electronic announcement board telling patients when their doctor was ready for them.

There were five people waiting, but after ten minutes the receptionist caught my eye and waved me through.

The passage leading to David's room was decorated with photographs and posters of racing cars, pictures which he had accumulated in his early twenties when he'd harboured a passion to become an amateur racing driver. Like most of David's more extravagant ambitions at that time – there had been schemes to fly hot-air balloons and buy into a yacht charter business in the Caribbean – it had fallen victim to the tight financial rein that Pa had kept us on. David had taken this restriction badly, as an unjust denial of his inheritance, yet Pa had always gone out of his way to explain how our trust funds were set up, telling us from a young age that there would be no capital until we were thirty. I could never work out whether David simply hadn't accepted this or had thought he could get round the old man. Either way he had been regularly, and to his mind unfairly, disappointed.

David came round his desk and gripped me awkwardly by both shoulders. I thought for a moment that he was about to embrace me, something that would have startled us both, but he gave me a small shake instead, a sort of rallying jolt. He stepped back, looking slightly cross with himself. 'What a bloody awful business,' he exclaimed finally.

I could only nod.

'Now how's Tingwall shaping up?' he asked, waving me to a seat like a patient. 'He's definitely the best lawyer you'll get locally – I've checked up on him again, asked around.' He pulled up another chair and sat next to me on the patients' side of the desk. 'But being the best around here may not be saying too much.' He rolled a despairing eye at the limitations of the provinces. 'You *are* considering people in London?'

'I'm getting advice on that.'

'Make sure you get the best,' he urged. 'And what about a QC? Tingwall's getting you a QC?'

We had already discussed these things on the phone at least once, maybe twice. Whether David had forgotten or was simply anxious to press his advice home I couldn't tell.

'And the medical side?' he continued systematically, like a chairman working his way through an agenda. 'That's under control, is it?'

'We're getting a letter from her asthma specialist, saying she's got to have bail for health reasons.'

'Anything else you need in that department?' he asked almost fiercely.

'That's what I came about, actually. We need a good psychiatrist. Someone who's prepared to say Ginny's not a suicide risk. Otherwise they might block bail.'

David's expression brightened at the challenge. He tapped his fingertips together while he pondered. 'There's a bloke called Jones. Based in Bristol.'

'He'll be all right, will he?'

'Oh, he'll do the necessary, if that's what you mean.' From the confidence of his tone, Jones and he might have been fellow mafiosi who traded favours in the form of foregone conclusions. 'I'll speak to him this afternoon.' He reached for a pad and made a note.

'Tingwall found a guy called Robertson, but' – it still disturbed me to say it – 'he seemed to think that Ginny might be a risk to herself.' Seeking reassurance, I lifted my brows and turned this into a question.

'Well, anyone would be a bit desperate in her situation, wouldn't they? *Christ!* Facing all *that*.' He grimaced at the thought, and gave a sudden shiver. 'But if she's a bit depressed the right drugs will soon sort her out.'

'You really think so?' I longed for Ginny to be released, but sometimes the prospect of looking after her on my own worried me.

'Oh yes. Jones will know what to prescribe.'

A pause, during which we exchanged a quick glance.

'Nothing else I can do?' he asked.

I shook my head.

Another pause as David prepared himself to say awkwardly, 'Look, it's none of my business, and the last thing I want to do is – *interfere* . . .' He contorted his face, waiting for objections, before continuing gruffly, 'But what have they got in the way of evidence, for Christ's sake? What *can* they have? They must have got something drastically wrong, it's crazy to think that Ginny—' He shut his mouth abruptly as if he'd already said enough.

I would never have foreseen David as an open champion of Ginny's cause, just as I could never have predicted the extent of his concern. I was touched. David had such a long history of detachment, he had always been so wary of gratuitous confidences that he usually steered clear of what he called 'situations'.

'They know Sylvie was killed on the boat,' I told him haltingly. 'And then they have a fingerprint of Ginny's, found on board. And some witness who saw her rowing out to the boat, on the Saturday afternoon.'

David frowned. 'A fingerprint? But what does that mean, for heaven's sake? Ginny's been on the boat often enough.'

'No. No... You see, it was in blood. Sylvie's blood.'

'Ah.' He absorbed this grudgingly. '*Ah*.' He stared beyond me in further consideration, then shook his head. 'But couldn't there be some other explanation? Couldn't she have – I don't know...' He threw a hand in the air. 'Come into contact with the blood some other way. After the event, or...' He ran out of ideas, just as I did whenever I put myself through the same exercise. Catching sight of my face, seeing with alarm that I was close to the edge of my emotions, he added briskly, 'The thing is, there's going to be a way of getting her off, Hugh. There always is. Some fact they haven't checked, some witness who hasn't come forward, some deal to be made with the lawyers. That's why you need the best defence team money can buy. Eh?'

But I wasn't in any mood to be cheered up. 'Ginny's simply not capable of this thing, David. She just couldn't have done it.'

He shifted in his seat. 'No.'

I held on to my voice with difficulty. 'She just couldn't.'

He nodded grimly.

'She . . .' But I couldn't speak, I was clenching my lips too tightly.

Leaning forward, David moved a tentative hand as if to comfort me before thinking better of it and sweeping his hand up towards his chin.

I pulled in my breath with a gasp. 'She has no violence in her. None at all. She couldn't hurt a fly. She just couldn't . . .'

'No.' Swinging to his feet, David fetched water and Kleenex, and, thrusting them at me, waited while I blew my nose and generally pulled myself together.

'I'm keeping your patients waiting,' I said at last.

'Oh, they're used to it,' he declared airily. 'Now what about you? Need anything to make you sleep? Anything to cheer you up?'

'Oh, I'm all right.' I rearranged my expression into something a little less morbid.

'Shall I give you something anyway, just in case?'

I stood up and gave my nose a final blow. 'David, they don't make pills for what I need.'

'You'd be amazed what Prozac can do.' He lifted a satanic eyebrow.

'I'd rather not find out just at the moment.'

'My patients live on the stuff,' he announced, poker-faced. 'High doses – keeps 'em nice and quiet.'

As so often, I wasn't quite sure whether David was spinning one of his darker jokes.

He walked me to the waiting room door then, resuming some of his old manner, gave an evasive almost irritated smile before turning quickly away.

I was unlocking my car when a horn tooted and I looked up to see Mary's car swooping in through the entrance. Parking untidily, she came striding over.

'I caught you! David told me you were popping in. I'm so *glad* I caught you!' She gave me a firm kiss on the cheek and, gripping my arm, surveyed me with fond concern. 'How are you?'

I pulled a so-so expression.

'Now you *are* staying tonight, aren't you?'

'Wish I could, but . . .' I gestured difficulties.

'Oh, come on. Come and stay!'

'I really can't.'

She made a face. 'Why on earth not? Where will you go, for goodness sake?'

'Oh, Melton. I have to go and see to the place.'

She shook her head at me. 'Well, come back for a quick coffee then!'

'Mary, I wish I could, but I have to rush.'

'But I so want to talk to you!' She gave a rapid smile to soften the rebuke in her voice. 'I've got important things to tell you.'

'What sort of important things?'

'I'll explain, but come and have a coffee. It'll be easier over a coffee.'

I couldn't hide my exasperation as I said: 'But what's it about, Mary?'

She sighed at me. 'Why, the case, of course!'

A flutter of hope. 'You've heard something? What is it?'

'It's hard to explain just like that.'

'Mary, just tell me! Tell me, please!'

She gave me a look of mock anger that wasn't entirely light-hearted. 'I can't see what's so difficult about coming home for a minute!' Her good humour had developed a sharp edge to it, and it occurred to me that she too must have been feeling the strain of our family's instant notoriety. 'All right! All right!' she declared suddenly, as though giving in to the whim of a child. 'Let's get out of the wind at any rate.'

We got into my car. Mary pushed her hair back from her face and I dimly noticed that she'd done something new and not entirely successful with the style. She had eye makeup on, too, a shade of blue that contrasted strongly with her pink cheeks and dark eyebrows.

'Right!' she declared forcefully. '*What* I wanted to tell you was that I've been doing some research. I went through my old legal tomes – the ones I still have, at any rate – *and* I went and looked through a friend's legal library which is more up-to-date. *And* I spoke to a friend of a friend in London who's a real ace on case law and precedent. Now it seems there have been some very significant cases in recent years.' She spoke fast and emphatically. 'There was one case where a wife killed her husband's lover and pleaded manslaughter on the grounds of diminished responsibility and only got *eight* years. Which means she served four. And *that* was a case where there were definite overtones of premeditation – the wife went round to the other woman's house with a hammer. *Said* she only intended to break the windows, *but . . .*' She made a knowing face before racing on. '*Then* there was another case. A wife discovered her husband in bed with another woman. She rushed down to the kitchen and got a knife and went up and stabbed him. Said it was PMT that drove her to it, temporary insanity. She virtually walked free—'

'Mary, what are you trying to tell me exactly?' I interrupted in a calm voice.

I had broken her flow. 'What I was *trying* to say was that in these types of cases the jury can often overlook the odd bit of premeditation—'

'I meant, your point. What is your point?'

'If you'd let me explain—'

'Mary . . .' I held up both hands. 'I'm grateful, but I don't think I'm quite ready for this.'

She gave a rapid empty smile. '*All* I'm trying to tell you is that if there's diminished responsibility and not too much premeditation then the sentence could be almost nothing! A few years!'

'I see,' I said tightly. 'I see. Well, thank you for going to the trouble.' Not trusting myself to say any more, I scrambled out of the car and stood looking down at the harbour.

I heard Mary's door slam. 'Hugh,' she cried, coming up behind me. 'Hugh! I just wanted you to

291

realise that it needn't be that bad. I mean – a few years! It's not so much, is it?'

It was suddenly a great deal to me, much more than it had seemed in Tingwall's office. And I was terribly hurt by Mary's presumption of Ginny's guilt, the way she seemed to be offering a few years' prison as some sort of consolation prize. In my mood of desolation it struck me that beneath David's show of concern he might also believe that Ginny was guilty. Perhaps everyone thought she was guilty.

But then perhaps I was reacting so strongly because, deep down, against all my wishes, it was what I believed too.

Ginny appeared at last, and, seeing me, cast her eyes down and wove her way slowly between the crowded tables. She was wearing something nice, I noticed, a flowing ankle-length skirt and matching top, and her hair was newly washed and combed so that it gleamed ochre and amber in the light.

We embraced briefly and sat facing each other across the formica table.

I searched her face. 'How are you?'

'Oh . . .' She pondered this. 'They gave me something. Tranquillisers, I think. They seem to even things out a bit.'

This was more than she had said to me during both of my previous visits put together, and I smiled, 'You look better.' This wasn't true: she looked thinner, her eyes appeared larger in her face and the skin of her cheeks seemed to cling more tightly to the bones. But the empty look that had disturbed me so much on my last visit had faded, and I recognised something of the old Ginny in her eyes.

'How's the room? Did they move you?'

She gave the faintest nod. 'I'm on my own. Not everyone's on their own.'

'Well, that's something!'

'It has sun.'

'That's nice!' I replied rather too brightly. 'Health all right? You've got enough inhalers? You've seen a doctor?'

She was slow to concentrate. 'More than one,' she said. 'Two . . . three. Psychiatrists, mainly.'

'I'm afraid that you might have to see another,' I ventured gently. 'A man called Jones. Did Tingwall tell you? It's to make sure we get this bail application through.'

She looked uncertain, as though her memory were playing tricks.

'We need someone to say that you're fit and well to come home. Tingwall should have told you.'

'I didn't know what to say,' she murmured. 'He kept asking me how I felt about the future.'

'Who? Robertson?'

'What was I meant to say?' She cast me a baffled look. 'I didn't know what to say.'

I reached for her hand. 'Darling, don't worry about it. Just leave it to Jones when he comes. He'll make sure it's all right.'

There was a commotion at the next table as a child started to scream.

When the child had quietened down a little Ginny asked dully, 'Will I get bail?'

I hesitated. 'Tingwall thinks there's an excellent chance.' I explained about the QC, and how Tingwall was aiming to pre-empt any objections the police or prosecution might have. But she had seen my hesitation and understood it; she realised it would be a mistake to count too firmly on her freedom.

'But listen,' I said, pushing optimism into my voice, 'I had a long session with Tingwall. We started mapping things out. We've got six months, maybe more, before the trial. That gives him plenty of time to prepare the best possible defence. Now I want you to be quite clear, darling – we're going to have the very best team, the best lawyers, the best experts and doctors – whatever it takes. There won't be a single thing that won't be covered. Not a thing!'

She thought about this but did not seem to draw much comfort from it.

I ploughed on. 'And as for tactics – approaches – there are all sorts of options. Tingwall went through them with me . . . Ginny?'

She had sucked in her lips, she was blinking rapidly: the signs.

'Darling,' I pleaded helplessly.

Pulling her hand away, she stared down at the table and shook her head. It was both an appeal and a warning. She did not want to discuss it.

Retreating, I cast around for safer ground. After a long pause I offered half-heartedly, 'Things at Hartford are still frantic. Everyone racing around . . .'

She nodded to show she was listening.

'But I've backed off for a while. Left them to it. Quite nice, being out of it.' I added for light relief: 'Might try it on a permanent basis.'

There was no flicker of an answering smile. 'And the buyout?'

'Oh, more off than on at the moment.' I shrugged: 'There was always a risk.'

'Sorry.'

'One of those things.' Another pause during which I became increasingly lost. 'Oh . . . The estate agent says there might be some people interested in Melton.'

'That would be good,' she said with visible effort. 'Before they next go over the place get Mrs Hoskins to put plenty of flowers everywhere, won't you? It makes such a difference.'

A couple of young children roared past. We lapsed into silence again.

I said, 'Nothing from the agents in France, though.'

She gave a long jagged sigh. 'I'm sorry,' she gasped, and I realised we weren't talking about houses any more. 'I know you were only trying to help.'

'Doesn't matter.'

'I find it so hard . . . You see' – she raised her eyes at last – 'whenever I think about it, I can't see any way out, and it frightens me to death.'

A spark of dread passed between us.

'Ginny, there *will* be a way out. Wait until you talk it through with Tingwall. He'll explain all the options. I promise – there *will* be a way out! Just tell him what he needs to know. I promise!'

She swung her head slowly from side to side. 'But what can I tell him?'

Aware that she might be on the brink of some irreversible revelation, feeling a terrifying blend of fear and curiosity, I led her slowly forward. 'You must tell him anything that could help. Like where you were on that Saturday afternoon, at exactly what time, and who might have seen you . . . Someone *must* have seen you, darling. At Glebe Place, or on the motorway, or . . .'

'But I was there.' This comment slipped into the pool of silence, a small ripple which grew and grew. 'I can't say I wasn't there. That's why they're never going to believe me.' She gave a ragged laugh, near tears. 'Never.'

My breath was tight in my chest. 'When you say *there*, you mean . . . you mean in Dittisham?'

She nodded bitterly.

'You . . .' I could hardly ask it. 'You weren't near the boat, though?'

'I thought you were on board, I went to find you.'

A cold horror settled in my stomach. I felt sick. 'And then?' I whispered.

I thought for a moment that she wasn't going to answer. Her eyes glistened with unshed tears. 'I found her.'

I could hardly speak. 'Found her?'

She put a hand to her head, as though it was causing her pain.

'Ginny, Ginny . . .' I tried to keep the shock out of my voice. 'What are you saying? Are you saying she was dead?'

She was silent.

'*Ginny?*' I pleaded. 'What are you saying?'

She rubbed her temples. 'It doesn't matter.'

'But is that what you're saying? For God's sake, *tell me.*'

She looked me straight in the eye then, and it was a look which contained resignation and defeat, and finally, a small but unmistakable flicker of confirmation.

My mind went racing off in several directions, most of them startling, all of them confusing. 'But, Ginny . . . why didn't you tell anyone this? Why didn't you report it?'

She shook her head slowly, and kept shaking it for a long time.

I leant across the table, I seized her hands roughly in mine. 'But you must tell them now! You must!'

'It wouldn't do any good.'

'Why not, for God's sake?'

'Oh Hugh . . .' And she gave me a pitying look.

'I don't understand.'

But she closed herself off from me then. Her face emptied, she dropped her eyes.

I struggled to make sense of it, I tried to grasp what she was telling me, but I was hurt and confused by her lack of faith in me, it was all a jumble, and for a while I felt as though I too were going mad.

Ten

IN ENGLISH courts there are two kinds of magistrate, Tingwall enlightened me. There are the stipendiaries, known colloquially as 'stipes', trained lawyers who sit alone on the bench as full-time professionals, and there are the lay magistrates, part-time justices of the peace who sit for a few days a month in a triumvirate with two fellow JPs.

Exeter had no stipendiaries, only JPs. I wouldn't have given this any thought, I certainly wouldn't have seen it as any kind of disadvantage if Grainger, our QC, hadn't commented to Tingwall within my hearing, 'Oh for a stipe.' Seeing I had picked up on this, Grainger elaborated derisively in his affected drawl, 'JPs can be dreadful old women. Paralysed by the fear of doing the wrong thing. And, as a consequence, of course, frequently doing precisely that.'

I did not fret about this for too long. Partly because I saw Grainger's concern as a way of covering his back. Partly because, by the time we had waited in the hall outside the court for an hour, I was beginning to think that Grainger himself might be a far greater liability. His arrogant overbearing London style seemed destined to rub the JPs up the wrong way, as it had so thoroughly irritated me. I tried to talk myself out of disliking the man, but the way he strutted about, his bombastic voice and imperious manner made me so angry that I had to take myself for a walk around the block. Tingwall reassured me that Grainger was one of the top criminal barristers in the country and that he hadn't won this reputation by chance, but by the time we filed into court I had convinced myself that Grainger was in every respect a terrible mistake.

I recognised one of the male JPs from a previous remand, but the second man and the woman were new. Both men were sixtyish, one a successful business type, the other, the chairman, a tweedy countryman, a landowner or professional man. The woman was younger, about forty, and stylish. They were the sort of people Ginny and I had occasionally met on Wiltshire weekends, though I couldn't decide whether to take encouragement from that.

Stairs led straight up into the dock from the cells below, and to the accompaniment of clanging subterranean doors and shuffling feet, Ginny appeared with officers ahead and behind. This sight disturbed me, it seemed grotesque, as though Ginny were the victim of some hideous identity switch.

She did not glance in my direction as she went to the front of the dock and sat down. The business quickly began. Grainger announced that he represented Ginny and made the application for bail.

The prosecution objected to bail due to the seriousness of the crime and the prison psychiatrist's report, which indicated that Ginny was in a frail state of mind and might be a danger to herself.

Rising, Grainger began his plea. I had to strain to hear him. At first I thought he was simply getting into his stride, working his voice up to a theatrical pitch, but then it dawned on me that this quiet unassuming tone was the one he had deliberately selected for the occasion. The actor-lawyer, appearing for this performance only as the sincere advocate without pretensions. As he pleaded Ginny's previous good character, her exemplary life, her charitable work, her poor health which, the doctors agreed, would suffer dramatically unless she were allowed home, I was forced to hand it to him, grudgingly at first, then with increasing admiration. It was a masterly show of moderation and restraint, with just the right dash of humility. If I hadn't met him beforehand, I would have thought he was an extremely nice man.

Without giving the slightest hint as to the way Ginny intended to plead, he managed to suggest that she was incapable of hurting a fly, and suddenly the idea of her innocence was floating gently and inoffensively on the air. He emphasised that Ginny would be returning to the bosom of her family, that she had the full support of her husband, family and close friends.

Calmly Grainger referred the bench to the report of the eminent psychiatrist Dr Jones, which granted that Ginny had been in a state of shock and depression for the first week after she had been charged, but declared that, with the commencement of treatment, she was now in a robust and sensible frame of mind, and constituted no danger to herself. Mrs Wellesley's mental health would continue to be closely monitored by Dr Jones, whom she would be seeing at least once a week. No good would be served by keeping Ginny in custody, he summarised, and no harm could possibly be done by allowing her out on bail. He offered the surrender of Ginny's passport, residence at Melton, and surety at the court's discretion.

Tingwall had warned me that the JPs would withdraw to consider their decision, so I was taken off-guard when, after a short discussion between themselves, and a brief consultation with the clerk, the chairman promptly announced that bail was granted, subject to residence at Melton, surrender of passport and surety of fifty thousand pounds.

Tingwall had the papers ready, the surety was approved, and with that the court rose for lunch.

I pushed my way out of the public gallery, past the usher and into the court. Ginny turned and met my clumsy all-enveloping embrace with impassivity. 'We're going home,' I said with considerable emotion, 'I'm taking you home.'

'You'll be there?' she said.

I wasn't sure what she meant. 'Of course. Where else would I be?'

Grainger came up and I shook his hand.

'Thank you. You were superb.'

He gave a faint smile, as though he was aware of what I had thought of him and took amusement from having proved me wrong. 'You might want to leave by the back way,' he commented, turning his eyes towards some reporters in a gaggle by the door. 'They can't bother you inside the building, but they'll try for a photograph outside. I wouldn't recommend draping anything over the head, it makes a very unfortunate impression. Dark glasses are not ideal, either. But the head averted, the hair hiding the features? Family on either side and in front?'

I had not been prepared for this. Automatically I looked to Tingwall. 'I'll go and find out,' he said doubtfully, and I realised that he hadn't been prepared for this either.

David's voice came from behind. 'Put me in the vanguard. I'm good barging material.'

'I didn't know you were here,' I laughed.

'Crept in late. Sat at the back.' He kissed Ginny fleetingly on the cheek. 'Why don't I go and get my car and bring it round to the side or wherever it is?'

Tingwall arranged for us to leave through the court office. David, with great seriousness, synchronised his watch with mine and went off to do a recce. Tingwall then took Ginny and me to the court office, as though to do more paperwork. Two sharp-faced reporters followed us across the hall and hung around the office door, making no attempt to conceal their purpose. Someone fetched Ginny's bag from the cells, we found reasons to open the door regularly so the reporters could see we were still in there, then, on the appointed minute, we ran for the side exit and jumped into David's Mercedes.

We would probably have escaped the worst of the press if the automatic barrier hadn't been slow in lifting. Forced to pause in full view of the front of the building, we were soon surrounded by photographers. As they lifted their cameras I called a warning to Ginny and raised my hand to shield her face. And so it was that the photograph that featured regularly in the newspapers over the days and months that followed showed Ginny's head largely obscured by my splayed hand, and, in the foreground, made prominent by the flashlights, my face wearing an ugly aggressive expression, teeth bared, eyes popping, like a dangerous maniac on licence from Broadmoor.

After seeing this photograph for the first time I stopped reading the newspapers.

From superstition or lack of forethought or a mixture of both, I had made no preparations for our arrival at Melton. I hadn't phoned Mrs Hoskins to ask her to turn up the heating, and I hadn't bought any food. So it was that we arrived to a cold dark house with nothing in the fridge but a few eggs, a half-empty carton of milk and some tinned pâté which had been open a dangerously long time.

Leaving Ginny in the kitchen with a cup of tea, I went through the place turning up thermostats, lighting fires, drawing curtains. Returning, I found Ginny sitting in the same position at the kitchen table, staring out of the window into the dusk.

'There's hot water,' I told her.

'I'll go and unpack.'

I carried her bag upstairs. In my pleasure and anxiety at having her home, I talked nervously about anything that came into my head: the food I would buy in the morning, the book I wanted her to read, the latest developments at Hartford, much of which

I had already told her during the journey from Exeter. I joked that unemployment was making me lazy, that I was enjoying not having to get up in the mornings, none of which was true, but which seemed to form a necessary part of the charade of normality.

One by one she took her clothes from the bag and dropped them into the laundry basket, except for two sweaters which she laid on the bed and folded neatly, following the inviolable pattern she always used. Placing the sweaters symmetrically on the shelf she regarded them for a moment before changing her mind and relegating them to the laundry basket with the rest. 'So dirty,' she murmured. 'I felt so dirty in there. I don't think I'll ever feel clean again.'

'Have a long bath,' I cried rousingly, like some ghastly team leader. 'I'll run it for you.'

She seemed to focus on me for the first time since we had got back. 'You're very good to me,' she said.

'Don't be silly,' I laughed awkwardly.

'I can't tell you how much it means, that you . . . that you're here.'

'Of course I'm here. Where else would I be?' I said lightly.

There was a pause. We both looked away.

'Would you like a drink while you're in the bath?' I asked in the same jovial tone. 'A glass of wine?'

It occurred to me that she had wanted to talk and that, in my present state of inadequacy, I had missed the opportunity, or avoided it.

Attempting to be useful, I took the laundry basket down to the utility room and, not sure what else to do with the clothes, emptied them onto the top of the washing machine.

Staring at the pile, unwanted thoughts rushed into my mind, thoughts of what Ginny had been wearing on the weekend that Sylvie had died. I dreaded these invasions, but I couldn't stop them, I couldn't stop trawling my memory for clues – denials or confirmations.

I tried to picture her in the doorway when she'd made her unexpected appearance at Dittisham that Saturday night. She'd been wearing trousers of some sort, not jeans exactly, more like tight slacks, off-white or cream, a pale shirt, and her favourite raspberry-coloured jacket. A long scarf had been jammed untidily into one pocket. But what I was really trying to see, of course, was the blood. Could I have missed it? Even at my least observant could I have failed to notice stains or spatterings of blood?

I threw the laundry basket down and, calling to Ginny to tell her where I was going, drove to the local pub and ordered chicken and chips to take away. The woman behind the bar, whom I recognised from my occasional visits, told me that strictly speaking they didn't do takeaway, but, casting me a collusive smile, said she would manage something if I didn't mind having it wrapped in newspaper. Waiting in a corner of the bar, I felt the scrutiny of the other occupants, and it struck me with renewed force that whatever happened, even if Ginny walked free, we would never be able to live our lives in the same way again. This realisation, though harsh, no longer intimidated me: there were worse things, for Ginny at least.

Returning with my hot newspaper bundle, I found Ginny curled up on the bed, sleeping the deathly sleep of the exhausted. I put the quilt over her and, though I checked her regularly and kept the meal hot in the oven, she didn't wake again, and at midnight I turned off the oven and crept in beside her. When I put my arm around her waist, she gave a small fearful cry like someone caught in a night terror, then, still without waking, gripped my arm and pulled me close against her back and did not let me move away until morning. It was strange to be together in our bed again, in the security of our large comfortable house, to possess the security we had always taken for granted, yet to have lost all certainty of the future. It was like an illusion, a giant exercise in double-thinking whereby nothing was what it seemed.

Listening to Ginny's soft breathing, an image stole around the edges of my mind, the one scene which I had until then managed to block from my thoughts: the vision of Ginny in confrontation with Sylvie. I could see fierce pride in Ginny's face, I could see jealousy and anger, even fury, but the deed itself – that eluded me completely. I could not picture the knife, nor the hand that drove it into Sylvie's flesh; I could not envisage the person who, having committed this cataclysmic act, coolly wrapped the body and bound it and slipped it over the side into the black water. I tried to give the scene substance and action and dialogue, but while it contained Ginny it remained dark and unformed. Maybe I simply lacked the courage for it.

During the first days after Ginny's arrest I had

latched on to the idea of her innocence as an essential survival mechanism which would enable us to get through the long months ahead. But since her declaration in the prison I had been forced to confront the fact that, though I longed to believe her, persistent doubts had settled painfully in my mind.

As I breathed the scent of Ginny's hair, and felt in the touch of our bodies the history of our long years together, one thing was certain. We would stay together in this, we would stick it out through thick and thin. I couldn't abandon her, and I certainly couldn't judge her. It seemed to me that my guilt was inseparable from hers, that, in terms of blame, my selfishness was indivisible from her desperation.

I woke early and made a shopping list: what Ginny would have called a man's list, heavy on luxuries, short on essentials. But then Ginny had always organised the food, the cooking, the staff, the maintenance. From the earliest days of our marriage she had actively discouraged me from involvement in anything remotely domestic. She had not wanted a liberated man, and she had not got one.

In town it took time to discover the best shops. Eventually I found olive oil, sun-dried tomatoes and endives to go with the wild salmon and fresh pasta. I bought a few bottles of Ginny's favourite Pouilly-Fumé, I remembered herbs and flowers, and it was only as I arrived home that I realised I had forgotten butter and fruit juice.

I found the house silent, the bedroom and bathroom empty. Suppressing a dart of panic, I hurried through the ground floor calling Ginny's name before emerging breathlessly onto the terrace.

She was standing looking out over the garden, wearing a Japanese wrap with a woollen coat thrown over the top. She said absently, 'I'm here.'

My relief was so conspicuous that she must have guessed what had been going through my mind.

'The roses haven't been dead-headed,' she commented in the same flat voice. 'Oh, and the agent called. The people want to have another look round the house this afternoon at three. They're going to make an offer, he says.'

'That's good.'

'If they do decide to buy, I was going to ask you . . .' She turned towards me, and I noticed how puffy her eyes looked, and how her skin, always so luminous, had lost its clarity and transparence. 'Could we move straight away?'

'Well . . . If that's what you want.'

'If you wouldn't mind.' Her politeness was almost formal.

'The upheaval . . .'

'It won't be so bad. And it'd give me something to do.'

Though she spoke dully, I was encouraged by the normality of our conversation and the re-emergence of her interest in practical matters, which had always been so important to her. As for moving, I didn't need to be persuaded of the benefits of living full-time in London. Quite apart from the cost of running more than one home, I was forever leaving clothes in the wrong place, not to mention documents and, once, an airline ticket.

'And would you mind . . .' The odd formality again. 'Could we rent something? A cottage?'

Hiding my surprise, I said levelly, 'You don't want to live in London?'

'I'd rather not,' she said. 'If you don't mind.'

'Well—'

'Just a cottage, something really small. Near London if you want. Or . . . near Hartford. It doesn't matter.'

Looking out over the long lawns and spiralling leaves, I began to warm to the idea of a cosy cottage without gardeners and housekeepers, a place where we could live anonymously, in every sense of the word. 'Yes, why not?'

'Wish we could get rid of Provence as well,' she said with a glimmer of her old agitation.

'Well, there's no hurry about that. We don't need to decide for the moment. Not until—' I was going to say, *until things are clearer*, but tried to make a small joke of it instead. 'Until I know whether I'm going to be gainfully employed or not.'

'But all that bother. You won't want the bother of running it.'

I noticed the 'you', the assumption that she wasn't going to be around to organise things any more.

'Let's cross that bridge if and when . . . Anyway, we might want to retire there. I was thinking about it – before all this, I mean. It might be something to plan for, don't you think?'

'Retire?' She looked at me as if I were talking gibberish.

'I mean, when the time comes. In ten years. Who knows? Lots of people retire at fifty. It might be rather nice down there,' I rambled on. 'No rat-race. Uncluttered days. Good people. Food and drink. Friends to stay.'

'Ten years.' She was blinking rapidly. 'Is that what Charles thinks I'll get?'

'*What?* No, *no.*'

'What does he say then?'

'Ginny, when I said ten years it was nothing to do with you and the – *case.*'

'But he must have some idea what I might get.'

'He can't make *any* predictions, Ginny. None at all! Anyway, we're going to get you off! Good Lord, Charles and I haven't even discussed anything else!'

Ignoring this, or accepting it, she looked away and said, 'I'm sorry if it's a nuisance, renting a cottage.'

'Don't be ridiculous!'

'The thing is, I feel that . . . if we can have a few months in a quiet place – just us – I think I'll be able to stand it, the idea of not coming back.'

'Ginny, you mustn't—'

'Otherwise I'm not absolutely sure I'll be able to cope,' she said gravely. 'Dr Jones has given me all these pills. He says I must be sure to take them, otherwise – well, he doesn't give me an otherwise. I think he thinks I'm half gone already. Sometimes I think I am too.' She gave an unhappy laugh. 'There've been times when it's been so hard just to keep going. It's as though . . . as though I can't take it all in. As though everything's too much for my head. And then I get frightened . . .' She was struggling to express it. 'Because if it's going to be like that, then I'm not sure I'll be able to hold on.'

I put an arm round her and pulled her against me. 'Darling, if you're feeling bad, you must talk to me. Promise you'll talk to me?' I kissed the top of her head, but my heart was plummeting at the realisation of how close to the edge she was, and how fearsome was the responsibility I faced in taking care of her. I wondered if it would ever be safe to leave her alone.

As if reading my mind, Ginny said, 'Oh, I'll be all right while I'm here. Honestly. It's after . . . It's the idea of being put away in that awful place.'

'You talk as though it were inevitable. It's not! Once Charles begins on your defence, once he gets your story—'

She moved away. 'My story? There is no story.'

'Ginny, you've got to tell Charles what happened.'

'There is no story,' she repeated with emotion.

I stepped cautiously. 'What about what you told me – about finding Sylvie dead.'

I always forgot how acute she was, how finely attuned to nuance and omission. She heard the doubt lurking at the back of my words and said ironically, 'But if you don't believe me, why should Charles?'

'I do believe you,' I said. 'I do! I just don't understand why you won't talk about it. I can't see why you have to make a secret of it. What possible point can there be?'

'It was a mistake. I made a mistake.'

Inside the house the phone began to ring.

'A *mistake*?' I exclaimed, as mystified as I was exasperated. 'What do you mean?'

Her lids drooped. 'I feel so tired. The drugs probably . . .' She turned and walked into the house.

I called angrily, 'Ginny!' but she didn't stop.

Crossing the hall, she seemed to hear the phone for the first time and, altering direction to pick it up, lifted the receiver almost to her mouth before changing her mind and holding it out to me.

It was George. Watching Ginny climb the stairs, I didn't at first gather what he was saying.

'. . . in the post. Should be with you today.'

'What's that, George?'

'Something from everyone here at Hartford, something that will speak for itself,' he said enigmatically. 'They feel very strongly, Hugh. Also – and I hardly like to mention it, I know how busy you are – there's a meeting with the Chartered Bank tomorrow. I don't want to press you, but it would make all the difference if you could make it.'

It was hard to focus on Hartford matters again. I had already spent a lot of the previous week persuading Zircon and the banks to hold their loans, and George had somehow talked me into attending several strategy meetings.

'Ten o'clock, in Cheapside,' George urged. 'Just an hour. Hugh – I know it's out of your way, I realise you'll have to come up specially, but it's critical.'

'What's happened?'

'They're threatening to turn us down. This will be our one chance to change their minds.'

'But they were okay last week.'

'Something's made them think again. It's really critical, Hugh.'

With George every meeting was critical, every plea for help the very last he would make. While part of me resented the relentlessness of this pressure, I knew that in his position I would do exactly the same thing, that if it weren't for my personal crisis I would be right there beside him, fighting from the front.

'I'm not sure I'll be able to get away,' I told him, already feeling torn. 'Can I let you know?'

'Of course. But Hugh – it would make all the difference.'

I went into the study where I could be more certain of not being overheard before calling Jones. His secretary said he was doing his hospital rounds but should be able to phone me back later.

Even as I rang off I realised I could have saved myself the call. Whatever the psychiatrist might say, however safe he might rate Ginny's mental health, I wouldn't be able to leave her on her own. It wasn't simply a question of watching over her, though that would be a factor for as long as she continued to talk in such disturbing terms; it was also a matter of trust. I had not forgotten the promise I had made to her on the night when we'd searched for the petrol receipt. I had promised that I would never leave her alone again, and though at the time neither of us would have interpreted this as a round-the-clock commitment, I felt I owed her as much now.

I called Dr Jones's secretary and cancelled the message.

The decision was straightforward, the implementation harder. Who would watch over Ginny when I wasn't around? While she had been away I had been opening her mail, and though there had been cards and messages from two or three of her London girlfriends, there was nothing that amounted to a wild rush of unconditional support. And the people who lived around Melton, the people who had been glad to dine at our table, had, whether from reticence or disapproval, been conspicuously silent.

But then friends might not be such a good idea anyway. The few I had seen in recent weeks had expressed the sort of embarrassed sympathy people normally reserve for those who are bankrupt or caught up in a messy divorce. So anxious were they not to seem in the slightest bit curious that they had been breezily distant, almost offhand. Such encounters were not likely to get any easier.

Our families offered even less choice. Ginny was an only child, her father long dead, her mother living abroad. On my side there were only David and Mary, both of whom had heavy commitments and couldn't get away at short notice.

It occurred to me then that Ginny and I had no one but each other, which was, perhaps, all that we had ever had. Despite the frantic pace of our socialising and travelling, neither of us had ever been deeply gregarious at heart. We had gone about our business, we had been surrounded with people much of the time, but at the end of the day we had been glad to retreat to the safety of our own company. Until things had gone wrong between us and we had lost our one safe haven. Then, it seemed to me now, we had both begun to drift.

I called Julia and asked her if she wouldn't mind coming down to work at Melton the next day. Julia, who was staying on until the buyout was resolved, not only had the benefit of being instantly available, but was loyal and discreet. While she wasn't someone Ginny would be able to talk to, she wouldn't intrude either.

The post brought the mysterious missive that George had hinted at. It was a giant greeting card packed with the signatures of the Hartford staff. Above the printed best wishes message had been written: *We're still backing the buyout all the way.* I was touched. At the same time I couldn't help wondering if this gesture of support and encouragement was entirely spontaneous, or something a little more Machiavellian, engineered by George who, in my absence, seemed to have developed unsuspected tactical skills.

I stood the card on my desk, a reminder, if I needed one, that life roared on in the world outside.

I went upstairs to check on Ginny, but she was asleep again, curled up in bed, her mouth slightly open, a faint frown showing above the mask. I glanced at the bottles of pills on the bedside table, but didn't recognise the names of any of the drugs. Taking the extension off the hook, I stole out and closed the door.

Tingwall was in court all morning, his office told me, and it wasn't until after noon that he returned my call.

'How is she?' he asked.

'Very tired.'

'When do you think she'll be up to seeing me?'

'I don't know. But Charles – she won't talk to me. She won't talk about what happened. And I have the feeling she won't talk to you, either.'

'Well . . . it's early days yet. And, Hugh, sometimes people tell their solicitors things they don't tell their own families. Sometimes it's easier to talk to a stranger, particularly when that person is duty-bound not to tell anyone else.' He didn't say: even the husband, though that was what he meant.

'I hope you're right.'

We arranged for me to bring Ginny down to see him in two days' time.

'Dr Bagnall's preliminary report came through.'

The pathologist. The post-mortem. Sylvie's body cut up on a slab. The stench of formalin, like the lab at school. 'And?'

'Nothing very startling, I'm afraid. He agrees with the cause of death, and there's nothing to suggest that the attack couldn't have been carried out by a woman of average height.'

I saw a flash of it then, an image so violent and graphic that it caught me like a panic. Ginny thrusting a knife up under Sylvie's ribs, forcing it home.

To drive the picture out I said quickly, 'But it doesn't prove anything?'

'It certainly doesn't prove that any particular person did or didn't commit the crime.'

'It could have been a man then?'

'Well . . . yes.' That caution had come into his voice again.

'What about the rest of the forensic stuff?'

'I've tracked down a DNA expert, and there's a top fingerprint lab in Wolverhampton. The DNA man isn't free for a couple of weeks, but the fingerprint people can get onto it straight away.'

'And if they don't find anything?'

'Then I think we have to accept there's nothing to be found.'

'We don't have to say that in court?'

'What? No, no. Our barrister will decide what evidence to use, and he'll only use what will actively *help* our case. What did you think of Grainger, by the way?'

'I thought he was pompous and conceited and overbearing,' I said without hesitation.

'Oh.'

'And surprisingly effective.'

'Well, we don't have to commit ourselves to him yet. When the prosecution serve their evidence we could ask him for an opinion, and take it from there.' A pause. 'While we're on the subject – have you come to any decisions about me?'

'You?' I said, knowing perfectly well what he meant.

'Do you want to retain me?'

'You'd better ask Ginny that.'

'Yes, of course. It's just that the real work's about to start and I thought . . .'

'As far as I'm concerned, you'll do, Charles.'

And he laughed, because it was in his nature to take this as a compliment.

I had put out some feelers about Tingwall among my barrister friends but even before the word came back that he was considered competent I had made up my mind to keep him. As a lawyer Tingwall had a rare advantage: he was prepared to become emotionally involved. Let the QC be the bleak professional; for this stage of the case Ginny needed someone who was prepared to go the extra mile.

'Are you married, Charles?' I asked.

'What? Yes. Six years now. Twin boys of two and a half. A real handful.'

I thought: Then you understand. You understand the need to believe that there is going to be a way out.

'I must tell you,' he said, resuming his lawyer's voice. 'The strangest thing. A witness has come forward to corroborate your story.'

'*My* story?'

'He saw you just outside Totnes, driving south, at about six-forty on the Saturday evening of the murder. He was away on holiday when you were arrested. He only heard about it when he got back. Contacted me through your brother last night. His name is Horrocks. An assistant harbour master, I believe.'

I remembered Horrocks. He was one of the men I had stood a drink in the pub when I was trawling for information about *Samphire*.

'He was absolutely adamant about the identification. Knew your car, recognised you. Even waved to you, he said. And – the dream witness – he was in no doubt about the time, because he was due at his sister's silver wedding party and was already ten minutes late. Anyway ... there we are. Just thought you might be interested.'

'Does Henderson know?'

'I doubt it. But I wouldn't be in a hurry to tell him. Best not to offer information unless it's needed.'

'Ginny could do with a witness like Horrocks.'

'Yes,' he said, as though considering this afresh. 'It would help a lot.'

I woke Ginny for lunch and came down to prepare pâté and smoked salmon and salad. I hadn't tackled a french dressing in years, but I made a passable effort with a combination of the balsamic vinegar and olive oil that Ginny always used, and a dash of mustard.

Ginny appeared and sat down obediently at the kitchen table, like a guest in someone else's house. She looked no less exhausted than she had done that morning. While I cajoled her into eating, we discussed her health. Or I talked about the importance of taking care of herself while Ginny agreed in a vague placatory way. When this subject lapsed I led us on to the practicalities of selling Melton and we discussed it for the rest of the meal. The disposal of the furniture seemed to be the one topic that roused a spark of interest in Ginny, as though she were eager to rid herself of non-essential possessions.

To avoid meeting the prospective purchasers we arranged for Mrs Hoskins to let them in, and drove up onto the downs for a walk. The wind wasn't cold but it was blustery, and Ginny took my arm as we climbed slowly up the rabbit-tracked hill.

'Do you remember that holiday in Brittany?' I asked, resorting to the comfort of nostalgia. 'When we got caught in that downpour?'

She gave a single nod.

'God – the weather!' It had been overcast and rainy for all but two days of our stay. But then La Baule with its long sands and *belle époque* hotels had not really suited either of us. I'd found myself hankering after the craggy coast of North Brittany which had been the scene of so many childhood holidays on *Ellie Miller*, while Ginny had missed the warmth of the Mediterranean and having friends to dine with.

'Not the most successful holiday in the world,' I smiled.

'You wanted to be sailing.'

'Oh, I don't know,' I said with half a laugh. 'Did I?'

'I think so.' She corrected herself: 'I know so.'

'But I still enjoyed the holiday.'

'No, you didn't,' she said with a directness that was quite new to her. 'The holiday was the worst of both worlds. Trying to please each other and ending up doing what neither of us wanted. You should have said, you know. What you wanted. So should I. Perhaps that's where we went wrong.'

She had never spoken like this before. While I welcomed the opening of these dusty attics, I was faintly apprehensive as to what might emerge next.

'But you didn't like sailing,' I ventured.

'Not the long trips, no. But I could have flown across the Channel and joined you in France. I

320

wouldn't have minded going from harbour to harbour.'

'I felt it was too much to ask.'

'But I would have fitted in, I was desperate to fit in,' she said almost to herself. 'I felt it was a necessary part of loving someone, to fit in.'

This thought settled over me uneasily as we climbed the last few yards to the ridge of the hill and paused to look out over the prairie of ploughed fields below.

I said, 'But we were happy in Provence, weren't we?'

'Oh yes,' she agreed without hesitation. 'It was the one place where you were free of it all. The business. And your family.'

'My family?'

She cast me a glance, gearing herself up to voice something that I wouldn't like. 'Your family,' she confirmed. 'Your father mainly. But David and Mary too.'

'But I didn't need to be *free* of them.' Even as I said it, the idea lodged in my mind as a startling and disturbing possibility, made all the more real by the realisation that I had never allowed myself to consider it before. 'Why do you say that?'

'Because you were the one they expected things from. The business. The tradition. All the rest.'

'But my father never interfered. My father never asked anything of me.'

'No?' Her tone betrayed her doubts. Then, attempting to close this unsatisfactory argument: 'But Provence – yes, we were happy there.'

'Hang on,' I said, not ready to let go. 'Are you

saying my family put pressure on me? Because you'd be quite wrong, you know.'

The wind spun her hair across her face and she pushed it back and held it against her head. 'Not pressure like that. Not . . . *open* pressure. But it was still there, wasn't it?' She looked at me with a touch of her old uncertainty. 'You having been groomed to take over. Being your father's favourite. The way he made the business into this great and holy thing. This sacred inheritance. I always felt' – the thought emerged bitterly – 'that you were doing it for him.'

'For him? But it was for us too! Always for us! I don't know how you can think that.'

She gave up the argument with a submissive twist of both hands and walked on. But as we tramped along the undulating ridge her words still rankled.

'How could you think I wasn't doing it for us?' I asked hotly.

She came to a slow halt, as though in her tiredness she could not concentrate and walk at the same time. 'Because you went on and on pushing yourself, spending more and more time away, hardly being at home. Not choosing to be with me. It didn't look to me as though you were doing it for us.'

'It was only because it was all going wrong, Ginny. The business, I mean. I was desperate to save it. I thought if I just kept trying harder . . . And then I seemed to get *overwhelmed*.'

She absorbed this silently and looked away into the wind. 'And all that time I was feeling useless, you see. As though I had nothing to offer you any more.'

'That's ridiculous.'

'No!' she argued, a harsh edge to her voice. 'It's not ridiculous. You always say things like that, you always brush things off as if that'll make the subject go away. But I'm telling you – that was how I *felt*. I felt I had nothing to offer you any more.' She stated this with exasperation, as though I had never made any real effort to understand her. 'Oh, it took me ages to work out that I wasn't getting it right, that you hated the people and the parties and the social scene. It took me ages to realise it wasn't what you wanted. I was as bad as you were, you see – I clung on. When things began to go wrong, I just kept trying harder. Because it was the only thing I was good at, organising things, making things happen. I didn't know any other way.' She gave a small shudder. 'But I got there in the end. That weekend when you rushed off to Dittisham, I finally got the message. But by then . . . it was too late.'

'Oh Ginny.' All the accumulated misunderstandings of the years seemed to hang over us like so many missed opportunities. 'What a pair.'

Something in this brought her emotions to the surface and, turning swiftly away, she made a move for home.

'It wasn't too late, you know,' I said after we had walked in silence for a time. 'Not for me.'

But she wouldn't answer that because we were talking about the summer, and the summer was Sylvie.

When we got back she went into the sitting room and dozed off in front of an old film. As I scrubbed the potatoes for supper, her comments rolled round my mind. I accepted that I might not be able to judge my family too objectively – who could? – yet had I really understood so little about myself all these years? Had I really been driven by my obligations to them rather than my own needs, or Ginny's? I had always striven to please my father, certainly, and that had never diminished. And given the choice I had preferred David's approval to his annoyance, which could be fearsome. But had I really been driven by the fear of letting them down? It was a dispiriting thought.

I overcooked the salmon and undercooked the potatoes. Ginny assured me that she wasn't very hungry and wouldn't have eaten much anyway. She drank some Pouilly-Fumé though, two full glasses, and was halfway through a third before she slowed down.

'Tingwall – Charles – needs to see you some time this week,' I told her. 'I have to go down to Hartford on Thursday so I could drop you in Exeter on the way. Will that be all right?'

She took a long troubled breath.

'You have to see him, darling. You have to trust him.'

She nodded stiffly.

'He's really thorough, you know. In fact, I'm pretty impressed with him. I think he's well up to the job.' I added tentatively: 'So long as we give him all the help he needs, of course.'

She was staring out beyond the window, focused on some inner world, and gave no indication of having heard.

Suppressing a creep of frustration, I said, 'You will talk to him, won't you, darling? You can talk to him in confidence, you know. I mean, he won't tell *me* anything you don't want him to.'

I found it impossible to read what was going on in her mind. She gave me nothing back. After the revelations of the walk, the sudden burst of communication, she had put up the shutters again.

'He's been busy,' I said in an effort at conversation. 'Getting hold of experts to check the evidence . . .' Lumbering on, searching for points of interest, I added, 'Oh, and would you believe it, a witness has come forward, confirming my arrival time in Dittisham that day. Ironic, really. Henderson was always so transfixed by that missing journey time. Thought he could catch me out, like some Agatha Christie detective.'

I had her attention at last. 'A witness?'

'A man called Horrocks. An assistant harbour master. Saw me just outside Totnes.'

Her eyes burned brightly, urging me on.

'Saw me at twenty to seven, apparently. Absolutely positive it was me. Knew the car and so on. Even waved at me, though I didn't see him.'

'So . . . So . . .' She was blinking rapidly. 'Does that mean you're in the clear?'

A long confused pause followed.

'Did you think I wasn't?'

'I was worried in case . . . You know, I thought . . . They'd think that we'd . . . together. That you were involved . . .' She dismissed the rest of this thought

325

with an agitated shake of her head before repeating more forcefully, 'Does that mean you're in the clear?'

Conflicting thoughts raced uncomfortably round my brain. 'I would think so, yes.'

'What about afterwards? After you arrived? They won't think you could have got down to the boat then and helped me?'

I was struggling to catch up, to fill the gaps in this startling new scenario. 'No. David saw me in town, remember.'

'And after that?'

'Well, you were there. And David dropped in.'

'That's right, that's right. Yes . . . You had no time, did you?' Without warning she began to blink back tears and laugh at the same time. 'I was so worried. I thought . . .' Now she was laughing more than she was crying, an odd overwrought sound. 'Thank God.'

I went round the table and sat next to her.

She kept repeating, 'Thank God.' Then, with a flash of doubt, 'But can we be sure? Can we really be sure? That it'll be enough?'

'Charles can find out, I imagine.'

'Can he?' She seized on this. 'If he can . . .'

I tried to make light of my next question. 'You thought Henderson might come back for me then?'

'What?' From a state of near-apathy she had become taut as a wire, as though hit by the effects of some fast-working drug, and I wondered if the pills she was taking had interacted with the wine. 'Yes. *Yes*,' she insisted. 'There was always a risk, wasn't there?'

Maintaining my tone, I smiled, 'Was there?'

Caught up in her frantic relief, she was barely listening again.

'Ginny?' I prompted. 'There was a risk that he'd charge me?'

'Yes. *God*. It was my nightmare. My worst nightmare. I thought they'd come back for you. That we'd both end up in prison.' And she half winced, half laughed at the thought.

I was missing something fundamental here, something which both alarmed and electrified me. 'So . . .' I felt my way cautiously, aware of how quickly the shutters might close again. 'If this chap hadn't seen me, if I'd had the time to' – I searched for innocuous words – 'get down to the river . . . then Henderson might have suggested that I'd . . . that I'd . . .?'

'Oh, that you'd killed Sylvie, of course. And that I helped you to get rid of her afterwards.' She went on: 'You see . . . That's what *I* thought too. That you'd killed her.'

I was very still now. I was hovering on the brink of understanding, but I still needed to hear it from her mouth.

'But I didn't kill her,' I prompted softly.

'I know that now. But by the time I realised . . . it was too late.' She shook her head again.

'Why was it too late, Ginny?'

Through her tears, she gave me a beautiful lost smile. 'Because by then I'd got rid of her. I'd put her over the side.'

Eleven

'OH, I knew the theory. I knew I should sit tight and let it blow over,' Ginny began in a brittle voice. 'Let you get bored with her, get her out of your system. I knew that's what clever women did. But I wasn't feeling clever, not about that sort of thing anyway. And you see – I wasn't at all sure it *would* blow over. In fact the longer it went on, the more convinced I became that I was losing you for ever, that you'd never come back. And I couldn't quite . . . *deal* with that.'

We had come to the smallest of the three living rooms at Melton, the room we called the sitting room, a low-lit room with book-lined walls, soft sofas and a fireplace which threw out plenty of heat. We sat side by side on the smaller sofa, staring into the fire, wine on the low table in front of us.

'It was one thing to suspect that something was going on. But actually knowing, seeing . . . That was *awful*.' And her voice rose to a gasp. 'When I saw you together that weekend, watched you go off in the boat – well, I thought that was it. I could see she was younger. Prettier. And she knew how to sail. Well . . . I couldn't see what possible reason you could have for staying with me. And I didn't need to ask you how you felt about her. I could read the signs. I could see you were completely smitten.'

I forced myself not to say anything, not to offer the kind of instant denials which Ginny seemed to find so meaningless.

'So there I was,' she declared harshly. 'Another weekend on my own, another weekend knowing you were with her. I simply couldn't sit there any more like some animal to the slaughter. The more I thought about it, the more I felt I had absolutely nothing to lose by following you down and making a fool of myself. I'd have gone mad if I'd stayed at home a moment longer. Literally mad.' She stole a nervous glance at me before reaching for her wine and taking a gulp. 'I went through this great debate as I drove down – trying to decide on confrontation versus the oh-so civilised discussion. You know – do you love her, Hugh? Do you intend to leave me? Oh well, in that case, good luck old thing. I knew I'd never be able to carry that one off. Never have been able to deal with things in that way. *Coolly*. Not when I'm . . .' She wrestled with this thought only to leave it unfinished. 'So it was going to have to be the great confrontation. Burst in, have a scene, give you an ultimatum. I knew I'd probably end up behaving . . . *pathetically*. Crying. Making a fool of myself. I knew you'd probably hate me for it, I knew I risked losing you altogether – the hysterical wife, no humiliation untapped – but I couldn't see any other way. At least the whole thing would be out in the open. At least I wouldn't have this feeling that I wanted to die the whole time.'

Catching my expression, she said, 'Oh, please don't think I'm saying all this just to make you feel bad, Hugh. I'm not. Really. I just wanted you to understand how I was feeling, how desperate I was.'

I nodded rapidly, determined not to speak.

She pushed her head back against the sofa before starting off again in a voice that was increasingly unsteady. 'I thought you'd gone straight down to Dittisham that Saturday. When you said you were going into the office for a few hours I thought you were just saying that – you know, to discourage me from joining you, to keep me away. So as soon as I thought you were well on your way I set off. And all the time I was planning what I'd say when I caught you together. I was going to wait until I did catch you together, you see. Awful, I know. Awful to set out to make a scene. But I was hurt. Angry. Off my head with worry. I felt like *killing* you.' She flung me a fierce look. 'Or myself. More likely myself. Anyway . . . You weren't at the house, of course. I didn't drive up. I parked in the village and took the path through the garden. I crept round the house, looking in through the windows like some awful nutter, and then I saw that your car wasn't there, and immediately thought of the boat. I went to the terrace and looked across, and I saw it – the dinghy. Tied up to *Ellie Miller*. To me that meant only one thing, of course. That you must be there with *her*. That if I was quick I'd catch you in the act. Well – I'm not sure I actually wanted to find you in bed with her – I wasn't that masochistic. But together, anyway. I wanted to have a good look at her, you see. I wanted to know just how pretty she was. And I wanted to confront both of you, to make you feel – I don't know – *bad, guilty. Something*. Stupid, of course.' She gave me a scornful sigh. 'Never does any good, that sort of thing, does it? Never makes people change their minds.'

I couldn't let this pass. 'My mind never needed changing. I wanted to finish it. I knew there was no future in it.'

'But I didn't know that, did I?' she argued with a spark of resentment. 'I thought you were mad about her. I thought you were about to leave me. Oh, I tried to tell myself it mightn't be that bad, I tried to be . . . *sensible*. But it never did any good. I couldn't think of any reason why you should stay with me, you see. No confidence. Never have had. Hopeless.'

A pause while she dealt with this thought and put it behind her.

'Anyway . . .' Her voice was flagging. 'I couldn't get out to *Ellie* fast enough. I couldn't bear the thought of missing the two of you together. I rushed down to the quay. I hadn't thought about transport, of course. But there were quite a few people about. A load of people were just getting into a rubber dinghy and I was about to ask them for a lift when I saw *Ellie*'s dinghy, sitting there at the pontoon. The name and everything: *Tender to Ellie Miller*. Well, that drew me up short for a second. I wondered if I'd got it all wrong. I wondered if someone else was on the boat – a repair man or whatever. Then I thought: On a Saturday afternoon? They never work on Saturday afternoons, do they? So I got going again. I hadn't forgotten how to row. You taught me too well. In the days when I pretended to love boats.' Her voice softened a little. 'Well, I loved being with you, doing what you enjoyed, so in a way I did love it, while it lasted.'

Reaching for her wine she cradled it in both hands as if it might warm her. 'By the time I reached the boat I was shaking like a jelly. I could barely tie the dinghy up. And of course I was trying not to make any noise. My heart was hammering so hard I could scarcely breathe. And then I remembered that I'd left my inhaler in the car. God!' She rolled her eyes at the memory. 'So I stayed in the dinghy for a while, trying to catch my breath, trying to prevent an attack. Sat there like a dummy doing my breathing exercises, listening, half expecting to be discovered at any second. Nothing happened, of course, no sounds from the boat.' This thought created its own silence. 'When I'd finally calmed down a bit ... I climbed aboard. I—' The horror was revisited on her face. 'I went into the cockpit. I looked into the cabin. I ...' She could barely speak. '... *saw her.*'

I waited for a long moment. Finally I murmured, 'And she was dead?'

Her face contorted. 'Yes.' And she turned her gaze onto me, searching my expression, desperate for some sort of reassurance.

I nodded, urging her on.

'She *was* dead.'

'Yes,' I said hastily. 'Yes, of course she was.'

'But they're not going to believe me, are they? They're never going to believe me.' And the despair sounded in her voice.

332

'Of course they will! Why shouldn't they?'

She was drawing great gulps of air. 'You believe me, though?'

'Of course!'

'Really?'

'*Yes*, Ginny. Really. I wouldn't say so if I didn't!'

But for Ginny no amount of reassurance could ever be enough, and she continued to scrutinise my face before she drew sufficient confidence to go on. Even then she kept casting rapid glances at me, never quite satisfied, never entirely convinced.

'I had a terrible attack, of course,' she sighed, picking up the story again. 'Thought I was going to die. Lay in the cockpit. One of the worst ever. I almost blacked out at one stage. I've no idea how I managed to keep breathing. Thought it would never end. God, I really thought I was going to die! I even said my goodbyes. But then – well, it began to ease. And when it was finally over I lay there for a long time, not daring to move – not wanting to move. Sort of hoping I could put the moment off, hoping I could keep lying there and not have to face up to what was in the boat. Then through it all – the shock and everything – I began to think about what I was going to do. Was I going to row ashore and report it? Was I going to shout and wave from the boat until someone saw me on the bank? Then suddenly . . . *suddenly* . . . it came to me. I mean, like a bolt from the blue. That I couldn't report it. I *mustn't*. Because . . .' She made a statement of this: 'Because.'

'I had killed her.'

Her mouth seesawed, she lifted one hand, the

333

beginning of a plea. 'Don't think too badly of me, don't . . . But I couldn't think what else – *who* else – it could have been.'

'No.'

'The way you'd been behaving. Frantic. Off your head. I couldn't think . . .' Again she put it to me, 'Who else could it have been?'

'No, I can see . . . I would have thought the same thing.'

She grasped at this. 'Would you? Would you really?'

'Definitely.' Again I tried to give her the reassurance she craved. 'Finding her there on the boat. You thinking I'd been aboard . . . I was the obvious person.'

'Yes!' she affirmed fiercely. 'You *were*, you *were!*' She jerked her arm so violently that she spilt her wine. I took her glass and, putting it on the table, went to the cloakroom to find a cloth and dampen it with water.

She dabbed at her sweater, breathing heavily, clenching her lips. I fetched a glass of water which she drank greedily.

When we had been quiet for some time, she repeated reproachfully, 'It had to be you. It had to be.'

Her eyes flicked towards me, and I quickly agreed, 'Yes. It had to be me.'

Gathering some comfort at last, she prepared to go on. 'I fell apart for a while,' she said shakily. 'The whole thing seemed so ghastly, so totally un—' the word eluded her 'so un-*saveable*. You know how

334

something can happen which is so ghastly that there's nothing you can do to make it right again. Once it's happened, it's happened. However much you may wish it different, there's no *un*doing it, ever, *ever*. Except this was twice as ghastly as anything I could ever have imagined. But then I thought— Then I thought—' She straightened up in her seat and some of the life came back into her voice. 'Perhaps I *can* undo some of this. Usually I pretend that difficult things aren't happening, don't I? I just push them out of my mind.' She held up a staying hand as if I were about to disagree. 'Oh, I do, I know I do! All my life . . . always. But this time – well, I *could* make things right again, couldn't I? Oh, not totally, of course. But almost right. For *you* anyway. For us. And Hugh—' She opened her eyes wide. 'It thrilled me. I mean – I felt glad. Glad that I had thought of it. Glad I was going to do it. I was absolutely determined, you see. Determined not to be weak and pathetic. Determined to carry it through to the very end.'

The phone was ringing but neither of us made a move to answer it and eventually it stopped.

Ginny was still lost in her story. 'I imagined you'd rushed off in a state of shock. Rushed back to London. It seemed to me that I had plenty of time – time to do the thing properly. So I planned it! I thought it through! I sat in the bottom of the cockpit where no one could see me, and I thought about every detail. I was determined, you see, not to forget anything.' Her mouth fell. 'It wasn't possible, of course – not to make any mistakes. But I didn't realise that then.' Suddenly her control deserted her and she clamped a hand

335

to her eyes. Just as abruptly she pulled her hand away again and went on, as though any loss of momentum might sabotage her chances of finishing.

'I knew there was blood – I'd seen it,' she began at speed. 'I knew I'd need something to wrap her up in, to stop the blood and keep it from— So I looked in the cockpit lockers and found some plastic sheeting and a rope. Then I braced myself to go below. The strange thing was that it wasn't as bad as I thought it would be. Partly because I'd geared myself up for it. Partly because I'd made up my mind that I wasn't going to *let* it bother me. Mind over matter,' she exclaimed with a hint of pride, 'like doctors and operations.' She paused for breath before racing on. 'I didn't look at her, though. I half shut my eyes. And I kept talking to myself, blabbering away, which seemed to help, God only knows why. The hardest thing was getting the plastic all the way round her. Not getting any blood on the *outside*—' She jerked to a halt and cried in sudden anguish, 'God, you don't want to hear all this, do you! You don't want all the ghastly details!'

Part of me wanted to hear everything, but it was a part of me I didn't trust. 'Don't tell me anything you don't want to,' I said.

'Nothing I don't want to,' she repeated with irony, blinking back the hovering tears. 'The awful thing was – half of me was proud of what I was doing! So methodical. So efficient. Not forgetting a single thing!' And she gave a sad empty laugh. Blowing her nose, she continued with attempted toughness, 'So! I put her in the plastic, I wrapped the rope round several times, I knotted it. Then I cleaned up as best I could. I was already planning to come back the next day and scrub the floor, scrub every inch of the boat. With bleach – I knew bleach was the only thing. But there wasn't anything more I could do that night, not until dark, so I sat in the companionway and waited. That was the worst, waiting. The darkness seemed to take for ever.' The pretended toughness had vanished. Large splashy tears dropped silently onto her sweater and dripped off her nose. She had run out of tissues so I went and fetched some more. She blew her nose and wiped her eyes ferociously, as though this might be enough to stem the flood.

'It was hard. Moving her.' The effort of speaking was very great and between gasps her voice was all over the place. 'I used a rope – a halyard or something – to hoist her up. I tried using a winch but the rope got into a terrible mess. It took me ages to unravel it. So in the end I just put the rope over the boom and hauled that way. God, it was hard – *hard*. But somehow, *somehow* . . . I got her up. I got her onto the deck and . . .' She trailed off and with a low moan leant forward and sank her head into her hands.

I put an arm round her shoulders, I murmured vague words of comfort, but I hardly knew what I was saying, the images that crowded my mind were so overpowering. I saw Ginny pulling the body onto the side deck and forcing it under the guardrails, I saw it hanging out over the edge of the boat before it finally broke free and slid into the blackness, I heard it hit the water with a low splash, I saw it bobbing up and floating away on the tide. I saw all this and began to realise what a massive undertaking it must have been for Ginny. I felt astonished at her strength of mind, at the sheer force of her determination.

Not trusting myself to say anything useful quite yet, I resorted to offering tea. Ginny nodded from the depths of her hands. When I came back with the mugs she was sitting up again, blowing her nose.

'Sometimes in the night I dream that it didn't happen,' she breathed. 'I dream that it was just – well, a dream. And then I wake . . .' She took the tea and her hands were trembling.

'You'll tell Charles the whole story, won't you?'

She gave a tight shake of her head.

'*Ginny* – for God's sake.'

'Oh, I *suppose*,' she surrendered wearily. 'For what it's worth. But it's not going to do any good, is it?'

'Ginny, don't be—' I caught myself on the brink of saying *ridiculous*. 'There must be a way of proving what happened. But we can't expect him to even *begin* to help us until he knows the truth.'

'But everyone's going to think I'm making it up, aren't they? They're going to think I'm lying. I mean, who's going to believe that I did what I did if it wasn't to cover up for you? I mean, why would I bother, if *you* hadn't killed her? Or if *I* hadn't killed her? If neither . . . then why . . .' In her weariness she was confused by her own argument and put a hand to her head. Emerging from her daze, she said simply, 'It's no good – I've thought it through, I've thought it through a million times. And Hugh—' Her gaze was like a baffled animal's. 'I can't see any way out. And it frightens me to death.'

I tried to keep my own fear out of my face as I pulled her against my shoulder and murmured reassurances which sounded empty even to my own ears.

We lapsed into the silence of exhaustion, and when I finally spoke again I realised Ginny was beyond further talk. I took her up to bed and watched her count out her tablets and wash them down. As we lay in the darkness she grasped my arm and whispered apprehensively, 'Thank you for believing me.'

Knowing what she wanted to hear, knowing she wouldn't sleep until she heard it, I said, 'I never doubted you for a moment, darling. Not for a moment.'

Later as I lay awake with no chance of sleep, I found myself believing almost too much of what she had said: I found myself believing that there was no way out.

'That's right, isn't it?'

I wasn't sure what George had just said, but I gave an authoritative nod.

We were sitting in one of those conference rooms that looks identical to every other conference room in the City, with vertical slatted blinds at the picture windows, neutral walls and an ostentatious elliptical table that stretched almost the length of the room. Our small band was scattered round one end of the table. There was George and Alan and myself, one of our lawyers, and three Chartered Bank people. Significantly – or otherwise – the Chartered party did not include either of the two grey-suited executives who had smiled their way round Hartford on the conducted tour. Instead we had graduated to two full directors.

Now that I was listening properly I realised that George was labouring a point that he had already made twice that morning. The bankers had not been impressed by his argument the first two times around and, hearing it a third time, were looking distinctly po-faced. George was asking them to knock a point off the interest rate they were demanding. He couldn't see why we should pay over the going business rate. He couldn't see that we were in a poor negotiating position, and that the bankers, having let themselves be talked into granting us the loan virtually against their better judgment, were in no mood to do us any more favours. The meeting had gone on too long, we were losing ground. Risking George's wrath, I interrupted him in mid-stream. 'Suppose we agreed to carry this premium for a period of one year?'

They didn't commit themselves, but they didn't turn it down either. They'd probably offer four years, and we'd settle on three, two if we were lucky, which wouldn't be bad under the circumstances. They said they'd come back to us the next day.

I could feel George looking daggers at me as we went down in the lift. He managed to restrain himself until we reached the street.

'It would be nice not to have the ground cut from

under my feet,' he said with barely concealed indignation.

'We were never going to win that one, George.'

'Maybe not, but it would have been nice to discuss it, feel we had a *strategy.'*

'We had to concede something.'

'Why the hell should we pay over the odds?'

'Because we have no choice, that's why.'

'It's another twenty grand a year!'

'We'll have to live with it.'

'I'm not sure we can!'

'In that case we shouldn't be here at all.'

He retorted acidly, 'Well, that's a thought!' Then, sighing hard, he shuffled his unwieldy feet and made an apologetic face. 'It gets me, that's all, the way they squeeze us dry.'

'I know.'

He cast a scornful eye over the glass canyons. 'It's not as if they actually *make* anything, is it? Apart from fat salaries. You know, I'm never bothered by anything the factory throws at me. Employees' problems, suppliers, later deliveries – you name it. No trouble. But this lot! They'd screw their own grandmothers, wouldn't they? And then ask for another meeting to renegotiate the terms. You just never know where you bloody are with the slippery buggers. That's what I can't take!'

'Won't be long now, George.'

'Ha! That's true enough! Death or glory.' He rolled his eyes, then, with a conciliatory expression, asked cautiously, 'Look, Hugh . . . can you spare a couple of hours? I wouldn't bother you, but Cumberland's lawyers are trying to throw a whole new set of spanners in the works. And that's only a half of our problems.'

I hesitated, and in hesitating it came to me that a great deal hung on this small and apparently insignificant decision. A couple of hours would undoubtedly stretch into three, and then the whole afternoon would be gone and I wouldn't get back to Melton until nine or even ten. Tomorrow I was due at Hartford for a late-morning meeting which, given half a chance, would run into the afternoon. Before very long I'd be back on twelve-hour days and fast-evaporating weekends. And Ginny would be on her own with time to think and brood.

'No,' I said. 'I'm sorry.'

George stuck out his chin. 'Tomorrow then, after the meeting?'

'It won't be possible, George. I can't give you any more time at the moment.'

'Just for the next two weeks, until after the EGM? Until we sort out the lawyers?'

'I'm sorry.'

'If I came to Wiltshire?'

I knew I was sounding unreasonable. 'No.'

He exclaimed, 'This is our one chance, Hugh!'

'Don't think I don't know it.' If we didn't win the backing of the Cumberland shareholders at the EGM then the buyout would finally be dead and buried.

George clamped his mouth shut and looked away. Then, with a sigh that seemed to settle in his stomach and swell his considerable girth, he said in an alto-

gether softer tone, 'I didn't mean to be, you know –
unsympathetic. You've got your priorities.'

'I'm sorry I can't do more.'

'You *will* put the motion at the EGM though?'

'Oh, I'll put the motion.'

'See you tomorrow then.' He touched my arm as
he left.

Walking to the car, I wondered how I would feel
if the buyout failed at the eleventh hour through some
avoidable error, if I discovered too late that George
had missed some obvious move. It would exasperate
me, it would hurt me, but it wouldn't kill me. Responsibility had its limits, and I had reached mine. In
making the decision to distance myself from Hartford,
I was wrenching my life out by the roots and shifting
it to new ground. But it was my own choice, made
on my own terms. Perhaps, if Ginny were right, the
first independent choice I had ever made.

Setting off homeward, I called Melton. Julia told
me Ginny was having a short sleep and seemed fine.
This news took the edge off my concern, but like an
ache temporarily suppressed by an analgesic, the
throb of apprehension soon returned. I couldn't
entirely rid myself of the idea that the prison psychiatrist might have got it right and Ginny might be
close to some act of desperation.

The answering machine at Furze Lodge referred
calls for Mary to a mobile number which didn't
answer the first few times I tried it.

'I didn't know you had a mobile,' I remarked
when I finally got through to her.

'Ah, well, you don't know everything about me,'

she teased. 'A girl's got to stay in touch, hasn't she?'
She was speaking from some quiet place with no
background noise. 'Let me guess,' she said. 'You're
on the M4 somewhere. Heading west.'

I laughed, 'How did you know?'

'I cheated. I spoke to Ginny at lunchtime.'

'Mary – thanks for doing that. *Thanks*. How did
she sound?'

'Oh . . . fairly shattered. But then, that's not too
surprising, is it? She *is* seeing someone good, isn't
she, Hugh? The psychiatrist?'

'Yes. Well, David thinks he's good.'

'It's Jones, is it?'

'Yes.'

'He *is* the best. And the drugs – they're really
amazing nowadays. Prozac and all that. Ginny tells
me you might be looking for a cottage somewhere
on the edge of Dartmoor,' Mary continued in some
seamless train of thought. 'I could keep an eye out
for something, if you'd like me to. I hear of places
from time to time.'

'Oh . . . would you? Thanks.'

A pause while we waited for me to come to the
point of my call. 'Mary, I want some help.'

'Anything.' Behind the warmth I caught a hint of
wariness.

'Blackwell Cottage – do you know who owns it?
Or more to the point, who arranged to let it, and who
exactly they let it to?'

The silence that followed was aflame with objections. 'Hugh, I don't think that sort of information is
going to help anyone.'

'I only want a name, Mary.'

'Yes, but *why* do you want it, Hugh? Contacting witnesses can get misunderstood.'

'I only want to talk to someone.'

'I really don't think it's a good idea.'

Sometimes I forgot that Mary was a lawyer by inclination as well as training, and that in situations like this her caution was liable to come bustling to the fore.

'Fine,' I said, giving in without a fuss.

A sharp pause, and she muttered in a mock head-mistressy voice, 'I suppose that means you'll go and find out anyway, from somebody else?'

I didn't say anything to that. The connection faded as a lorry overtook in the fast lane and she asked: 'Are you still there?'

'I'm still here, Mary.'

'Who do you want to talk to anyway?' she said, trying to maintain a disapproving tone. 'Don't tell me – the long-haired lout?'

'Yes.'

'You realise he's likely to be a prime prosecution witness?'

'I doubt it. He was always completely stoned.'

She gave an admonitory groan. 'All the more reason to stay away. What are you hoping to find out anyway?'

'I'm not sure,' I said, partly playing her at her own game, but also responding to some instinct for caution, a wish to protect Ginny and her story from perfunctory judgments.

'Whoa,' Mary sang. 'If I were to help you – and

345

I'm not saying I am – then I'd need to know what you were letting yourself – and me – in for.'

Still unwilling to give away too much, I offered a limited version. 'I want to find out about Sylvie's drug-taking, the dealers, the people she mixed with. Joe was around most of the time, he must know.'

'And this is going to help Ginny?' she asked in a voice of concern.

'I think so.'

'How, Hugh?'

I wondered if she meant to sound quite so sceptical. 'By digging out some of the facts the police never considered,' I said doggedly.

'How do you know what they considered?'

'Well – we've got a fair idea,' I bluffed.

'This is something for your solicitor, Hugh. *He's* the person to judge whether something needs investigating, not *you*. And he'll have someone he uses for these things, a retired copper, someone who's used to making these kind of enquiries. Someone,' she added heavily, 'who can speak to witnesses on a professional basis.'

'I don't think Joe's likely to talk to a policeman, retired or otherwise,' I said, for the sake of argument.

'I'm getting signals here,' Mary sighed. 'And the signals are telling me that you're determined to do this your way.'

'Well, I can't leave it, Mary, that's for sure.'

'But where's it going to get you, Hugh? What are you hoping to achieve?'

I felt a swell of resentment at this unrelenting flow of difficulties. 'I'm trying to help Ginny,' I said stiffly.

She didn't speak for so long I began to wonder if she was still there. Finally I heard a long sigh. 'Oh, *Hugh*. The things I do . . . All right, I'll see what I can find out. But on one condition. That if I do find an address for Joe-the-long-haired-loon that you don't go near him yourself. That you pass the address straight on to your solicitor – what's his name – ?'

'Charles Tingwall.'

'Tingwall. And that you leave him to deal with it. Promise me, Hugh?'

I heard myself say, 'Okay.'

'You won't make me regret this, will you?' she murmured as she rang off.

I thought hard before making my next call. I thought of all the objections Mary would make to it if she found out.

David's laconic bark announced that I was inter-rupting him with a patient.

'Won't keep you,' I promised, 'but could you give me Jean-Paul's address.'

'Jean-who? *Oh*,' he said in the next breath as it came back to him. 'Oh, yes. Hang on . . .' I could imagine him leaning across his desk and flipping open his address book and going down to the 'M's. He gave me an address in the Clifton area of Bristol, and a phone number as well.

'Thanks,' I said. 'And, David, it might be best if you didn't mention this to Mary.'

Whether he simply didn't have time to query this or it would never have occurred to him to discuss it with Mary anyway, he agreed impatiently.

'Anything else?' he asked in a more considerate tone.

'Not at the moment, thanks.'

Then, almost kindly, 'Will we see you soon? On the weekend? I think we should see each other on the weekend. I'll speak to Mary.'

'That would be lovely,' I said automatically, wondering as I rang off how Ginny would feel about the invitation.

I let myself into the house and, hearing laughter, paused uncertainly on the threshold. Following the sound, I found Julia and Ginny at the kitchen table. Ginny was still smiling, her head on one side, her hair falling onto her shoulder in a cinnamon curve.

Seeing me, she stretched out a hand. 'You're home early,' she declared, and the laughter had made her lovely again. She gave me a kiss and didn't let go of my hand. 'We're celebrating,' she said, and something in her tone put me on my guard.

'Why?'

'The people have made an offer for the house.'

I felt a wash of relief. 'That's wonderful.'

As she gave me the details I examined her surreptitiously. She seemed more alert, far less tired. But there was something else, something I couldn't put my finger on.

Julia stood up and looked diplomatically at her watch. 'Better be going. Messages in your study.' She sent me a well-practised eye signal, and I followed her into the hall.

'Howard called,' she said. 'Wanted to speak to you *urgently*. I told him you weren't available. But it was like talking to a rhino, all thick skin and pea brain, so be warned. He may call this evening.'

'Thank you for coming.'

'Any time. I mean that. Just let me know.'

'Maybe a couple of days next week?'

'Of course. I look forward to it.'

Ginny was loading the dishwasher when I got back to the kitchen.

'You seem much brighter,' I said.

'I am.'

'Having Julia wasn't too much trouble then?'

She flashed a glance at me. 'Don't be silly. I know why she was here.'

'Ah.' I made a contrite gesture. 'It was just . . . Jones thought it best. Until we could be sure the medicines were the right ones for you.'

'I've stopped taking them. Except one.'

My anxiety lurched to the surface. I stuttered, 'Is that wise?'

'They made me feel like a zombie.' She began to hunt through the fridge.

'But darling . . .' I came round the table. 'Wouldn't it be best to discuss this with Jones first?'

'I won't change my mind,' she said, her voice rising a notch. 'My head's so much clearer, I feel I can cope. They were doing me no good.'

I watched her long fingers pulling at some cling-film and her movements seemed jerky and uncoordinated.

'If that's what you feel.'

She put the packet of food down and said, 'Nothing's going to stop me feeling desperate, Hugh. Nothing.' And her voice rang nervily. 'But I'd rather feel alive and desperate than half dead all the time. Anyway, I'm still taking a touch of the librium. Well, I think it's librium. It's the other stuff that makes me feel so wretched. Really – I feel so much better.' She must have read the doubt in my face because she said with a touch of indignation, 'I'm not going to kill myself, you know.'

I pulled a stupid smile. 'Promise?'

'I'll give you notice, all right?' she said. 'If I start planning anything.'

I nodded, not encouraged by the knowledge that this was the one bargain a dedicated suicide would never keep.

Ginny insisted on making the supper. I opened a bottle of Chablis for her, what we called cook's rations, and when I wandered back into the kitchen half an hour later I noticed that the bottle was nearly half empty.

Ginny caught my glance and said, 'Yes, I'm drinking. Got to have something to make me sleep.'

'Fine,' I said.

She picked up her glass and, keeping her eyes on mine, took a long defiant gulp. 'You might have to carry me to bed,' and there was both humour and gentle entreaty in her face.

We kissed, and there was stored-up passion in her mouth, and urgency too, as though time for her were already running short. She pressed herself against my body in a way that was for her quite unusual and brazen. 'See what drink does to me,' she said in a low excited voice, and I kissed her again, much harder than before. We stumbled hurriedly upstairs like two teenagers, leaving a scattering of clothes across the bedroom floor. She did not close her eyes as we made love, but watched my face with unwavering intensity. At first I thought she was doing this to bring some greater reality to our lovemaking, to banish whatever demons came to her when her eyes were closed, but in the moment before I was lost in my own sensations it seemed to me that she was searching out something in my face, a truth or a confirmation that she was half afraid to find there. She cried out as she came.

As we lay side by side, panting softly, shoulders touching, I whispered, 'I love you,' and prepared myself for the expressions of doubt that this simple statement had often engendered in the recent past. But she only said, 'It's a long time since we made love before dinner.'

'Lack of time rather than lack of ambition,' I said. My memory searched lazily back. 'We used to quite a lot, though, didn't we? In the old days, at your flat.'

'*God*.' The memory didn't please her. 'I hated that time.'

I made a show of taking offence, twisting my head to give her a mock glare, and laughed accusingly, 'I don't quite know how to take that.'

'Oh, I loved the excitement of it all, of course I did. But I hated loving you so much and not knowing if I was going to keep you. I was so desperate to marry you and I began to think you'd never ask me.'

This was one of those situations where it was going

to be impossible to say the right thing. I ventured, 'Well, you know how I was. Cautious Charlie. One step at a time. Not really appreciating I was on to a good thing.' The truth was that I had hesitated long and hard over making the final leap. There had been a neediness in Ginny which had unsettled me and which instinct had told me would not easily be satisfied. And while she had never been openly possessive she had still managed to make me feel guilty for spending time away from her. I'd known that no marriage was ever perfect, that many of my friends had compromised and settled for a rough measure of contentment, I'd known that Ginny loved me more than was good for her, and probably for me as well; yet I hadn't been able to decide whether my quota of misgivings was normal, whether it formed a suitable basis for a workaday marriage or reasonable grounds for retreat.

'And once we were married?' I asked lightly.

'Then I was terribly happy.'

'So was I.'

'Were you really?' It was a straight question with no apprehensions attached.

'Oh yes,' I replied. 'I felt much more relaxed. I *liked* being married.'

She said in a distant reminiscent tone, 'Then I went and spoilt it all.'

'That's simply not true, darling.'

'Oh, it is, I know it is. I tried too hard, didn't I? Trying to make up for all the things I couldn't do, like have babies. I was always worrying, wasn't I?

Always fussing. And about *things,*' she exclaimed in disgust. 'Really! Such a lot of time wasted on *things*.'

'Really, Ginny, you're being far too hard on yourself. I've had no complaints.'

She turned her head and gazed at me with the same fierce intensity as before. 'I wish we were starting again. I wish it were all different. I wish I could show you how I'd love you now, without all that – *nonsense.*'

Touched by this strange declaration, I said without thinking, 'We've got six months.' Then, in a clumsy attempt to cover my tactlessness: 'I mean, just for a start—'

'No, don't say that!' she interrupted with a shudder. 'Please . . . *don't*. Let's just settle for six months. Don't let's think about anything more.'

And with that she gave me a rough kiss before swinging off the bed and reaching for her clothes. I watched her walk into the bathroom and it struck me that from this crisis Ginny was drawing a measure of, if not confidence, then self-possession. It lent her a strength I had never suspected. I was proud of her for it, and maybe a little in awe of her too.

While Ginny made something exotic with chicken I laid the kitchen table with crystal and candles. As we sat down to eat I thought how far away six months sounded at the moment, and how very quickly it would pass.

Choosing what seemed like a good moment I said gently, 'I won't ask again but . . .' She had already stiffened. 'What happened to the other dinghy? To Sylvie's . . .?'

She looked down at the table, she twisted her knife, she brought herself slowly to the subject. 'I took it back to the pontoon, tied it there.' She gave an ironic smile. 'I'd worked *that* one out all right. I just . . .' she raised her head and looked beyond me, lost in memory ' . . . didn't clean enough. *Thought* I had. Scrubbed the floor. And the sides of the bunks. And the seat covers. And the table – the legs, everything. Used a ton of bleach. Didn't want to miss anything, you see. Went over it all again, to be absolutely sure.' She grimaced. 'Wasn't as thorough as I thought, though, was I?' She inhaled sharply as if to put this behind her. 'Then . . . I found her bag. A small shoulder bag. I hadn't noticed it the night before. I couldn't decide what to do with it. I couldn't very well chuck it over the side, in case someone saw me and picked the bag straight up again. So . . . I brought it ashore and put it in a rubbish bin in the village.' Something about this memory made her wince, and I wondered if she had been seen. 'Then I got rid of the cleaning things in a skip. And then I came back. To you.'

At this, we drifted away on our separate thoughts.

'There was nothing else on the boat?' I asked eventually. 'No signs of anyone else?'

'What do you mean – signs?'

'I don't know really. You didn't see anyone rowing near *Ellie*?'

She shook her head.

'On either day?'

'No.'

'Not on your way out that first time, before you

found the body?' I heard myself say 'the body' as though it had never been Sylvie.

'No.'

Hearing the strain in her voice, I said placatingly, 'It was just a thought. That was all.'

She nodded, then, eyelids fluttering nervously, she braced herself to ask, 'Was Sylvie looking for you? Was that why she was there?'

This was the question I had asked myself countless times since her death. 'I don't think so. We hadn't spoken in ages. Two weeks, in fact. We had – broken off communications.' Ginny flinched a little and fiddled with the knife again. 'I can only think...' I paused to examine the idea again, to test it against my knowledge of Sylvie. 'I can only think that she'd stashed some drugs on the boat and gone out to pick them up. Or to leave some more. She knew where the key was kept, she knew how to get into the boat.'

'But why would she do that?'

'Because she was dealing in drugs, or running them, or both. I think she and her friends brought them over from France and sold them on. I think she didn't dare keep them at her place. She was incredibly organised where drugs were concerned. She planned her life around them.' I thought of the parcel tape she had used to bind the package to her back, and the waterproof material she had wrapped it in. 'She used every opportunity, every person she met. Including me. Well – *especially* me. That trip to France,' I admitted with an undimmed sense of shame, 'it was all about drugs.'

Ginny looked away and, following some logic of her own, said, 'As soon as I got back to the house that night and found you there, saw you so normal, so un- . . . un-*bothered*, I *knew!* Deep down somewhere, I knew it couldn't be you! But I couldn't bring myself to face it. I couldn't face up to the ghastly thought that I'd done all that – that I'd done everything I'd done – for nothing. *Nothing!*' Reliving this thought she contorted her face as if in pain. 'But then, of course, I realised! I *realised . . .*'

'Realised?'

'That it made no difference.'

And still I didn't get it.

'They would still *think* it was you. Whatever I said, whatever you might say – they'd never believe it, would they? Why should they, after all? So I realised I'd still done the right thing. The only thing.'

I stared at her.

Locked in her memory, she rushed on, 'I still had to finish the job the next day, didn't I? I still had to go and clean the boat out. The floor – the floor was the worst. Bleach was the only thing. Lots of bleach. And the bunks too. It was a nightmare, trying to find every spot—'

She was still in full spate as I reached across and took her hands. 'It's all over,' I soothed her. 'All over now.'

She came to a halt with a final indignant echo: 'It was still the right thing to do.'

The right thing? I didn't know what to say. She had done all this for me. She had succeeded in protecting me – if protection was the word – but at what cost? Could it be worth all this?

'I think I should go to bed now,' Ginny breathed at

last. 'Too much wine.' And she gave a single uncertain laugh.

Clasping her hand, I tucked her arm ceremoniously under mine and, leaving the dinner uncleared, we turned off the lights and headed across the hall. The phone began to ring. We paused and looked at it.

'Might be Tingwall,' I said.

Howard's voice said, 'Hugh! There you are. You're really very difficult to get hold of, you know.' He gave a humourless chuckle to show that he was prepared to forgive me this lapse.

I mouthed 'Howard' to Ginny and cast my eyes heavenward.

'Now listen – this EGM business,' Howard said without pause. 'It's a waste of everyone's time, you know. You should pull your hounds off and save yourself a lot of trouble. Really, Hugh, it's not going to get you *anywhere*.' He was using his this-hurts-me-more-than-it-hurts-you voice. 'We've done a straw poll of the institutional shareholders. And I have to tell you that they're going to back the board all the way. I think you'll find this'll do your little consortium a lot of harm, you know. And the publicity. Well, it's bound to be bad, isn't it' – he hesitated for dramatic effect – 'what with one thing and another . . .'

A mixture of anger and exultation stormed through my veins: for once I knew exactly what I was going to say to Howard.

'Aren't you forgetting something?' I began quietly. 'One small detail? Aren't you forgetting that I don't have to listen to you any more, Howard? That I don't have to take any more of your claptrap? The delights of working with you are now behind me. The Cumberland board now have that pleasure – and good bloody luck to them! You have no rights over me, Howard, and the sooner you realise that, the sooner you might also realise that nothing you say is going to make the blindest difference to what I choose to do. *Since* you mention the EGM, thanks to the terms *you* negotiated for all of us, both David and I have shares in Cumberland, so we have every right to call an EGM if we so wish. And we *do* so wish. Along with all the other shareholders who don't like what's going on.' My heart was pounding with savage excitement. 'I also take exception to your gratuitous and insulting attempt at intimidation. Don't talk to me about publicity or any other of your bully-boy tactics. Your threats don't hold any water with me, Howard. And finally – while we're talking about what I take exception to – I take exception to your calling me at home late in the evening. I have a perfectly good office and daytime phone number, and I don't want my evenings interrupted by you, on the telephone or in any other form—'

The line buzzed in my ear.

'Damn – he's rung off,' I said.

Ginny was laughing gently. 'Well, you told him all right!'

'You think so?'

'Great stuff!'

'There's one thing I wish I'd said.'

'What was that?'

'I wish I'd told him to fuck off.'

But I was pleased all the same.

Twelve

TINGWALL'S SECRETARY looked up from her work. 'Are you sure you don't want him to know that you're here?'

'No. I'll wait, thanks.'

Ginny's meeting with Tingwall had overrun by almost half an hour, but I didn't want to interrupt them, I didn't want Ginny to feel I was looking over her shoulder.

Flicking inattentively through *Country Life* I came across a full-page advertisement for Melton. The photograph had been taken in early summer, with the wistaria and lilac in full bloom, a last flush of blue-bells under the trees and razor-sharp mowing tracks striping the lawns. The house looked idyllic with its wide bays, mellow brickwork and comforting Georgian symmetry, the sort of place that features in glossy picture-books peddling quintessential dreams of English rural life. Nobody is immune to dreams, and being a workaholic I'd probably been more susceptible than most, beguiled as I was by visions of instant tranquillity. Yet for all the ambitions Ginny and I had attached to Melton, the dream hadn't been impossible, just a little too wearing perhaps, just an inch or two beyond the grasp of our busy lives.

Tingwall put his head round his door and called, 'Come in, Hugh.'

I met Ginny on the threshold, on her way out. 'Back in a moment,' she murmured. I couldn't read anything in her face as she passed.

Tingwall's expression was more transparent, a blend of gravity and apprehension.

'She's told you what happened,' I said when he had closed the door.

'Yes.'

'Well? What do you think?'

He considered for a long moment before saying, 'Not for Ginny's ears, Hugh, but I have to say that as a defence it would worry me a great deal. You mustn't go entirely by what I say, of course, you must take Grainger's advice, but for what it's worth I can't help thinking it'll be an extremely difficult defence to pull off. Far more difficult than – well, the other alternatives.'

'What are you saying then?' I said in alarm. 'You're not suggesting she should plead guilty?'

'No,' he replied carefully, perching himself on the edge of his desk. 'No, I would never do that. But pleading not guilty has certain risks – a harsher verdict, a heavier sentence. And if on top of that you're asking the jury to believe that an unknown third party committed the crime – well, it's going to present some serious problems, Hugh. To plead that sort of defence successfully one needs hard evidence, you see. Something to back up one's story. Now Ginny might come over well in the witness box – in fact, I've no doubt she'd come over very well indeed. But that in itself –

well, it's not likely to be enough. Not when the opposition have what seems like unassailable forensic evidence.' Glancing towards the door, he lowered his voice. 'And then – who is this third party? Are we saying it's someone completely unknown? If so, why didn't Ginny report the murder straight away? What was to stop her? That's what really bothers me,' he declared unhappily. 'If she tells the jury that she thought *you'd* killed Sylvie and was trying to cover up for you – well, that's not going to look too good, is it? To put it mildly. In the eyes of the world you'd be branded guilty without ever standing trial. It's a Catch-22 situation for Ginny.' He didn't attempt to conceal his dismay. 'She'll be damned if she tells the truth, and damned if she doesn't.'

'But if we could show that someone else had been there? The killer.'

Tingwall lifted his hands and raised his eyes heavenward: if only.

'What evidence would it take?'

He blew out his lips. He began to speak, he paused glumly, he folded his arms only to unfold them again. 'I'll have to think about that,' he said finally. 'A witness, I suppose. Someone who saw a third party going to the yacht before Ginny got there. Or . . . some forensic evidence, something to show that this third party was aboard at the time of the murder.' His tone was not abounding with confidence. 'I'll have to think about it.'

Faced by Tingwall's loss of heart, I found myself faltering. 'What about hiring an investigator?' I asked. 'Someone who can find witnesses the police might have missed? Who can search out Sylvie's druggy friends – the ones the police never bothered with?'

Whether he suddenly appreciated my argument or, faced by the inadequacies of Ginny's story, was all too ready to grasp at straws, Tingwall showed his first real interest in the idea of a drug connection. 'We can give it a try,' he agreed, talking himself into it by the moment. 'There's a chap I use occasionally, here in Exeter. And another in Bristol, ex-CID man. In fact he'd probably be a better bet for this sort of thing. Rather more high-powered. His name's Pike. Not cheap, I'm afraid.' Catching my expression, he said, 'I'll get on to him straight away then.' He added, 'Of course, the prosecution might be lining these people up as witnesses against us. You do realise that?'

I made a show of absorbing this.

'Mind you,' he said with some of his old spark, 'even if they're with the other side it'll be no bad thing to sound them out. At least we'll get a better idea of what we're up against, won't we? So . . . Any thoughts on where Pike might start?'

'There's a man called Hayden. He owns the boat Sylvie used to go sailing on. *Samphire*. Moored on the river. According to the local grapevine Hayden's a professional yacht skipper who lives, or used to live, near Totnes.' Tingwall was making notes. 'And then of course there was Joe who shared the cottage with Sylvie. Or just dossed there. Probably known to the police. Well, I'd imagine so, the way he dosed himself with drugs. Out of his mind most of the time. I'm trying to get his surname and an address.' If Tingwall thought I was overstepping the mark with my amateur detective work he didn't say so. And if he was wondering at the number of facts I hadn't previously disclosed to him or the police, he didn't remark on that either.

'There was another girl who sailed on *Samphire*, but I don't know who she is.'

He was waiting for more, so I told him about the drug running. 'I don't know how regularly they brought drugs across the Channel, but Sylvie had a contact in Cherbourg. He supplied her with a large packet containing some sort of powder. Heroin or cocaine, I imagine.' Tingwall shot me a dart of surprise and what might have been disapproval.

'I have no idea what she did with the drugs once she got them to England. But I have a theory – I think she may have kept them on *Ellie Miller*. I think she may have been using *Ellie* as a – what's the word? – a cache. And *that's* why she went to the boat that day. And that's why she was killed. Maybe she fell out with someone further along the line. Maybe she hadn't paid someone. Maybe she'd been bringing in extra drugs that she hadn't been telling them about.'

Tingwall had stopped writing. 'You've no evidence for this?' he asked quietly.

'No. But I can't think of anything else. She was bright, you see. She knew they were sniffing around.'

'They?'

'The customs.'

Tingwall put his notebook down. 'I wish you'd told me some of this before,' he murmured.

'Didn't think it would look too good on my CV,' I replied flippantly. 'You know – aiding and abetting the smuggling of drugs. And if I were to say that I'd got involved unwittingly, that I didn't know what was going on – the innocent abroad – well, do *you* ever believe that old chestnut when you read it? No, neither do I.'

Tingwall was contemplating this with a dispirited expression when Ginny reappeared. He straightened up, shuffled his feet and smiled boyishly. Which seemed to make two of us who were rather in love with her.

I drove Ginny straight on to Bristol for one of her twice weekly appointments with Dr Jones. During the journey she fell into a listless uncommunicative mood, and I couldn't make out if it was the bad night she'd had or a sudden bout of depression. As we'd got ready for bed she'd become restless and preoccupied, and several times during the night I'd woken to find her gone from the room. Her absences weren't good for my jittery imagination, and twice I'd set off in search of her. The first time I'd found her in the kitchen, staring out of the window into the darkness while the kettle boiled untended on the Aga. An hour later I'd discovered her scrubbing the kitchen table. 'It hasn't been cleaned properly,' she'd complained matter-of-factly. 'Liquid and bleach. You can never get rid of the grease marks without liquid and bleach.' She'd seemed completely unaware of the echoes in this, there was no glint of comprehension, and a warning had begun to tick away in my mind. Feeling out of my depth, I'd remembered the forthcoming visit to Jones with a rush of relief.

The psychiatrist had his consulting rooms in a semi-detached villa in the Kingsdown area of Bristol, not far from the university and the hospitals. Drawing up outside, I said to Ginny, 'If I'm delayed, you won't mind waiting a bit?'

She shook her head and fumbled with the contents of her handbag. I went round and opened the door for her and helped her out. She kissed me absently on the cheek before climbing the few steps to the door and ringing the bell. Watching her pass into the house, I wondered if she would come clean with Jones about the self-appointed reduction in her drug regime, and whether I would be betraying her trust if I contacted him later to find out.

With a street map of Bristol propped against the wheel, I set off in the direction of Clifton. I got lost almost immediately, going down a hill I had climbed just minutes before, but after stopping to get a new perspective on the map managed to put myself back on the right road, and within ten minutes was crawling along the busy street where Jean-Paul lived, squinting at the street numbers. Number nineteen was a flat-fronted terraced house, three storeys high with grimy windows and peeling white stucco and rubbish spinning around the front steps. There were names against three of the bells, none of them Mathieson, so I pressed the fourth, which was labelled Flat 2.

A dog yapped frantically somewhere near by, a succession of heavy vehicles shuddered past on the road behind. I pushed the bell again. I was wondering whether Jean-Paul had changed his mind when the door swung open and he was there, a tall figure standing well back from the threshold. I was surprised at how little he had changed. He was still a string bean of a man with a pinched face, a thatch of dark hair and heavy brows drawn into a permanent frown. He still wore his hair long and his jeans tight, though after fifteen years he had less of the hungry student about him and more of the lean cerebral air of the academic. I saw no resemblance to Sylvie until he stepped back to let me in and then something in his profile, the set of his mouth, gave me a shudder of remembrance.

'Good of you to see me,' I said as he pushed the door shut with a slam that shook the house.

Jerking his head towards the stairs he led the way up to the first floor. His flat consisted of one large room spanning the full width of the house with an open-plan kitchen in one corner, a bed in another, and a door leading to what was presumably the bathroom. Overloaded bookshelves sagged along every wall, and more books were stacked in untidy piles in and around the massive Victorian desk which stood before the windows, its surface almost lost in paper. Mozart was playing softly in quadraphonic sound.

Jean-Paul faced me in the middle of the room. 'So?' he said abruptly.

I hadn't planned this in any detail. 'First, may I say how sorry I am—'

He flicked an impatient hand. 'Think we can skip that bit.'

I understood this, perhaps I had half expected it. I

began again, no more confidently, 'I assure you that my wife did not do this terrible thing. They've got it all wrong. It's the most appalling mistake.'

'So you said on the phone.' His manner was cold.

'The thing is ... I'm trying to find some of the people who knew Sylvie, to see if they can think of anyone ... of any reason ... I was wondering if you could put me on to some of her friends, people who saw her this summer. I thought they might be able to tell me – I don't know – whether anyone had been bothering her in any way ... following her ... That sort of thing.'

He raised a dubious eyebrow and, perching himself on the edge of the desk, said in a voice that was heavy with indifference, 'She didn't tell me much. I didn't see her that often.'

'Anybody you can think of. Anything she told you.'

He exhaled irritably as though he was already regretting having agreed to see me. 'All I knew was that she was living in Dittisham, that she was doing her sculpture or whatever it was.'

'Did she mention Hayden, the person she sailed with?'

'May have. Don't remember.'

'Or Joe, the chap she shared the cottage with?'

'A bit.'

'What was his second name, do you know?'

He gave an exaggerated shrug. 'Wilson. Willis. Wilkins. Something like that.'

'You don't know how I could get in touch with him, do you?'

His eyes glimmered coldly. 'Maybe.'

'You've got a number?'

'He may not want to talk to you.' His tone made it clear he thought this highly likely.

'But could you ask him anyway? Explain how important it is.' Before he could refuse, I pulled out a card and, balancing it on my hand, scribbled my home and mobile numbers on the back. 'I'd be most grateful.'

With the bad grace that seemed to be habitual to him, Jean-Paul dropped the card onto the clutter of papers on the desk behind him, where it sank, a small white rectangle, into a sea of white.

'Did she mention any other people?' I asked. 'Not just in Dittisham, but elsewhere. In London perhaps.'

'Not really. She had friends all over the place.'

'What about business associates?'

'*Business?*' he repeated scornfully. 'What sort of *business?*'

I plunged in. 'Drugs.'

He tossed his head angrily. 'Oh, *please!*'

'They say she was involved in hard drugs.'

'Who says!' he retorted. 'That's crap. She was into hash, a bit of speed maybe. Nothing more. Who says?'

'The police.'

'Rubbish. They never told you that. Who told you that?'

'The hash,' I said, avoiding the question, 'where would she have got it from?'

'Where anyone gets their stuff from.' He was talking to me as if I were a complete imbecile. 'Everywhere.'

'I wondered if perhaps she could have fallen out with the dealer.'

He gave a harsh contemptuous laugh. 'You've been watching too many bad films. People don't get killed by their hash suppliers, otherwise half the university would be decimated. What were you thinking – that she owed somebody money and they killed her for it? Listen, hash costs nothing, and everyone pays up front anyway. Or if they do get credit, it's never for very long or for very much, believe me.' He gave his derisive laugh again. 'Christ, what a pathetic idea.'

I hesitated, remembering the feel of the package around Sylvie's waist the night she dived into the water. 'Once she had something else. A powder.'

His eyes flashed with hostility. He was trying to gauge whether I'd sprung this on him on purpose. 'So?' he said tightly.

'I thought she might have got mixed up with the dealing side.'

He buttoned down his mouth and glared at me by way of a reply. The Mozart came to an end, and there was only the faint rumble of traffic and the tick of a central-heating pipe.

'Her friends,' I said, bringing us back to less contentious ground. 'Was there anyone she was particularly close to?'

'I expect so.'

'Who, do you know?'

'I told you – she had friends all over the place.'

'What about boyfriends?' I asked, holding my expression.

'She told me about one, yes.'

Concealing my leap of curiosity, I said, 'Oh? Who was that?'

'You.' He had enjoyed that moment, he had enjoyed catching me out.

I gave a slow nod which he could take as a tribute to his little coup if he wanted to.

'Well, I *assumed* it was you,' Jean-Paul said, milking the moment a little longer. 'Sylvie said she had a lover, and he was in *glass*. I didn't know what a lover in *glass* was. So she told me. She said the family *made* glass. I asked if it was you – I remembered something about the glass.'

'Was there anyone else? Any other lover?'

'Should there be?' he asked with a spark of sarcasm, and I realised that while Jean-Paul might be tolerant of his sister's hash smoking, he wasn't quite so relaxed about her love life.

I looked away through misty windows to threadbare trees and spotting rain. 'Did she say anything else about me?' I asked, not quite sure why I wanted to know.

'No,' he said dismissively. Then, tiring of his own animosity, he gave the question some consideration. 'She said you had a boat. She said she was going on it. What else?' He blew out his lips. 'It was a long time ago. I really don't remember.'

'When was this?'

'Oh, April, I suppose. Early May. Thereabouts. Oh yeah,' he said as something else came back to him, 'she talked about some trip you were going to make.'

'To France?'

He frowned at me. 'Maybe. I can't remember.' For

no obvious reason he became cross again. He straightened up and folded his arms meaningfully; the interview was over.

'Well, thanks for your help,' I said. 'If you could speak to Joe?'

He made a gesture that was intentionally ambiguous.

'Perhaps I could call you in a day or so?'

'No thanks,' he said bluntly.

'I meant—'

'If Joe feels like making contact, I'll get him to call you direct.'

At the door I said, 'A while ago my brother told me you wanted to see me.'

'That was then.'

'I just wondered . . .'

'I had very little to say to you then,' he declared with a rancour that was all the stronger for having been temporarily forgotten, 'and I've got even less to say to you now.'

The door closed sharply behind me and reaching the ground floor I heard the muffled clamour of strident orchestral music drifting down the stairs after me. As Jean-Paul's last remarks reverberated caustically in my mind, I had the feeling I would not be hearing from Joe.

'I'm glad you were able to come,' Jones smiled, gesturing vaguely towards a chair. He began to search for some errant object, patting his outer pockets several times before swinging open a jacket front and starting on the inner realms, only to return once again to the outer pockets, dipping his hands into the same slots time and again like some bemused rap dancer. He spread a palm and smiled in benign defeat, 'My glasses . . .'

He was a man of indeterminate age, somewhere in his fifties or sixties, short and balding. I couldn't work out if this absentmindedness was genuine or part of some stratagem for putting patients at their ease.

With an exclamation of victory, Jones scooped up his glasses from under some papers and, settling himself behind his desk, cast me a diffident smile.

'I hope it wasn't inconvenient,' he said with a strong Welsh lilt, 'but I felt a chat would be useful.' He had called me late the previous evening after Ginny's visit, to ask if I might be able to come and 'discuss a few things', a request which had sent profound and irrational fears shivering through my heart.

'You worried me,' I told him now. 'You made it sound serious.'

'Did I? Well, I don't think it's anything to be too concerned about,' he said with a caution that managed to convey precisely the opposite impression. 'I just felt there were certain problems which you should be aware of.'

'I know she's not taking all her drugs.'

'Ah.' His eyebrows flew up.

'She didn't tell you?'

'No,' he said with the lack of surprise of a doctor who is used to his patients following their own ideas about what is good for them.

'She's still taking the tranquilliser, I think, but not the Prozac. She said it made her feel worse.'

'I'll have a word with her next time,' he said, making a quick note. 'See if I can find her something that suits her better.' There was a pause in which he gathered himself to tell me what was on his mind. 'Yes, the thing is . . . We had a useful session yesterday, Virginia and I. On the face of it she seems to be coping. She doesn't appear to be too overwhelmed by her situation. She seems to be able to contemplate the future – even the idea of prison – with some degree of composure. But at the same time I'm not absolutely sure that her view of the future, or indeed of the past, is based on reality. I'm not sure she's able to determine what is real and what is not, or to separate what is true from what she would like to be true. Sometimes people evade the truth as a way of managing their fears – evade it, but deep down never lose sight of it. In Virginia's case, however, I think she *has* lost sight of reality. I think fact and fantasy have become profoundly muddled in her mind.'

This was an alien sea, and I was floundering. 'But she's been perfectly – *clear* with me. She's never been confused about anything.'

'Oh, she expresses herself articulately, certainly,' he agreed with alacrity. 'But she's clear on an interpretation of events that deep down she's really quite confused about – if you appreciate the distinction. She would like certain things to be true, but she's not sure whether they are or not. It's not simply a matter of blotting things out, of suppressing unpleasant events, but of having painted herself an alternative picture of events and being unable to distinguish this version from the real thing.'

I was still struggling. 'Are you saying she's not telling the truth?'

'I'm saying she's telling the truth as she sees it, which, as I'm sure you'll appreciate, is rather a different thing. It may well *be* the truth, there's nothing to say it isn't, but she has no way of determining whether it is or not, no way of sorting it out in her mind, you see. And in the end that's what might disturb her.'

I felt as though I had stumbled into an emotional bog, a murky impenetrable place with no points of reference. 'She's told you, then, about Sylvie's death?' I asked, half afraid of what he might say.

'She's told me something,' he said guardedly.

'She's told you she's innocent?'

He made an apologetic gesture. 'I'm sorry, Mr Wellesley, I would be breaking her confidence if I were to discuss that.'

I suppressed a bubble of frustration. 'But what I'm trying to understand is how you've arrived at this view of her? How do you *know* she's getting things muddled?'

'There are certain procedures one can use to determine a patient's state of mind, to establish his or her grasp of reality. These techniques involve discussions of all sorts of existing situations – relationships, family, work, whatever. Now in the course of these discussions Virginia has consistently revealed a confused grasp of existing realities, even of everyday truths. And if someone loses their grasp on mundane matters in this way it's invariably symptomatic of a general and pervasive loss of reality. The delusions they show in small matters extend *to*, and stem *from*, the original trauma and its attendant delusions.'

Delusions. One of those terms like paranoia or psychosis which belong to other people, to strangers with real problems, not to someone you know and love. Fighting my own sense of confusion, I asked fretfully, 'But what sort of things does she get wrong?'

'Wrong is too strong a word,' he commented in his measured Welsh tones. 'But let me think ... Well, to give you an example, she told me she was an expert sailor, that she'd sailed a lot with you, gone over the Channel many times. But that's not quite accurate, is it?'

He read the answer in my stricken silence.

'I guessed it wasn't, from something she'd said earlier. Now I never dispute her on these matters – I'm very anxious not to undermine her confidence in any way – but if I should inadvertently question something she gets very disturbed. She cannot deal with the idea of being challenged, even on the smallest things. She becomes quite agitated.'

I looked into his bland benevolent face and felt as Ginny must have been feeling, caught between several baffling truths, each distinct, each so fatally blurred that there was no way of knowing which to believe. A man I had only just met was telling me that my wife was mentally unwell and, in trying to gauge the validity of this, all I had to go on was the fact that he had a clutch of qualifications and seemed reasonably well-intentioned.

'Okay,' I sighed. 'Okay. So Ginny wants to pretend. So what does it matter? What's the harm?'

'There's no harm for the moment,' Jones said kindly. 'But if the situation is allowed to continue she will start to find the strain unbearable. Delusions may seem like an excellent self-defence mechanism, but they carry an enormous burden of guilt and confusion. And the real risk comes when and if she is forced to confront her delusions before she is ready, before she's able to come to terms with them in her own way.'

'Risk? What do you mean?'

Jones said in a voice that was suddenly very professional, 'She could become seriously ill.'

The room seemed to crowd in on me and, clambering to my feet, I went to the window and stared unseeing into the back yard. 'So I mustn't say anything to upset her?'

'That's one thing, certainly.'

I turned back. 'What else?'

The light was in his eyes and he blinked up at me from his desk like a dazzled owl. 'It would help if she could get to see me more often. Three times a week if that's possible.'

'But what can I do?'

'You could look for signs of distress. Obsessive behaviour. Worrying excessively and continuously about insignificant problems, like whether the windows are properly closed or an object is correctly placed on a shelf. And repetitive behaviour. Going back to the same task time and again. Frequent hand washing, showering, skin scrubbing.'

I thought: Or table scrubbing, and wished the idea hadn't flown quite so smoothly into my head.

I thanked him before he could come up with any more unsettling thoughts.

As I was leaving I asked: 'She will get better, won't she?' and saw from his face that this was the one question he could not answer.

'Hello, darling.' Ginny planted a kiss somewhere close to my left cheek. 'You're early.'

It was four, precisely the time I'd said I'd get back. 'The meeting went well,' I murmured. Taking on a life of their own, my eyes strayed inexorably to the kitchen table, examining the bare pine surface for signs of recent scouring. I couldn't see anything, no patches of damp, and, though this proved nothing, it seemed to postpone the moment of reckoning.

'Julia had to leave half an hour ago,' Ginny reported as she slid the kettle onto the Aga. 'There were lots of messages. George called at least twice. And several business people – lawyers and accountants, so Julia said. Oh – and *Mary*. She wants us to go down on Sunday to have lunch with them and look at a cottage.' Ginny turned to face me and said in a voice sharp with some emotion I couldn't read, 'You've been plotting behind my back.'

'What – the cottage? Mary offered to keep an eye open, that was all.'

'I'd rather you hadn't asked her,' she said tightly. 'I'd rather you didn't involve Mary in anything to do with us.'

377

'But she volunteered.'

'She would. She enjoys interfering.' I'd never heard Ginny voice such strong criticism of Mary before. Her eyes narrowed with sudden suspicion. 'You haven't talked to her about *us*, have you?'

'No,' I said unconvincingly.

'My God, if you *have* . . .'

'No, I told her about Sylvie, that was all. Nothing else.'

'About *Sylvie*,' she gasped. 'What did you tell her, for God's sake?'

'Ginny, does it matter?'

'*Yes*, it matters!'

I sat wearily on a chair. 'I told her about the summer. I told her what happened.'

Ginny's chest started heaving. 'What – *everything?*'

'More or less.'

Ginny clamped her lips together and, holding on to her self-control with an effort which distorted her face, she shook her head at me. 'How could you!'

I lifted my hands helplessly. 'Mary's a friend. She was *there*. I needed someone to talk to.'

'But – God, you just don't see it, do you?' she cried through the pull of her breathing. 'You think Mary's so *special*. You think she's such a *friend*. Well, let me tell you, she's no friend of ours and she *never* has been!'

'Oh, *Ginny—*'

'No, *no!*' And suddenly she was in a fury. 'I tell you, she gives this great impression of being so – so – *saint*-like, so sympathetic, but it's all a big act. It's all a front! Oh, she seems like the great Lady Bountiful all right, she seems so caring – but only while it suits her! She's not Howard's sister for nothing, oh *no*. It runs in the family – all this getting people where she wants them, all this playing one off against the other.' She gave a gasp of frustration. 'Oh, you can't see it, I know you can't! For you she can do no wrong. For you she's this perfect person. But let me tell you, she *uses* people, she worms her way into people's confidence as a way of keeping a hold over them. It's *all* about control.' She glared at me. 'You look at me as though I'm mad, but it's true! You just can't see it. Good old Mary! Generous kind Mary! All that charity stuff, up on her high horse. But there's only one thing Mary really cares about in the whole world, only one thing she even *thinks* about – and that's her beloved David, and how she's going to hang on to him. Everything after that – well, it's all a front.' She waved a fierce hand at me. 'Oh, I can see what you're thinking. You think I'm just jealous of her or something. You think I just hate her! But it's not that – it's . . .' She seemed to pull the thought out of the air: 'It's that I'm *frightened* of her. I'm frightened of her little schemes. She'll go behind your back without a second thought, she'll use anyone and anything to keep herself up there as the great and good Mrs Wellesley. She'll—' Words and breath failed her simultaneously, and striding to a drawer she opened it with a bang, pulled out an inhaler and drew on it.

After a long pause I said quietly, 'I have to say I don't agree, I think Mary's always been a good friend to us. But if that's the way you feel . . .' I stood up. 'I assume you don't want to see them on Sunday?'

'All I want,' Ginny laboured, 'is for you to stop telling her about *us* and our private life. That's all. I don't *mind* going to see them, I haven't *minded* all these years, have I? I can deal with her so long as she doesn't start interfering. And I certainly don't want to get the blame for stopping *you* from seeing them.'

I rubbed my face ferociously and said nothing.

She came back to the table. 'Perhaps I should have said all that a long time ago.' She gave me a redeeming look, subdued and penitent.

'Perhaps.'

'It's what I feel.'

'Yes, I can see that.'

Her lids began to flutter, she twisted her fingers into a knot. 'It would be nice . . . if you felt you could tell *me* all those things.'

'I would. I do. Really.'

A silence, during which her eyelids continued their feather-dance. 'Will you tell me what Dr Jones said then?' Catching my expression, she said, 'Oh, I guessed that's where you'd gone. He phoned last night, didn't he?'

I didn't attempt to deny it. 'Oh, he didn't say a lot really,' I began. 'He just wants me to keep an eye on you, that's all.'

'He doesn't think I'm going barmy?'

I smiled. 'No.'

'What *does* he think, then?'

'He thinks . . .' I shrugged while I struggled to find something approaching the truth. '. . . that the strain might get to you.'

Her expression softened. 'You know one of the

things I love about you, Hugh? You always try to protect me, don't you?' She cast me a crooked smile that managed to contain affection and rebuke in equal measure. 'Oh, I know what Dr Jones thinks,' she stated robustly. 'Dr Jones thinks I'm a total case. He thinks I'm making it all up. He thinks that I won't face up to what I've done. He thinks I killed Sylvie but I'm suppressing it all, or whatever you do when you're a basket case. He made up his mind right at the beginning. I *knew* it, I sensed it, and now when I see him it's like talking to a brick wall.' She gave a ragged sigh. 'Nice to have your shrink believe in you.'

'He wants to see you three times a week.'

'Oh, does he?' Her voice wobbled. 'Yes, I bet he does.'

'You don't have to. The bail condition is only for twice.'

'But twice a week is quite enough for what he wants!' she exclaimed darkly. 'That's all he needs to wear me down.'

'Can we let you know about Sunday?' I asked Mary when I called her. 'It might be rather last minute.'

'Of *course*,' she cried. 'Don't even think about it. I've booked a restaurant but it can easily be cancelled. But you just *have* to see this house some time! It's absolutely sweet. Beautifully furnished, wonderful view, gorgeous garden, and only a few miles from the motorway.'

'Well, if not Sunday . . .'

'I heard about it through a friend, someone who

owes me a favour. The owners want some people who're going to take good care of it while they're abroad. They won't expect much rent.'

'Sounds good.'

She gave a knowing murmur. 'But you're doubtful.'

'Well, it'll be up to Ginny.'

'Of course.' And her tone managed to convey both sympathy and pity.

'Any luck with that address?' I asked.

'Address?' She knew perfectly what I was after. 'Oh, the long-haired creature, you mean? Look, I did try, Hugh. As much as I could without getting into trouble anyway. I found the people who own the cottage. Live in Somerset somewhere. Phoned them, but all they did was put me on to the letting agents and – well, it was *difficult*, Hugh. I mean, I couldn't very well say what it was really about, could I? So I waffled on a bit about the last tenants owing me money and could they let me have an address for the chap, Joe whatever-his-name-was, and they told me they didn't know anything about him, that the place had been let to the lady who was now deceased. That's how they put it – *deceased*. So there we are. Sorry.'

'Thanks for trying.'

'Will you try another way?'

'Tingwall's got a private investigator on it.'

'Ah, that sounds better,' she said approvingly. 'Best to keep your distance, Hugh. Best to keep well clear.' She added brightly, 'What's his name, this chappy?'

'Umm, Pike. Based in Bristol.'

'*Pike*.' She made thinking noises. 'Don't know the

name. But keep me posted, won't you? Let me know how he gets on. You never know, I might be able to help somewhere else along the line. You *will* keep me posted, won't you?'

'Yes, Mary.'

'And Hugh? I think you're amazing, you know that? Absolutely totally amazing.'

I said goodbye before she could explain what she meant by that.

George sat with his back to the study window. Even allowing for the gloom of the rain-swept day, his complexion had an unhealthy grey cast, the pallor of exhaustion and worry, and watching him talk his way through the latest sales figures it occurred to me that with his straining belly, exercise-free lifestyle and rocketing stress levels he was prime heart attack material. Even now he was wading into the chocolate biscuits, washed down by a second cup of Ginny's powerful French coffee.

I interrupted him in mid-sentence. 'What will you do if we find ourselves out of a job, George?'

'Do?' He tried to look surprised at the question, but I could see he'd given it some thought. 'Well, Dorothy fancies a cruise. The *Oriana*, she's keen on the *Oriana*. And me, I fancy some golf. After that . . .' He made a wry face. 'Fifty-five isn't the sort of age when they beat on your door, is it?'

'Retirement, then?'

'I suppose. But I might do the odd thing. I thought – a small garden ornament business.'

'Ornaments?' I couldn't suppress a smile. 'Not gnomes, George?'

'Yes,' he said with perfect seriousness. 'But mainly birdbaths, larger statuary. They've developed this composite that looks like the finest stone but comes in at half the weight. I think there's a market. At the right price.' And we exchanged a smile. 'At the right price' had been a catchphrase of my father's.

'And you?' George asked.

'Me? Ahh. Well, I used to paint. I wouldn't mind having another go at it. Oh, I don't mean professionally – too late for that – but for my own amusement. Watercolours, I expect. Landscapes, like every other amateur.'

'And work?'

In the garden a rain squall was flailing the leaves from the rose bushes and ripping the petals from the last spindly blooms. Grasping at a half-considered thought, I said, 'Something hands-on. Something *impractical*. A vineyard. A small farm.'

'Abroad?'

'Probably.' I let the thought expand and settle. 'Won't make me rich, of course.'

'You wouldn't want something more challenging?'

'More challenging? You mean, more stressful, more time-consuming? No.' And I was surprised and reassured by my own certainty. 'No, I wouldn't want all that again. I've been on the roller coaster too long, George. I want out for a while. I want time to dawdle a bit. To remember each day. To notice its passing.'

George considered this with slight puzzlement

before returning his weary gaze to the sales figures. 'Not off the roller coaster yet.'

I almost said: More's the pity.

As we came to the monthly financial summary the phone buzzed and Ginny said, 'There's someone on the direct line. Joe somebody. You asked him to call you, so he says.'

My stomach clenched. I said with false calm, 'Put him on, would you?' I took the phone across the room to the length of its cord.

'Joe?'

A curt 'Yeah'.

'Thanks for calling. I was wondering if I could come and see you.' Silence. I felt a momentary panic. 'Joe?' I said into the silence.

'Yeah.'

I repeated, 'I need to see you.'

'Gimme one good reason.'

'Jean-Paul must have told you—' Aware of George, I lowered my voice still further. 'They've got it all wrong. My wife is not the person.'

'Yeah, well. You would say that, wouldn't you?'

'Maybe,' I said carefully. 'But that doesn't stop it being true. And I can tell you why.'

'Yeah?' The scorn again. 'And why should I listen?'

I sighed, 'Because we both want the same thing. I assume. We want the person who killed Sylvie.'

He exhaled grudgingly into the phone. 'Yeah, well . . . But if you're windin' me up, I'll fuckin' kill you. Okay?'

*

Heavy rain and Saturday night theatre traffic had reduced the western approach roads to a crawl, and by the time I had battled my way along the Marylebone Road and into the dripping labyrinths of Camden Town I was half an hour late. In the glimmer of the tawdry shop lights the *A to Z* offered obscure advice, and after negotiating the one-way system twice, I worked my way onto the Camden Road and, more by chance than design, found the right street.

Joe's place stood at the end of a terrace of identical Victorian houses with blackened brickwork and sullen windows with unshaded light bulbs and drooping curtains. The porch was unlit and if there were names against the cluster of bells I couldn't see them in the feeble glow of the streetlamps. I began to press each bell in turn and, reaching the third, the door sprang open with a loud buzz.

The hall smelled of old frying and new damp and mouldering carpet. Unclaimed letters and circulars littered the floor and a scribbled message on one wall informed the world that Jake and Janey had moved to another address.

I made my way up to the top of the house but no doors opened. Turning back, I followed loud music to a door on the first floor and knocked. A Rastafarian with a knitted hat gave a wide shrug at the name of Joe and waved me doubtfully up the house again. Climbing the last flight of stairs once more, I looked up and saw Joe standing on the landing above.

Through the crack of the open door behind him I glimpsed shabby wallpaper and a Monet exhibition poster, but he didn't invite me inside. Instead he leant against the doorframe with one arm folded and a cigarette held dart fashion in the other. His hair fell in lank waves over his shoulders while a dark stubble crawled unevenly over a thin jowl and scraggy neck. He didn't give the impression of having washed too recently.

'I wanted to ask you about the people Sylvie knew,' I began haltingly. 'Whether there was anyone who might have had reason to harm her.'

'You goin' to crack the case all on yer own, are yer?' he scoffed with an ugly laugh.

'Maybe not,' I admitted. 'But at least I'll have tried.'

'The fuzz been through all this a thousand times, asked loadsa questions. So why should they be wrong all of a sudden?'

'Well, they damn well are,' I said. 'My wife just . . . Well, she found the body, that was all.'

He pitched me a do-me-a-favour look and, drawing on his cigarette, funnelled the smoke expertly out of the side of his mouth. 'And I suppose you don't know nothing about it either.'

'I'd hardly be here otherwise.'

'You'd hardly be here,' he echoed in a mocking imitation of my accent.

Ignoring this, I said, 'I wondered about the drugs. Who Sylvie dealt with, whether she'd got on the wrong side of anyone. A dealer, perhaps.'

Suddenly he was still, his eyes wary behind the wafting smoke. 'A *dealer*?' He shook his head. 'She never got on the wrong side of any dealer. She hadn't been near a dealer.'

'Who did she get it from then?' I added: 'And who did she pass it on to?'

He searched my face as though he suspected me of laying some elaborate trap. 'Pass it on?'

'She collected some stuff in France. Enough for an army.'

He took a last drag of his cigarette before dropping it onto the pockmarked carpet and grinding it in with his heel. 'That wasn't any big deal.'

'It was a large packet.'

'So she got stuff for everyone. So.'

'Everyone?'

'People. Friends. We all forked out for it. It was like a co-op. She made the collection.'

I took a long breath and tried another tack. 'The man she got it from, the man in Cherbourg, was he a regular – *supplier*?'

'Nah. Friend. Doing us a favour.' Now he was watching me with lazy curiosity, wondering how far I would take this, and perhaps also wondering how far he would let me go.

'What about Hayden?'

'What about him?'

'Do you know where I can find him?'

'Why d'yer wanna know?'

I mustered my patience. 'To ask him the same questions.'

'Yeah?' he shrugged. 'Well, he's abroad some place, isn't 'e? Greece. Turkey. On some fat-cat yacht.' Taking some pity on me he added, 'Listen, he can't tell you anything.' I noticed that Joe's grammar, like his accent, came and went, that occasionally the politically correct yoof mumble slipped to reveal the unmistakable education beneath. Minor public school, I guessed. Home counties upbringing.

I said with a small gesture of defeat, 'So if he can't help me, who can?'

Through bleary eyes he gazed at me appraisingly and, with a long lumbering sigh, seemed to come to some kind of decision. 'Look ... We got stuff in France, okay. Elk knew this geezer in Cherbourg—'

'Elk?'

'Charlie Hayden – Elk. The stuff came from Paris. But it was only, like, twice. A favour, that was all. No big deal.'

Putting a casual note into my voice, I asked, 'What was it, the stuff?'

He looked away crossly, he wasn't certain he wanted to answer that. 'Coke,' he admitted finally. 'And some junk, too.'

Some instinct told me. 'Sylvie was on heroin.'

He raised his eyebrows slightly in agreement. 'She was clean when she went down to Dittisham, she'd done the treatment, the full bit. NA, therapy sessions. But then ...' He raised a dismissive shoulder and pulled a battered pack of Lucky Strikes from his shirt pocket. I waited silently while he found a light and coughed over his first pull. He tucked one arm under the other and settled into his bird-like stance. 'Then someone started giving her stuff again.'

'Who?'

'Dunno. I wasn't around then. But whoever it was kept it coming.'

'A *dealer*, then?'

He shook his head. 'Nah. Not a dealer. A friend.'

'What sort of friend?' But perhaps that was a stupid question. 'A lover?'

'Maybe.'

'She had a lover?' And the thought sent a sudden tension into my belly.

'I guess. But like I said, I wasn't around then.'

'When did you get down there?'

He blew out his cheeks with the effort of memory. 'Jeese . . . Umm, June? Yeah, some time then.'

I wasn't sure where this was leading, or how best to pursue it. 'Who would know?' I asked eventually. 'Who was around before you got down there?'

He chased something round his teeth with his tongue while he thought about that. 'Yeah – Elk. Elk might know. Yeah. He was around then.'

'But Elk wasn't the guy?'

'What? Nah. Not Elk. Elk never did junk.'

'Was he her lover, though?'

He guffawed, a coarse braying sound. 'Nah. He and Sylvie, they didn't get on. I mean, like they hung out together but they fought. Nah,' he said adamantly, 'not Elk.'

'What about the woman who worked in the pottery shop? Would she have known about Sylvie's friends?'

'Doubt it.'

'What was her name?'

'Liz.' He waved his cigarette vaguely. 'Never knew 'er second name.'

I was drained of ideas. I murmured, 'And there was no one else you can think of . . .'

'What, that mighta killed her? Nah.' His expression grew sly. 'Only you.'

'Don't be bloody stupid,' I said in sudden anger. 'You know it wasn't me.'

He snorted, 'I dunno that! Why should I know that?'

'Because I hadn't seen her in weeks. Because she wasn't coming to see me that afternoon.'

'She said she was goin' out to the boat.'

So that was what he had told the police. 'Not quite the same thing,' I pointed out.

Suddenly he was in no mood to concede this or anything else. 'Yeah, well, you would say that, wouldn't you?'

The place was lovely, a sturdy farmhouse in grey stone with a sheltered garden and views of Dartmoor. It wasn't too large, hardly more than a substantial cottage, and it had a tranquil comforting air, the sort of place where you could imagine yourself hidden from the world.

It seemed promising to me. Mary thought so too because she kept extolling its virtues in ever more extravagant terms, but as David and I followed the women into the garden a certain futility seemed to settle over the expedition. I sensed that Ginny had taken a dislike to the place and that nothing any of us could say was likely to change her mind.

'How do you think she looks?' I asked David quietly.

'Ginny? Oh . . . Surprisingly well, really. Getting on with Jones all right, is she?'

We paused by a weathered sundial. I hesitated, caught between loyalty and a painful need for reassurance. 'He thinks she's suffering from some sort of delusion.'

'Christ, aren't we all?'

'You don't think it's serious then?'

'Look, I'm not the right person to ask,' he protested. 'Doctors know damn-all about psychiatry. We just shove patients towards the men in white coats and breathe a sigh of relief when they're willing to take them on. And then again, most of us are a bit worried about being found lacking in the mental department ourselves.' He gave a dry bark of a laugh. 'You know how the statistics go – doctors sky-high in the suicide league, not to mention the alcohol stakes.'

'It's just that I find it hard to judge how good he is.'

'You and me both. There's not one of them that ever agrees. They argue like crazy between themselves. I can only say that Jones seems to be the best around.'

'He thinks she might find the strain too much.'

'Well, I *would* take notice of that. Psychiatric claptrap aside, it's the one thing he's likely to get right.'

Absorbing this as best I could, we strolled on through an arch into a paved herb garden. The women were a long way ahead, disappearing around the back of the house.

'How's the case coming along?' David asked with sudden awkwardness. 'Anything I can help with?'

'Not really. Everything's on hold until the prosecution present their evidence.' We came to a halt again. 'There was something though . . .' I framed the question with care. 'I know you said that you only saw Sylvie a couple of times, and there was no way of telling she was on drugs, but what about heroin? Can't you tell with that?'

David looked away towards the rise of the moor. 'In women they say the skin gets a luminous look – quite beautiful, apparently – but unless you know the person . . .' A dismissive lift of the shoulders. 'Otherwise needle marks, of course. But you would have to *see* them.'

'So no one would have known?'

'Not by looking at her, no. Why?'

I wasn't terribly sure why I was asking. 'Just wondered, that was all.'

David grunted, 'She was definitely on heroin, was she?'

'Yes.' We both studied the view again. 'Where would she have got her drugs from if it wasn't from a dealer?'

David threw me a sharp quizzical look. '*Not* from a dealer? Well . . .' He did a mental double-take. 'You know it wasn't a dealer?'

'Apparently not.'

He went through the motions of thinking about this. 'Well, it could have been legally, from a doctor. So long as she was a registered addict. But she wasn't registered with me. Though . . .' He frowned. 'She could have been registered with another doctor, I suppose. When she signed on with me her notes were forwarded from some private doctor off Sloane Square, but she could easily have had a second doctor somewhere else. One she'd persuaded to give her a long-term repeat script. There are some doctors who specialise in signing up drug addicts to boost their lists, and then go and hand out scripts like confetti from a gravy train, with no intention of weaning them off anything.'

'If she had prescriptions she must have used them locally then?'

David missed the question. 'Otherwise another registered addict,' he mused. But he didn't sound convinced. 'Someone who was willing to share their quota. I've got four or five addicts on my books, but they're all on methadone.' He gave a sardonic grunt. 'I will persist in this crazy idea that they'll get off drugs one day, you see. I go through the motions.'

'A local chemist would notice a prescription for heroin then?'

'For diamorphine – that's the name – well, he *might*. Normally it's only used for terminal cases – cancer. Largely dispensed through hospitals and homes.' He cast me a sidelong glance. 'You think this could be important?'

I gave a wide shrug. 'Who knows? But yes. Yes, I do.'

'You think . . .' He wore the irritated expression that always overtook him when he was forced to voice something that might make him look foolish. 'You think the drugs are something to do with her death?'

'Well, it has to be as good as anything the police have come up with, doesn't it?'

David eyed me thoughtfully, as if appreciating for the first time that I had not given up on the idea of Ginny's innocence. He pushed out his lips and nodded sagely. 'I'll see what I can find out.'

The offer surprised me. 'Would you?'

'Sure. There aren't that many chemists in the area. They're always calling me up.' He grunted disdainfully, '*Say* they can't read my handwriting.'

'Thanks, David.' Then, as if I needed to justify myself further: 'I feel I have to try.'

'Of course.' And I recognised the tone in his voice that signalled fast-waning interest.

The women reappeared at the far end of the garden. Ginny was hugging her arms to her stomach, looking cold.

'This EGM,' David said in a voice that was so remote and abrupt I could only wonder at his ability to switch mood. 'Is it going to come off?'

'Yes. You should have been notified. Next Friday.'

'Isn't it all a waste of time, Hugh? I mean, wouldn't we do better to just take the money and run? Or rather, *keep* our money and run?'

'We have very little to lose, David, and an awful lot to gain.'

'*Do* we? You could have fooled me. It seems to me that Cumberland must know what they're doing. They've made their decision and we should accept it.'

From across the flowerbeds Ginny caught my eye as she listened inattentively to something Mary was saying, and it was a plea for rescue.

'They'll close the factory, David. They'll put a lot of people out of work. Isn't that reason enough to give it a try?'

'No.' Warming to his indignation, he protested, 'No, it damn well isn't. That's the way *bad* decisions are made.'

'Look, it's not long to wait now,' I said appeasingly. 'It'll all be settled on Friday.'

He growled uncompromisingly, 'Once a ship's sinking . . .'

Mary and Ginny were moving towards us again.

I touched David's arm. 'One last thing – when did Sylvie join your list?'

'*What?*' He was thoroughly incensed now. 'What's that got to do with anything?'

'I wanted to know when she arrived in Dittisham.'

'Oh.' He allowed himself to be slightly mollified. 'March. Beginning of March.'

Ginny came up and fastened herself to my side.

'You're cold,' I said and, taking off my jacket, put it round her shoulders.

'Well, what do you think?' I asked as we followed David and Mary back to the cars.

She whispered, 'I don't like it.'

'Fine.'

'And it's *not* because Mary's so crazy about it, if that's what you're thinking.'

'No, no – I wasn't. No, don't worry about it. We'll find somewhere else.'

'It's got something spooky about it,' she shivered. 'I feel as though someone died here.'

Suppressing faint alarm, I squeezed her hand. 'In that case . . .'

She stopped suddenly and looked up at me, her eyes burning fiercely, and said for no apparent reason, 'I do love you, you know. Sometimes I don't know what I did to deserve you.'

I kissed her softly on the lips. 'It's me that's the lucky one,' I said.

I glanced up and saw Mary at the corner of the house, looking back at us. Instantly, she gave a broad smile and called, 'David and I both know the way to the restaurant. Why don't we split up in case we get separated?' She put on a comically doubtful expression and laughed, 'If that makes any sense!'

I turned to ask Ginny but she was already shrugging her agreement.

David led the way in his Mercedes, and as I fell in line behind I saw him turn his head to Ginny, asking her something, or replying.

'Ginny didn't like the house,' said Mary, fixing her seat belt.

'I'm afraid not.'

'Oh well. Worth a try.' She didn't seem in the least perturbed. 'How's everything else going?'

'Not a lot of progress at the moment.'

'How's the investigator doing – Mr *Pike*. I must say, it's a rather unfortunate name. Aren't pikes terrible predators, gobbling up everything in sight?'

'No word yet. It's only been a few days.'

'So he hasn't tracked down the dreaded Joe yet?'

I answered the question truthfully. 'No.'

She cast me a sidelong glance. 'Awfully glad you

didn't get involved, Hugh. It really wouldn't have done, you know.'

'I can see that.'

We drove on in silence for a time.

'Tell me,' I asked casually, 'do you know the woman who worked in the pottery shop with Sylvie? Liz something? I tried to phone the place but it must have closed down. The number was discontinued anyway.'

'Haven't a clue! Don't even know which shop it was! But *Hugh!*' she exclaimed, attempting to moderate her disbelief and exasperation with a laugh. 'Same warning applies, for God's sake. Could be a prosecution witness!' She sighed at me as if I was beyond redemption. 'Why do you want to know anyway?'

'I thought she might know who Sylvie's lover was. The one before me.'

'The *one?*' she questioned drily. 'I thought she never had less than a *bevy* on the go.'

'There was one in particular.'

'Well – who knows then? Any red-blooded male in the area, presumably.'

'This one supplied her with drugs.'

Mary gave me an abrupt glance. 'Oh really? *Really.* Well, there you are then. She was always on to the main chance, wasn't she? Addicts are all the same. Dragging people down into their own little cesspool. Polluting everything in their path. They commit most crime nowadays – did you know that? Muggings and burglary. The new scum of the earth.'

I had nothing to say to that.

'You think you'll find this *lover?*' Mary asked.

'No idea.'

'If you ask me you should try your Mr Pike. He'll know all about that little world. He'll know all about the rot at the bottom of the muckheap.'

Thirteen

Tingwall's office lights blazed in the darkened building. A hastily departing staff member let me in and I made my way down the passage and through the dimmed outer office to Tingwall's door, which was open. Catching sight of me, Tingwall stood up in the act of swallowing a hot drink and promptly choked. Spluttering, he put his cup hastily down and waved a voiceless welcome.

'I'm sorry I couldn't make it earlier,' I said. 'A crisis at Hartford.' It would have been truer to say, another crisis in a succession of emergencies. This time it had been a last-minute panic over the documentation for the EGM.

Still speechless, Tingwall clutched his throat and gestured me to my customary chair. I perched on the edge of my seat and, making no attempt to hide my restlessness, looked straight at the clock. Catching this, Tingwall gestured remorse for the delay and, coughing heartily, went to the side and poured himself a glass of water which he downed rapidly and refilled.

'It's just that Ginny will be waiting,' I explained.

'I wouldn't have bothered you . . .' Tingwall gasped. 'If it hadn't been . . . important.' He drew up a chair and, clearing his throat, sat on the very edge of his seat, arms on knees, hands clasped, eyes grave. 'Look, what I'm about to tell you – well, I think we *must* treat it with caution until everything is confirmed and clarified, until we can get a third opinion and be really sure of our ground, *but* – well, it's possible we may have something on the forensic front.'

'What sort of thing?'

He held up a hand as though to pre-empt some excessive reaction from me. 'I really do think it would be a mistake to get too excited about this,' he warned. Yet behind his calm veneer I realised it was Tingwall himself who was quietly excited. 'It's the fingerprint expert – chap called Armstrong—'

'Our expert?'

'Oh, yes – *our* man. He's looked at the fingerprint that the police took from the boat and he's found two things. First, that it's a pretty poor print – a fragment from an index finger, and lifted off natural wood with a strong grain, which means the print is fairly broken up. Well, I'm not sure if that's the correct technical term, but you can imagine – wood isn't the smoothest of surfaces. *But* even more importantly, he's found only fourteen points of similarity between this print and Ginny's, which is two short of the number which is needed for a positive identification in an English court of law.' He paused to let me absorb the full significance of this. 'What it all boils down to, Hugh, is that in his opinion this print cannot be positively identified as Ginny's. If he's right – and he *is* a top man – then the implications are absolutely—' Losing

the word, he wheeled an impatient hand before settling on: 'Crucial.'

Many different thoughts jostled in my mind as I
heard myself ask, 'But these points of similarity –
fourteen, was it? Isn't that rather a lot?'

'Sixteen is the absolute minimum required in law
for a positive ID,' Tingwall repeated, weighing each
word authoritatively as though he were in court.'
Armstrong explained it all to me – we'll have to wait
for his report, of course – but his conclusion was
unequivocal, Hugh. He says that in his opinion it
would be unsafe to say these prints were from the
same person.'

At some point in the last few weeks I had lost
the capacity for hope or joy, and, while part of me
recognised the importance of this news, my emotions
failed to respond. 'Where do we go from here then?'

'We get another expert. I've tracked down a chap
called Benyon in London. Meant to be the best independent. He can get back to us in a few days, though
he said it could be longer if it's a complex job.'

'And what happens if he doesn't agree? What happens if he thinks the print is Ginny's?'

Tingwall wasn't ready to allow such negative
thoughts. 'Armstrong seems sure, Hugh. And a man
of his experience doesn't offer an opinion like that
without very careful consideration.'

But part of me wanted to deflate his optimism, if
only to protect myself from disappointment. 'What
about the police expert – why should he be wrong
and our people right?'

'Ah!' Tingwall declared, flipping open one palm

like a flashy magician about to produce his best trick. 'We're dealing in reasonable doubt, Hugh. If we manage to cast reasonable doubt on the reliability of the evidence, if we have two top experts saying that they think a match would be unsafe, then the police evidence will be fatally undermined. Reasonable doubt, Hugh. In a case of murder the judge will bend over backwards to make sure that reasonable doubt is understood and acted on by the jury.'

I said ironically, 'But I'm not to get excited?'

Tingwall, whose excitement had become increasingly apparent, had the grace to smile. 'Perhaps I shouldn't have told you at this stage. I'm sorry if you would have preferred me not to. But Hugh, the thing is that if Armstrong is right, and Benyon agrees with him, it will alter our position significantly. The prosecution will be left with nothing but the eyewitness sighting, and eyewitness evidence is always the weakest part of any case. However impressive this eyewitness may be – and we know nothing about him yet – we're back to reasonable doubt. It only needs one small inconsistency, one small hesitation, and a good defence counsel will expose the flaw and rip the evidence apart. Grainger has a reputation for that, you know – demolishing star witnesses.'

Instinct told me that it couldn't be as simple as that. And by way of endorsement, a troubling thought hovered at the edge of my mind and swooped home. 'She cleaned up the boat, Charles. They'll still have that. Why would she want to clean up the boat? Or,' I suggested heavily, 'are we going back to the idea that she was covering up for me?'

'The boat cleaning, that's circumstantial. Not enough in itself, Hugh. And as for Ginny thinking you were the murderer, hopefully we won't have to use that, and certainly not if the case never even gets to trial.'

'Don't tell me they're likely to drop it!' I said, by now so thoroughly unsettled that I took a harsh satisfaction in arguing against my own interests.

'No, but . . .' An inner debate flickered over Tingwall's face. Finally he ventured, 'We'd have to take advice, of course – *plenty* of advice – but it's *possible* we might want to go for an old-style committal in front of a stipendiary, and try to get the case thrown out altogether. But, look,' he cautioned hastily, 'don't take it from me. I mean, I may be way off the mark!'

Two things struck me: that while Tingwall might be meeting the challenge of the case, he was also feeling the full responsibility of it, and that, for all his dedication and tenacity, he was not as confident as he made himself out to be.

Tingwall hurried on, 'I thought that as soon as we have Benyon's fingerprint report and the prosecution's statements, which should come through any day now, we should have a conference with Grainger, sound him out, see if he thinks an old-style committal's a starter. What do you think?'

I looked out into the black November night, aware of how long Ginny had been alone and the time it would take me to get back to her. 'Can I phone my wife?'

Tingwall looked dubious. 'Do you think it's wise to tell her?'

'I'm not going to tell her over the phone, Charles, if that's what you mean.' It wasn't what he meant, of course. He meant that it might not be wise or fair to tell her anything at all. But it occurred to me as I went to make the call in the outer office that raising her hopes might be no bad thing, that hope was a fairly harmless commodity when you didn't have much else to hold on to.

I could never speak to Ginny on the phone these days without listening for sounds of strain in her voice, for some sign that her self-control was wearing thin, and hearing her now I knew with a small lurch of alarm that something had happened. 'What is it?' I asked.

'Nothing.'

'You're upset. Was it Jones?'

She exhaled fiercely into the phone. 'He *refuses* to believe me. He just won't *listen*. He's treating me like an idiot!'

I cursed my weakness for staying at the Hartford meeting for longer than I had meant to. 'Okay,' I said soothingly, 'we'll sort it out. Somehow we'll sort it out, I promise.'

'He's trying to wear me down, just like I said he would. He undermines everything I say – *everything*. Even you and me – he tries to make me say that I'm angry with you, that I was out for some sort of revenge, that I was really trying to get my own back at you and – oh, I don't know – lunatic things!'

'I'll tell him to lay off.'

'Will you?'

'Of course. I'll tell him to lay off or we'll take our business elsewhere.'

'Oh, will you? Will you really? He makes me feel so dreadful. He makes me want to crawl under a stone.'

'Ginny – rise above it, ignore it. Believe in yourself.'

'But I'm so angry, Hugh, I'm so *angry.*'

I searched for words that might have some meaning for her but could only plead impotently: 'I promise I'll sort it out, darling. Just hold on. Please – don't get upset. *Please.*'

'I'm all right,' she said in a calmer voice. 'I'm always better after I've talked to you.'

Tingwall walked me out to my car. 'It must be a hard time for Ginny,' he said as though he had divined something of my conversation. 'It's always so much harder for innocent people. They feel they're battling against the assumption of guilt. I had one chap up on a rape charge and even when he got off he never stopped feeling hounded. It's an awful lot easier being guilty.'

'I'll take your word for it.'

Climbing into the car, I remembered what I had meant to tell him and opened the door again. 'I forgot – your man Pike needn't bother with Sylvie's friend Joe. I found him.'

'Don't we want to talk to him?' Tingwall asked.

'No.'

'No?' Catching some hint of what had been going on behind his back, he shot me a look in which curiosity, disapproval and the sense to ask no more were neatly fused.

'Has Pike made any progress with Hayden?' I asked.

'Nothing yet.'

'Could you let me know the moment he finds anything?'

'Sure.'

He was still giving me a speculative narrow-eyed look as I drove away.

I had a picture of what I would find on my arrival home. Rooms in semi-darkness, Ginny by an unlit fire picking the skin at the edges of her nails – she had already made them raw – and an air of anxiety which she would expect me to alleviate; the rest of the evening bolstering her confidence, a tricky chat with Jones and finally to bed, to find peace of a sort for a few hours. Another day survived.

The lights were on in the drive, the floodlights around the front of the house too. As I parked, Ginny came out to meet me. She was dressed in a simple black dress with a heavy gold necklace and matching earrings. When I kissed her I caught a waft of *Je Reviens*.

'Did I forget something? Are we having a party?'

'Absolutely,' she smiled, taking me into the house.

'Who's coming?'

'Just you and me.'

'Sounds all right to me.'

Passing the kitchen I caught the smell of wonderful things cooking and saw that she had laid the small circular breakfast table with a white cloth and candles and flowers. She led the way into the sitting room and poured me a glass of champagne.

'You look uncertain,' she said.

'No,' I said rather too quickly. 'No, just – surprised.'

'I wanted us to have a jolly evening for a change. You must get fed up with all my moaning.' She flung me a bright smile. 'I want you to feel you've got something to look forward to when you get home. To know that you're going to be spoilt a bit.'

'But I do. I am.'

'Liar,' she smiled. There was a glow in her face which I hadn't seen in a long time. Part of it, I realised, was makeup, a clever mix of colour and shading that lifted her features and intensified her eyes, and which she hadn't bothered to put on for weeks; but there was an inner spark, too, some new resolve.

I gave up with a laugh and raised my drink. 'Here's to jolly evenings.'

As we drank she caught me watching her over my glass. Some of the doubt must have shown in my eyes because she said, 'What *did* Jones tell you? Did he say I was going off my head? Is that what you've been thinking all this time?' Her voice managed to be brittle and fluid at the same time. 'Oh, don't worry, I wouldn't blame you if you had. He's very persuasive. God – sometimes he's had *me* wondering if I'm going barmy. *But*' – she gave me a conspiratorial grin – 'I've finally done what I should have done ages ago. I plucked up all my courage and half an hour ago I called him! I told him what I thought of him!'

I had paused in the act of drinking. 'What did you say to him?' I asked nervously.

'Say?' Her eyes gave a dark triumphant flash. 'I told him that he'd been out of line. That he'd been intimidating me – well, *bullying* me, really. That he'd been making assumptions that weren't his to make. *Undermining* me. That I didn't deserve that. That no one did.' Reliving her own temerity, she gave a strange high-pitched laugh. 'I can be so much braver on the phone – no eye contact, none of those awful silences that he uses to make me feel guilty!'

I was still immobile, the glass just short of my lips. 'And what did he say to that?'

'Well, he didn't want to admit he was wrong, did he? He said he'd never disbelieved anything I'd said, never made up his mind about anything. But he had – he knew he had. He didn't want to admit he'd been . . . *pressuring* me. I made him promise that in future he'd listen without *deciding*, that he'd listen and accept what I had to say. Just *accept*.' And her jaw hardened, she spoke with a sudden vehemence that made her shudder visibly.

I sat down and said, 'Gosh.'

Finding her mood again, she tipped up her chin. 'I felt so much better afterwards, I can't tell you! I felt as though I'd got a little bit of my life back. Oh, I know you would have waded in for me,' she remarked affectionately. 'You always do. But for once I needed to say it for myself, I needed to feel I was fighting my own battles. And I'm glad I did, *glad*. It's done me so much good!' And she sparkled at me, all shaky confidence and new determination.

'There's something else.' She came and knelt on the floor at my feet and rested her arm on my knee. 'I've been thinking that I really must be much more positive! Things are far more likely to go right if one thinks positive, aren't they? And misery's such a bore. So wearing. I should be remembering all the good things and making the most of what I have!' She gave an excited laugh and – a pang of disloyalty – I couldn't help wondering what she'd been taking. 'I want us to plan like mad,' she declared. 'Everything, all the way through to our old age. Every house and holiday and job and – oh, I don't know! But as though I'm going to be around. I need that, I need to believe it's all going to happen.'

'Ginny . . .' I put my drink down. 'Something came up today.' And I told her about the fingerprint expert, how nothing was definite yet, but if all went well and the two experts agreed then her chances would significantly improve.

She listened attentively, she asked a couple of questions then shrugged carelessly, 'There you are. See what a bit of positive thinking can do!' In her sparky optimism I saw the Ginny of years gone by, the Ginny I had fallen in love with, and in apparent awareness of this, she looked up and we exchanged a glance of shared memory.

I was leaning forward to kiss her when the phone rang.

David's voice said, 'Not interrupting dinner?' Without waiting for a reply, he reported, 'The chemists look as though they're going to be a dead loss, I'm afraid. I got four or five to look back through their registers but nothing out of the ordinary in the way of diamorphine scripts. Without asking them for chapter and verse there's not a lot more I can do, I'm afraid.'

'Oh well.'

'Anyway, I was thinking – she's far more likely to have got her stuff on the open market, isn't she? Bristol's seething with drugs. Buy them on every corner. It's not far, after all.'

Bristol made me think of Jean-Paul. Time had not lent him credibility, and I found myself wondering if he had told me anything approaching the truth. 'No, it's not far,' I agreed. 'Thanks anyway.' I hesitated. 'There was one other thing. The woman who worked in the pottery shop with Sylvie. Liz something. Fifty-ish, ethnic clothes, beads. You wouldn't have any idea who she was?'

He made a doubtful sound. 'I know who you might mean. Seen her once or twice. Retired hippy type. Long gypsy skirts. But no – not a patient of mine, not someone I know. Useless again, I'm afraid.'

'Thanks anyway. And thanks for lunch yesterday.'

'Oh, for heaven's sake.' David regarded social niceties as superfluous at the best of times and positively ridiculous within the family. He rang off with a sharp admonitory grunt.

I took the champagne bottle into the kitchen and found Ginny at the table, doing last minute things to some beef that smelled of wine and garlic and herbs. She nodded enthusiastically when I offered to refill her glass. 'Heaven.' And she smiled in such a way that I wasn't quite sure what she was referring to. I was trying another kiss when the phone rang.

'Doomed by the bell,' I muttered.

'Caressus interruptus.'

I snatched the receiver off the hook and was met

by the howl of a child. 'Sorry to bother you, Hugh,' Tingwall said over the din, 'but it's Pike. He's found this chap Hayden.'

'Where?'

The screaming reached a terrifying pitch. 'Nothing I can do about this, I'm afraid,' he shouted, sounding harassed. 'In sole charge. Wife at a girls' night. Well, that's what she tells me.' He laughed to show it was a joke. 'No, when I say *found*, it's not quite as good as that. Apparently Hayden's on his way to Heathrow at this moment, heading for the Far East. Pike just missed him in London.'

'Damn. Can he catch him at the airport?' I shouted back.

'He's going to try. He's on his way there now.' Tingwall made some cooing noises off-stage and for a moment the screaming subsided to a succession of wails and sobs. 'At best he might only get a few minutes with Hayden. I've given him some questions to ask, but I wanted to check with you to make sure I hadn't missed anything obvious.'

'Can I speak to Pike direct?'

'What? Sure. He's got a mobile.'

I took down the number and repeated it back to him through the renewed caterwauling.

'Won't be a minute,' I called to Ginny as I rang off and disappeared in the direction of the study.

The number didn't answer first time. When I tried again two minutes later an expressionless voice announced itself as Pike. I explained who I was and Pike told me he was on the motorway, just minutes from the airport.

'If you do manage to find him,' I said, 'try to stop him leaving, will you? Any way you can.'

'I'm not sure I understand you.'

'Offer him whatever it takes to delay his flight.'

'What's your limit?'

'I don't know – five hundred? Two thousand? Whatever it takes.'

'Some people won't be bought at any price.'

'This one will,' I said, though I couldn't have said what gave me such confidence.

'Right. I'll keep in touch.'

I gave Pike my number and went through to dinner. I tried to enter into the spirit of Ginny's evening but I must have been a poor actor because Ginny's intuition soon caught me out.

'The phone. Something's happened,' she said.

'I may have to go out later. If I do, will you be all right?'

'Of course.' But she didn't sound at all convinced.

'I may be late. Well – very late.'

That unnerved her. She didn't like being alone in the house at night. The animation fell from her face. 'How late?'

'I don't know. I might have to go to the airport to talk to someone. I could try to get Mrs Hoskins to come over if you like.'

'It can't wait, this thing?'

I shook my head. 'It's someone who might have information, you see. About Sylvie.'

She gave me a searching, almost hostile look. 'I thought Charles was dealing with all that.'

'He's tied up, and this man's about to fly off some-where. It's the only chance.'

She was very still. 'Where's all this leading, Hugh?'

'Leading?'

'What's the point of it all?'

I stared at her, baffled by her attitude. 'The *point*?' I heard the impatience in my voice and argued more reasonably, 'Well, someone killed Sylvie, didn't they? So someone has to know *something* about it. The people she mixed with, the dealers ... If we don't make an effort to find out, then, then—' But mystification blocked my words.

'I think ...' She hesitated for a long moment. 'I think it would be a mistake to hope for too much.'

'I'm not hoping for *too much*—'

The phone rang and, pushing my chair back roughly, I got up to answer it.

'Bingo,' said Pike's voice. 'But you'll need to bring some cash.' Five minutes later, armed with a batch of traveller's cheques and credit cards, still smarting a little from my discussion with Ginny, I was heading for the motorway.

Pike had booked Hayden into one of the smarter hotels on the airport periphery, a newish place with a lobby designed in what Ginny would disdainfully dub the mid-Atlantic country-house style, with garish chintzes and hunting scenes and dimpled leather sofas. Pike hadn't stinted on the room either. He let me into a suite with a lobby, three doors leading off it, and a large display of fresh flowers.

Pike was a nondescript man, dead-eyed and stoop-shouldered, with an unhealthy complexion and lugubrious expression. Closing the door behind me, he murmured in the professional undertone of a copper, 'He's friendly enough, but greedy, I'd say. He finally agreed to a grand, cash in hand, plus a replacement air ticket at seven hundred, plus overnight expenses, but I reckon he'll be after more. Shall I sit in?'

'Please.'

Pike led the way into a sitting room with a mirrored bar complete with counter and stools. Hayden was lying back on a sofa watching television, his feet on a low table, drink in hand and a bowl of nuts balanced precariously on his stomach. Removing his eyes unhurriedly from the screen, he disentangled himself from the sofa and rose to a hefty six foot three or four.

'Hi.' His steely handshake was accompanied by a broad lazy smile that was all the more startling for the contrast between his teeth, which were numerous, even and exceptionally white, and the depth of his golden tan. With his springy sun-bleached hair, athletic shoulders and model-boy looks, he might have come straight from a Californian lifestyle commercial. He was the same man I had watched through the binoculars on *Samphire*, but coloured more vividly.

While Pike made the drinks, Hayden grinned some more before sauntering back to the sofa and sinking into the cushions with his eyes fixed on the television again, as though the business session hadn't yet opened and he was still at leisure. When I sat on the chair opposite he didn't hurry to tear himself away from the blaring comedy but waited for some raucous punch line at which he laughed in a loud contrived way before finally operating the remote control.

He turned his smile on me again, and it was a facile smile without warmth. 'Good trip?' he asked as though we were small-talking at a party.

'Fine, thanks.'

'Great.' He nodded a lot, though not as much as he smiled. 'Going straight back?'

'I expect so.'

'Great. I'll be needing cash, did, ah, he tell you?' He indicated Pike with a movement of his head.

'He told me.'

Pike brought the drinks.

Hayden was watching me indolently, like a man with all the time in the world, and I realised he was waiting for the cash to appear on the table.

I produced the traveller's cheques.

He gave an exaggerated theatrical wince, all regretful head-shaking and raised shoulders. 'Ah – *sorry.*' And behind the knowing eyes I recognised someone who was used to getting his own way. I remembered the scene I had witnessed on *Samphire,* the way Sylvie had stood her ground against him.

Pike caught my eye. 'I'll go and see if the management can oblige.' I passed him the cheques and my Amex Gold Card.

'You won't mind if we start?' I asked when Pike had gone.

'Sure.' His tone told me what I already knew, that

416

he wouldn't be telling me anything of real importance until the money arrived.

'I assume Pike's told you what this is about?'

He started picking at the nuts again and popping them expertly into his mouth. 'Sure.'

'Have you spoken to the police at all?'

'I've been away,' he said in a conversational tone. 'Gib, Turkey, Italy, delivering boats. They couldn't've found me if they'd tried.'

'But you were in Devon until – what, August?'

'I was coming and going. I got this dinky little cottage up near Totnes. For my, ah, old age, you know.' And the idea amused him in the way some equally distant prospect like going grey or bald might amuse him. 'Bit of a ruin still. Done the roof. No heating, no light.' He shrugged. 'Next year, I'm hoping.'

'And *Samphire* – you got to do quite a bit of cruising?'

'Sure. Always take the old girl out when I can. Otherwise she rots – you know?' And he smiled his empty affable smile.

Rather than risk questions that he was unlikely to answer, I threw it open. 'Tell me about Sylvie.'

'Sylvie?' He laughed as if I had said something unexpected. '*Yeah* . . . Well, we went back quite a way, Sylvie and me. South of France, Ibiza . . .' He waved a hand, indicating other times, other places. 'Hung out in the same crowd. So when she came around she, ah, got in touch. You know.'

'What brought her to Devon?'

He spread an open palm. 'New start? I guess.'

'She was happy?'

But this question obviously had its price, and his face took on an impenetrable look.

'I saw Joe the other day,' I said, watching for a reaction which I didn't get. 'He told me all about Sylvie's drug—' I almost said 'problems', but amended this to: 'habits. And he told me about the trips to France on *Samphire*, to the dealer there.' Hayden's bland expression did not alter. 'What I need to know – when our business is done' – I offered my own version of a hollow smile – 'is who else she got her stuff from.'

He showed no surprise at the question. Taking a swig of his drink, he creased up his eyes with the effort of some mental calculation and asked, 'When did you come on the scene with Sylvie? I was trying to work it out.'

'Me? What's that got to do with anything?'

'After Easter, was it?'

'June,' I answered reluctantly.

He began his slow nodding again, and did not stop for a long time. 'Yeah,' he said at last, as though he had finally solved the puzzle. 'Yeah.'

Pike reappeared at last with the hotel night manager in tow, and after signing a batch of traveller's cheques and credit card vouchers I took delivery of a thousand pounds in cash.

I plopped the notes onto the table in front of Hayden.

Unhurriedly he leant forward and scooped them up.

'Well?' I demanded.

'Well?' Hayden repeated in the lazy amused manner that appeared to be his stock in trade. 'Where d'you wanna start?'

'The stuff. Where did she get it?'

And still Hayden took his time. 'Can't tell you where she got *everything*. Sylvie had a lot of contacts – you know? But some of the time, back last winter anyway, she had prescriptions. Nicked, I guess. But she never had any trouble with them. Never got thrown out of any chemist or anything. But she was clever about that sort of thing – you know? Used to ring the changes. Sometimes Dartmouth, sometimes Exeter, sometimes Bristol when she was up that way.'

'They were made out to her, the prescriptions?'

'Nah,' he said without hesitation. 'She used to fill in the names herself. She had three of her own to choose from, you know. Mathieson and a couple of married names.' He chuckled, 'Or do I mean divorced names?' Enjoying his own joke for a moment, he finally sauntered on, 'She had two passports anyway, one French, one British, in different names. That way she could always produce ID.' While I was absorbing this he added, 'The prescriptions, she had plenty last winter. Must have had a whole pad of the things. Cost her, I bet. Well, that's what I thought—'

'Cost her?'

'Sure. Junk isn't my scene, you understand. But – yeah, she'd have bought them.'

I was being slow, but I had to understand this. 'You mean, pads get stolen and sold on?'

Deferring to the expert, Hayden tipped an amused glance at Pike.

'They get stolen all the time,' Pike confirmed in his bleak voice. 'Doctors' cars, surgeries. Though the thieves don't get much joy a lot of the time because the chemists are on the lookout. Lists of stolen pads get circulated. The chemists check up on anything suspect.'

Hayden drained his drink and wiggled his glass hopefully. Pike got grudgingly to his feet and took the glass for a refill.

Hayden yawned.

'So?' I urged.

'Yeah, well . . . the prescriptions, they seemed to run out in . . . I guess it must have been Easter time, and then she, ah, started on at me to go to France all the time, to pick up stuff there. But listen, that wasn't my scene. I mean, the occasional little trip, a bit of hash, that's okay, you know what I mean? But regularly, for junk?' He blew disapprovingly through his lips. 'Well, that's asking for it, isn't it? And I've got my reputation to consider.' He angled his head a little, as if to show his best profile. 'One run-in with the customs and I'd never work again. Like, *never*. So I just told her to jump. I told her that wasn't my game. Then . . . I can't be sure, you know? But I think she got her stuff from Bristol. Well . . . Let's put it this way, she never came back from Bristol without quite a stash. That's all I can tell you, really. That's all I ever knew. Sylvie – she was, like, quite tight about those little things. Protecting her sources, you might say.'

I groped back in search of a loose end. 'You were

going to say something just now,' I reminded him. 'Something about the prescriptions . . .?'

But the thought had gone, and neither Pike nor I managed to prompt his memory.

'What about boyfriends, lovers?' I asked. 'Who was she seeing in the early spring?'

Hayden's face took on an odd gloating look. 'There was some bloke, yeah. She saw him all the way through last winter. That's what our deal was, she used my cottage at weekends, like as a retreat, in exchange for, you know, keeping an eye. She came down from Bristol every weekend, hacked wood, built fires, put buckets out to catch the leaks.'

'She was living in Bristol?'

'Sure. Her brother was there.'

'And the lover, who was he?'

'She never told me. No names, no pack drill,' he smirked. '*But* . . .' He paused for dramatic effect. 'I did see him once. He bowled up at the cottage when I was there. Made off smartish when he realised his mistake. Good dresser, smart car – spanking new Mercedes. Money, definitely.'

It wasn't what I had expected.

'Was he local?'

He said with heavy irony, 'That would have been difficult to say, wouldn't it, seeing him like that.'

'What did he look like?'

He made a face. 'Affluent. Oldish. Your average Mercedes owner.' It was hard to tell if he was being deliberately evasive, but in the silence that followed I began to think I had wasted my time and money.

Hayden let me fret a little longer before announcing lightly, 'Saw him again, though.'

I didn't like being strung along, especially by the likes of Hayden. 'Oh yes?' I said harshly.

'Might even be able to place him for you.' He spread his hands like a market trader producing the best goods from the back of the barrow.

'Place him then.'

A look of sly calculation came over Hayden's face, I spotted the light of avarice in his eyes, and with a stab of cold anger I barked, 'Don't even think about it.'

With an expression of injury, Hayden looked around as if to plead his innocence to a wider audience, but behind this extravagant show he was using the time to gauge his position. 'I wasn't thinking about a *thing*,' he protested, laughing to cover his retreat. 'I'm just trying to tell you, that's all.'

'Tell me then.'

'The guy had a boat on the river. I saw him launching a dinghy from the pontoon.'

A small warning sounded in my brain.

Hayden was watching me closely now. 'The dinghy was the tender to a boat called *Ellie Miller*.'

My heart gave a single beat, a thump against my chest. I held on to my expression, I showed nothing in my face, but Hayden, with all the perception of a habitual dissembler had picked something up. 'Someone you know?' he enquired.

'You're sure it was the same man?' I asked, revealing some of my turmoil.

'*Yeah*. It was him all right. And then I went and

422

asked someone at the yacht charter place who he was, and they said he was the local doctor. Seemed pretty sure. Like I said, you should be able to place him, right?'

The blood seemed to burst in my veins, I was filled with a terrible heat. I held tight to my drink to stop it from spilling. Then a miraculous liberating thought struck me, and it was so obvious that I almost laughed. 'Sylvie was his patient. He was probably making a call when he came to the cottage!' And the relief was already rushing through me.

'His patient. Yeah, that would make sense, wouldn't it?' he said knowingly. 'With the prescriptions, I mean. That was what I was going to say before – right at the end something she said made me think she was getting those prescriptions on tap. Like, on request.'

'You're not hearing what I'm saying,' I said, holding on to my temper with difficulty. 'I'm saying he must have gone to the cottage to see Sylvie as a patient. She must have been ill.'

He reflected on this. 'Could be,' he conceded. 'Just one problem.' And he grinned abruptly; he was enjoying himself. 'The doctor had a key.'

I didn't attempt to sleep when I got back to Melton. After going up to check on Ginny I shut myself in the study to sit out the remains of the night in silence and darkness, with a brandy at my elbow and misery in my heart.

The more I tried to make sense of the thoughts that

bumped and veered around my mind, the more the few remaining certainties of my uncertain life seemed to trickle away, and I had the sensation of slipping headlong towards more appalling upheavals and calamities. On leaving Hayden I had been dazed by disbelief and a smarting sense of betrayal, as though on the subject of duplicity I had anything to be proud of. But now in the long quiet hours of the night the incredulity had begun to fade and, coming to terms with Hayden's revelations, I was left with the most terrifying uncertainty of all: What had I really stumbled across? David had been Sylvie's lover, David had deceived me and, it would appear, everyone else: this much seemed inescapable. But what did it mean? It might mean nothing; it might mean everything. It could be nothing more than an extramarital affair, or something so frightening that I couldn't begin to imagine where it might lead without pulling up in an agony of doubt.

Out of long habit part of me rose to David's defence. David, who had suffered my father's disapproval for so much of his life, who had increasingly felt the bitter dissatisfaction of his own failures; David, the eldest but second son, who had somehow never quite managed to pull his life together. Pa had always judged him harshly, and I did not want to do the same. I told myself that nothing terrible had happened, that, like me, he had simply snatched at temptation; that, like me, he had been used and discarded by Sylvie. These were not heinous crimes, yet for David with his thorny pride, they would be enough to account for his silence. I told myself that this was all there was to it. Now and again I even managed to convince myself. But I couldn't entirely rid myself of hideous black thoughts which came screeching at me out of the darkness, like birds out of the night, and then I was seized by such a combination of misery and dread that it was all I could do not to pick up the phone and call David there and then.

At about six I showered and changed and, leaving a note for Ginny, set off into the gloomy dawn.

The road was clear, I was through Totnes just before eight. I did not stop at Furze Lodge but went straight on to Dartmouth. David's car was not in its place outside the surgery, but the receptionist told me he was due in at nine and had a steady stream of appointments until eleven. I left him a curt note, saying I needed to see him urgently, and drove slowly to Dittisham to wait.

Drawing up outside the house I sat in the car, absorbing the silence, wishing it would last. At nine my mobile began to ring: George on his first call of the day. As soon as he had given up I phoned Julia and told her to keep everyone at bay for the morning.

'Do you want me down at Melton?' she asked.

'I think Ginny's all right.'

'Shall I check?'

'No, I'll call her myself.'

'If you're sure.'

Ginny didn't answer the first time I tried, nor the second, and then the line was engaged for a while, and then it didn't answer again. Reading more into this than was good for me, I called Julia back and asked her if she wouldn't mind going down after all.

For a time I sat in the quiet again, then, breaking free of my trance, got out of the car and, taking the key from its ledge in the porch, let myself into the musty hall. I made my way slowly through the house, examining each room with a new and jaundiced eye, as though it might contain traces of the past which I had not previously had the wit to see.

If David had brought Sylvie here, then it must have been soon after Pa's death. No qualms about that then.

Pausing outside the kitchen I remembered how Sylvie had made her way here unhesitatingly, how she had known where to find everything. Had they drunk coffee here together, kissed, made love? I saw them making love everywhere, on floors, on sofas, upright, naked, clothed.

And the study: I remembered the way she had appeared at the french windows, as though she were used to coming through the garden and arriving unannounced.

These fragments of proof gave me great bursts of misery but also a kind of masochistic satisfaction and, unable to stop myself, I trudged up the stairs and stood on the landing, taking mental measurements of the distances to the various doors. Had Sylvie pulled me into David's room because it was fractionally the closest, or out of some perverse desire to take a second brother to the same bed?

I glanced over the shelves by the bed, I opened the drawers of the bedside table and angrily closed them again, not even wanting to think of what I had expected to find there. I stood at the window and looked down the river to where *Samphire* lay at her mooring, and felt an unexpected gratitude to Hayden. At the end of the day, knowledge, however bitter, gives you some sort of grip on the future.

Returning to the study, I remembered the night when Sylvie and I had made love with the curtains undrawn, and the sound I had heard from the terrace, a memory which until last night I had pushed from my mind. Trying to give the sound substance now, it seemed to me that it was a garden chair being accidentally bumped across stone. In a trick of the imagination I saw not Ginny but David stumbling across the chair in the dark.

hearing a car in the drive, I opened the front door and watched David get out and walk towards me. Looking up, his face darkened and he paused in front of me as if to demand what was going on before changing his mind and passing silently into the house. Automatically he made for the study, the room which he, more than anyone, associated with inquisitions and retribution.

I sat at Pa's desk while David pulled a chair away from the wall and, placing it by the french windows, settled himself warily. 'What's up then?'

Now that the moment had come I could only say, 'You and Sylvie.'

In the pause that followed his mouth twitched but his eyes were steady. 'Yes,' he exhaled abruptly. 'So.'

'You don't think you should tell me about it?'

'What do you want to know?'

427

'Everything.'

'I don't think you mean that.'

'Don't bloody tell me what I mean!' I blazed with sudden anger. 'Don't bloody talk *down* to me, David. For once, for *once*' – I splayed a furious hand at him – 'just tell me the bloody truth!'

If my anger had taken me by surprise, David met it impassively. Looking away towards the river, he began in a dispassionate voice, 'I met her about a year ago, down on the quay. Pa wasn't too well, I'd been out to look at *Ellie*. I was stacking the dinghy when Sylvie walked up and said, "You're David." That was it, really. We went for a drink. It started from there. We met at weekends. She was living in Bristol. She'd borrowed this cottage near Totnes – Hayden's cottage. Then in March she moved down to Dittisham, rented a place—' He glanced towards me, 'Well, you know about that. Then she broke it off in, oh . . . about May, I suppose. We got together again briefly, but . . .' His shrug indicated that it hadn't worked out. 'I didn't know about you, I promise. Well, not for a long time. Not until I saw you together on *Ellie*. Can't remember when that was – August some time? But until then I had no idea. Really.' He gave a caustic smile. 'Otherwise I would have warned you.'

Another pause, like darkness. David lifted a shoulder as if to say: Well, that's it.

'Haven't you left rather a lot out?' I said.

He examined my face in the sombre light, searching for my meaning. 'Ahh,' he said heavily. 'You mean, our arrangement?'

'The prescriptions.'

He nodded stoically. 'This was Hayden, was it?' Immediately he dismissed the question as of no importance. 'Yes,' he said with a long sigh, 'it's amazing what one does when one's – how shall I put it? – not thinking too cleverly. Enough to get me struck off ten times over, and then some. At first it was just to *help* her, you understand. One last fix, and then she was going to take the cure. She'd been on a cure just that summer, but it hadn't lasted long. She thought she could control it, you see. Take a hit now and again. You can't, of course – control it. Also she had no real will to stop. She never believed it was doing her any harm. They never do. She didn't think about the future. She thought she could just go on—' He broke off suddenly and his mouth turned down. 'Anyway . . . one thing led to another. She kept asking for more. And I kept handing out. The risk was ludicrous. I got calls from chemists a couple of times, thought there'd be trouble, but somehow nothing ever came of it. Sheer luck. I knew it was madness.'

'So why didn't you stop?'

He raised an eyebrow, and his expression seemed to say: Are you sure you really want to hear this? Reading my determination, he announced bluntly, 'Because I wanted her. It wasn't that I couldn't stop – it was that I didn't want to.' His eyes glittered at the memory. Catching an echo of some powerful and voracious emotion, I felt a tremor of jealousy.

I said sharply, 'And Mary?'

'What about Mary?'

'For God's sake – did she know?'

'If she did, she never mentioned it to me.' He added casually, 'She's never said anything to you?'

'No.' And now I had the feeling he was trying to deflect me. 'You got together again, you said, Sylvie and you?'

'What? Oh yes . . . June. July. She wanted some more scripts. But by then it was what you might call a business arrangement.'

'Business?' And suddenly I was having trouble with my patience again. 'Spell it out for me, David.'

Once more he gave me the do-you-really-want-this look, the raised eyebrow and the down-turned mouth. 'She wanted some drugs, I wanted a good lay. I think that more or less sums it up.'

I couldn't work out if this harsh judgment was designed to punish me or himself. Whatever, there was something in his manner that rang false, and I thought I caught a hint of bitterness.

I asked, 'And this was all the way through June and July?'

'No, no,' he exclaimed, irritated at my dull-wittedness. 'We managed without each other very well, believe me. Sometimes I didn't see her for weeks.' He retorted, 'Really.'

I recognised this display. He was using the blend of intimidation and defiance that he had always employed as a child to try to bluff his way out of trouble. I suspected him then. I suspected that he was lying.

I said tersely, 'You were still seeing her when she died.'

There was a pause while we stared at each other across the expanse of the window. 'No, Hugh,' he said very deliberately. 'And I didn't kill her either.'

'Come on,' I argued with a semblance of control. 'She was going to the boat to meet someone. It wasn't me, so it seems fairly obvious that it must have been you. Because when you think about it, there wasn't anyone else it could have been. You couldn't use the house any more, could you, because I was always turning up there. You couldn't go to her cottage – too many people to see your car outside and Joe hanging about all the time. Too far to Hayden's place. So it had to be the boat, didn't it?'

He watched me gravely without attempting a reply.

'Well? Have I got this wrong?' I demanded stiffly. 'I mean, where did you meet? *Tell* me.'

He looked away again, and still he was silent.

'The boat. *The boat*,' I chanted back at him. And for a moment my throat seized, I couldn't speak. And still he said nothing. '*Christ* . . .' My eyes had misted up, my lips were trembling. 'What happened – did Sylvie try to blackmail you or something? Did she get nasty? Did she go mad? Did *you* go mad? Tell me!'

He was looking out at the river, his eyes screwed up against the light. 'It wasn't like that,' he murmured.

'*Well*? Tell me what it *was* like, for Christ's sake. Tell me something – *anything*.'

He made a mildly dismissive movement of his head, as though any comment would be a waste of time.

I shot to my feet and stood over him, and now I was shaking with rage. 'Tell me why the hell I shouldn't go to the police! Give me one good reason! Just *one*, you bastard.'

He considered this with an air of great weariness. 'For one thing it would be a mistake, because I didn't kill her. For another, it would destroy my career.' He added ironically, 'For what that's worth.'

'I don't give a stuff about your career,' I exploded again. 'What's your goddamned career compared to *Ginny!*'

He looked up at me. 'I'm sorry it's got this far with Ginny, I really am.'

I gave an ugly shout. 'Well, I tell you something – Ginny's not going to prison to save your miserable neck.'

He stood up with an air of infinite dejection. 'I didn't kill her, Hugh.'

'And I'm meant to believe you?'

He gave a distracted nod. 'Yes.'

'Jesus.' I sank back on my seat.

'But listen, Hugh – I'm not sure yet, but I think there's something I might be able to do to help Ginny.'

'Excuse me,' I jeered, '*something you can do?*'

'Yes. But I'll need a bit more time.'

I was momentarily incapable of speech. In his more imperious moments David had always had this ability to reduce me to a state of mute frustration.

'Just give me a bit more time,' he repeated solemnly.

'More time – for *what?*' I burst out at last. 'The only *help* she needs is to get off, for Christ's sake.'

'That's what I meant.'

'Oh, for God's sake get out of here!' I cried, overtaken by a new wave of anger. 'Just bloody get out of my sight.'

Fourteen

To judge by the seating arrangements, the Cumberland board were not expecting a massive turnout. No more than two hundred chairs had been set out in short rows at the far end of one of the hotel's larger conference rooms, giving the effect of emptiness and insignificance, while stacks of spare seats stood idly at the periphery, in the unlikely event of a sudden rush.

George, aided by Julia, was setting up shop outside the door, with piles of Hartford brochures and information sheets for any shareholders who for some reason had not received them through the post. There were also copies of the resolution that I had drafted and formally tabled for the meeting, requiring the Cumberland board to explain why they had not accepted the highest bid.

George looked harassed and downcast, and I guessed that our final tally of proxies hadn't exceeded the discouraging eighteen per cent we had logged last night.

'Press coverage.' George passed me a folder of cuttings.

Most of it was small stuff, paragraphs tucked away on business pages, but one of the tabloids had run a longer piece just that morning, an emotional David and Goliath story in which Cumberland was portrayed as a heartless monolith, needlessly and cruelly consigning a skilled workforce to the scrapheap.

George commented gruffly, 'Every little helps – so they say.'

But we both knew that publicity wouldn't be enough to win us our resolution, let alone the vote of confidence. Nor would the support of the private shareholders who were beginning to trickle in through the doors. The real control lay in the hands of the institutional shareholders, the pension funds and unit trusts whose vast blocks of equity gave them dominant voting power. Knowing George and Alan had spent the whole of the previous day phoning around some of the institutions, I asked, 'Any luck yesterday?'

'A lot said they'd given their proxies to Cumberland.' He shrugged.

'But some might still be uncommitted?'

George gave me a look that said: If only.

Julia handed me an envelope and began to tell us about a pension fund manager she had been in touch with, but recognising the handwriting on the letter I moved to one side and opened it. *Dearest Hugh, I've got all my fingers and toes crossed for you!* Mary had written. *But look – if it's simply a question of more money, please count me in! Probably too late for all that, but if you do need any more, then I'd really like to help. Went to my trustees – yes, I've still got trustees – and found I have bags more to spare than I thought. Up to half a million. I really mean it, Hugh. If it'll make any difference*

435

to winning, it would be the proudest moment of my life. Really! With tons and tons of love, Mary.

My first reaction was profound gratitude; my next sharp suspicion, made all the more mortifying by the affection that had come before. Where had Mary suddenly found such an enormous sum of money? Why had she left the offer so late? In fact what had prompted her to offer it at all? Giving my darkest thoughts full rein, it seemed to me that this could only have come from David, that only David could possibly have this sort of money lying around. Following on from this came a further rush of unwelcome thoughts: that David was trying to buy me off in some way, and that, being him, he was confident of succeeding; alternatively, that in his proud inarticulate way he was simply trying to help and did not like to do it in person. I wasn't sure which idea made me most uncomfortable. Either way, it was shabby to use Mary.

And then again, perhaps the demons in this were all of my own making. Perhaps this offer was exactly what it seemed. Perhaps Mary in her generosity was simply trying to help and had told David nothing. Perhaps I was simply becoming paranoid, like Ginny. Two frightened people, reacting badly. It was an oddly heartening thought.

Thrusting the note into my pocket, I headed back towards the doors to be intercepted by Julia, brandishing her mobile phone. She hissed under her breath, 'Howard.'

I moved out of earshot.

'Hugh?' came the smooth tones. 'Listen, can you spare a few minutes?'

'Is this business or social, Howard?'

'Something we might want to discuss. Something that might be helpful to both of us.'

'You're sure about that?'

'Would I bother you otherwise? I'm upstairs. Suite 223.'

'I'll need to bring George with me.'

'Fine.' Ever the orchestrator, he was already sounding pleased with himself.

George pulled an astonished face when I told him. 'What, *now*? We've only got twenty minutes.'

'That's probably the whole point.'

As we headed for the stairs, George said, 'But what can he want?'

'It'll be an offer of some sort, I imagine.'

'God,' he chuckled nervously. 'A *deal*?'

'A softener, more like. A consolation prize, Howard-style. Which means,' I said caustically, 'that there won't be much in it for us.'

Howard was waiting at the door of the suite. 'Welcome,' he smiled, at his most gracious. He appeared to harbour no animosity towards me over my telephone tirade, but then Howard had always regarded people who got angry with him as having a personality defect.

He waved us to a seat. 'Coffee? No? Are you sure?'

As he went and poured himself a cup at a pace that was deliberately unhurried I could see George beginning to fret over the time, but I knew that

Howard would have calculated it down to the last minute and there was no point in rushing him.

Sinking elegantly into a chair, Howard smiled, 'Well, I must say, you've mounted a most impressive campaign. Very thorough. The shareholders, the press and so on. Excellent stuff.'

George, taking this at face value, said, 'Thanks.'

'Pity it had no hope of success. From your point of view, I mean. But, well – it was hardly to be expected, was it?'

'You've got your fifty per cent, have you?' I asked: the proxies he needed to carry the day.

'Of course,' Howard smiled as though it had always been a foregone conclusion.

I wanted to say: Then why are we here? But I knew better than to ask such an obvious question.

'However . . .' Howard sipped at his coffee and gave us a beneficent gaze. 'The situation has changed somewhat. New considerations have come to light. And, without wanting to go into detail – without being *free* to – suffice it to say that events have shifted to the extent that the board might be prepared to review your bid in a more favourable light.'

Startled, I tried to imagine what could possibly have changed. Donington's share value? As far as I knew it hadn't dropped significantly. Or maybe Cumberland's lawyers had uncovered something they didn't like, some fancy footwork in the small print of Donington's offer.

I could see George sparking with excitement but, deliberately failing to catch his eye, I asked Howard, 'What are the terms?'

'Terms?' Howard echoed with the air of cool surprise he assumed when someone spoiled his timing. 'Oh ... as before,' he stated as though this should have been obvious. 'As before. With an adjustment for the differential between the two bids, of course. To make good our shortfall. You know how it is,' he beamed. 'Duty to the shareholders.'

I had known there would be a catch. 'But our bid was as good as Donington's,' I pointed out. 'If not better.'

'Ah, but you have to allow for the appreciation of the Donington shares. A steady-growth company. We were banking on an annual stock appreciation of at least seven per cent.'

This was rubbish. No one could bank on steady growth at the moment, particularly in china and glass, which had always been a volatile performer in times of economic uncertainty. It was a load of nonsense, but then Howard knew this as well as I did.

'This *notional* differential,' I said. 'What did you have in mind, *allowing* for the fact that our offer is already pitched at, and maybe even beyond, the maximum value of the company? *Allowing* for the fact that we couldn't justify going to our backers and asking them to invest a penny more? *Allowing* for the fact that we have precisely ten minutes to sort this out? *Allowing* for the fact that brinkmanship goes both ways?'

Howard grinned quietly. He liked nothing better than a good fight. 'Well, we're prepared to compromise, to forego some of this *notional* gain, as you put it. We're prepared to settle for half a million.'

I felt a pull in my stomach, a chill of disbelief. I told myself that it was a coincidence. I told myself that stranger things had happened. I tried to keep calm, to conceal the resentment and suspicion that had rushed into my face.

'Can't be done,' I said.

'Oh?' Howard affected surprise. 'We'd give you two weeks to arrange the funding.'

'Not at that price.'

Howard looked pained. 'Couldn't square any less with the board. Or indeed the shareholders. The figure's been agreed, you see, as the most generous we could possibly offer. It's not open to negotiation.'

'There's no more money.' And the violence in my tone made them stare at me.

George ventured at last, 'Perhaps we could have a few minutes?'

'Surely.' Howard finished his coffee and pulled himself lazily to his feet. 'I'll be next door.' Scooping up his mobile, he disappeared through a connecting door.

'It's extortion,' I protested before George could say a word. 'Blackmail. And we're not going to pay a single penny.'

George began to make hasty calculations on his notepad. 'But all this publicity might make it easier to raise the money—'

'It's not the money, George, it's the principle!'

George threw me a baffled look, then another, as if he really couldn't work out what I was talking about. 'Maybe they'll come down a bit.'

'But we'd still be paying over the odds, damn it!'

'Yes, but not much. And this is going to be the end of it, isn't it? They won't be able to go back on their word a second time, will they? We'll be home and dry.'

He was right, but I wasn't in any mood to hear the truth, and while he continued to play with numbers I paced up and down the room, nursing a sense of betrayal and impotence, made all the worse for knowing that my feelings were irrelevant.

'The additional interest wouldn't kill us,' George announced. 'But look, we should grab Alan and get him to go through this—'

'No time. That's the whole point, for heaven's sake. We have no time.' I stopped by the window and stared out into the featureless London street, and in that moment the last of my resentment trickled away like so much useless energy, and I gave in to the inevitable. Yet if I had been outmanoeuvred somewhere along the line, if I had been set up, I told myself that I had not yet been bought, and if anyone thought otherwise they would quickly discover the difference.

'We've got the money,' I admitted.

'*What?*'

'We have the promise of the money. A private investor.'

'*Good God!* You mean— Then—'

As if on cue a soft knock announced Howard's return. 'Don't mean to hurry you,' he said in his most honeyed tones.

'Just supposing we were able to reach an

441

agreement now,' I said immediately, 'what would happen downstairs?'

'Ah . . . The board would announce that we were reconsidering your bid in every expectation of reaching a favourable outcome.'

'And Donington?'

'By implication, that bid would have run into difficulties, wouldn't it?'

'And our resolution?'

'You'd want to withdraw it, I imagine.'

I turned on my heel and headed for the door. I waited at the top of the stairs for Howard to catch up. 'Half a million is a ludicrous sum,' I said as we started down.

He gave a small laugh. 'That was our valuation, Hugh.'

'Don't give me that crap, Howard. It's just a face-saver, isn't it? A way for your board to go back to the shareholders and say they're getting them a better deal. Anything less than half a million would make you look stupid, wouldn't it? Isn't that more like it? So what's happened to Donington, Howard? Have they pulled out altogether? Have they discovered they can't do business with you?'

'Nothing like that,' he asserted confidently. 'They still have their hat very much in the ring.' Howard was such an excellent liar that it was impossible to tell if this statement bore any relation to the truth.

We halted short of the conference room, and still I was bothered by the fact that I didn't understand what the hell was really going on.

Howard lifted both palms questioningly. 'Are we agreed?'

'No going back,' I warned.

'*Hardly,*' he exclaimed with a look of injury.

I held out my hand. 'You take my hand at your peril, you shit.'

Grasping it, he smiled with something like affection. 'I knew we could do business, Hugh.'

Watching him walk away, I had the sensation of having travelled a long way only to return to the same point. Howard's deviousness did at least have a comforting familiarity.

Julia caught me on the way into the meeting. 'Two unit trust managers have turned up!' she whispered excitedly. 'One I've been talking to all week. He introduced himself just now and pointed out another one. If two have actually bothered to turn up, they can't have given their proxies! And there might be more. Maybe some pension fund managers. I contacted all the unions, you know, every single one. There might be a whole *slab* of votes going begging.'

Maybe that was it. Maybe Howard had lied to me. Maybe the Cumberland board hadn't got the vote in the bag. Maybe we could have won the day on the no-confidence vote and saved ourselves half a million pounds.

'Maybe a lot of things,' I murmured to Julia.

Going into the meeting, I touched the note in my pocket and Ginny's words floated reproachfully into my mind. *Mary isn't Howard's sister for nothing.*

*

Grainger's chambers were situated in a dark building overlooking a secretive courtyard of the Inner Temple, just beyond the soot-stained buttresses of the church. The recessed doorway with its ladder of names reminded me of my old staircase at Trinity, but once inside all resemblance to college was dispelled by the lavish carpets and speckling of spotlights, the rag-rolled walls and confident glow of the reproduction furniture.

Grainger's room had extravagantly draped curtains over matching roman blinds, large Impressionist prints, a scattering of bulbous table lamps with pale silk shades, and a large gas log fire. The effect was of a drawing room seconded for office use, and only the wall of legal tomes behind us and the oversize desk ahead of us with its stacks of papers and box-files gave the lie to the mood of elegant inactivity.

Tingwall was already there and kissed Ginny warmly on both cheeks.

'Mrs Wellesley.' Grainger bowed over Ginny's hand and showed her to a chair at a narrow table which abutted the giant desk in a T-shape. Tingwall and I found seats opposite her, while Grainger ostentatiously took his place behind the desk, like a lecturer facing his students.

As soon as the coffee had been poured Grainger fastened his eyes on Ginny and said without preamble, 'We're faced with a difficult decision, Mrs Wellesley. I expect Mr Tingwall has explained something of it to you?'

'Yes,' Ginny replied in a voice so low it was barely audible. She had been looking tired for some days, despite – or possibly because of – the sleeping pills she had been taking with increasing regularity.

'Well, I would like to explain it to you again, if that meets with your approval.' The formality of Grainger's address, the charcoal pinstripe three-piece with the gold watch chain, the calmly intertwined hands, the neat greying hair and patrician features, all served to create an air of effortless authority which was entirely intentional, and, according to Tingwall, entirely appropriated. Apparently Grainger's grand style and Eton drawl obscured a childhood of poverty and deprivation as the son of an unemployed York-shire coal-miner. I didn't care for his chosen persona, but I couldn't blame him for it either. He depended for his living on impressing his clients and intimidating his opponents, although I suspected that he didn't always achieve them in that order.

'Mrs Wellesley,' he began fluidly, 'the decision is a difficult one because it involves risk, and however clear-sighted we try to be, however critically we approach the facts, it will be impossible to assess those risks with any degree of accuracy. All I can do is set out the situation as I see it, explain what is involved in the two principal strategies which are open to you, and give you my opinion as to your best course. After that, the decision must be yours. I cannot make it for you.' In the seclusion of his chambers Grainger's voice, while maintaining the affectation which had so annoyed me at the bail hear-ing, had lost its hunting-field stridency and taken on an intimate almost melodic tone.

Ginny nodded, 'I understand.'

Grainger assumed an expression of exaggerated concentration. 'Now, our *first* option is to offer *no* defence at the committal stage and let the case go unopposed to crown court. This means a wait of perhaps six months and a full hearing before a judge and jury. Of course, in those six months circumstances could change and cause the prosecution to alter its stance, or indeed for us to alter our position in some way, but let's assume for the moment that we will be pleading not guilty to the charge as it stands – that is, to a charge of murder. The first thing to understand is that this is an extremely serious charge and that if you are found guilty you will go to prison for a long time.' His face took on a suitably grave aspect, his voice resonated sympathetically, and I couldn't help thinking what a performer he was, how he relished every moment.

'The second thing to know is that a jury is a thoroughly unpredictable body, and there is no determining in advance how they may or may not be swayed by any particular piece or body of evidence. The only sure thing about a jury is their ability to surprise.' A pause to allow us to absorb what he intended to be a daunting truth. 'Now, for us the *advantage* of letting the case go unchallenged to crown court is that the prosecution will not have the chance to test our defence in advance, nor indeed to appreciate and shore up the weaknesses in their own case. We will, so to speak, have kept our cards close to our chest. That way we can hope to spring a few surprises on the opposition' – his eyes glinted at the thought – 'to discredit a witness or two, to work away at the flaws in their case, without giving them too much warning of our strategy. For the defence advocate this is an important weapon and one he is loath to give away without good reason.'

Ginny broke the short silence that followed. 'I was wondering . . .'

When she failed to continue Grainger prompted briskly, 'Yes, Mrs Wellesley?'

'Would I give evidence?'

'That is something we would not decide until much nearer the time. It is something which would require very careful consideration. Though it is possible, just possible, that we might decide against it.'

'Against . . .' Ginny echoed with what might have been a touch of relief. Blinking rapidly, she said, 'Sorry – I interrupted.'

Grainger smiled faintly and rearranged his hands into an elegant display of interlaced fingertips. 'Now, for the *second* option,' he drawled. 'The second option is to defend the case at committal stage with the object of getting the case thrown out before it ever gets to crown court. This means going for what is termed an old-style committal. Here all the evidence is brought before, usually, a stipendiary magistrate sitting alone, the important witnesses appear in person, the evidence is open to challenge under cross-examination. Clearly the *only* reason for choosing this option is if you think you have a good chance of persuading the magistrate that there is no case to answer – *no case at all*. He must be persuaded that the prosecution's evidence is so insubstantial or unreliable that at crown court no reasonable jury, properly directed, would be likely to return a verdict of guilty. Lack of reliable evidence is *sufficient* in itself for the case to be stopped, *but'* – he raised a finger – 'if the bench can also be persuaded that we have a valid defence then clearly our chances become that much stronger.'

He raised his eyebrows at Tingwall. 'Now, what we have, do we not, are some promising developments.'

Taking his cue eagerly, Tingwall's eyes darted back and forth. 'I took a bit of a gamble. Armstrong – our fingerprint expert – asked if he could talk to the prosecution's expert. Apparently it's quite common when experts of this calibre disagree for them to what they quaintly call "compare notes". Armstrong said it's done to avoid wasting court time, but – well, perhaps they prefer to avoid looking incompetent as well. Anyway, I told him to go ahead, and the upshot of it was that Armstrong gave the prosecution's man chapter and verse on where he thought he'd gone wrong, and the chap went back and had another look at his opinion' – he paused for effect – 'and he's *conceded* on one of the points of similarity.' He tightened his lips as though he didn't trust himself not to break into a grin and give too much away. 'Which means that the prosecution won't be able to use him as a witness because fifteen points of similarity between two prints are not enough!'

Grainger said smoothly, 'We can't of course rule out the possibility that the prosecution will find another expert or two to back them up.'

Tingwall allowed this reluctantly. 'It's *possible.*'

'But let us assume for the *moment* that the Crown is unable to present any fingerprint evidence whatsoever.' Grainger lifted his head to the thought. 'Then we have a situation where the prosecution would be left without any forensic evidence to link us to the scene of the crime. None at all. I need hardly say that this would improve our situation considerably. *However* . . .' He slid his elbows onto the desk and clasped his hands under his chin: his cautionary look. 'Cases can and do get sent up to the crown court on non-forensic evidence alone. That's the first point. Second, the prosecution will still have this eyewitness of theirs.' He picked up a batch of stapled papers and, hooking some half-moon glasses onto his nose, leafed through them. 'It is impossible to tell from a witness statement how a witness will perform in court, how convincing he will be, but if we are to take this statement at face value it would seem that the witness is confident in his identification of Mrs Wellesley. He is saying' – Grainger skimmed the lines – 'that he was by the river on the Saturday afternoon of the weekend in question, at about five, and that he saw this woman get into a dinghy and set off across the water, and that he recognised that woman as Virginia Wellesley. He recognised her because apparently . . .' His eyes darted over the pages again. 'Apparently he had worked at Dittisham House as a gardener some years ago and knows all the family by sight.'

Astonished, I tried to think who it could be. 'Old Gordon?'

Grainger flipped back to the first page. 'His name is . . . Gordon Latimer.'

'Old Gordon,' I affirmed. 'He must be seventy-five, eighty, if he's a day.'

'Age is not yet a barrier to providing evidence,' Grainger commented drily.

'But surely his eyesight can't be too good—'

'It would be pointless to conject on that until we have the opportunity for cross-examination,' Grainger argued firmly. 'For the moment we must look at this statement as it stands, and I have to say that in my *opinion*, unless the witness is manifestly unreliable, it is likely that his evidence will be sufficient to send the case to trial. You see—' He removed his spectacles in a deft movement that was so reminiscent of David that for an instant I had the strange sensation of facing my brother. 'In your statement to the police, Mrs Wellesley, you said that you went to the boat only once during the weekend – on the *Sunday*. There is no mention of going on the Saturday. So we are left with two options. Either we deny the eyewitness's version of events, which will leave us in a his-word-against-ours situation. Or we accept his evidence and offer an explanation as to *why* we went to the boat on the *Saturday* and *why* we failed to tell the police about it.' He made a neat gesture, a small overturning of the hand. 'You appreciate the problem?'

'I explained,' Ginny said. 'I told . . .' And she indicated Tingwall.

'Indeed,' Grainger said smoothly. 'I have read your account of events, Mrs Wellesley. I have read it very carefully indeed. However, if we are going to say that we went out to the boat on the day of the murder and found the body and disposed of it into the water then we face great difficulties. *One*,' he began remorselessly, 'why didn't we report the finding of the body at the time? Two: if we are going to admit to the disposing of the body, then this is going to cast us in an extremely unfortunate light which will undoubtedly do us very great damage. After all, what motive could we have for committing this deliberate and dangerous act if it wasn't to protect ourself or someone extremely close to us?' He left this thought in the air for a second. 'Three: if we say we were trying to protect our husband, only to discover that he was miles away at the time and couldn't have done it, then what suspects are the jury left with? Who are they meant to cast as the murderer?' This, too, hung in the silence for a moment. 'Four: not to put too fine a point on it, Mrs Wellesley, are we likely to be believed?'

Ginny flinched slightly and looked down at her hands before nodding readily. 'Yes, I see the problem . . .'

'If there was a reasonable explanation for your presence on the river on the Saturday,' Grainger reflected, 'and a reasonable explanation for your having failed to mention it to the police, then we *might* think about putting that forward. But I fear that to put forward your account of events as it stands without any evidence to back it up is . . .' He inhaled delicately. 'Well, it is not likely to be the most rewarding approach. You understand what I'm saying, Mrs Wellesley? You see the difficulties?'

If I had been harbouring any hopes of a way out for Ginny they evaporated then. With a stab of alarm

451

I realised that her situation was bleak, that, even without the fingerprint, the evidence was still stacked against her.

I asked Grainger, 'What *is* our defence then?'

The eyes dropped languidly but when they came up again they were very sharp. 'From what we have so far it would seem to me that our most effective defence would be character-led. The impossibility of someone as respectable, virtuous and fragile as Mrs Wellesley committing such a heinous crime; how her life has been exemplary, etcetera etcetera; how it would have been completely out of character for her to hurt a fly; how she, a chronic asthmatic, was seen to suffer no anxiety or nerves or other ill-effects at the time of the crime, and indeed appeared perfectly normal in every respect. Your brother, Mr Wellesley, will be an excellent witness in that regard, having seen both of you that Saturday evening. Then, on the practical side, if Mrs Wellesley had committed this terrible crime, why was she not covered in blood? Indeed, how could she have appeared later that evening without so much as a bloodstain on her? You will attest, Mr Wellesley, as to how normal and indeed immaculate she looked. And so on, and so on. In this way we would hope to appeal to both the hearts and the minds of the jury, we would hope to cast some doubt on the evidence of the eyewitness. We would *chip* away. We would be going for the reasonable doubt. And don't forget – that's all we need: reasonable doubt.'

Tingwall piped up, 'The old-style committal, are you ruling that out then?'

'We have to balance the likely benefits against the more certain costs,' Grainger ventured with an air of great sagacity. 'It all hinges on this eyewitness. If we want to gamble on his unreliability – and I use the word "gamble" advisedly – then we should go for the old-style committal. The stakes would be high. If he turned out to be an uncertain witness, we stand to gain everything – the total collapse of the Crown's case. But if he turned out to be an unassailable witness then we would gain very little – at the great expense of having revealed much of our defence. A risky business indeed. The *alternative* is to play safe. To keep our cards close to our chest, to hope to catch the prosecution off-guard, and to go for the hearts and minds of a jury in the way I described – in which case we should wait.'

'So what's your advice?' I asked.

He tapped his fingers together while he thought about it. 'It's hard to give such a thing as *advice* when one is dealing with a key eyewitness who is by definition an unknown quantity. However, going by the witness statement . . .' He looked upwards as though searching for a last drop of inspiration. '. . . my instinct – and that's another word I use advisedly – my *instinct* would be to let it go to trial. Trust to the twelve good men and women, and maintain our element of surprise.'

I asked, 'When do we have to make up our minds?'

Grainger addressed Tingwall. 'Perhaps you would like to discuss the matter further with Mrs Wellesley, come back to me with any questions, and perhaps we can make a decision in the next week or so?'

We all stood up and Grainger moved fluidly to open the door. Ginny paused beside Grainger and said in an undertone, 'I have one question.' She frowned over the thought. 'If Old Gordon is a good witness, if he's going to be absolutely certain that he saw me, then . . . wouldn't I do better to plead guilty?'

'Absolutely not,' I protested over the taut silence which followed.

Grainger observed Ginny for a long moment. 'In some cases a guilty plea to a lesser charge can prove the best course. But, Mrs Wellesley' – he fixed her with cold eyes – 'only *you* can decide if this option is open to us.'

'Why on earth did you say that?' I demanded, taking an aggressive weave through the traffic.

Ginny looked ahead, her profile unreadable. 'Because in the end it might be best.'

'But you can't plead guilty to something you didn't do. It's ridiculous.'

'It could be the least bad thing to do. You heard what he said.' And there was a nervy finality in her voice, an attempt to shut me out.

'The least bad thing. For Christ's sake, Ginny – how can you even *think* of it?' I kept glancing across at her but she didn't reply. 'Promise me you won't even think of it.'

'But Old Gordon was there,' she argued finally. 'He saw me all right. He even nodded to me. We were just feet apart. He's not going to be mistaken in court.'

'Ginny, for *heaven's sake* – it's still early days yet.

Anything could happen. All sorts of things might turn up. I don't know – witnesses, somebody who . . . somebody who . . .' I broke off in sudden misery, knowing I couldn't put the problem of David off any longer. I had spent most of the last two days persuading myself that there was no point in dragging him into our nightmare, that he had nothing to contribute to Ginny's case. Yet his story had left out too much, the gaps and evasions had left me with the wretched suspicion that he had given me something less than the truth.

Grasping some of my turmoil, Ginny had turned to look at me. I hadn't told her about David, partly because I'd been coming to terms with it, partly because the implications of what he'd told me had frightened me too much. 'Listen, something's come up,' I began unhappily. 'I didn't have the chance to tell you before. Well – I *did*,' I admitted, 'but I couldn't, I was feeling too bloody sick about it, too . . . The thing is' – and my throat tightened, I could hardly say it – 'I wasn't the only one having an affair with Sylvie.' I felt a fresh surge of incredulity. '*David* was. David was having a great big affair with Sylvie. All the way through last winter and most of the summer too. They used to meet on the boat – some of the time, anyway. And I think—' I had to force the words out: 'I think he was on the boat that day. At least he didn't deny it, for Christ's sake! I think he was there, and I think – oh *shit!*' And suddenly all my emotions shot to the surface and I couldn't see the road, it had become so blurred.

'Stop,' Ginny begged, casting nervous glances at the speeding traffic. 'Stop, *please.*'

I drew into the kerb amid a storm of protesting horns. I pulled out a handkerchief and rubbed it furiously across my eyes.

'*David?*' Ginny echoed as though she'd only just understood what I was saying. 'All through the winter?'

'The summer too.'

She digested this. 'It was serious then.'

'Serious? Well,' I scoffed, 'I don't think it was *love* exactly. From what he told me, more like lust. Lust and drugs. He used to supply her with drugs.' I had made it sound sordid, but then maybe I had intended to. 'He swears there was no more to it, he swears it was just an affair, he says it fizzled out. All I bloody know is that they met on the boat regularly and he didn't bloody deny he was there that day. He didn't – *Christ*, I don't know!' I suppressed a fresh burst of emotion. 'If he's lied to me I'll bloody kill him.' And even as I said it I felt the old ache of responsibility, the old instinct to defend him.

Ginny was looking blankly ahead. 'Tell me,' she murmured in a reminiscent tone, 'what was so special about her? What was it that made you both forget everything – everybody – else?'

I blew my nose savagely, I took my time but in the end I could only say, 'I don't know.' I added, 'But perhaps that was it, perhaps it was the very fact that she was impossible to know, that she was anything you wanted her to be. She gave this great impression of freedom, of anything being possible.'

Ginny gave an ironic murmur as if to say: And I didn't, I suppose; I was the one who held you back.

'And the sex?' she asked calmly. 'Was that especially terrific?'

There are some truths that must never be told. Bracing myself for the lie, I replied, 'I think it was like they say – it's the secretiveness of these things that gives them an edge, the danger of discovery. So, in that way – yes, it was exciting, I suppose.'

'She didn't do anything amazing that I didn't do?'

'No,' I said, trying to push pictures of Sylvie at her most adventurous and uninhibited from my mind. 'Nothing like that.'

'*David*.' Turning the idea over in her mind again, she shook her head. 'He always seemed so – immune. So unemotional. Well – she must have had something.'

I thought: What she had was allure without conscience.

Ginny took a puff on her inhaler and coughed a few times. A new phalanx of traffic roared past and the noise seemed to invade the car. I restarted the engine and pulled out.

Ginny asked unsteadily, 'So you think that . . .?'

'I don't know what to think!'

She kept looking at me. 'What will you do?'

Making up my mind, I said, 'I'll go and see him.'

'And then?'

'And then I have no idea!' I answered sharply, not wanting to imagine what would happen to David's life if he were interviewed by the police.

She was quiet for a time, then: 'Don't assume too much, will you?'

Jerking my head round, I almost jumped a red light. 'What do you mean?'

'Don't think the worst.'

'I'm not thinking anything!' I exclaimed, feeling a dart of indignation because she had touched on the truth.

As we came up the drive in the twilight the figure of Julia appeared at the front door with three brilliantly coloured helium balloons in one hand and a bottle of champagne in the other. She waved them energetically and called out to us, 'The deal's been done!' Then with upstretched arms, in loud theatrical tones as if announcing it to the whole county: 'Hartford is yours!'

'Good God,' I laughed uncertainly.

'The most deserved event of the year!' And she hugged me enthusiastically, champagne, balloons and all. 'George just called. It's in the bag!' She went to embrace Ginny. *'And . . .'* She made another grandiose gesture, a flourish of both arms. 'You have exchanged contracts on the house. It was sold at three this afternoon. I tell you – it's all happening!'

I smiled because everyone else was smiling, and because deep down I did feel glad: glad for George and everyone else at Hartford, glad for Ginny because she could finally get to grips with the move, and, if I thought about it, glad for myself, though, in the shadow of everything else that was going on, the pleasure emerged as a rather pale and inconsequential emotion.

David's surgery said he was out on a call, so I left a message on his pager, and then, with some hesitation, tried Furze Lodge.

Mary answered. 'I gather hearty congratulations are in order!' she cried. 'I'm *so* delighted, Hugh! What a triumph! You must be thrilled!'

'I am. All thanks to you, Mary.'

'Well . . . I'm proud to be part of it all, Hugh. *Proud*. And I know you'll make a success of it. I never had any doubts.'

'I'll do my best.'

'You must be over the moon!'

'Yes.'

Her tone shifted. 'You don't *sound* very happy.'

'I'm just incredibly tired, that's all. Hasn't sunk in yet.' I tried to relax my voice as I said, 'Is David around tonight?'

'Tonight? Hang on . . . The diary, the diary.' She made searching noises. 'Here we are . . . He's in after seven-thirty. In theory anyway.'

'If you speak to him, can you tell him I need to see him?'

'What – tonight?'

'I should be with you about eight.'

A short pause. 'Can I say what it's about?' And her voice was taut with curiosity.

'Oh – just—' I said the first thing that came into my head. 'A legal thing.'

'To do with the buyout?'

Feeling cornered, I said, 'Pa's estate, actually.'

'Pa's *estate?*' She didn't try to hide her surprise. 'And it's urgent?'

'I want to get it out of the way.'

'But you sound so grim, Hugh. Is there something the matter? Not Ginny, I hope?'

'No. No, really.'

'Well, if you don't want to tell me . . .'

'Nothing to tell,' I said stubbornly.

Her reproach hung in the air. 'You'll have some supper at least?' she said.

'No, Mary.'

'I'll tell David you're coming then.' And when she rang off her tone contained a note of faint injury.

I stayed long enough to make a quick congratulatory call to George, who from the sound of it was holding a party for the entire Hartford staff, and to glance through the mail and messages, which Julia had laid out in order of importance. I skimmed the letters until I came to an unopened envelope marked Strictly Private. It was from Jones. I sat down and read it quickly, then again more carefully. '. . . *nothing has happened to change my original opinion . . . she has developed severe paranoid delusions with marked persecutory tendencies . . . increasingly retreating into unreality . . . convincing herself of plots, including the notion that I am opposed to her and scheming to give evidence against her. I am concerned that if she continues to refuse medication she may suffer a major crisis . . .*'

With a chill in my heart, I read the letter a third time before locking it away in a drawer.

Charged with a new sense of urgency, I went through to the sitting room to find Ginny.

She looked up from her conversation with Julia. 'You're going now? It wouldn't be better to wait until tomorrow?'

'No. No, I must go now.'

She tilted her head to be kissed.

I asked, 'You'll be all right?' Feeling traitorous, I examined her expression for signs of impending crisis.

Sensing this or something close to it, Ginny frowned, 'I'll be fine.'

'I'll bag a bed for the night, if that's all right,' Julia announced from the far side of the room. 'Not safe on the roads.' She raised her glass and cast me a meaningful look.

Ginny got up suddenly and followed me into the hall. 'You won't forget,' she breathed nervously.

'What about?'

'About keeping an open mind.'

'You make me feel that I'm being unreasonable,' I said accusingly. 'For Christ's sake, Ginny, somebody killed Sylvie!'

She dropped her eyes. 'Yes.' She kissed me again and her lips were cold against my cheek.

'He's been delayed. Some emergency.' Mary closed the door behind me. 'Come and have a large drink. You must be exhausted.'

She led the way into the drawing room and threw open the drinks cupboard.

'Whisky,' I said. 'Please.'

She poured a glass and, bringing it over, came up

very close and smiled up into my face. 'Now what on earth's this about?' she asked. 'What's the matter?'

'The matter?'

'Why you're here.'

'I told you.'

'Come on.' She cast me a reproving smile that suggested I could do better than that.

I exhaled unhappily. 'It's rather complicated, Mary.'

'You can tell me, surely,' she said coaxingly. 'David and I have no secrets.'

I felt like saying: Everyone has secrets. Instead I murmured, 'In that case he can tell you himself, can't he?' I hadn't meant to sound dismissive, I raised my hand as if to take it back, but a purposeful expression had already settled over Mary's face. Taking my hand, she led me to a chair by the fireside and, pulling up a stool, sat facing me, knee to knee, as she had done all those weeks ago at Dittisham House. Recalling my uninhibited outpourings about Sylvie, I felt an abrupt and belated vulnerability, a sense of having disclosed too much.

'Hugh . . .' She flashed me one of her warmest smiles. 'You're very dear to me, you know. After David and the children . . . well, you're probably the most *precious* person in the whole world to me. I want you to be all right, I want you to be happy, I want you and Ginny to be over this whole ghastly business.' The smile again, which somehow failed to illuminate her heavy features. 'But Hugh darling' – a dipping of the voice – 'it would be quite wrong of you to think that David has the answer to your problems.' Her avid eyes searched my face to see if I had grasped her message.

She had caught me totally off-balance. 'My problems? I don't understand,' I stammered, having a suspicion that I might understand rather too well.

She gave me an appraising look and began again. 'Hugh darling – I believe you have ideas about David that are quite mistaken.'

'Do I?'

'*Indeed* you do,' she said firmly. Then, disdainfully: 'Oh, he got waylaid by that woman' – she gave a scornful laugh – 'if that's the right expression. He had his head turned – but then I don't need to tell *you* about that. But that's *all*, Hugh.' She shook her head emphatically. 'That's *all*.'

I stared at her. 'You knew?'

'Of course,' she declared with a touch of pride. 'All that stuff about a wife being the last to know? Well, I knew immediately. I may be many things, but I'm not stupid. There were a thousand things.' She gave a tiny snort. 'I knew.'

'You never said anything?'

'Oh *no*. The thing was bound to burn itself out quickly enough. She was such a user, wasn't she? Off to the next man, off to the next meal ticket. I knew she'd disappear sooner or later.' She gave a dismissive shrug. 'And I was right. She ditched him, didn't she? Oh, he was upset for a while, went around looking like a whipped dog, but it was just his pride, wasn't it? Feeling his age, needing to know he could still *pull the chicks*' – she used the expression derisively, with a roll of the eyes – 'all that stuff. He was over it in no time. I knew he would be. But Hugh—' she leant forward, arms on knees, eyes locked on mine '—that's all it was. He doesn't deserve to have his career ruined, his life wrecked. He doesn't.'

I felt a terrible tension, a warring of instincts and loyalties. I screwed up my face and managed to say, 'But *someone* was on the boat that day.'

She gave me a soft pitying look. 'Not David, Hugh. Couldn't have been. He was seeing patients all morning, and then he had lunch with me, and then he went to a partners' meeting which lasted most of the afternoon.' She was very gentle with me now. 'There wasn't a moment of his day which wasn't accounted for.'

Part of me tried to accept this, but another confused part of me wanted to shout: But you're bound to say that, aren't you?

'I know the way it must look to you,' Mary conceded with the same patient note of understanding, 'but I *promise* you – he wasn't there. He couldn't have been there.'

I can't have looked terribly convinced because a spark of exasperation passed over her face and she argued with more determination, 'You would be ruining his life, Hugh! And for what? For an *affair*. With someone like *that*. It's too ghastly. Too – unfair. Don't repay me this way, Hugh – *please*.'

I felt a sudden coldness. 'Repay you?'

She dropped her eyes and fanned her fingers as if to withdraw the remark. 'Just promise me,' she said, returning her gaze to mine. 'Promise me you won't ruin his life – *our* lives – for *nothing*.'

I thought of Ginny, I thought of everything we had been through, and I hardened my heart. 'I can't promise that, Mary. I just can't.'

A succession of violent emotions passed over Mary's face, her features seemed to swell. Finally she said in a voice that trembled with feeling, 'I've gone out on a limb for you, Hugh. I've protected you, supported you, *lied* for you. Don't do this to me. Don't repay me this way.'

'If it's a question of repayment,' I said tightly. 'You can keep the money. I don't care about the money.'

She threw me a furious look. 'It's not the *money*, for God's sake.'

We glared at each other, separated by the depth of our misunderstanding.

'*Lied*,' I echoed as her words came back to me. 'I'm sorry you feel you had to *lie* for me as well.'

'Not for *you*.'

'Who for then?'

She shook her head, as though she had already said too much. 'Leave it. Please. Let's just leave it.'

But something in her manner drew me forward, a suggestion of momentous revelations, and I was filled with a strange beating fear. 'You can't say something like that and expect me to ignore it.'

She kept shaking her head. 'If only you could understand that David wasn't involved. If only you could *believe* me, then—' Her eyes sparkled with unshed tears. I had never seen her upset before.

'Mary, don't.'

'I'm sorry,' she said, pulling herself together with an effort. 'I didn't mean to . . .' She fumbled in her sleeve for a handkerchief. 'But Hugh – promise me, please.'

'I can't do that, Mary. I can't promise something like that.'

She gave a shudder that shook her whole body. 'How I wish I didn't have to do this!' she cried. 'I never wanted to have to *say* anything – ever! Ever! I wanted to *save* you that at least. Oh Hugh, how I wish—' She sniffed hard and wiped her eyes, and when she looked up again her makeup had run, a streak of blue that leached down one cheek. 'And, believe me, you *must* believe me, it's *not* an either-or thing – I would *hate* you to think that! It's not as if I'd *ever* go to the police! I'd rather die! I'd rather die than tell them! But Hugh – you *have* to understand that it wasn't David! You *have* to realise!'

As she made her circuitous way towards the point, my sense of foreboding grew.

Mary said again, 'I'd never tell! Never!' Calming herself visibly, she dabbed her eyes again. 'In fact, I'd lie to them again. I'd lie to them every time.' She took a sharp breath. 'I did lie, you see. I lied to them straight away. When David and I gave our finger-prints to the police, they asked me about the day the woman died, whether I knew anything, whether I'd seen anything. And I said I hadn't. But – it wasn't true.' She paused and looked at me in anguish, as if we might yet escape this moment of truth. 'I saw Ginny, you see. I was at Dittisham House with Mrs Perry, and I saw Ginny.'

I kept staring at her.

'I was up in David's old room,' she began slowly. 'I looked out at the river and I saw a dinghy tied up to *Ellie*. I knew it couldn't be David – he was at the partners' meeting. I thought maybe it was someone from the yard. There were some binoculars there by the window. I was looking through them when I saw someone come up on deck.' She gave a tiny shudder. 'It was the woman. There was no mistaking her – the long hair, the tight clothes. It was definitely her. I thought – well, you can imagine. I thought she was hanging around in the hope of seeing David. I thought she was trying to get him back or something. I was ready to get hopping mad. But then – *then* – oh, *Hugh*.' Mary's face crumpled, she clenched her lips together, when she finally spoke her tone rose in despair. 'Ginny . . . came. In a dinghy. She . . . rowed up to the boat. She rowed up to the boat and . . . they talked, she and . . . *her*. For a minute or so. Then—' Her mouth moved but no words came.

'Then?'

She forced herself on. 'Then . . . Ginny climbed on board. And . . . they talked some more. I think they were— No,' she suppressed some unspoken thought, 'no, I couldn't tell from that distance. No – they *talked*. And then . . .' Each word was dragged from her with terrible effort. 'Then . . . they both . . . went down below. Into the cabin.'

My mind was cold and clear, but my imagination was blurry. I saw the two figures climbing down the companionway, but they remained a long way off, I

467

couldn't bring them into focus. I said, 'You're sure it was Ginny?'

Mary nodded sadly.

'From so far away?'

'Hugh, believe me, she was the *last* person I was expecting to see. I couldn't believe it at first, I kept looking. But that hair – no one else has hair like Ginny's, no one. And she was wearing that jacket of hers, the dark pink one – sort of raspberry-coloured. I'd remembered it, it was such a lovely jacket. And she had the same long floaty scarf she'd worn with it before, sort of cream and raspberry mixed. She wasn't really dressed for the water. So smart. And then she turned towards me.' She exhaled sharply. 'It was her.'

I didn't say anything for a while. 'Go on,' I murmured at last.

She continued in a flat voice, 'Oh ... I waited a while, but Mrs Perry needed to get home and I had to get on. It was after five. I kept going back to the window, looking, but there was no sign of anybody. I thought – well, I didn't know what to think. Maybe that Ginny knew her, that they had arranged to ...' Suddenly dissatisfied with this idea, she abandoned it with a small movement of her head. 'I had a last look before I left, but I couldn't see anything.' Her final words emerged as a murmur: 'Just the two dinghies.'

The silence that followed was broken only by the sound of Mary's sighs. 'Oh, Hugh,' she said at last, 'I'm so sorry you had to know.'

I pictured Ginny as she had appeared at Dittisham House that night, I saw the raspberry jacket and the long floaty scarf jammed halfway into one pocket, and a strange calm spread through me, and it was the calm that comes at the end of a long and troubled journey.

Fifteen

L IKE AN icy hand the cold had stolen in off the
 blackness of the moor. Climbing out of bed I
caught the glint of frost on the window panes. The
freeze had begun two weeks after Christmas and, ten
bitter days later, was showing no sign of a thaw. I felt
my way to the bathroom and, turning on a light,
peered blindly at my watch. Not yet seven. Pulling
on a robe I went down the narrow cottage stairs to
the boiler to see if I could entice it into action. I
twisted the thermostat to and fro, checked the setting
on the time controller and gave the pump a solid
whack. With a shudder of complaint, the ancient fur-
nace roared capriciously back into life.

The boiler wasn't the only primitive contraption in
the rented cottage – the cooker was slow, the fridge
antique – and in this weather the steep track leading
up from the road was icy and treacherous, but Ginny
liked the place, she felt safe here, and it was only
twenty minutes from Hartford, so, all said, it still had
a lot to recommend it. We wouldn't be here for very
much longer anyway. With Melton gone and Glebe
Place virtually sold and the various loans and mortgages almost settled, we could think about buying a
new place in the spring. I spent a lot of my time on

such practicalities nowadays, I positively over-whelmed myself with details of every kind. That way I maintained an illusion of usefulness.

Making myself some coffee in the still-unfamiliar kitchen, I heard creaking floorboards above and set out a tea tray for Ginny, with some fruit and a couple of Ryvita, which was about all she ate these days. I found her running a bath. Her nakedness alarmed me, she had grown so very thin, and I had to make an effort not to say anything. She greeted me with a pale smile.

'Would you like your tea here?' I asked.

'Please.'

The morning tea tray was one of our little rituals, along with Ginny's pretence at eating. Normally I was first in the bathroom so as to be ready to leave the house by eight, but since the committal proceedings had begun we had altered our timetable and now Ginny bathed first while I drank my coffee in front of the breakfast news.

'I'm out,' she announced ten minutes later, going past me to the wardrobe. 'I'm not sure what to wear. What do you think?'

We stood before the rail of clothes. We had already decided against anything too bright, and she had worn grey for the first day and navy blue for the second.

'The black?' I suggested.

'Mmm. But it needs something to soften it up a bit.' She pulled out a scarf in muted blues. 'What do you think?'

'Perfect.' But then Ginny always looked perfect. I

thought of the stipendiary magistrate who had been sent down from London to hear the case, and, while he was doubtless the most scrupulous of men, I couldn't believe that he would be immune to appearances and that Ginny, with her frail understated femininity, wouldn't make a favourable impression.

When we had dressed we got ready to leave for Exeter. After two days these departures had also developed a certain ritual. I asked Ginny to check that she had two full inhalers with her; she asked me if I had my briefcase. I was certain she wouldn't be warm enough; she told me I worried too much. By such solicitous concern did we conduct our relationship, by such scrupulous consideration did we maintain a veneer of composure.

The track had been gritted but a fresh sprinkling of snow had formed an ice sheet in the night, and, though I took the slope very gingerly, I felt the wheels slip at the last turn. The next instant the back of the car thumped into the earth wall and we began to slither crabwise towards the road. At the last moment the brakes gripped and the car slid to a halt a couple of feet into the road. I reversed back onto the track just as a car sped past, blowing its horn.

'I'll get it gritted again,' I said when my nerves had quietened down a little.

Ginny had her head pressed against the back of the seat, eyes screwed up, breathing sharply.

'Are you all right?'

'Yup,' she rasped.

'Breathe,' I said. 'Keep it slow. Calm thoughts. Plenty of time. No hurry.' I made her unclench her fisted hands, I pressed her shoulders gently down, I lifted her coat collar higher around her neck.

She gave a small gasping laugh. 'What would I do without you?' Taking long steady draughts of air, she opened her eyes and turned her head towards me. 'I really don't know, you know – what I'd do without you. I certainly couldn't have gone ahead with the court thing. Not if you hadn't believed in me.' She lifted my hand and pressed it against her cheek. 'Sometimes I get the feeling that Grainger doesn't. Believe in me, I mean. Oh, he doesn't actually say anything of course, but ever since I asked him if I'd do better pleading guilty he's never quite looked me in the eye again. I think he thinks I *did it!*' She vamped the words and gave an ironic little laugh that didn't quite come off. 'And Charles,' she added with sudden bewilderment, 'sometimes I think he has his doubts as well.'

'That's just not true,' I argued, 'Charles has no doubts at all. Honestly.'

She frowned, not entirely sure whether she could take this protestation of honesty at face value. 'Anyway,' she said with forced brightness, 'you're the only person who matters. So long as you believe in me, then the rest of the world can—' She dismissed the rest of the world with a shake of her head.

I maintained my gaze as best I could. I couldn't think of anything to say.

She brought her face close to mine. 'Thank you, darling. Thank you for giving me the most important thing of all.'

I saw the need in her eyes, and the vulnerability,

and my mouth jerked into a smile, I gave an indeterminate shrug. 'Dear heart,' I murmured, gripped by emotions so disturbing that it was all I could do to keep them out of my face.

'Love you,' she said fiercely.

'Love you too.'

Her eyes didn't leave my face but took on a glint of faint puzzlement, as though she had caught something in my expression which confused her.

I said quickly, 'It'll be all right, darling. I have a feeling about it.'

Her lids fluttered, she nodded jerkily, then, hugging her arms against her body, settled back in her seat.

I fumbled with the heating controls and we set off again. Worried about ice, I concentrated hard on my driving, but the road had been salted, it seemed safe enough, and when we had been silent for some time I offered, 'I'm sure you're wrong about Grainger, you know. I think he's right with you.'

She thought about this. 'Oh, he may be with me. But that's not quite the same as believing in me, is it?'

'Well, he seems optimistic enough. I think he's glad you decided on the committal.'

'Oh he just likes the gamble, whatever he may say,' Ginny remarked, loosing one of her perceptive darts. 'He enjoys the risk.'

I had been careful to take a back seat in the decision over the full committal. I had left Ginny to talk the whole thing through with Tingwall and said almost nothing during a second conference with Grainger. I had listened to Ginny's agonised deliberations, I had commiserated with her dilemma, but I had managed to offer no firm opinion. I felt the loneliness of the priest who has heard too much and must now remain silent.

Once the decision to go for the full committal had been taken and the date set, Ginny had started to show signs of strain, as if she had only just appreciated what lay ahead. She had spent the intervening weeks fighting asthma and other obscure nervous attacks which frequently sent her to bed for hours at a time. The weight had continued to drop off her, and the fluttering of her eyelids had become more pronounced. Often she cried out during the night, sudden shouts that had me waking with a racing heart.

Yet as we walked into Tingwall's office none of this was apparent. She assumed her public mask, a look of serenity and quiet acceptance, and I could only wonder at her extraordinary self-control.

Tingwall was also showing his nerves. As we sat down for our daily recap, he didn't so much smile as expose his teeth, and his eyes danced excitedly. 'So, all the police evidence is out of the way now. I thought Grainger made some good points off Inspector Henderson yesterday. Getting him to admit that you had been totally consistent in everything you'd said, Ginny. That you'd never made a single admission in all those hours of questioning. And asking him how he thought a woman of your build might have lifted a body up a steep ladder – well, it all adds up.' He bared his teeth again in the semblance of a smile.

'But the main thing, of course, is the lack of forensic evidence. That will hardly have gone unnoticed. So!' He clasped his hands together, a troop leader boosting morale. 'It's just the eyewitness now.'

The *just* lingered uncomfortably in the air, and Tingwall quickly corrected himself. 'It's Gordon Latimer now.'

I asked, 'Will his evidence take long?'

'Impossible to say. And then there'll be Grainger's cross-examination. Really impossible to say. But I can try to get the occasional message out to you.'

I made my usual face. 'Thanks.' As a defence witness I was not permitted to sit in court, so rather than hang around the door in a state of anxiety I had spent much of the last two days at a nearby hotel, doing business on the phone and waiting for occasional calls from Tingwall's assistant.

At twenty to ten Tingwall drove us to the court. As the building came into sight Ginny delved into her bag and took a puff of her inhalant. She had not forgotten the mass of press who had greeted our first appearance on Monday morning, thrusting their lenses against the car windows and jostling us as we entered the building. Ginny hadn't attempted to hide her face. We had decided that, as someone with nothing to hide, she should hold her head high. But the aggressiveness of their behaviour had shaken her and once inside she'd suffered a massive asthma attack.

There was only one photographer today, a down-at-heel man in a faded anorak who waited until we had got out of the car before taking a few desultory pictures. Inside the building we were left alone: for this hearing reporting restrictions were in place, and no word of the proceedings nor comment of any sort was permitted to be published.

In the hall was a motley gathering: defendants and their supporters destined for other courts – according to Tingwall mainly traffic offenders and TV licence evaders, with a sprinkling of shoplifters and drunks; and then, to one side, Henderson and his henchmen in their best suits, watching us with their unblinking policemen's eyes; and, far to the other side, visible in an adjacent lobby, Grainger, holding court with his junior and Tingwall's assistant.

Grainger greeted us with his usual air of melancholic authority. 'The Crown present their Mr *Latimer* today. Now, Mrs Wellesley, my cross-examination could be long and detailed, but don't be surprised if it is rather less comprehensive, covering only a few major points. Much will depend on how the witness appears, and the strength of his evidence. You appreciate?' He cast a peremptory glance over us all, looking for questions but expecting none. 'All must be decided as the situation reveals itself . . .'

My attention was diverted by the sight of a figure making his way perilously across the hall, a man who was both familiar and strange, someone I knew but couldn't place. It was another moment before I realised with a slight shock that the emaciated bow-backed figure was Old Gordon. His tweeds may have fitted him in younger sturdier days, but now they hung on him like sacking. He walked unsteadily, with a marked shuffle, and leant heavily on his companion, a middle-aged woman whom I dimly recognised as his daughter. It was hard to believe it was the same man I had last seen a year ago at my father's funeral. He seemed to have aged twenty years. His narrow skull was exceptionally bony and his sparse lifeless hair floated above it like down. The skin hung heavily on his cadaverous face and his pouchy eyes had the watery look of advanced sickness.

Grainger must have caught some of my astonishment because when I looked back at him he raised a mildly inquisitive eyebrow.

I said in an undertone, 'Gordon Latimer.'

He followed my gaze. 'The one leaning on the woman?'

'Yes.'

He watched while Old Gordon took a seat, and when he turned back to me a closed uncommunicative expression had settled over his face. 'You're sure?'

'Yes. Though he looks absolutely terrible, poor chap. I can't believe it.'

Grainger murmured as though to himself but pitched for my hearing too, 'Nothing is certain in this life but uncertainty.'

Without explaining this, he summoned his team and moved towards the court. Ginny and I embraced briefly. Watching Tingwall lead her away I couldn't rid myself of a creeping unease, an irrational sense of approaching doom.

A familiar voice said, 'Hi there,' and Julia swooped up to peck my cheek.

'What are you doing here? I thought you had a decent job to go to.'

'Decent jobs – curse of the upwardly mobile. No, I thought I'd come and see if I could be useful.'

'Not a lot to be done,' I said flatly. Then: 'Have you been fired or something?' She'd only started her new job two months before.

'Not that I know of,' she said airily. 'No – I'm on sick leave. I've got flu.'

I peered at her. 'I'm sorry.'

She touched my arm. 'Hugh – not really.'

'Oh. *Oh*. Sorry, I'm a bit slow today.'

'Come and have a coffee.'

There was a trolley selling drinks and snacks, and we carried two cups of watery coffee to a corner.

'How are things at Hartford?' Julia asked.

'Umm . . .' It was an effort to think of Hartford. 'Pretty good. No – *more* than good. Orders up twenty per cent. Packenhams have re-listed us – did I tell you?' She nodded. 'They even gave us a window display at Christmas. And . . . well, the staff have been wonderful. Productivity up. Costs down . . .' I trailed off, easily distracted.

'So ya-boo to Howard!' Julia crowed.

But I was hardly listening. I was watching Old Gordon, and my disquiet returned, a niggling worry that I couldn't quite name. 'Would you do something for me, Julia? Would you go and sit in the court when it starts and come and tell me what's happening?'

'You'll be here?'

In saying yes I realised I had taken the decision not to go and work from the hotel.

'Do you want full notes or—'

'No – just the gist of it.'

She gestured towards the people accumulating around the entrance to the court. 'Never mind about later,' she growled. 'I'd better go now if I'm to get a seat.' She hurried away and, sweeping past the queue, spoke to the usher and, without seeming to incur any objections, stationed herself at the head of the line.

I was about to go and find a quiet corner when I glanced back and paused. Julia had turned to talk to another woman just behind her, and the woman was Mary. I kept looking, I waited until the woman turned her head again, but there was no doubt about it. For an instant I felt put out, even a little indignant, that she should have turned up without telling us. In the next instant I was ashamed of such uncharitable thoughts. Mary would be here out of the best of motives, to support us, and as if to confirm it she turned and, catching sight of me, clasped her hands together in a gesture of encouragement and solidarity. I waved back.

When the hall was almost deserted I chose a seat not far from Old Gordon. The old man was hunched in his chair, staring vacantly at the floor. When his daughter spoke to him he lifted his rheumy eyes and peered vacantly about him. His gaze passed over me without focus or recognition.

An usher called his name. His daughter roused him and helped him to his feet. Watching him walk arthritically into the court, my disquiet took new shape, bringing regular beats of alarm that had me on my feet, then sitting again, then pacing restlessly up and down until Julia finally emerged twenty minutes later.

'He's very doddery,' she whispered, 'and a bit vague. I wouldn't say he was doing too well.'

'Where are you sitting?'

She gave me a sharp look. 'Me? At this end, in the back row, by the door. Why?'

'Who's next to you?'

'No one special.' Reading my mind only too well, she hissed, 'Look, is this a good idea?'

'Choose a moment when there's something going on. Some distraction.'

'I really don't think this is a good idea,' she muttered as she went back into the court. Two minutes later she reappeared and waved me hastily past her and through a second door, which led into the public gallery.

My arrival went unnoticed amid some general movement in the court. Only one head turned as I sat down. Some sixth sense had made Mary glance round from her place in the front row of the gallery. Her eyes widened slightly at the sight of me, then with a quick bright smile she looked away again.

I slid down in my seat and shaded my eyes with one hand. In the witness box to one side of the room Old Gordon was settling himself on a chair and being offered a glass of water. Ginny was sitting in the dock with her back to me. Ahead of her were the lawyers, also with their backs to me. Only the magistrate was facing the gallery.

The magistrate leant forward. 'Are you well enough to continue, Mr Latimer?'

The old man's eyes swivelled nervously. 'Aye.'

The magistrate, an owl-faced man with pebble glasses and thick grey hair, nodded to the prosecuting counsel, who rose to his feet.

'Mr Latimer, could you once again cast your mind back to the thirtieth of September last year?' the prosecutor began. 'You were telling us where you were in the afternoon at approximately five o'clock. You said you were down by the ferry, is that right?'

Old Gordon appeared to concentrate hard. 'By the ferry, aye.' His voice was thin and reedy and breathless.

'When you say the ferry, Mr Latimer, you mean the ferry that crosses the River Dart from Dittisham village?'

The old man's mouth moved several times before murmuring: 'Aye.'

'Mr Latimer, what were you doing there by the ferry that day?'

Gordon's hooded lids blinked heavily and his jaw slackened, and it seemed to me that he was having difficulty in comprehending even the most basic question.

'Sitting,' he muttered at last.

'You were sitting where exactly?'

Gordon's eyes wandered anxiously. 'By the pub.' Then after another pause: 'Always sit by the pub.'

'This is the pub called the Ferry Boat Inn?'

Another pause. 'Aye.'

'You were sitting on a bench, were you?'

He nodded distractedly.

'If you could say yes or no, Mr Latimer,' the prosecutor reminded him gently.

Gordon hesitated for a long moment, as though he had forgotten the question. 'Aye,' he said finally.

'Thank you. And this bench overlooks the ferry pontoon?'

The old man seemed beset by a growing air of apprehension, as if each question were leading him further on to perilous ground. 'Aye.'

'While you were sitting on the bench that day, could you please tell us what you saw?'

'Saw . . . Mrs Wellesley,' he whispered, and his eyes were agitated.

'You mean Mrs Virginia Wellesley?'

The pause stretched out.

'Mr Latimer? This person was Mrs Virginia Wellesley?'

'Mrs Hugh,' Gordon said at last.

'By that you mean Mrs Hugh Wellesley? Virginia Wellesley?'

This seemed to confuse him for a moment. 'Mrs Hugh,' he repeated in a voice that was increasingly quavery and fearful.

'Quite. Mrs Hugh Wellesley. Do you see her in court, Mr Latimer?'

The rheumy eyes registered something like bafflement, the mouth began a gasping fish-like motion.

'Mr Latimer, do you see Mrs Wellesley in court?'

A measure of understanding dawned. He began to cast about uncertainly. His glance came past the gallery, stopped momentarily before drifting away and roaming the room. Screwing up his eyes, leaning forward slightly as if to focus better, his gaze finally settled on the dock. 'Aye.'

'You can see Mrs Wellesley? Could you point her out to us, please, Mr Latimer?'

Gordon raised a hooked finger at Ginny.

'Let it be shown that Mr Latimer was indicating the defendant. Now, Mr Latimer, could you tell us what Mrs Wellesley was doing when you saw her that day?'

The jaw sagged again. The effort of memory seemed almost beyond him. 'A boat. Took a boat.'

'Did you see her go to this boat?'

Pause. 'Aye.'

'Where was she when you first saw her?'

His brows pulled down, he seemed to glower.

The prosecutor tried again. 'Did she pass close by you?'

Gordon gave a slight nod. With the bent shoulders and gaping mouth, with the bony head hanging forward on the scrawny neck, he had the look of an ancient bird.

'Was that a yes, Mr Latimer? If you wouldn't mind speaking out . . .' Getting no response, the prosecutor urged, 'Did she pass close to you, Mr Latimer? If you could say yes or no?'

'Yes.'

'How close would you say?'

This question troubled him. 'Close,' he offered tentatively.

'As far as she is from you now, in this courtroom? Further? Nearer?'

'Same.'

'So, two yards at the most. And did you get a good look at her?'

'Aye – Mrs Hugh.'

'You were sure it was her?'

The eyes were fearful again. 'Aye.'

'Now this boat she went to, what kind of a boat was it?'

He thought for a long moment. 'Small boat.'

'A rowing boat perhaps?'

He nodded vaguely.

'Was it a rowing boat? If you could just say yes or no, Mr Latimer?'

'Aye . . . yes.'

'And Mrs Wellesley went off in it, you said?'

Another pause: 'Aye.' The old man reached out for the glass of water. The prosecutor waited while he grasped it with clawed hands and brought the rim unsteadily to his lips. As he drank, water spilled down his chin and fell onto his jacket. An usher came forward and took the glass from him and placed it back on one side. Old Gordon made no attempt to mop up the spilt water and it formed a darkening stain on his lapel.

The prosecutor continued, 'So she rowed off, did she, Mr Latimer?'

Old Gordon's concentration seemed to have drifted again, and the question had to be put to him a second time. 'Aye,' he said at last.

The magistrate, who had been making notes much of the time, was now watching Gordon intently.

'Which direction did she row off in?' asked the prosecutor.

Silence.

'Was it up river, or down river, or across river?'

Gordon frowned a great deal before breathing, 'Up.'

'Up. She rowed off *up* river.' The prosecutor glanced down at his papers and, coming to what looked like an abrupt decision, said, 'Thank you, Mr Latimer,' and, nodding to the bench, sat down.

Grainger rose to his feet. 'Mr Latimer,' he began in a kind unhurried tone, 'you are fond of sitting there by the pub, are you?'

Pause. 'Aye.'

'You like to watch the world go by?'

The empty colourless eyes seemed to focus momentarily. 'Aye.'

'And there's quite a bit to see, is there? The ferry, the pleasure boats coming and going, and so on?'

A whisper. 'Aye.'

'You go there regularly?'

Grimacing, Gordon sucked in his thin lips. 'Not so much.'

'Not so much now. What about last autumn, Mr Latimer, in September at the time you say you saw Mrs Wellesley on the pontoon – did you go there regularly then?'

Much thought again. 'Some.'

'How often did you go in a week, Mr Latimer?'

The troubled look again, the groping for words. 'Sundays. Other times. When it were fine.'

'You would invariably go on a Sunday?'

'When it were fine.'

'So last autumn, if it was fine, you would go on a Sunday. And other days too, if it was fine?'

The old boy was flagging. His shoulders bowed further, his chin descended almost to his chest. 'Aye.' And it was little more than a gasp.

'I'm so sorry – did you say yes, Mr Latimer?'

'Aye – yes.'

'So how often might you go and sit by the pub then, Mr Latimer? As often as three times a week? Four? If it was fine.'

He had to think about that for a long time. 'Sundays. Tuesdays sometimes. An' Fridays.'

'As many as three days a week then? What about Saturdays?'

Gordon seemed uncertain about that.

'Did you go there on Saturdays at all?'

'At my daughter Saturdays.'

'Ah. So you generally visited your daughter on Saturdays?' A pause. 'Have I got that right?'

Gordon's mouth began to work in increasing agitation. 'Aye, to my daughter.'

'Where does your daughter live, Mr Latimer?'

Another long pause. 'Primrose Cottage.'

'That's in Dittisham village, is it?' When he had his reply Grainger said in a pleasant almost reminiscent tone, 'So on a day when you went to visit her, you would stay until what time?'

'Teatime. Leave after tea.'

'*After* tea? And what time did tea finish?'

This was the one answer which came without hesitation. 'Half past six.'

'So on the days you visited your daughter you wouldn't leave until after six-thirty?'

'Aye.'

'Now on a day you went to see your daughter, would you also find the time to go and sit by the pub?'

The old man looked thoroughly bemused at this. His pale eyes cast anxiously about, his mouth drooped at the corners and his lower jaw reverted to its strange gasping motion.

Grainger repeated the question carefully.

No one moved. The court seemed to hold its collective breath.

Finally the thin voice rasped, 'At my daughter Saturdays.'

'Forgive me,' Grainger said, selecting a compassionate tone, 'I just need to be clear. Last September you were in the habit of visiting your daughter every Saturday until seven. So are we to understand that you never went and sat by the pub on a Saturday?'

The old man's face crumpled further, he seemed thoroughly confused. Eventually he gave an odd movement of his head.

'Can I take that as a yes, Mr Latimer?'

Another indeterminate movement.

Grainger turned towards the bench, as though for assistance. The magistrate leant forward and said in the ringing tones that people usually reserve for the deaf, 'Mr Latimer, do you understand the question?'

Old Gordon's mouth went through its frantic motions.

'I'll ask Mr Grainger to put it to you one more time, shall I? Mr Grainger, if you please.'

Grainger repeated, 'Last September you were in the habit of visiting your daughter every Saturday until seven. Can we take it, then, that you never went and sat by the Ferry Boat Inn on a Saturday?'

Old Gordon closed his mouth and nodded distinctly. 'Aye.'

'Thank you.' And Grainger's tone left no doubt that he had made his point. 'Now, Mr Latimer, if I may I'd like to take you back to the occasion when you saw Mrs Wellesley setting off in the boat. Which day of the week was that?'

It was as though the old man suddenly appreciated his predicament. He became increasingly distressed, his face contorted into a grimace of woe and confusion, his mouth wobbled. Finally he shook his head.

The tension was like an electric charge. My mind told me that it was all over, logic insisted that we had won, but the consequences of this thought were so overwhelming that for the moment my emotions refused to follow.

Grainger was driving his advantage home. 'You can't say?' he repeated. 'So it could have been a Sunday?'

The old man lifted a bent hand to his chest as if his breathing were giving him trouble.

'So it might have been a Sunday?' Grainger pressed with the urgency of a man who senses he is running out of time. 'Mr Latimer?'

'Can't say.'

The magistrate leant forward. 'Mr Latimer, are you feeling unwell?'

'Can't say,' Gordon echoed miserably.

'Mr Latimer.' The magistrate raised his voice again. 'Are you feeling all right?'

'Can't remember like I used to,' Gordon cried plaintively.

'Is it your memory that's troubling you, Mr Latimer, or are you feeling unwell?'

'Memory . . . bad.'

'So apart from your memory you're feeling all right?'

Old Gordon nodded despairingly, and he seemed close to tears.

'In order that the court can be absolutely clear,' the magistrate continued with great deliberation, 'you are saying, Mr Latimer, that you cannot be sure which day of the week it was when you saw Mrs Wellesley go off in the boat?'

The old man's mouth turned down almost to his chin, he blinked rapidly and shook his head. 'Memory . . . it's terrible.'

The magistrate took his time writing his notes before looking towards Grainger. 'Any more questions, Mr Grainger?'

'No, sir.'

There was a pause as the usher helped Gordon from the witness box. The old man's corrugated cheeks were streaked with tears, and his eyes held the terrors of bewilderment.

The prosecutor stood up briefly and said disconsolately, 'Sir, that completes the case for the prosecution.'

The magistrate looked expectantly at Grainger, who rose and announced in a firm voice, 'Sir, I would like to move that there is absolutely no case to answer. The Crown has offered no forensic evidence *whatsoever* that links my client to the scene of the crime. Nor has it produced a *single* piece of forensic evidence to link her to the victim. Indeed, its case relies solely on Mr Latimer's eyewitness evidence, and Mr Latimer *cannot remember* which day it was that he saw my client rowing off "up river". Now we do not dispute the fact that my client took a dinghy from the pontoon and rowed out to the yacht *Ellie Miller* on the day *after* the murder, on the *Sunday*. My client herself volunteered this information to the police at her first interview, and was happy to repeat it in her subsequent statement. What we dispute utterly is that she was anywhere near the water on the day before, on the *Saturday*, and indeed the prosecution have entirely failed to prove that she was *anywhere* in the vicinity on that day. Thus, sir, I submit that there is simply no case to answer and that it would be unsafe in every respect to allow this case to proceed any further.'

Grainger sat down. The magistrate studied his notes before bending forward to have a word with the clerk. Looking out over the court, he said with a long sigh of exasperation, 'I agree with you entirely, Mr Grainger, for all the reasons you have stated—'

There was a startled cry, and a banging of doors as some people hurried from the gallery.

'The prosecution have failed to produce any reliable evidence to connect Mrs Wellesley to this crime—'

I buried my head in my hands.

'. . . In my view it would be unsafe in the extreme to allow this case to proceed to the crown court. I find that there is no case to answer, and the defendant is therefore discharged.'

He addressed Ginny then – something about being free to go – but I couldn't hear his words for the violence of my own emotions. Julia's voice sounded in my ear and her arm came round my shoulders, and she may have been crying too.

Even before the magistrate had left the court, the place erupted into noise and movement. Someone close by began shouting, a man pushed roughly past me. Julia led me out of the gallery and into the well of the court. In the midst of the people congratulating her, Ginny looked small and dazed. Reaching her, we embraced uncertainly as if neither of us could quite absorb what had happened, and then her arms tightened around my waist and she was gasping, and laughing a little too.

Tingwall was hovering, grinning all over his squinty-eyed face.

'Not too late to fire me,' he chuckled.

'I always said you were too young for the job.' And I embraced him.

I heard Mary's voice. 'Ginny!' she cried, and, sweeping past me, enveloped Ginny in a large hug. 'I'm so, *so* glad!' she declared. 'I'm so pleased! Oh, Ginny! I'm going to phone David this minute! We're so thrilled!' Throwing up her arms as though lost for further words, she laughed in an odd overexcited way and enveloped Ginny again.

I went over to Grainger who was packing his papers away. 'Thank you,' I said simply, and shook his hand.

'It would have been hard to lose,' he said with a sigh of disappointment, like a prize fighter cheated of a good bout. 'That old man . . . In the circumstances it was a lucky thing that your wife is something of a gambler.'

'You still handled it brilliantly.'

His eyes narrowed. 'Did I? You were in court?'

I smiled at how easily I had been caught out. 'Just at the end,' I admitted.

'Oh, Mr Wellesley.' He shook his head with an ironic show of disapproval. 'If we had gone to trial, that little escapade could have made our lives very difficult.'

'Perhaps I'm a gambler too.'

He thought about that. 'Yes,' he drawled in his unfathomable accent, 'I think you probably are.'

Before I could ask him what he meant by that Tingwall came bustling up with something he wanted me to read.

'I prepared this for the press last night. A statement.' Waving the paper in the air, he giggled like a child. 'I knew, you see. I knew!' Waiting for my grin of acknowledgement, accepting it with a small swagger, he read from the handwritten sheet. 'Mrs Wellesley has protested her innocence most vigorously ever since she was charged, and with the throwing out of the case her position has been entirely vindicated. There was never the slightest evidence against Mrs Wellesley, yet she has been forced to suffer months of needless distress as a result of a charge that from every point of view should never have been brought. Her family would now ask that she be left in peace.' He looked up. 'I would have liked more time on it, but what do you think?'

'I think it's fine.'

I turned to find Mary at my elbow. She drew me aside and whispered fervently, 'Hugh – you've no idea what this means to me. *No* idea. I've been *praying* for this from the very beginning.' Her eyes with their garish blue lids looked fiercely into mine. '*Praying!*'

'I know.'

'What we need to do now is forget,' she said in a confidential tone. '*Forget* we ever had that talk. *Forget* what I said.'

I stared at her in open astonishment, wondering how she could possibly imagine I could forget something so devastating, something which was going to darken my life for ever. '*Forget?*'

She grasped my arm. 'As far as we can, of course.'

I shook my head.

'All in the past now, Hugh,' she insisted. 'The *past.*' She laughed suddenly, the same odd laugh again. 'Well – I must go and phone David! He'll be so thrilled.' With a jolly wave, she hurried off.

The next few hours were a confusion of downward-floating emotions. Tingwall went to the front of the court building and read his statement to the horde of waiting press who had materialised, as always, out of nowhere. Then when Tingwall's assistant had brought his car round to the front we left the shelter of the building and launched ourselves at the jostling photographers and shouting reporters for what I fervently hoped would be the last time. Ginny ignored their questions until, on reaching the car, a BBC reporter put a microphone under her nose and asked how she felt. 'I feel immensely glad that it's all over,' she replied.

Back at Tingwall's office we drank champagne, made a few calls to spread the news and took the congratulations of the firm's partners before going to lunch at a nearby restaurant. Tingwall and Julia chattered excitedly, but Ginny and I were rather more subdued, too drained of feeling for such straightforward emotions as joy or relief. I drank too much wine and compounded the error with two brandies, so that when we set off for home it was Ginny who had to drive through the gathering dusk.

The cottage was icy. I thumped the boiler to no avail while Ginny answered a steady stream of calls from friends and well-wishers. Finally, at nine, we took the phone off the hook and huddled side by side in front of the fire with a sandwich and a glass of wine.

'I think back to last winter,' Ginny murmured reminiscently. 'I think of everything we had then and how unhappy we were. And then I think of what we have now, and – well, I wouldn't change all this for anything, not for *anything*. I wouldn't be anywhere else but in this freezing little dump of a cottage with you. I feel so lucky, Hugh. The luckiest person in the world.

Most of all' – and her voice was rough and low – 'I feel so terribly lucky to have you.'

'Darling.'

She pulled back a little and looked into my face. She asked softly, 'I do have you, don't I?'

'Of course.' I added a smile. 'Of course you do.' And something in my heart felt infinitely weary.

'It's all I've ever wanted, you see. You and me. For us to be happy.'

I put my wine down, then hers, and we wrapped our arms around each other. I saw the future stretching out before us, and it seemed to go on for ever. I saw Hartford growing steadily, I saw us in a pretty house near by, I saw summers in France and, when Hartford didn't need me any more, I saw us going to live there amid the vineyards: I saw all these things, and none of them could assuage my loneliness.

Ginny moved against me, her lips travelled across my cheek, she opened her soft mouth to mine. Soon we went upstairs to the warmth of our bed and, as Ginny's passionate body pressed itself against mine, I felt a surge of love, and a chasm of emptiness.

Sixteen

Entering the silent house, breathing the musty blend of furniture polish and wood smoke that took me lurching back to my childhood, I thought: This is the last time I will stand here, this is the last time I will feel so close to my past.

The remains of the furniture had been removed during the week, organised, like everything else to do with the sale, by Mary. Two geometric patches of deeper colour marked the spot on the study carpet where Pa's desk had stood, and ancient scorchmarks long hidden by a well-placed rug fanned out from the grate, from the days when Pa had favoured blazing open fires. The shadowy outlines of pictures lined the stairs, and in my old room the dusty curtains framed unwashed windows clouded with the grime of the long winter.

The bed had gone, the side table too, but, as Mary had forewarned me, everything that neither she nor Ginny had claimed and which was otherwise destined for jumble sales had been stored here, an accumulation of old lamps, rickety chairs and cardboard boxes stacked high with kitchen utensils, chipped china and battered paperbacks: the family detritus of fifty years.

I found my old paintings in a cardboard box half crushed by a pile of *Eagles* dating back to the sixties. The Winsor & Newton watercolours, the set of sable brushes which at fourteen I had saved up for so carefully were not with them however, and, though I hunted desultorily through a few of the neighbouring boxes, I soon realised the search was hopeless. My old lamp with its parchment shade lay on a chair but when I picked it up the top lurched over and I saw that the shade had acquired a second split.

Shutting the door, I carried the paintings down to the car and, after one last look around the hall, locked up the house. Touched by a last bout of nostalgia, I took a wander round the side of the house to the terrace. Dark shadows dotted the flagstones where the flower urns had stood, and one of the flowerbeds showed signs of fresh digging where a plant had been removed. That would be Mary, who was always on the lookout for additions to her garden.

The river was grey under a cold March sky, and an exceptionally high tide had lifted the water almost to the branches of the trees overhanging the opposite bank. Another boat lay at *Ellie Miller*'s mooring, a modern tub with its name displayed garishly down the side. *Ellie* had been taken to Plymouth to be refitted, renamed and, in due course, we hoped, sold. There would be no buyers for her here.

I went down the steps to the middle terrace and on to the lower garden. Under the bare trees the last of the crocuses lay flat like fallen warriors, and in the rough grass the daffodil shoots stood stiff and tall, awaiting their moment.

I glanced up and saw beyond the summerhouse a bowed figure standing among the apple trees, head canted upward in contemplation of something above his head. He had his back to me but as I made my way towards him I recognised the bony head and the bent shoulders under the baggy tweed jacket.

'Hello there,' I called.

Old Gordon turned. 'Mr Hugh!' he exclaimed amiably.' 'Day to you.' He raised a gnarled hand in salute and gestured on upwards at the trees. 'Need a good prune. Won't get much fruit without a good prune.'

'Aha.' I inspected the branches dutifully. 'I'm afraid everything's been rather neglected.'

'Not too late, if it's done quick.' He nodded and hummed a little. 'Mrs Bennett – she's keen on her fruit. Likes makin' apple pies, she does. Does 'em for the fête.' He chortled, 'Dozens o' the blessed things.'

'Ahh.' The Bennetts, who had lived on the other side of the village for some years, were the new owners of Dittisham House. 'You'll be working here then? I thought you were retired, Gordon.'

'Ah, yes and no, yes and no. Still do bits and pieces. Can't risk the prunin' meself, o' course. I'd be no sooner up a ladder than sailin' off it again.' He cackled at the thought, showing a fine set of false teeth. 'But I don' mind a bit o' diggin' and weedin'. Keeps me goin'.'

'You're feeling pretty fit then?'

'Can' complain, Mr Hugh. Can' complain at all. Good to be back on me feet again, I can tell yer.'

'I, er . . . I'd heard you hadn't been too well.'

He made an exaggerated grimace. 'Bad winter. Bad.

Rheumatics. Heart. *Angina*. Felt somethin' terrible. *Terrible*.' He blew out his sunken cheeks at the memory, before brightening suddenly. 'But I'm all set now.'

'I'm so glad.'

The old man's face puckered again, and he cast me a troubled glance. 'Sorry about the court business, Mr Hugh.'

'It doesn't matter, Gordon. Really.'

'They kept askin', the police. Never stopped askin'. Dates, times. Dates, times. On and on. What a palaver.' He rolled his drooping eyes and jerked a clawed hand in a gesture of disbelief. 'Then they got me makin' this statement. Puttin' me name to it. And all the time I thought maybe I was helpin' out, yer see. Thought I was doin' good. An' then, next thing I know, they says they want me in court, and, I tell you, Mr Hugh, if I'd 'a' realised . . .'

'I understand, Gordon, really.'

'I didn' know I was sayin' things against Mrs Hugh. They never told me that.'

'No, I'm sure they didn't.'

'If I'd 'a' known, well . . . I'd 'a' kept me mouth shut.'

'But you couldn't have known. Honestly – we didn't blame you, Gordon. Not for a moment.'

He was lost in his reminiscences again. 'They kept sayin' ter me – just say it like you said it before, in the statement. But comes to it, comes to the day, an' I couldn' get a darn' thing straight in me head. I was feelin' so bad with me heart. Been bad for weeks.

Between you and me, Mr Hugh, thought I was on the way out. Thought me number was well and truly up.'

'Gordon, don't worry about it. After all, everything worked out fine in the end.'

He grunted, 'Gets so you can't be sure of anythin'.'

Nodding solemnly, I contemplated the truth of that remark. I looked up at the trees. 'Hope you get a good harvest.'

'Better, hadn' I? All those pies to fill!' The cadaverous face split into a quiet grin.

'Take care, Gordon.'

He laughed, 'That's one thing you may be sure of, Mr Hugh.'

I drove away at a crawl while my thoughts circled restlessly, stirring up long-suppressed ideas that I had almost persuaded myself to forget, converging on a single unhappy notion which proceeded to worry at me like a cracked tooth. Absorbing the idea, allowing it houseroom, it seemed to me that truth was a terribly overrated objective, that in going after it you ended up not with the hoped-for sense of resolution but with yet another bout of turmoil and unhappiness.

But there was one thing more unsettling than an unhappy truth, and that was the kind of uncertainty which was eating away at me now. Accelerating to the next junction, I took the turning for Furze Lodge.

The house was open. No one answered my calls and I wandered from room to room until, coming into the kitchen, I spotted David through the window, digging a hole in the lawn.

Coming closer, I saw it was a long shallow trench.

'Drainage?' I asked.

He spun around, looking startled, and flashed me a reproachful look. Calming down just as rapidly, he offered, 'Electricity cable.'

'Floodlighting?'

'Mary wants a summerhouse in the far corner there, and maybe one day a swimming pool, though I think they're a total waste of time myself.' In a movement that was almost violent, he plunged the spade into the ground and shovelled some earth. 'How's Ginny?'

'She's fine.'

'And the new house?'

'Oh, dust and mess. We're camping at the builders' convenience – you know.'

'And Hartford?'

'Fingers crossed, going better than I ever dared hope.'

David said drily, 'That must please Howard no end.'

He shifted a few more feet of earth before resting on his spade. 'I should have hired a digger.'

'I'd help if . . .' I gestured as though for a second spade.

David swung his gaze on me and I could see that he was in a prickly mood. 'So what brings you here after all this time? I was beginning to think the Cold War had set in.'

'I was just picking up some stuff from Dittisham. I thought I'd pop in.'

He raised a sceptical eyebrow and waited for me to tell him something nearer the truth.

'I wanted to ask you something,' I confessed. 'I wanted to ask if Old Gordon was a patient of yours.'

'Of course.' He gave a small snort. 'How else do you think I fixed him? And to answer your next question, it was a mixture of codeine, antihistamine and a tranquilliser called thioridazine. Guaranteed to addle the brain in the right doses.' He snapped irritably, 'And you don't need to look so bloody disapproving. It wasn't going to kill him. He's perfectly all right now.'

There is an instant after a truth is confirmed when, though you've known what was coming, the facts still seem bald and shocking.

David growled, 'Besides, his memory had been dodgy for years. He'd probably got the whole thing wrong anyway. The wrong day, the wrong person – who knows? So it wasn't as if I was perpetrating a great miscarriage of justice, was it?'

I didn't say anything.

David cast me a scathing look. 'You didn't realise?' he asked, working himself up into some kind of fury.

'I half guessed. When I saw him at the court . . .'

'Come on, you must have known! I'd promised, hadn't I?'

'Promised?'

'I said I'd help.' He repeated almost crossly: '*I said I'd help*. You must have realised!'

'I suppose I didn't want to think about it. I didn't want to . . .' I shrugged, 'deal with it. But now . . . well, I can only say thank you. *God* – that's totally inadequate, isn't it? What I mean is – I'll never be able to thank you enough, David. Never.'

'Stuff your gratitude, Hugh,' David said with sudden vehemence. 'I may be an adulterer and a liar and a few other things besides, but I wasn't going to let Ginny go to prison for something she didn't do. Even *I* thought that was a bit much. You know – something I might *just* have difficulty in living with for the rest of my life. I may be a shit, but not *that* much of a shit.'

'It's all right,' I said quietly. 'I know what really happened. Mary told me.'

I had caught him by surprise. He stared at me in dismay or alarm or both. 'What did Mary tell you?'

'Oh . . .' I still found it hard to say. 'That she saw Ginny go out to the boat and talk to Sylvie and go aboard and—' I cut myself short with a sharp gesture.

'She said *that?* My God.' He shook his head incredulously. 'God.' He gave an unsteady laugh that was suddenly quite devoid of assurance. 'You should know better than to believe anything that Mary tells you.'

I felt a momentary disconnection from the conversation, as though it were happening at some other time in my own past or future. 'She'd seen Ginny,' I argued hoarsely. 'She must have. She described what she was wearing. She . . .' But I was silenced by the look on David's face.

'You poor sod,' he murmured pityingly. 'You thought . . . all this time . . .'

Doubts roared through my mind. I felt a tug in my chest, a sudden heat, followed by the first stirrings of a fearsome anger. 'What the hell are you saying?'

'Hugh – I'm saying that Mary was lying.'

'She never saw Ginny?'

'She never saw Ginny,' he sighed. 'Not then anyway. Ginny arrived a lot later. I'm sorry. I'm really sorry.' He sounded genuinely shaken. 'When was this? When did Mary tell you this? Were you about to go to the police? Was that what it was? She'd have done anything, I'm afraid, to stop you doing that. Was it the police?'

I didn't trust myself to speak.

'I'm really sorry, Hugh.' He raised both shoulders in an exaggerated appeal for understanding.

'*You bastard!* She was protecting *you!*' I exploded at last.

He flinched, he was halfway to making a contrite face when my anger burst over me in a hot wave and I lunged for him. Grabbing him by his shirt, I twisted it tight under his chin. 'You bastard! *You bastard!*' My rage was huge and ugly and inconsolable. I was overcome by the lust for revenge. I wanted to inflict the most terrible pain and suffering on him, as he had done on me, and at that moment no punishment could possibly have been too terrible. I pushed my fists higher and higher under his chin, driving his head back until he was forced to twist away. As he straightened up, I aimed a punch at his face but my swing was wild and hopelessly wide and, seeing it coming, he lashed out with an arm and deflected my blow. I came in with a weak left hook but he ducked under that and my fist swished uselessly through the air. In my rage and frustration, I became more cunning. I dropped my arms to my sides as if in surrender and the moment he relaxed I sent a sharp little jab into his stomach which doubled him over. As his head came up for air I splayed my feet, dug in my heels, and put all my weight into a low upward swing that whistled up under his chin. Even before my knuckles made contact I knew it was going to be a powerful blow. There was a loud crack, the impact sent a sharp jabbing pain into my hand, David cried out and jerked back before falling slowly onto one knee. Clasping a hand to his chin, panting hard, he looked up at me with what might have been a plea for truce, but if he thought I was finished he had another think coming.

He staggered to his feet and we faced each other warily. He tried to say something but I wasn't listening and I went for him again with a tight swing of my left fist, a feint which I intended to follow with another solid blow from the right. But he caught my first arm and held onto it and tried to twist me off-balance. I shoved my shoulder under his arm in a half-remembered wrestling manoeuvre but he hooked his foot behind my ankle and the next moment we fell untidily to the ground. For a few seconds we grappled ineffectually. I became aware of a frenzied barking and growling from one of David's dogs. Perhaps it was the fear of being bitten that gave me new strength but I managed to push David over onto his back and land a quick knuckle on his face. I didn't think I'd hit him very hard until I saw his nose spout a stream of blood. While I stared at the blood spreading down his face, his fist came out of nowhere and caught me high on the cheek, just under one eye. I felt my head snap back, I saw stars and, falling sideways, rolled slowly onto my back.

There was a silence broken only by the sound of our panting. After a second or two I heard a different sort of panting and felt a wet nose snuffling at my face. I pushed the dog away and it went to inspect David, who murmured, 'Piss off, Bodger,' so I knew he couldn't be too badly hurt.

My face was throbbing painfully, and my hand too. I touched them gingerly, but as far as I could tell nothing was broken. I'd only ever got into one serious fight, at school, and that had ended in defeat after one blow. I was rather surprised that I had managed to land any sort of a punch on David, let alone a couple which had found their target. But I felt no sense of satisfaction, far less triumph, only a depressing futility.

Pressing a hand to my burning cheek, I sat up cautiously and looked across at David. He was still lying flat on his back. Opening one eye a crack he peered blearily at me before closing it again. The dog stood nearby, wagging its tail sporadically.

'Couldn't let her go,' David said without warning.

My breath caught high in my chest. I kept very still, as if by ignoring him he might leave the subject alone.

'Just couldn't do without her.'

'For Christ's sake shut up!' I retorted furiously. 'I don't bloody want to hear.'

'Please,' he asked simply. When I didn't reply he continued with a gasp, 'Never thought anyone would ever get such a hold on me. I'd never . . . in all my

507

life . . . Never been so – *taken*. So – *mesmerised*. Or perhaps I mean obsessed,' he said in the bemused tone of someone who still hasn't quite worked things out. 'Hardly knew what to do with myself. Got so I couldn't even *think* when I was away from her. Couldn't function. She was so – *different*. So – *crazy*. Made me laugh. Made me feel— *Okay*,' he conceded as though I'd put up some sort of argument, 'Okay, it was sex to begin with. I mean, I hadn't strayed for a long time, I'd forgotten how . . . well, how bloody fantastic it could be.' His voice shuddered at the memory. 'But then . . . then it was more than that. Much more. I always felt so good when I was with her. For the first time in my life – good, *good*. I thought, so *this* is what it's all about, this is what people go on about. She made me feel alive, Hugh. That was the thing – ' the gasp again ' – *alive*.' His tone dropped. 'I thought we had a future. I thought I could cure her, you see. I thought I could get her off the drugs. I thought she would do it for *me*. That's the worst thing, thinking that someone's going to change because you want them to. But I really believed—'

He broke off suddenly. I looked across at him and his blood-smeared face was so contorted with grief that I quickly looked away again.

'I believed she'd do it for me,' he whispered at last in a raw voice. 'But I was wrong. She was never going to change. I didn't give up trying though. I never gave up trying. I had this plan. I was going to take her away. We were going to make a new start, somewhere completely different. America. Italy. Somewhere

where she wouldn't know people in the drug world. Somewhere she could do a sculpting course and study her New Age stuff. We made plans. Lots of plans.' He made a harsh sound, a sigh that was also an expression of despair. 'Right up until the end, until the last day. More plans.'

The dog, who had been sitting down, got up and, whining softly, tried to lick David's face. Holding it at bay with one hand, he went on, 'I stopped her drugs when I realised she was making no effort to cut down on them. Well, that was the reason I gave for stopping them – because she wouldn't cut down – but really I was trying to force her into coming away with me. I couldn't think of any other way. She'd never agree on a date, she was always wriggling out of it for some reason or another. It had got so she wouldn't even talk about it any more. I began to imagine the worst – imagine that she was going to finish the whole thing. I was terrified she'd just up and off one day and I'd never see her again. I thought that if I cut off the drugs she'd come crawling back.' He grunted at the idea. 'Of course, crawling back wasn't Sylvie's style. She just found other ways of getting what she wanted. Her brother in Bristol. That chap Hayden and the excursions to France.'

And me, I thought. Don't forget me.

As if reading my thoughts, David said matter-of-factly, 'I didn't cotton on to you for a long time, honestly. Amazing what you miss when you're not looking. I thought you were simply having troubles with Ginny. When you kept coming down to the boat I thought you were just trying to get away from it all. I didn't realise until the very end, really. Until just before . . .'

Cautiously, patting his nose gingerly, he pushed himself up onto one elbow. Then, just as slowly, he sat up and, pulling his feet towards him, rested his forearms on his knees and stared out across the garden. Our breath formed puffs of vapour in the cold, the ground was very damp, but neither of us thought of moving.

'She was furious with me,' David went on. 'When I stopped the drugs. I saw the wild side of her then, and how. But it didn't change anything. It didn't stop me wanting her,' he said gruffly. 'Nothing could do that. She was my drug, you see. I could never get enough of her, even after all those months. Could never *imagine* getting enough of her.' His voice cracked, he shook his head as though he himself scarcely believed the power she had exerted over him. 'Part of me knew what she was like, knew she wasn't too good at commitment, that she'd never stayed with anything for very long. But I thought it would all be different once we got away, once she was off that bloody poison.'

He raised a weary hand and rubbed his eyelids. 'She always came back,' he said dully. 'Always. Oh, sometimes it was to wrangle a script out of me, sure. *Sure*. But most of the time she came back because she needed to see me, just like I needed to see her. Because we couldn't stay away from each other. Underneath it all we had something, you see. Something *strong*. We were two of a kind. She always said so. Two of a kind.' His voice rose and he stalled momentarily. 'I think we could have made it together, you know. I think we could have been happy. I think – I think—' He could hardly say it. 'I think I loved her. I think I really loved her.' He dropped his head into his hands and snatched at his breath.

I looked away and watched a magpie prowling through the trees. After a while I said, 'What about Mary?'

He brought his head up heavily, dragging his hands down his face as he did so. 'Mary,' he sighed. '*Mary*. At the beginning – well, what she didn't know wouldn't hurt her and all that. But then – yes, I would have left her, I would have left her like a shot if Sylvie had ever got her act together, if she'd ever committed herself.' A slight shrug. 'I can't say our marriage was bad exactly, but it was pretty mechanical. It had never been much else, really. In those days I thought you just settled for a nice efficient person who shared some of your interests and who'd do a good job with the children. That sounds pretty unfeeling, I suppose, but that was what I thought it was all about. I never minded the fact that Mary wasn't a great beauty – I never thought that mattered. I wanted someone who'd be a good wife, who'd fit in with my life, back me up.'

When he showed no sign of continuing, I said, 'She found out.' It was half a statement, half a question.

'I guess so,' he breathed distractedly. 'I guess so.'

He turned away, and we sat in silence for a time. Only the dog stirred, cocking its ears to some far-off sound and lifting its nose to the air.

My anger had evaporated; only the sour aftertaste

of violence remained. I had no feelings left for David, except perhaps pity. And, for the moment at least, gratitude for having told me his story and set me free. I almost left then, I almost got up and walked away to start the miraculous new existence which unexpectedly stretched before me, the new life with a Ginny whose only crime was to have tried to save her worthless husband. I almost got up and walked away, but something made me hesitate.

'I had no idea. No idea at all,' David murmured at last, giving voice to some thought of his own. When he next spoke, it was with new emotion. 'I'd arranged to meet Sylvie on the boat that day. Most of the summer we'd been meeting at someone's house, a chap who'd gone away for a few months. But that day we decided to meet on the boat.' He paused, and it was only with a visible effort that he forced himself on. 'I got delayed – a stupid meeting – then they paged me – a heart attack. By the time I got down to the river I was almost an hour late. But I knew she'd wait. When she'd called she'd sounded really happy, really keen to see me. I knew she'd wait.' He rubbed his head, close to misery again. 'But when I got down there I couldn't find the dinghy oars. Then I couldn't find the *dinghy*. Thought someone must have pinched it. I was about to borrow someone else's when' – he inhaled sharply – 'when I looked up and saw someone rowing the dinghy towards me. I thought it must be Sylvie, that for some reason she'd taken my dinghy instead of *Samphire*'s. I almost called out to her. It took me ages to realise that it was Mary. She was wearing this baggy old oilskin, one of Pa's relics, with the hood up. As soon as I realised it was her, I knew she could only have been to *Ellie* – I mean, there was nowhere else she could have been. At first I persuaded myself that Sylvie would have made herself scarce in some way, that she would have seen Mary coming. That's what I wanted to believe anyway, that's what I told myself . . .' He screwed up his eyes, his mouth turned down, he said bleakly, 'Although deep down . . . deep down I had an awful feeling, even then.'

I had been avoiding the moment of confrontation, I had been shutting it out, but there was no escaping it now. Feeling emotionally sick, I gave the thought life. *Mary*.

'Mary never went out to *Ellie* normally,' David was saying, 'she could hardly row a dinghy. There had to be a *reason*, and the only reason . . .' But he couldn't cope with this thought and pushed it aside. 'So there I was . . . I couldn't face a scene there on the river, so I went up the road and round a corner where Mary wouldn't see me. As soon as she'd landed, she rushed off, went straight past me. I couldn't decide what to do then. I looked for Sylvie, of course. I'd bought her a mobile phone but she never remembered to take it with her, she was always leaving it in the wrong place, so I wasn't surprised when it didn't answer. And then I looked for her dinghy. I couldn't see it at *Ellie*. I couldn't see it at *Samphire*.' Quite suddenly he began to cry, awkwardly, with great contortions of his face. A trickle of tears mixed with the drying blood and dripped in a pink stream off the end of his chin. 'It must have been there, of course, at *Ellie* – I just didn't see it. I can't stop thinking that if only I'd gone out there, *if only I'd gone and had a look* then maybe I could have saved her.' And he gave a loud sob, a howl of irretrievable loss that made the dog recoil and whimper uneasily.

I stared at him, this brother I hardly knew. I reached out and gripped his arm. 'You mustn't think about that—'

'I can't help it!' he cried helplessly. 'It's all I ever think about! If only I hadn't been late, if only I hadn't been called out, if only— Oh God, oh *God*,' he wailed, 'it's all I ever think about!'

I shifted closer and put an arm round his shoulders. In my mind's eye I pictured the shadowy figure spying on Sylvie and me from the terrace at Dittisham House, and I saw Mary there in the darkness, I saw Mary creeping up to the window and bumping the metal chair across the stone flags, and I wondered how often she had crept up on David and Sylvie, how often she had seen them together.

'Afterwards I couldn't get rid of this – this *feeling*,' David said despairingly. 'I knew . . . I just *knew* something was wrong. I drove around most of the evening. I went to her cottage, I went to Dittisham House and found you and Ginny. And I couldn't find her, I couldn't find her anywhere. And then, next day when they found her . . . When they found her . . . *Christ* . . .' Weeping again, he shook his head and kept shaking it. 'But I needed to know, you see. I needed to know for sure, so before Mary went out I went and looked at her car. And the oilskin was there in the boot, in a plastic bag. With some clothes. And the clothes, they were . . . covered, absolutely covered . . . '

A wind had sprung up, intensifying the cold. My hands were frozen and I thought I felt David shiver. 'Come inside,' I said.

'I wouldn't have let Ginny go to prison,' David said as I helped him to his feet. 'I swear it.' He faced me for the first time since I had hit him, and I saw that one eye was swelling badly. 'I swear it,' he repeated.

'I know that.'

He nodded emotionally.

We walked towards the house.

'Does Mary realise?' I asked.

'That I know? That I saw her? No. We've never spoken of it, or anything to do with it. I don't think she has any idea. But I'll be leaving quite soon,' he said firmly. 'I thought it wouldn't be safe to leave before, in case the police thought – well, whatever they might think. But I'll leave quite soon now. In a week or so. I'll miss the children, of course . . .' He made a hopeless gesture.

We went into the kitchen and David reached a hand into the serving hatch and pulled out a bottle of cognac. He poured two measures and we knocked them back.

'You'd better go and clean yourself up,' I told him as he refilled our glasses.

He ran exploratory fingers over his face, and raised a critical eyebrow. 'You too. You're going to have a real shiner, I'm afraid.'

I drained the last of my drink. 'I'll wash on the way out.'

We faced each other.

'Don't think too badly of her,' David said with a bitter ring to his voice. 'She worked very hard on Howard, you know, to get him to bring the Cumberland board round. In fact, I'm pretty sure she swung it for you.'

'Swung it? But how?'

'Oh, I think she knew things about Howard that he didn't want the world to know.'

Ginny's words came to me again: *She's not Howard's sister for nothing*, and the sick feeling crept back into my stomach.

We heard the car at the same time.

I touched his arm and hurried towards the downstairs cloakroom to splash water over my face. Glancing back, I saw David pouring himself another drink. Looking up, he raised his glass in an ironic salute and his battle-scarred face took on its habitual mask of sardonic indifference.

I emerged from the cloakroom as the children burst noisily into the house. They gave me a happy unsurprised wave before roaring on towards the kitchen.

'Hugh! How lovely!' Mary advanced rapidly on me. 'Good God!' she laughed. 'What *have* you done to yourself!'

'I walked into something,' I said.

And mustering a smile, fixing an expression of pleasure on my face, I bent down to kiss her.

Living up to their reputation for maximum disruption, the builders had left a pile of gravel just inside the gates. Forced to abandon the car, I loaded the box of pictures under my arm and strode up the drive. Fumbling with the door handle, I sent the half-painted door against its stop with a bang.

'Is that you?' Ginny called, appearing round the kitchen door.

I dropped the box on a chair and faced her.

'Oh!' she cried, clamping a hand to her mouth. 'Good God! Whatever happened to you?' She came and raised gentle fingertips to my face.

'I've been stupid.'

'*Have* you?' She had a wonderful way of making it sound the most unlikely thing in the world.

'I can't believe how stupid I've been.'

Looking alarmed, she took a fearful breath. 'Not the car? You haven't had an accident?'

'No. Nothing like that.'

Her worst fears allayed, she pressed a hand to her chest, she took a series of sharp breaths. 'What then?'

'I walked into something.'

'Into *something*?'

'A large man in a pub?'

But her anxiety wasn't going to be bought off by thin jokes. 'Oh yes?' she said sternly.

'Okay,' I laughed, preparing to parade my stupidity. 'It *was* the car – but not while it was going anywhere. I opened the door to put something inside and I turned round too quickly – I just wasn't looking – and the door swung back in my face and the corner got me right here.' Pointing at the swelling, I put on a gormless expression: the complete idiot.

She frowned, not entirely satisfied with this, I could

see the questions hovering, then with an obvious effort she put her doubts behind her, and a smile bubbled to her lips. 'A large man in a pub is going to get you far more sympathy.'

'In that case, the large man has it.'

She raised herself on tiptoe and kissed my bruised cheek.

'Was that the sympathy?' I asked.

She slipped an arm round me. 'You might get a raw steak for the eye if you're lucky.'

I would have said I loved her then, but just at that moment my heart was too full.

Clare Francis
Deceit £5.99

In this brilliant and frightening novel, Clare Francis turns to crime.

Always secretive. Always a loner. Harry had gone missing at sea – presumed dead. But it is only at his memorial service that Ellen's doubts about her husband begin to take shape. As fellow MPs, old army friends and business associates come to pay their respects, a web of financial and political scandals begins to surface, and the Harry that Ellen knew and loved turns out to have had several hidden lives.

As Ellen struggles to salvage what she can from the tangle of legal and emotional problems, Moreland, a colleague of Harry's from the Falklands War, enters her life and tries to uncover the truth about Harry's death – a truth which Ellen would prefer left undisturbed. But the more he tries to help, the more the finger of suspicion points inexorably in her direction.

Powerful and unrelenting, *Deceit* marks the spectacular crime début of this internationally best-selling writer.

Clare Francis
Red Crystal £6.99

THE ANGER IS THERE, THE INJUSTICE, THE REPRESSION, THE
SITUATION JUST NEEDS TO BE POLARISED –
CRYSTALLISED . . .

Out of the savagery of the Paris barricades there was born the
most sinister of all the terrorist groups of the 1960s. Secretly
funded by Moscow, trained in subversion and assassination in
Italy, the Crystal Faction came to England. To wage war . . .

For Nick Ryder of Special Branch, finding and infiltrating the cell
presented a daunting challenge. Hampered by the deviousness
of his own superiors and lack of cooperation from MI5, he was
drawn slowly but inexorably into a tangled web of sex, drugs,
murder, intrigue and lost innocence.

And at the centre, the beautiful Gabriele Schroeder, leader of the
Crystal Faction. A tough, daring, utterly ruthless woman for
whom killing had become a pleasure . . .

'The climax is agonising, and made only too horribly likely by the
author's careful groundwork and ability to maintain suspense'
Books & Bookmen

'A sexy as well as a fast-paced thriller'
Daily Express